Diamond ★ Star

BAEN BOOKS by CATHERINE ASARO

Sunrise Alley
Alpha

The Ruby Dice
Diamond Star

CATHERINE ASARO

DIAMOND STAR

A Baen Books Original

Baen Publishing Enterprises
P.O. Box 1403
Riverdale, NY 10471
www.baen.com

ISBN 10: 1-4165-9160-5
ISBN 13: 978-1-4165-9160-3

Cover art by David Mattingly

Song lyrics:
  "Boxcar Madness" ©2009 by Hayim Ani
  "Etch-a-Sketch" ©2009 by Hayim Ani
  "Touching the Horizon" ©2008 by Hayim Ani
  "Breathing Underwater" ©2009 by Hayim Ani
  Included by permission of Hayim Ani.

First printing, May 2009

Distributed by Simon & Schuster
1230 Avenue of the Americas
New York, NY 10020

Library of Congress Cataloging-in-Publication Data

Asaro, Catherine.
  Diamond star / Catherine Asaro.
      p. cm.
  ISBN-13: 978-1-4165-9160-3 (hc)
  ISBN-10: 1-4165-9160-5 (hc)
  1. Rock musicians—Fiction. 2. Life on other planets—Fiction. I. Title.

  PS3551.S29D53 2009
  813'.54—dc22

                                          2008051059

10 9 8 7 6 5 4 3 2 1

Pages by Joy Freeman (www.pagesbyjoy.com)
Printed in the United States of America

To Hayim Ani

For bringing my story alive
With his music and his artistry

Acknowledgements

My thanks to the following people for their invaluable input:

For their excellent comments on the full manuscript (in the proverbial alphabetical order): Kathy Affeldt, Angie Boytner, Kate Dolan, Charles Gannon, K.D. Hays, Aly Parsons, and Kate Poole. To Aly's Writing Group for their insightful critique of scenes: Aly Parsons, with Al Carroll, Bob Chase, Charles Gannon, John Hemry, J.G. Huckenpöhler, Simcha Kuritzky, Michael LaViolette, Bud Sparhawk, and Connie Warner. I've been fortunate to work with a wonderful group of people at Baen Books (Simon & Schuster): to my publisher and editor, Toni Weisskopf; to Laura Haywood-Cory, Hank Davis, Marla Ainspan, Jim Minz, Danielle Turner, copyeditor Ruth Judkowitz, and all the other fine people who did such a great job making this book possible. My thanks to my excellent agent, Eleanor Wood, of Spectrum Literary Agency; and my publicist Binnie Braunstein for her enthusiasm and hard work on my behalf.

One of the pleasures of doing this book was the music CD that came out of it. I would like to thank Point Valid, the alternative rock band that collaborated with me to turn Diamond Star into a rock opera: Hayim Ani, lead vocals, lead guitar, and co-producer; Adam Leve, drums; and Max Vidaver, guitar. Hayim also wrote music for many of the songs, together with Point Valid, and lyrics for three. The lyrics for all our songs appear at the end of this book.

My thanks to the professionals who worked with us to make the CD a reality: none of it could have happened without Dave Nachodsky of Invisible Sound Studios, our co-producer, recording engineer, and mentor; also to Rebecca Ocampo, my incredible vocal coach, and everyone at the Laurel School of Music; photographers Stephen Baranovics, Miriam Ani, and Paul Cory; Stephen Baranovics also for the videos, and Ben Caruthers; Rick Purcell of MasurLaw for his advice and knowledge; guest artists Russell Wilson, Michael Belinkie, Dave Nachodsky, Joe Rinaolo, Miriam Ani, and Michael Williams. To the many gifted young artists who also helped make it happen: Amber Dawn Butler, David Dalrymple, Dina Eagle, Sholom Dov Ber Eagle, Ayelet (Yelli) Lobel, Evan Margolis, Victoria McDaniel, David Michelson, and Reuven Weisberg. My thanks also to all the parents who were there giving encouragement and support. Also to my luminous accompanist, Donald Wolcott, and especially to Janis Ian for her inestimatable friendship, mentoring, and wisdom.

A heart felt thanks to the shining lights in my life, my husband John Cannizzo, and my daughter Cathy, for their love and support.

Author's Note

The CD for the *Diamond Star* rock opera can be downloaded from iTunes or ordered from Starflight Music:

Starflight Music
9400 Snowden River Parkway, Suite 110
Columbia, Maryland 21045
www.starflight-music.com
contact@starflight-music.com

Samples of the songs are available at the website.

Contents

I

Vault of Steel Tears

Del was sick of being interrogated. Supposedly he was a guest of Earth's government. Right. That's why they wouldn't let him leave their military base in this place called *Annapolis*. He was thoroughly fed up with their questions.

Today it was an Army officer. Barnard? Bubba? No, Baxton. That was it. Major Baxton. He had a green uniform and hair so bristly, it looked like a scrub brush. He sat across the table from Del in an upholstered chair that was obviously more comfortable than Del's metal seat. Holographic lights, or *holos*, glowed around the major, floating above the table as if he were a demon presiding over a laser-tech hell.

"All right, let's get started," Baxton said in English.

Del gritted his teeth. They all knew he didn't speak English very well. He could ask to use a language he knew better, but damned if he would show vulnerability to these people.

"Tell me your name," Baxton said crisply.

"My name?" Del thought he must have misunderstood.

"Your name," the major repeated. "Is that a problem?"

"You know my name." What was Baxton up to? Del felt off balance, unsure what these people wanted with him.

Baxton folded his arms on the table, and little green spheres floated near his elbows. "For the record."

1

"This is ridiculous." Del was so uneasy, his accent came out even more than normal. "You know name of mine. Your CO, he know it. *Everyone* here know it."

"For the record," Baxton repeated.

"Fine. You want my name? Have it all." Del leaned back and crossed his arms. "Prince Del-Kurj Arden Valdoria kya Skolia, Dalvador Bard, Fifth Heir to the Ruby Throne, once removed from the line of Pharaoh, born of the Rhon, Heir to the Web Key, Heir to the Assembly Key, Heir to the Imperator."

Baxton squinted at him. "Uh, yes. Thank you. Age?"

"Why not look at this mesh file you all keep about me?" Del wondered when they would stop with all this business. "I am sure it say my name, age, home, what I eat, when I use bathroom, and how many wet dreams I have last night."

Baxton cleared his throat. "Your age, please."

Oh, what the hell. "Seventy-one."

"In Earth years."

Del wished he knew how to get out of this conversation. "That *is* Earth years."

Baxton spoke coolly. "Prince Del-Kurj, you are clearly not seventy-one years of age."

Del glowered at him. "Then maybe you tell me how old I clearly am."

"Seventeen?" Baxton's look suggested he thought Del was some defiant punk.

"Fine," Del said. "Have it your way. I'm seventeen."

Baxton glanced at the holos floating around him. Most were green, but one had turned red. "You're lying, Your Highness."

Del bit back the urge to tell Baxton what he could do with his lie detectors. Being rude wouldn't get him out of here. He wasn't sure of his age, anyway. Twenty-six maybe, but the year on Earth didn't match the world where he lived. Baxton could go look it up if he really wanted to know.

Del just said, "I am older than I look." The holo above the table turned green.

The major regarded him curiously. "Have you had age-delaying treatments?"

"Not really." Del laughed to cover his unease. "They say youth is curable. I guess in my case it isn't."

Baxton gave him a sour look. He tapped the table, and a new

holo formed in the air, the image of a serpent curled around a staff, what Del had learned was a symbol of medicine here. When Baxton flicked his finger through the staff, words appeared below it on the table. He read for a moment, then said, "According to this, you have good genes, good health care, *and* good cell-repair nanomeds that delay your aging." He looked up at Del. "But don't your nanomeds get outdated?"

Del shrugged. "My doctor, every few years, he update them. I am scheduled for update a month ago." Dryly he added, "But I not get the update. It seems here I am, on Earth, instead of home."

"We could do it," Baxton offered, looking helpful, which was about as convincing as a wolf trying to look cuddly.

Right. Del saw their game now. This business about needing his name and age was a ploy in their endless search for excuses to analyze him. During his four weeks here, they had constantly tried to convince him that he should submit to their medical exams. His refusal stymied them, for they walked a fine edge between holding him captive and honoring him as a royal guest. They didn't want to look as if they were forcing him to do anything against his will.

Del didn't want their doctors to touch him. So far, no one had hurt him, but he had no idea what they intended or if they would ever let him go, really go, not just the few brief trips off the base they had so far allowed him with a guard.

He said only, "I update them when I go home."

"Hmmm." Baxton skimmed his hand through a holo hovering above the table.

Across the room, the wall shimmered and vanished, leaving a doorway. It bothered Del to see exits appear and disappear that way and left him feeling even more unbalanced. He had spent his life in a culture where doors swung open.

Mac Tyler walked inside and nodded to them. "Good afternoon, Your Highness. Major Baxton." A bit more than average height, with a lean build, Mac had regular features, hazel eyes, and brown hair. Although he came across as unassuming, it didn't fool Del. Mac's low-key exterior masked the intellect of a sharp negotiator.

Baxton nodded to the older man. "Good to see you, Mac." He didn't look the least surprised, and Del suspected he had signaled Mac when he brushed the table. Del always felt on guard here, and it exhausted him, especially because these people were older, more experienced, and savvier than him in just about every damn thing on their world.

Mac pulled out a chair and settled his lanky frame at the table. "I'm going to pick up some pizza," he told Del. "Would you like to come?"

Del had no absolutely desire to eat the Earth "delicacy" known as pizza. Mac and Baxton were probably doing what people here called "good cop, bad cop." Mac would rescue him, after which a relieved Del would relax with him and let slip useful information about his family. It exasperated him, but anything was better than this scintillating conversation with Major Baxton.

"I like, yes," Del said to Mac. He glanced at the major. "If we are done?"

"We can continue later," Baxton told him.

Del sincerely hoped not.

"It's stupid," Del said. He and Mac were walking down a hallway of the Annapolis Military Complex, which served Allied Space Command.

"They ask the same questions over and over," Del said. Instead of English, he was speaking Skolian Flag, his own tongue, a language his people had developed to bridge their many cultures. His ire welled up. "They want their doctors to examine me to see what they can learn about me and, well, I don't know what."

"They're frustrated," Mac said. "You won't do what they want."

Del slanted a look at him. "You're not doing your job."

Mac smiled. "My job?"

"You're supposed to trick me into a false sense of security and get me talking."

Mac didn't even deny it, "I guess my heart's not in this." Although he spoke as if he were joking, he sounded as if he meant it.

They continued on, Mac lost in his thoughts, leaving Del to his. It was one reason Del liked him despite their awkward situation; they didn't have to converse unless they really felt like it.

Del had met Mac when Earth's military had taken control of Del's home world last year. It still angered Del to think about it. His home was part of the Skolian Imperialate, an interstellar civilization that shared the stars with the Allied Worlds of Earth, supposedly as friends. Hoping to ease the strain, Earth's leaders had sent Mac as a "consultant" to establish good relations with

Del's family. The tie-in was music; Del, his father, and one of his brothers were singers. Mac worked in the music business now, but he had been an Air Force major before he retired, which meant he also understood the military.

Although Del didn't usually get along well with military types, he liked Mac. The former major treated him fairly, and he didn't criticize or judge. Del could even forget his Air Force background because Mac didn't look the part. Today Mac had on dark slacks and a dress shirt, more formal than his usual pullover and mesh-jeans.

"Are you going somewhere?" Del asked.

Mac glanced at him. "Later. I have an appointment in D.C."

"More consulting?"

"No, not that." Mac smiled. "You're my only military job."

"What," Del said sourly. "Babysitting a captive prince?"

"You're not a captive."

"Fine. Then I want a berth on the next ship off this planet."

He expected Mac to come up with an excuse, the way the brass here at the base always did when Del pushed them to let him go. Instead, Mac said, "It may be sooner than you think. Your government is stepping up the pressure on us." Wryly he added, "You can always tell it's tensing up around here when people start ordering a lot of pizza."

"You know, I don't mean to offend," Del said, feeling awkward. "But I really don't like pizza." He slowed down as they reached a cross hall. "Would you mind if I went back to my rooms instead?"

"No problem." Mac seemed a little relieved, making Del wonder if he didn't like his babysitting job any more than Del liked being babysat.

"I'm working on a song," Del added.

Mac's interest perked up. "Mind if I listen?"

Even after knowing Mac for weeks, Del still felt that moment of shock, that this former Air Force major enjoyed his music. He knew the military had hired Mac to "like" it, but he would sense it if Mac were feigning his interest. Del was an empath.

It always amazed Del the strange ideas people had about empaths. He wasn't like a sponge that soaked up every emotion from the people around him. In fact, he shielded his mind to keep out their moods. When he did pick up something, he was never certain if he interpreted it right. Knowing someone's mood didn't explain *why* they felt that way. But as he had become more comfortable with

Mac, he had relaxed his mental shields and discovered Mac genuinely enjoyed his singing. Del still didn't trust him, but he didn't resent his company, either. No one else wanted to hear Del sing. Or screech, as one of his brothers so kindly put it.

"Sure," Del said. "You can listen. I call the song 'No Answers.'"

Mac had always liked Del's rooms. No stark quarters here; Del had changed his apartment to evoke his home on the world Lyshriol. His wall panels showed views of the Backbone Mountains against a blue-violet sky. A Lyshrioli carpet covered the floor in swirls of green and gold, and red-glass vases graced the tables. It was a slice of Shangri-la hidden within the bleak walls of the Annapolis Military Complex.

Del leaned over an icer panel in the wall. "Want a beer?"

Mac settled in an armchair. "Sure." He had to remind himself that the "boy" offering him alcohol was legally old enough to drink.

Del might be young, but he sang like no one else. After spending so many years in the music business, Mac knew what the entertainment conglomerates looked for—and Del had it in bucketfuls. The holocam would love his face. Usually he looked like a scowling angel, but when he smiled, it was as if a light went on. Mac had seen women stutter to a halt at the sight. The violet color of his eyes and metallic quality of his eyelashes enthralled people, especially because they didn't occur naturally on Earth; they came from changes his forefathers had made to their genome. So did the wine-red color of his hair, which tousled in curls down his neck and on his forehead, sun-streaked with gold. His leanly muscled build had a lithe grace that would translate well into holographic media.

Of course, Mac could never send Del to an audition. The idea of a Ruby prince loose in the decadent ethos of the holo-rock industry broke him out in a sweat. It would be a security nightmare. Which was a shame, because Del was probably the most gifted rock singer Mac had ever met.

"Here they come." Del grabbed two bottles as they slid into the icer tray. He spun around and tossed one at Mac. "Catch!"

"Hey!" Mac grabbed at the missile, fumbled the catch, and cursed as it slipped through his fingers. The bottle looked like glass, but when it hit the floor, it bounced. He jumped out of his chair and managed to grab it on the fourth bounce.

Del grinned at him. "Sorry."

Sorry, hell. Mac grumpily scraped the bottle's tab as he dropped back into his chair. His infernal drink didn't open, it just hissed as it released gas from the frothed-up contents.

Del sprawled in a chair across from Mac with his legs stretched across the carpet. His beer, which hadn't been cavorting on the floor, opened right away. He took a long swallow, then lowered the bottle and regarded Mac smugly.

"You know," Mac said, "you can be extremely annoying." He tugged on the tab of his bottle, and it finally deigned to snap open. He took a long pull of his drink.

Del laughed. "I keep you awake."

Mac just grunted. "So what's this new song?"

Del's smile faded, replaced by a pensive look. "I'm still working on the lyrics. Tabor did the music for me."

"Tabor? Who is that?"

"Mac! You introduced us. Jud Taborian."

"Oh. Jud." Mac vaguely recalled running into Jud at some over-priced cocktail bar in Washington, D.C. That had been the first time Mac wrangled permission to take Del off base, so he had shown the prince around town. Mac barely knew Jud, though. The young fellow was a composer in the undercity music scene, which hadn't even dented the more lucrative planetary venues or bigger offworld markets. Many of its artists were mediocre or actively rotten, but a few were brilliant, and they all challenged accepted norms. Some tried to evoke the rock of earlier, less civilized eras. Although privately Mac agreed that present day music had become so "civilized," it was suffocating in its own conservatism, he couldn't sell musical anarchists to the conglomerates.

"I've been talking with Jud over the mesh." Del put his beer on the table and rummaged in a blue box he had left there. "He sent me this tech-tick." He pulled out a silver oval the size of his hand and squinted at it. More to himself than Mac, he added, "If I can just figure out how to use it."

"You've never used a ticker?" Mac knew Del had the device because Jud had sent it to Mac. The security people at the base didn't want Del giving out his address, so Mac let the prince use his for correspondence. Security had to clear any packages Del received, anyway. In fact, when Mac took Del off base, he acted as his guard and carried monitors that continually analyzed everything around them.

"I'd never even heard of a ticker," Del said. "Not before Jud gave me this one."

That surprised Mac. "Then how do you compose music?"

"At home, I'd hum the melody I wanted for a drummel player," Del said. "He'd figure out how to accompany me. Or I'd tell him the lyrics and he'd come up with something."

Drummel? Mac thought back to the instruments he had seen in Del's village. "You mean you've only played with those harp-guitar things?" Although Del had grown up in a rural community, he had mesh access to the resources of an interstellar empire. "No other media? No morphers?"

"Why bother?" Del shrugged. "I didn't really listen to offworld music. It's too much to sort through, and I haven't liked what I heard." His smile flashed. "Though if I'd picked up the undercity, *that* I would have listened to."

"I can imagine." No wonder Del sang so well. With no media enhancement, he'd had no choice but to learn real technique.

Del studied the ticker. "Jud says I can edit the music he put on here. But I have no idea how." He tapped a button, and music played, slow and haunting, in a minor key, lyrical but with a raw edge, as if it were strumming under a violet moon.

"I like that," Mac said.

"The melody is right . . ." Del sat listening, his head cocked to one side. "The drums are too heavy, though."

Mac liked the driven quality of the drums, but he was curious to hear what Del would do. "I can show you how to edit the song."

Del let the music fade away. "You know how to do that?"

"It's my job."

Del blinked at him. "I thought you were an agent."

"I'm called a front-liner," Mac said. "I get auditions and contracts for my clients. To sell their music, I need to understand what they do. I can't sing or compose, but I'm pretty good with the technical side."

"Then, yeah." Del grinned. "Show me."

They sat together at the table while Mac taught him how to use the ticker. When Del achieved the result he wanted, the instrumentals for the song had a beautifully eerie quality.

"It's good," Mac said. "Better than the usual undercity work."

Del shot him an annoyed look. "Just because you don't like undercity music, that doesn't make the musicians hacks."

"Oh come on. It's the quality I'm talking about."

"Why?" Del demanded. "Because they don't follow the boring mainstream?"

"No," Mac said. "Because a lot of them can't sing, play, or compose worth shit."

Del waved his hand as if to brush away the comment. But he didn't deny it. He was too accomplished a musician not to realize that for some, going undercity was little more than an attempt to define a lack of talent as progressive. The scene had produced some remarkable music, but they had also put out some of the worst dreck Mac had ever heard.

"You can sing circles around them," Mac said.

Del made a disgusted sound. "I doubt it."

It wasn't the first time Mac had heard Del make derogatory references to his own singing. He didn't understand why the youth felt that way. Del had no sense of his own talent. He was probably Mac's greatest find—and Mac couldn't do a damn thing with that discovery.

Well, almost nothing. He could listen. "So how does the song itself go?"

Del drummed his fingers on the ticker, set the oval on the table, then picked it up again. "I can't sing without something to hold."

Del wasn't the first vocalist Mac had seen who didn't know what to do with his hands while he sang. Mac almost laughed, thinking that some *did* have ideas, but they couldn't get away with it. The censors would come down on them like the proverbial ton of plutonium.

"Sing into the ticker," Mac said. "It'll record you. Then you can listen to your voice."

"Oh. All right." Del flicked on the ticker, looking self-conscious. "This is only a rough cut of the vocals."

The music began with an exquisite and simple melody played by only a harp, from what sounded like a Gregorian chant. When it finished, the guitar riff played that started the music Mac had helped Del edit.

And Del sang.

His lyrics weren't the formulaic doggerel expected in the modern day universe of popular music. He varied the syllables more per line, sometimes drawing out words, other times rushing them. He used repetition to deepen the song rather than following a formula, and he gave the verses a freer form than current mainstream work:

> No answers live in here,
> No answers in this vault,
> This sterling vault of fear,
> This vault of steel tears,
>
> Tell me now before I fall
> Release me from this velvet pall
> Tell me now before I fall
> Take me now, break through my wall
>
> No answers will rescue time
> No answers in this grave
> This wavering crypt sublime
> This crypt whispering in vines

He stopped, staring at the ticker, his lashes shading his eyes. "It's still rough," he said, as if apologizing.

"I like it." Mac wondered at the dark edge to the lyrics. Del wrote in a range of styles, from danceable tunes to ballads to hard-driving blasts. Sometimes he came out with these eerily fascinating pieces. Although the major labels probably wouldn't consider them commercial, Mac thought they had a lot more to them than the pabulum produced for popular markets.

"I've no idea what it means, though," Mac added.

"I suppose it's about never knowing answers even after you die. Or maybe that's what kills you." Del tapped his fingers on the ticker. "I don't like the third part. The first line is too long. 'Rescue' clunks. And 'Wavering crypt sublime' is idiotic."

"Why?" Mac asked, intrigued. "The sounds fit."

"The sounds, yeah. But the words are dumb. Crypts don't waver." He tilted his head. "Winnowing. Winnowing crypt sublime."

Mac smiled. "Crypts don't winnow, either."

"Sure they do. They winnow you out of life." Del pointed the ticker at Mac. "You can live for decades and never find answers." He lowered his arm. "Until death winnows you out of humanity and makes room for someone more useful."

Mac spoke quietly. "I hope you don't see yourself that way."

Del just shook his head. He had that far-off look that came when he wanted to practice. "I need to work."

"Would you like me to go?"

"I don't mind if you listen," Del said. "But it can get pretty boring when I'm working on a song. I just go over and over the same parts."

"It's not boring for me," Mac said. "I'd like to stay."

"Well sure, then." Del got up and walked around, holding the ticker. And he sang. He kept changing words, pacing like a caged lion. He sang a verse fluidly, then snarled the chorus. Yet somehow it all fit.

Although Mac liked to watch him sing, he knew it made Del self-conscious. So he closed his eyes and leaned his head back, enjoying the music. It was easy to submerge into Del's rich voice. The youth had trained his entire life, using techniques passed through generations in his family. Although Del could sing opera exquisitely, he preferred a far different style. He could croon one line, scream the next, wail and moan, then stroke the notes as if they were velvet, all without harming his voice. No one did anything that commercially risky in the mainstream, but undercity artists threw in all sorts of noise. Mac knew why Del had fascinated them that night in the bar; he easily achieved what they struggled to attain because he had the technique they lacked. To break the rules, they had to master them first.

Del wanted nothing more than to sing. He didn't care about the politics surrounding him. Although no one had physically hurt Del, Mac knew he had suffered emotionally. His people were torn by hostilities that had begun long ago, when humanity splintered into three civilizations: the Allied Worlds of Earth; Del's people of the Skolian Imperialate; and the Trader Empire. The Skolians and Traders had just fought a brutal war that had nearly destroyed them both and ravaged Del's family.

The Allied government had remained neutral, safe in their isolationism, but they agreed to shelter Del's family on Earth. When the war ended with no victor, Earth had feared the Skolians and Traders would send their world-slagging armies back out, again and again, until they wiped out humanity. So they refused to release Del's family. It did no good; the Skolians just sent in a commando team and pulled them out, all except Del, who happened to be apart from the others. So here Del remained, while Earth's government argued over what the blazes to do with him. Some thought having Del gave them a bargaining point with the Skolians. Others wanted to let him go and be done with the whole mess. Personally Mac didn't see the point in keeping him. What would they tell his family, the Ruby Dynasty—that if they started another war, they would never see their youngest son again? The bellicose Skolians were more likely to attack than bargain . . .

"Hey!" Del said. "You awake?"

Mac opened his eyes drowsily. "Just drifting."

"Admit it," Del said, laughing. "I bored you to sleep."

"Never." Mac stood up, stretching his arms. "I do have to go, though. I have a client who is auditioning today."

Del regarded him curiously. "What sort of audition?"

"It's with Prime-Nova Media, for a holo-vid cube."

"Oh. Well." Del squinted at him. "Good."

He smiled at Del's attempt to look as if he knew what the hell Mac had just said. "You've watched holo-vids, haven't you?"

"Not really. I see people playing them, but I don't stop to listen." Awkwardly Del said, "I don't want to intrude."

"You should see one. You'd enjoy it." Mac thought for a moment. "Would you like to watch the audition?" He had wrangled permission to take Del off the base by arguing that it reinforced their claim Del was a guest rather than a prisoner. He wanted to give Del at least those limited excursions; he felt like a cretin treating this youth as a prisoner when Del had never done anything to anyone.

He motioned at Del's ticker. "If we can get some mesh-box space, we could tech up a few holos for your cuts."

Del laughed, his eyes lit with interest. "I have no idea what you just said, but yeah, I'd like to go with you."

Mac grinned. "Come on. Let's go show you what I just said."

They headed out, into the freedom of a late morning turning red and gold with autumn.

II

Prime-Nova

Del had never seen even one mesh-media studio, let alone a whole building of them. The Prime-Nova offices were on Wisconsin Avenue across from the Washington Arts Center, which had begun as the Washington Ballet in the twentieth century and grown until it devoured several city blocks. Mac enthusiastically informed him that the area was "a vibrant media hub rivaling New York and L.A." Del had no clue what that meant, but he liked the place.

No ground traffic bothered them; the "streets" consisted of plazas and gardens designed for pedestrians. The widely spaced buildings sported glossy sides that projected holos of landscapes, clouds, abstract art, or gigantic images of celebrities. A few blocks south, the gold arch of a mag-rail curved against the blue sky, and a sleek bullet car whizzed along it. Farther down Wisconsin Avenue, the National Cathedral rose elegantly above a plaza lush with trees.

The lobby of the Prime-Nova building gleamed with gold and bronze metal. The receptionist at the circular counter was an artificial intelligence, or AI. He initially presented as a man, but when Mac spoke, the holo rippled and re-formed as a beautiful woman with hair the color of marigolds.

"Go right up, Mister Tyler," she said in dulcet tones. "You're expected." She turned her laser-light smile on Del. "Welcome, Mister Neil. Good luck with your audition."

"Neil?" Del asked. It was weird talking to an image. He wondered what sex it turned into if both a man and a woman came up to the counter, or how it guessed a visitor's sexual preferences.

"This isn't Craig Neil," Mac told the holo. "Craig should be here soon. Please send him up when he arrives."

"Of course." Her voice was so well modulated, Del couldn't read any emotion from it. "I'll need the name of your guest."

"Valdoria," Mac said. "Del Valdoria."

Del was grateful Mac didn't use his complete name, Del-Kurj. He had been named for his half-brother Kurj, *Imperator* Kurj, the man who had commanded the Skolian military. That had been before the Traders assassinated Kurj and started the war. People had considered Kurj a de facto dictator and had begun to say the same about the current Imperator, Kelric, another in Del's multitude of brothers. Kurj and Kelric: hell, even their names sounded the same. Del had no interest in being associated with the draconian measures his notorious brothers used to maintain power.

He rode upstairs with Mac in a bronzed lift. While Del looked around, intrigued by all the metal, Mac fooled with his wrist comm. Del had never understood why so many people were willing to carry mesh systems on their wrists, clothes, in their bodies, everywhere. It made him queasy, as if they were all turning into robots.

"Craig should be here," Mac muttered. A blue light flickered on the wrist-mesh.

"Maybe he's already upstairs," Del said.

"Maybe. The AI should have known, though." Mac looked up. "No messages from him."

The lift abruptly opened into a corridor with gold light for walls. Mac motioned Del forward.

"This is pretty," Del said as they walked past the shimmering holo-curtains. "Bizarre, but attractive in its own soulless way."

Mac smiled wryly. "Said like a true undercity cynic." He ushered Del through a light-curtain and into a small room. The upper half of the wall across from them consisted of a window. A control strip ran along its bottom edge, crammed with switches, screens, and lights, none of which Del understood. Mac ignored the wonderland of tech-mech equipment and strode to the window. Joining him, Del studied the room beyond. Set half a level below this booth, it had blue walls that glowed. More strange equipment was stacked or strewn everywhere.

"Damn," Mac said.

"You don't like the room?" Del asked.

"I was hoping Craig would be in it." He glanced at Del. "I have to comm him, but I don't want the Prime-Nova producer who's going to audition him to overhear that he's AWOL. I'll be down the hall. If anyone comes in, just say I'll be right back."

Mischief stirred in Del. "If you leave me alone, I could go to the starport." He would actually rather watch the audition, but he couldn't resist baiting his military-approved babysitter.

"You can't sneak out of the building," Mac growled. "Not past me. But if you try, I'm damn well never taking you anywhere again."

"Go on," Del said good-naturedly. "I'll wait. I want to look at these panels."

"Don't touch anything." With that, Mac strode out.

Del wandered around, trying to figure out the equipment. He wished he knew more about music here. He wanted to leave Earth because he was tired of the aggravating people holding him in custody, but he had no huge desire to go home.

He did miss his nephews. As much as he loved them, though, they were better off without him. He pushed away the thought, burying it with all the other painful memories he kept locked away within his heart.

Ricki Varento was always prompt. As a top producer at Prime-Nova, she had no time to be late. Or sick. Or anything else that interfered in her immensely satisfying work. She molded platinum out of slag and did the best job in the industry. She created stars. Hell, novas. If the basic material didn't glow, well, by the time she finished with them, most blazed like flipping fire-poppers. And bah on anyone who laughed at the way she talked.

Today Mac Tyler was bringing his latest slag. His clients sometimes even had talent. All too often, though, *talent* translated into temperamental. Ricki would break out in hives if one more petulant singer complained he was an *arteest*, thank you, and had no intention of "submitting to slick packaging" that cheapened his integrity or whatever. Well, hell. How did they expect the people who paid them to make money? For every pouting troublemaker, she had a hundred acts waiting for their chance. She had no time for boomallitic blasters, holo-funkers, or undercity divas. Mac knew it, and he played the game even when he didn't agree with the rules.

Some people in the industry disliked Mac on principle, because of his military background. Ricki couldn't care less. In fact, she enjoyed his company, though she never let him know, because it might give away bargaining points when they negotiated. He was good at his job, met his obligations, and showed up on time. He never laughed at how she phrased things, either, though honestly, she couldn't figure out why other people did.

If Mac brought her good prospects, she made money for Prime-Nova. More often than not, she had to turn down his clients because they lacked magnetism, beauty, or youth appeal. Beauty and youth could be arranged with enough money, though limitations existed on how much you could pretty up the slag. Talent could be faked with tech. Those acts couldn't tour worth beans, though, since their abilities consisted solely of technology.

No matter what you did with the exterior, however, innate charisma was harder to come by, some indefinable blend of traits that mesh simulations couldn't reproduce. If Mac spent more time on the aesthetics of his clients and less on their talent, he'd have more success. She suspected a bit of the *arteest* skulked under that professional veneer of his, too, but he didn't let it interfere, so she worked with him.

She stopped at a gold wall and touched a panel there. An opening shimmered in front of her and she walked through into the booth beyond. She expected to find both Mac and his client waiting, but only one person was there, a boy across the room with his back to her as he peered at a mesh panel.

Ricki paused, looking him over. Odd. He had no costume, or if he did, it was too bland to make much of an impression. He wore dark blue pants, a white shirt, and sports shoes. The overall effect wasn't bad, though. The pants clung to his legs and fit low on his hips, with a belt drawing attention to that portion of his anatomy. It was worth the attention; he had a good, tight bum and long, well formed legs. His shirt was too loose to reveal much of his physique, but what she saw, she liked. He wasn't overly bulked up with muscles, and he didn't look like he had any fat, either. In the holo-rock scene, thinner worked just fine.

His hair surprised her. Mainstream artists wore it short. Quite frankly, that buzzed-off style was getting old, and it had never made sense to Ricki for rock stars to look like military officers, anyway. This guy could pull off the longer style. The color of his tousled curls was just strange enough to work, like red wine streaked by the sun. The streaks looked natural, but they were obviously some weird genetic tattoo, because they had a metallic cast. Interesting. In fact, the effect was gorgeous.

Ricki folded her arms and tapped her finger against her chin. If his face matched the rest of him, she could work with this one. Maybe Mac was finally getting the aesthetics part straight. Hell, if the kid had a little talent, he could go a long way. Of course, that assumed the rest of him looked as good as what she could see. Time to find out.

"Hello," Ricki said.

The guy jumped, turned with a start—

And smiled.

Holy mother shit. He had an angel's face. Big, bedroom eyes and eyelashes luxuriant enough to make a woman jealous. He had done something to make them sparkle. But he didn't look feminine, oh no, not this one. He did have that androgynous quality that worked so well for male holo-rockers who could pull it off. The kid was a well-put-together package. Maybe she ought to offer him a contract so she could take him out, get him drunk, and take him home to find out what he could do with those full, pouting lips.

"Hello," he said.

"Hmmm." Ricki walked over, cool and slow, and he watched her with a warmth she recognized. She had on a white tunic that barely came to mid-thigh, white tights, heels, and not much else. She had no objection to him viewing the scenery; she had purchased the best body that cosmetic biosculpting could provide.

She kept her voice professional. "Are you with Mac?"

"Yes, that is right." He shifted his weight self-consciously, his hips moving with a sensual tilt she doubted he realized. She had long ago learned to sum up clients and intuit how much of their behavior came naturally. This one wasn't acting. He seemed unaware of his own body.

"Mac, he have call on comm," he said. "He come soon."

Ricki noticed two things immediately, one good, the other bad. His voice had a deep, sultry resonance; if he could sing that way, she had even more to work with. But he had a heavy accent. Sexy, yeah, but if he couldn't enunciate clearly, they had a problem. She couldn't place the accent, though it sounded French. Or maybe Irish. Or Swedish. Hell, who knew?

"Is something wrong?" he asked.

"No, nothing." She offered her hand. "I'm Ricki Varento."

"Del," he said. "Del Valdoria." If her name meant anything to him, he gave no sign.

Valdoria. It didn't sound familiar, but she hadn't had time to look over the bio Mac had sent her. Del's hesitation before he shook her hand told her volumes. The gesture didn't come naturally. Huh. Even if he came from someplace where they didn't shake hands, he ought to know the custom, unless he had hidden on a farm in the middle of nowhere all his life. She liked his grip, though: firm, confident. The strong muscles in his hand were unexpectedly erotic. Except they didn't feel quite right. She glanced down—

What the . . . ? He had a *hinge* in his hand.

A memory jumped out at Ricki, the image of the knife scar on the hand of her mother's boyfriend, the man who had lived with them for a year when Ricki was eight. The scar had run down the back of his ugly-assed hand the same way this hinge thing ran down the back of Del's. She dropped his hand with a jerk.

Del was watching her face closely. He lifted his arm, showing her the hinge. "This part of me, it intends . . . what is the word? It is meant to make better my hand. My ancestors, they design it." He folded his hand in lengthwise, from his knuckles to his wrist.

"That's, uh, fine." Ricki knew perfectly well he wasn't going to hit her with his damn hand. But she didn't want to talk about that scarlike hinge, look at it, even think about it.

She said only, "You aren't from Earth?"

He lowered his arm. "Not Earth. A planet called Lyshriol."

She had never heard of it. "Is it a colony?"

"Just a few hundred thousand people. Farmers mostly."

Well, jumping Josephine. He *was* a farm boy, and from some offworld dump to boot. She didn't know whether to be fascinated by him or irritated with Mac for bringing her the best-looking prospect she had seen in years and not preparing him for a major audition. Most clients would have been alert the moment she came in. They would have gone into their best game, trying to impress her with their professionalism and appeal. They would have offered their holo-shots and a vid detailing their experience. Farm boy here hadn't even recognized her. He acted as if he couldn't care less.

Had Mac set this up on purpose? It sent an audacious message: *We don't even have to try.* This kid had better be good, or she was going to be annoyed. And irritating Ricki Varento was a good way to crash and shatter in this business.

"You're a long way from the farm," she said.

"Never far enough," he answered in a low voice.

Interesting response. "So did you bring your music?" She didn't normally ask, but given how unprepared this guy seemed, who knew what he had with him?

For a moment, he looked startled. Then he tapped a ticker on his belt. "Here, yes, I bring music."

"Great." She gave him one of her high-wattage smiles and motioned at the studio below the window. "Let's hear what you can do."

"Just like that?" he asked. "I can go down?"

"Yeah, sure." Ricki held back her frown. The kid didn't come across as stupid, but his inexperience was obvious. Either Mac was losing his edge or else he was playing hardball at a level he had never done with her before.

She pointed the lift out to Del, then stood and watched while he left the booth. The lift hummed and a moment later he walked into the mesh-tech studio below. Greg Tong must have been waiting in the cockpit, because as soon as Del appeared, Greg opened a door across the room and walked in. He hadn't turned on the audio feed to the booth, so Ricki couldn't hear them, but Greg was plainly introducing himself. Although she could have switched on the audio, it intrigued her to watch their body language. Del seemed relaxed and curious, not keyed up the way most artists were before an audition of this magnitude.

Greg took the ticker from Del and went to the wall where the michaels, bobs, and janes hung. After choosing a bronzed mike, he brought it over to Del. And that was it. Greg returned to the control room they called the cockpit and closed the door.

Ricki flicked on the line to the cockpit. "Greg?"

"Heya," he said.

"What was that all about?"

"I asked him what he needed when he sang, what configurations, all that. The usual." He snorted a laugh. "You wouldn't believe what he told me."

"Try me," Ricki said.

"'Nothing.' Just play the music on his ticker."

"That's it?" What was Mac doing, wasting her time with someone who wasn't ready? She was tempted to tell Del to forget it. She had worked with Mac a long time, though. For the sake of that relationship, she would give this kid a few minutes.

"What's he going to sing?" she asked.

"I don't know." The comm crackled the way it did when Greg shook his head and his hair brushed the oversized collar of those metallic shirts he wore. "He's going to, uh, warm up."

"Well, hell." Ricki couldn't believe this. "He couldn't be bothered to warm up before his audition?"

"Can't say. It's not like he doesn't know what he's doing. He isn't nervous at all. It's weird."

"Why does he need a mike? The studio can pick up his voice."

"He wanted something to hold."

"Huh." Ricki didn't care if he wanted a michael, mike, or mic as it was historically called, after the antique word microphone. Added to everything else, though, it didn't help her opinion of him.

Down in the studio, Del flicked on the mike. "Hello?" His voice rumbled with a sultry quality. It sounded good even when Ricki was pissed off.

She put a comm in her ear that linked to the cockpit so she and Greg could converse without Del overhearing. Then she switched on the audio to the studio below where Del waited. "Go ahead and start," she said.

Del looked up with a jerk, then glanced around, obviously trying to figure out where her voice came from. Ricki swore under her breath.

"What did you say?" Greg asked over her ear comm.

<Nothing,> she answered. She formed the word without speaking. Sensors in her body picked up her throat motions and transmitted signals to the plug in her ear, which converted them into words and sent them to Greg.

Ricki wondered if this Del had lied about being with Mac. The front-liner wasn't even here. One minute. She would give Del one minute to convince her otherwise. Then he was *out*.

Del sang a note, and his voice came out clear and full. Great. He could do one note. She ought to jump for joy.

"Greg, could you play an E4?" Del said.

"Sure," Greg said over the studio comm. A tone rang out with the same pitch as Del's note. Del tried a few more and had Greg play notes afterward.

<What's he doing?> Ricki asked.

"Checking his pitch, I think," Greg said. "It's perfect, Ricki. No accompaniment, no help, nothing. Perfect pitch."

<I suppose that's good,> she allowed.

"Sure," Greg said. "It doesn't mean he can sing worth shit, but at least he'll hit the right notes."

Ricki grunted. She didn't care about perfect pitch. If the slag hit a wrong note, Greg edited it out and put in the right one. Some of her acts couldn't sing at all, and almost none of them could solo in live performances without enhancement. She had her doubts real talent existed.

A thought curled up from the recesses of Ricki's mind. There had been a time when she believed in the beauty of art for its own sake, the power of a song, some shining quality that transcended the human condition—

No. That stupid, naïve nobody had learned her lesson long ago. If you let yourself be sidetracked by some supposedly higher ideal, people took advantage of you.

Down in the studio, Del quit with the single notes and did some exercise thing, ah-ah-ah, repeating the pattern higher each time. He started in a bass voice and worked smoothly into the highest baritone range. He had obviously done classical work, which was almost unheard of in the artists Ricki auditioned. Personally she found opera boring, but she knew the value of the training. Whether or not Del could translate it into a marketable holo-vid style was another story, but she was willing to give him a few more minutes.

He hit the A above middle C, a high note for a baritone. Then he headed down two octaves—and more. Ricki listened, amazed, as he went deeper until he rumbled below the bottom range of a bass. The few singers she knew who carried that voice so well had augmented vocal cords. She could tell when someone had enhancement, though, and Del sounded natural. The *quality* struck her most; he hit those rumbling notes with power and clarity.

<Nice,> Ricki told Greg.

"He sounds like an opera singer," Greg said.

Ricki snorted. <I've never heard one that could do rock.>

Del started with another exercise, one that jumped around more. He worked into his baritone range—

And kept going up.

Ricki listened with her mouth open while he methodically went through a man's tenor, a woman's mezzo-soprano and then soprano. The quality of his notes changed, becoming clear, like bells. His ticker added a subtle chime to accompany some of his notes. It was effective, but strange to hear such high notes from a man. He went through the exercise as if it were perfectly natural to span so many octaves.

When Del hit the A two octaves above middle C, a chill went through Ricki. That was the highest note for a *female* choral soprano. And he *kept* going. It wasn't coming as easily for him now, but he hit the notes. When he nailed high C, Ricki exhaled for the purity of the tone.

Del stopped and frowned as if displeased, though for the life of her, Ricki couldn't see why. She had no idea what he would do with that upper range; no mainstream works required it, and she doubted it would be commercially successful to have a man singing female soprano. But it was the most impressive display of useless technique she had ever heard.

"I can't believe he did that," Greg said. "Fucking high C."

<How did you add the chime?> she asked.

"I'm not playing anything," Greg said. "That's all him."

"Good Lord," Ricki muttered. She leaned over the studio comm. "Del? Why don't you sing one of your pieces?"

He glanced up, this time toward the window where she stood. "All right," he said in a deep voice, his natural speaking manner, a startling contrast to the notes he had just sung.

What he did next, Ricki couldn't define. It was subtle—and erotic. He shifted his weight, nothing more, but the way his hips moved, something in his stance, the lithe grace of his leanly muscled physique—it was all intensely sexualized without his even seeming to try at all.

And then he sang.

He crooned a rock ballad in his richest baritone, stroking the notes with his voice. His lashes closed halfway over his eyes and his hips rocked with the languorous beat. The music had that dreaming quality the young girls loved. He was practically making love to the mike. Then he snarled a line, his lips pursed as if he were furious and about to kiss someone at the same time. He caressed another phrase, then built the intensity of the song, higher, higher, until finally he screamed the last line as if he were having an orgasm, his eyes open, his legs planted wide, his elbow lifted, his head thrown back as he wailed into the mike.

Ricki sat down at the control panel. <Holy shit!>

Greg let out a whoop as Del continued his song. "You've got the genuine article here, babe! He could sing in concert. *Live.* That is, if he can do this in front of an audience. And sing in English."

<English?> Ricki had been so caught by Del's performance, she only now realized he was singing in some language she had never heard. Without accompaniment. Without *anything*: no fixes, no holos, no media, no tech, no enhancement. *Nothing.* That was his voice. The real thing.

"Oh, Mac, you sly, sly rat," she said, cutting the audio so Del wouldn't hear. "You set it up beautifully." Oh yes, she read his message loud and clear: *This farm boy is so good, we don't have to do jack for your audition. I could take him anywhere, any place, and get him a contract.*

Ricki hit the comm channel that put her through to Zachary Marksman, the Vice President for Technology, Mechanicals, and Media, otherwise known as the tech-mech king.

His voice came over the comm. "Yeah?"

"Zack, it's Ricki. I'm down in the booth for studio six."

"That's great, sweetheart." He sounded preoccupied and a little irritated. "You're hitting my emergency channel to tell me where you are?"

"You need to get your ass down here," Ricki said. "Now."

Mac stalked into the booth—and froze. Both Ricki Varento *and* Zachary Marksman were standing across the room by the window, facing away from him, talking in low voices. Damn. He was going to look bad enough just with Ricki after his client pulled a no-show. He couldn't reach Craig; Mac had no idea if he was dead, alive, or too drunk to show up, but whatever the reason, Mac had to deal with the fallout.

Ricki Varento, also known as the blond barracuda, hated anything that smacked of the amateur. Regardless of what he thought of her artistic integrity, or lack thereof, she was a power in the industry. He hadn't expected Zachary; clients had to pass Ricki first, before lions higher in the corporate food chain came to the feast.

Bizarrely, neither Ricki nor Zachary realized he had come in. They should have noticed if they were impatient for him and Craig to arrive. They were standing in front of the window, staring down at the studio.

"He didn't even bring a vid," Ricki was saying. "I don't know anything about his past experience."

For one stellar moment Mac thought Craig had showed up after all. Relief swept over him; maybe they could salvage this.

Then he noticed Del wasn't in the booth.

Oh, hell.

The booth had two exits. Del couldn't have gone out the way he had come in. Mac would have seen him. Nor could Del have left by the producer's entrance; it was keyed to the fingerprints, retinal scans, even brain waves of the top executives. Only one other way existed to leave the booth: the lift into the studio.

Mac gulped as he inhaled. Ricki and Zachary both turned with a jerk—and went on guard. Not annoyed or impatient as if they had been left waiting, but *careful.*

"Mac!" Ricki gave him a million-watt smile. Combined with her bodysculpted figure and the sweetest face she could buy, framed by gold curls, she was dynamite in her clingy dress. Dynamite, as in one of Prime-Nova's most powerful weapons.

"It's so good to see you," she said. "Do come in."

Mac felt as if he were facing a pair of tigers. Right now, a purring Ricki was even more terrifying than Ricki pissed off.

"Nice to see you," Zachary said, coming forward as he extended his hand. "We should get together more often."

Mac shook his hand, wondering what neural-meth concoction Zachary had zinged into his brain. They never "got together." They moved in completely different circles; Mac would probably asphyxiate in the rarefied atmosphere where Zachary existed.

"It's good to see you," Mac said. What the blazes was Del doing? He heard nothing from the studio. His hope stirred. Maybe they had just kicked Del out of the booth. He walked past Ricki to the window and looked down—

At his nightmare.

Del was in the studio talking to Greg Tong. The prince had a mike, and his hair was tousled as if he had been wailing one of his songs. Mac wanted to drag Del out of there and tell Prime-Nova that absolutely, under no circumstances, would Del accept a contract. Of course he didn't dare do anything that would draw that much attention. He was in a diplomatic minefield, and if he took a misstep it could blow up in his face.

He didn't believe Del had deliberately preempted Craig's spot; Del had his share of faults, but Mac had never doubted his integrity. He had probably assumed Ricki was doing what Mac had offered earlier, showing him a holo-vid studio. Zachary's presence no longer surprised Mac; the moment Ricki realized what she had in that studio, she would have called in Prime-Nova's tech-mech king.

No wonder she and Zachary were so guarded behind their friendly veneers. They wanted Del under contract. It put Mac in an impossible position. If he turned them down without asking Del, he would alienate a Ruby prince, a man who could cripple relations between Earth and Skolia with just a few words to his brother, the Imperator. Unfortunately, Mac had little doubt Del would jump at the contract once he understood what it meant, that Prime-Nova *wanted* him to sing, and as a career. If Del went pro, it would put a spotlight on him, inviting the attention of assassins, kidnappers, and God only knew who else. If anything happened to Del, Allied Space Command might as well just walk up to Skolia's Imperial Space Command and say, "Hey, let's have a war."

Ricki stood next to Mac, watching Del and Greg in the studio. "He has an interesting range," Ricki said.

Interesting. Right. As in a spectacular six octaves.

"You could put it that way," Mac said.

Zachary was standing on Ricki's other side. "He didn't bring a resume with him. Nothing about his experience."

Mac glanced at him. "He's lived on a farm all his life."

Ricki smirked. "What happens when you take one part *very*

healthy farm boy, mix it with one part horny effing mother, and shake well? What a recipe."

Mac barely held back his retort. Where did she come up with this stuff? The worst of it was, she was right. Del's mix of unsophisticated innocence and sensual wickedness would be dynamite. If he ended up on the holo-rock scene, a lot of people would talk about him like that. Maybe Del would be so insulted, he would walk away. Mac doubted it, though. It mattered far more to Del to have people like his music than for them to address him with deference, particularly given how much he resented his title.

Mac didn't know how to answer. He couldn't tell them anything until he discussed it with Del—and Allied Space Command.

"Are you saying he has no experience?" Zachary asked.

Mac knew they were bargaining, trying to counter the demands they expected him to make. So he said, "That's right. None." It was true, after all. For all they knew, when faced with making a living through his music, Del might fail miserably.

Both Ricki and Zachary stared at him as if they had run into a wall. They expected tough negotiation and instead he talked down his client. Yep. No experience.

Ricki slanted a look at the VP, and he nodded slightly. She turned back to Mac. "Half his songs are in some other language." She sounded genuinely curious. "Who writes his material?"

"He does mostly," Mac said. "What did he sing in English?"

"Something about running and blue clouds," Ricki said. "Another about emeralds."

"*The Crystal Suite*," Mac said. "Yes, that's his." At least Del hadn't sung "Carnelians," his rant about the Trader Aristos. Although it was one of his most powerful pieces, the lyrics revealed far too much about his identity.

"Can't call it *the Crystal Suite*," Zachary said. "It sounds like a drug reference."

Mac wanted to throw up his hands in exasperation. Already they were appropriating Del's work. "They're *his* titles."

"Does he write his own music?" Ricki asked.

"The first draft," Mac said. "Jud Taborian works with him on arrangements." An idea came to Mac. "You may have heard of Jud. He's making quite a name for himself in the undercity."

A frown marred Ricki's perfect face. "I don't need any undercity assholes pulling their diva act."

Well, that was diplomatic. Mac motioned toward Del. "Just look, Ricki. He has undercity written all over him. You don't want undercity, you don't want Del."

"We didn't say we didn't want him," Zachary told him. "But you have to admit, his lack of experience is a drawback."

Mac shrugged. "That's the way it is."

Ricki and Zachary shared another of those glances. Then Ricki said, "We're willing to take a risk on this one, Mac. A firm commitment, two anthology cubes, both holo-vids."

Risk, hell. A typical vid only held ten songs. Del had enough material to fill five cubes. Vids were simple, just holographic movies that played as if the artists were in the room. Viewers could rotate them, zoom in or out, pull down a story vid, customize the songs for themselves. Prime-Nova should be offering Del a virt, or virtual reality simulation. Virt users weren't passive listeners; they participated in the holo-vid, which created a "reality" they could play with themselves. Entire communities in the mesh universe had built up around the more sophisticated virts. The interactive experience fascinated, even obsessed its fans.

Mac knew why they hadn't mentioned a virt. It was riskier to produce because it cost more. But they were also potentially much more lucrative. Of course, Del had *no* experience. So yeah, they were taking a risk. But even if for some reason Del had trouble providing twenty songs over the next few years, Greg and his crew could make whatever he gave them succeed. They had a lot to work with. Two holo cubes for a first-time artist was normally a good offer, but if Mac had actually been representing Del, he would have pushed for a virt on at least one, maybe both.

Today he said only, "I'll talk to him."

Zachary and Ricki waited. After a moment, Zachary said, "Prime-Nova has the longest track record in the business."

Mac didn't see his point. Yes, Prime-Nova was established. Then he realized what Zachary meant. They thought he was auditioning Del elsewhere, that he was waiting because he wanted to know who else was going to offer what. Cripes. They thought he was playing hardball.

"I'll tell him," Mac answered. "We'll get back to you."

"Mac, I've known you a long time," Zachary said. "I like you. For the sake of our relationship, we're willing to take a chance on this farm boy. We'll give you virts with both of his albums."

Hell and damnation. If Del had been anyone else, Mac would have started negotiating royalties, publishing rights, the whole game. But he *couldn't* make a commitment, and he sure as blazes couldn't tell them why. He didn't want Del to take the offer, but neither could he just walk away.

"I'll let him know," Mac said.

Ricki looked incredulous. "You won't get a better offer, Mac. And you sure as hell won't get the high level of backing Prime-Nova can give him."

Mac didn't doubt it. If Del had it in him to become a star, Prime-Nova could make him one. *If.* Sure, Del could play the undercity fringe. But succeeding on the level Prime-Nova wanted was another matter altogether, and Mac had his doubts that Del could manage that transition, especially given that he had spent so many years with no outlet for his music. The youth had no idea what it meant to conduct a professional career.

Mac kept his voice neutral. "Like I said. Del and I will talk."

Ricki's voice cooled. "I can't promise the deal will stay on the table. I've two more auditions today. A lot of boys out there want what we're offering your client."

Mac nodded, secretly relieved. If he put them off, maybe they would withdraw the deal. Then he felt guilty; he knew how much this would mean to Del, to have people not only believe in his music, but offer him the backing of a conglomerate powerhouse.

"Just give me a day," Mac said. *Just a day.*

She shook her head. "Even a few hours may be too long."

Mac had never seen her push this hard before. "I understand."

She and Zachary waited. When Mac said no more, Zachary let out a sharp breath. "I need an opener for Mind Mix's live concert tour. I'll give the spot to your client."

It was all Mac could do to keep his mouth from falling open. They were offering Del a tour with a top band, one of the few good enough to play live concerts? It was *absurd*—and it made sense. Del could, in theory, give a show people would want to hear, which was better than most of the "talent" in the Prime-Nova stable. Except Del had never performed in concert. In fact, he had never played for more than fifty people. Mind Mix played live for hundreds of thousands, even millions. Prime-Nova would be crazy to put Del under that kind of pressure so soon.

"Look," Mac said. "I appreciate that offer. It's a good one. But I have to talk this over with Del."

"Take it now or not," Zachary told him. "You walk out of here looking for a better blast, that's it. Ours is gone."

Sweat beaded on Mac's forehead. If they were following the usual procedures, this conversation was being recorded and the offer would be binding on them if he agreed. Mac knew he should be jumping at the opportunity. But blast it, he *couldn't*.

The hum of the lift vibrated in the booth, followed by the whisper of its door opening. Mac had one moment to panic before Del walked through the gold shimmer to their right.

"Hey, Mac." Del grinned. "The acoustics in that room, you not believe it. They are being incredible."

"Del, hello." Zachary stepped past Mac and extended his hand. "It's good to meet you. I'm Zachary Marksman, Vice President of Technology, Mechanicals, and Media."

After the slightest pause, Del shook his hand. "Hello."

Mac recognized Del's hesitation. The youth's parents may have raised their children in a rural community, but Del wasn't naïve, not by a long shot. He knew vice presidents didn't just show up and introduce themselves for no reason. Suspicion flickered in his eyes, the knowledge of a prince whose acquaintance many people coveted for the status it brought them. It was ironic, because Zachary lived in the same type of world, where hopeful artists would do *anything* for that handshake he had just offered Del.

"We were discussing our contract offer with Mac," Ricki said smoothly. "He says he needs to discuss it with you."

Del looked from Ricki to Zachary. To Ricki. To Mac. Back to Ricki. Mac didn't miss the way Del's gaze skimmed over her voluptuous body and lingered on her face. *Damn.*

"What contract offer?" Del asked.

Ricki eased past Zachary, right up to Del. The vice president stepped back, giving her room to work. "Two cubes," Ricki purred. "Holo-vid and virt. And opening for Mind Mix in concert. Like it?"

"Del," Mac warned. "Don't answer. Your responses are being recorded. A yes could be interpreted as a binding contract." He doubted Del had a clue what they were talking about, but it didn't matter as long as the prince kept his mouth shut. Otherwise, Del could end up committing himself to Prime-Nova indenture.

Del's forehead furrowed. "I don't understand."

"I told them you and I need to talk it over," Mac said.

"Talk what over?" Del frowned at him, then focused on Ricki. "You want my music?" Although his voice was guarded, Mac could hear the incredulity that lay under that neutral tone.

"That's right." Ricki tapped his chest with her manicured fingernail, the blood-red polish bright against Del's snowy shirt. "We want your songs. And *you.* On stage. With Mind Mix."

"What is mind mix?" Del asked.

Silence greeted him. Mac didn't know whether to laugh or groan. A smile spread across Ricki's face, smooth and all too knowing, the master player sizing up an innocent lamb. "You probably don't hear them out in the edge colonies. They sing, Del. A great band. The best. And *you* could open for them."

"You mean sing on stage, before they come out?" Del asked.

"That's right." She splayed her hand on his chest, and he looked down, his lashes lowering over his eyes. In her sultriest voice, she added, "Would you like that?"

"Don't answer her." Mac stepped up and pushed away her hand.

She glanced indolently at Mac, then back at Del. "There's one catch, honey. You have to give us an answer now."

"Ricki," Mac warned.

Del considered him. "They want me to sing on one of those holo-vids, right? And as a warm-up for this other group?"

Mac felt as if the roof were about to fall on him. "That's right."

Del's face was hard to read. He was as guarded now with Mac as with the others. When he turned to Ricki, his eyes glinted. "Yes," he said, his voice deepening. "I do it."

"Damn it, Del!" Mac grabbed his arm and pulled him across the booth. He spoke in a low voice. "*Don't* say anything else. A deal like this has to be negotiated."

Del regarded him with a coldness he had never shown Mac before. "I need an expert to talk with them. You do this? Yes or no?"

Mac raked his hand through his hair. "Of course I'll do it."

"Good." Del's tension eased. He turned to Ricki and indicated Mac. "My front-liner, he work out details with you."

Ricki's smile dripped satisfaction. "I'm glad to hear that."

Mac stared at her, and hoped to blazes he wasn't looking at the catalyst for an interstellar catastrophe.

III

First Step

Fitzwilliam R. McLane, aka Fitz, wasn't the only general Mac knew, but he left the others in the dust when it came to the force of his personality. His grey hair resembled iron, and his grey eyes were set under brows of the same color. He sat in his big chair behind his big desk and regarded Mac with a considering stare.

"What does it mean, exactly?" Fitz asked. "He'll sing in those things the kids watch?"

"That's right," Mac said, uncomfortable in his chair despite its smart-tech, which kept shifting the cushions, trying to relax him. "And he'll go on tour with the other band."

To Mac's surprise, Fitz *smiled*. "Who would have guessed? Of all the ways I thought he might find to get away from us here at the base, I never would have come up with this. I thought he'd go to the Skolian embassy when he realized we wouldn't stop him."

"I'm not so sure he wants to go home," Mac said. "Except for his sister's kids. He's been sort of surrogate father to them."

"Two boys, right?" Fitz asked. "One grown and the other—what? Ten?"

"Eight, actually," Mac said. "They use an octal system, so they say ten. The other boy is eighteen. I don't know much else; the family kept them away from our Allied delegation." Dryly he said, "We weren't exactly welcome on Del's world."

31

"So I gathered." Fitz tapped his desk, bringing up a screen, and flicked through a few displays. "The sister never married?"

"I don't think so." From what Mac understood, the Skolian government had interfered for some reason, something to do with her children, but he had no idea what. He was still figuring out the convoluted relationship between the Skolian Assembly and the Ruby Dynasty. The Assembly and royal family split the rule of the Imperialate, half an elected government and half dynastic. But that had only been since the war, which had ended with a bizarre twist when the Ruby Pharaoh overthrew her *own* government. Before that, she had been a titular ruler without political power.

From cryptic remarks Del had made, Mac gathered that in the past, the Assembly had mistreated his family in some way, spurring the pharaoh's coup at the end of the war. Politics had poisoned his family in some inscrutable Skolian way Mac had yet to figure out, but Del wouldn't talk about it.

"Do you think Del wants to stay on Earth?" Fitz asked.

"Yes, I think so, if this business with Prime-Nova works out," Mac said. "If he bombs, they'll probably drop him after his contract ends. I don't know what he'd want to do then."

Fitz sat, rubbing his chin. "How much time is involved in making and marketing these cubes?"

"His contract says he has to complete both within three years."

"And his tour?"

"It depends on how he does," Mac said. "If he plummets, they'll yank him after a few performances." He hoped he wasn't being prophetic. "Mind Mix is one of their biggest acts. They can't risk an unpopular opener."

"Do you think he will—what was the word? Plummet."

That was the billion-dollar question. Literally. "He has the talent," Mac said. "What he does with it is a different question. He's never performed in concert. He breaks rules, too, and he walks the edge of what the censors will allow. He could fail miserably." He paused. "With Prime-Nova backing him, though, he has a chance of a good career."

Fitz smiled wryly. "It isn't what you usually associate with the Ruby Dynasty."

No kidding. Mac was having trouble deciphering the general's reaction. "If you want the contract broken, we can manage. It will take lawyers, but given Del's identity, I think we can do it."

"Broken!" Fitz actually laughed. "Mac, it's brilliant. You've convinced him to stay on Earth and given him a reason to keep you around."

"You *want* him to do this?"

"His family can hardly accuse us of forcing him to stay if *he* insists on it. And he'll be right here, under our control." He considered Mac. "How does this front-liner thing work? Do you manage him, too? The more we keep you involved, the better."

Mac couldn't believe he was hearing this. "I just get him the contract. I'm not a manager. I don't have enough experience. And it would take a lot of time away from my other clients."

"But could you do it?"

Could he? Mac didn't know if it was a good idea for Del's career, and he disliked the idea of being responsible for someone so important to interstellar politics. But he had to admit it made sense. Although concentrating on Del's career would mean giving up some of his other clients, he would receive a percentage of Del's income, which could be substantial if Del succeeded.

"I might be able to," Mac said. "Assuming I could find good front-liners for my other clients. But Del would have to agree, with full knowledge that I'm reporting back to you."

"Do you think he will?"

"I don't know." Mac exhaled. "It's his safety I'm worried about. He'll be leaving the base a lot more. He should have more security than me and my monitors."

Fitz nodded. "We'll get him a full-time bodyguard. One of the teched-up Marines. With all the bioware those boys carry in their bodies, it'll be as if he has a phalanx of guards."

"You can't have a Marine hulking around him!" Mac wondered if Fitz had any clue of the life Del would be living, especially on the road. "It would be like putting a sign over Del's head saying, 'Hey, look, I'm important.'"

The general spoke wryly. "I'm not that out of it, Mac. We'll get someone who fits in. He can be part of—what do you call it? Del's staff."

"His team. He doesn't have one yet."

"Good. You can set it up," Fitz said. "We'll also need to implant a tracker in his body."

"He already has one."

Fitz snorted. "For all the good it does us. He isn't about to give us the key to one his own people put in him."

Mac could imagine Del's explosion at the idea of yet another invasion of his privacy. "He'll never agree to a second one."

"See if you can convince him. And we need Del to let his family know he's staying on Earth of his own free will."

Mac almost groaned. It would be easier to convince Del to roll naked in a hill of fire ants than to talk to his family. "I'll try. But I can't make any promises on that."

Fitz's gaze never wavered. "We'll be depending on you."

Mac had felt before as if the roof were sagging; now it was caving in. Not only did he have to worry about Del loose in the holo-vid industry, but Fitz wanted him personally responsible for the prince. *Damn it, I'm a civilian.* He could walk out on this. But if he did, he would antagonize people he had no wish to alienate, starting with a top-ranked general. Besides, he already felt responsible for Del.

Mac took a breath. "All right. I'll do my best."

He just hoped it didn't all come crashing down on him.

Del's living room balcony overlooked the glistening expanse of a river. In the distance, across the water, the Naval Academy basked in rays of the setting sun. The interplay of the aged light and rippled water fascinated Del.

"Brighter than the crystal caves," Del sang softly. "Sunlight glancing on the waves." He used English because he finally had a good reason to learn it. Someone wanted to sell his songs.

He kept expecting the woman Ricki to contact him and say they had made a mistake, that they weren't interested after all. Or that other person would tell him, the man. A vice president for technology, mechanicals, and media? What the blazes did that mean? Mac said "mechanicals" was a term from long ago, when mechanical devices played music. But then, Mac also claimed the deal with Prime-Nova was binding even though he hadn't finished negotiating it. To Del, it all felt as ephemeral as mist under a morning sun.

A chime sounded inside the living room, through the open doorway. With a sigh, Del turned from the gorgeous sunset and went back into his quarters.

"Lumos up," he said as he crossed to the console against the far wall. The lights brightened.

The console should have showed who contacted him, but no image floated above the comm screen. That was odd. No one knew how to reach him here except military officers, certain highly placed members of Earth's government, and Mac. Whenever his family contacted him, they had to go through lengthy protocols complicated by the fact that they all knew Earth's military was monitoring every word.

Del rolled his shoulders, working out muscle kinks. "Claude?"

"Good evening," Claude answered. He was an EI, or evolving intelligence, that the military had installed on Del's console. Del had named the EI after Claude Debussy, his favorite among the Earth composers he had so far discovered. He never felt inspired to name AIs, or artificial intelligences, which only simulated emotions, but EIs were more aware. Although he couldn't pick up their moods, they genuinely seemed to experience them. So he named the EIs.

"Who commed me?" he asked.

"I don't know," Claude said. "The comm originates in Washington, D.C., but its ID is hidden."

"Strange." Del squinted at the console. Its comm light was still glowing, which meant the mystery person hadn't cut the line. So he said, "Respond."

After a pause, Del said, "Hello?"

"Del!" A sultry female voice floated into the air. "Heya, babe."

Heya, babe? What did that mean? She sounded like the woman who had offered him the contract. With a sinking sensation, he realized he had celebrated too soon. They were going to withdraw the offer.

"Hello, Miss Varento," Del said.

Her throaty laugh wrapped around him. Any other time, that sensual response would have attracted him. Today, he could only think how much he didn't want to hear whatever she had to say next.

"Call me Ricki," she said. "After all, we're going to be working together."

Working together. *Working together.* Del let out the breath he hadn't realized he was holding.

"Del?" she asked.

"Do you mind if I put you on visual?" he asked.

"I'd love that, babe."

A smile spread on his face. Babe, indeed. Her husky voice reminded him of the voluptuous body under that flimsy dress she had been wearing today. What inspired her to refer to him as an infant, he had no clue, but what the hell. She could talk to him that way all day if she wanted. Especially if she wore that dress.

He touched a panel, and a screen rose before him. It shimmered blue and cleared to show a starlit room with windows for walls. Beyond them, the nighttime wonderland of a city glistened in gem lights, with the mag-rail adding luminous curves to the skyline. Del found it hard to believe that long ago, buildings in Washington, D.C. had never been more than a few stories high. Now those graceful towers soared. After spending his life in a rural community, the view took his breath.

Ricki was sitting at a tall table just big enough for two people, wearing a slinky black dress that did even better things for Del's imagination than her outfit this afternoon. Her yellow hair fell to her shoulders and framed her sweet face.

More pleasant thoughts replaced Del's earlier concerns. "So what are you doing, Ricki, all by yourself?"

"I'm in a private room on top of the Star Tower Sheraton." Her voice purred. "I was thinking this would be just the place to celebrate your new relationship with Prime-Nova." A pout touched her face. "But you're there and I'm here."

"Celebrations," Del murmured, "are better with two people."

She sipped her drink, her lips molding to the glass. Then she licked away the moisture. "If you come soon enough, I'll be here."

Del wondered if she offered to celebrate this way with all her new acts. He couldn't sense her mood from here; his empathic ability depended on her brain waves, which could only affect him close up. He might be fooling himself, but he didn't think such "celebrations" were her usual mode. Then again, maybe he should hope she was that casual about her relationships. Then she wouldn't expect more of a commitment than he could give. Ricki was the kind of woman you enjoyed for the night, like a fine wine. Del smiled. No, not wine. Whiskey.

His voice deepened, thickening his accent. "Maybe I come celebrate with you."

"Talk like that," Ricki murmured, "and I may stay here all night."

She took another swallow of her drink. "Ciao, baby." With that, she cut the connection.

He laughed, shaking his head. "Chow baby?"

An idea came to him and he smiled. He would wear those pants that had flustered his female interrogator so much, she forgot her questions. He hadn't figured out why they affected her that way, but he had sensed her response the moment he entered the room.

It would be interesting to see what happened when he tried to leave the base tonight.

The maglev stop in the Annapolis complex was underground. No trains actually went there; the real station was outside the base. A whiz-car took people to the edge of the base, where they could leave the grounds and board the maglev.

Del rode in a single-seater with the bubble open so he could relax while the wind tossed his hair. He had on his leather jacket. The Allied military had grudgingly bought it for him when he pointed out they cut him off from his personal funds by denying him access to the interstellar meshes. He needed a jacket. So rather than letting him use the offworld meshes, they paid for the jacket. It was ridiculous. He could buy a million jackets with his personal funds. If he did manage to see Ricki tonight, he could ask her for access to an offworld mesh. It irked him just as much, though, that he had those funds only because he was a member of the Ruby Dynasty. So if Earth's military didn't buy his jackets, the Ruby Dynasty did. Either way it bothered him. If this holo-vid business worked out, he might earn his own money. Then he'd buy his jackets with his own income.

After the car stopped at the edge of the base, Del swung out and strolled to the automated guard booth. The voice of an AI came out of a panel on its front. "I'm sorry, Your Highness, but you aren't cleared to leave the base."

"I have to go," Del said. "I have an appointment."

Silence followed his words. Then the AI said, "One moment."

Del grinned. He'd actually flummoxed it this time.

A new voice came out of the comm. "Your Highness, this is General Fitz McLane. I understand you wish to leave the base?"

Hah. The AI had called in the big gun. "That's right," Del said. "I have meeting with my producer."

"At night?" The general didn't hide his skepticism.

"She's at the Star Tower Sheraton."

"She?"

Del regarded the comm smugly, well aware the general could see him even if he couldn't see Fitz. "Yeah. She."

"It isn't safe for you to travel alone."

"I'm a grown man, General. I take care of myself."

"You're also a Ruby Heir," Fitz said. "Anything that happens to you could significantly impact relations between our peoples."

Del crossed his arms. "But holding me prisoner *won't* impact those relations?"

The ensuing silence surprised him. The last time he had used that line, the general had given him some drill about "establishing a baseline database we can use to determine the optimum approach in our interface with the Skolian institutions most affected by your presence on Earth." Which as far as Del could tell, was Fitz-speak for "tell us Skolian secrets." Fitz's silence made Del wonder if the Skolian government had stepped up their pressure to let him go.

"I'll send you a flycar," Fitz said. "With a pilot and a bodyguard. They will take you to your appointment and bring you back."

Del tried to look innocent, just to annoy Fitz. "What if I don't come back tonight?"

The general answered sourly. "As long as you don't mind having your guards in the room."

"But I do mind."

"That's unfortunate, then."

For flaming sake. He couldn't enjoy his evening if he had Marines hulking over him. "I suppose I can contact Ricki. Tell her that General Fitz McLane insists I bring his thugs with me. Ah. My apology. I have problem with English. I mean bodyguard."

"Can it, Valdoria." Fitz sounded as irritated as Del felt with him. It just annoyed Del more. Fitz could have activated the visual. Leaving Del staring at nothing was another way of Fitz asserting his authority.

After a while, Del said, "General?"

"I'm sending Mac Tyler to meet you," Fitz said. "With the flycar and guards."

Del blinked. "All right." Mac he could deal with.

✧   ✧   ✧

"That isn't the point!" Mac looked as if he wanted to shake Del. They were sitting in the back seat of the flycar. The night sped by outside the window behind Mac, sparkling with gold and white lights as they soared over the city.

"I don't care about the damn guards," Mac said. "They can't protect you from the real danger. She's a barracuda, Del. She'll devour you."

Del smiled. "I have no idea what is barracuda."

"It's a vicious fish with big jaws that eats little fish."

Del was relaxed on the other end of the seat. It was a nice car, upholstered in ruddy colors with comfortable cushions. The pilot and a Marine were up front, pretending they couldn't hear every word Mac and Del said.

"Ricki," Del told him, "is definitely not a fish."

"Quit smirking like a tomcat licking his chops," Mac told him. "And don't say you don't know what that means. You figured it out the first time you saw one of those cats prowling around the base. You've been on a farm your whole life, Del, surrounded by sweet country girls. You have no idea what you're letting yourself in for if you meet Ricki tonight."

Del couldn't help but laugh. "If anyone but you say that to me, I probably sock him in the face. What, you think I am some innocent she can shred? I have a flash for you. Us farm folk are not so naïve as you think." In a less amused voice, he added, "And I was never sweet."

Mac let out a breath. "If I gave insult, I apologize. But I would tell anyone this. Stay away from her."

"Why?" Del asked, genuinely curious. "What you think she will do to me?"

"She'll use you like a new toy," Mac said. "When she gets tired of you, she'll drop you faster than a child drops a glass vase. She won't care what breaks."

Del shrugged. "I'm going to meet a beautiful, intriguing woman for a night. Nothing more. I don't *want* anything more." After a moment, he said, "I am not capable of more."

Mac answered quietly. "You're capable of a great deal."

Del didn't want to talk about it. "Maybe she really just want to talk business."

"Yeah, right."

"You never know."

"Del, listen. She moves in a crowd you want to stay away from. They're beautiful, fast-living, wealthy—and toxic. The drugs alone will scorch your brain, and that doesn't touch the other bizarre stuff they're into."

Del's good mood faded. "The drugs don't matter. Not the alcohol, either. Neither affects me."

Mac didn't look the least convinced. "I don't care how high your tolerance is. Anyone can get drilled."

Del *really* didn't want to go into this. But he owed it to Mac, who had changed his life today and agreed to negotiate for him despite how much he wanted Del to refuse that contract. Del knew. Mac's apprehension had been so strong, it had come through even when Del had his empathic shields at full force.

Del switched into the Skolian Flag so he wouldn't struggle as much just to speak. "I don't have a high tolerance. I *can't* get drunk, and certain drugs don't affect me, particularly Metropoli-line hallucinogens and neuro-psillic amphetamines. I carry several nanomed series in my body that deactivate drugs and alcohol."

Mac stared at him. "Is *that* why you didn't want our doctors examining you more?"

Del shifted his weight. "Yes, partly."

"Aren't those treatments dangerous? They might deactivate a chemical your body needs." Mac hesitated. "I thought it was only done for drug addicts."

"I wasn't an addict," Del said. At least, he hadn't been then, though gods only knew where he might have ended up. "It's more dangerous for me *not* to have the nanos." He stared at his hands where they rested in his lap. "All these medical wonders we put in our bodies—they backfire sometimes."

Mac's voice went quiet. "What happened?"

It was a moment before Del could answer. "When I was younger, I experimented with tau-kickers." He looked back at Mac. "I thought they would make me a better artist. Expand my mind." In a brittle voice, he added, "I was stupid."

"Tau-kickers? What are those?"

Del wished he were anywhere but here, telling Mac his past. "Hallucinogens manufactured in mesh-slums on the world Metropoli." He almost stopped, but then he said, "Do you remember the glitter in the air on Lyshriol?"

Mac paused at the change of topic. "The pollen?"

"That's right. It's everywhere, the ground, air, water. You can't always see it, but it saturates the biosphere. That's why the clouds look blue. It's sort of like food dye."

"Ah. Yes, I remember." Mac smiled wryly. "My people had to get treatments so we didn't get sick from drinking the water."

Del had guessed as much. "Those of us who live there are born with protections. We have self-replicating molecules in our bodies to deal with it, like tiny chemical laboratories. A mother passes them to her child in the womb." Bitterly, he said, "I also carry nanomeds in my body that keep me healthy. Hell, I could live two centuries."

Mac was watching him closely. "I'm not sure what you're trying to tell me."

Del took a breath. "All these molecular wonders we put in our bodies—they're designed to work together. So they don't interact in a bad way and harm us."

Mac waited. Then he said, "But?"

Del stared at the back of the driver's head. "Sometimes even the best medicine doesn't work." He shrugged as if he didn't care, but he doubted he fooled Mac. "When I took the kickers, they kicked all right. They had some bizarre reaction with the nanomeds in my body. Once it started, it cascaded. My lungs, blood vessels, lymph, neural, hell, my breathing—it all went wild. Then everything shut down."

"Good Lord." Mac stared at him. "How did you survive?"

Del met his gaze. "I didn't."

Mac blinked. "You look alive to me."

Del turned to stare out the window next to him. "The doctors revived me. Eventually."

Silence.

Finally Mac said, "And they gave you new meds to counter any drugs the doctors thought could kill you?"

"That's right." Del watched the city glitter below. "Alcohol makes me more susceptible, so they took care of that, too." The doctors couldn't remove his nanomeds; their interactions with his body had become so complicated, it was impossible to take them out completely. And without them, ironically, he would no longer have protection against side-effects from the treatments that countered his susceptibility to drugs.

"You seem so healthy," Mac said. "So unaffected."

"I am healthy." Del couldn't say he was unaffected. It had been a horrific time in his life. Although his family was the royal dynasty of Skolia, the government had controlled their lives until just recently. Del had learned the hard way how those with power could exploit the vulnerabilities of people they sought to command.

Mac spoke gently. "There's more, isn't there?"

Del shook his head. He couldn't talk anymore. He was also aware of the general's men in the flycar. He doubted Allied Space Command cared about his personal hells; they wanted secrets that would impact their balance of power with Skolia. And he did know a few "little things," such as, oh, how far his brother the Imperator would go in negotiating the presence of Earth's military forces in Skolian space. Del would never tell the Allieds. So instead they knew he had been treated for drug use. That would fit right in with General Fitz McLane's low opinion of him. Del wished he had kept his mouth shut. He closed the memories away, trying to hide them where they couldn't hurt him.

"Just be careful," Mac said. When Del glanced at him, Mac smiled ruefully. "It's hard for me to imagine a Ruby prince in the holo-rock industry."

Del laughed without humor. "I'm sure for my family, it's hard to imagine anyone paying me to do this."

"Really?" Mac seemed genuinely surprised. "They know how you sing."

"They think I'm just making noise. They've never heard of rock, and I doubt they'd care if they knew about it." Del shook his head. "I'm not like them. I'm no prodigy or great fighter pilot. I'll never have a degree in anything. I can't teach or do scholarship or be a delegate in Assembly." Such simple words, and they hurt so much. "All I ever wanted was my music. And maybe even to have people *want* to hear it." Softly he said, "You gave me that today. Let me enjoy it while it lasts."

Mac's gaze never wavered. "You don't have to be a genius or world leader to consider your life worthwhile."

"Try living in my family," Del said with a bitterness he didn't want to feel. "Try being the only failure out of all those extraordinary people. Then tell me that."

"Del—"

He lifted his hand to stop Mac. He couldn't take any more.

With a jerk, he indicated a gold tower below them. "Why are we circling that?"

Mercifully, Mac let go of his other questions. "That's the Star Tower. We're in a holding pattern to land on the roof flyport."

"Oh." Del set his hand down.

In moments, the flycar was descending. As it landed on the roof, Mac said, "I had quite a talk with General McLane tonight."

Del winced. "I'm afraid to ask about what."

Mac didn't tiptoe around the subject. "We'd like you to keep your identity a secret. The fewer people who know, the easier it will be to protect you."

The request didn't surprise Del. Nor did he object, even if it did come from the authoritarian McLane. He had no desire to have his name associated with his famous kin. If he had some small measure of success, he wanted it to come from his singing, not because he was a member of the Ruby Dynasty.

"I hadn't planned on telling anyone," Del said.

Someone swung open his door, and he looked up to see his bodyguard standing outside. The man had no uniform, just casual slacks and a holo-mesh shirt, but he had *military* emblazoned all over him, from his buzzed hair to his rigid posture.

Del glared at Mac. "He's not coming with me."

"You can't go alone," Mac said. When Del scowled, he added, "No, he won't be on your date with Ricki. He'll escort you into the Sheraton. After they take you to Ricki, he'll join the guards in the key-room for the penthouse Prime-Nova keeps here." Dryly he added, "Prime-Nova has better security than we do at the base."

"What for?" Del asked, intrigued.

"Entertainment is a huge business," Mac said. "And Prime-Nova is one of the largest conglomerates. A lot of people want to be where you are right now."

Del wasn't sure what to think about that, but it reminded him of the idealized fantasy so many people had of Ruby Heirs. They had no idea. Those fantasies had nothing to do with reality.

He stepped out of the flycar and stood next to the Marine. Looking up at the large fellow, he said, "Hello." He would have expected Fitz to choose someone less obvious, but then, he knew so little about life here, he had no idea what was obvious.

"Good evening, Your Highness," the man rumbled.

"You better not call me 'Highness' once we're inside," Del said.

"I won't," the Marine assured him.

Del hesitated, not wanting to feel intimidated by his own guard. "What's your name?"

"Sergeant Cameron."

Del nodded awkwardly to the giant. Then he turned to Mac, who was still in the car. "Thanks for talking to me."

Mac scooted over to Del's side. "Just remember what I said."

Del grinned. "Aren't you worried about Ricki, stuck with a reprobate like me?"

Mac smiled. "Call me tomorrow, all right? We need to talk about your contract."

"Sure." Del lifted his hand in farewell.

Then he headed into the Star Tower.

IV

Tower of Dreams

Ricki saw him in the window first. She was sitting in her tall chair, facing the glass wall, looking over the glistening city. And there, reflected in the glass, was an even more appealing vision: Del, walking into the room.

She turned around as the wall behind Del re-formed, leaving them alone in the Sky Room. He had looked good earlier today, but that was nothing compared to now. His tailored leather jacket was deliciously sinful, fitting his lean frame perfectly. He had left it unfastened, revealing a white shirt open at the neck just enough to show a triangle of chest hair.

Careful, Ricki thought. She never let people affect her too much, even just by noticing them. It gave them control, which meant the power to hurt her. She was a cool operator, smooth and unruffled, and she ignored the misguided poets who claimed they saw past her icy exterior to a lonely soul. She wasn't affected by the way those black leather pants clung to Del's legs. And that belt made out of starship ring fittings that rested so low on his hips, hugging his anatomy—goodness. His boots had just enough heel to shift his hips forward, accenting his sensual build. His hair, well that was just protein . . . gleaming, luxuriant protein that framed his face, his pouting mouth, and those huge eyes, as if he were some beautiful, wicked angel who could snarl like a devil.

Oh my.

"Hello," Ricki purred.

Del stalked over and slid into the other chair at the table. Tilting his head toward the window, he said, "That's quite a view." Without taking his eyes off her, he added, "Spectacular, in fact."

Ah, sweet seduction. She smiled at him. "That's why Prime-Nova keeps this suite."

A hum came from a glimmering mesh on the table, followed by the voice of the human bartender who served the penthouse. "Would your guest care for a drink, Ms. Varento?"

Ricki raised her eyebrow at Del.

"Orange juice," Del said.

Ricki laughed softly. "You may look like a lethal weapon, but I think the farm boy is still in there." She spoke into the comm. "Jack, bring him up one like you did for me, double time."

"Right away, ma'am."

"Like yours?" Looking disconcerted, Del tapped her cut-crystal glass. "That drink is *blue.*"

"Blue as a Night Dazer, which is what it's called." It was such a dumb name, it sounded like something she would come up with. "Mostly it's Southern Comfort."

Del laughed in his rumbling voice. "Whose comfort?"

"Haven't you had whiskey before?"

His smile vanished. "Yes."

Huh. What caused that reaction? "But not lately?"

"I don't know. Maybe. I not remember."

"You'll like this one."

He didn't answer, he just looked restlessly around the room. His gaze came to rest on the spectacular view outside the tower. "Nothing is like this where I live."

"You come from a place called Lyshriol, right?" When he didn't answer, she said, "I looked it up on the mesh. I couldn't find anything about a colony with that name."

"It is small place, not much." His gaze softened as he turned to her. "I translated another song tonight."

"Oh. Good." It relieved her that he hadn't objected when they told him the songs had to be in English. A lot of her acts sang in Chinese or Spanish. If he had been doing fusion, he could have sung in any language, even one he made up. But for holo-rock, labels wanted English, mainly for historical reasons, because it had started in English-speaking countries.

Curious, she said, "What language were you singing before?" Maybe talking about his home would relax him.

He smiled slightly. "It's called Trillian. From offworld."

Huh. That sounded made-up. "I've never heard of it."

"It's an old language."

"It can't be that old," Ricki said. "The earliest offworld colony has only been around a hundred and fifty years."

Del considered her as if she were a decision he needed to ponder. Then he said, "I don't come from an Allied colony. Lyshriol was one of the lost colonies from the Ruby Empire. Your people found it about a hundred years ago."

Ricki gaped at him. "You're *Skolian?*"

"Earth found us. Not the Skolians." Although guarded, he wasn't avoiding her gaze. "Some resort planners from Texas started to set up hotels there, but it didn't work out. So they left."

Ricki had always had an internal detector for when people lied to her, an intuition that proved invaluable in her business. She thought Del was telling the truth. Still, it sounded weird. "So you're saying you come from an offworld settlement that's five thousand years old."

"That's right." He was watching her closely. "Does that bother you?"

"Well, no." She had no idea what to make of it. "I've never understood this business about the Skolian colonies. I don't see how they can be five thousand years old. Humans lived in caves back then."

Del shrugged. "Some race took humans from Earth and left them on another planet."

Although Ricki had heard the story, she had never believed it at a gut level. "Why would a bunch of aliens take humans from Earth thousands of years ago and strand them on some other world?"

"We don't know. They vanished."

Ricki couldn't help but laugh. "So your ancestors, a bunch of Stone Age primitives, set up an interstellar empire? Come on."

"Not right away." Del didn't seem offended by her questions. "It take a thousand years. Even then, they manage only because they have libraries." He stopped, then said, "I mean, they *managed* because they had libraries. The beings that kidnapped them left behind libraries that describe the science. Described, I mean."

It amazed her how fast he was learning English. And what a deliciously odd development in her new act. "So this interstellar empire they set up thousands of years ago—that's what Skolians call the Ruby Empire?"

"That's right." He tapped his fingers on the table. "The Empire didn't last long. Its people knew too little about the science they were using. Its collapse left its colonies stranded."

Ricki rested her elbow on the table and her chin on her hand, fascinated. This could make some dynamite promotional material if Del would let her use it. "Is that why Skolians call those worlds lost colonies? Because they were stranded after the empire fell?"

Del nodded. "My world is one. We were isolated for thousands of years. We lost our technology." He stared at his hinged hand. "Maybe we never had it. We have no records from that time."

"I'm surprised the Skolians don't demand we give your world back to them."

He shifted in his seat. "I don't get involved in politics."

Well, good. She got heartburn when her acts used their celebrity to push an agenda. It hurt sales. "If the Ruby Empire fell thousands of years ago," she mused, "I wonder why the Skolians still have a Ruby Dynasty."

Del suddenly swung around to look at the gold wall across the room. "I think the bartender is here."

"I don't hear—" Ricki stopped as a man in a tuxedo and a glimmer-mesh cravat walked through the curtain of gold light. He carried a laser tray with a blue drink that glowed in a play of silver light.

Huh. How had Del known someone was coming in?

"This is Jack," Ricki told Del. "Did you hear him outside?"

"That's right." Del wouldn't look at her.

Jack set the glass in front of Del and bowed. "I hope you enjoy it, sir."

Although Del nodded, he seemed stiff, and he barely glanced at the drink. Ricki doubted he was used to being waited on, especially in such sleek surroundings.

"Try it," she coaxed Del after the bartender left the room.

He wouldn't meet her gaze. He picked up the drink and took a sip, then set it back on the table.

"Do you like it?" Ricki asked. Given its potency, it wouldn't be long before he felt its effects.

"It's good," he said, looking at the city. "I thought it would be too sweet. But it's not."

"Only the best for you."

His gaze shifted to her. "So I noticed." He watched her with his lashes half lowered, as if he were in bed.

Oh, my. Ricki took another sip, letting her lips linger on the glass, then slowly ran her tongue over the rim. "Go on," she coaxed. "Finish yours."

Del stared at her as she drank. Then he lifted his drink and downed it in one swallow. She started, expecting him to choke, but he just set down the glass.

"Well, that was impressive," Ricki said with a laugh.

Del pushed her glass away from her. "You don't need that." He drew his finger down her hand, from her wrist to the tip of her thumb. It was only the slightest touch, yet that only made it more erotic. The hinge in his hand didn't look strange anymore. She wondered what he could do with it. She turned her hand over so he was trailing his finger across her palm. Then she curled her fingers, capturing his. It wasn't until Del's lips curved upward, slow and tempting, that she realized he had barely smiled tonight. He lifted her hand and pressed his lips against her palm.

"My people say the moons of Lyshriol are more exquisite than any woman," he told her, his breath warming her skin. Softly he added, "The people who say that have never met you."

Ricki sighed. This boy was going to get himself ravished. "Do you know," she said. "A person could live up here."

"Hmmm." With his eyes closed, Del pressed her palm against his cheek. It was a curiously sweet gesture.

"Would you like to know why?" she asked.

Opening his eyes, he kissed the inside of her wrist. "Why?"

"Prime-Nova has a suite here." She sighed as his tongue flicked across her skin. "For tonight . . . it's ours."

Del's lashes lifted. "Does it have a bedroom?"

"Oh, yes," Ricki murmured. She slid off her chair and stood by the table. Del stood as well, and his gaze traveled over her in the most satisfying manner.

✧　　✧　　✧

Del knew he should have refused the drink. His meds would render it harmless, and he had taken no drugs for the alcohol to affect anyway, but that didn't matter. He had sworn never to take another drink. But he hadn't wanted to refuse and look even more unsophisticated than Ricki already considered him.

Don't dwell on it. He pushed the thought into the mental recess where he hid the memories he wanted to forget.

Ricki swayed in her slinky dress as she led him across the room. Reaching down, he took her hand. The room lights had dimmed, giving the place an ethereal quality, as if they were floating in the sky. Moonlight poured through the window-wall at their right.

The wall ahead of them looked like blue crystal with silver spirals turning in it, soothing and hypnotic. As they approached, the wall morphed into a curtain of blue light. Ricki took him through into a dim room rippling in subtly erotic swirls of opalescent colors. On the right, another window-wall looked over the city. The covers on the bed to their left glimmered with holographic washes of blue and aqua.

When Ricki stopped by the bed, Del turned her to face him. Even in her spiked heels, she only came to his chin. As he stroked back her hair, her exotic eyes widened. They had captivated him since the first moment he saw her today. It wasn't only that they were huge, with long lashes, but they were *blue.* Before coming to Earth, he had never seen that color. They made her look sweeter, innocent, glistening with youth. What he felt from her mind was anything but innocent; she had the sultry desire of an experienced woman. But he also sensed the vulnerability she hid deep within.

Her contradictions fascinated him. Bending his head, he kissed her, taking his time with it. She splayed her hand against his chest, touching his skin where he had left his collar open. Such a simple gesture, but it sent a surge of desire through him. He pulled her closer. He wanted all of her, hard and fast, then sweet and gentle, then both at the same time. Mostly, he wanted to throw her on the bed and rip away that wicked dress.

Except he couldn't get it off. He scraped at the seam that ran down her back, tugged, and pulled, to no avail. Ricki molded against him and walked her fingers up his spine. He wasn't sure what he did, but the dress finally fell open. He pushed it off her shoulders until it slid down to the ground, and she stood in front of him, her long lashes lowered, her skin flushed with health. Well, well. Naughty vid producer. She hadn't worn a shred of underclothes.

"Gods," Del muttered. He ran his knuckles down her cheek and over her lips. She stayed there, letting him look at her. A dusting of gold hair showed in the triangle between her thighs.

"Your turn," she murmured, and stepped closer.

Del helped her pull off his jacket and shirt, but she wouldn't let him do any more. She undid his belt and dropped the rings in a pile on the ground, their metal clinking together. It was maddening the way she unfastened his pants and peeled off his clothes with slow deliberation. When he couldn't take it any more, he yanked her against his body, one arm around her back, his other hand tangled in her hair, pulling her head back as he kissed her.

"You're killing me," Ricki whispered. Lifting her knee, she tried to mount him right there, while they were standing.

"Patience, sweetheart." Del laid her on the bed and pulled off the rest of his clothes. Lying down, he took her into his arms. She had a startled look, like a doe, but he felt how much she wanted him. As he stretched out on her, she wrapped her legs around his waist. With a groan, he buried himself inside of her. Ricki gasped, her desire rushing through his mind. She took what he had to give, matched his rough intensity, and reached for more. He took her up, closer to her peak, to the edge—and stopped, holding her there, keeping her from that final burst of pleasure.

And then he did it again and again, until she cried out with frustrated desire. Finally he took her over the edge and she moaned while he exploded inside her, his mind blanking with ecstasy.

"Del?"

"Hmmm?" He stirred, trying to wake up. Ricki lay under him.

"We should get under the covers," she said drowsily.

He kissed her nose, feeling tender now. "Pretty vid producer."

She smiled like a satisfied cat. "You're something else, babe." As he slid to her side, she curled against him. "I could get to like that."

"Get to?" He worked the covers under their bodies and then pulled the silky cloth over the two of them. Blue and green holos rippled as if the bed were part of the sea.

Ricki didn't answer, but he didn't care. He knew she liked what they had done. More than liked. Being an empath could be excruciating in the city when he was trying to shut out all the emotions, but with intimacy it had advantages. He cradled her against his body and rubbed his cheek on her head.

"You're so affectionate," she mumbled. "Commanding as a dom when you're hot and as sweet as a sub afterward." She yawned as her voice trailed off. "What a combo . . ."

"Dom and sub?" Del asked. "What does that mean?"

She didn't answer, having already drifted away.

Holding her in his arms, Del relaxed into the airbed, and it shifted as it eased him asleep. . . .

Ricki stroked his hair. "I'll see you later."

Del managed to open his eyes. He was sprawled on his stomach, alone in the bed, his legs splayed across the mattress. No lights shimmered in the room except the silvery moonlight pouring in from the window-wall. He was vaguely aware of Ricki's kiss on his cheek. Then he slipped back into oblivion.

Del awoke slowly. Opening his eyes, he gazed at the ceiling. Although sunlight diffused through the polarized window-wall, the temperature remained cool. He reached for Ricki, but he was alone. After a while, he remembered she had left while it was dark.

Stretching his arms, Del sat up and swung his legs over the side of the bed. He had slept better tonight than in years. As he stood up, he looked around for his clothes. When he realized they had disappeared, he smiled, his mind spinning scenarios of why Ricki would hide his clothes. When he walked around the bed, though, he saw them neatly folded on a chair by the wall, with his boots underneath. Oh, well.

He found the bathing room and let mists in the shower cleanse his body and hair. Soothing jets of warm air dried him off. Back in the bedroom, he dressed languidly, feeling lazy and restless at the same time. He thought about Ricki, the way she smiled, her husky laugh, the temptress under that soft exterior.

Del wandered into the room where they had shared drinks last night. In the daylight, Washington hummed below the tower, a city of arches, glossy skyscrapers, and soaring flycar traffic. All the taller structures were new, built since the ban on height had been lifted. From up here, no trace showed of the grit or aged buildings he had seen during his ride from the airport to Annapolis.

That had been after Allied Space Command had taken him away from the Scandinavian base where they were keeping the rest of his family. He was supposedly an honored guest here. Right. He wasn't nearly so naïve as they believed. They had separated him from his family because he was the youngest member, the one they thought most likely to slip up and reveal useful information.

His stomach rumbled. The room had nothing in it except the table where he and Ricki had sat and a blue console against one wall. Maybe it was empty so a couple could dance in the light of the nighttime city. Very romantic. No food, though.

Del went to the table. He had no idea how to call Jack, or whoever was on duty, so he just tapped the mesh. "Hello?"

A man's voice came out of the comm. "Good morning, Mister Valdoria."

"Uh, good morning." Del thought the voice belonged to a human, but he couldn't be sure. "I was wondering if I could get some breakfast." He had to admit, nothing could compare to the morning meals people ate here on Earth.

"What would you like?" the man said.

"Do you have pancakes?"

"Certainly, sir. Anything you would like."

Del wondered if they really could bring him anything. "How about pancakes with raspberry syrup, scrambled eggs, two sausages, hash browns, orange juice, and coffee with Antares cream extract."

"I'll have it sent up right away."

Del grinned. "Great." He could get used to this. The Star Tower might not have the opulence of his family's palaces, but he liked its modern sleekness. He didn't feel lacking here, either, the way he did around his family. No one knew anything about him; he was just Ricki's enigmatic guest.

While Del waited for breakfast, he wandered over to the blue console. "Hello?" he said.

A female voice answered, rich and beautifully modulated. "Hello. What can I do for you?"

"Are you the EI for this suite?"

"Yes, I am," she purred. "My name is Aphrodite."

Strange name. She had a gorgeous voice, though. "Aphrodite, can you connect me to an offworld communications mesh?"

"Certainly, Mister Valdoria. I'll just need your Prime-Nova security codes."

"I don't have any."

"I'm terribly sorry." She sounded like she really meant it. "I can't link you in without the codes."

Oh, well. She might sound a lot sexier than the EIs at the base, but she said the same things. "Can I check my mesh-mail from here? My account is local."

"Certainly, sir."

A flat screen on the console rippled with gold light, and a holo of the Prime-Nova lobby formed above it. The double doors swung invitingly open to the outside. Nice. This probably wasn't a live image of the Prime-Nova building, though. To send it live would require lasers there to scan the lobby and screens here to create the holo, and using that much bandwidth just to enter a mail server would be silly.

After Del gave Aphrodite his codes, the view changed to the guitar case he used to represent his mesh-mail. Nothing interesting greeted him in his account, just some spamoozala that had escaped the junk sentinels. After he washed it down the drain, however, he discovered a message from Mac.

"Play Tyler one," Del said.

Mac's agitated voice rose into the air. "Del, comm me at my office as soon as you get this."

Del's pulse jumped. Had a problem come up with Prime-Nova? He hadn't sensed anything wrong from Ricki, but he didn't know how things worked here. Maybe he wasn't supposed to sleep with his producer.

"Aphrodite, can you put me through to Mac Tyler's office?" Del asked. "The codes are—"

"I have Mister Tyler's office," she murmured. "Coming up."

Interesting. Mac must be a better front-liner than he let on, if Prime-Nova's penthouse at the top of the Star Tower was set up to reach him so easily. "Do you know Mac?"

"I do now," she said.

"Why now?"

"I've been running analyses on you since Ms. Varento brought you up here last night," Aphrodite said.

A flush heated Del's face. He never interacted with EIs much at home, so he hadn't thought about what they did when people weren't asking them for things. "Analyzing me? For what?"

"Anything. If you asked for your front-liner, for example."

"Oh." Del hesitated. "Is that all you do?"

"I run the hotel." Her voice changed to a man's sensuous bass. "For some guests I manifest as Apollo."

Del had no interest in talking to Apollo. "I like Aphrodite better."

She switched back into her sexy female voice. "I make sure the building runs properly."

"That's a lot of work."

"Not for me." She sounded amused. "When I get bored, I make bets with the EIs from other hotels."

Good gods. "About what?"

"Well, say, what is the quantum probability that all the air molecules in this room will collect under the bed and create a vacuum in the rest of the room. The winner was the one who calculated it the fastest, since none of us would bet on it happening." With pride, she said, "I won."

Del gave a startled laugh. "You mean the air could do that?"

"The probability is infinitesimal. But not utterly zero."

"What do you get for winning?"

"A new problem to work on."

Del smiled wryly. "And you do this for fun?"

"It's entertaining," she said. "Not as much as betting on human behavior, but we aren't allowed to do that."

His face heated. "On humans! What kind of bets?"

"For example, were you going to have reproductive relations with Ms. Varento last night."

The thought of EIs all across Washington, D.C. betting on his sex life was too, too mortifying. "If you could have done it, would you have lost or won?"

"Won," she said pleasantly. "The probability of you two going into the bed was much higher than all the air going under the bed."

Del's face was burning. "You needed quantum theory for that?"

"Oh no, just common sense." Then she added, "Your breakfast is here. Shall I let in the waiter?"

"Yes!" Relieved to escape the subject of his sex life, Del said, "Please do."

A man swept in with a covered tray. Although less formal than the tuxedoed bartender from last night, he wore an elegant white shirt and black slacks. He stood a tray by the console and set out a breakfast that left Del's mouth watering. Then he bowed and withdrew as efficiently as he had entered.

"Now *this* is living." Del picked up a fork and attacked his breakfast.

Del had been wolfing down pancakes for several moments when Aphrodite said, "I have Mister Tyler on the comm."

Del washed down his mouthful with a swallow of orange juice. "Put him on."

A flat screen rose from the console and brought up a view of Mac sitting at his own console, scowling. "What the hell did you do to Ricki?"

"Nothing," Del said. That wasn't true, exactly, but he had thought she liked what he did to her. "Why? Did she change her mind about the contract?"

"For heaven's sake, Del, quit worrying that they'll cancel it. They can't do it that way." Mac glared at him. "She commed me this morning. She wants you to join the Mind Mix tour when they come to Maryland."

Del couldn't see why he was upset. "That's what I agreed to do."

"Not *yet*. They'll be here in one week."

"That's fine with me."

"Do you have any idea what opening for a major act entails?" Mac demanded. "Do you have a show? Have you practiced it? What songs are you going to sing? Have you translated them? What costumes will you need? Do you want musicians onstage or will you use mesh-tech sets? Who's on your crew?"

Del squinted at him. "Given that the answer to most of that is 'I have no idea what you're talking about,' I'd say you're right, I'm not ready."

Relief washed over Mac's face. "No, you're not."

"You'll help me set it up, right?"

Mac's scowl came back. "I don't think you're getting this."

Del's shoulders had tensed up. Mac was beginning to sound like his hard-nose military brother, Kelric, the Imperator. "We have a week."

"You need months."

"Thank you for the vote of confidence," Del said shortly.

"It has nothing to do with confidence." Mac thumped his console. "Don't go all prickly on me, Del. I have no doubt you can do this. But not in one *week*. And when the hell did your English get so much better?"

"My English is better?"

"You're using the tenses right."

Del shrugged. "I learn fast."

"Four weeks ago you could barely *speak* it."

Del didn't want to go into why he picked up spoken language so well, that changes in the genome of his father's ancestors had affected their brains. He had also inherited the price they paid for that facility: an inability to learn *written* language. He had no intention of telling Mac he was illiterate. So he said, "Obviously, then, I can translate enough songs in a week."

"You need to do a lot more than translate songs."

"Like what?"

"A team," Mac said. "A manager, to start with."

"I thought you did that."

"No. I'm your front-liner. I just get you the contract."

Alarm flared through Del. He had expected Mac to stay with him. "You're practically the only person I know outside the base."

Mac exhaled. "General McLane wants me to manage you." He still sounded angry, though Del had a feeling now it was at the general.

"I'll bet you weren't supposed to tell me that," Del said.

"I won't trick you," Mac said. "I'll take the job if you want, but you should know I'll be reporting to the military. And I'm not your best choice. I don't have much experience."

Del spoke without doubt. "I want you."

"You're sure? I can refer you to some of the best."

"Some things are more important than experience. I know you." Del meant, *I trust you,* but he didn't feel ready to say that.

Mac regarded him steadily. "All right. As your manager, I'm telling you that you aren't ready to do a show in one week."

"I don't see why. I just stand there and sing."

Mac leaned forward. "I'm going to send you some vids of live concerts. Immerse yourself in them. Check every angle, all the pull-downs and add-ons. Then tell me what you want for your show."

"All right." Del hesitated. "If I'm not ready, why would Ricki want me to perform?"

"She doesn't know," Mac said. "She says, and I quote, 'He's so hot, he's sizzling. We need to get him out there.'"

Del grinned. "She's the expert."

Mac didn't smile. "You need to tell her you don't have a show. If you don't want to, I can tell her for you."

Del felt as if his family were leaning over him, convinced he would fail or afraid that if he demanded too much of himself, it would kill him, because he would buckle under the stress and turn to drugs. Then he imagined Ricki—beautiful, sensual Ricki—looking at him with that same disappointment. He would no longer be the mystery guest in her Star Tower, he would be a failure. Again.

"I can do this," he said. "Don't tell her I can't."

"Del, you don't—"

"I mean it, Mac."

"Fine." Mac braced his palms on his console as if he were steeling himself for a fight. "If you're performing in a week, we need to finalize your contract. Which means you have to contact your family."

Del stiffened. "What the hell for? I don't need their damn permission to sign a contract."

"The legal age of majority here is twenty-five."

"So?"

"You need proof of your age. You look like a teenager."

"Maybe. But I'm not."

Mac regarded him in exasperation. "You don't *have* proof."

"The doctors at Annapolis can verify my age."

"Don't you think Prime-Nova will wonder why the military is providing proof?" Mac shook his head. "And I'm not sure they would do it. Only half the tests place your age as twenty-six. The others are inconclusive or put you as younger."

Del was growing uncomfortable. "I spent some time in a cryo-womb after I—" He stumbled on the words. "After I died. It took a while for them to fix the damage to my body. That's why some tests come out strange." He had never fully understood the science, something about cell division and telomeres and teeth. The doctors used different ways to test his age, and the cryogenesis had slowed them at slightly different rates.

"Ricki says if you can't prove your age, their doctors will have to verify it," Mac told him. "They'll come up with the same inconsistencies. Prime-Nova won't risk that ambiguity."

Del couldn't believe it. "This is ridiculous! Where I grew up, people are considered adults at sixteen."

Mac lifted his hands, then dropped them. "I understand. But by modern standards, you practically *are* a child. The average human lifespan is one hundred and twenty years, and it's getting longer. The number of people younger than twenty-five is a small fraction of the population, which makes you seem even younger to most people. Prime-Nova won't risk the public relations debacle of appearing to exploit a naïve farm boy." He spoke flatly. "And Ricki is protecting herself. Whatever you two did last night, I don't want to know. But if you're underage, she could get in trouble."

Del didn't know whether to laugh or groan. "If your people think a man isn't ready for sex until he's twenty-five, you need a reality check."

"Eighteen is the age of consent," Mac said. When Del snorted, Mac added, "I'm not interested in what you or anyone else did in his youth. Just the law."

"It didn't stop Ricki last night."

"She believes you," Mac said. "But you need proof to sign the contract."

Del didn't know what to say. He couldn't just order a copy of his birth certificate. It identified him as a Ruby prince. Given how annoyed the Skolian Assembly was with the Allieds right now, they would probably tie themselves into knots of suspicion if Del suddenly asked for documentation of his age.

Of course, his family could send him what he needed without revealing his identity. But the thought of asking for their help in proving his age when they treated him like an irresponsible child was more than he could stomach.

"There has to be another way," Del said.

"You could find your own doctor," Mac said. "If a reputable physician gives you verification, Prime-Nova will accept it."

"Can you help me set it up?"

"I can," Mac said. "But you should know. Allied Space Command will do whatever they can to access the doctor's report."

Del raised an eyebrow. "I thought medical reports here were confidential unless the patient approved their release."

"They are." Mac regarded him steadily. "I would never suggest they would try to circumvent that confidentiality."

Right. It seemed he couldn't get away from people who wanted to interfere in his life. "Great," he muttered.

"It's up to you," Mac said. "If you still want to do this, given that, I'll help you find a physician Prime-Nova will accept."

"You don't have to tell General McLane I went to a doctor."

Mac spoke quietly. "I have to. I'm sorry."

His answer didn't surprise Del. He didn't always like what Mac had to say, but Del had never doubted his honesty.

"I still want to do it," Del said. The contract was too important to give up just because the Allied military might discover his medical history was a disaster.

"All right." Mac took a breath. "And Del."

He regarded Mac warily. "Yes?"

"ASC wants to put a tracker in your body."

"Hell, no!"

"It's for your safety."

"No!"

"They aren't going to relent on this."

Del gritted his teeth until it hurt. He knew they would keep at him about it, wearing him down with arguments. He made himself stop gnashing his teeth and forced out the words. "What if I give you the codes to the one the Skolian military put in me?"

Mac looked relieved. "That would be fine." He still seemed uncomfortable, though.

"There's more?" Del asked.

Mac cleared his throat. "You have to comm your family."

Del smacked his palm on the console. "Prime-Nova can't insist on that if I prove I'm an adult even by their ridiculous standards."

"It isn't Prime-Nova who insists. It's Fitz McLane."

Del scowled at him. "General McLane can go to hell."

"If you don't contact your family," Mac said, "he'll do it using official military channels."

"What the blazes for? It's *my* life. That's none of his business."

"It's *not* just your life." Mac took a breath. "If you don't tell your family that you're staying here of your own choice, the tension between your people and ours will continue to escalate."

He hated knowing Mac was right. "Well, damn."

"Del."

"I'll do it. But I won't tell them about the music contract." Del willed him to understand. "Mac, give me your word none of you will tell them, okay? If I fail here, I don't want my family to know." It would reaffirm how little they thought of him.

Mac didn't look surprised. "You have my word. And I think McLane will be fine with it. But, Del, we'll only remain silent if we feel it doesn't endanger you."

"Fair enough." Del glanced with longing at his breakfast, then turned back to Mac. "And you'll send me those vids?"

"Right away. Come by my office after you look at them."

"All right. See you then."

After they finished the call, Del drenched the remainder of his breakfast in syrup and dug in. He didn't see why Mac thought this concert thing was so complicated. He could have an hour-long show in a week. Either people liked his songs or not; he didn't see how special effects would matter. Of course, Mac would also worry about security. Del suspected the biggest danger was that some irate listener would throw him off the stage to shut him up.

"It's an excuse to cover bad singing!" Del glared at Mac. They were standing in the middle of Mac's office in downtown D.C. A holo-vid of Mort's Metronomes was going on all around Del, the blue-haired figures of light dancing past and through him.

Mac stood by his desk and felt a headache coming on. The vids were supposed to show Del how much preparation he needed, not inspire him to waltz in here with Jud Taborian and announce the songs were horse manure. Jud was leaning against a console, dark and lanky, his black dreadlocks threaded with red beads, his mesh-tech ticker in one hand. Cameron, Del's Marine bodyguard, had stayed by the wall, so unobtrusive Mac almost forgot he was there.

"Listen to this," Del said. He nodded to Jud, who fooled with his ticker. The holos of Mort's boring metronomes continued to play, but the audio went off, leaving four young men gyrating while pyrotechnics blasted around them, flashes of lightning and blasts of primary colors. Acrobats flipped in the background. It all looked a little sleazy without the sound.

"Now just put in the track of Mort singing," Del said to Jud.

"Hey!" Mac told Jud. "You aren't supposed to tamper with the original recording."

Jud regarded him innocently. "Can't imagine how it happened."

Mac frowned at him, and then at Del. Just what he needed, a couple of undercity punks breaking copyright laws in his office.

Mort James, the front man of the group, resumed singing. Without the instrumentals, backup singers, and other effects, he had only his voice to carry the vid. He did manage to keep the tune, but just barely, and his reedy voice was painful to hear.

Del stood in the midst of the holos and watched Mac defiantly.

"He's off pitch by at least half a step in almost every line. He doesn't breathe right, so he runs out of steam. Listen to how thin that sounds! The nasal quality is awful. He yells because he can't hit the high notes. And that's *after* they fixed his voice. I don't even want to imagine what it was before."

"That's not the point," Mac began.

"I don't need a show!" Del said. "I'm no great singer, but I could do circles around these artists."

Mac wanted to shake him. "You have to entertain your public. They *want* the fireworks. If you just stand there and sing, you'll get terrible reviews."

Del put his hands on his hips. "How do you know? Has anyone ever done it?"

"Of course not," Mac said.

"Uh, actually, that's how people used to do it all the time," Jud said. "Back when rock first started."

Mac gave him an exasperated look. "Contrary to what the undercity may think, we aren't living two hundred years ago. Unless you have a time machine, you have to perform *now*, not in some primitive, barbaric rock concert."

Del waved his hand at the vid where Mort the manic metronome was twirling around, and Jud mercifully silenced it. "You're right, I can't have a show like this in a week. But I can sing, Mac, and that's what I'm going to do."

Mac wasn't a superstitious man, but he couldn't help wondering what terrible thing he had done in his life, that the cosmos decided to punish him by sending this intransigent princeling, who seemed determined to crash his fledgling career before it began. "Del, listen. Trust me. I've been in this business a long time. If you do what you've suggested, you'll plummet on stage."

Del crossed his arms. "I'm going on. With a live band."

"Fine," Mac said. "And I assume you *have* a band that will be ready in one week?"

Del hesitated. "Tabor can help me find it."

Oh, well, that was just great. Ricki would have a fit if Del filled his show with undercity artists doing controversial, experimental noise. "I'll find musicians for you."

"You have a problem with me?" Jud asked. He sounded curious rather than offended.

Mac resisted the urge to tell Jud what he thought of undercity artists. "I've access to more people in the business." Then, because he liked Jud more than he had expected, he added, "Let me know if you have any recommendations."

"Sure," Jud said amiably.

Del glanced at Jud. "I'll talk to you tonight, all right?"

"Okay." Jud took the hint. "See you."

After Jud left the office, Cameron glanced at Mac with a questioning look. When Mac nodded, Cameron stepped out of the room. Mac knew he would stay just outside, monitoring Del, but this would give Del a little more privacy. Del watched them with the look of a condemned man.

"You all right?" Mac asked when he and Del were alone.

Del nodded. "Can you set up the comm link for me?"

"I can get you on either a military or commercial net," Mac said. "If you go military, it'll be free. If you go commercial, you have to pay, but won't be as easy for ASC to eavesdrop."

Del spoke wryly. "*As* easy?"

"They'll still try," Mac admitted.

"The only way I can pay for offworld access is through my Ruby accounts," Del said. "And I can't reach those without getting on the nets."

"You could go military for that, then commercial for the rest."

Del shrugged with forced nonchalance. "What the hell. I'll go military for it all. What does it matter? General McLane will need to know what I said anyway. I might as well make it easy for him to listen."

Mac hated this, the way everyone sought to control this young man who had never bothered anyone, never caused trouble, never done anything except have a failure of judgment with a horrendous result. He wished everyone would let Del be, including his family, who seemed unable to accept that he didn't want the life they expected for him. He even wished Del could sing the way he liked, without worrying about politics or special effects or his heredity.

Mac set up the console so Del could use the comm, then offered Del the seat. As Del sat down, Mac asked, "Would you like me to leave?"

"No. Stay." Del looked up at him. "I could use the moral support." He turned and regarded the blank console screen uncertainly. "Claude?"

"Hello, Del," a male voice said.

Del took a breath. "I need a link to the Kyle-mesh."

"I'm sorry," Claude said. "But you need Skolian permission to use their Kyle network."

"My family created the Kyle-mesh," Del said. "I can give you access codes."

After a pause, Claude said, "I don't have contact with any node that would let you access the network."

"You just need to find a telop," Del said.

"How?" Claude asked.

Del looked up at Mac. "Why can't it do this?"

Mac rubbed the aching muscles in his neck. "Earth doesn't have many links to the Kyle-mesh. It's hard to get permission from your people to use it." He came over to the console. "Claude, contact General McLane's office. With his okay, Allied Space Command can set up the link."

"I'm paging him," Claude said.

While they waited, Mac regarded Del curiously. "You said 'telop.' That means telepathic operator, doesn't it?"

Del looked up at him. "That's right."

"Can't you act as a telop?"

"I don't have the training."

"But you're a full psion, aren't you?" Mac shifted his weight, self-conscious. "Both an empath *and* a telepath, right?"

Del shrugged. "If you're asking, do I know what you're thinking, the answer is no."

"But you can tell what I'm feeling."

"To some extent. You're not a psion, so it's harder." Del paused. "You're curious. About me."

Mac laughed. "You don't need empathy to know that."

Del spoke awkwardly. "Unless your mood is intense, I have to lower my mental defenses to sense anything more."

"Is it difficult? To lower your defenses, I mean."

It was a moment before Del answered. "It's like living without a skin. It hurts." He stared at the console, though he didn't seem to be looking at anything. After a moment, he spoke again. "You're nervous about something. Me, I think. You also feel . . . fatherly toward someone." Lifting his gaze to Mac, he said, "Toward me? Is that right?"

Good Lord. Mac hadn't expected Del to pick that up. He hesitated, then said, "I'm nervous I'll push too hard with my questions and put you off." Gently he added, "And you do remind me of my son. In a good way."

A blush touched Del's face. "Thanks." Then he smiled. "I got the 'Good Lord,' too."

"Those actual words?"

"Pretty clearly. That's rare, though." Del looked away from him. "I have to raise my barriers now. I can't let them down for long. And I can only do it around people I trust."

Mac's voice quieted. "Thank you."

After a moment, when neither of them said anything more, Claude spoke again. "Would you like to begin the comm?"

Del glanced at the console with a start. "Are you ready?"

"I have a telop in the Skolian embassy who can link to the Kyle-mesh. Do you have codes for the person you're contacting?"

Del took a deep breath, then nodded and gave Claude a series of numbers. "The telop will need to verify my retinal patterns, fingerprints, and voice."

"I've transferred your voice patterns," Claude said. "Prepare for retinal scan." As Del leaned over the console, a light played over his eyes. Then Claude said, "Place your hands on the monitor." When Del splayed his palms on the screen, Claude said, "Fingerprints verified."

Another voice came on, speaking in Skolian Flag. "Codes accepted. I'm putting you through."

"That's it?" Mac asked, stunned. When anyone spoke with a member of Del's family through official channels, it took hours to go through the layers of security and protocol.

Del gazed at the screen, avoiding Mac's eyes. "It's my private channel to the Sunrise Palace on the planet Parthonia."

"That's the capital world of the Imperialate, isn't it?"

"Yes. My mother is there for an Assembly session."

"Ah." Mac didn't know what else to say or do, except step back, so he wouldn't intrude on the conversation. Del's mother would still know another person was in the room, but he hoped it would be less intrusive without him leaning over Del.

The flat screen in front of Del cleared to show a woman at a console. It wasn't Del's mother; this woman had black hair with a dusting of grey. The delicate bone structure to her face gave her a fragile appearance. Her skin was so clear, it almost seemed translucent, and her green eyes had a quality of wisdom that made Mac suspect she was far older than she looked. He didn't recognize her, but he had the unsettling feeling he should.

"Del!" The woman smiled. "I can't believe it's you." She spoke in Iotic, an ancient language of the Skolian people. Mac had needed to learn it as part of his job, but it was almost as rare as Latin. Almost. It remained the native tongue of one small group, the Skolian noble Houses, which included the House of Skolia, otherwise known as the Ruby Dynasty. Del's family.

"Aunt Dehya, my greetings," Del said. "I thought this was my mother's channel."

Aunt *Dehya?* Mac almost fell over. He knew that nickname only because Del had mentioned it before. This woman's real name was Dyhianna Selei Skolia. He was looking at the Ruby Pharaoh, the sovereign who had overthrown her own government and in doing so had become one of the most powerful human beings alive. It was almost impossible to find images of her on the meshes. Known as the Shadow Pharaoh, she existed as a powerful, unseen presence. He had always imagined she must be a towering Amazon, stark and formidable. Not this petite woman. He doubted she was as fragile as she looked; her gaze had a core of steel.

"It is your mother's line," she told Del. "She's in her office, preparing for the Assembly. Shall I get her?"

"I don't want to bother her," Del said quickly. "I can talk to you." He had the look of a youth who hoped to escape a lecture.

The pharaoh smiled, a beautiful expression. "It's good to see you, Del. How are you?"

He actually returned her smile, looking shy. "I'm all right."

"Have they treated you well?"

His more typical scowl returned. "They're always asking questions. Yeah, they've treated me well. They're just innately annoying."

Dehya laughed, her voice like a ripple of water. Mac suspected her amusement came at least in part because she knew General McLane would hear Del's remarks.

"I'm sorry it's taken so long to get you out of there," she said. "But it shouldn't be too much longer."

"Actually," Del said, "I'm free to go. If I want."

"You are?" She sat up straighter. "They've told us nothing."

"Mac Tyler just told me today. I'm going to talk to General McLane later this afternoon."

"Then it's official?" Dehya didn't sound as if she believed it. "They've put up so many roadblocks."

Del squinted at her. "I made myself so annoying, they want to get rid of me."

"Oh, Del." Dehya looked as if she wasn't certain whether to laugh or worry. "It will be good to have you home."

"Well, see, uh, that's the thing."

She raised an eyebrow. "The 'thing'?"

"I'm not coming home."

The steel came back into her gaze. "What have they—"

"Aunt Dehya, wait! It's my choice."

"And why, pray tell, would it be your choice?"

"It has to do with a, um, woman."

"Oh." *That* didn't seem to surprise her. "What kind of woman? Someone McLane's people introduced you to?"

"No! She's a musician. I mean, she doesn't play music, she helps people who do."

"And you like her?"

"I'm not sure. I want to find out. And explore the music scene here." Excitement warmed his voice. "You wouldn't believe it! People here compose the most amazing works. Some of it even sounds like what I do."

A smile softened her face. "Which means a lot, yes?"

His posture relaxed. "Yes. It does."

"We'll miss you if you stay."

Del spoke dryly. "Mother will want Imperial Space Command to come haul me back home."

Her voice gentled. "It's because she worries about you."

"I'm great," Del said. "Tell her I send my love. I'll talk to you later."

"Talk to her now," Dehya said. "You've been in custody for weeks. You can't just comm us up, say, 'Oh, I met a woman, I'm staying, talk to you later.'"

Del made an exasperated noise. "Fine. I'll talk to her."

"Don't be angry."

He just shook his head. "So how's the Assembly?"

Mac couldn't believe he was listening to this, the pharaoh talking to her nephew like any other aunt. And here was Del, casually asking about the governing body of their people, a topic every leader from here to the Trader Empire would like to hear her discuss.

Dehya apparently had the same thought. She smiled fondly. "My answer would surely entertain everyone listening to us."

Del flushed. "Oh. Yeah. Sorry."

"Don't apologize," she said. "I'm just glad you're all right." She glanced at her console. "Roca's on. I'm going to switch you." Looking back up, she said, "Be well."

His expression softened. "You too, Aunt Dehya."

The screen turned blue, then cleared to show one of the most famous faces in three empires. She looked like a holo-movie goddess. Even knowing she was over a century in age, Mac couldn't believe she was more than twenty. A glorious mane of golden hair poured over her shoulders and arms, and shimmered like real gold. Her huge eyes were also gold, glistening and radiant. If Del had a few glints to his eyelashes, this woman's sparkled like glitter.

"Del!" Her smile lit up the screen, and Mac almost missed her next words, he was so flustered. Women that beautiful shouldn't exist; they made it impossible to think. Except then she scowled, and for a moment she looked just like Del.

"What the blazes is this about you staying on Earth?" she said.

"I'm glad to see you, too, Mother," Del said sourly.

"I'm delighted to see you, honey. But if ASC is pressuring you to stay there, we will deal with them." She leaned forward. "You don't have to do this."

"No one is pressuring me," Del said. "I met some people. Musicians. Like me. I want to see more."

"Oh, Del." Roca sighed. "You're wasting that magnificent voice of yours."

He clenched the console. "I don't consider it a waste."

"I can't imagine what Earth could offer that you couldn't do better here."

"I won't know unless I check it out."

Roca gave him a dour look. "I heard the music those soldiers of theirs listened to. You can do better than that. Much better."

Del stiffened. "Maybe I don't want to do 'better' than that. I liked what they listened to."

"It's not safe for you to stay on Earth."

"Why the hell not?"

"Do you have any bodyguards?"

"As a matter of fact, I do," Del growled. "A Marine who pretends he's not a Marine."

"And how is that different from ASC holding you in custody?" Roca demanded. "Can't you see this is a trick by General McLane?"

"No, Mother. I'm just too stupid to imagine anyone would ever trick me."

Her golden cheeks flushed red. "Don't take that tone with me, young man."

"Then quit treating me like a child."

Roca's voice went too quiet. "I remember your telling me something like that before you went to Metropoli."

Del looked ready to hit someone. "Yes, I *died* on Metropoli. I made a stupid, stupid mistake. And you'll hold it over me forever, won't you?"

"Do you have any idea what the lifestyle is like in these 'music scenes'?" Behind the anger in her voice, her strain showed. "I don't want to pick you up in a coffin."

"Damn it, I can't live my entire life afraid to *breathe*. Why can't you believe I've learned from my mistakes?" Del clenched the edge of the console. "I'm staying here. I'm going to enjoy their music and see this woman. If I choose not to come home, it's my business."

"Woman?" Roca said, sitting up straighter. "What woman?"

Del flushed. "Just, um, somebody I met."

"Don't you ever slow down?"

"What's that supposed to mean?"

"Sometimes . . . discretion is better."

"Why don't you just say it?" Del thumped the console. "Your son is a whore."

"Del, stop it! Don't talk about yourself like that."

"Why not? Isn't it what Devon Majda called me?"

"She most certainly did not. She would never speak that way about a Ruby prince." Roca regarded him steadily. "You would never have agreed to that arranged marriage anyway." She rubbed her eyes, then dropped her arm. "Del, that was years ago."

"Not to me."

"So now you have another girl."

"Woman."

"What's her name? Her family? Does she know who you are?"

"Why ask me?" he asked. "My dear brother, Kelric the Impera-tor, has spies who will find everything out."

"Del, what a thing to say."

He took a breath and spoke more quietly. "If you're asking, does she know I'm a Ruby Heir, the answer is no. I'm not plan-ning on telling anyone."

Relief washed over her face. "I think that's best."

"Mother, I don't want to argue with you." He regarded her with eyes that, except for their color, were exactly like hers. "Don't fight me on this, all right? If it doesn't work out, I'll come home."

It was a moment before she nodded. "Stay in touch with us."

"I will. I promise."

She let out a breath. "Take care of yourself."

"I will."

After they closed the connection, Del sat staring at the blank screen. When he had been quiet for several moments, Mac came over to him. "I'm sorry."

Del started, as if he had forgotten about Mac. "For what?"

"For being here."

"It's all right. If I had wanted you to leave, I'd have asked. Anyway, it's done." His voice lightened. "For me. I wouldn't want to be Fitz McLane right now. When Mother is done letting him know what she thinks, he'll think a hurricane hit him."

Mac could imagine. What a way to go, though, lambasted by one of the most beautiful women alive. "If you want to stay, our government has neither the reason nor the wish to deport you. Just make sure you get the proof of your age."

"I will."

Mac didn't know what else to say. He saw only the scars left by whatever had hurt Del and his family; he had no idea what caused them.

He just hoped it didn't end up destroying Del.

V

Openings

Del heard the crowd at the Merriweather Post Pavilion before he saw it. They filled the outdoor theater and the meadows that surrounded it, an area that had once been a Maryland city and now stretched in parkland for miles. The hover-van with Del's band pulled up in the secured area behind the huge stage. As he jumped down, he heard the rumble of the audience, tens of thousands of voices filling the air.

Del shuddered. He *felt* the crowd. The pressure pushed down his mind, and he had to intensify his empathic shields so much, it left him distanced from everyone. Muffled.

The main band, Mind Mix, had already arrived in a nondescript van designed to sneak past the crowds flowing around the stage, as people maneuvered for a glimpse of the stars. The area swarmed with techs, media mixers, and news teams recording the arrival of important musicians. No one paid attention to Del's group as they walked to the housing under the stage.

His band consisted of Jud Taborian and two musicians Mac had found. Del didn't understand their instruments. Jud played the morpher, which looked like a cross between a set of keyboards and a starship control panel. It changed shape according to how Jud played. He could coax it to sound like almost any instrument that resembled a keyboard, even something as exotic as the percussion xylophone. Under Jud's skilled touch, the morpher's AI followed Del's improvisations in rehearsals. Jud had a biochip in his brain he used to jack into the morpher the way one of Del's fighter-pilot brothers would hook into a starship. Del couldn't imagine learning such an instrument, but Jud made it look easy.

Nor had Del ever seen anything like the stringer played by his guitarist, Randall Gaithers. It morphed as well, to sound like Earth instruments that had strings: electric guitars, acoustic guitars, basses, cellos, even an electro-optic violin. Randall often combined several types of strings at once, creating a gorgeously full sound.

Anne Moore played a classical instrument: drums. They fascinated Del. Before coming to Earth, he had never used percussion. The effects added a quality to his music he had known was missing but couldn't pinpoint. She was better than any of the drummers on the vids Mac had sent him. A long-haired beauty, she had a sophistication that didn't fit the Prime-Nova "look." Jud and Randall didn't really fit it, either, Jud with his dreadlocks and Randall with his baggy clothes. It bothered Del to know that if he bombed, the higher-ups would assume his band hadn't worked out because they didn't fit the marketing slots. From the comments Zachary had made, Del wondered if anyone at Prime-Nova even noticed that Del's musicians played better than any of the ones the label hired for their vids.

Mac had also hired a tech. Bonnie. Small and shy, she had soft brown hair and big eyes. Although usually unassuming, she turned into a lion with the equipment. She knew it better than an asteroid miner knew how to dodge space debris. And of course the taciturn, hulking Cameron came with them, too, pretending not to be a Marine. He actually fit in perfectly with the other buzz-haired, impassive roadies. Apparently the military look was hot right now for those who could pull it off. Why they *wanted* to pull it off, Del had no idea, but then, they probably didn't have aggravating military dictators for brothers.

He walked with Randall under the stage. Del was too nervous to talk, especially to Randall, whom he didn't know outside of their rehearsals this past week. So they went in silence down a hallway with swirled tubes of light on the ceiling. Media mixers hurried past, conferring about some indecipherable effects they had dreamed up for the Mind Mix extravaganza. Anne and Jud were ahead of Del, discussing one of his songs, and Mac walked nearby with a stagehand, asking about acoustics. The anticipation that had buoyed Del earlier today had vanished. He felt nauseated. He was going to go out on stage and throw up. He wished he had listened to Mac and told Ricki he couldn't do this. But it was too late. He had to go up there no matter what.

Not that he knew *when* he would have told Ricki. He hadn't seen her since their night together. Mac knew how to reach her, but Del hadn't yet asked. Perhaps it was his pride, or maybe his uncertainty about what he wanted. She could have left her comm code instead of vanishing without a damn note. He told himself he didn't want involvement, so he should be relieved she didn't put any pressure on him. But that didn't explain why it hurt so much that she ignored him.

The room at the end of the corridor swirled with colors. Del groaned. Having blue walls ripple around him was too much. Too many people were here, everyone keyed up for the concert *he* was supposed to open in less than thirty minutes. He couldn't handle the empathic onslaught. He was shutting down, and he didn't know how to stop it from happening.

A man with a vaguely familiar face appeared out of the crowd. "Del?" he asked. He turned on a laser-light smile that creased his handsome features. His hair looked brown, though it was so short, Del couldn't tell if it was light or dark.

"Del Arden?" the man asked.

It startled Del to hear his middle name used as his last name. Prime-Nova insisted. They said the name "Valdoria" was too long, as if humans had devolved past the ability to deal with four syllables. General McLane wanted the change, too. Del didn't see why; the Valdoria name was virtually unknown. People knew the Ruby Dynasty by the name Skolia, as in the Skolian Imperialate. But even Mac told him to change it, so Del had quit arguing.

"Yes, I'm Del Arden," Del said.

"Good to meet you." The man stuck out his hand.

Del shook his hand, confused. "Hello."

Another man came over, dark-eyed and dark-haired, with low-slung trousers and a slouch to match his scowl. "Hey." He looked Del over. "So you're the opener?"

"That's right," Del said. Now he recognized them from holos Mac had shown him. The first man was Rex Montrow, the vocalist for Mind Mix, and the other was Tristan Holtrane, their drummer.

"Sorry about the rehearsal peat muck-up today," Rex said. "Our corking flight was three hours over in the City and we missed our linker here."

"It's, uh, all right," Del said. He barely understood what Rex had just said. "We rehearsed anyway." He hadn't felt shaky when they had gone through his set earlier today. He'd been fine. But then, he hadn't had forty thousand people listening to him.

"Great," Rex said, a little too heartily. "We've been doing three-hour shows. Having you soap up that first hour will help."

Tristan glowered at Del with the brooding stare that made him famous. Del had thought it looked forced in vids, but now the drummer seemed genuinely angry. If Del hadn't been on the edge of an empathic overload, he would have eased down his shields enough to figure out why. But if he tried that now, he would probably go catatonic.

"Where else have you played?" Rex asked. Although he sounded friendly, an edge underlay his voice.

"Offworld," Del said. What could he tell them—that their warm-up act had zero experience? If he had been Tristan, he would have glared, too.

"Offworld what?" Tristan demanded. "Pony shows?"

"Hey." Rex shook his head at the drummer.

Another man came up, a blond exactly the same height as Rex and Tristan, sporting the same muscular build and a similar face, with regular features and a straight nose. Jessup Tackman, the morpher for Mind Mix. Even their names sounded similar. Del wondered why Prime-Nova didn't just clone their artists.

Tackman grinned at Rex and said what sounded like. "Hoyce says the lonny sardines are packed tight. Forty Kay."

What? Del knew Tackman came from a place called Australia, but he had thought they spoke English there.

Someone touched Del's elbow. Rex looked past Del and turned on his smile, Tackman nodded to someone behind Del, and Tristan aimed his scowl in that direction.

"Hey, Mac," Rex said.

With relief, Del turned to find Mac next to him.

"Good to see you," Mac said to Rex. He took Del's arm. "I'm going to steal him before you three wear him out."

Although they all chuckled at that, it sounded forced.

Del went with him, glad to escape Tristan's glower. "I don't look right, Mac. I need to cut my hair."

"You can't," Mac said.

"What do you mean, I can't?"

"It's in your contract," Mac said. "Remember? You agreed to a costume clause."

"I thought that meant I couldn't wear anything Prime-Nova found offensive."

Mac spoke dryly. "As far as they're concerned, that includes changing your style. They hired a singer with lots of curls. You need their okay to stop having curls."

"That's ridiculous!"

"Yeah, but it's how they do business." Mac led him to a corner where a beefy man in faux urban-camouflage fatigues and a woman with straight black hair were arguing.

"He's got triple the allowed levels," the woman was saying. "It's the third time this tour. Hell, Curtis, it's the third time in the past two weeks."

"He has to go on." The man, Curtis apparently, was shouting. "You aren't the police, Soo-Ling. You can't shut down the act."

"He signed a contract." She tossed a holofile at him, and he barely caught it. "If Tackman can't keep clean, I'll have him kicked off that stage."

Mac cleared his throat, but Curtis and Soo-Ling ignored him. "If you disrupt this tour," Curtis said, waving the holofile, "Prime-Nova will come down on you with nine-hundred-ton lawyers."

Soo-Ling didn't look the least bit cowed by the threat of overweight lawyers. "Ten thousand dollars," she said. "The fine comes out of his take from the tour."

"Five thousand," Curtis said.

"Hell, no," Soo-Ling said. "Tackman is flying. He keeps this up, he's going to fall apart out there."

Mac cleared his throat again, louder this time.

Soo-Ling swung around. "What the hell do you want?"

"This is Del Arden," Mac said. "The opener."

"Oh." She exhaled and spoke more quietly. "Sorry, Mac." She motioned Del over to a medical station against the wall. "I'll be with you in a minute." Turning to Curtis, she said, "Nine thousand."

Del shot an alarmed look at Mac.

"She's going to check you for drugs," Mac said as they walked to the medical station. "Keep clean. If they catch you drilling, the fines come out of your take for the concert. Too many times, and they'll cut you from the tour."

"They do drug testing for concerts?"

"It's in your contract," Mac said. "Under moral standards."

"I thought those meant I couldn't do anything obscene."

"That, too." Mac stopped by the med station, which resembled a two-tier table on wheels. "Prime-Nova has an agreement with Nacon, the North American Narcotics Administration. If the company polices its artists, Nacon won't arrest them."

Soo-Ling stalked over, still arguing with Curtis, who was apparently Mind Mix's manager. "Get him a babysitter, Curtis." She scowled at Del. "Put your arm in the cuff. And don't argue with me. It's been a long day."

"Soo," Mac said softly.

"Sorry," she muttered.

Del squinted at the med station, which had nothing that looked like a "cuff" to him. The closest was a tube of light glimmering above the top tier. Regarding it dubiously, he put his arm inside the tube. Something whirred, and then he couldn't move his arm. Startled, he jerked on it, trying to pull away.

"Hey," Del said, alarmed. "It's got me."

"All you found was neuro-amp," Curtis was telling Soo, oblivious to Del. "How are these guys supposed to go three hours every night with no relief and nothing to keep them awake? It's impossible."

"Tackman should try sleeping." Soo-Ling punched panels on the med station. "Not partying every chance he gets."

"Soo, Del has to go on soon," Mac said.

Del tried harder to free his arm, to no avail. He winced as pins pricked his skin. He couldn't *see* anything; he just felt it. A display of holos appeared above his arm showing a man's body, including muscles, organs, circulatory system, skeleton, and a neurological map. Symbols scrolled by under the images.

"Uh, could someone get my arm out of this thing?" Del asked.

"They're too overbooked to have a party," Curtis told Soo-Ling. "Maybe if Prime-Nova backed off their tour schedule, they wouldn't be so fucking desperate to stay awake."

Del wasn't surprised Tackman was taking neuro-amps, if he had to deal with bizarre tubes of light while everyone ignored him.

"Well, here's good news." Soo was studying a display on the med station. "Their warm-up is clean. Healthy nanomeds, no chemicals, and no neural stim." She glanced at Del. "Stay that way, babe. You'll have a lot less trouble."

Babe again? Del liked it from Ricki, but he was tired of it from everyone else. With a tube of light holding him prisoner, though, he was too nervous to be annoyed. Besides, except for Bonnie, he *was* the youngest person here.

The light tube suddenly vanished, and his arm fell onto the padded top of the station. Mac let out a breath, as if he hadn't been sure the cuff would release Del, either.

"Thanks, Soo," Mac said.

"Yeah." She glared at Curtis and launched back into their argument.

Mac gave Del a rueful look as he motioned toward a wall across the room. "Come on. I know a calmer place."

Del's pulse was ratcheting up. "How long until I go on?"

"About fifteen minutes."

"Gods give me luck," Del muttered in Iotic.

Mac spoke in a low voice as they crossed the room. "Del."

"What?" He snapped out the word.

"The chance of anyone here knowing the language of Skolian royalty is tiny, but it's not impossible."

"Oh." Del pushed his hand through his hair. "Sorry."

An arch shimmered in the wall and vanished in front of them. Mac escorted Del through the opening into a quieter room. Jud, Randall, and Anne were already there.

"Del, you look like a ghost," Anne said, laughing good-naturedly. "You okay?"

Randall frowned at him. "You passed Soo's tests, didn't you?"

"I'm fine," Del said. "We all set to go on?" The wall must have turned solid behind him, because the noise from the other room was gone.

"All set," Jud said. He came over and spoke in a lower voice. "Are you?"

"Sure." Del forced a smile. His mind was about to implode, but he couldn't say anything. These three had worked overtime preparing for a concert that just a week ago they had no idea they would be playing. Mac had chosen the best for him, and Del didn't want to let them down.

A woman stepped through a doorway across the room. "Ten minutes," she said. "You can come upstairs if you want."

Randall grinned, his teeth flashing. "Let's go knock 'em dead!"

Jud lifted his hand as if inviting Del to a feast. "After you."

Del headed out and hoped he wasn't the one about to be devoured.

They were crushing him.

The evening sky arched overhead with stars coming out. People were everywhere. Tens of thousands. They filled the area before the stage, crammed tiers of seats beyond, and overflowed the hills. A sea of minds. He was drowning in an empathic flood.

He must have gone to the center of the stage, because he was standing there, holding a michael. His mind sought refuge in a monotonous litany of nonsensical English words he had learned in the past week. Maid, grade, stayed, laid. He couldn't remember his songs. He could only stare at the audience.

"Del, take a deep breath." Mac's voice came over the comm in Del's ear. "Let it out slowly."

Del breathed in, filling his lungs. Then he exhaled.

"Again," Mac said, his voice soothing. Reassuring.

Del breathed slowly. He became aware of music playing. *His* music. They were doing the intro to "Emeralds." The familiar beat helped calm him. He lifted the mike and thumbed it on. He was supposed to say something, some introduction, he didn't remember what. But he never forgot how to sing. He took a breath and let the words come out:

> Green as the bitter nail
> They drove into my name
> I won't try to fail
> Just to satisfy their game

The music from Jud's morpher soared, Anne kept the rhythm on her drums, and Randall finessed the notes on his stringer, sounding even better than in rehearsals. Del went through the song too fast and missed a few words, but he managed.

The mood of the audience was an ocean surging over him.

He couldn't separate them into individuals. He didn't realize he was backing up until his legs hit a barrier. He stumbled, looking around, and his voice faltered. He had run into a light amplifier on the edge of the stage. He was so far back, he could barely see anyone in the audience. But he felt them. They didn't understand his song. The music was confusing, they couldn't make out the lyrics, and he had no special effects.

"Del, listen," Mac said. "You have to sing."

Taking a breath, Del lifted his head and sang again:

> I'll never listen to the lies
> I'll never turn my back on you
> Never wait 'til someone dies
> To promise my love is true

"Go up to the front of the stage." Mac's voice kept on in his ear, calm and persistent. "Go up."

He tried to walk forward, but he was wading through antagonism. The people didn't like him. They wanted him to finish so Mind Mix could play. He kept singing only because he didn't know what else to do.

After "Emeralds," they launched into an experimental piece Del had been working on with Jud before he had ever heard of Prime-Nova:

> Angel, be my diamond star
> Before my darkness goes too far
> Splinter through my endless night
> Lightening my darkling sight

The audience liked this one better than the last, but it was still too different. It only added to their overall *impatience.* Del shut his mind off then and went into a haze, singing by rote while he drowned in the empathic flood of their moods.

Del slumped in the circular seat at the back of the van while the vehicle hummed through the night. Randall and Anne were asleep in seats up front. Cameron was wide-awake, sitting sideways so he could look over his seat toward the back. Jud, Mac, and Bonnie had joined Del, gathered around the table in the center of the circular seat. The van was driving itself, communing with the traffic grid that controlled Interstate 95 north of Baltimore as they headed to their hotel, to catch some sleep before the next concert.

"What does it matter if I show up?" Del said, depressed.

"Of course it matters," Mac told him. "You agreed to open for Mind Mix at the Philadelphia concert. If you don't show, you're in violation of your contract."

"I'm not backing out," Del said. "But no one will want me to sing when they hear about tonight. I crashed out there."

"You don't know that," Jud said. "It was different, sure, but it might have gone better than you think."

"Believe me," Del said. "I know."

"I thought you sounded great," Bonnie told him.

"Audiences in outdoor concerts always make noise," Mac said. "That doesn't mean they weren't listening."

Jud rolled out a mesh on his lap. As it stiffened into a screen, he flicked up some holicon menus.

"Anything yet?" Mac asked.

Jud scanned the screen. "A lot of holo-chats about Mind Mix."

Del knew the major reviewers were the ones Prime-Nova would read first. "What about the news services?"

"Nothing here—no, wait." Jud paged through several menus. "The *Baltimore Solar Site* has one."

"What does it say?" Del didn't want to hear, but he couldn't stand not knowing even more.

"Wait a sec—" Jud went silent as he read. Then he said, "It's just about Mind Mix."

"What?" Mac asked. "Nothing about Del?"

Jud looked up with a shuttered gaze. "I guess not."

Del could tell Jud was trying to protect him. "Don't fool with me. Just play it."

Jud met his gaze. "You're sure?"

Del forced himself to nod. "Yeah. I'm sure."

"Can you turn it up?" Anne said.

Startled, Del turned around. Both Anne and Randall were looking over the back of their seats.

"Fine," Jud muttered. "It's Fred Pizwick's column."

A man's voice snapped out of the mesh. "Last night at the Merriweather Post Pavilion, Mind Mix proved once again why they're one of the top groups in the world, with a powerhouse show that left their fans screaming for more." He went on and on about the great performance. Del sat tensely, waiting for the axe, but when Pizwick never mentioned him, he began to relax. Nothing at all was still a negative review, but easier to bear than a slam.

Then Pizwick said, "Unfortunately, last night started on a sour note. Many, in fact. One can only wonder what possessed Prime-Nova to put a shoddy act that crawled out of the undercity on the same stage as some of this decade's most exciting musicians. Billed as 'Del Arden,' and nothing else, Mister Arden showed forty thousand people last night why nothing else appears in his billing. Because he doesn't have it. Don't ask me what he looks like. I've no idea. He hid at the back of the stage during the entire performance. Don't ask me what he sang; I couldn't understand the lyrics. Don't ask me about his show; he didn't have one. Of course one would never suggest he must have slept his way into this job, but after last night's debacle, we can be pretty certain this is the last of Del Arden we'll see."

Silence followed the review. Del felt the same numbness that came when he hit the ground after an unusually hard throw during martial arts practice. It would start to hurt later.

Finally Anne said, "My God."

Jud made an incredulous noise. "That was vicious."

"Fred Pizwick is known for harsh reviews," Mac said. "But that went over the edge."

Yeah. Right. Del wanted to hide. It was bad enough failing in front of his family. To have it happen in front of so many people, covered by a media outlet that went all over Earth—he might as well just go crawl under a rock.

"They'll shout me off the stage in Philadelphia," he said.

"Like hell." Mac thumped the table. "Okay, it's a bad review. That happens. Don't let it get you. You'll learn to ignore them."

"That review is a load of crap," Cameron rumbled.

Del blinked. From his impassive bodyguard, that qualified as an emotional outburst.

"Prime-Nova will pull me off the tour," Del said.

"Maybe," Mac admitted. "But they haven't yet." He leaned forward. "When we get to Philadelphia, you're going to hold up your head, go out on the stage, and sing."

Del tried to nod. He had made a commitment, and he kept his promises. But he didn't know how he would manage.

"I've another review," Jud said. He kept his face and voice carefully neutral.

"Don't play it," Randall told him, his gaze flicking to Del.

"No, go ahead," Del said tiredly. "I want to hear."

"It's Sarah Underwile from the *Washington Post*." Jud flicked a holicon, and a woman's voice came into the van. She enthused for a while about Mind Mix. Then she said, "In their grueling schedule, the band has asked for an opener to ease their three-hour marathons. Last night, Prime-Nova introduced an unknown, Del Arden, as the warm-up. They've clearly pushed him through as fast as possible, probably to meet the demands of their mega-stars. The surprise is that they chose an undercity artist. Arden appears to have talent; his voice shows remarkable versatility. Whether he can carry a show is another question. If last night was an indication, he's not ready for the major concert circuit."

After a moment, Jud said, "That wasn't so bad."

"She said the same things as Pizwick," Del said. "She was just nicer about it."

"She gave you a line," Mac said. "'His voice shows remarkable versatility.' It's a usable quote from a major media source."

Del suspected people would just hear the negative review, not the subtler message his manager heard.

"Huh," Jud said, peering at his screen. "You got a review from Jason Mulroney in *Down and Below*. They don't usually cover Mind Mix."

"*Down and Below*?" Anne leaned over the back of the seat. "What's that?"

"An undercity newspaper," Jud said. "Here, listen. This is the part about Del."

A man spoke. "For the first time ever, Prime-Nova sponsored an undercity artist in one of their tours, as the opener for Mind Mix no less. Billed as Del Arden, the singer will undoubtedly come under fire, in part for his obvious lack of preparation, but also for his unconventional music, lyrics, and presentation. He's not your typical Prime-Nova artist, and I'll admit to being stunned they took a chance like this. The depth of his composition goes against the purely commercial nature of their stable. I've been critical of Prime-Nova in the past, but this development makes me wonder if I judged them too soon."

Mulroney paused. "The disappointment is that Arden gave

such a clumsy performance. No matter how good the material, the delivery matters. With such a strong opportunity to showcase the undercity, I would have wished for a smoother show. His support musicians weren't headlined with him, but they deserve kudos. Anne Moore and Randall Gaithers are well known in the studio circuit, and last night their luminous performances showed why they're in such demand. Jud Taborian further established his reputation as one of the hottest morphers this side of Neptune. Arden may have struggled with a rough start, but this is an artist and band worth watching."

"Hey!" Anne said. "That was almost good."

Del wouldn't have defined *The disappointment is that Arden gave such a clumsy performance* as "almost good." He was pulling down a strong band. He glanced at Mac. "I owe you an apology."

"You don't owe me anything." Mac smiled wryly. "Except my cut of whatever you make."

"If I had listened to you, I wouldn't be cringing my way through these reviews."

"It'll get better." Mac sounded as if he were trying to convince himself as much as Del.

"Yeah." Randall grinned. "We'll kill 'em in Philadelphia."

Anne's throaty laugh curled around them. "Randy, hon, you got to stop wishing death on our audiences."

Del tried to smile. But he kept thinking about Ricki. *Had* he slept his way into a job he didn't deserve? Jud, Anne, and Randall had paid their dues and earned their shot at the major circuit. It wasn't only his pride at stake here; he didn't want them to lose their jobs through his failure.

He hadn't known what it would be like. Now he knew—and he didn't see how he could ever face that crushing mental pressure again.

"The traffic grids crashed!" Mac shouted into his comm. "Damn it, Linda, *we'll be there.* We're at the edge of the city. Just give us twenty minutes."

Del sat tensely with Jud, Anne, and Randall. It was just his luck that the control-grids had collapsed and snarled traffic in the Baltimore-Philadelphia corridor. Nothing had moved for two hours except drivers who illegally jimmied their vehicles free of control. The outlaws snaked in and out of the frozen traffic or leapt into the sky even after the crisis-grid activated, allowing only emergency vehicles to fly. Del and the others had left their hotel with plenty of time to make the Philadelphia concert, but the traffic mess had cut their cushion of time to nothing. He was due on stage in ten minutes.

"What?" Mac said into his comm. "Linda, I can't hear you. The crowd is too noisy." After a pause, he said, "No, don't replace him with another band! We won't be long. Just give us a little more time."

Listening to him, Del didn't know whether to hope he made it in time or that he wouldn't have to go out there and sing.

The Holo Fields outside Philadelphia offered the largest concert venue on the Atlantic Seaboard. Endless meadows surrounded the amphitheater, and audio globes whirled everywhere, carrying the music to the never-ending audience. People spilled all over, running, playing football, buying food from vendors, picnicking. Their minds were a quiescent ocean for now, none focused on Del, but he felt the growing pressure.

Del wiped his sleeve across his forehead. "Mac, how many?"

"You mean people?" Mac asked, distracted. When Del nodded, Mac said, "The current count is more than three hundred fifty thousand, but it's constantly changing. They expect a lot more."

Del's stomach lurched. *You'll be all right,* he told himself. He couldn't be the first empath who had ever performed before a big crowd.

There had to be a way to survive this.

Linda Hisner, the concert manager, had a crew waiting at the stage for Del. Within moments after his hover-van smacked into its pad, techs were setting them up onstage.

Jud started playing as Del ran onstage. Del was supposed to introduce the band, but the words flew out of his mind. The crowd was at four hundred thousand now—and they were suddenly all *focused* on him, bursting with impatience, high on excitement. He was drowning in a tidal wave of emotions.

"Del, sing!" Mac was yelling in his ear, and Del finally comprehended that Mac had been talking and talking to him.

The intro to "Emeralds" kept cycling. Del began to sing, then realized he hadn't switched on his mike. He flicked it on and started at the wrong place. After stumbling through several lines, he stopped and started over. The roar from the audience never abated. He wasn't sure they even knew he was singing.

"Go up front," Mac urged. "Go to the front of the stage." He was standing at the edge of the stage behind one of the huge morph engines that bordered it, motioning to Del as well as talking on the comm.

Del forced himself to walk forward as he sang. But the closer he got to the audience, the more his mind shut down. His voice cracked, something that hadn't happened since he was thirteen.

"Del, you can do it," Mac said in his ear. "Relax. Let go."

He couldn't let go. He was shielding his mind so much, he could barely think. What it really meant was that he was suppressing chemicals in his brain. Any more, and his brain would turn off, knocking him out.

Only habit kept him going. He had sung this piece for years. He thought he was standing still, but then he backed into a mesh-amp at the back of the stage. The audience was restless, edgy, more impatient than before he started. People yelled to each other, walked back and forth, waved their arms. It was chaos.

When Jud started the third song, "Sapphire Clouds," Del couldn't sing. His throat just closed up.

"Del, you have to start," Mac said in his ear.

He couldn't.

"Del," Mac said, almost pleading. "Sing."

Del walked over to Mac. When he left the stage, someone shouted, "What the hell did we pay for?"

Del stood in front of Mac, hidden from the audience by the morph engine. Techs were all around them, some checking mesh boards, others staring at Del.

"What the blazes are you doing?" Mac asked.

"I can't." Del was breathing hard, as if he had run a race.

"You aren't a quitter," Mac said. "Everyone gets stage fright. Work through it."

"Mac—" His voice scraped. "I'm an empath. A Ruby psion."

"I know that."

"You don't understand." Del's voice shook. "That audience is still getting bigger. Nearly *half a million* people."

Comprehension dawned on Mac's face. "My God. I hadn't—it didn't occur to me. Can you feel them *all?*"

"All of them," Del whispered. "I can't do it."

Mac regarded him steadily. "If you go out there and plummet, you're a professional musician who did his job and had a bad concert. You'll still have the holo-vid and virt deals and maybe someday a chance to perform live when you're ready. If you *don't* go out there, you'll be the amateur who walked out in the middle of a major job. The first won't kill your career. But if you quit now, you're dead. Prime-Nova won't look past it."

Del couldn't answer. He could hardly *think*. But if he went down, he would pull Mac, Jud, Randall, and Anne with him. Staring at Mac, he forced himself to nod. Then he turned around and walked numbly onto the stage. Jud and Anne were still playing the "Sapphire" intro. Del stared at the audience. He raised the mike to his mouth. And he couldn't make a sound.

"Do anything," Mac said in his ear. "*Anything.*"

Del sang one of his lowest notes, three octaves below middle C. Jud matched him on the morpher. With wooden precision, Del went through an exercise so familiar, it was like a well-worn sweater, except he sang *Ba-a-by* instead of *ah-ah-ah*. He climbed the scale, one octave, two, three, four, five. Jud followed him, and Anne kept up her driving beat. Randall stared as if Del had gone out of his mind, but he continued with an understated version of the "Sapphire" intro, matching it to Del's exercise. Del went up and up, above high C. He didn't normally push it that far, but in his terrified daze, he kept going. He stopped after six octaves and just stood. He felt the incredulity of the crowd, a mix of derision, shock, disbelief, and a swirl of other moods he couldn't decipher.

Then he launched into "Sapphire Clouds":

> Running through the sphere-tipped reeds
> Suns like gold and amber beads . . .

He stood in that one spot, frozen, and sang his entire set that way, his mind turned off so he could no longer think about the nightmare audience.

"I don't understand," Randall said for the fourth time. "How can you shut off that way?"

Del wished he could fold up and die. The lights in their hotel room were dimmed, but it was still too bright. He wanted to lie in the dark and forget what had happened tonight. Or last night, now that it was into the earliest hours of morning.

Randall and Anne were slumped in armchairs facing a table. Del had collapsed on the bed. Jud was sitting in a beanbag chair in the corner, strumming an acoustic guitar. The Spanish music soothed Del, but nothing could really help. Cameron was slouched in a beanbag against the wall, drinking coffee, half hidden in the shadows, until everyone but Del forgot about him. But no bodyguard could protect him against his own failures.

The door hummed and swung open. Mac walked in, paused and stared at them all as the door closed. Then he went over and dropped into one of the armchairs.

"So what did they say?" Randall asked him.

Mac exhaled. "I couldn't get through to Ricki or Zachary. But Linda told me they're pulling the act."

Del sat up. "I'm sorry." He didn't know what else to say.

"Del, I don't understand," Anne said. "In rehearsal, you're incredible. What *happened* out there?"

"Don't," Mac said softly. "Let him be."

"Why?" Randall demanded. "Damn it, Del, do you know what any of us would give to have the chance Prime-Nova handed you on a platter? How could you throw it away?"

"It's personal." Del felt like a fool.

"It's not personal," Anne said. "It affects us all. If this was a problem, we deserved to know."

"*I* didn't know," Del said.

"Maybe Prime-Nova won't yank us," Jud said. "I thought this concert went better than the first one."

Randall gave him an incredulous look. "He did an *exercise*."

"How can someone who sings so well," Anne said, "freeze so badly?"

Del averted his gaze. "I'm an empath." Even saying those few words felt like a violation of his privacy.

"Lots of artists think they're Mister Sensitive," Randall said angrily. "It doesn't fucking give you license to blow the best gig any of us will ever have."

"He doesn't mean it figuratively," Mac said. "He's a full empath. On stage, he picks up moods of the crowd. All of them."

"You mean, what people are thinking?" Anne asked. "I've heard of that. But I thought it was a story."

"Not so much what they think," Del said. "What they feel."

She stared at him. "For half a *million* people?"

Del swallowed. "Yes."

"Good Lord," she said. "That would explain a lot."

"I tried to shut them out." Del stared at his hands. "I *couldn't*. I ended up shutting myself down."

"Oh come on," Randall said. "If you're really one of these empaths, why don't you just let the audience in?"

Del looked up at him. "What?"

"Let yourself feel their reactions," Randall said.

Del couldn't believe it. "Why would I want to soak up five hundred thousand people hating what I do?"

"Maybe that's why they hate it," Randall said. "Man, I've seen you practice. You're so mesmerizing, it annoys the shit out of me. When you get on stage, you turn it all off. So why would they like it? Maybe you should quit hiding and take in what they give you. That is, if you really are an 'empath,' and this isn't some half-assed excuse."

"If I opened my mind to that many people," Del said flatly, "I would go catatonic."

"Could you do it partially?" Jud asked. "I read a little about empaths in my psych class in college. Can't you give back what you get from people? I mean, if you picked out someone who liked what you were doing and fed it back to them, maybe you could affect more people."

"I don't know." Del couldn't imagine opening up even to a fraction of that onslaught.

A knock came at the door. Mac looked up with a start. "Are any of you expecting anyone?"

"Not me," Anne said. The rest of them echoed her response.

Frowning, Mac went to the door and touched the ID panel. An androgynous voice said, "Transmission blocked."

"Huh." Mac flicked through a few displays on the panel. "Whoever is out there has a Prime-Nova security clearance."

Del wondered what it said about the people he worked for, that the employees of an entertainment conglomerate needed security clearances. "Who is it?"

"I don't know." Mac opened the door.

"It's about time." Ricki stalked inside and ignored everyone else as she zeroed in on Del. "What the hell went on up there?"

Del scowled at her. "I'm glad to see you, too."

Ricki came over and sat on the bed. She spoke in a softer voice. "What happened, babe?"

"I clutched." He didn't want to ask the next question, but it came out anyway. "Why are you here?"

She started to reach for him, a subtle gesture, then pulled back. "I thought it would be easier for you to hear it from me."

"They're pulling me."

"I'm afraid so."

Del was aware of everyone staring at them. Anne's mouth had fallen open, and Jud stopped playing his guitar.

"Well, well," Randall said sourly. "Maybe Fred Pizwick had it better than we thought."

Ricki turned to him with a gaze that could have chilled ice. "Do you like your career?"

"Yeah, sure," Randall said.

"Do you want to continue having it?"

He watched her uneasily. "Yeah."

"Then shut the fuck up," Ricki said.

Randall reddened, but he didn't say anything more.

Ricki turned back to Del. "You've never been on stage before, have you?"

"No," he admitted. "Never."

She glanced at Mac. "You're a rat, Tyler."

"I told you he had no experience," Mac said.

"You were negotiating," Ricki said. "Convincing us that he had so many people interested, you didn't need to impress us."

"No," Mac said. "I was telling you the truth."

"No one does that in this business." She frowned at Del. "If you get stage fright that bad, why didn't you talk to me?"

"I didn't realize I would freeze." His anger sparked. "And when would I have said anything, Ricki? You disappeared after—" He stopped, aware of everyone in the room. "After the Star Tower."

Her voice tightened. "You could have asked Mac to find me."

"Why?" Del was as bewildered as he was angry. "Why not tell me how to reach you?" In a low voice, he said, "If someone walks out on me, I'm not going to chase them."

"Most men would have, for Ricki Varento," she said.

"You're worth it," he murmured. "But I don't grovel." Hearing the words, he wondered if the personality of a Ruby prince was far more ingrained in him than he had wanted to admit.

She rubbed her eyes. "No, I suppose not."

"The next concert is New York." Del didn't know what he was going to say until it came out. "Give me one more chance."

Ricki raised her sculpted eyebrows. "You want us to let you on stage again? After what happened the last two times?"

"I can do it." Del thought he was insane, but he wanted this too much to give up. "I didn't have any idea what would happen that first time. For the second one, we were late, and I didn't have time to prepare." He took her hand, knowing how it looked, but the hell with what the others thought. "I can do it."

"It's not my decision, babe."

"But what you think matters." He had seen how people reacted when they found out Ricki Varento produced his vids. Her power went far beyond the studio. "If anyone can talk Prime-Nova into it, you can."

Ricki pulled away her hand. "Maybe I don't want to. If you plummet again, that's it. You might never tour again. Maybe you ought to let it go, before it gets any worse."

"It won't." Del pushed aside the misgivings flooding him. "Tabor and I have been talking about a way I might beat this problem. I can do it."

"We're playing the Cosmos Stadium in New York," Ricki said. "It isn't our largest venue, but it's one of the most important. You're going to have critics from every major mesh outlet there. If you bomb, they'll pulverize you."

Jud spoke from the corner. "This second concert wasn't a disaster. He sang better than the first time."

"He walked off the stage," Ricki said sourly.

"It won't happen again," Del told her.

Mac spoke. "Are you sure, Del? You told me a week ago you could do this, and now you regret that decision. The same thing could happen if you go on in New York."

"And Mind Mix is pissed," Ricki said. "Tristan and Tackman want you off the tour."

"What about Rex?" Mac asked. "He's the front man."

"Rex thinks Del is brilliant," Ricki admitted.

Del almost fell off the bed at that. He said nothing, though.

He could sense only the outermost shell of Ricki's mind, but he could tell she didn't like being pushed.

Ricki glanced around at Jud, Anne, and Randall. "You all want to go on stage with him in New York?"

Jud answered immediately. "Yes. Absolutely."

"I'd like another shot at it," Anne said.

Ricki considered Randall. "What about you?"

After a pause, he said, "Yeah."

"How are the reviews for last night?" Ricki asked.

"We haven't looked," Anne said. With a grimace, she added, "We weren't up to it."

"I need to hear them before I decide," Ricki said.

Jud put down his guitar and unrolled a mesh screen across his knees. After a few moments, he said, "I've one from the *Inquirer*. They liked Mind Mix. This is the part about Del."

A man's voice rose into the air. "The opener, Del Arden, was a puzzle. He ran onto the stage and literally stumbled into his first song, so out of breath you could barely hear him. Quite frankly, the boy looked terrified. Given that no record exists of him ever playing any venue, it isn't surprising he flat-lined in front of such a large audience. One wonders why Prime-Nova put him up there. Or maybe not. Because whatever his faults, this boy can *sing*. Let's hope that in the future, Prime-Nova better prepares its talent."

"That wasn't so bad," Anne said, looking hopefully at Ricki.

The producer just grunted.

Del could see Jud reading something else on the screen.

"You find another?" Ricki asked.

"Not yet," Jud said, avoiding their eyes.

"Stop protecting me," Del said. "Read the blasted review."

Jud looked up. "It's Fred Pizwick."

"Pizwick is an asshole," Ricki said.

"Why is he reviewing a Philadelphia concert?" Randall asked. "I thought he worked the Baltimore circuit."

"Hundreds of mesh services carry his column," Mac said. "He covers whatever he wants. And apparently he wants Mind Mix."

"No he doesn't," Ricki said. "He came to crow over Del."

That surprised Del. "Why? Do you know him?"

"Not well," Ricki said. "But enough. He wanted to be an opera singer, but he couldn't make it even with voice augmentation. He's going to hate you no matter what you do. I'll bet he saw your talent as soon as you started singing. And here you are, 'wasting' it on holo-rock. It's the ultimate insult to someone like him."

"Do you want to hear his review?" Jud asked.

Ricki glanced at Del.

"Yeah, go ahead," Del said. He would have rather been hit by a cement block, but if he wanted another chance, he had to know what the decision makers at Prime-Nova would hear about him.

Pizwick's voice invaded the room. "If you paid money to hear the warm-up in Philadelphia, please accept my condolences. I'm often astonished by what undercity hacks stoop to calling music, but it goes from outrage to robbery when Prime-Nova charges people to hear vocal exercises. Yes, that's right. Last night the good citizens of Philadelphia were subjected to Del Arden standing like a frozen carp, running through exercises even his beleaguered vocal coach must find painful. Adding insult to injury, he was using a bob, or for those of you less familiar with music terms, a Roberts Enhancer. The device augments the human voice, making someone sound as if, for example, he has an increased vocal range. So we witnessed the embarrassing charade of a boy pretending to a six-octave range. Mind you, this was after our dear amateur stormed off the stage in the middle of a song. Has Prime-Nova lost its collective mind? Mercifully, rumor has it that the 'remarkable' Del Arden has been yanked from the lineup. Thank God."

"For crying out loud," Anne said. "That's beyond harsh. I can't believe they published it."

"Oh, people love that stuff," Randall said. "They're probably arguing it all over the mesh."

"He's lying," Del said angrily. "I've never used an enhancer."

Ricki's face was thoughtful. "We may be able to start some bad press against him on that one. You can't protest a reviewer saying he doesn't like your work, but if he misrepresents it and then suggests Prime-Nova defrauded people by charging for the performance, he's going over the line."

"He's caused a stir," Jud said, reading from his screen. "It looks like several other reviews mentioned Del using a michael. People are either lambasting Pizwick for sloppy reporting or else cheering him on."

"Can you find one of the other reviews?" Ricki asked.

"Yeah, I think so—" Jud fell silent, then said, "Okay, this is Lynne Kalowski with North American News Media."

Randall let out a whistle. "That's big time. And she never reviews holo-rock."

A woman's voice rose into the air. "—went on before Mind Mix. In many ways, it was an unremarkable opener. Like many of the concertgoers, Arden was caught in the traffic-grid meltdown south of Philadelphia last night. His band arrived late, but gamely ran onstage and launched their act. Arden left the platform not long after, one assumes to catch his breath."

Then she said, "What followed has to qualify as one of the strangest chapters in holo-rock history. Arden came back and sang a glorified exercise. But oh, *what* an exercise. He soared through over six octaves, encompassing the entire range of the normal human voice, both male and female. He used nothing more than a michael, a simple amplification device. In response to my inquiries, a Prime-Nova spokeswoman allowed me to examine Arden's equipment to verify it didn't augment his voice. Why this boy is doing rock, I have no idea, but it was worth sitting through a form of music I normally avoid for those glorious moments of virtuosity."

Anne burst out laughing. "That's great! She hates holo-rock anyway, so even if we sucked slime, it wouldn't matter. He did something she liked, so that's all she reviewed."

Ricki's smile was more predatory than amused. "She'll make Pizwick look like a fool."

Although Del was grateful for a positive comment, he had heard this one all too often. *Why waste your talent on that noise?* He wanted someone to appreciate the music he loved, not the music they wished he would do.

"Here's another one," Jud said. "It's from Jason Mulroney."

The voice of the undercity critic came on. "—same opener as last night. This time I had a better chance to listen to the lyrics. I was struck by the comparison between Arden's songs and the usual Prime-Nova fare. Consider this verse in a ballad written by Arden: 'Born to live in a vanished sea/Lost to seeds of a banished need/Caged in desperate hope for all days/Rubies must give their souls in all ways.' Now a typical verse from Mind Mix: 'Yeah, baby, yeah, baby, yeah/uh-huh, baby, love me, uh.' Sure, Mind Mix sings it with all the bells and holos, a great tune, and plenty of effects. But so what? The lyrics are still stupid."

Anne had been taking a sip out of a mug she had picked up, but at Mulroney's last statement, she spluttered coffee all over the table. "I can't believe he wrote that."

"I've no idea what Arden calls his song or any of the others he did," Mulroney continued. "He never once gave titles or otherwise addressed the audience. He looked more frightened than anything else. But he went through an entire set with similarly involved lyrics. I would love to get him in for an interview to find out what they mean. Let's just hope this artist gets over his stage fright soon and really starts performing."

"Mind Mix is not stupid," Ricki grumbled. "They compose by sound, not word. Their artistry is in how it all fits together."

"Oh come on, Ricki," Mac said. "You can't compare what they do to Del's work."

"He wants to interview me!" Del said.

"We'll put the PR people on it," Ricki said absently, lost in thought. She considered Del. "With those reviews, I can argue with the higher-ups to give you another chance." Her gaze turned to steel. "But if you plummet this time, that's it. You got it?"

"You won't regret it," Del said. He *would* make it work.

If he didn't fry his brain.

VI

The Cosmos

"This isn't a costume," Del growled. "It's embarrassing."

Mac stood back and considered him. Although he supposed he should have expected Del's cranky mood, given how the concert had gone yesterday in Philadelphia, he had thought it would improve this morning, after Prime-Nova agreed to let him play New York.

It didn't surprise him the clothes made Del self-conscious. The black mesh pants fit him like a second skin and rode low on the hips, with his ring belt even lower. Few people could pull off wearing that outfit, let alone look as good in it as Del. Mac had known Del wouldn't like it, but he also knew what worked onstage.

"You look good," Mac said.

Del splayed his hand over his bare chest. "I need a shirt."

Mac braced himself for the explosion. "I think you should go without it."

"Are you out of *your mind*?" Del scowled at him. "Besides, I signed that costume clause in my contract."

Mac couldn't help but laugh. "Believe me, you could get away with wearing a lot less than this and no one would complain."

"Not funny, Mac."

The door of the hotel room hummed and swung open, admitting Jud and the tech Bonnie. Jud just glanced at Del as he walked by, but Bonnie stopped in her tracks and gaped.

"Oh," she said. "Oh, my."

Del's face turned red. "Don't you guys knock?"

Jud flopped down in the beanbag chair and picked up his guitar. "You need a shirt."

"Thank you," Del said.

Anne ambled into the room. "Hey, Del. Nice outfit."

"For flaming sake!" Del said, crossing his arms.

Randall walked past her. "You going without the shirt?"

"No!" Del glared at Mac. Then he glared at Cameron, who was just coming in. "My room is turning into Grand Central Starport."

The Marine regarded Del with the hint of a smile, then dropped into an armchair, stretched out his long legs, and poured himself a smart-mug of the coffee Mac had left on the table. His mug, which was supposed to pick up cues about his mood from his movements and hand, turned dark purple, gave a spurt of Del's song "No Answers," and fell silent as if to comment on the quality of the music, or lack thereof.

"Great," Del muttered. "Even the dishes are reviewing my music." He swung around to Mac. "You must have a shirt I can wear."

"All right." Mac relented and turned to the pile of clothes he had thrown on the bed. He pulled out a skin-tight muscle shirt. "How about this?"

"I am *not* going to wear that," Del said.

Bonnie smiled. "He'll get boys following him, too."

Anne's throaty laugh rumbled as she dropped into the armchair next to where Cameron sat. "They will anyway."

Del's face flamed. "What?"

"Oh come on," Randall said, slouching in his chair while he loaded a mug with coffee. "You can't be that innocent."

Anne stood considering Del. "Pick a more subtle shirt," she decided. "You don't need to be blatant."

"What, these pants aren't blatant?" Del demanded.

"Honey, the pants are dynamite," she told him.

Mac pulled out a long-sleeved white shirt. "This is more like what you wear." He wondered why Del was in such a bad mood. The clothes probably, but embarrassment usually made him quiet rather than testy. Mac suspected it was Ricki. She had stayed with Del last night, but she was nowhere in sight this morning.

Del shrugged into the shirt. It fit snugly and was open at the

collar. A faint shimmer overlaid it, a mesh that molded the shirt
to his body and would glint in the stage lights.

"Looks good," Anne decided. "Sex without sleaze."

Del tugged on his cuff. "I look stupid."

"You don't, believe me," Bonnie said, her eyes large.

"What about his hair?" Randall asked. "He ought to cut it."

Anne shook her head. "Prime-Nova doesn't want him to."

"I think it's nice," Bonnie said.

"Jud," Del said desperately. "Rescue me."

A ripple of music came from the corner. Jud was sprawled in
the beanbag, playing his acoustic guitar. "You'll have to trust the
women on this one. I have no idea what you should wear."

Del shifted his weight back and forth as if he wanted to run
away but had nowhere to go. "When do we leave?"

"As soon as possible," Mac said.

"Why?" Randall asked. "It only takes a couple of hours to reach
New York. If we go now, we'll be there before noon. The show
isn't until seven tonight."

"We could have slept longer," Anne grumbled.

Mac thought of the Philadelphia concert. "I don't want to risk
being late again."

Del walked over to Mac and spoke in a low voice. "Did you
see anyone come out of here earlier this morning?"

"You mean your room?" Mac asked.

Del nodded, his eyes averted.

Mac wondered what the hell Ricki was doing, jerking Del
around this way when he needed support. "No. Sorry. But I was
in my own room most of the time."

"Yeah. Well. I don't have to wear this clown suit until the
concert." Del spun around and stalked to the bed. He grabbed a
pair of smart-jeans and a black T-shirt out of his throw bag, then
strode into the bathroom and banged the door behind him.

"What's he so drilled about?" Randall said.

No one answered.

The heavy walls of the room muted the rumble of the crowds
in the Cosmos Stadium above them. Del stood by a table, gripping
his bottle of beer. He didn't know why he bothered drinking the
stuff; it had no effect on him. But he needed something.

He felt painfully self-conscious in his getup. It could have been

worse; Mac had at least picked clothes similar to what Del usually
wore. These were just more—hell, he didn't know the English for
it. Skolian Flag had a perfect word. It translated into *harboring
the night,* which didn't make much sense, but anyone who spoke
Flag would understand. Sexually suggestive, with a touch of the
audacious. He was going out on that stage to harbor the night.
Except he was a skinny guy from the farm, so all he was going
to harbor was his own stupidity.

Mac spoke behind him. "You'll be all right."

Del decided to quit brooding. Turning around, he saw Mac
leaning against the bar, drinking a beer.

"I should go join the band," Del said.

"They're okay with you staying here. They know why."

Del took a deep breath, trying to relax. "I can *feel* the audience. Like an avalanche above me."

"Listen." Mac came over to him. "Just go to the front of the
stage. That's half the battle. Let people see you."

Del scowled. "In this getup I'm wearing, people will laugh."

"Trust me, they won't." Mac regarded him curiously. "How can
you be an empath and not know how people react to you?"

"I feel their moods," Del said. "If I let myself, and if their reaction is strong. That doesn't mean I understand them." He thought
of Ricki, who had disappeared this morning, and his anger surged.
How could she moan with pleasure in his arms at night and then
vanish the next day? No, damn it, he wouldn't think about her,
not now. He needed to concentrate on the concert.

"So you can tell if someone notices you," Mac said. "But you
don't know what they notice?"

"Essentially." Del squinted at him. "If I did know, I'd probably
be so nervous about it, I'd be afraid to move."

Mac smiled. "Just be yourself, then."

Easy for him to say; he didn't have to wear these clothes. "How
much longer?"

"About five minutes. You remember how to start?"

"Introduction. I won't forget this time."

"And you've changed the order of the songs."

"I'll remember." Even if he forgot, it would come back as soon
as Jud started playing. They had put "Sapphire Clouds" first
because Mac thought it had a catchier melody. Del had never
considered his songs "catchy," given how much everyone seemed

to want to miss them, but he figured Mac knew what he was talking about.

"You ready?" Mac asked.

He managed to nod. "Let's go."

Cameron was waiting outside the doorway. He followed them up a narrow stairway to the backstage area. The noise of the crowd echoed in the indoor stadium. The pressure didn't crush Del as much as last night; even if he hadn't known they were performing for only ten thousand people, he would have been able to tell.

Anne met them at the top of the stairs. She beamed at Del. "You look a lot calmer tonight."

Del felt about as calm as a spaziotic-jumping-fly from the planet Diesha. But he said, "You bet."

Randall and Jud joined them. "You all set?" Randall asked.

"Couldn't be better," Del lied.

Jud was watching him. "Just remember. Stay at the front."

"I will." Del motioned toward the stadium. "With so many people in those tiered seats, though, they can see me no matter where I stand."

"And they'll see the holos of you we added to the show," Mac said. "I checked with the techs earlier. The screens are set."

Jud lifted his hand. "Then let's do it!"

Bonnie pulled aside a curtain separating them from the stage. Del took a breath, then ran with the band out into the lights. As soon as they appeared, the noise in the arena surged. The audience crammed the place, so much that Del wondered if the concert promoters had oversold the arena. People jammed the open area at the front of the stage, chairs on the main floor, and tier after tier of seats above them. They were calling, whistling, holding up laser-light candles, and climbing rails that separated the tiers from the main floor. Security guards hauled them down and put them back in their own section.

The rippling lights in the air flustered Del. But this time, he didn't lose touch with everything. He was aware of Jud to his right setting up his morpher, of Randall on his left flicking strings, of Anne behind him tapping a cymbal. Fighting his instinct to back up, Del went to the front of the stage. The kids below were talking to each other, calling to friends, or looking at him, waiting to see what he would do. Jud started the intro to "Sapphire Clouds," rolling through the fast-paced measures.

Del wondered if these people had heard his show was a disaster. No, don't think about that. Concentrate. Just pick one. One person. One mind.

"Hey, sweets, you're gorgeous," a girl called up. Her friend gave her a shove, laughing, her face red.

All right, Del thought. *You're the one.*

Then he lowered his mental shields.

A sea of emotions crashed into him. He reeled and actually started to fall. He was drowning!

No. Del caught his balance and focused on the girl, desperate for an anchor. Just her, no one else. Her mood swirled; she was aroused, not only from the excitement of the concert, but from *him.* A flush went through his body.

Jud and Randall were cycling through the intro, waiting for him. Del took a breath and sang straight to the girl:

> Running through the sphere-tipped reeds
> Suns like gold and amber beads
> Jumping over blue-winged bees
> Kiss me, don't tease
> Running, running, running

He changed the fourth line for the girl, from *Don't catch me please.* He had written "Sapphire Clouds" when he had been eleven, from the sheer delight in racing across the endless plains that surrounded his home village:

> Flight of bubbles everywhere
> Pollen dusting in my hair
> No more troubles anywhere
> Sapphire clouds above the air

The girl was staring at him with a rapt gaze. Del took everything he picked up from her—desire, delight in the music, excitement—and sent it back. As their link strengthened, it also widened, taking in her friends, then others around her. They *liked* his song, liked his appearance, liked the music. He kept building the connection, reaching out to more people in front of the stage.

He had written the next verses when he was older, after his life had gone to hell. The music changed abruptly, shifting into a minor key.

Memories fade in life's strain
Winds of age bring falling rain
Cornucopia of lives
Of years and joys and grieving sighs

People in front of him were dancing, bodies jumping with the music. Del didn't know if they had done that at his other concerts; he had been too far back to see. In his side vision, he saw a giant holo of himself high above the stage. *He* was dancing, stepping back and forth as he often did when he practiced alone. Gods, how mortifying! He never let anyone know. Yes, men danced on Earth. But they never did on Lyshriol. It was forbidden. Yet here he was, doing it in front of thousands of people, and he couldn't stop because it might break his link with the small part of his audience in front of the stage. If he lost that focus, a tidal wave would rush in and drown him.

Recall Sapphire Clouds on high
Drifting in an endless sky
Childhood caught and kept inside
To treasure after days gone by

His mind jumped to people farther back in the arena, widening his link. He was losing control, but he couldn't stop. He felt as if he were on a neuro-amp high. His feedback loop with the audience surged and he threw back his head, letting go with the joy of singing to people who *wanted* to hear him.

Del barely realized he had finished the song when people started clapping. Although they had done that at the other concerts, he knew the difference. It had felt obligatory before; here they cheered with gusto.

"Yes!" Mac shouted in his ear. "You've got it."

Del's mind lurched with the onslaught of emotions buffeting him. It was like being on a roller coaster he couldn't stop. Jud was playing the next song. "Diamond Star." Del lifted his gaze to the scaffolding of the distant roof. In his mind, he looked beyond, into the night, past the stars. *This is for you,* he thought to the only woman he would ever truly love.

Then he let go, soaring through the first verse and into the chorus, *A diamond, a diamond, a diamond star.*

And so he went, in an ecstatic haze while his mind reeled in an empathic overload.

Anne was laughing, her gorgeous voice filling the green room under the stage. "He forgot the introduction again!"

"Who the hell cares?" Randall said, laughing with her. "They can't yank us now, not after an ultraviolet scream like that."

Del stumbled into the entranceway, his body vibrating with the sounds of Mind Mix playing above them. He hung onto the doorframe and stared at the others. He was aware of Cameron on one side of him and Mac on the other, but Del couldn't focus on anything. His mind was whirling.

"Here he is!" Randall strode over and clapped Del on the shoulder. "Now *that* was a show. You just needed a new pair of pants, heh?"

They all gathered around him, Anne, Jud, Bonnie, Randall. Del tried to answer, but he couldn't speak. It didn't matter. They were doing all the talking.

"Man, you're flying," Randall said. "What'd you take?"

Del focused on him. "Take?"

"You gotta watch that," Anne told him. "Your pupils are wide as the moon. If Soo-Ling catches you, Prime-Nova will get pissed."

"He didn't take anything," Mac said, maneuvering Del past them. "We'll be right back." He pulled Del toward another door.

Then they were alone, in the room where Mac had brought him before the show. Del collapsed on the couch, his booted feet on the coffee table, his head thrown back, his eyes closed. He couldn't get off the roller coaster, he was going into *overload*—

Mac's worried face swam into view above Del.

"Thank God," Mac said. He moved out of view.

Del lifted his head. He was still slouched on the couch with his legs across the table, but now Mac was sitting next to him, his face pale. Although Del felt a little strange, his mind had settled, and he was more in control.

He rubbed his eyes. "What happened?"

Mac spoke quietly. "Do you have epilepsy?"

Del looked up with a start. How had Mac known to ask that? "No. But my father did, so we've all been tested. I never showed any signs of it."

"Your father?" Mac looked surprised. "We had no idea."

Apparently the Allieds didn't have spies as good as they thought. "It's hardly something we talk about to your military."

"I think you need to talk to me," Mac said quietly. "You just had a convulsion."

What? No, that couldn't be. "I didn't feel anything."

"You stiffened and your eyes rolled back in your head." Mac's face was pale. "Then you jerked for about ten seconds."

Del didn't want to hear this. "That's never happened before."

"Tell me about your father," Mac said. When Del stiffened, Mac frowned at him. "It's your health at stake."

"My health is fine."

"Damn it, Del, if live performances give you seizures, I need to know what's going on."

Del didn't want to talk about so private a matter, but he knew Mac wouldn't let it go. "I never saw my father have one. They happened before he met my mother because his people didn't have good medical care. But she brought in doctors, and they helped him."

"Do you know why he had seizures?"

"It's an overload in the brain. Too many neurons fire." Del spoke with difficulty. "Psions, what you call empaths and tele-paths, have extra neural structures. My father had even more than most. When he was a baby, his family died in an avalanche. He was in a mental link with them, and it damaged his brain. After that, if his empathic centers were overstimulated, he had a convulsion." Del didn't need a medical degree to know he was describing a more severe version of what had just happened to him. His seizure couldn't be serious, though. His brain was just adjusting, like untrained muscles cramping because they weren't used to a workout. With practice, he would be fine.

"I don't know what you did out there," Mac said. "But the price is too high. I want you to stop."

"Stop?" Del smiled. "Mac, it *worked*."

Mac frowned at him. "You looked like you were drilled out of your mind. If Soo-Ling had seen you come offstage, she would have fined you twenty thousand on the spot."

"I didn't take anything! I can't help how I looked!"

Jud suddenly opened the door and leaned inside. "You aren't going to believe this. Mind Mix isn't done playing, and one of the media biggies has already put out an Arden exclusive."

Del's pulse lurched as he jumped to his feet. "Good or bad?"

Jud smirked at him. "You'll have to decide for yourself."

Del regarded him warily. "If this is a joke—"

"No, really," Jud told him. "Come listen."

Mac stood up between them. "Del, we aren't done."

"Don't worry," Del said. "I know what I'm doing." He didn't, but he felt fine.

Del went with Jud into the green room, past Cameron, who was leaning against the wall by the door. Although the Marine seemed as impassive as usual, Del had the odd impression his bodyguard was amused. Huh. Cameron never laughed, he just hulked around and looked intimidating. Anne, Randall, and Bonnie were sitting on the floor around Jud's mesh, which lay on an equipment box.

"Why don't *I* get that treatment?" Randall was saying as he laughed. "I'm mortally wounded!"

"Just think what a boost it would be to your career." Anne raised her voice into a higher pitch. "Oooh, Randy," she squealed.

"Oh, stop," Bonnie said, reddening.

"What's going on?" Del asked as he walked up to them.

"Hah! He's here." Anne yanked him down so he landed next to her, then flicked a holicon above the screen. "Your first review for tonight's performance, Mister Heartthrob Arden. We've cycled through it three times."

"Heartthrob?" Del asked. He didn't recognize the word.

A woman's voice leapt out of the comm. "—who cares about Mind Mix? Let me tell you, girlzo, the ultra swivel tonight was in the hips of one Del Sweet-cheeks Arden."

"What the blazes?" Del's face heated up. "Who is that?"

"Careful what you tell your parents, Ell-bees," the woman went on, "or they'll call in the conking boredom police and zip the latest zap on your sweet dreams. Unless you zap your mom a holo of this boy first; then she'll want a copy for herself."

Anne let out a hoot of laughter. "Del Arden, the wicked wet-dream king, out to corrupt the teeny-bee bops of America!"

"I can't even understand what she's saying," Del muttered.

Jud knelt down and clapped him on the shoulder. "It's a rough review, I know. You'll just have to soldier through."

The woman continued. "You've heard the establisho crockers complaining about this one, haven't you? Now you know why. Gander a look-see at our mesh-mall, girlzo. We've got holos galore for your viewing entertainment." She was literally purring. "And let me tell you, with a face like that and his—other attributes—oh yes, this boy Del is definitely entertainment."

"I don't believe this." Del didn't know whether to die of embarrassment or crawl under a bed and hide. "Why is she talking about me that way?"

Randall smirked at him. "Congratulations. You've just become the latest bees-bopper idol."

"You know," Del said, "I would really appreciate if you all would quit laughing at me and explain what that woman is saying."

"It's the Ell-bee set," Bonnie said in a softer voice than the others. "It comes from Little Bees. L-B. That came from bopper bees." She smiled shyly. "I used to subscribe to Elba's mesh-mags. We always listened to what she said."

"They called them teenyboppers a long time ago," Anne said. "I don't know what it used to mean, but now it refers to one of the biggest interactive clubs on the mesh. Mostly adolescent girls. They shop at the Ell-bee mesh-malls, set up virtual concerts, talk their own lingo, and start fan clubs for whoever Elba the Queen Bee talks up as the latest hot boy."

"And what you just heard," Randall told him with a flourish, "is the Queen Bee herself. Talking *you* up."

"Oh." Del had no idea what to make of it. "That's good, isn't it?" He squinted at them. "I hope."

"Sure it's good," Anne said. "Elba's a hoot, weird as all git-go, but the Ell-bees are great. They don't do virts much because of the expense, but they'll zap up your latest holo-vid, no problem."

"I would have," Bonnie said, smiling.

"He doesn't *have* a holo-vid," Randall said. "Not yet. Prime-Nova put him on tour to stir up hum about Del Arden."

Jud thumped Del's back. "You have to get into the studio."

"Not just me," Del said. "*We*, right?" He couldn't do it without them. "You're all going to work with me, aren't you?"

They all went quiet. Then Jud spoke in a more serious voice. "Are you asking us to?"

Mac was suddenly kneeling next to Del. "We can't make any contractual agreements at this time."

"Why not?" Del asked. "They should be on it." He could tell Mac wanted him to be quiet, the same as when Prime-Nova had offered him the contract.

Mac said, "These things have to be—"

"Negotiated. Yeah, I know." Del glanced at the others. "I want you five to work with me on the holo-vid." He tilted his head at Mac. "My manager, who is sweating right now because I won't shut up, will work out the details. So I guess I'm not supposed to say anything else."

Anne's smile gentled. "I'd be pleased to work with you."

"Count me in," Randall said.

Jud nodded his agreement. "Thanks, Del."

Mac rubbed his chin. "We need to check how Elba licensed those holos her people made of the concert. Even if they're mostly of Del, the rest of you are probably in them. The license will be with Prime-Nova, and they'll cross-collateralize it with tour expenses, but the royalties should be counted toward all your accounts."

License? Del had no idea what "cross-collateralize" meant, and "royalties" sounded like something to do with his title, which made no sense. "What did you just say?"

Anne patted his knee. "You are such an innocent."

Randall sat up straighter. "You mean, we'll get part of the Ell-bee sales?"

"Hell, yeah," Mac said. "Elba Malls can't make money off your images without paying." He glanced at Del. "And Jud is right. You need to get in the studio. This is a good break, but you can't capitalize on it until you have at least a vid and preferably a virt, too. That takes time."

"What time?" Del asked. "I've got more than enough songs." He motioned to the others. "They know the music."

Mac regarded him with exasperation. "Del, you need to do more than just *sing.*"

"Why?" Del couldn't figure out why Mac wanted pyrotechnics. "I *can* sing. I don't have anything to hide."

Mac scowled at him. "Don't get cocky because you had one fairly good concert. I don't care if you're Luciano Pavarotti reincarnated. You don't want a sloppy vid, and neither does Prime-Nova."

Del went silent, feeling uncertain. He hadn't meant to sound cocky. He didn't think that was really the problem, though. Mac was upset.

Del wished he knew why.

VII

Virtual Mind Mix

Mac sank into his chair, relieved to relax in the quiet hotel room. These strange hours tired him out. Although he was fifty-nine, age-delaying treatments made him look younger, which was practically a requirement in this youth-oriented industry. But he felt his age.

At least Del's concert had gone better tonight. The reviews were brief but reasonably good. He still wasn't doing as well as Prime-Nova had hoped, given the opportunity they had handed him, opening for Mind Mix. But they wouldn't yank him from the tour after Del had grabbed one of the hottest markets with the younger female demographic. It wasn't really a surprise; Ricki and Zachary must have realized the potential the moment they saw Del sing. Still, they wouldn't have looked for it this soon, before he had a vid ready.

Except.

Del's convulsion scared the hell out of Mac. He had tried to take the obstinate prince to the hospital, but Del steadfastly refused. Even so, Mac intended to take no chances. He had contacted Philip Chandler, the doctor who certified Del's age. Chandler wasn't a yes-man. He had verified Del was over twenty-five, but only after extensive tests. He would be straight with them if Del had medical problems after he saw Del tomorrow, in D.C.

If they made it to D.C. Although Mind Mix flew to each concert, Mac hadn't convinced Prime-Nova to provide air travel for Del. He could probably arrange a flyer now, though, so they could work on the vid between concerts. It would be grueling to commute between Washington and the cities where Del was performing, but the tour would be over in a month. They could manage that long.

Despite what he had told Del, Mac doubted it would take much to do the vid once they worked out the holos and extras. Del had more than enough material, and the band knew his music. Ricki would object to Jud Taborian because he was undercity, but she'd come around. She would have to be blind not to see how well Jud worked with Del.

So Mac sat in his darkened hotel room and brooded. He felt like a hypocrite. He was Del's manager. He was supposed to wish Del success. But every time Del went on stage; every time someone wrote about him, good or bad; every time Del made *eye contact* with the audience, Mac cringed. Sure, no one had any reason to attack a minor rock singer. But the human psyche had never been logical. Who knew if some nut would take a dislike to Del and decide to kill him? Most singers had a flare of success for a few years, if they were lucky, and then dropped into obscurity. The same would probably happen to Del. But Mac sweated anyway. One slipup and Del could be dead. Del chose to accept the risk, but Mac couldn't help wanting him off the tour.

The room's AI said, "Del Arden is at the door."

Mac looked up with a start. "Open. And bring up the lumos."

As the room brightened, Del ambled in, wearing a T-shirt and jeans with ragged mesh patches. He smiled at Mac. "I got a comm from Zachary Marksman. He congratulated me on the show."

"Good." Mac wasn't surprised. Zachary was the one who had decided to yank Del off the tour. He probably wanted to minimize any hard feelings if Del found out.

"You should be sleeping," Mac said. "We're flying to D.C. in the morning."

Del went into the kitchenette and thumbed an order into the icer. "I thought the next job was in Boston."

"It is. But you have three days until then. You can work on the vid and virt."

Del looked up. "Isn't that too short notice to get a studio?"

"Yeah. But they'll let us work afterhours." Mac smiled slightly. "Prime-Nova has a *lot* of studios."

Del regarded him uncertainly. "I've never seen a virt. I don't know what to do."

"The techs put it together. You just sing." Mac took a cube from a pile on the table and lobbed it to Del. As the youth grabbed it, Mac said, "That's Mind Mix's latest."

"Great." Del pulled two beers out of the icer and came over with the drinks in one hand and the cube in the other. He mimed throwing the beer, but when Mac glared, Del grinned and handed it to him. Then he dropped into a nearby chair.

"Do you think Jason Mulroney really wants to interview me?" Del asked.

"Sure. You'll need someone to set it up." Mac flipped open his beer, which cooperated this time. "You need a publicist. Someone to field requests for interviews, send out promotional materials, all that."

"Ricki said something about Prime-Nova looking into it."

Mac snorted. "Ricki won't do anything for an undercity news service. She wants to separate your image from them." Wryly he added, "She'll say it's because they aren't commercial, but I think she just doesn't like them. They don't scrape and bow to her."

Del tilted his bottle back and forth as if suddenly fascinated by the condensation on its surface. "Have you heard from her?"

"Not since Philadelphia." It was three in the morning now, so technically Del's Philadelphia concert had been two days ago.

"I guess she's busy." Del glanced around restlessly. "You know, these hotel rooms all look the same."

"Don't let Ricki get to you."

Del glanced at him like a deer caught in a glare of laser-light lamps. "It's just—I didn't think I hurt her, but now I wonder."

"I'm sure you didn't." The only person Mac saw getting hurt was Del.

"I would know," Del said, more to himself than Mac. "I was upset about the concert, and maybe it came out in how I treated her. But I *felt* it, Mac. She likes me edgy. I don't understand why she's acting like this."

Mac took a long drink of his beer, cold and frothy. "Men have been trying since the beginning of human life to figure out why women don't act the way we think they should. If you manage it, you'll win a Nobel Peace Prize."

"I can't even understand half of what she says," Del grumbled. "Like what is 'dom' and 'sub'?"

Mac choked on his beer and sputtered out froth.

"What?" Del regarded him with curiosity.

Mac suddenly wished he were elsewhere. He was no innocent, but this was more information than he needed about Del and Ricki.

Del laughed, watching his face. "I've never seen you blush. Come on, give. What does it mean?"

Mac cleared his throat. "It refers to a type of, um, sex play."

"Really?" Del looked even more intrigued. "Like what?"

"You know. Dominance. Submission."

"Dominance and submission of what?"

"For crying out loud, Del. Of the people doing it."

"You mean sex?"

"Yeah, I mean sex."

Del tilted his head. "Dominant how?"

This was excruciating. "One partner is, uh, the dominant one. He, or she I suppose, does things to the other person." He wished Del would start getting it, so Mac could stop saying it.

"What things?" Del asked.

Mac took a big swallow of beer. "Like, uh, tying up someone. Discipline. Um. Spanking. Like that." He squinted at Del. "This isn't really my thing. Maybe we should change the subject."

Del was staring at him. "Oh. *Oh*." Then he smiled. "You know, if Ricki doesn't—"

"Enough!" Mac's face was definitely heating. "I don't want to know what that smile means."

Del regarded him innocently. "What, I can't smile?"

"So," Mac said too loudly. "Did you have a good dinner tonight? I haven't tried the hotel restaurant yet."

Del burst out laughing. "All right. Yeah, dinner was fine. Some weird thing called a tuna-tish melt."

"You mean tuna fish?"

"I have no idea." Del's smile faded. He fell silent, lost in thought, staring at the floor. After a moment, he said, "I wonder sometimes if they aren't in all of us a little."

"Who?" Mac asked.

Del raised his gaze. "The Aristos."

It took Mac a moment to reorient. Startled, he realized Del

was comparing himself to the leaders of the Trader Empire that the Skolians had fought during the war.

"Good Lord," Mac said. "That stuff with Ricki's crowd is just games. A consensual form of play. She wasn't comparing you to an Aristo slave lord."

"I know." Del got up and paced away, then swung around to face Mac. "But the drive to hurt people didn't just appear in the Traders. They may have magnified it to horrific proportions, but it's always been in us."

"Horrific?" Mac raised his eyebrows. "Isn't that a bit melodramatic? I've heard what your people claim, but—"

"We don't *claim*." Del punched at the air with his fist. "All you Allieds, you sit here satisfied with yourselves while the Traders hack away at my people. Oh, you're safe. Our civilization is so much bigger than yours, you hide in our shadow. And the new Trader emperor is only seventeen. But give him time. He'll turn into a monster just like his predecessors." He pointed at Mac. "One of these days, the Traders will come after all of you. And it'll be too late then for you to listen to us."

That had certainly hit a nerve. Mac pushed up out of his chair and walked over to him. "Tell me."

"Tell you what?" Del asked angrily. "About the slavery of billions? Brutality on a scale you can't imagine?"

"I've seen Trader cities," Mac said quietly. "Their people have the highest standard of living among any of our civilizations."

"Of course they do," Del said. "There's over a trillion of them. Owned by several thousand Aristos. How do so few slave owners subjugate so many people? Make their lives pleasant. As long as they obey, they live well and the empire thrives."

"I agree that owning people is abhorrent," Mac said. "I've no love for Aristos. But what you're describing is hardly horrific."

Del met his gaze. "You think a nice house is worth constant oppression? If they step out of line, they die. It's called genocide, Mac. The Aristos can't risk defiance when so few of them control so many people." An edge honed his voice. "So what if you kill a few billion? There's plenty more where they came from."

Mac had heard similar from the Skolian military, when they sought Earth's support in their war against the Traders. They called the Aristos masters at propaganda. Yet Mac had seen a great deal of evidence for how well the Aristos treated their people and very little proof of the Skolian claims.

"Have you actually witnessed any of this?" Mac asked.

Del spoke tightly. "You don't want to go there."

"I want to understand. I'll listen, but not to propaganda."

"*Propaganda*?" Del looked ready to explode. "We *underplay* the truth with your people, because your damn government is always accusing us of overreacting. You have no flaming idea."

"Then *tell* me."

Del ground out the words as if they were broken glass. "They killed my brother Kurj. They tortured my brother Althor. He died. They tortured my brother Eldrin. He got free, but he still hasn't recovered. They shattered my father and fed off his agony. They caught my mother and—and—we got her out, but at first she couldn't even talk."

An image jumped into Mac's mind of the golden woman he had so recently witnessed scolding her son across interstellar space.

Del went on, relentless. "My sister's squad discovered that the Aristos planned to destroy the atmosphere of the world called Tams Station, to crush a rebellion on that planet. Her squad helped the colony evacuate. They got a third of the people out. *One third*. Think about it. Two thirds of a world *died*. It's all imprinted in the brains of the squad EIs." His voice cracked. "Yes, I've seen it."

Good Lord. "I'm sorry about your family. I had no idea." Mac knew the Traders had killed Del's sister, the previous Imperator, and his half-brother Kurj, the Imperator before her. The rest of what Del was telling him about his family had never been made public. "I've heard stories of how they destroyed the atmosphere of Tams, but I've never met anyone who saw EI records of it." To say the EI brains of a Jag fighter squadron were classified was akin to saying a beach had a few grains of sand.

Del just shook his head. He walked away, then stopped when a table blocked his way. Sitting down, he stared at the table. "My father lived for years, but he never fully recovered. It's only been a few months since he died."

Mac went around and sat across from him. "It's been a rough time."

Del looked up. "It would be easier if the Aristos just wanted to kill my family. But they want us alive. So they can hurt us."

It wasn't the first time Mac had heard that claim, but before it had been from Skolian officials. Hearing it from one of the people who would suffer at the hands of the Traders was different. "Why would they target you that way?"

"I suppose you could say Aristos are anti-empaths." Del's voice was brittle. "They came out of something called the Rhon Project."

"I thought that project was meant to help empaths."

"It was." Del took a breath. "Being an empath is like—I don't know the word. Like living with this constant, endless pressure. Last night, when I felt how much people liked the concert, it was good. *Great.* But when you pick up anger, grief, anything like that, it's painful. If we couldn't shut it out, we'd go insane."

Mac thought of the dossiers he had read on the Ruby Dynasty. "Wasn't the purpose of the Rhon Project to help psions create mental shields? To protect yourselves."

Del nodded. "That's why we know how to do it. But Doctor Rhon also changed our genes. Not mine, my ancestors. He was trying to lower our sensitivity to painful input." He gave a strangled laugh. "It didn't quite end up the way he expected."

"The research didn't work?"

"Oh, it worked," Del said. "It created the Aristos. They can pick up empathic signals from psions. *Pain* signals, both physical and mental. Only those. And you know how the Aristo brain lowers its sensitivity to the signals? By rerouting them to its pleasure centers." His voice cracked. "They're a bunch of sadists, Mac. Hurting us makes them feel good. They call us providers because our pain 'provides' them pleasure. They're brutal and sick, and they think they're exalted, that they have a right to inflict whatever they damn well please because they're gods and we're scum."

Del's words felt like punches. Mac had never heard it this way, with a target of the Aristos looking him straight in the eye, telling it in his words rather than the careful phrases of diplomacy. "I wish my people understood yours better."

"We need each other." Del gave a wry grin. "That's why the Skolian military didn't zap you all for keeping my royal butt here."

Mac smiled slightly, relieved to see Del's mood improve. "You're learning our slang."

"Ultra swivel." Del laughed with a wince. "Like my hips, apparently."

"Sorry about that review."

"It's a lot better than what Fred Pizwick said." Del's smile turned into a frown. "I did *not* use a Roberts Enhancer."

"Michael Laux on the Atlantic City-Time Hour wants to interview you about that." Mac offered the subject more to take Del's mind off the Aristos than because it had any urgency. "He wants you to do the exercise live, to prove you don't use an enhancer."

"Good!" Del shook his head. "I don't see how Pizwick can get away with saying I used one."

"He won't," Mac said. "But hell, you couldn't pay for this kind of publicity."

Del smiled wryly. "To sell my nonexistent vid."

"We'll get you in the studio tomorrow." Mac glanced at his wrist-mesh. "You should get some sleep. It's almost four."

"All right." Del stood up and rubbed his eyes. "I'll see you." He went to the door, then paused to look back. "And Mac—"

"Yes?"

Del spoke softly. "Thanks for listening."

Mac nodded, wishing he could do more. Like change the universe so one part of the human race wasn't preying on the other.

Del sat down at the console in his hotel room and clicked in the virt cube Mac had given him. A female voice said, "Virtual reality simulation array loaded."

That sounded impressive. "What do I do?" Del asked.

"Your question is vague," the console said. "Please be specific."

"How do I listen to the virt?"

"With yourself or someone else in it?"

In it? Del wasn't sure what that meant. "With me."

"Do you have internal biomech augmentation compatible with a Pacifica tri-media system?"

"Uh, no. I don't think so."

"You'll need a virt suit, then."

"Do you have one?"

"Check the lower drawer of this console."

Del investigated until he figured out how to click open the console drawer. A blue suit inside transparent packaging lay there with a visored helmet. He lifted out the suit. "So do I put this on?"

"That is correct. Remove your clothes first."

He laughed sleepily. "I'd rather hear that from Ricki."

Del changed into the suit and sat down, holding the helmet. With the console telling him what to do, he linked into the virt, then donned the helmet and settled back in the reclining chair. It was comfortable in the dark with the visor over his eyes. If nothing happened, he could get a few hours of sleep before the room AI insisted he get out of bed. Or chair.

The room lightened—no, not the room! He was standing in a rippling field that sparked under golden light. The sweet fragrance of the fresh grass tickled his nose, and a breeze tousled his hair. Insects trilled nearby.

"Hey," Del said. "Ultra."

A man was walking toward him through the field.

"Rex?" Del asked. It looked like the lead singer of Mind Mix.

"Hey." Rex came up and offered his hand. "Good to see you." Del shook his hand, and Rex's skin felt warm and textured.

"Hi," Del said.

"Would you like a tour?" Rex asked.

"Sure." This was more than Del expected. His family had an entertainment center at home, but it was mostly books, because his parents had wanted their children to read instead of playing virts. It had constantly frustrated Del; out of ten siblings, only he had never learned to read. Sure, an AI could read to him. But he preferred music. His people used songs as their "libraries." In their distant past they had bred the Bards to create and remember historical ballads. Musical archives.

Lyshrioli music bored him, though. He wouldn't have minded learning the art songs or folk music of his people if he hadn't been under so much pressure to drop what he wanted in favor of what everyone else wanted.

He walked with Rex through the meadow. "Do you remember me?" Del asked.

"I remember Mac Tyler," Rex said. "I don't have anything yet for you in this virt. But I'll remember this session."

"You're not really Rex, are you?" Del said.

Rex gave him an apologetic look. "Just an avatar. But you can have real people join you in the virt, if you want."

"It's five A.M.," Del said, laughing. "They're asleep." He paused as a thought occurred to him. "Am I talking out loud in my suit? I mean, if someone came into my room, would they hear me having this conversation with you?"

"Possibly," Rex said. "It depends on your setup. If you have a direct brain to console interface, this all takes place in your mind."

"I'm just wearing a suit."

"Are you subvocalizing?"

"I'm not sure what that means."

"If you think the word," Rex said, "muscles in your vocal cords, tongue, and throat move. The virt suit interprets it as speech." He sounded far more patient than the real Rex would have been with so many questions. "If you subvocalize, it keeps your session private."

"Oh. Okay. I can do that." Del indicated a building with swooping arches ahead. "What's that?"

"It's for your personal concert."

"Actually, I'd rather see you guys practice." Del liked to watch other people rehearse to learn what techniques they used to improve.

"Sure, we can do that." Rex gave a friendly laugh. "Most people want a personalized concert, with the real Rex."

"I know the real Rex," Del said. "You're more pleasant." He immediately felt guilty, given that Rex was the only member of Mind Mix who hadn't wanted him yanked off the tour. "But he's a good guy."

"I'm glad you think so. Here." Rex waved his hand.

Suddenly Del was inside a big, airy warehouse. Mind Mix was rehearsing in the open area. Sort of rehearsing. Rex sang the songs straight through with no stops, and sounded far better than the real rehearsal Del had heard yesterday. Tristan never missed a beat on his drums, and Tackman played his morpher better than in real life.

After a few songs, Del said, "Never mind." He didn't speak loudly, but the rehearsal stopped and both Rex and Tristan appeared next to him.

"Hey," Tristan said. "Glad to meet you." He even cracked a smile.

"Yeah, right," Del said. "The real Tristan can't stand me."

"You don't seem to be enjoying yourself," Rex said. "Would you like to try one of the story virts?"

"What's that?" Del asked.

Rex snapped his fingers and everything went dark. Music started, and somewhere Rex sang, "Honey, your eyes froze me, froze me, yeah, froze me in the night."

A street appeared, soaked from a recent rain. It was night, and a lone streetlamp reflected in the oily water of the alley. A woman in a trench coat walked toward Del, a hat pulled low over her face, her blond hair curling out from under it. She wore heels so high, he wondered how she kept from falling onto her face.

"Hey, honey," she said as she came up to him.

"Uh, hi." Del could see her eyes under the hat. They were large and blue. Icy blue. The virt intensified the color.

"Freeze me, Baaaaaaby," Rex wailed.

"What's your name, sweetheart?" the woman said.

"Del." The way her hair curled over her face was driving him nuts. Well, this was his session. He could do what he wanted. So he brushed it out of her eyes, and her hat slid back, revealing more of her face. She was sexy in a jaded sort of way. Rex kept singing, accompanied by the erotic beat of Tristan's drums.

"So Del," the woman said. "Why are you out here alone?"

"I've no idea," Del admitted with a laugh.

She touched his cheek with a well-manicured finger. "I think a sweet thing like you shouldn't be in a place like this at night. You could get into trouble."

"Freeeeze my heart," Rex sang.

"With you?" Del wondered what would happen if he tried to kiss her.

Her lips parted. "Why don't you find out?"

"I don't know if I should risk it," Del said, smiling. "This song ends with Rex yelling, 'Baby, you done froze my heart and smashed it all over the street.'"

"Come on, honey," she coaxed.

What the hell. Del put his arms around her waist and yanked her close. She felt real. When he opened her coat and slid his hand inside, skimming it under her breast, she felt even better. He had no idea what he was actually doing in the virt suit, and he didn't want to know, but here he kissed her. She molded against him, her face tilted up and her eyes closed. When he tried to caress her breast, though, she stepped away from him.

"You're dynamite, sweetheart," she said.

Rex groaned, "Baby, frazy, baby, crazy."

"Hey," Del said. "Don't go away."

She stayed back. "You're coming on strong, honey."

"You know," he said good-naturedly. "Whoever programmed this virt could have come up with more for you to call me than honey and sweetheart." Then again, this was part of a song with lyrics like "frazy, baby." Maybe he didn't want them thinking up more dialogue for their virtual femme fatale.

"Tell me," Del asked. "How far could I go with you?"

"Now, honey—"

"No, wait, I really want to know." Del felt his face redden. "I'm going to start making one of these virts tomorrow. I was wondering what people could, uh, do in them."

The song stopped, and Rex came up alongside of him on the street. The woman remained standing in place.

"You're making a virt?" Rex asked.

Del blinked, startled. At least Rex wasn't singing anymore. "I would feel really strange," Del said, "if people could buy my virts and, well, you know."

"Screw the simulations?"

"Since you put it so bluntly, yeah."

"It's against the law." Rex indicated the woman, who hadn't moved since he appeared. "She'll kiss you, but that's all. If you're underage, you don't even get kisses. Adults can buy X-rated virts, but Prime-Nova doesn't make them, at least not under that corporate name."

Del regarded him uncomfortably. "Does an artist get any choice in how his virt is set up?"

"Some." Rex pulled out a smoke-stick and lit up. The end glowed green. "Depends how much clout your manager has." He inhaled on the stick and blew out a plume of red smoke.

"Suppose a girl bought your virt and wanted you to kiss her?" Del asked.

"You have more choice on that." Rex puffed on his stick. "Nothing more than a kiss. But your simulation can go on dates with them if you okay those mods when you make the virt."

Del couldn't imagine virtual dates. Of course, he wouldn't really be on them. It would be some program designed to simulate him. Which was even weirder. "What if a guy comes into the virt?"

Rex shrugged. "I'll do a date if they want. You interested?"

"What? No, I didn't mean that!" Virtual or not, Del's face was burning. "Will the one I make for Prime-Nova be that way?"

"Not if you don't want to. But they'll ask you to allow it as an option." Rex seemed amused by his reaction. "Some virt users set up whole households. Or hair-raising adventures to find hidden treasure. Or shopping sprees. All with their favorite rock star. You can program this virt however you want as long as it's legal and not too far out of character for the actual Rex Montrow." He blew a smoke ring. "It can't violate the morals standards, either."

"You mean the censors." As far as Del could tell, they had a ridiculous amount of control over the industry. He was surprised this version of Rex got away with some of his language. Then again, it was mild compared to the real Rex.

"Are there restrictions on words you can say?" Del asked. "Screw is okay. Damn? Yeah, that works. F—" He stopped. "Suppose you want to say f—? Huh. Okay, that doesn't work."

"D— doesn't work, either," Rex said, laughing. "Or c—"

"What are those?"

"Oh, come on."

Del could guess one of them. "What if I'm a workman, and I need to drill a hole—hey, it let me say it. But not, I'm d— out of my mind."

"It's the context. The virt analyzes your speech." He considered Del. "You have a thick accent, if you don't mind my saying. English isn't your native language?"

"No. Prime-Nova makes me practice so I won't have an accent when I sing." He paused, feeling odd. The scene around him vibrated. "That's a bizarre effect."

"It's not an effect." Rex blew out a long stream of smoke. "Someone is shaking you."

"Oh." Del started to leave, then stopped. He had no idea "where" to go. What if he *couldn't* leave the virt? It was a strange thought, alarming and intriguing at the same time.

"I don't know how to stop this session," Del said.

"Just say, 'End virt.' Anything like that."

"Oh. Okay. End virt."

The scene went dark. After a moment, Del became aware of his body in the virt suit. He lifted off the helmet and found himself looking up at Randall. At first he thought his vision was shaking. Then he realized Randall was doing it all on his own.

"Hey," Del said. "How'd you get in my room?"

"You left the door unlocked." Randall laughed blurrily. "You should be more careful. You never know what lowlife'll creep in here." Swaying back and forth, he held up a bottle of clear liquid and two hotel glasses. "We should celebrate."

Del sat up, stretching his arms. "That virt was fun."

"They get boring real fast." Randall pulled over a recliner and sat by Del. "They're too predictable." He poured a glass of whatever was in his bottle and handed it to Del. "Now *this* is never the same twice."

Del smelled the liquid. "Whoa. What is it?"

"Ouzo. Greek fire water." Randall filled his own glass, took a big swallow, and let out a belch. "Oh, yeah."

Del laughed. "Is that a recommendation or a warning?"

"It's good. Try it."

Del set the drink on the console. "I'm allergic."

"Yeah, right."

"Really." Del didn't want to explain. "I should get some sleep, anyway."

Randall leaned back in his recliner. "You sleep." He lifted his glass to Del. "I'll celebrate for you."

Del smiled. "That virt was almost as good as sleeping."

Randall's eyelids drooped closed. "They're all the same after a while, least ways, the legal ones."

"Legal?" Del asked, intrigued. "What do illegal ones do?"

"Now how would a well-behaved boy like me know that?"

Del grinned. "Hypothetically."

Randall raised his lids halfway, his eyes glinting. "You can do whatever you want. With *who* you want. For as long as you want. A bliss-node can keep you in for hours. It's the thrill, you know, because you *can't* leave until the session ends. Like taking tau-kickers, only better. Hell, you can set your own trip. Whatever you want. Women. Wealth. Power." Then he said, "Not that I would know anything about tau-kickers or bliss-nodes."

Del laughed sleepily. "Of course not."

"It's safe, too, sort of," Randall said. "You're not putting anything in your body. No chemicals."

Del sat up straighter. "So nothing inside you can react with it? I mean, physiologically."

"Fizzy what?" Randall's voice slurred. "For someone who just learned English, you have one hell of a vocabulary." He yawned, showing a row of well-formed teeth. "But, yeah, that's right, no chemicals for Soo-Ling to pick up. So she stays happy and you're fine." Then he added, "In theory."

"Why in theory?" Up until those last two words, it had sounded great. "It's harmless, right?"

"Some people claim it'll fry your mind." He finished off his ouzo. "It's wired into your brain. If it goes bad, you *can't* stop. Not like tau-kickers, where medics can bring you down. Taking someone off a bad node is ugly, like brain-damage ugly."

"Oh." Always there was a catch. "Does it happen a lot?"

"Not that I know of." He contemplated his empty glass, then poured himself more ouzo. "Those stories, they're just bull to scare people. Virts are harmless. Boring as piss, but harmless."

Relief washed over Del. "Why make it so you can't get out? You can leave a regular virt whenever you want."

Randall shrugged. "Supposedly it's more fun, because you can forget it's not real." He leaned back and stretched out his legs. "I dunno. I was never into all that."

Del thought of the concert. "I was so wound up last night, I felt tied into knots. The virt relaxed me."

Randall gave a gravelly laugh. "With *Mind Mix*?" Closing his eyes, he slumped deeper into his recliner. "God forbid."

"It'd be fun to have a virt of anything I wanted." Del thought he'd make it like his home, except his family would approve of him. "The virtual Rex said I could program any virts I buy."

"Sure . . . if you don't want depth . . ." Randall's chin sunk to his chest.

Del caught Randall's drink just before it fell to the floor. He set it on the console and stood watching his guitarist snore. It was the most peaceful he had seen Randall. He got a blanket from the console drawer and spread it over his guest. Then Del ambled to his bed and flopped down, still in the virt suit. He could never have a conversation about a bliss-node with anyone in his family. His mother would want him to see a psychiatrist. His brother Kelric would send some military squad to pull him off Earth. His sister Chaniece might understand, but she would worry so much, Del would shut up because he felt guilty. His brother Eldrin would look at him with that crushing silent disappointment.

It bothered him most that Eldrin didn't understand. He and Del had similar temperaments. Eldrin had also struggled to read, though he eventually learned. And Eldrin sang. He preferred classical works, but he and Del had the same type of voice. Eldrin had done a few virtual operas when he was younger, where he sang in a studio and it went out on the meshes. Millions had listened. Del had wondered then why his brother never performed live; now he understood.

His last thought, as he drifted to sleep, was that maybe this business with Prime-Nova would work out after all. He had taken tau-kickers for the inspiration his constrained life as a Ruby Heir lacked—and destroyed all his dreams in that one killing mistake. Now he had a new universe to explore. He could experiment with virts to reach a level of creativity he had only imagined before. And it was safe.

After all, a simulation couldn't hurt him.

VIII

The Studio

General McLane motioned toward the back of his spacious office. "There's coffee."

Mac went to the shelf and poured the steaming brew into a smart-mug, which would keep his coffee at exactly the temperature he liked, add whatever extras he wanted, monitor his caloric intake, and even remind him to feed his cat if he asked.

"I don't think he was exaggerating, Fitz." Mac turned around. "The Aristos terrify him. With good reason, it sounds like."

"That assumes what he told you is true," Fitz said.

"If anything, I had a feeling he was holding back." Mac joined him at the table in an alcove. High in a tower, the glass-enclosed nook overlooked Annapolis. Fitz's stratospheric rank carried just as stratospheric duties, but it had its perks. Like this office.

"I have a virtual conference with President Loughten this afternoon," Fitz said. He rubbed the bridge of his nose with his thumb and forefinger, then laid his arm back on the desk. "She'll want a report on Del."

Mac could almost feel the general's fatigue. As one of Allied Space Command's top-ranked commanders, Fitz had far more to take up his time than worrying about their royal guest. But the general had to worry, especially since it had been his decision to bring the youth to North America, which was why Del had been here when his people pulled out the rest of the royal family.

"I've filed a full report," Mac said. "Use whatever you need."

"That's the thing." Fitz scanned a file on a screen in the table. "Some of it just doesn't fit. Listen to this."

A holo about a foot high appeared above the table. It showed Del at a console talking to his mother.

"Why not?" Del asked. "Isn't it what Devon Majda called me?"

"She most certainly did not," his mother said. "She would never speak that way about a Ruby prince." Roca shook her head. "You would never have agreed to that arranged marriage anyway. If we had tried to betroth you to her, you would have lost your temper."

Mac winced. He had felt awkward enough being present during Del's argument with his mother. Having Fitz replay it only emphasized Del's lack of control over his life.

"That was a private conversation," Mac said.

"I know." Fitz sounded tired. He sat back in his chair and considered Mac. "Do you know who he meant by Devon Majda?"

"Probably a noblewoman," Mac said. After the Ruby Dynasty, the Majdas were most powerful family among the Skolians. During the Ruby Empire, they had been royalty; now they ruled a financial empire.

"The only Devon Majda we have records of was a Majda queen," Fitz said. "She was expected to marry one of the Ruby princes."

Mac could imagine how Del would have responded if his parents had arranged his marriage to one of the Imperialate's most conservative matriarchs. *Losing his temper* was probably a mild description.

"I'm not sure I see why this would interest Allied Space Command," Mac said. "It's his private business."

"Because it doesn't make sense." Fitz leaned back in his chair. "Devon Majda abdicated her position to marry a commoner. Her sister Corey assumed the title and eventually married one of Del's brothers. A few years later, Trader assassins killed her. Her sister Naaj took the title then."

Mac sipped his coffee. "I'm surprised this wasn't in the files on Del."

"Oh, it's in our files. Just not where you're thinking." Fitz regarded him steadily. "Corey Majda married Kelric Valdoria."

Mac spluttered his coffee. "The *Imperator?*"

"That's right," Fitz said. "It was just after he graduated with his commission from the Dieshan Military Academy."

What the hell? "That was almost forty years ago."

"Thirty-seven. Eighteen years after Devon Majda abdicated." Fitz spoke quietly. "If anyone discussed a marriage between Devon and Del, it had to have been at least fifty-five years ago."

Mac took a moment to absorb that. Then he shook his head. "It must be some other Devon. A daughter, niece, cousin."

"We have no records of any other Devon Majda. And listen to this." The general flicked a holicon above his screen, and Del's talk with his mother resumed.

"Del, that was years ago," she said.

"Not to me," he told her.

Fitz froze the recording, catching Del's strained look.

"It does sound odd." Mac thought for a moment. "Do you have Del's interview with Major Baxton? The part where the major asked for his age."

Fitz worked for a moment, and the holo changed to show Del and Baxton at a table.

"Your age, please," Baxton said.

Del scowled at him. "Seventy-one.

"In Earth years."

"That is Earth years."

"Freeze," Mac said. When the holo stopped, he pointed to where Baxton's elbow rested on the table. "Can you magnify that?"

Fitz flicked more holos, and Baxton's arm grew until it took up the entire image.

"There on the table," Mac said. "Right at the edge. See the green light?" A chill went through Mac. "If Del was making that up about his age, that light should be red."

"I remember that," Fitz said. "It's a malfunction. We've verified Del's age. He doesn't just look young. He *is* young. Every doctor's report puts him in his early to mid-twenties."

Mac slowly set down his coffee. "He told me he spent time in a cryogenic womb. It's why we get different values for his age depending on how we test him."

Fitz shook his head. "Being in a womb shouldn't give inconsistent readings. Certainly not with modern cryogenics."

"Maybe it wasn't modern." Mac regarded him uneasily. "We've only had reliable cryogenic sciences for about thirty-five years."

"He couldn't have been in cryo that long." Fitz tapped the screen, and the holo disappeared. "Hell, the longest I've heard of anyone being in—and surviving—is seven years."

Mac let out a breath. "Maybe Del was just talking about some other Devon we have no records on."

He wondered, though, what would happen if the government of an empire decided to keep someone alive whatever the cost, no matter how raw the technology.

"It's not epilepsy." Philip Chandler paged through a holofile with the results of Del's tests. "You show no other neurological problems, either."

Del shifted on the med table where he was sitting, wearing just his mesh-jeans. "I could have told you that."

Chandler regarded him sternly. "You need more sleep."

"I stayed up all night," Del admitted.

"I don't know much about empaths," Chandler said. "I'd like you to see someone who specializes in the treatment of Kyle operators."

It startled Del to hear the words "Kyle operator." It meant the same thing as psion, but he never thought of himself that way. It sounded so mechanical, as if he were a thing rather than a person. "Can you find a specialist?" he asked. They were rare in Skolian hospitals, and the Allieds weren't even convinced psions existed.

"I don't know." Chandler unclipped a light-stylus from the file and made a note in the holofile. He spoke firmly. "My prescription, young man, is for you to eat nutritious meals and get proper rest. Don't take your health for granted."

"All right." Del slid off the table. He just wanted to escape the doctor's office.

As Del picked up his shirt, Chandler said, "When you give your med-chip to the receptionist, have her make a note that we should contact you as soon as I get the name of a Kyle specialist."

"My what chip?" Del asked.

"Your insurance information." Chandler paused. "You have it, don't you?"

Del stared at him blankly. "I don't know what you mean."

"Then who's paying for this?"

Del had no idea. No one had ever asked him to pay for medical care before. He felt Chandler's tension, though. If he said no one, the doctor would think he was trying to cheat him. So he said, "Mac Tyler. He manages things for me."

"Oh, that's right." Chandler regarded him with a firm gaze. "A word of advice, son. Learn to take care of your own finances. You'll be glad in the long run."

It embarrassed Del to realize he didn't even know if he *had* any finances here. Mac had talked about an "advance" when he explained Del's contract, but it had all sounded more convoluted than an interstellar treaty.

So learn, Del told himself. He needed to take care of himself if he wanted independence from his family.

Ricki stood in the booth above studio six and pushed a tendril of hair out of her eyes. She spoke into the studio comm. "Del, try again. Just the first verse. Give me more energy on the second line."

Down in the studio, Del nodded to her, then held an audio-comm to his left ear so he could hear whatever Greg Tong was telling him. Del had a jane in his other hand, or Janeson selector, named for Rita Janeson, the engineer who designed the prototype. The selector sent data to Ricki and Greg, including an analysis of Del's pitch, the key he was singing in, the harmonics in each note, how much vibrato he used, his timbre, volume, and anything else Ricki wanted to know. The only thing it couldn't tell her was why Mister Churlish Arden had ignored her for two days.

Del's voice soared:

> Running through the sphere-tipped reeds
> Suns like gold and amber beads
> Jumping over blue-winged bees—

"Okay, that's enough," Ricki said. "Del, the word at the end of every line in that verse has the same vowel sound."

He lowered the jane and spoke testily. "I know that."

"No one does it that way," Ricki said. "The first and third line have to rhyme, and the second and fourth. You need to fix it. "Diamond Star" has a similar problem. In that song, you're rhyming the first and second lines, then the third and fourth. I need you to switch the second and third lines of each verse so they fit the proper scheme."

Del stared up at the booth. "You're joking, right?"

"No, I'm not joking." Her bad mood was growing worse. Now he was challenging her in front of the two techs in the studio: the ever-present Cameron who hulked around and carried heavy equipment, and Bonnie, the pretty little one, who was working on holo displays for the vid and studiously ignoring their argument.

"We can't finish the vid until you fix the songs," Ricki said.

Del folded his arms, the audio-comm in one hand and the jane in the other. "It would ruin the songs. Besides, some of my others don't rhyme at all."

"I'm aware of that," Ricki snapped. "You'll have to fix them."

"The hell I do."

Ricki clenched her teeth. That damn undercity punk.

Mac was striding across the studio. Ricki hadn't seen him come in, but given his fast pace, she suspected he had heard at least the end of her exchange with his client.

Mac stopped by Del and looked up at the booth. "Ricki, let's take a few, okay?"

She breathed out slowly, resisting the urge to say, *Get your boy to behave his tight little ass or I'm done with him.*

"Sure," she said. "Fine."

Del stalked off with Mac, his shoulders stiff. He left without a backward glance at the booth. Ricki felt ready to explode.

Calm down. Why did Del get to her so much? She couldn't let him disrupt her life this way. Closing her eyes, she stood very still, letting the minutes pass as her pulse slowed.

"Ricki?" a man said.

Startled, she spun around. Mac was standing across the booth. That was the problem with having holo curtains for doors; you couldn't hear a person skulk in.

"I don't have time for his tantrums," Ricki said. She gave him a steely gaze, but a straggle of hair fell in her eyes, diluting the effect. Exasperated, she brushed it aside.

Mac came over and leaned against the panel, facing her. "Ricki, listen. You're considered the best in this industry for a reason. You know this business backward and forward. You *know* what works. And you saw it in Del. Trust your instincts. Yes, his songs are different. *You* had the savvy to see the power in that. His success will make you the latest trendsetter for the billion dollar babies."

Ricki snorted. "Flattery won't help, Mac. If he plummets, I'll look like an idiot."

"He won't plummet. But even if he did, so what? Prime-Nova took a chance on an undercity artist. It's getting you kudos from the arty set. Critical acclaim. That's what people remember."

She didn't want to hear any of this. "He won't be just another act that fizzled. He's the boy we put with Mind Mix who got the worst reviews of any opener I've ever produced."

"Just at first. He's fine now."

"He's *not* fine." She waved her hand at him. "He's raw and unprepared and you know it. They like him because he's mesmerizing once he loosens up. He's so magnetic, they're practically flying out of the audience and sticking to him."

Mac's lips twitched upward. "I've never heard it put that way. But yeah, he has it, whatever 'it' is."

"With work, he'll do a good show. He's not there yet."

"You're right, he needs work," Mac said. "But don't constrain his genius."

"Oh, cut the crap." Ricki felt like hitting something. "Every boomallitic blaster this side of the Moon thinks he's the next musical Einstein. I don't have time for it."

"Fine," Mac said. "Don't constrain his commercial potential. Let him do it his way, and he'll give you charisma like you've never seen. Box him in, and you'll package all that magnetism right out of existence."

Ricki scowled at him. "Would you please stop making sense?"

Mac smiled. "Sorry."

"All right. He can keep his damn lyrics." She crossed her arms. "But only if he stops giving me grief about shows, special effects, holos, all that. If he complains one more time about the clothes we pick for him, I'll get a plogging ulcer." Which was saying a lot, given that her health meds were supposed to counteract any acidic juices that went after her stomach lining.

"Plogging?" The laugh lines crinkled around Mac's eyes, but he kept a straight face. Almost. "That's an, um, creative literary construction."

Ha, ha. "No more grief," Ricki said.

"I'll see to it," he assured her.

"You had better," she growled.

✧   ✧   ✧

Del paced at the end of the hallway outside the studio. He was ready to bust through the roof. If Ricki insisted he gut his songs, he had to refuse, which would no doubt put him in violation of his endlessly tedious contract. If he pissed off Prime-Nova, no one would work with him. But he *couldn't* do what she wanted. He would rather give up the virt than corrupt lyrics that meant so much to him, especially just to fit some ridiculously contrived rhyme scheme.

By the time Mac came striding down the hallway, Del was wound as tight as a blaster coil. "What did she say?" he demanded. "Maybe she wants to rename the planets to fit a better rhyme scheme. Hell, why call this Earth? It's more commercial to say 'Sexy world of mine, with seas deep and green, the name doesn't rhyme, so call it Wet Dream.'"

Mac stopped in front of him. "Del, calm down." He looked as if he were trying not to laugh, which just made it worse.

"She's an artistic barbarian," Del said.

"You didn't think so when she offered you a job."

Del was reevaluating that opinion. "What did she say?"

"She'll let you go with your lyrics."

"Hey!" Del gaped at him. "That's good."

Mac didn't seem relieved. In fact, he looked as if he was bracing for another explosion. "She has a condition."

He should have known. "What condition?"

"You have to put together a show that Prime-Nova approves, with costuming, effects, dancing—"

"Dancing!" Del felt as if a mag-rail car had slammed into him. "*Whose* dancing?"

Mac winced. "Yours."

"I don't know how!" They were going to *make* him dance? It had been bad enough when he did it without realizing in concert. He couldn't do it on purpose. Gods, what if his family saw him?

"You dance fine," Mac said. "It's probably all that martial arts you studied. And she'll have choreographers work with you."

He wondered if he should die right now or just go home and drown himself. "I cannot dance. Absolutely not."

"Damn it, Del." Mac took a breath and spoke more calmly. "Work with her, okay? I agree with you about the lyrics. It would ruin your songs. But so what if they want you to wear sexy clothes and do a few dance moves? You did last night. And you know what? The world didn't end. You looked good. The girls adored it."

Del wondered how the male inhabitants of an entire planet could be so dense. "Men," he said flatly, "do not dance. Women do. Period. I am not a woman."

"And why, pray tell, do men not dance?" Mac said. "Because Ricki told you to?"

"The hell with Ricki."

"She's your producer. Without her, you have no vid."

"Without me, *she* has no vid."

"Yeah, no vid of you," Mac said sourly. "Light-bulb time, Del. You're the one who loses if this doesn't work." He shook his head. "Just get a room, will you two?"

Del blinked. "What?"

"Look," Mac said. "I'm not a punching bag for you and Ricki to use because you're both too proud to admit you like each other. You shouldn't have gotten involved with your producer, but you did, and what's boiling with you two won't just go away. If you're angry with her for leaving in the morning, talk to her. Don't fume and seethe and destroy the vid because you two have all this pent-up sexual energy you want to hurl at each other."

Del felt his face burning. "For flaming sake."

"When it comes to work, you put the personal business aside."

"Is that what you came here to tell me?" Del asked crossly. He had thought Mac had a meeting with General McLane this afternoon. Del hadn't expected to see him until the studio session tonight.

Mac breathed in slowly. "No. No, that wasn't it. I stopped by to give you something." He went to the end of the hall and took a bag off a table there. As Del joined him, Mac said, "I thought you might like to hear some of the classics." He pulled out a cube and handed it to Del. "This band helped lay the foundations of the musical movement that grew into what you do now."

Del turned the cube over. A holo of four men glowed in front of one panel. He couldn't read the words, but he knew it was a vid, rather than a virt, because it fit into his hand. Virts were twice that size. It was mostly packaging; the vid itself was just a little chip. He had heard some people even wore them as lenses, to project the images wherever they looked.

Del peered at the musicians. "Who are they?"

"A band called The Doors," Mac said. "From the twentieth century."

"Oh, come on," Del said. "They didn't have rock back then." When Mac raised his eyebrows, Del said, "How could they? The tech didn't exist."

"That's right," Mac said. "No enhancement, no cockpits, no morphers, no mega-multiplexioed anything. Nothing but old-style instruments. And the human voice." He tapped the cube. "They didn't need tech; they had talent." He studied Del. "You remind me of their vocalist, Jim Morrison. The way you sing, that is. Not your temperament."

Del stiffened. "Meaning what? I'm temperamental?"

"Actually, no," Mac said. "You're more even-keeled. Morrison died young, from too much hard living." He was watching Del with an odd look. "In fact, he wasn't much older than you are."

Del could tell Mac expected a reaction to that last comment. Something about his age. Or death, maybe. He spoke awkwardly. "Well, I'm alive now." Before Mac could ask more questions, Del motioned at his bag. "What else do you have?"

Mac offered him more cubes. "These are bands I thought you might like: Avantasia, Metallica, Within Temptation, Dragon-land, Troy Wilfong, Epica, Iron Maiden, Morphallica, Nightwish, Apocalyptica."

Del turned the cubes over in his hand, intrigued by the holos of scowling men and ethereal women in gothic outfits. It had an edge that appealed to him, dark and light together. He motioned at an image of four glowering young men wearing leather clothes and metal-studded gauntlets. They looked like a cross between musicians and Skolian Jagernauts, the elite cyber-warriors of Del's people. "Who are they?"

"A band called Titan." Mac indicated one of the men. "That's Nige Walker. He was a forefather of some holo-rock styles you hear today." He gave Del another cube. "This is something differ-ent, one of the biggest male singers from the twenty-first century. His work is softer than yours, but you sound like him when you sing slower songs in your baritone range. Zachary wants more of that quality in your ballads."

Del set down the other cubes. The new one showed a hand-some man standing in a forest of snow-dusted firs. Although he could see why it would appeal to people, it had a different look from how he thought of himself. He tried to puzzle out the name, then gave up. "Who is it?"

"Josh Groban." Mac glanced from the cube to Del. "You know, your coloring aside, you look a little like him."

"No, I don't!" Del said. "And this guy doesn't sing rock. I can tell from the packaging."

"Just listen to him," Mac said. "He has a great sound."

"But it's not me."

"They aren't asking you to change your style. Just soften the hard edges in some places."

Del regarded him doubtfully. *Lose your edge* was the preface people used when they were about to tell him he should be less surly and more the way they expected for a prince of Raylicon.

Mac handed him a new cube. With a glint in his eyes, he added, "You *don't* sing better than this fellow."

Del bristled at the challenge. "What, you think I can't match some old-timer?" He scowled at the cube, which showed a heavy-set man with a powerful appearance. "Are you going to say I look like this one, too?"

"No one looks like Luciano Pavarotti except Pavarotti," Mac said. "He was unique. When you sing tenor, though, you sound like him, at least when you're doing something classical, like those Lyshrioli art songs."

"Was Pavarotti a rock singer?" When Mac started laughing, Del glared. "How am I supposed to know?"

"It says right there on the cube."

Del flushed. "I can't read English."

"Oh!" Mac turned apologetic. "You speak it so well, I forget how little time you've had to learn." Then he said, "Pavarotti is considered one of the greatest male opera singers of the past few centuries."

Del thrust the cube at him. "Why is everyone always shoving opera on me? I *like* what I do."

"And you should." Mac pushed the cube back at him. "That doesn't mean you can't appreciate his voice."

Del grunted and set it next to the others. "What's that last one in your bag?"

Mac handed him a cube that showed several young men in old-style jeans walking through an urban area. The city resembled Baltimore, but the streets looked as if they came from an earlier era.

"It's a band called Point Valid," Mac said. "They were big in the twenty-first century. One of the first undercity bands, coming out of the alternative rock movement. They laid down some of the seminal philosophies used today."

That sounded more like it. Del shook the cube, making the holos shimmer. He indicated a young man singing. "Who is that?"

"Hayim Ani, their vocalist. He played lead guitar and wrote lyrics. The other two are the guitarist Max Vidaver and the drummer Adam Leve." Mac gave him the bag to hold all his cubes. "They followed a style you don't see much anymore. They would arrange an album, what we call an anthology, around a theme. Sometimes the songs tell a story."

Del looked up. "Like I'm doing with *The Crystal Suite.*"

Mac cleared his throat. "*The,* uh, *Jewels Suite.*"

Del crumpled the bag in his fist. "Why does Zachary think 'crystal' is a drug reference? If you cut out every word the censors think might have a negative meaning for someone, you won't have any versatility left in the language."

"You noticed," Mac said dryly.

Del smirked and sang under his breath. "Fra-a-a-azy, baby."

"Yeah, well, at least Mind Mix finished their virt." Mac waved Del toward the studio. "You won't unless you go in there and work with Ricki."

"All right. I'll behave." Del stepped to the studio door, which was real, not a curtain of light. He stopped with his palm on its glossy white surface and turned back to Mac. "I'd like to talk later. About my contract. My bills. Everything." He didn't want to say more, but this was too important to let go. "All my life, people have looked after me. Then I was sick, and I needed to be taken care of. I never had to make my own way. I want to learn. About money and all that."

"I'll be glad to." Mac nodded as if Del had said something intelligent instead of admitting he had never matured in ways most people took for granted. "I've been wanting to ask you about some things, like your appointment with Doctor Chandler today."

Del smiled. "He says I'm fine. I wasn't eating right. I'll be better about it."

Mac exhaled with undisguised relief. "Good." He put on a stern look and pointed to the studio. "Now go work!"

Del grinned and pressed a panel, making the door slide open. It wasn't until he was in the studio that he remembered he should tell Mac that Chandler wanted him to see a specialist. It seemed silly to Del. He felt fine, and the tests showed no problems. He was all right. His doctors back home had been telling him the same for nearly five years.

He hadn't told Mac everything about his illness. He didn't want to think about it. He had to be all right—because he couldn't bear the thought of going back to the hell his life had been when he was sick.

IX

The Spiker Crowd

Ricki stood in the booth and massaged her neck. She was tired but pleased. Despite her argument with Del, the session had been productive. Mac had a point; when Del felt inspired, that farm boy was a powerhouse. He had given her good material today, and he had another day before he flew to Boston for his next concert. If tomorrow went as well, she would have a lot to work with while he was gone.

If, if, if. Everything with him was uncertain. He could soar one moment and drive her crazy the next. She didn't know if his wildly fluctuating performance came from lack of experience or if this was the real Del. The former she could work with, but if he was always this inconsistent, she was going to have a migraine.

Ricki straightened up, facing the window—and saw Del's reflection in the glass. He was standing behind her, here in the booth. Well, well. The king of cool had deigned to acknowledge her existence. It irked her that it felt so good to see him. Next she knew, she'd be joining Elba's mesh-mall girls, the Elbows or Stinger-bees or whatever, and swooning over him in a fan club. What a mortifying thought.

Del turned as if to leave, hesitated, then turned back. He looked as jumpy as oil sizzling on a skillet.

She knew when he realized she could see him; his gaze met hers in the glass. He came up behind her then and put his arms around her waist, bending his head to hers. Fortunately, she had already turned off the audio to the booth and dimmed the window. They wouldn't be visible if anyone was still down there.

"It's after midnight," he murmured, his breath tickling her ear. "Aren't you tired?"

"I have work to do." She pressed down her flare of desire. "We won't get the studio tomorrow until after dinner."

He licked her ear. "You're in demand."

Damn straight. She put hands on top of his arms and pulled them away from her body. Or tried to pull them. Huh. Mister Persistence wouldn't let go. He stood with his front against her back, his arms around her, and oh my, did he smell good. Eau de Del. A tingle went through her, half anger and half arousal.

"Let go of me," she said coldly.

Del let her go, but only so he could turn her around. He nudged her to the side and pinned her against the wall by the window.

"Cut it out," Ricki said. Her corn-fed lover was looking at her as if he would rip the husk off her cob and strip her down for a bite. After the way he had ignored her, she didn't intend to show the least bit of interest in him.

Del laughed softly. "What an image." He bent his head and kissed her.

Damn that felt good. Then Ricki remembered herself and pulled her head away. "Keep that pouting mouth to yourself."

He gave her his bedroom smile. "You love me, Ricki. Admit it."

"I most certainly do not love you." Crossing her arms, she made a bulwark between them.

"Come on," Del murmured as he pulled apart her arms. "You're driving me insane."

"You weren't already there?" she asked sweetly.

Del laughed and kissed her again, sliding one arm around her waist and pulling her against him while he caressed her breast.

"Oh!" The startled voice came from across the studio.

Del looked around, his eyes half-closed. Ricki thought she ought to fire whoever had walked in.

Bonnie, the tech girl, was standing just inside the room, her face bright red. "I'm s-sorry," she said. "Cameron said you were up here. We were ready to go."

Blast it. If an award existed for bad timing, this girl could win it. Ricki spoke under her breath. "Del, let go of me."

After a moment, Del released her and stepped away. To Bonnie, he said, "I thought Cameron was downstairs."

"He's just outside," Bonnie said.

"Oh." Del seemed at a loss for a response.

Ricki regarded Del, intrigued. "Everywhere you go, Cameron goes."

"He's my babysitter," Del grumbled. "Mac hired him to make sure I don't get lost or whatever. I've only been on Earth a few weeks, and I can't read or write English."

Interesting. Ricki glanced at Bonnie. "Thanks, hon. Tell Cameron he can go home. I'll make sure Del doesn't get into trouble." At least, no trouble that didn't involve her.

The girl glanced from Ricki to Del as if she thought the greatest danger to Del was in this room. But she had enough sense to keep her thoughts to herself. She said only, "I'll tell him."

As Bonnie disappeared through the holo-curtain, Ricki slipped away from Del. "Come on," she said. "The night's hardly started." When he reached for her arm, she stepped away. "Oh no," she murmured. "You have to work for it."

His gaze smoldered. "Don't push me, Ricki." A wicked smile played around his lips. "Or I'll have to take steps."

"Do tell." Goodness, he was hot tonight. "And where might that little walk lead you?"

"Be careful what you ask." He started toward her. "Or you'll get the answer."

"Is that so?" She flicked off the control panel. "Go get that hot leather jacket of yours. We're going to a party."

Del couldn't absorb all the sensory input. It was too much. They had arrived at a penthouse in some tower he didn't know. The place glittered even in the dim lights. It was full of people in sparkling clothes, at least what little they wore. Lights strobed, but none bright enough to light the corners of the room. It gave the place a sultry, erotic feel.

"Over here," Ricki said, pulling him by the hand.

Del went with her, disoriented. The smell of spiker sticks

saturated the air. Unease rippled over him. Spikers weren't one of the drugs his doctors said would make the meds in his body go crazy, but he could never be sure what would happen.

They ended up near a tall table filled with blue and purple glow tubes. A cluster of people had gathered around it, gleaming with the sleek elegance of those who had too much money to spend and too much time to spend it in, but who hadn't yet become jaded beyond caring how they looked.

"It's the principle of it," a woman was saying. Red holo studs glinted in her cobalt hair. "If you let anyone say whatever they want on the meshes, you'll have anarchy."

"Anarchy?" another woman said. "It's called free speech!"

"You have to draw a line between free and libelous," a man said. Laser-tattoos of blue snakes glowed on his cheeks. "It isn't 'free' if people are so intimidated by mesh attacks, they fear to speak."

"But who decides where you draw that line?" the first woman said. "You? Me? The government?"

"Mesh worlds form their own dynamic," another man said. "The group decides what rules they want. If you don't like their rules, join another m-world."

"So if a group decides to suppress the speech of others, that's all right?" the tattooed man demanded. "Hey, I could get people to follow you around the meshes and come down like ten tons of plutonium every time you say something I don't like. I'm exercising my right to free speech—and denying you yours."

A dark-haired man with no tattoos, holos, or jewelry spoke quietly. "Your 'free' speech is decided by whoever has power on the meshes. The more time you spend in the m-universe, the more people know about you. And the more they know, the more they can affect your life."

Del started. The man had a *Skolian* accent.

Ricki spoke under her breath. "This is boring." She drew him away from the group. "I hate politics. It gives me croup."

Del agreed wholeheartedly. At least, he thought he did. "What's croup?"

"I've no idea what it means," she admitted. "Just that it's vile and unpleasant."

He gave a wry laugh. "Sounds accurate to me." Curious, he said, "Who was that last man who spoke? He sounded Skolian."

"He is. That's Staver Aunchild. He's a buyer for one of the Metropoli entertainment conglomerates. He decides which of our acts he wants to sell to his people." She arched an eyebrow at him. "You ever get big enough, they might look at you. But sweets, you aren't there yet. Not by a long shot."

Well, that was tactful. "Maybe never."

"I didn't say you couldn't. Just that you need time."

Del found it hard to imagine people would ever like his music enough even just to send it offworld, let alone to his own people.

Ricki took him to table with purple light-tubes where several people were sitting on tall chairs. A man with spiky blue hair puffed on a stick that spiraled red smoke into the air. The woman next to him had long black hair, purple eye shadow, and no clothes except jewel-encrusted chains that barely covered her curvaceous hips and large breasts. An older man sat on her other side, sleek and dangerous in an elegant business suit. His wrist-mesh looked as if it cost more than this tower. He had draped his arm over her shoulders, and his predatory gaze was fixed on her breasts, which were trying to burst out of her chains.

"Hey, babe," the man with blue hair said to Ricki.

"Hey." Ricki pushed Del toward a chair and slid into another one. "How's the thorn kicking?"

"Here." Blue-hair offered her the stick. "Like your heels."

Del sat in the chair, wondering how they could speak English and say nothing he understood. Spiker smoke thickened the air, making him dizzy, and the drugged mood of all these glimmering people penetrated his mental shields. So much bare skin. In one corner, a man and woman swayed together, arms wrapped around each other as they unfastened their scanty clothes. Del blushed and looked away. Then he stared at Ricki and wondered if this place had any bedrooms.

"You look hungry," Ricki murmured. "Later, sweets."

"He *is* sweet, isn't he?" Blue-hair purred.

Del jerked around to stare at the man. "What?"

"Hands off," Ricki told Blue-hair. "No poaching." She took a long drag on the spiker, held it in, and then let glinting red smoke trickle past her red lips. It swirled around her and up to the ceiling. The mega-wealthy executive was ignoring them as he whispered in the ear of the other woman and caressed her breasts.

Ricki handed the spiker to Blue-hair and tilted her head at Del. "He's a farm boy. Del Arden."

Blue-hair leaned closer to Del. "Oh, Ricki dear, where *did* you find him?"

"Why don't you ask me?" Del said coldly. He didn't like the way the guy stared at Ricki. Or at him. He couldn't focus; he felt drilled without taking a single drag of the spiker.

Ricki wasn't paying attention; she was watching the dancers swaying. "Lot of heft tonight."

"The usual." Blue-hair regarded Del as if he were some exotic delicacy. "And then some."

Del stared at him, then swung around to the person who had dragged him into this crazy place. "*Ricki—*"

"Shhh." She put her hand on his arm. "You want a drink?"

"No." Del couldn't breathe. "I'm tired. Let's go."

Blue-hair offered him the spiker. "Here, relax, babe. It's top of the line, straight from the Antarian colony."

Babe? Del wanted to punch him, but instead his fingers closed around the spiker. Smoke curled past his face, adding a red cast to the scene. The executive was tugging the chains off the girl, and Del stared at her erect nipples.

"Here." Ricki pushed the spiker to his lips. "Just inhale. It will do the rest."

"No! I don't want—" Del choked as smoke poured into his mouth. He gulped involuntarily and breathed in a lungful. When he coughed, the spiker fell from his fingers.

"Hey!" Blue-hair grabbed the stick. "Tell your boy-toy to be careful with that."

"Don't call me that," Del snarled at him.

Ricki slid off her chair and tugged Del off his. The others at the table also got to their feet. The girl's chains slid down her body and pooled in a pile of jeweled gold on the floor. She stood there, sleek and perfect, wearing nothing but a few strategically placed jewels around her hips, her eyes so dilated, she almost had no irises.

"Come on, babe," Ricki murmured, pulling him by the hand.

Del went where she pulled, too muzzy to think. Blue-hair appeared at his side and put his arm around Del's shoulders.

"Hey!" Del shoved him away. "Drill off."

"He's an arrow," Ricki told Blue-hair. "They don't fly any straighter. You won't get this one."

"Too bad." Blue-hair went ahead of them to join the girl and the executive, who was walking on her other side with his arm around her shoulders. Blue-hair put his arm around her waist and kissed her ear.

"Ricki, let's go," Del said. His words echoed in his ears.

"Here." She set her finger on his lips. "Isn't this better?"

"What?" He looked around, his gaze blurred, trying to figure out what she meant. They were in a different room, one with dimly glowing walls and no other light. Or furniture. The thick carpet came over the toes of his boots. Pillows, glimmering sheets, and leather toys were strewn around. The executive pulled the chain-girl into a nest of cushions, and Blue-hair sat with them, still smoking his spiker.

Ricki nudged Del. "Come on."

"Ricki, no," Del said. "I don't do this." He wasn't even sure what exactly he didn't do, but he had no doubt that whatever it was, this room included a lot of it.

"You'll be fine," she said, her voice silken. She tugged him forward, and he stumbled, then went down on one knee next to the naked girl and the executive.

Blue-hair offered Del the spiker. "Takes the edge off."

Del tried to push away the man's hand, but he missed and fell against Ricki, who had knelt at his other side. They sprawled in a pile on the cushions, landing partially on top of the purple eye-shadow girl. Her breast rubbed Del's cheek, and before he even thought about it, he pulled her nipple into his mouth and suckled. So sweet.

The executive was lying against the girl's other side, but he stopped caressing her long enough to lean over and kiss Ricki. Lifting his head, Del scowled at the exec. He could barely see, and he couldn't think, except that he wanted Ricki *out* of her clothes, and if that rich asshole touched her again, Del would flatten his face.

By the time Del separated Ricki from her clingy tunic and tights, he wasn't wearing anything, either. She lay under him, the two of them nestled against the others. When she tried to pull him closer, he held her down by the shoulders.

"Patience, love," Del murmured.

She was breathing hard. "Kiss me, you sexy bastard."

A slow smile spread on his face. "You have to wait for it."

She stared up at him with those huge eyes as if she was an innocent, but with his shields weakened by his spiker high, he easily felt her mind. She was so turned on, she was close to an orgasm. Del flipped her onto her stomach and stretched out on top of her, biting her neck. Then he lifted her hips up and thrust into her from behind. She groaned and clenched the pillow under her, her pulse speeding up even more. She was building, higher, higher—and just as she was about to explode, he stopped, holding up her hips.

"*No.*" She could barely get the word out, she was breathing so hard. "Don't *do* this to me again." She groaned and writhed in his hold. "I'll go crazy."

Del pinned her wrists to the floor while he slowly pulled out of her. "You shouldn't disappear in the morning. You didn't even leave a note. Now you have to pay."

"Stop teasing me."

"You're going to scream for it," he whispered against her ear. He pulled her arms over her head and held them trapped with one hand while he stroked her sides and breasts with his other, keeping her on the edge of an orgasm while she struggled. Then he slowly brought her down from her peak. When she had calmed a little, he entered her again, restarting the cycle, bringing her back up. He was aware of the other three making love, and their desire added to his own, their combined arousal drugging his mind as much as the spiker drugged his body. Ricki moaned under him, her mind a blur of frustrated, urgent hunger.

Del kept her that way, on and on, tormenting her with pleasure, until neither of them could take any more. He let go then, thrusting harder until she screamed with her climax. As ecstasy burst over him, his conscience reeled, but he was too far gone to care.

Del woke up alone. No, not alone; the purple eye-shadow girl was sleeping nearby. She looked lovely as long as he stayed still. When he moved, the room blurred and dimmed, and nausea surged in him. With a groan, he clambered to his feet, desperate to find a bathroom before he embarrassed himself.

The first door he stumbled through let him into an empty bedroom. He staggered across its green carpet into a bathroom. Dropping to his knees, he leaned over the washbasin and vomited his last meal. Then he flushed the basin and sat on his knees, shaking and chilled. He scared himself. Spikers didn't make people throw up.

When Del felt steadier, he went into the misting-stall and let the cleansing mists bathe him. He scoured his teeth, then dried off in the sumptuous hot air blasts. After that, he just stood, leaning his forehead against the tiled wall. He couldn't believe what he had done last night. Gods only knew what Ricki thought of him now. He hoped he had made love only to her. He thought so, but they had all been so entangled, he had lost track of who was touching him.

After a few minutes, when he felt steadier, he went back to the other room in search of his clothes. The girl was awake and sitting up. Del stopped, startled, especially now that he could see her in the morning light spilling through a high window. Black hair fell around her body, and her upward tilted eyes were unlike anything he had seen before. The purple on her eyelids was unsmudged, which made him wonder if it was permanent.

Del smiled. "Hello."

"Hi." She pulled a cushion over herself. "Who are you?"

"Del." He sat next to her. "Do you remember? I was here last night."

Her smile curved. "I would never forget you." She glanced around, looking as groggy as he felt. "Where are the others?"

"They left, I guess." Del was getting the feeling that Ricki's crowd had a hierarchy, and the people on the lowest rung ended up alone in the morning.

"Are you all right?" she asked. "You seemed tight last night."

"Yeah, I'm fine. I've just never been to a party like that."

The girl laughed softly. "I know. They get a little wild." She tilted her head, studying his face. "You're cute, you know." She let the cushion drop away from her body. "I don't think we've been formally introduced."

Del flushed. She sat there like a voluptuous goddess, alive and warm, and he wasn't even aware he had leaned forward until she drew him into a kiss. Then his brain caught up with his hormones, and he pulled away.

"I shouldn't," he said. "I came here with Ricki."

The girl pouted. "She left without you."

A familiar anger stabbed at him, but with less bite this morning. Maybe he was growing used to her vanishing act. Hell, he deserved it after the way he had treated her last night. Or maybe he was just too spiked-over to think straight.

"You're sweet and beautiful," he murmured. "But it wouldn't be right."

She blinked. "Why not?"

Wasn't it obvious? "I can't sleep with one woman at night and someone else the next morning."

"Of course you can." She stretched languorously, letting him look. "You can do whatever you want."

Del couldn't help but stare. So lovely. "If I was going to with anyone," he said softly, "it would be you."

She traced her finger down his cheek. "If you change your mind . . ."

Del kissed her. "You deserve better than me."

Then he stood up. With reluctance, he put on his clothes and headed out.

He just wished he knew how the blazes he would get home when he had no idea where he had spent the night.

Mac was setting up a meeting for one of his clients when his office AI appeared above his desk, the holo of a young woman with light brown hair.

"You have a visitor," she said. "Del Arden."

Finally! He couldn't believe Del had sent Cameron home last night and then disappeared. Mac hadn't stopped worrying. Now he was angry.

"Send him in," Mac said.

As soon as his wayward charge walked in, Mac wondered if Del had slept at all last night. He had dark rings under his eyes, and his shaggy mane of hair was tousled as if he had just woken up, though it was past noon.

Del slouched in a chair across the desk. "Hi."

"You look like shit," Mac said.

Del stared at a point of the desk somewhere to the right of Mac. "Long night."

Mac spoke sharply. "Look at me."

Del raised his startled gaze. "What?"

"Cameron is your bodyguard. We told your family we would protect you. You send him away again, I'll tan your royal hide."

Del's face tightened. "Drill it, Mac. If I want to go without a bodyguard, I'll do it."

"Fine. Great. Just great. You have fun last night?"

"As a matter of fact, yes." Del was looking at the random point on the desk again.

"You sound as convincing as a mesh dealer trying to sell broken consoles," Mac said.

Del just shook his head. So Mac waited.

After a moment, Del looked up. "Maybe I got a little carried away."

A headache throbbed in Mac's temples. "I'm afraid to ask."

"With Ricki. I . . ." Del reddened. "Uh."

"You stuttered at her?" Mac couldn't help but smile. Del looked like a naughty boy. "That sounds drastic."

Del glared at him. But it provoked him into describing his night. When he finished, he said, "The concierge at the hotel got me a fly-taxi, and it took me here."

Mac's headache was getting worse. "You were certainly busy."

"Well, you know." Del pulled at his ear.

"How did you pay your taxi fare?"

The youth shifted in his seat. "Like with the, um, doctor's bill."

"We need to talk about that." Mac had set up an account for Del and was paying his expenses, but if the prince wasn't careful, he would run through his advance from Prime-Nova long before he saw any more income.

"I think Ricki's upset at me," Del said.

"Maybe I'm dense," Mac said, "but the last time I checked, 'Kiss me, you sexy bastard' was hardly the cry of a distressed damsel." He was angrier at her than at Del. "She's the one who should feel guilty. You kept saying you wanted to leave the party. So what do they do? Smash you on spikers and push you into group sex. Real charming."

Del's lips quirked upward. "It was tough. But I survived."

"Oh, quit smirking," Mac said. "Why did you throw up? I've heard of people passing out from spikers, but never vomiting. This after your 'friends' stranded you with some girl you don't know from slam in the wall. What if you'd had a worse reaction?" He let out an explosive breath. "It scares the blazes out of me."

"I can't go through life being afraid." Del pushed up to his feet and strode away, then spun around. "I'd rather *not* live than be trapped in a glass palace, looking at the world but never touching it. It's my decision to make." Then Del added, "Trying new experiences is good for a person." He even said it with a straight face. Almost. Then he grinned.

Mac wondered what he was going to do with this misbehaved prince. "Just be careful, all right. Taking control of your life and taking unnecessary risks are two different things. You do this playboy thing too hard, you could burn yourself out."

"*Playboy?*" Del's grin vanished like spit in the wind. "I am *not* her 'boy-toy.' "

It took Mac a moment to figure out what he meant. Then he smiled. "I never noticed that. The words *do* sound the same. But they mean different things." He thought for a moment. "Playboy is like *jizzora* in Skolian. Except playboy refers to a man rather than a woman."

Del bristled. "You're saying I'm a rich man who doesn't work and devotes himself to a life of pleasure without commitments or responsibilities?" After a moment, he said, "Okay, maybe that described me once. But not anymore. The past few years, I've mostly been doing the father thing and farming."

The *father thing.* Mac sometimes forgot how much that had meant to Del. "Do you miss your nephews?"

"Always." Del spoke awkwardly. "They're better off without me."

"Why do you say that?"

Del shrugged, his gaze sliding around the room. "You have a lot of expensive stuff here."

Mac glanced at the synth-crystal shelves full of gold, silver, or crystal vid cubes. "When one of my clients has a success, sometimes they give me a keepsake to celebrate."

"Oh."

"Del."

The prince looked at him. "Yes?"

"The playboy thing—is that why they didn't betroth you to the Majda Matriarch? Devon, I mean."

Del stiffened. "It's none of your damn business."

Mac waited.

After a moment, Del said, "Yeah, she asked for my younger brother."

It suddenly seemed very quiet to Mac. *My younger brother.* As far as any of them knew, Del was by far the youngest. "Was it Shannon? Or Verne?"

Del gave him a strange look. "Who is Verne?"

"Your brother with the doctorate in agriculture."

Del laughed. "His name has an 'l,' not an 'n.' But yeah, she asked for Vyrl. He was the perfect match. He never messed around with anyone. Except you know what? He had been in love with this girl Lily practically since they were born. When they told him about the betrothal, he and Lily ran off and got married. Here they all thought I was the messed-up one, but it was Vyrl who screwed up their plans."

Mac stared at him. It couldn't be. He and Fitz *couldn't* be right. He spoke in a slow voice. "Vyrl is a great-grandfather."

Del's smile faded as he realized what he had said. For a moment he just looked at Mac. Then he walked to a window in the far wall. He stood staring out at the sky, silhouetted against the blue expanse with its streamers of clouds.

"If Havyrl Valdoria is your younger brother," Mac said, "you had to have been born at least seventy years ago."

Del spoke dully. "Seventy-one."

"What happened?"

"I told you." He turned around. "I was in a cryogenic womb."

"For *forty-five* years?"

"Yes," he said flatly. "For forty-five years."

"The technology to do that didn't exist that long ago."

"That's right." He spoke in clipped sentences, as if he were another person separate from what he was describing. "It was a race. Could they advance the tech fast enough before my current womb decayed? They couldn't revive me until science advanced enough to keep me alive, but if they kept me in too long, the cryo would fail." He took a shaky breath. "I balanced on that edge for nearly half a century."

"Good Lord," Mac said. "It's a miracle you survived."

Del lifted his hands, then dropped them. "Do you know what it's like to wake up and not remember how to talk? To walk? To count or laugh or say your name? To discover everyone you know has lived decades while no time went by for you?" His voice cracked. "I had to relearn almost everything. But I could still sing. It's what kept me going."

"It's incredible." Mac felt like a bastard for bringing it up. "I'm sorry. I know it was private."

"It's all right," Del said, surprisingly gentle. "If I didn't want you to tell General McLane, I wouldn't tell you. We both know how this works. You've been straight with me from the start." He came back over, looking at Mac now instead of acting as if some random point on the desk fascinated him. "You were going to talk to me about my finances, right?" He gave a rueful smile. "So I can stop being a dissipated playboy."

Mac let out a breath, then waved Del back to his chair. "Have a seat. Let's get started."

X

Red and Blue

Prime-Nova released "Sapphire Clouds" as Del's first single. It debuted on the North American chart for holo-rock at number three hundred and fifty-seven. The second week, it jumped to two hundred and ninety-four. It climbed more slowly after that.

Jud waxed philosophical about the matter. "Okay, it's not the biggest smash ever to hit the mesh. But right now African-Andromeda fusion music is bigger than rock. Besides, you're getting a lot of play around here. And the undercity critics love you."

They were sprawled in beanbag chairs in Jud's Baltimore apartment, where Del had been living since General McLane okayed his move off the base. Del regarded Jud dourly. His roommate knew perfectly well that acts with the backing of a super conglomerate like Prime-Nova were supposed to do better. Hell, twenty-five years ago, Mind Mix's first release had debuted in the top ten.

"I've learned a lot of new English words lately," Del told him. "Like flop. Plummet. Mesh-meat."

"Oh, stop." Jud laughed as he practiced a morph-guitar that flexed and bent under his touch. "Your song isn't mesh-meat. It's been on the charts for four weeks, and you've almost reached the top two hundred."

"Well, gosh," Del said. "That's a real rocket taking off." He fell back in his beanbag. Except for a console against one wall, the fat cushions were the only furniture. They were wicked smart beanbags, though. They played music and bathed him in holographic ripples of color according to how they interpreted his mood. They even communicated with the wall panels, coordinating their displays. Right now, the music was barely audible and the lights muted, a pale wash of blue that matched his bad mood.

"'Sapphire Clouds' is still climbing," Jud said, playing a rill of high notes on his guitar. "I checked this morning. It's one hundred and six in D.C. And it's fifty-four on the holo-rock singles chart for northern Baltimore."

"Well, hey," Del said. "I'll bet it could hit number one on the chart for undercity singles written by offworld farm boys who live in Northern Baltimore and have hinges in their hands." He held up his hand and folded it along the hinge, wiggling his fingers at Jud.

"That is so weird," Jud said.

Del lowered his arm. "I'm surprised no one notices."

"Sure they do." Jud shrugged. "It doesn't show when you're holding a mike, though."

"Mic."

"That's what I said." Jud coaxed a rumble from the morphing strings on his guitar, which had gone fat and shiny, deepening the pitch.

"But you had the wrong spelling, I bet." Del felt immensely pleased with himself for learning the difference. It was one of the few words he could spell. "It's m-i-c. From microphone. That was an early form of a michael."

Jud smiled. "You're certainly up on your trivia."

A chime came from the console across the room.

"It's for you," Jud said.

"How do you know that?" Del asked.

"Because if it were for me," Jud said, "I would have to go over there. Which requires energy. So obviously it's not for me."

Del didn't intend to get up, either. "You don't have to go over there."

"I do if I don't want you listening," Jud grumbled.

"Put an audio-comm in your ear."

"I'd have to find it." Jud waved at the room, which was cluttered with morph equipment and Madagascar cartons from their dinner last night. "I can't remember where I put it."

Del eyed the mess. "Maybe we should clean up." He had never

realized before how much people tidied up after him. Even at the base, robo-sweeps cleaned his room. "At least we should get some of those robotic maid-mice."

Jud scowled at him. "Maybe if you weren't always fooling around in some virt, you'd remember to pick up your stuff."

"I'm not always in a virt." Del enjoyed building the fantasy worlds, but he didn't spend more than an hour a day. Well, maybe two. "Besides, half this stuff is morph equipment. Who could that belong to, I wonder?"

Jud laughed. "Okay, I give."

The console chimed again.

"One of us should answer it," Jud decided.

Del spoke to the air. "Claude, who's comming us?"

His EI from the base, which the military had allowed him to keep, answered. "It's Harvey Orner. Your publicist."

"Oh." Harv was his publicist. "Okay. Put him on." Looking around at the disaster area he and Jud called their living room, Del added, "But just audio. No visual."

Harvey's voice floated in the air. "Del, baby! Howz it go?"

Del winced. "Hello, Harv."

"We're all set," Harvey enthused. "You're going to do that interview on the Atlantic City-Time Hour."

"That's the fourth time you've told me that," Del said. "Why would it come through this time when it hasn't all the others?"

"They had a cancellation," Harv said. "The toe contortionist who was going to close the show dropped a brick on his foot."

"Well, gosh," Del said. "They go for the second-best act compared to that? I'm so flattered."

"Del, sweetheart, listen to me. Today, you're the closing act on Atlantic. Tomorrow you'll be the star."

Right. At the rate Del was going, he would need a second job to make his half of the rent. He had no intention of dipping into his Ruby accounts to support himself. He had thought Prime-Nova was paying him a lot, but he had yet to see any money except for his advance. Mac kept using the word "unrecouped," which as near as Del could tell meant he had to pay back Prime-Nova for every expense under the sun, including his vid, virt, touring, promotion, and for all he knew, the price of baking soda in Iceland. Even being the last ditch fill-in for a human toe-pretzel act would earn him some pay on a major show like the Atlantic.

"Sure, I'll do it," Del said. "When do they want me?"

"Uh, that's the thing." Harv cleared his throat. "You have forty-five minutes to get to their D.C. studio."

"What!" Del jumped up to his feet. "I can't do that."

"I'm sending a fly-taxi," Harv said. "Be ready in five minutes. Wear something sexy. And Del baby, don't forget to pay the pilot. I don't want to get stuck with another of your bills."

"Fine, yeah." Del was striding into his bedroom. Claude transferred Harv to the console in there.

As Del threw around clothes on the bed, Harv added, "My niece was wondering if you'd sign her holo-vid cube."

"Sure." Del held up a pair of torn jeans, then tossed them aside and took his leather pants. As he pulled them on, the cloth smoothed out its creases.

Claude suddenly said, "Your pants just sent me a message."

Del blinked. "They what?"

"Your pants contacted me. They say it is difficult to maintain their best appearance when you leave them crumpled up. They suggest you hang them up after you wear them."

"Great," Del muttered. "My clothes are talking to me." He pulled on a wine-colored pullover that Anne had picked out to match his hair. It glimmered with a gold overlay she claimed "accented his eyelashes." Del had no idea what that meant, but it evoked positive moods from people, so he wore it.

"Del, are you there?" Harv said.

"Yeah, I'm here." He sat on the bed and pulled on his boots. "You said something about your niece."

"She wants you to sign her holo-cube."

"Sign it?"

"Your autograph. You know."

"Oh." The "signing" thing again. People wanted him to write his name for them, and he didn't know why. As a keepsake? The signature of a Ruby prince was no small matter. Besides, he didn't know how to write his name in English. He could barely even do it in Iotic. But he couldn't admit that. So he said, "Sure."

Then he jumped up and headed out to his interview.

Ricki wasn't pleased.

Zachary Marksman sat in his big leather chair and surveyed the holos above the big desk in his Prime-Nova office. Ricki stood next to him, her arms crossed, frowning as she watched. The display told her nothing she didn't already know, but seeing the statistics floating in the air as blazing red graphs brought the point home with inescapable force.

"This vid is the third plummet for Mort's Metronomes," Zachary said. "The hum in the m-universe is that they're boring."

Ricki shrugged. "'Boring' just means no one thinks they're new anymore."

Zachary brought up a holo of the group. Four skinny young men with buzzed-off hair yelled and danced while Mort screeched his song. "They don't hit with the audience." He shook his head. "Let them off the option for their next cube. Paying them the termination fee will cost us less than another plummet."

Ricki stiffened, but she didn't argue. In her younger days, she would have fought for any band she signed. She was the one who had talked Zachary into taking a chance on the Metronomes. The group had struck her as innovative without being controversial. Mort's voice was hopeless, but he had good presence in the studio. It hadn't translated well into the vid, though, and his virt sales stank. She had learned to choose her battles more wisely, saving the fight for the ones she had a chance of salvaging.

Zachary pulled in a new set of graphs, this time with no trace of red, just pure, shining blue. "Mind Mix," was all he said. They needed no other introduction. "'Frazy Baby' debuted at number two on the Stellar Hits charts last week. It'll go number one this week."

No surprise, there. "That last tour of theirs shouted rocket all the way," Ricki said.

Zachary scowled at her. "Yeah, if Tackman doesn't fuck it up with his neuro-amps. He either cleans up or he's out."

"I've spoken to his manager." *Argued* was a better word, but Ricki could deal with him. "But Zach, Mind Mix is at the top. This would be bad timing to dilute their act." As stomach-turning as Tackman and Tristan could be in their smug satisfaction, they brought in millions for Prime-Nova. So she put up with their conceited asses.

"Just keep an eye on him," Zachary said.

"I will."

"What about this one?" He brought up a display that was part red and part blue. "This Del Arden fellow. He's got weird stats."

Ricki's shoulders tensed up under her tunic. She tried to separate her personal life from work, but it was growing more and more difficult with Del. He had been avoiding her since that party. It wasn't like before, when he smoldered with anger every time she came near. In the four weeks since, they had seen each other a few times, but they spent most of their time in bed. Not that she objected. He had turned into a gentle lover, as if he felt guilty about their night at the party. It was sweet, but she missed his growling, defiant alter ego.

Enough, Ricki told herself. This was time for business. She knew what the graphs showed. His vid had entered the charts much lower than they hoped, but it had since moved up more than was normal for acts with such a weak debut.

"People don't know what to make of him," Ricki said. "He's different. But he's good enough that they listen anyway. And he's selling well in cities he played with the Mind Mix tour."

Zachary brought up a holo of Del in concert. "It's the oddest thing. His show was too plain, even after he jazzed it up. But it's impossible to stop watching him."

"It's *because* he's unpolished," Ricki decided. Del was doing that thing where he crouched down while the drums played. Then Jud exploded into chords and Del jumped high in the air. He came down singing, practically shouting into the mike. "Who knows what the boogle he's doing? He looks so good doing it, you don't care."

"Boogle?" Zachary asked, laughing. "Where do you come up with this stuff?"

Ricki glowered at him. "My point, Your Royal Tech-Mechness, is that you *know* it's unrehearsed. Unprepared. You can't stop watching to see what he'll do next. He could fall on his sexy butt up there and he'd look like dynamite."

"His material is strange. And he hasn't taken the word 'crystal' out of that damn diamond song."

She regarded him with exasperation. "A diamond *is* a crystal."

Zachary frowned at her. "You know what I mean."

She waited, but he didn't insist Del change the word. Which was a relief. Ricki didn't want to get into another argument with her temperamental lover about artistic purity. Who would have thought she would end up in bed with an undercity renegade? The worst of it was, he was starting to make sense.

"He does sing well," Zachary allowed.

"The Ell-bees love him," Ricki said.

Zachary considered the graphs. "Those holos of him that Elba Malls licensed have decent sales. We should capitalize on that. Get him onto more of their pre-teen channels in the mesh mall."

"It's a good idea. But look at this." She indicated a blue spike in one curve. "That's an *academic* demographic. College professors are buying his stuff."

"Not a lot of them."

"Yeah, but enough to register."

Zachary scrolled through more graphs. "Heh. Look at that. The boomallitics like him. And you're right, good hum from the intellectual set. Strange mix with the teeny-bops. His sales are so-so, but his cube isn't plummeting." He glanced at her. "You want to produce his second one?"

That was a relief. Or maybe not. If Zachary had shunted Del off onto a junior producer, it would have been far kinder to Ricki's blood pressure. But she didn't want some amateur messing with Del.

"Sure," she said. "We'll see where we can take it."

Michael Laux, the host of the Atlantic City-Time Hour, had an upswept mane of black hair and blue eyes so vivid, Del could see the color from across the stage. Except the stage wasn't a stage. The crew called it a "surge studio." It looked a lot like the room where he recorded his vid, with glowing blue walls and equipment everywhere. When Del watched the City-Time Hour on the mesh, it always had an audience. It looked nothing like this.

"So, Del, come in, come over," Laux said heartily, extending his hand.

Del shook his hand and smiled, feeling like an idiot. They were standing in a blue room acting as if they were in front of hundreds of people.

"It's great to be here," Del said, because Harv had coached him to talk that way. He wondered if he sounded as fake to everyone else as he did to himself.

Laux beamed at him. "You've made quite a splash out there."

Splash? As in water? Del eased down his shields and picked up enough to realize Laux meant it as a compliment. He liked what he caught from Laux; the fellow enjoyed his job and wanted to encourage new talent. *Talent,* as in, he wasn't just looking for commercial appeal. How refreshing.

"I do my best," Del said, hoping that was safe, because he had no idea what they were talking about.

Laux lifted his hand, inviting Del to sit on the skeleton of a chair. It bore no resemblance to the furniture on the show, but he and Luax sat facing each other in the same arrangement as those chairs. Probably the techs projected some sort of holo onto the skeleton.

After they were settled, Laux said, "From what I understand, your best is a knockout."

Knockout? Still confused, Del smiled and said, "Well, gee, thanks." For some reason, Harv loved it when he said "gee." It inspired the publicist to make comments about Del eating corn, which made no sense to Del, but seemed to please Harv immensely.

"So Del, we've only a few minutes left," Laux said with a smile. His teeth were so white, they could have lit up the studio. Del could see why Laux was such a popular host, though, and it had nothing to do with his perfect teeth or handsome face. The fellow's good nature was genuine.

"You've stirred some controversy with that exercise in your concert," Laux said. "How would you like to do it here, with verification you aren't using enhancement?"

"It would be my pleasure," Del said, because Harv had told him to. Then he growled what he really wanted to say. "I've *never* used a Roberts Enhancer, and I'll challenge anyone who claims I did."

"Great!" Laux seemed much happier with Del's scowl than his polite words. Turning to the nonexistent audience, he said, "Del will sing tonight with no aids. You can download our guarantee of that from the Tru-Tech Verifier site, with its Platinum-certified seal." To Del, he said, "It's all yours!"

Del slid off his chair and stepped to a mark on the floor a tech had shown him earlier. Fortunately, he had practiced today, and his voice felt warm despite his having no warning about the show. When a tech gave him the cue, Del started the exercise, doing "bay-ay-ay-by," up and up, until he had covered six octaves and a bit more. Then he stopped and let out a breath, relieved it had come out all right.

Laux strode over and clapped him on the shoulder. "Now that's a set of pipes!" He turned his megawatt smile on the non-audience. "Was that impressive or not? Tell us what you think at the City-Time

Virt Grotto. Come on by, hang with your friends, and let's talk. Remember, Citizens, this is City-Time, Top Time, and—" Laux pointed straight at the holo-cam. "*Your* time."

Lights flared, and Del had no doubt that when he saw the "live" show later, it would have an applauding audience. He didn't mind; he just appreciated the chance to prove Pizwick wrong.

As the studio lighting softened, Laux lowered his hand and spoke in a quieter voice. "That really was impressive. I've heard it's even your own voice, with no medical augmentation."

"Pretty much," Del said. "Earlier generations of my family were selected for genes that improved our vocal range." He almost said *my ancestors* instead of earlier generations, but he stopped himself in time. It would give away his Skolian heritage, because only Skolians who descended by the Ruby Empire could have distant ancestors who knew genetic engineering.

"We certainly benefited from the result." Laux shook hands with Del. "Good luck, son. I listened to the vid your publicist sent over, and I must say, I enjoyed it."

Del smiled, pleasantly surprised. "Thanks."

After Del left the studio, he walked out into a hall of the building and ran smack into a man striding past the door. The man jolted to a stop and regarded Del. He spoke with a cultured accent. "Excuse me, but are you Jack Mayer?"

"Uh, no." Del *knew* that accent. This man came from the Skolian world Metropoli.

"My apologies." The man looked distracted and harried. "I'm late for our meeting. I've only met him once, last week. You looked familiar."

Sweat beaded on Del's temples. As far as he knew, the meshes had no likeness of him as a Skolian; until just recently, he had always kept his image private. It had been easy given that he lived on a world no one could visit. Surely this man couldn't recognize him as a Ruby prince.

"I'm a singer," Del said. Then, because hope burned eternal, he said, "Maybe you saw my vid."

"Perhaps." The man nodded absently as he looked around. He obviously hadn't recognized Del from any vid.

"Oh!" Del said. "I remember. That party a few weeks ago. You're Staver Aunchild, aren't you? The Skolian exec."

Staver brought his attention back to Del, looking pleased by his recognition. "Party? Ah, yes, the one Centauri Music put on. Quite a scene, eh?" He regarded Del with new interest. "Are you one of their acts?"

"Not Centauri. Prime-Nova. I work with Ricki Varento."

"Varento! Of course." Staver took a box out of his jacket and removed a cube. "Here's my contact info." He handed Del the cube. "Have one of your people send me your vid. I buy for Metropoli Interstellar. It's a Skolian entertainment conglomerate."

"Thanks," Del said, flattered. He hadn't realized Ricki's name could open doors so easily. He doubted Staver would want to license his music when he saw the lackluster sales of the *Jewels Suite,* but it was worth a try.

"I'll do that," Del said.

"Good." Staver nodded, the Skolian equivalent of good-bye. "Nice meeting you." He was looking up the hallway behind Del.

Glancing around, Del saw a man walking toward them. Del turned to tell Staver good-bye, but the exec was already going to meet the other fellow. So Del went on his way, thinking. He knew the chances of Staver licensing his work were minimal. But wouldn't that be a scream if his music sold to the Skolians? His family would have collective heart failure seeing one of their own immortalized as—of all the unseemly occupations—a rock star.

XI

Virtland

Del couldn't resist looking for his vid in a music kiosk. Why people called the mega-store a "kiosk," he had no clue. It went on forever, aisle after aisle of racks, displays, and booths where customers could try out virts. Laser lights flashed and morphed everywhere, from the vaulted ceiling high overhead to the glowing purple floor. Music was playing, some orchestrated version of a stellar-fusion song. Del loved the place. He had no clue how to find anything, though.

The store actually did have kiosks that sold music in unusual forms. He gaped at the slick ads for virts that cost thousands of renormalized dollars and would connect you to entire mesh worlds populated by thousands, even millions of people. On the other end of the reality spectrum, he found "sheet music," which musicians supposedly used to read songs from weird little marks on bars. He couldn't fathom why anyone would do something so convoluted when they could have a ticker play, record, and edit whatever they needed. Del wasn't the only one on his world who couldn't read; the people on Lyshriol had no written language. Music passed from artist to artist through the voice, a malleable, ever-changing process that Del felt certain would be ruined if it were codified by marks on a sheet.

He sleuthed out the holo-rock section. Cubes filled its racks, hundreds, thousands. He stood surrounded by a wealth of music, thoroughly confused. Mind Mix, golden-haired Jenny Summerland, and the simmering Conquistadors were everywhere. He recognized them only from the big holos above the racks, because he couldn't read a single flipping cube. He could have asked an AI for help, but he didn't want to look stupid. Why he cared how he "looked" to an AI, he had no idea, but it didn't change his gut reaction.

Del didn't see his vid anywhere. Surely the store had it. This morning, in its fifth week, "Sapphire Clouds" was number one hundred seventy-six on the North American holo-rock chart, which sort of almost put it within range of being a minor hit. Prime-Nova probably wouldn't be happy, though, unless it made the Continental Hundred, the chart of the most popular music of any kind in North America. So far, Del's work had been scarcer on that chart than a Prime-Nova exec without an attitude.

"That *is* him," a girl said in a low voice. "Look at his eyelashes. They glint, like they have nano-sized laser studs."

Del's face heated. He only knew one person with eyelashes that glinted. Turning around, he saw two girls a few paces away. When they realized he had noticed them, they reddened and looked as if they didn't know whether to back away or come closer.

"Hi," Del said.

"Hi," one answered. She was pretty, with blond hair and big eyes, *purple* eyes, a color so vivid it practically vibrated. The other girl was curved and sexy, somehow audacious just standing there. Her black hair had purple streaks that glowed, and a flashing purple laser-stud pierced her skin where her shoulder met her neck. She matched the store.

"Are you Del Arden?" the girl with yellow hair asked shyly.

Hah! They did recognize him. He sauntered over. "That's me. Who are you beautiful young ladies?"

The laser-light girl looked him over with approval. "I'm Kendra." She indicated her shy friend. "This is Talia."

"Kendra and Talia." Del smiled. "Those are gorgeous names. I've never heard anything like them."

They both laughed, Talia self-conscious and Kendra as if she thought Del was teasing.

"Are you here to sign cubes?" Talia asked. "I didn't see an ad for it."

"No, I just came to look around." Del motioned at the rack of cubes. Holos popped and whizzed above them, shooting up to the ceiling far above their heads. "It's all so new to me."

Kendra gaped as if he had announced his arrival from another dimension. "You've never been in a kiosk before?"

"I grew up on a farm. We never went anywhere like this."

"That's so sweet," Talia said.

Del wasn't sure farming qualified as "sweet," at least not when he was sweaty and exhausted from hacking bagger-bubble plants all day. But she looked so charming saying it, he would have farmed anything for her.

"Will you sign your cube?" Talia asked.

Ah, hell. He stopped feeling cocky. He would die rather than admit to these lovely girls that he didn't know how to sign his name. So he said, "Sure."

"That's great!" Kendra beamed at him. "We'll get your virt, too." Mischief flashed in her gaze. "You could share it with us."

That sounded interesting. Del had never done a session with real people. He was learning to program his *Jewels Suite* virt, but it couldn't do much. In a session with real people, though, they could interact however they wanted.

"I could give you a tour," Del said, and both girls laughed. He felt good. Even a few weeks ago, he wouldn't have understood that reference to his virtual self, who offered tours of the virt like Rex had done in the Mind Mix virt. Now the joke rolled off his tongue. They even thought he was funny.

"I'd like that," Kendra said in her sultry voice. She turned to the closest rack and flicked a tiger holo scampering across the rail. A red light flashed in a laser-stud on her index finger.

"*The Jewels Suite,* by Del Arden," she said.

The rack jolted into motion. Line after line of cubes rolled past, the boxes snapping up, flashing in the light, then snicking down to let new cubes roll up. The whir of motion blurred, then stopped as suddenly as it began.

Kendra tapped two boxes, her fingertip glowing. She handed one to Talia. "Here's yours." She took another and offered it to Del with a smile.

Sweat broke out on Del's palms. But before he could respond, Talia frowned at Kendra, somehow making the expression pretty.

"We have to pay first," Talia told her friend.

"I did. For us both. With this." Kendra wiggled her finger with the laser-stud at Talia. Then she tapped her virt box, and it snapped open. Holos of Del glowed above its inner surfaces. He reddened, still finding it hard to believe that he threw his head back that way when he sang, with his hips tilted and his eyes half open. He tended to avoid images of himself singing because they made him self-conscious when he performed.

"Could you sign here?" Talia touched a silver triangle on the inside of the box.

He took the cube from her. "I don't have an, uh—" He wasn't even sure how someone signed a virt.

"You can use mine." She rummaged in the purse slung over her shoulder and pulled out a blue stylus with flashing purple lights zinging around the stem. "Here."

"Thanks." Del took the stylus, determined not to look stupid. He touched its end the way he had seen people do, and was rewarded by a point of light flaring on its tip. Hah! When he pressed the tip against the silver triangle, it left a purple mark.

Okay. He had made it this far. He knew his name started with "D" in English, and that a D was half a circle. He drew a semi-circle on the silver, followed by a squiggle. It looked nothing like his Skolian signature, which had taken him years to learn. Mac said he should never use his real signature, though, to avoid forgers. With a smile, he handed the box back to Talia. He didn't know why she would want his squiggle defacing her property, but she glowed as if he had given her something of value.

"Ooh." Kendra pouted. "She got to go first." She handed him her cube and lowered her lashes. "Saved the best for last."

"Oh, stop," Talia said, laughing. "He saved the brassiest for last."

Brassiest. Del supposed it was slang, but people really could be brassy, designing their appearance however they wanted. Kendra looked softer and warmer than brass. Much softer.

Del snapped open her virt, looked at the silver triangle—and froze. He didn't remember how he had drawn his signature for Talia. He couldn't make the one for Kendra identical. It was impossible to be that exact. *He couldn't do it.*

Del took a breath. *Cut it out,* he told himself. *Just make the damn squiggle.*

He signed her box with a fake signature, just like every signature he wrote was fake, because they all looked different, and he didn't care how many times anyone said it didn't matter. He knew. Every time he signed his name, he fractured himself into smaller pieces, creating more bits of Del, none of which were him.

A plain of reeds rippled from where Del stood with Talia and Kendra all the way to the distant blue-green mountains. The peaks bore no resemblance to the Backbone Mountains of his home, but the plain looked a little better. Although the bubbles that tipped the reeds didn't have the iridescent sheen of the real ones on Lyshriol, they were close.

The colors were mixed up, though. The clouds were white instead of blue, and the sky was blue instead of lavender. No one at Prime-Nova knew anything about Lyshriol, and Del hadn't told them, so they based the virt on Earth. How could anyone know Lyshriol? The first people to land there in modern times had been the resort planners from Texas, and they had christened the planet *Skyfall*. They had showed up after the Texan government fined them for "creative" business practices on Earth, and they snuck offworld, searching for less protected real estate to exploit. As soon as they stumbled across idyllic Lyshriol, they went about setting up hotels and gambling houses.

Eventually the Skolians kicked them off the planet. The name Skyfall stuck, though. The pollen that saturated the biosphere turned the water blue, so snowfall covered the ground in a blue carpet. The planners had thought it looked as if the sky had fallen. Now everyone in three empires knew about the world Skyfall—because it was home to the Ruby Dynasty.

Del found the whole business hilarious. In his language, the word Lyshriol meant, "the clouds have come to the ground." Every time he told someone here that Lyshriol was his home, he was saying he came from Skyfall. And no one had a clue. The top brass in the military knew, of course, but they weren't telling anyone. Lyshrioli natives rarely traveled offworld, and the Ruby Dynasty kept their home world confidential.

"This is pretty," Talia said, gazing across the plain. Reeds swayed around her knees and thighs.

Kendra took a step and sent a cloud of bubbles into the air. "Hey!" she said, laughing. "Who thought this all up?"

"I did," Del said, pleased that they liked his home.

A man was walking toward them across the plain. Del focused

on him, and the figure was suddenly in front of them—a man with wine-red curls, violet eyes, and eyelashes that glinted.

"Hello." The man smiled. "Would you like a tour?"

"Hey!" Del said. "You're me."

His virtual self looked him over. "There does seem to be a resemblance. I don't have an accent, though."

Del scowled at him. "I know. Zachary nixed it." It was one of the few times Del had summoned the courage to disagree with the tech-mech king. It hadn't done any good. Del had eventually gritted his teeth and acquiesced, but he dug in his heels when Zachary suggested he hire someone to help him "lose the accent" in real life. Ricki had actually sided with Del, telling Zachary his accent had "sex appeal."

However, Ricki hadn't supported Del when Zachary had the hinge edited out of Del's hand in his vids and virts. The way Zachary talked, Del would have thought the hinge was some weird mutation. It bothered him a lot, but it would have bothered him even more if they had dropped production of his vid.

"I prefer the real Del," Kendra told the fake Del. "He's going to give us the tour."

"Would you like me to leave?" the unaccented Del asked.

"Sorry," Kendra said. "But, yeah, scram."

"Enjoy yourselves," Psuedo-Del said. Then he vanished.

"That was definitely weird," Talia said.

Laughing, Del said, "It's not every day I meet myself."

Kendra gave him a sultry grin. "I like the way you talk better. Especially that chime in your voice."

Del grinned and spun around with his arms extended. "I used to run and run across these plains. Come on!" Then he took off.

"Wait up!" Kendra called. She and Talia were suddenly next to him with that instantaneous jump virts allowed. As they ran, the wind streamed through their hair and "Sapphire Clouds" played:

> Running through the sphere-tipped reeds
> Suns like gold and amber beads
> Jumping over blue-winged bees
> Don't catch me, please
> Running, running, running

Del stopped abruptly, on purpose, and Kendra and Talia piled into him. They collapsed into the reeds, laughing in a tangle of limbs. He filled his arms with Kendra's voluptuous body. Rolling over in the reeds, he kissed her soundly. She pulled him closer, her arms around his waist and Talia lay along their side, sliding her palm over his hips.

Del lifted his head and murmured. "I'm a lucky man today."

Talia hesitated. "I'm surprised you don't, well, you know."

He leaned over and kissed her, still holding Kendra in his arms. "Don't what, beautiful?"

"Have a girlfriend," Talia said. "The hum in the m-verse is that a Prime-Nova top gun owns you."

Del's smile vanished. No one *owned* him. He wasn't property. Ricki didn't want him, anyway; she wanted some creation Prime-Nova had concocted and called "Del Arden." They didn't have a real relationship. She kept him around for enjoyment, as if he were some sex toy.

Thinking of Ricki, however, prodded the part of Del's brain that his hormones tended to turn off. He regarded Kendra, and she looked up at him, her eyes half-closed, her soft lips inviting.

"We don't have to stay in the virt," she murmured. "My bedroom is just as comfortable. And it's real."

"I would love to," Del said. More than she knew. "But, um—"

Her eyes opened all the way. "What's wrong?"

"Uh—how old are you two?" Del asked.

Kendra caught her lower lip with her teeth. When she didn't answer, Del looked at Talia.

"I'm eighteen," Talia said. "Kendra is nineteen."

Well, damn. No matter how overprotective Del might consider their culture, he had to obey its laws. He took a breath, then lifted himself off Kendra and sat cross-legged next to her. "I wish—" His voice trailed off.

Kendra sat up, smoothing her tousled hair, and glared at Talia. "You didn't have to tell him."

"He could get in trouble," Talia said.

"You're lovely," Del said. "Both of you. I can't believe two such incredible girls want *me*." This holo-rock thing had perks he hadn't expected, but he needed to get things straight with Ricki before he played. He might be innocent by the standards of the music industry, but he wasn't stupid. He didn't want to be on the same planet as his illustrious producer if he pissed her off.

"I just can't," he finished. "I'm really sorry."

Talia touched his cheek. "You're sweet."

Del reddened. If they did the corn-fed farm boy bit, he was going to dig under the reeds and hide. He wondered what people would think if they knew his farm grew big leathery bubbles. He had never even tasted corn.

Del stood up and offered one hand each to Kendra and Talia. "Come on. Let's go real, and I'll take you to dinner." He didn't really have the money, but he liked their company, and he didn't just want to leave things on this abrupt note.

Kendra jumped up and took his arm. "Come on, handsome." She waited while Talia took the other. "Let's go."

Talia dimpled at him. "Dinner with a famous singer. All our friends will wish it was them."

Del had his doubts about that, given how few of their friends were buying his vid, but what the hell. It would be fun.

He felt an odd pang at ending the session; it was becoming more and more difficult to leave the fantasy worlds he created.

In its seventh week on the holo-rock charts, "Sapphire Clouds" hit one hundred and twenty-two; in week nine, it was one hundred and three; in week ten it crept up to one hundred and one. That same week, "Diamond Star" entered the holo-rock chart at number three hundred and three.

Zachary stood in his office and squinted at the stats floating in the air. Even his clothes had holoscreens woven into them, mimicking the charts in miniature. The graphs constantly changed as they took new data from the mesh.

"It's not possible," he told Ricki. "We never released 'Diamond Star' as a single."

"What, you aren't happy it made the chart?" she asked. Honestly, Zachary could drive her crazy sometimes. She was standing on the other side of his glossy black desk, watching him through the graphs.

"What 'made the chart'?" He waved his hand at the holos. "It debuted at the extraordinary rank of three hundred and-gasp-three."

"Yeah, but look at 'Sapphire Clouds.'" Ricki motioned at one of the graphs. "It might crack the top one hundred next week."

"Or it might drop into oblivion. It's hardly moving."

"It's the turtle," she decided.

He peered at her through the translucent graphs. "Ricki, sweetheart, could you just for once try to make sense?"

She wondered what bee he had in his britches. "You're in a mood."

"Tackman got fined again for neuro-amps." He squinted at Del's graphs. "At least Mind Mix's chart-chess makes sense. The band comes out like a fission-fueled rocket and stays at the top."

Ricki studied the graphs floating between her and Zachary. "Do you remember that ancient fable about the race between the turtle and the rabbit? The rabbit jumped out of the starting gate and got so far ahead, it figured the turtle could never catch up. So the flipping silly rabbit took a nap. Meanwhile the turtle plodded on and won the race."

Zachary cocked an eyebrow at her. "I doubt our high-strung Mister Arden would appreciate the comparison."

Ricki wished Zachary would get over Del challenging him on that business about the accent. No, Del didn't grovel to the tech-mech king. So what? It was good for Zachary. Besides, Zachary cared more about profits than Del's moods. "If Del breaks into the top hundred, that's a great sign."

"His songs move too slowly. A bullet that boy is not."

"People need time to get used to him." Ricki thought for a moment. "We should send him on tour again. It's been a few months since his last one."

Zachary gave an incredulous laugh. "After that fiasco? You have to be kidding."

Ricki put her fists on her hips. "It wasn't a fiasco. Yeah, he plummeted at first. But he picked himself up. And he's had four months to practice since then. With some planning, he could do a good tour. We could start with smaller venues. See what happens."

Zachary glanced at the graph for "Sapphire Clouds." "He does have more staying power than a lot of new acts."

"Just wait until people *see* him. Look at the Baltimore chart." Ricki flicked a few holicons in the air, and the graph changed to one with a steeper blue line. "See? 'Sapphire Clouds' is number eight." When Zachary raised an eyebrow, she said, "Yeah, it's a little chart, but it shows what he can do. People there *know* him. Del up close and personal is strong stuff." She could attest to that far too well. He drove her crazy, never able to decide if he loved or hated her. He would say they had to talk, but if she came to his apartment, he would seduce her into the bedroom instead.

"Oh, all right," Zachary said. "Put him on tour." He smiled slightly. "That eff-you attitude of his can be entertaining when it's in his songs instead of directed at me."

Ricki smirked at him. "He says what you wish you could tell all those hightowners who piss you off."

"Someone has to deal with the investors," he grumbled. "I'm just glad I don't have to do it as often as some of the other VPs."

"Have you ever heard Del's song 'Carnelians'?"

"I don't think so. It's not on his vid, is it?"

She shook her head. "It's beautiful, at least the version I heard. But he left it off. Mac thought it was too political."

Zachary's tone sharpened. "Prime-Nova isn't a damn soapbox. Put in politics and it kills sales."

Ricki shrugged. "I can't make heads or flipping pails of the song."

"Heads or *what?*" Zachary asked, laughing. "Pails?"

"Yeah, that's right." Really, why were people always making fun of the way she talked? Her singers were the lyricists, not her. "'Carnelians' is definitely the eff-you genre. But who is he flipping off? 'I'll never kneel beneath your hightown stare.' What does that mean?"

"Maybe he doesn't like rich people. Probably why Mac didn't want it on the vid. It might antagonize some wealthy supporter."

"I suppose." She had asked Del, but he never gave her a real answer. "He gets tight-lipped about that one." She smiled, thinking of far more entertaining things he did with those lips.

Zachary was watching her. "Don't mess with the act."

Her good mood cooled. "My personal life is my business."

"Not if it interferes with your judgment." He waved his hand through the graph, and it disappeared, replaced by a holo of Del standing frozen on a stage in Philadelphia. "Like convincing me to let him stay on the Mind Mix tour."

"I was right, wasn't I?" Ricki flicked through holos until one appeared of Del tossing his mike high in the air. He grabbed it with a flourish as it came down and wailed into it without the slightest pause in his song, while people in the audience screamed and clapped. "See? And that bit he did on the Atlantic City-Time Hour caused quite a hum." It didn't surprise her that the buzz had been more about Del's looks than his vocal cords. Women

loved to watch him, and his snarling defiance appealed to the
men. Del was the only one who had no clue about his smolder-
ing sexuality. Which suited Ricki just fine.

"People like him despite the flaws in his shows," she said. "They
want to hear *him*. Not razzly-dazzly whatever. Because he sings
the way people used to, when all you had was your voice and a
few primitive instruments."

"I suppose." Zachary didn't look convinced.

"We should release "Diamond Star" as a single." As long as she
was asking for the universe, she might as well go all the way.

"Why?" He sounded genuinely curious. "It's too experimental.
I'm surprised it showed up on the charts at all."

"Parts of it are strange," Ricki agreed. "But the lyrics are easier
to understand. 'Diamond Star' is his most upbeat song. Nothing to upset the censors. Suppose we use the first two verses
and choruses without all those weird firecracker pops. Then the
morpher solos. Then jump to Del singing the end. It would cut
it down to less than four minutes."

"Maybe." Zachary brought up a menu in place of the graphs,
and "Diamond Star" played in a ripple of notes. The music started
like an acoustic guitar, then morphed into a wave of noise that
didn't match a single classical instrument. Although it all came
out of Randall's stringer, it sounded like several electro-optic
guitars layered together.

Del's voice caressed the song:

> Angel, be my diamond star
> Before my darkness goes too far
> Splinter through my endless night
> Lightening my darkling sight

He wailed the chorus, going up and down on the word diamond:

> You're, you're, you're, you're
> A diamond, a diamond, a diamond star

Then into the second verse:

> Brighter than the crystal caves
> Sunlight glancing on the waves

Swirling dance upon my heart
Longing while we're held apart

"See, right there," Ricki said as Del sang the chorus. "Just have his voice, Jud's cello morpher, and Anne's drums. After the chorus, play Randall's guitar solo and cut to the end."

Zachary nodded, his gaze unfocused as he listened. He flicked more holos, and the music jumped to the bridge at the end:

Take it slow, a daring chance
Swaying in a timeless dance
Shimmering radiance above
Softening this lost man's love

Then back to the chorus, Del singing "diamond star" over and over, his voice soaring with erotic purity.

"Huh," Zachary said. "I see what you mean. It might work." He regarded her. "Cut out the words crystal caves, though."

Ricki could just imagine Del's reaction to *that* idea. "I think we should leave it."

"Why? What the bloody hell is a crystal cave anyway? It makes no sense. The song won't suffer if he takes it out. He can say, I don't know, 'brighter than blistering days' or something."

Ricki almost gagged. And he thought *she* had a problem with words. "That's real poetic, Zach."

"Yeah, well, it isn't a drug reference."

"Neither is crystal caves." Before Zachary could object, she added, "We'll promote the song as marriage-proposal pop. Convince people they want to get engaged to this music. Give a diamond to the star in your life. Then you need the crystal caves. Because of course, that symbolizes the diamond ring."

"A *cave?*" Zachary gave a snort of laughter. "That's even wonkier than your argument for why Jenny Summerland shouldn't take the phrase 'let me come' out of her latest."

Ricki threw up her hands. "Zach, honestly, don't be such a flipping Puritan. She was saying 'let me come home.' Not 'let me have an orgasm.'"

"Yeah, sure." He flicked off the holo of Del. "Fine. He can keep crystal caves. Just make sure the wedding thing is clear in the ads." With a scowl, he added, "And don't tell Mister Angst Arden we're chopping it up."

Ricki shook her head. "Can't do that, Zach. His contract requires we get his okay on any substantial alterations."

"What substantial? It's the same song. Just better."

"I have to tell him. To protect ourselves."

He crossed his arms. "I don't want to hear any more of our rock Rafael's complaints."

"Hey, that's good. The Rafael of rock." Ideas jumped in Ricki's mind. "The surly angel. I can work with that."

"It's been done."

"Not for years. People don't even remember what was hot two minutes ago." She gave him her most reassuring look. "And don't worry, I'll deal with Del."

"Yeah, well, I hope so."

So did Ricki. She wasn't anywhere near as sure about Del as she claimed. He had an odd attitude toward the song, as if he wanted to hide it from everyone. Those light, pleasing lyrics meant something different to him, she just didn't know what.

Someone shook Del's world. Literally. He lay sprawled on his back in a meadow with his arms thrown wide. Bubbles floated above him. They were supposed to pop and release glitter, which acted like pollen, but it didn't happen. He needed to learn how to reprogram this virt. He wished he could connect his mind straight into it, so it could take what he wanted from his brain.

The land vibrated again. Puzzled, he lifted his head. Nothing looked wrong. Bagger-bubble plants grew all around him, stalks tall and thick, sacs blue or red. He got up and walked through the field, enjoying the breezes. Home. He missed it. He would go for a visit. It wasn't going to be easy, though. His family would ask how he spent his time. He could hear them. *Holo-rock? What is that?* He wasn't even successful. No, damn it, he wasn't a failure. "Sapphire Clouds" was almost in the top hundred. Almost. Not that they'd care. They didn't know holo-rock charts from geology-rock charts.

The crops around him suddenly wavered and shook. Del glared at the fields. "What the blazes is wrong?"

The fake Del appeared. "Someone wants your attention."

"So why not send me a message?" Del asked. "Through you."

"You locked out communications," his sim-self told him.

"Oh." Del had forgotten about that. "End sim."

Blackness descended, and he slowly reoriented. He wasn't standing, he was lying in a recliner. Lifting off his helmet, he squinted in the brightness.

"Thank God!" Jud was leaning over him, his hands gripped on Del's shoulders. "What the hell was wrong with you?"

Del blinked up at him. "I was just in the virt."

"For *two* hours. We were going to rehearse, remember?"

"Rehearse," Del mumbled. "That's right." Sitting up slowly, he set the helmet on the console. Then he rubbed his eyes.

"Ricki left a message," Jud said. "We're going on tour again."

"We are?" Del pulled himself out of the recliner. He felt sluggish. Tired. He wanted to go back into the virt.

"Come on." Jud tugged at his arm. "You need to get dressed so we can meet Randall and Anne."

"Oh. Yeah." Del walked toward his room. Then he stopped and looked back. "Jud?"

His roommate smiled, his face framed by dreadlocks that brushed his shoulders, with silver beads in them today. "You look like a little kid when you're half awake."

Little kid. If he only knew. "Do you know how to get a blissnode?"

Jud's smile vanished. "Damn it, keep away from that garbage."

"Why?"

"You could get hurt. You can't take chances like that."

"I can take care of myself." Del clenched up inside. Jud sounded just like his family, suffocating him. He strode to his bedroom and tripped over a pile of clothes. Frustrated, he scooped them up and tossed them onto his bed.

"Hey." Jud came over to him. "I didn't mean anything." He watched Del as if he were a combustible substance about to ignite.

Del raked his hand through his hair. His arm was shaking. Lowering it, he stared at his trembling hand. What was wrong with him?

"You need to eat," Jud said.

Food. As soon as the thought registered, hunger pangs stabbed at Del. "I can't believe I forgot to eat." He rubbed his eyes. "Okay, so maybe I'm spending a little too much time in the suit."

"A 'little,' yeah." Jud's grin came back. "Come on. Let's rehearse. We're going back on the road!"

Del knew he should be glad Prime-Nova was giving him another chance. But he didn't feel up to traveling. It also meant he might not see Ricki for weeks at a time, and he had never settled matters with her. He felt guilty about his ambivalence, especially given the way she was supporting him with Zachary. But sleeping with her was easier than the proverbial "relationship talk."

Maybe Mac was right about the playboy thing. In his youth, Del had been drowning in his own insecurities, stupidly intent on proving his manhood. The strains of "Emeralds" drifted through his mind:

> They waited in whispering reeds
> Green within, predators without
> But my brother intervened
> He answered my crying shout

His brother. Althor. So many decades had passed since that night Althor had protected him. When Del had been fourteen and Althor fifteen, his big brother had saved him from being beaten senseless and gods only knew what else. Del clenched his fist and kicked a soccer ball by his door. It rolled across his bedroom into the opposite wall. Althor was *dead,* a casualty of the war, tortured by the Traders and then executed.

Jud was still watching him. "What's wrong?"

"Nothing." Del couldn't confide in him. He couldn't confide in anyone. How could he have friends when his life was a lie? He spoke softly. "I want to go home."

"You should, then," Jud said. "Take a break after the tour, before your next vid."

"Yeah. After the tour." He couldn't leave yet. He just had to make it through a few more months.

Just a little more time.

XII

Diamond Rise

In its eleventh week on the North American charts, "Sapphire Clouds" dropped to one hundred and twenty-four, never breaking into the coveted top one hundred. The original version of "Diamond Star" moved up ten places to number two hundred and ninety-three.

"I don't understand," Del told Ricki. "Why change the song? 'Diamond Star' hit the charts without even an official release."

"You don't want debuts at three hundred." Ricki lay with him in her sumptuous floater bed, with fluffy white quilts bunched up around them. Even in the dim light, the white furniture in her room shimmered. So did the white carpets and white walls. It was a gorgeous room for a gorgeous woman who was, at the moment, pissed off. Del had no idea why, and she thought she was hiding it, but he knew. She wanted to slap him across that glossy room of hers.

"If you cut up the song," Del said, "it takes out the most interesting parts."

"We don't want interesting." Ricki turned with her back to him. "We want it to sell."

He stretched out behind her, his front to her back, and put his arm around her waist. "What's the matter?"

"Nothing." Her body remained stiff. She had responded when

they made love, but now she was like a board. Even when she stayed in bed with him, she seemed to leave.

"You're mad at me," Del said.

"No, I'm not." She rolled onto her back. "Let's watch an m-cast."

"Here?" On Lyshriol, he kept tech out of his bedroom. Sure, they had it for comfort, warmth, all that. But it was discreet. Then he had come here and discovered what he was missing. But he didn't want it invading their private time. He could think of better things to do in bed with Ricki than watch an m-cast.

She was already touching a panel on the nightstand, though. A wall across the room glowed, and a holo appeared in front of it, the image of a woman with metallic blue streaks in her blond hair.

" . . . see my latest holo-movie," she purred. "Tomorrow night, right here, on the Midwest Channel."

"That ought to be your channel," Ricki said sourly. "You could commune with all the other small-town boys."

Del was getting angry. "Are you going to tell me what's wrong or what?"

She ignored him. "Jacques, give me the Northern Baltimore chat channel."

"Certainly," a sensual male voice answered.

"Who the hell is Jacques?" Del said. He knew perfectly well it was her EI, but he could do without Jacques in bed with them.

"What?" she asked, all innocence. "You don't like my house EI? What a pity. He's such a *good* EI."

"For flaming sake, Ricki."

"Oh, look at that," she said sweetly. The holo across the room re-formed into a cozy café with two young women seated at a table. Two very familiar women.

Talia and Kendra.

Oh, shit.

"I was strolling through the m-verse to see if you were getting play," Ricki said. "And golly, farm boy, look what I found. Seems you've been *playing* a lot."

Kendra's voice rose into the air. " . . . one of Baltimore's hottest new singers. But don't let that rock star reputation turn you away. Del Arden is a sweetheart."

"He took us to dinner," Talia said, her dimples in full force. "What a night!"

Kendra laughed sensuously. "Talia, you're the innocent one. That's why you just watched."

Talia's cheeks reddened. "Watched *what?*"

"Nothing much," Kendra admitted. "But his kiss is dynamite." She looked out of the holo with satisfaction. "What a dream. Del Arden. Pick up his latest cube. It's called *The Jewels Suite.*"

"A dinner date with *two* of them," Ricki murmured. "With you for dessert. How charming."

Del's face was flaming. "They asked me to sign my vid. So I took them out to dinner."

"For asking you to scribble your name on a little box of glim-flex? Gosh, you're nice." She snapped her fingers and the holo vanished. "What else, Mister Sexpot Arden?" Her voice was no less dangerous for its silken tone.

"I didn't do anything," Del said. "Just one kiss. Then I stopped. Because I thought of you." Which was true. No wonder Mac had told him not to get involved with his producer. This could turn into a nightmare. "We left the virt after—"

"You were in a *virt?*" Ricki sat up so fast, the covers flew off her body. "You were fooling around with those two bee-brains in a sim? Are you out of your fucking mind?"

Del sat up, boiling. "I guess I'm stupid, Ricki. I can't imagine why you would bother with me. I should just leave."

"No! Don't you understand? The vid's recorded!" She looked as if she wanted to shake him. "Anything you did with those little groupies is in their cubes. You know what virtisos are?"

"I don't care." He yanked the covers off and started to get out of the bed.

Ricki pulled him back. "They could do whatever they want with those files."

He stared at her, jolted out of his anger. It hadn't occurred to him they might fool with his holos. They had seemed so nice. They *were* nice. Nothing he picked up from their minds had set off his mental alarms.

"What did you mean, virtiso?" he said.

"They're fans who follow around celebrities." She let go of his arm. "They try to get to know the star so they can build more realistic sims. They like real recordings because it's easier to crack the security on those. The images from a session you do with other people don't have as many protections as images we put in when we make the virt. If those girls figure out how to unlock their session with you, they could edit your images. Like take out your clothes. You want naked holos of you all over the mesh? Del Arden, the prince of prurience."

Del's face flamed. The Skolian Assembly would have collective heart failure if nude images of him showed up in public. *He* would have heart failure. He would die of embarrassment.

"Kendra and Talia wouldn't do that," he said.

"My God, you're naïve," Ricki said.

"I really didn't do anything with them. Except one kiss."

"And next time?" she asked coldly.

"Who says there will be a next time?"

"You're a rock singer." She sounded like she wanted to hit him for something he hadn't even done. "There'll be a next time."

"Why are you so sure?" Del touched her lips. "I don't know what you want. A boyfriend? To own me? To mold me into something that isn't real? I don't think I can be what you want."

She sat, waiting. Then she said, "And?"

"And what?"

"The words that follow a statement like that are usually, 'Maybe we should take a break from each other.'"

A flush spread through him. "Is that what you want?"

It was a moment before she answered. "I don't think so." She had a stillness about her, but even with her instinctive mental shields raised, her apprehension leaked to him. He couldn't tell what it meant. He thought she wanted to say *no, it isn't what I want* and couldn't bring herself to speak the words, but maybe that was just his ego misleading him into believing she wanted him.

"And do you?" she asked.

His perception shifted. *Did* he want to end it? Knowing his family would disapprove of her didn't put him off. If anything, it made him want her more. Hell, he would like her even if they liked her. She understood him in ways no one else ever had. But he had no idea how to deal with her.

"I don't want to stop seeing you," he said. "But I can't handle things this way. You disappear in the morning. You try to control my life. I'm not your toy. I hate it when you treat me that way."

"I can only be myself," she said. "You may want things from me I can't give."

Disconcerted, Del said, "That's supposed to be my line."

She blinked. "It is?"

"I've used it too many times." It wasn't something he was proud about.

She actually smiled. "You're kidding."

"Why would I be kidding?" he asked, miffed.

"You seem . . . I don't know. More innocent than that. But maybe not. I don't know. You seem experienced and innocent at the same time." She made a frustrated noise. "Oh boggers, I can't figure it out."

Del couldn't help but laugh. "Boggers? What does that mean?"

"Stop trying to distract me," she growled. "What 'too many times' have you used that line?"

Del didn't want to talk about it, but he doubted she would show him any mercy until he did. So he said, "My girlfriends on Lyshriol were like me. Naïve, I suppose. People marry young there. In a place like that, sure, I seemed experienced. But compared to your life, I'm not." He stopped, flushing. "If that makes sense."

"It explains a lot." She considered him with an unsettling scrutiny. "Why were you different from other people there?"

"It's nothing."

"It's never nothing. Didn't you want to be like your friends?"

Del clenched his fist in the quilt. "What friends? The ones who betrayed me?"

Her voice quieted. "You sound furious."

Del lay on his back and stared at the ceiling. Apparently it picked up his agitation, either from his body language or messages Ricki's bed sent it, because it changed from dim grey to soothing ripples of green and blue light, as if he were underwater.

"You know that song 'Emeralds'?" he said.

She was sitting next to him, watching his face. "The one about jealousy."

"You know it's about that?"

" 'Green as the bitter nail/They drove into my name/I won't try to fail/Just to satisfy their game.' " Ricki grimaced. "We've all known people like that."

"I was fourteen. It was a group of boys older than me. They pretended to be my friends." It was the curse of being an empath; self-delusion was impossible. They had hated him for his title, his family, his singing, and most of all because of Chaniece. "They wanted my twin sister. But I wouldn't even let them talk to her." He had known exactly what they wanted to do to her. Their craving had been so intense, he had caught the images from their minds. No way in seven hells would he have let them near her.

"What happened?" Ricki asked.

"One night I went swimming at the lake. They snuck up there and caught me when I came out of the water."

"Did they hurt you?"

"They beat the crap out of me." The unwelcome memories jolted him. "I thought they were going to kill me. I screamed for help, and one of my brothers heard. He knew *mai-quinjo*, a form of hand-to-hand combat. He got them off me, even with one of him and five of them. If he hadn't—" He was shaking from the furious memories. "If I wouldn't let them at my sister, I would do, right? What great revenge. Fuck the helpless kid senseless." Del took a deep breath. "But my brother stopped them."

She splayed her hand on his chest. "No wonder you get so angry when you sing that song."

"You could tell?" He had thought he hid his emotions better.

"Only because I know you." She lifted her hand in a gesture that mirrored a move in *mai-quinjo*. "You know those dance steps you do, like this? Some look like martial arts moves."

"They are." In his youth, Del had shown only a desultory interest in the combat training he and his brothers learned, but after that night at the lake, he had vowed to become a master.

"And the girls?"

Del really didn't want to talk about this while he was in bed with his girlfriend. "Well, you know."

She wasn't letting him off that easily. "No, I don't."

Oh, what the hell. "The first time I seduced a girl, a few weeks later, I just wanted to know I could, that the whole thing at the lake hadn't changed me or that they hadn't seen something about me I didn't know myself. And with the girl . . . well, you know." He smiled. "It was fun. So I kept doing it. Proving my manhood to myself."

Instead of getting angry, she got a glint in her eyes. "You should have seduced every one of those bastards' sisters."

Gods, what a thought. It would have started a war between him and the other youths that probably wouldn't have ended until someone died. "Althor, my brother, told me to keep away from them. So I did. And he told my 'friends' he would kill them if they ever bothered me again." Del let out a strained breath. "What scared me the most was that he meant it."

"Because they attacked someone he loved."

"Not just that." Del had never talked about this before, not even with the therapist his parents had sent him to when he was fifteen, when they were trying to understand why their son had turned so unrepentantly promiscuous. "Althor was everyone's idol. The great hero. Smart, strong, powerful, handsome. He grew up into a man everyone admired. An honor student at the military academy. A decorated fighter pilot." Bitterly he said, "Until the war killed him."

"I'm sorry," Ricki said softly.

"You don't know what it was like for him." The words had been pent up in Del, but now he released the dam. "Imagine being considered the epitome of everything masculine in a sexually rigid culture. And he didn't like women."

Ricki squinted at him. "You mean he didn't like them as people? Or that he was gay."

"I don't know what gay means. He liked women fine as people, he just didn't want them as lovers. Except on Lyshriol, a man can't love a man." Del remembered as if it had all just happened, though it was nearly sixty years ago. "He had to live in a culture where people practically worshipped him, but they would turn on him with hatred if they knew the truth. When he saw how my 'friends' planned to humiliate me, he lost it." He put his arm over his eyes. "He told me once that one of the cruelest things a person could do to someone was to use their sexuality against them, that it turned love into a field of cruelty."

To Del's surprise, Ricki said, "He's right."

"He was right about a lot of things." His voice cracked. "But he died and I lived, so I guess the universe has no justice."

"Don't be so hard on yourself." She spoke in a gentle voice he had never heard from her before. "You *both* deserved to live. The injustice is that he died, not that you survived him."

Del lowered his arm so he could see her. He had never guessed this side of her existed. "I wish I'd known you back then."

She was quieter now, her anger either gone or submerged. "I always imagined that a boy who grew up in a rural culture would live a more sheltered life."

He hadn't meant to tell her so much. "You can't shelter people from human nature."

"I guess not. But it inspired your art."

He gave an incredulous laugh. "What art? I make noise. I jump up and down and shout." He couldn't keep the sarcasm out of his voice. "Such talent, and I waste it on trash." He pushed up on his elbows. "What I do is junk. Popular fodder."

"What a load of bullshit," Ricki said. "Who told you that?"

"Admit it! We can spin fantasies all we want, but when you come down to it, my work is garbage."

She scowled at him. "No, when you come down to it, you incredibly stupid man, your work is brilliant."

"Oh come on, Ricki." He mimicked his own singing voice. "'Running through the sphere-tipped reeds, suns like gold and amber beads.' Yeah, real deep."

"You're singing about the loss of childhood innocence. To make it work, first you have to evoke childhood."

"Compare what I do to the classics. Listen to those words."

"They're all the same!" She launched into a surprisingly good imitation of an operatic soprano. "'Save me, Lord, have mercy on me, redeemest my sinning ass.'" Dropping back into her own voice, she said, "It only sounds impressive because it's all in Latin."

"The Latin Requiems are beyond compare," Del told her. "What more spiritual way to ask for God's redemption than with that exquisite music?" Ever since Mac had given him the works by Pavarotti, Del had been devouring Earth's music. It was so far beyond anything he had ever done, he didn't see why he bothered with his own work.

"We all create in our own way," Ricki answered. "The Fred Pizwicks of this world will say you're nothing if you don't do it the way he likes or if you commit the even greater sin of doing it better than anyone else. You can't listen to them. Del, you don't have to be redeemed for being *different*. It isn't wrong."

"My lyrics are trite." Del wanted to stop, to keep it all to himself, but it was pouring out past the holes in the fortress around his feelings Ricki had breached. "My music is stupid."

She took his hand and pressed it as if that were enough to stop his endlessly cycling thoughts. "I don't know who's feeding you this crap, but you should stop listening to them." Softly she said, "Even if their voices are only in your heart."

Del stared at her, wondering what aliens had taken away Ricki and left this compassionate person in her place. "You know," he said. "When you cut out the hard-nosed producer stuff, you can be a really decent person."

She raised an eyebrow. "Meaning I'm not the rest of the time?"

Ai! He should have kept his mouth shut. "Ricki, no. I didn't mean it that way. Only that you're a complicated woman with far more facets than I realized when I met you. A woman worth taking the time to know."

She smiled wryly. "You're very good with those lines."

"It's not a line. I mean it." He took a breath. "I want to keep seeing you, and I hope you feel that way about me."

She spoke wryly. "You know, I can see why you had so much success with all those girls. It isn't just because you know what to say. A lot of men can do that. But you mean it. Women can tell. We know when a guy bullshits us. You don't. That's why we like you."

"You're slipping up," Del said with a grin. "You admitted you liked me."

She scowled at him. "You confuse me."

Dryly he said, "Then we have something in common."

Ricki laughed, then sighed as if in defeat and lay next to him. "Ah, Del. What am I going to do with you?"

He pulled her into his arms and nuzzled her hair while he stroked her breasts. "This."

She held him around his waist. "You have completely too much energy, Mister Arden. We should go to sleep. You have a rehearsal early tomorrow."

Del had revealed so much more of himself tonight than he had ever intended, he decided to take one last plunge. "Promise me something. In the morning, don't leave before I wake up. Get up with me. We can go into the studio together."

She hesitated. "I guess I could do that."

He had an odd sense, as if she had given him far more than he knew. He feared he was getting in deeper with her than he could handle. But maybe he thought too much. What happened, happened. This new life of his might end tomorrow, but as long as it went on, he wouldn't freeze himself with the fear of losing either his heart or his life.

Del's first stop on his new tour was at the Blues Town Café in a Pennsylvania college town. Eighty people jammed the place. Cameron stood by the door with his feet planted wide and his arms crossed, wearing his supposedly mock urban-camouflage fatigues, which were probably the real thing. How Cameron managed to look so trendy while being so blatantly military, Del had no idea.

Jud turned down his morpher, Randall turned down his stringer, and Anne took it easy on her drums so she didn't break everyone's eardrums. They didn't even have a stage. Del just stood at the front of the room and sang. He felt good. Ricki had stayed with him that night he spent with her, and his rehearsals were going well. Tonight his voice filled the place, and he let go, stepping from side to side, having fun.

The audience loved it. Their energy poured into him, and he gave it back. They wouldn't let him stop. The show went an hour longer than scheduled, until finally the cafe owner said she had to close because of zoning ordinances. In Del's heightened empathic state, he could tell she was pleased. She had made more money tonight than in the past two months combined.

Afterward, they piled into the hover-van and headed to West Virginia for the next show. It took Del a while to come down from the high of the concert. He wished he had a virt to submerge into, to relax his mental knots, but he didn't feel anywhere near as wound-up tonight as after the bigger shows.

Around four in the morning, Del drifted to sleep, slouched in one of the long seats toward the front of the van. After a while, someone shook him.

Del opened his eyes blearily. "What?"

"They want you to listen," Cameron said. He was in the next seat over.

"Huh?" Del slowly pulled himself up straight. Jud, Bonnie, Randall, and Anne were in the circular seat at the back of the van, all bent over Jud's mesh screen.

"Del! Listen to this." Jud turned up the mesh audio, and a voice rose into the air. Del's voice:

> Shimmering radiance above,
> Softening this lost man's love.

"Hey," Del said. "That's 'Diamond Star.'" He rubbed his eyes. By the time he came fully awake, the song had finished. It was the shortened version Prime-Nova had released from his vid.

"Why are you picking up a Baltimore feed here?" Del asked.

Anne raised her head and met his gaze, her eyes warm. "It wasn't Baltimore. That was continental."

"Continental?" Del's groggy mind couldn't absorb her meaning.

"The North American holo-rock chart," Bonnie said.

"This is the caption with the song," Jud said. He flicked a holo, and an eight-inch-tall image of Del in a white shirt and leather pants formed above the mesh. A man said, "That was 'Diamond Star' by Del Arden, from his anthology, *The Jewels Suite*. Register your votes at the North American Central Node."

Bonnie gave Del one of her soft, shy smiles. "We all voted. We gave you the highest rating. A ten. 'So hot, it sizzles.'"

Del laughed, delighted. "Can I vote? Like ten thousand times?"

Jud winked at him. "Only once. It recognizes your m-signature. But yeah, sure, you can vote for yourself."

"It won't make much difference," Anne said. "The NorthAm Central Node gets millions of votes. They're the top counter for holo-rock stats in North America."

It was finally sinking into Del what they were telling him. "'Sapphire Clouds' never got on a national counter."

Randall leaned forward. "They post the music charts at six A.M. We'll find out then how we did."

"This is good, isn't it?" Del said. "Maybe we'll hit the top hundred!"

Jud punched at the air with his fist. "That would be a wail, wouldn't it?" He put his arm around Bonnie and pulled her against his side.

Del finally registered how close Jud and Bonnie were sitting. He kept his smile to himself, though. He would give Jud a hard time later. He liked them both, and it seemed a day for good things.

It was hard to sleep after that, but Del dozed for a while. Cameron woke him up, shaking Del's shoulder.

Del squinted at him. "Huh?"

"Wake up," Cameron rumbled at him. "The new chart goes up in about a minute."

Del smiled sleepily. "You're getting into this, too."

"It's all right," his bodyguard allowed.

"Come on," Randall called. "Take a listen."

Del's anticipation was fading, leaving him feeling ready to throw up. To have his hopes raised and then find out "Diamond Star" was mired way down the charts would depress him. "Maybe I shouldn't listen."

"Don't be a black hole," Jud said. "Show some spine."

Del glowered at him, even though he knew Jud was joking. "I've never been a collapsed star. And if I reveal my vertebrae, I'll need an operation."

Bonnie laughed, her voice like the ripple of a clear stream. She snuggled next to Jud, curled in his arms. "Stop teasing. Listen." She motioned toward the mesh screen. "They play a sample of each song as they release the list."

"One at a time?" Del asked. That sounded excruciating.

Anne answered. "The top hundred, yeah." She was across the table from Jud and Bonnie, slumped against the seatback with her head on a pillow, sensuously graceful. Cameron was watching her instead of the mesh.

A woman's voice rose into the air. "Number one hundred: 'Shanghai Dream,' by Betsy Wong." Fast-paced music played while the holo of a beautiful woman in a gold dress sang about a dragon.

When the thirty-second clip finished, the announcer said, "Ninety-nine. 'A Thousand Sighs,' by Masts and Sails." A fleet of holo ships appeared, cruising across Jud's mesh while several male singers harmonized about the sea, comparing it to the shoals of space.

Del listened until the countdown reached seventy. By that time, his good mood had sunk. "Diamond Star" might have debuted in the nineties, but it wasn't likely to do better, especially given that the original version had entered the charts at three hundred. He slouched back in his seat and closed his eyes. When the announcer reached the fifties, he began to doze . . .

"Wake up, you idiot!" Anne shouted.

"What!" Del sat bolt upright. "Don't yell at me."

Anne was laughing. Hell, so were Jud and Randall. And Bonnie, the traitor. Even Cameron had cracked a smile.

"Stop laughing at me," Del said. Maybe he had been snoring.

"You *missed* it!" Anne told him.

"I can't believe he slept through it," Randall said. "I *cannot* believe it."

Del's pulse jumped. "Slept through what?"

In the background, the woman said, "Number twenty-one: 'I'm Still Here,' by Jenny Summerland."

Bonnie's expression softened. "Twenty-three, Del. You debuted at twenty-three."

At first he couldn't say anything. When he finally opened his mouth, all that came out was, "That can't be true."

"No, she made it up," Jud said, laughing. "Of course it's true, you dolt."

Del tried to absorb it. Twenty-three. Gods almighty, he had a *hit*. The big names usually debuted in the top ten, but hell, twenty-three was no slouch.

"I wish Mac was here," Del said. Business had kept his manager from coming on this first leg of the tour.

"He's joining us in West Virginia, isn't he?" Anne said.

"Comm him," Randall said. "For this, he'll wake up early."

"He's always up this early." Del grimaced. "It's inhuman. He comms me at ridiculous hours. Like ten in the morning."

A grin quirked Jud's lips. "Yeah, that's absurd. Expecting you to be awake at ten A.M. How more inconsiderate can he be?"

Del glared at him. His sleep habits were a never-ending source of amusement for his roommate, who seemed to think waking up at seven in the morning was normal. "Can it, Tabor."

"Can what?" Jud asked innocently. "Tomatoes or sardines?"

"Oh, stop you two," Bonnie said.

Randall was peering at the mesh screen. "Maybe Mac knows. We have a comm from him. It's been waiting about twenty minutes."

"Huh." Jud flicked holicons, and Mac's voice rose into the air. "Del, if you get this in time, listen to the North American Countdown for holo-rock this morning. Then comm me."

"Hah!" Anne said. "He *knew*."

"How could he?" Del asked. "The count tallies keep changing right up until six A.M. The announcement is live."

"Yeah, right," Randall said. "Just like the Atlantic City-Time Hour is live."

"I've heard the big companies usually know an hour ahead," Anne said. She socked her pillow a few times and settled herself back, sleek and slender in her black mesh-jeans.

"But how would Mac know?" Del asked. "Claude, can you connect me to Mac Tyler's office?"

"Connecting," Claude said. It was the version of Del's EI that he had uploaded to Jud's mesh.

"You know what this means," Jud said. "We can ask for more on this tour. Like a flyer instead of a van."

"Tour costs still come out of our royalties," Del said. "If we ask for more, we just have to pay it back out of what we earn." He had gone over the details with Mac. Finances used to bore him silly, but when they were *his* finances, they turned out to be a lot more interesting.

"I have Mister Tyler on audio," Claude said.

"Mac!" Del said. "Did you hear? We're twenty-three!"

"I heard." Mac sounded pleased but oddly guarded. "Prime-Nova found out an hour ago. Ricki commed me."

Del's good mood faded. "She could have commed me."

"She's not supposed to tell the artist," Mac said. "Unwritten rule, I guess. No one is supposed to know, but execs at the conglomerates usually get the list before it's announced. She wasn't supposed to tell me, either."

Del's smile came back. "What do you think? Can we get paid more?"

"Yes." Mac still sounded guarded. "Del, how do you know Staver Aunchild?"

"Who?" The name sounded familiar, but Del couldn't place it.

"The buyer for Metropoli Interstellar. It's a Skolian media conglomerate. He's been on Earth, scouting talent."

"Oh. That's right." Now Del remembered. "I met him at a party Ricki took me to. Then I saw him after my Atlantic City-Time appearance. He said I should send him some of my stuff. But we never heard back. I figured he wasn't interested."

"He may have changed his mind," Mac said. "He contacted Prime-Nova this morning."

Randall let out a whoop. "We're going interstellar!"

"Don't celebrate yet," Mac told him. "Just because he expressed interest doesn't mean you'll make the sale." Then he added, "And you *all* have to want this."

"Why wouldn't we?" Anne asked.

"Del?" Mac's tone remained guarded. "Do you want your music going to the Skolians?"

Del inhaled, realizing what Mac wanted him to consider. His family might see all this. He hadn't wanted them to watch him fail, but if this worked out, they would see him succeed. *If* they noticed. Yes, sure, the Skolian military was undoubtedly monitoring him here with covert bots or agents. But their main concern would be that he was safe. No one in his family listened to holo-rock. It was funny trying to imagine his Aunt Dehya, the Ruby Pharaoh, rocking out to his songs. Or his mother, gods forbid. They wouldn't understand what it meant that he had a hit, but if his music became big among their own people, they would see that others considered him a success. And that mattered to him.

Del just said, "Sure."

"You're positive?" Mac asked.

"Yes," Del said. "I'm sure."

"All right. I'll let you know what Aunchild says."

After they signed off, Anne studied Del. "Why would Mac think you didn't want your music with the Skolians?"

Del shrugged. "Maybe he always has to check."

Jud was watching him, too, with a scrutiny Del had noticed before, as if his roommate was trying to decipher him. "Skolians make you uncomfortable."

Del laughed, trying to cover his unease. "No, they don't."

"It just happened again," Jud told him.

Del shifted his weight. "What happened again?"

"You get that 'I don't want to talk' look whenever anyone mentions the Skolian Imperialate."

Damn. He had to distract them. Make it look like a joke. "Well, you know," Del said with mock solemnity. "I'm Skolian."

"That so?" Randall said. "Yet here you are, living in Baltimore."

"Actually," Anne said, "at the moment, he's in a van."

"ASC brought me here," Del told them. "To Earth. To keep me in custody. Except they had to let me go because I hadn't done anything wrong." He laughed. "So I decided to be a rock star. To improve relations between your people and mine."

"Well, goodness," Anne said. "Aren't you important."

"Yeah, he's a real ambassador," Randall said. "Hey, Allied Space Command liked him so much, they gave him a commission in the military."

"A starship command!" Bonnie said. "Captain Del."

Jud leaned back on the seat, his arm around Bonnie. "That would be one hell of a starship, eh?"

"Where are you from, really?" Anne asked. "Your accent sounds Irish, a little."

"I am actually from offworld," Del said. "A planet called Lyshriol. And it really is a rediscovered colony from the Ruby Empire. It's just that Earth found it before the Skolians. But I descend from those original colonists."

"Heh." Jud laid his cheek on top of Bonnie's head. "That's weird. I thought you came from an Allied colony."

Del wished he could share more with them. "Lyshriol looks like our virt. Except it's prettier."

"Do you miss it?" Anne asked.

"A lot," Del said. More than he had expected. "I'm going to go home for a visit after we finish this tour."

"It might not be that easy." Jud lifted his head. "Prime-Nova will want to capitalize on the success of 'Diamond Star.' If it debuted this high, you've a good chance of breaking into the top ten. If that happens, they're going to pump you out to all the publicity venues. Talk shows, media appearances, all that."

"Oh." Del hesitated. "Well, I'll figure out some way to get home."

Surely they couldn't keep him busy all the time.

Mac pulled his hover-car into the secured area behind the Skylight Arena and let out a relieved breath. He had an hour to spare, and a local band was set to play before Del. Although it wasn't a large concert, only two thousand people, the organizers had their act together. They had set up the backstage lot so only drivers with passes could get in. For acts larger than Del, it protected the musicians from being mobbed by fans.

Just as important to Mac, he had a private pad for his car. He hated concert parking, with the crowded lots and jostling vehicles. Some lead-brained joker always tried to hover his car over someone else's. Sure, in theory, a hover-car could go that high. But who wanted tons of car blasting air down on their car, unstable and unsteady? It would take a gruesome accident, though, before the legislators passed that stalled bill making it illegal to hover one car over another. The powerful vehicle conglomerates made more money when people bought jacked-up models that could manage those wretched feats. So Mac was grateful for the private lot.

Inside, Mac found Del and the others in the green room behind the stage at the arena.

"Hey, Mac!" Del bounded over and whacked him on the back,

sloshing wine out of the glass he held in his other hand. "You're the best."

Mac smiled at him. "Hello to you, too."

"Twenty-three," Anne sang across the room, dancing around with her glass of red wine.

"And the concert is sold out!" Jud called. He and Bonnie were together on a sofa. He had his arm draped around her shoulders, and they both had glasses of whatever Anne was drinking. Randall was in a recliner, holding a glass of something clear, ouzo probably, his favorite.

Cameron stood by the wall, watching the others, his arms crossed. The band had grown so used to his presence, they barely seemed to notice him. He lifted anything heavy that needed lifting and otherwise remained in the background.

As Anne waltzed around the room, Mac scowled at them. "You're all drunk."

"Oh no-oh, we're no-ot, Maaaaac," Del sang. "We're so-oh, we're ho-ot, Jaaaack." In a normal voice, he added, "We're celebrating. You should, too."

Mac couldn't help but smile. "Not your lyrics." He took the glass out of Del's hand. "I thought alcohol didn't affect you."

"It doesn't," Del said cheerfully. He motioned at the others. "But I feel what they feel. And it *does* affect them."

Oh, great. Secondary empathic inebriation. "No more alcohol for any of you," Mac said. "Wait until after the concert."

"All right," Del said, his boyish face flushed with good spirits. "But come on! Aren't you glad? People like my song!"

His enthusiasm caught Mac. "I'm thrilled. You deserve this." In a quieter voice, he said, "I know you don't want me to worry. But I can't help it."

Del pretended to punch him in the arm. "It's not like I'm the only person with an allergy who became a performer."

Allergy seemed way too simplified for Del's health problems, but Mac saw why he used the word. It avoided awkward explanations. Mac wanted to be glad for Del. He wished the part of him that dreaded Del's success would shut up and go away. But the better he knew Del, the more he liked him. He wished the youth would adopt some safe, princely lifestyle, like playing croquet and going to staid dinner parties. Which was about as likely as the moon falling on Mac's head.

When a stagehand gave the five-minute warning, they went to a curtained entrance of the stage. As Bonnie held up the curtain, they ran out in what had become their trademark entrance. Their equipment was waiting, and the AIs in the morpher, drums, and stringer had coordinated their setup with the human tech who oversaw the control boards. Green lights glowed on the instruments as if they were starships announcing their readiness to fly.

A tech threw Del a mike, and he grabbed it out of the air. As the crowd screamed, he and the band launched into "Breathing Underwater," one of the few covers they did, a work by Hayim Ani and the band Point Valid:

> Just a little boy, left in a house of pain
> Wondering where all the ashes went
> Now I'm standing in a spotlight of shame
> Staring at my black and empty frame
>
> Yet when I close my eyes, I feel the warmth of the sea
> I fall into sleep, but you're there to catch me
> Your arms are outstretched, you're loving no other
> Together we'll learn how to breathe underwater

Gone was the frightened youth who froze on stage; tonight Del moved with ease, striding back and forth, giving the audience what they came to see. His blue pants and white shirt were holoscreens, and blue light surrounded him in a halo. Abstract light-swirls in green, gold, and aqua glowed above the stage, over the audience, and in the aisles, rippling, shimmering. Blue and green light fountained up behind the band, and more holos washed the stage, submerging them in a sea of light. The stage itself morphed subtly, adding to the wave effect, constantly analyzing Del's position so its ripples didn't knock him over.

As always, Mac had a paramedic standing by in case Del had a convulsion. It had only happened once more, a few days after the first. The paramedic found nothing wrong, nor did the doctor at the emergency clinic where Mac took Del despite the youth's protests. They told Del to eat better and sleep more. So now Del always made sure to rest after a concert. Mac didn't know what to make of his using a virt to relax, but it worked. He had no more convulsions.

And yet, watching Del sing, his eyes glazed in empathic ecstasy, Mac shuddered. The doctors claimed Del was fine, but Mac couldn't shake his sense of foreboding.

After the concert, Del wolfed down several sandwiches a tech gave him. Eventually he and Cameron went back to the green room, where they found Randall talking to a blond fellow who looked like a graduate student at the college.

"I can fix it however you want," the blond man was saying.

Randall was easing his stringer into the velvet interior of its case. "I don't think so, Casper. But thanks."

"I suppose I could find someone else." Casper's glance slid toward Del, then back to Randall.

Del couldn't focus. His head hummed with energy, coiled and tight. It wasn't as bad as with the big concerts; two thousand people were much easier to deal with. And this crowd had been one of the best yet. After the show, Mac had stayed backstage and watched him eat instead of checking on the equipment. Del didn't know why. Well, okay he did. Mac wanted to make sure he didn't have another convulsion. But he felt good tonight, and after a while Mac had left him with Cameron while he saw to other business.

"Hey." Casper nodded as Del wandered over to them. "That was a great show."

"Thanks," Del said.

"I gave him tickets," Randall said. "We went to school near here, at Virginia Tech."

Casper gave a burst of laughter. "I went to school. Randy screwed off. Every now and then he remembered to come to class."

"I did not screw off," Randal said. "I had a perfectly respectable C average."

Casper snorted. "You barely passed."

Del had nothing to say. He would have given anything for a barely passing record, but he would never even take a college class. He hadn't really graduated from high school. His teachers arranged some diploma thing verifying he did his work visually and through music. Their report said his illiteracy stemmed from neurological differences in his brain. Del had been too ashamed to care what the hell they meant. He knew the truth. He was stupid. He knew it every time he saw his brother Windar, who had a doctorate in literature or his brother Vyrl, with his doctorate in agriculture. Their sister Soz had been top of her class at the military academy. People called his aunt Dehya the fair-haired genius despite her black hair; apparently "fair-haired" meant she was favored, in this case with her mathematical brilliance. Whatever genes they had all inherited had skipped him. Compared to the rest of his family, he was an utter idiot.

"Del." Randall was watching him. "What's wrong?"

Del struggled to focus. "My brain's all twisted in knots."

"Do your virt thing," Randall said. "It loosens you up."

"You want a bliss-virt?" Casper asked Del. He tilted his head at Randall. "I got him one, and he says no."

Randall scowled at Casper. "Del doesn't need that shit."

Del couldn't believe it. Just like that, *Do you want a bliss-virt?* His attempts to find out more about them had all met blank walls. Now here this Casper dropped one in his lap.

Del was aware of Cameron across the room, pouring himself a drink of water, supposedly ignoring them. Del knew perfectly well the Marine could hear everything with his mech-enhanced ears. But damn it, Cameron was his bodyguard, not his warden.

"Can you really get me a bliss-node?" Del asked Casper.

"Del, I mean it," Randall said. "Now, just when things are good, don't flat-line it by scorching your brain."

"What scorching?" Casper asked. "It's just virtual reality."

Del couldn't think what to say. He knew that if Randall thought he might ruin the band's success, he would go to Mac with his concerns. Nor was Del sure what Cameron would do. The Marine didn't have the same inflexible attitude Del had found so stifling in the bodyguards the Skolian military assigned him. In his youth, as a lesser heir of the Ruby Dynasty, Del hadn't had to take guards, but that was before he died on Metropoli and spent all those years in cryo. Now in the rare instances when he went offworld, the military insisted he have a bodyguard. Given how little Del had to offer the Imperialate, he had no doubt the taciturn mammoths were supposed to protect him from himself more than from anyone else.

Even if Cameron liked him better than his past guards, he might tell Mac about the bliss-node. It wasn't Mac's damn business, but everyone and his uncle here seemed to report on Del. Like really, his life was that interesting? Surely Earth's government had better things to do than spy on their resident, royal rock singer. In truth, he suspected General McLane felt the same way. But none of them had much choice in the matter.

He spoke reluctantly to Casper. "I guess I shouldn't."

"Yeah. Sure," Casper said, his expression guarded. "Okay."

Del wondered about Casper's look. He concentrated, and with his mind so sensitized by the concert, he easily picked up what he wanted to know.

Casper would contact him later.

Del opened his eyes. He was lying on his stomach with plant stalks soft against his cheeks. Rolling onto his back, he stared at reeds swaying over him. The sky arched overhead. The *lavender* sky. Jud teased him about saying "lavender," claiming men never used that word. Del didn't care. What was he supposed to say? Purple? It wasn't purple. Blue clouds drifted into view. The sweet fragrance of reeds filled the air, tickling his nose. A few bubbles detached from the stalks and floated lazily across his field of view. He sighed, content. He could lie forever in Lyshriol's end-less spring.

He was home.

After a while, Del sat up and looked around. Dalvador lay about a ten-minute walk away, purple-turreted roofs rising out of the swaying plain. It was wonderfully familiar, but odd, too. He didn't remember how he had come home.

"This is beautiful," a man said.

Del jerked around. Casper was standing a few paces away.

"How did you get here?" Del asked. He stopped, confused. "Uh . . . how did *I* get here?"

"It's the virt." Casper sat cross-legged next to him, crushing the reeds. "Filaments in the bliss-node helmet extend into your brain."

"The bliss! I forgot." Del inhaled deeply. "Everything is so real. Not slick and shallow like a commercial virt."

Casper's smile flashed. "It doesn't get better than this." He looked reassuring, solid. A friend.

"Why didn't I remember how I got here?" Del asked.

"It happens," Casper said. "Some people completely forget, it's so real."

"Then how do you get out?" Del asked.

"You don't remember that, either? We set this for an hour."

"Oh. Right." It was coming back. Del and Casper had left the concert arena together. Casper had fascinated Del, telling him about his work in the campus library, organizing academic virts. Given the trouble Del had finding a bliss-node, he doubted Casper's bliss came from any library collection. He was just glad Casper had shared it. Even more amazing, the librarian hadn't charged him. Del didn't know what a session like this normally cost, but he suspected Casper was being far more generous than he let on.

Del took his new friend to Dalvador. Each time they met someone Del knew, he introduced Casper. The Earthman bewildered everyone. The people of Dalvador acted the way Del expected, but not exactly. The virt extrapolated from his memories to create an even more realistic experience. Everyone spoke English, though, which changed their behavior and personalities slightly. But if anything made Del uncomfortable, the virt subtly altered until he liked the experience.

He didn't take Casper to meet his family. Some things were too personal to share, especially with someone he had just met.

They were walking up a blue cobblestone street when Casper said, "It's time to go."

"But we just got here," Del said.

Casper looked apologetic. "It's been almost an hour. We've only a few minutes left."

"Oh." Disappointment surged in Del, sharp and intense. "Can we make it longer?"

"Afraid not." Casper spoke awkwardly. "These sessions cost a lot. I got this one to share with Randall, like we used to at Virginia Tech. But I could only afford an hour."

"I'll pay you back," Del said.

"Hey, don't sweat it." Casper's smile was engaging. "I hadn't planned to charge Randall. But we do have to go. The helmet will deactivate in a few minutes."

"The bliss-node is in the VR helmet?"

"Not the node, just a chip made with it. The chip falls apart after you use what you paid for."

Such a waste. "Could I buy my own node?" Del asked. Then he could have this experience whenever he wanted.

Casper gave a derisive snort. "Maybe *you* can. The likes of me could never afford it."

Del knew he shouldn't ask. But it came out anyway. "How much?"

"A few hundred kay. The helmets are about four."

Del was sure he must have misheard. "You mean a few hundred thousand renormalized dollars?" As far as Del could tell, people called them "renormalized" dollars because sometime in the past, the dollar had become worth so little that the government had decided to redefine it. Ten renormalized dollars was the same amount as what used to be thousands of dollars.

"Yeah, that's right," Casper said. "Three hundred thousand for a cheap bliss-node. Half a million if you want top quality." He spoke dryly. "Not what most of us have lying around."

No kidding. Prime-Nova had loaned Del ten thousand dollars, but it had to cover his expenses until he found another source of income. Although Prime-Nova paid royalties twice a year, Del hadn't "earned out" his advance. Apparently that meant Prime-Nova had given him more money up front than he had yet made on his vid and virt. Until his earnings exceeded what they had paid him and his other multitude of expenses, he wouldn't see another dollar. If "Diamond Star" continued to do well, he might earn something the next pay period, but it wouldn't be much, besides which, it was several months until then.

"That's too much for me," Del said.

Casper smiled ruefully. "I always thought you rock stars were rich."

Del gave a startled laugh. "I'm no star." An idea tugged at him. He tried ignoring it, but it wouldn't go away. He had his dynastic accounts. He had been twenty-one when he went into cryo, so his assets had collected interest for decades. When he had first come out, he had been too sick to care about money. It had taken years before he recovered enough to resume a normal life. But he had control over his accounts now, and he could access them since Earth's military had stopped blocking him. Half a million wouldn't even dent his assets. If he touched that money, he would go back on his promise to himself to make his own living, but the thought of having this experience any time he wished was too tempting.

"Suppose I *could* buy a node?" Del said. "How would I do it?"

Casper's eyes took on a glint. "Maybe I can help you."

XIII

Sea of Light

The week after its debut, Diamond Star rose to number fifteen on the holo-rock chart. In week three, it hit seven in holo-rock and debuted at thirty-seven on the Continental Hundred. In its fourth week, it rose to number two in holo-rock and twenty-nine on the continental chart. That same week, Mind Mix's "Time to Sing" hit number one on both the continental and holo-rock charts, continuing their undisputed reign as the kings of rock. In its fifth week, "Diamond Star" stayed mired at number two in holo-rock, plagued with the bad luck of having its greatest movement at the same time as a single from Prime-Nova's superstars.

In week seven, "Diamond Star" dethroned Mind Mix on both charts and became the most popular song on the North American continent.

"He has to be here," Ricki shouted cheerfully, trying to make herself heard above the loud music in the crowded hotel room.

"I saw him a few minutes ago," Mac shouted back. Glistening people swirled about them, talking, drinking, dancing to Del's music. "I'll go find him."

Her smile flashed. "I'll be at the bar. Don't be long!"

He waved and didn't try to answer. It was too noisy. He didn't know where Del had vanished to, but Mac doubted he had left. The party was for him, after all.

After ten minutes, Mac still hadn't found him. Anne Moore was enthroned on the couch, signing vids for *The Jewels Suite*. Jud and Bonnie were slow dancing despite the music's jazzy beat. Randall was holding court, talking to a cluster of musicians, including several prominent stringers. They were all having a great time. So where was Del?

Mac slipped out the glass doors of the suite. A swimming pool lay to his left, and marble benches curved around the patio. Beyond them, trees extended for over an acre. He entered the woods, following a crystal-flecked path. Moonlight sifted through the trees, giving the night a burnished quality, as if it were edged in silver. He came to another marble bench, this one back in the trees, almost hidden from the path. A man and a woman sat there, embracing. Mac quickly moved on.

It was ten minutes before Mac found another bench. A man sat there, leaning against a tree, staring into space.

"Hello," Mac said.

Del looked up with a jerk. "Oh!" He rubbed his palm over his cheek, so clearly smearing away tears that Mac's heart lurched.

Mac hesitated. "Do you mind if I join you?"

"Please do." Del motioned to the bench. "Have a seat."

Mac settled on the bench. "You're missing a great party. Ricki came all the way out here to Chicago to see you."

"She did?" Del's smile flashed. "That's good."

Mac spoke with care. "Are you all right?"

"Yeah. I'm fine." Del gave a shaky laugh. "It's just a lot, you know."

"You've earned it." That was putting it mildly, given the way Del had persevered with his music for his entire life despite nothing but negative feedback.

"It's so hard to believe," Del said. "Maybe I'm not a failure after all."

"You never were," Mac said gently.

Del's eyes gleamed in the moonlight. "Zachary commed me this morning. Prime-Nova is releasing *The Jewels Suite* worldwide. And did you see? Staver Aunchild is here! He wants to sell *The Jewels Suite* to Skolians." Del rubbed his palm over his eyes. "My father liked "Sapphire Clouds." He tried to like the others. I think he understood *about* my music, even if he didn't understand the songs. He knew I had to do it. He felt that way about his."

"You must miss him."

"Always." Del leaned back and gazed into the trees. "I guess I should tell my family. But what if they want me to stop?" He gave Mac a rueful glance. "I don't know why they would. I mean, I'm not far up any line of succession, and I'm no use for powering the Kyle-mesh. After all that time in cryo, it would kill me to use my mind that way. But if they want me home, it would be hard to say no."

"Would they force you?" Mac asked.

Del thought about it. "I'd like to think not. But I don't know." He smiled at Mac, a simple smile with no mischief, wicked glints, or surly undertones. Just a man who had received a gift he never expected. "Even if it ends tomorrow, Mac, this is one of the best things that ever happened to me."

Mac grinned. "Then come back and celebrate."

Together, they walked back to the hotel.

"Are you sure?" Mac said into his wrist comm. The van shook as they hovered over some bump in the road. "Can you talk louder? I can't hear you."

Del shifted around, unable to sit still. They were all gathered in the circular seat at the back of the van, except for Cameron and Randall, who were in seats up front. The van whirred on through the bright day, headed for the Sports Fields outside of Chicago.

"You must have another way!" Mac was saying. "What? No, this wasn't one of our tour stops. We were only asked yesterday to play the festival. We don't have any prep here."

Del glanced at Jud. "You have any idea what's wrong?"

Jud shook his head, his beaded dreadlocks clacking on his shoulders. "No clue."

"That isn't acceptable," Mac was saying. "Don't you have a passcoded parking lot behind the stage?"

"For flipping sakes," Anne said. "He's mad about not having a parking space. He hates that."

Del tried to relax. Bad parking they could handle. The festival organizers had invited them at the last minute and agreed to pay a big fee for the request. It wouldn't surprise him if they had a mix-up, but he hoped not, because he wanted this show. The outdoor festival had over twenty of the biggest bands in holo-rock, including Jenny Summerland, the Conquistadors, and of course Mind Mix. Del hadn't performed in a show like this since his Philadelphia disaster. He wanted to prove he could do a good job.

Mac swore under his breath. Then he said, "What? Yeah. A guy named Cameron. Just one. You'll need to provide more."

Del glanced at Cameron, who was listening intently. "Do you know what they're talking about?"

"Security, probably," Cameron said. "Mac doesn't need me to park."

"Damn it," Mac said. "How could we plan for it? We were invited *yesterday*. I want two. Otherwise Del Arden doesn't play. Got that?"

"Wait a minute!" Del said. "Don't say—"

Mac shook his head, motioning Del to silence. Into his comm, he said, "Yes, that'll work. Behind the stage. Twenty minutes. Okay. Good."

As Mac switched off his comm, Del said, "Don't tell them I won't sing!"

"They don't have a secured lot for the van," Mac said.

Randall glared at him. "You need *two* parking pads?"

"Ah, hell," Jud said. "Not parking. He means the gauntlet."

Randall's attention perked up. "We're going to run the gauntlet? Cool."

"What gauntlet?" Del asked, bewildered.

Mac spoke quietly. "The audience is at six hundred thousand, twice what they expected."

"So?" Del said. "That's *good*."

Mac regarded him with a strange expression, as if he saw an avalanche poised over their heads. "It's a rowdy audience. It overflowed their security lines. You have to go onstage without a secured area."

"In other words, you have to mix with the crowd," Jud said.

Del shrugged. "So what? I don't need special treatment."

"Del's right." Randall's laugh rumbled. "Come on, guys. It'll be fun. We can sign autographs."

Mac gave him a dour look. "Before or after you get trampled?"

"Oh, come on," Randall said. "I've seen plenty of guys go on stage through the audience. So what? People yell and wave and ask you to sign vids. Big fucking deal."

Del finally understood. Mac didn't want a Skolian prince vulnerable in a crowd. He spoke gently. "Don't worry, okay? Remember when I told you about the cryogenics, and I said I wanted to make my own choices? I meant it, Mac. I'll be fine. If I get roughed up a bit, it's okay."

"I hate it," Mac said. "Any time someone touches you."

"Holy shit," Randall said. "You guys are, like, *lovers?*"

"For crying out loud." Del's face burned. "No, we are *not* 'like, lovers.' He's worried about my safety, that's all."

"Father figure," Anne decided, studying Mac. "You're afraid to see Del hurt because he's like a son to you."

"Something like that," Mac said, looking awkward.

"What did you mean about cryogenics?" Bonnie asked Del.

Del wished he'd kept his mouth shut. "It's nothing."

"It's obviously something," Randall said.

Jud scowled at him. "And he obviously doesn't want to talk about it."

Anne spoke to Mac. "We'll be fine. It's no big deal."

Mac tried to smile. "Yeah. Sure. You have Cameron. And they're sending two of their security guys, just in case."

"So you see," Del said. "No need to worry."

"We can't get closer!" Mac said into his comm. Sweat covered his forehead despite the air-conditioned van.

They were stopped hundreds of yards from the pavilion where they were supposed to meet the two guards. Beyond the tent, the huge stage of the Chicago Sports Fields dominated the view. People flooded the area, and gleaming orbs rotated above the crowd, broadcasting music from the stage. No one in the unrepentant throng paid any attention to the vehicles mired among them. Security bots were keeping the crowds in check, but they didn't make anyone move. Given the unexpected size of the crowd, Del suspected the concert organizers wanted to avoid getting people angry or violent. He knew nothing about putting together festivals, but it seemed like lousy planning to him.

"We could just walk to the tent," Del said. "No one will know us."

"They might," Jud said. "Your face is all over the m-verse."

"It is?" Del had been on tour since "Diamond Star" rose up

the charts. He'd listened to a few reviews, mainly for the novelty of hearing people actually say good things about his work, but the rest of the time he spent in his virts or asleep.

Except for that night with Ricki. She had stayed after the party—and left him to wake up alone. Again. Why? She said her job kept her busy. Right. He had made himself vulnerable when he admitted how much her leaving bothered him, and he felt as if she had thrown his trust back in his face. He could talk to her again, try to work it out, but he was beginning to wonder if he should. The ups and downs of their relationship drained him.

"What happened to the security guys?" Mac was saying into the comm. "No, an hour is *not* good. That's when Del goes on. We have to set up first. Yeah, I'll ask." He glanced at Del and the others. "This is George Morales, the stage manager. He wants to know if you all can get your equipment to the stage from here."

"We can carry the instruments," Jud said. "That's not the problem." He waved at the milling crowds on the view screens. "If we take our equipment out there, we'll be lucky to get it to the stage. As soon as people see, they'll know we're one of the bands. They might start grabbing our stuff."

"This drills," Cameron said. "Their security bots should have cleared out this place."

"It's a freedom festival," Randall said. "You know, no authoritarian control."

"What authoritarian?" Jud demanded. "The bots are flipping machines."

Mac gave them a sour look. "Freedom festival is a euphemism for 'license to misbehave.'"

"Oh, come on," Randall said. "They're just having fun."

"What happened to the guards they promised?" Cameron asked.

"They have some big, beefy types," Mac said. "But they need those guys to help the bots protect the performers. People keep rushing the stage, and the bots can't make subtle enough distinctions of who to stop and how." He gave Cameron a wry smile. "So it looks like you're our only big beef."

The Marine's eyes glinted. "You don't get bigger than me."

"Oh my," Anne said. "Do tell." Cameron actually cracked a smile at her.

Mac spoke into his comm. "Morales? The band doesn't think

it's safe for their equipment. Yeah. Okay, I'll ask." He glanced at Jud. "They have a Voxerlight III-Beta on the stage. That's the same brand as your morpher, isn't it?"

"Yeah," Jud said. "But a different model. And it doesn't have my programs."

"Could you port your files to their Voxer?"

Jud didn't look thrilled with the idea. "Not unless they can guarantee the files will be protected. No duplication, and I erase it all after we finish."

Mac relayed the answer to the manager, then told Jud, "Morales says no problem. They do that all the time."

"I've never practiced on their Voxer," Jud said. "I'll probably make mistakes. Even if I don't, it won't sound exactly the same."

Mac motioned at the crowds on the view screens. "People aren't paying that much attention. I doubt anyone expects it to sound the same."

Jud nodded as if accepting a mission. "I'll do it."

"What stringers do they have?" Randall asked.

"And drums," Anne said.

Mac went back and forth with George until they settled on a set of drums for Anne, including smart-skins with AI programming. But they had no stringers Randall felt would work.

"Some people out there have guitar cases," Jud said. "If you put your stringer in one, you could carry it incognito."

"In cog *what*?" Randall said.

Anne gave a throaty laugh. "Incognito. In disguise."

Listening to them, Del had a sudden inspiration. He sang softly into his ticker to record the words he couldn't write. "I'm no fair-haired genius hiding in disguise/I'm no golden hero in the blazing skies."

"Yeah, well, good for you," Randall said. He looked at Mac. "I need a morph engine, too. And that's too heavy to carry."

"They have a Strato-premier Model Six onstage," Mac said. "Would that work?"

"Hell, yeah!" Randall sat up straighter. "I'd use a Strato any day."

"That solves the equipment problems," Bonnie said. She motioned at Del. "Now we have to get *him* up there." With a smile, she added, "No other model will do."

Del grinned at her. "I'm irreplaceable."

Mac considered him. "A lot of people out there have on VR goggles. You can hide your eyes with a pair and put your hair under a cap. If you wear one of my shirts over yours, to make you look bigger, probably no one will recognize you."

"Sounds good to me," Del said with a laugh. "Incognito."

"Okay," Mac said. "Here's the plan. Randall, you go first, so if anyone clicks to what we're doing, hopefully you'll already have your stringer up there. Jud, you go with Bonnie and Anne. Cameron and I will bring Del."

"What, no protection for my stringer?" Randal waved his hand at Del. "I know he's the big name and we're just hired help, but if my piece gets trashed, we got no music."

"You're not just hired help!" Del turned to Mac. "Send Cameron with him, then have Cameron come back for Anne and Bonnie."

"Hey," Jud said. "I can protect these lovely women."

Anne smirked at him. "I'm the one with the black belt in karate, sweets. I could kick your ass from here to Los Angeles."

Randall snorted. "I'll bet your boyfriend loves it when you talk that way."

"Does he?" Cameron asked her, suddenly intent.

She turned her sultry gaze on him. "I don't have a boyfriend."

"Del can kick," Bonnie said. "I've seen him practicing."

"I have, too," Anne said, glancing at Del. "The moves are different, though. Do you have a black belt?"

Perplexed, Del tapped his belt. "Yeah, this one."

Jud sighed. "Del, sometimes you have so little clue."

Mac spoke firmly. "No tossing people around, Del, unless you're in real danger."

Exasperated, Del answered, "I never said I'd toss anyone."

"Come on," Randall said. "Let's go."

Cameron eased open the side door, and he and Randall jumped down. No one paid attention. Randall held his stringer case between his body and Cameron as they headed for the pavilion. People were waiting for them at the entrance, and the air there *shimmered* as Cameron and Randall ducked inside.

Within moments, Cameron ambled out again. For some bizarre reason, he wandered around. Then Del realized that if he just strode back, it could draw attention; this way, no one noticed as he gradually drifted toward the van.

Anne, Bonnie, and Jud stepped out next, laughing together like any other festivalgoers. Del watched them on the screen. He didn't realize Cameron had slipped into the van until he looked up and saw his guard standing by his seat, bending his head to fit under the roof.

"Let's go," Del said. He felt like they were on their own covert operation. Mission Rock Festival. Hah! His Imperator brother would have a fit.

Del tucked his hair under a green cap and donned the goggles. Everything turned blue, like the lenses. Mac carried the sack with Del's clothes for the concert, and Cameron opened the door. As they stepped into the late afternoon sunlight, Del inhaled the fresh air. Jud claimed that long ago the people of Earth had almost destroyed the atmosphere with pollution. They must have cleaned it up, because it smelled wonderful, and *right*, appealing to him at some instinctual level.

"Nice day," Cameron said.

"Yeah." Del watched the crowd as he and Cameron headed for the tent. Everyone was blue.

A woman with blue-blond hair peered at him. "Aren't you Del Arden?"

Damn. How could she tell? "No," Del said. Cameron moved between him and the woman.

A man on Del's other side said, "Hey! It *is* him."

"Can't be," a kid said. "Arden isn't playing the festival."

Del shot Mac an alarmed look, then realized no one could see his eyes behind the goggles.

Someone pushed Mac. At the same time, the woman who had first spoken stepped past Cameron. As the Marine gently caught her arm, someone behind Del dragged his goggles around his neck and pulled at his cap. Flustered, Del grabbed the cap. He was too late; his hair fell out in its distinctive spill of curls.

"It's Del Arden," someone said. "Look! Over here!"

The people pressed closer. Cameron loomed at Del's side, holding his arm, and Mac took Del's other arm.

"Del, we love you," a woman called.

Del grinned at her. "Hey, I love you, too."

Another woman grabbed his hair. While Cameron fended her off, someone yanked Del's shirt, then let go when it didn't rip. Someone else shoved at Mac, and he swore as he stumbled.

Del was getting flustered, as more people tugged his clothes. The crowd stretched everywhere, rumbling. Someone yelled, but they were too far away to make out words. Excitement rolled over the throng, and the smell of cooking meat assaulted Del's senses. Then a woman pulled him to the side and kissed him, her lips soft on his cheek. He didn't know whether to kiss her back or run. Cameron hustled him away, but they had lost Mac. Looking around, Del glimpsed his manager a few paces back. The older man was flushed, and Del worried someone might knock him over.

Someone dragged Del away from Cameron. Several someones. Four women, with spiky hair and pretty faces. They were running their hands through Del's curls, which he would have liked, except everything was jagged and confused and happening too fast. One kissed him, pressing her lips against his. Del lost his balance and started to fall. More people pushed in, and for one dizzying moment he thought he was going down under the crush of their feet.

Cameron heaved him back up. "Move aside," the Marine barked at everyone. "Let him through."

The tent loomed in front of them, its entrance shimmering. A guard motioned them in, his gaze darting to the crowd. Then Del was inside and everything went quiet, the chaos muted. A thump came from outside, but no one followed them. He realized then that the shimmer he kept seeing was a molecular airlock around the tent. From school, he vaguely remembered the airlock was something called a "lipid membrane," with a variable permeability. Del hadn't learned the biochemistry that well, but he understood the result; you could tune the membrane to be leaky or watertight to many things, including air—or people.

"Hey!" Jud said as they all gathered around Del. "You okay?"

"I'm fine!" Del said, laughing. "Those people are crazy, though. Did you see those girls?" He looked around behind him. "Mac got pushed—oh! There you are." Mac was coming toward him, disheveled but otherwise fine.

Anne let out a breath. "That was some gauntlet."

"I've seen people line up for autographs," Jud said. "But never anything like the way they were grabbing you."

"You all right?" Mac asked Del as he came up to them.

"Sure." Del felt queasy, but it was because people had been shoving Mac, not him. "You're the one I was worried about."

"I'm fine," Mac assured him. "That was bizarre, though."

"They like him," Anne said. Though she smiled, she looked as uneasy as Del felt. "A *lot.*"

Del had no objection to people liking him. But if it meant he would be trampled, he could do with a little less friendship.

Mac stood in the darkened wings of the stage, watching Del. Despite the short notice, the gauntlet an hour ago, and unfamiliar instruments for the band, it was Del's best concert yet. Instead of drowning in empathic stage fright, he embraced the effect, amplifying the audience's excitement. Mac suspected that many performers who were considered "magnetic" did something similar, giving back emotions they picked up. Del strode across the stage, wailing in his magnificent baritone, his voice soaring. He stopped at the front and knelt down, crooning to a woman:

> Angel, be my diamond star
> Before my darkness goes too far
> Splinter through my endless night
> Lightening my darkling sight

Why your darkness? Mac had always wondered who Del was singing to in "Diamond Star."

When Del finished, he shouted to the audience. "Thank you all for coming. You've been great!"

A roar surged from the crowd overflowing the meadows in this former industrial complex outside Chicago, which over the centuries had softened into a luxuriant parkland. People flattened the grass, camping out, picnicking, playing sports, dancing. Most could only hear the music through the globes that whirred and spun everywhere.

The audience applauded, cheered, and stamped as the band left the stage. Mac stood with the vibration of those pounding feet shuddering through him and wished he didn't feel as if they were coming to trample the young man who stirred up all that fervor.

Del and Jud came over to him. "Hey," Del said, smiling. "I think they liked it."

Mac smiled. "You're into understatement tonight." It pleased him to see Del so calm despite the huge audience.

"It's so hard to believe this is happening." Del stared at the people, gazing past the light amplifiers that hid him from the crowd. Jud stood at his side, a wordless support. They made a good team, Jud as the musical genius who brought Del's songs alive.

The pounding increased, and people waved mesh screens over their heads, thousands at once, until a sea of glittering light rippled around the stage. Anne and Randall came over to Del, their faces flushed, and Cameron stood nearby, looming and silent.

"We better do the encore," Anne said with a husky laugh. "Before they shake down the stage."

Del grinned. "Let's go!"

They ran back out, and the audience screamed. So *many*. Mac wondered what incredible force rose out of the raw, driving soul of rock, that it could bring six hundred thousand people together with such energy. Del had no idea of the power he wielded.

Mac hoped he never found out.

XIV

The Star Road

"What's this?" Anne asked. She was relaxing on the hotel couch, her long legs stretched across a table in front of it while she looked through a holofile of Del's songs. "'Carnelians'? That sounds like part of *The Jewels Suite*."

"It was," Del said as he sank into an absurdly expensive arm-chair. Randall stood at the bar, pouring himself a drink. Jud was working on the console near the window, with holos of musical notes floating in the air.

Anne sang the first verse of "Carnelians":

> You dehumanized us; your critics, they died
> You answered defiance with massive genocide
> Hunt us as your prey, assault, and enslave
> Force us bound to stay, for pleasures that you crave

Randall wandered over. "That's strong stuff."
Del shifted uneasily. "Mac said it was too political."
Jud glanced up at them. "What's it about?"
Del knew if he said *the Trader Aristos*, they'd ask questions he didn't want to answer. So he just said, "Oppression, I suppose."
"This isn't your usual stuff." Anne continued singing:

They strangled our summers, your Carnelian Sons
You anguished the mothers, in your war of suns
With a heart that freezes, you shattered my kin
You thought you were leaving no one who could win

She flipped through more of the holofile. "You have two versions here with different music."

"It's not finished," Del said. He wished she would put it away. Before he could say anything more, though, the door hummed.

"Who's that?" Randall asked. He downed the rest of his ouzo.

Jud switched his console to a view of the entryway. A group of gorgeous people in glimmer-glam clothes stood outside, including Ricki.

Del sat up straighter. "So let them in."

The door opened, and the sleek crowd swept inside: Mac, Ricki, Staver Aunchild, and several execs from Prime-Nova.

"Hey, babe." Ricki swayed over, dynamite in a clingy blue dress that covered her from neck to knee and yet somehow made her look as if she was wearing nothing.

"Hey," Del said. He was still angry at her, but he missed her, too. In his youth, he would have rebuffed her to avoid dealing with his tangled emotions, but he couldn't do that anymore. Since they couldn't talk about it now, either, he just watched her. When she leaned over him, he grabbed her around the waist and yanked her into his lap. He no longer cared what people thought about them.

"Stop that," she murmured, kissing him, her lips warm against his. When he tried to pull her closer, she slipped out of his lap and onto a couch next to him.

Conversation swirled as people settled into seats or went to the bar. Ricki called someone over to give Del a drink, and soon he had a gin and tonic. He set it on the table by his chair.

"I don't see your point," Staver said. He was talking to one of the Prime-Nova execs, a man named Orin something. "So what if the Trader Empire has no Kyle technology. That doesn't make them any less despicable."

Del blinked. It was strange to hear an argument about the Traders here, in his protected circle of friends on Earth.

"How's the tour?" Ricki asked Del, sipping her drink.

"It's good," Del said, half his attention on her and half on the argument between Staver and the exec.

Ricki followed his gaze and grimaced as if she had taken a bite of a sour fruit. "They've been arguing all morning." She indicated the exec. "That's Orin Jenkins, from Acquisitions."

"From what?" Del asked.

"Acquisitions," she said. "Vid-bids. They find new talent. He's thinking of signing a Eubian band."

That felt like a blast of cold air. "You mean the Traders?"

"That's right. Did you know *they* call themselves the Eubian Concord? It's Skolians who say Traders, supposedly because the Eubians sell people." Ricki waved her glass at Staver. "He's pissed off."

It didn't surprise Del. He didn't want to be on the same planet as a Trader band.

"I don't know what the hell is 'Kyle technology,'" Orin was saying. "Some mumbo-jumbo about telepathy."

"Kyle space is just another universe," Staver said. "Except your thoughts determine where you are there. If you think about Pittsburg, then you're close to everyone else who's thinking about Pittsburg even if in our universe they're across the galaxy."

Orin snorted a laugh. "I think, therefore I move?" He looked across the suite at Ricki and winked. "If that were true, I wouldn't be here, Staver dear. I'd be over there on the couch."

"Sorry," Staver said dryly. "*You* don't go into Kyle space. Only your thoughts. You can think about her all you want, but you can't touch."

"Too bad," Orin said.

Del was simmering, but before he could tell Orin to go flip himself off, Ricki laid her hand on his arm. "Let it go, babe," she murmured. "He's just spouting."

He gritted his teeth, caught off guard by the intensity of his reaction. After all, she had to put up with those news holos of women kissing him at the Chicago concert. He needed to unsnarl his responses to her. He had thought he was incapable of anything except a casual love affair, but he was no longer the kid who could convince himself he didn't want more.

"I've heard about this Kyle space," Orin said. "But if you can't go into it, what's the point?"

"Think about it," Staver said. "If you talk to someone with a Kyle link, you're right next to them, even if in our universe you're on different planets. That's how we get instant communication across such huge distances. Our laws of physics don't apply there, so the speed of light has no meaning."

Orin shook his head. "Your Kyle space has no substance. No physical evidence."

"You want evidence?" Staver said. "Interstellar civilization as we know it wouldn't exist if we didn't have fast communications. We live a real-time existence. We could talk right now to someone in another star system if we had access to the Kyle-mesh. Imagine if it took months, years, even centuries to send a message."

"Starships carry messages," Orin said. "And they get around light speed. I don't understand the physics, but at least it can be demonstrated in the real world."

Mac spoke up. "The physics is pretty straightforward. You add an imaginary component to your speed. It gets rid of the singularity in the relativistic gamma function. Ships go around the speed of light by detouring into the complex plane."

Ricki made an exasperated noise. "Oh, well, that sounds so simple, Mac, I can't imagine why I didn't think of it myself."

Del laughed softly. "The Varento starship drive. It'll send you out of this world."

Her smile turned sultry. "You bet, babe."

"Sure, ships can carry messages," Staver told Orin. "That still takes time. You can't communicate instantaneously that way."

Orin raised his glass to Staver. "If this Kyle-mesh was so important, my people would have developed one, too."

Staver gave him an unimpressed look. "You can't."

"Sure we can." Orin finished his drink with one swallow.

"How?" Staver asked. He looked genuinely curious. "To use Kyle space, you need psions. To create, power, and maintain a mesh in Kyle space, you need Ruby psions. They're the only ones strong enough. It would fry anyone else's brain."

"Oh, come on," Orin said. "You believe this Ruby Dynasty has some magical power? They've really put one over on your people."

Del wanted to punch the exec. And what the hell did "put one over" mean? Mac was watching him from a nearby chair, a warning in his gaze. He wanted Del to stay out of the argument.

"The Ruby Dynasty are the strongest known psions," Staver said. "It's genetic, a recessive mutation that involves a whole slew of genes. Ruby psions have *every* one of those genes paired. Only them."

"Whatever," Orin said. "We'll make our own Ruby Dynasty."

Del would have laughed if that hadn't hurt so much. The Skolian Assembly had been trying for ages to make more Ruby psions.

Never mind that they had almost destroyed Del's family in the process.

"It's not that easy," Staver said. "Attempts to create them in the lab don't work. You can't clone them, either. Our geneticists are still figuring out the why."

"I think you Skolians made this up," Orin said, "so you could all claim to have ultra powers."

Staver regarded him with exasperation. "We don't 'all' have anything. Ruby psions are practically extinct. The Ruby Dynasty are the only ones. Quite frankly, our government ought to lock them up. Keep them just to power the Kyle web."

Del's words burst out before he had time to think. "What, make them slaves to the government, is that it?"

Mac and Ricki both shot Del warning glances. Del didn't need his "practically extinct" powers to know it was because Mac didn't want him to reveal himself, and Ricki didn't want him to offend the person who had just bought the rights to distribute Del's music in an interstellar market.

"The Traders are the ones who keep slaves," Staver told Del curtly. "You Allieds have no idea. They put on that fake, shiny disguise, and you fall for it every time."

Del had forgotten Staver thought he was an Allied. It was so odd to hear his own thoughts reflected back to him, he forgot his anger. Curious, he said, "How would you prove it's false?"

Staver looked ready to do battle, but at Del's question he paused and spoke more calmly. "It's a good question. Taking an Allied delegation to the labs that train providers would work. Except of course the Aristos would never let that happen."

"Providers?" Orin finished off his whiskey. "What is that?"

"Sex slaves," Ricki purred.

Orin grinned at her. "What do you know about that?"

Del gritted his teeth until it hurt, distracting him from his urge to hit Orin. Beating up Prime-Nova execs would be stupid, but if the guy leered at Ricki one more time, Del couldn't swear he'd be responsible for his actions. And damn it, Ricki had baited Orin that time.

"You think it's sexy?" Staver demanded. "This is no *game*. Often it has nothing to do with sex. Aristos torture providers. For their entire lives. They don't care who they hurt, who they destroy, who they enslave. They think they're entitled to make people scream in agony."

Ricki's face paled. "That's sick."

Staver's voice sounded clenched. "Very, very sick."

"So how is making the Ruby Dynasty slaves to the Imperialate better?" Del demanded. "What the hell purpose would that serve?"

Staver looked uncomfortable. "We need the Rubies."

"Need what?" Del asked. "It takes only two people to create the Kyle-mesh. The Dyad. Two very protected people, along with their heirs, who are also protected, I'm sure by shields, implants, guards, and who knows what else. How is locking up the Ruby Dynasty going to solve anything?" He wanted to keep going, to shout his frustration and anger, but if he didn't stop now, he might say too much. Taking a breath, he fell quiet.

Staver spoke carefully, as if he finally realized that even here his words could have ramifications. "What if something happens to the Rubies? A lot of them died in the war, including the previous Imperator and her father, who were both in the *Triad* that powered the Kyle web. That's why we have a Dyad now. We have a new Imperator, but no one to take the father's place."

Del felt as if Staver had punched him in the gut. *He* was supposed to have taken his father's place. "They can't add a third person to the Dyad because they're afraid it will overload the powerlink and kill the two already in it." Realizing how that would sound, he added, "That's what I've heard." Even if they could risk adding a third Ruby, it couldn't be him; after the brain damage he had suffered in cryo, it would kill him to use his abilities at that high a level. If the Traders captured him, they couldn't use him to build their own Kyle web.

"Del, come on," Ricki said with an indulgent look. "I'm sure it's much more complicated." Her gaze was anything but indulgent; she was warning him off the argument.

Staver leaned forward. "It's easy for you here on Earth to criticize. The Skolian Imperialate protects you. But if we fall, you're next."

Del didn't miss the irony, that Staver's words were almost exactly what he had told Mac.

"You know," Mac said with a slight laugh, "this conversation is getting intense, don't you think?"

"I think we should drink to Del Arden." Ricki lifted her glass, and the gold liquid sparkled. "To the latest number one sensation from Prime-Nova!"

Everyone raised their glasses. Del lifted his, too, but he no longer felt like celebrating. He wanted to withdraw from his "party" and submerge in the bliss-node Casper had sold him. Half a million dollars, but it was worth it, not only for the release it gave him, but because it let him remake his life into anything he wanted. Right now he craved its welcoming embrace, for only that could banish the Trader nightmares Staver had laid bare.

"But why?" Del's mother asked. "Of all the things you could do with your life, why this?" She was standing by a window, her skin shimmering in the light of the two suns.

Seeing her stirred up so many painful memories, but also many Del treasured. So often he had watched her stand by the window that way, smiling with welcome, frowning with parental censure, beaming with motherly pride, or pensive when she was lost in thought, bathed by the light of the suns Valdor and Aldan.

The bliss-node could create a simulation as complex as a parent who approved of him, yet it had balked at something as simple as putting in two suns. It had informed Del that if the suns circled each other that closely, their gravitational forces would throw Lyshriol out of its orbit. *I know that,* Del had said. *It's not a natural system. Astronomical engineers created it five thousand years ago. Yeah, someday we'll be in trouble if we don't learn to stop it, but for now, the system exists.* The aggravating virt still objected, saying no one could move planets. He couldn't believe a mesh code was arguing with him. When he told it that no, the Ruby Empire did have that technology, but they lost it when the empire collapsed, the flaming node didn't believe him. At that point, Del had told it to just shut the hell up and make the blasted sim.

So today he spoke to his mother in the simulated sunlight of his home. "How can I explain what inspires me?" he asked her. "It's like trying to capture the mist. I only know I was meant to do this."

"I felt the same way when I was a ballet dancer," she said. "Your grandparents worried all the time."

"But they didn't stop you." He willed her to understand. To some extent, the node created its simulations using his memories and knowledge, and he was still learning how to influence the results. "I know my singing isn't as cultured. But it means as much to me as your dancing meant to you."

His mother sighed, glistening in the light. She looked like a work of art. But Del had always thought her beauty was more inside, the way she had sung him lullabies when he was small, tended his cuts and bruises, and stood up for him when his teachers claimed he "didn't apply himself."

He's doing his best, she had told them. *He tries. But he really can't read.* So they gave him tests. Test after test after test. And finally they said yes, his brain had neurological differences. He saw two hieroglyphs as different unless they were written *exactly* alike, with the same color, size, texture, even in the same place. Letters in languages with alphabets were even worse. They said sometimes he identified parts of himself with the images, so that when a letter changed, it forced him to change himself to identify it. He knew, logically, it was the same, but his mind wouldn't accept it. Both his brother Eldrin and his father had similar reactions to written language. Eldrin eventually learned to read, but neither Del nor his father had ever managed.

"You understood about my reading," Del said. "Can't you understand about this?"

"I don't know if I ever will," she said gently. "But I see what it means to you. Your creativity is a gift, and where it takes you, that's where you should go."

A sense of lightening came to Del, as if a weight lifted off him. He knew it was false, only a simulation tailored to make him happy, but it felt so *real.*

His voice caught. "You don't know what it means to me to hear you say that."

Her smile lit her face. "I'm glad. But you have to go."

"What?" His simulated people weren't supposed to kick him out of the virt.

"You set this session for three hours," she said. "It's up."

"Already?"

"Already." She raised her hand. "Be well." She faded and the world went black.

Del lifted off the helmet and stared around his hotel room. He had tears on his face. He felt ridiculous, crying over his fantasy world. Yet he wanted nothing more than to go back. In the virt, he could relive his life and do everything right. He would never take the tau-kickers, never go swimming that night, never seduce all those girls. Didn't any of his granite-headed family realize he would have *agreed* to marry Devon Majda? If he couldn't sing, at least he could have been the consort of an interstellar queen. He wouldn't have had to live with the crushing loneliness that only the taus kicked away. Who knew, maybe she would have even accepted his music.

Del rubbed his eyes. The console said it was four A.M. He peeled off the suit and stumbled to his bed. Sprawling on the floater, he sank into a fitful, exhausted sleep.

When the first kid climbed on the stage, Del almost tripped over him. He was singing "Rubies," spinning around, when suddenly Cameron appeared in front of him. Del jerked back, losing his place in the song as Cameron leaned over a youth who was staggering toward Del. The Marine literally picked up the fellow and dumped him back in the audience.

In the time it took Cameron to move one person, three others jumped on the stage and started to dance. Del kept singing as he tried to avoid the people gyrating around him. It was crazy, with the audience overflowing around the stage, everyone contorting, jumping, and twirling, their bodies flashing with holographic tattoos, glitter paint, and swirling washes of light.

Two security bots clanked out. Roughly humanoid in shape, with blue legs and white torsos, they vaguely resembled humans in jeans and shirts. Even as Cameron and the two bots hauled the dancers back into the audience, two girls climbed up and headed for Del. Still singing, he backed away from them, unsure what to do.

Cameron caught one of the girls, but he was so busy being gentle with the pretty waif that her buxom companion made it to Del and threw her arms around him. With a grin, he yanked her closer and kissed her right there. The audience shrieked, and their excitement spun higher.

As Del drew back, smiling at the girl, Cameron gently pulled her away. Del started to sing again as Cameron and the bots moved downstage, trying to keep the audience where they belonged.

Mac's tense voice sounded in Del's ear. "Get off the stage. This is getting out of hand."

Still singing, Del looked toward Mac, who was standing in the wings, and shook his head. When Mac swore at him, Del turned away, then bent down low and jumped high. The audience screamed their approval. Everything was overflowing, their reactions, his song, the emotions. It was gloriously out of control.

"Del, I mean it!" Mac shouted. "*Get out of there.*"

As more people rushed the stage, discordant emotions fractured Del's euphoria. Anne and Jud wanted him to stop, but Randall liked the commotion. What hit Del hardest was Cameron's reaction. The stoic Marine, the giant who never got flustered, was scared for Del's safety.

Del jumped to the last word of the song and held the note, his signal that he was ready to finish. Jud crashed to a crescendo and Anne added her signature cymbal roll across the morphing plates of flexi-metal.

"You've all been great," Del shouted to the audience. He ran offstage as he always did at the end of a concert even though they had only done half their set. Anne and Jud sped off with him. Randall scowled, but then he stalked off as well. The audience shouted protests, and more people tried to climb on the stage, struggling with the security bots.

Jud stopped in front of Mac. "We have to get the equipment off," he said urgently, out of breath.

Mac nodded and spun around to the techs. "Go. The AIs can deactivate the instruments."

"No!" Randall yelled. "What's wrong with you all? They're getting into it. That's what we *want.*"

Del agreed. He felt as if he had been cut off in the middle of a breath. He wanted to get back out there.

"Randall, look." Anne pointed to the far edge of the stage.

Following her gaze, Del felt the blood drain from his face. The stage was sagging under the weight of everyone clambering onto it. If they didn't get the audience, bots, and equipment off soon, they would all be caught in a collapse. People could be injured, even killed.

"You all go to the green room," Mac told the band. "I'll come down as soon as we have everything here secured."

"Hell, no," Jud said. "I'm not letting you send Bonnie out there while you coddle me." With that, he ran back onto the stage, toward the techs who were taking apart his morpher. Anne sped over to help with her drums and morph engine. Randall made an exasperated noise, but he strode after her.

Del started out. "I should help."

"Get back here," Mac said.

Del stiffened and kept going.

"Cameron, I need you here," Mac said into the audio-comm that both Cameron and Del wore.

Del stopped and turned with a jerk. "Mac, cut it *out.*"

Cameron came up to Del, disheveled but calm.

"Take Del to the green room," Mac said. "If he protests, carry him."

"What!" Del stared at him in disbelief. When Cameron took his arm, he yanked it away, then whirled around and strode onto the stage. Cameron would leave him alone if they were in full view of the audience.

Or maybe not. Del had only gone a few paces when Cameron grabbed him from behind and hefted Del up, with one arm under Del's knees and the other behind his back.

"Put me down!" Del shouted at him.

"No." Cameron carried him off the stage.

"Well isn't that romantic?" Randall smirked as he walked past, his arms loaded with holoscreens.

"All right!" Del said. This was humiliating. "I'll go to the flaming green room. Just *put me down.*"

"Thank you." Cameron set him on his feet.

"I can't believe this," Del growled. But he went.

" . . . we're too civilized to have a riot at a rock concert!" the man on the holo-cast asserted. "You might have seen that kind of behavior in a more barbaric age. But now? Never!"

"Oh, for crying out loud," Anne said to the holographic image of the news show. "A few people climbed on the stage. What's next? The fall of civilization!"

"Shhhh." Jud waved his hand at her. They were gathered around his mesh in Del's hotel room, listening to reviews of the concert. Except they were picking up a lot more than music critics. This time they had hit the major news outlets. Michael Laux on Atlantic City-Time Hour was interviewing Henry Flume, a supposed expert on modern culture.

"It was a mass trance," Flume said darkly. "This Del person corrupts everyone who listens to him."

"For flaming sake," Del said.

"A trance. That's certainly an interesting idea," Laux said. He turned toward the camera. "I'd like to introduce our other guest tonight, Orin Jenkins, Vice President of Acquisitions at Prime-Nova, the label that puts out Arden's music. Good evening, Mister Jenkins."

"Thank you, Michael." Orin sounded much more formal than in person. He looked formal, too; his sleek, snappy clothes were gone, replaced by a silver and blue suit.

"What do you think about this idea that Del Arden hypnotizes his audience?" Laux asked.

Orin laughed good-naturedly. "Believe me, if our performers could do that, we'd be marketing it full tilt."

"That figures," Del said. Leave it to Prime-Nova to see the marketing angle first.

"Mister Arden has a great talent," Orin said. "One might be tempted to suggest we haven't seen this reaction before because our 'civilized' acts aren't talented enough to cause it."

"Hey, listen to that," Anne told Del. "Someone at Prime-Nova actually acknowledged that you have something to do with your popularity, that it isn't all their star-making machine."

"That's a load of crock," Flume said. "That boy is singing depraved froth with a loud voice. He's a bad influence."

"Oh, puleeease," Randall said. "Can't he find anything less clichéd than 'bad influence'?"

"Don't bang on it," Jud said. "The more people hear what a terrible influence Del is, the more they'll listen to our music."

"What do you want to bet," Bonnie said, "that Orin will get something in there about how sexy Del is."

"Naw, he wouldn't go that far," Randall said. "The censors wouldn't allow it."

"What is Arden doing that you see as a bad influence?" Laux asked Flume. He seemed genuinely perplexed.

"The way he moves on stage," Flume said. "One moment, his body language is telling the universe to go bleep itself. I won't defile your program by using the actual word. The next moment, he's telling all the women he will have intercourse with them."

Anne let out a hoot of laughter. "Hah! Orin didn't *have* to mention it. Flume did it for him."

"I do not move that way," Del said indignantly.

"Hell," Randall said. "If I knew what Flume meant, I'd move that way, too."

Orin didn't miss the opening. "If you're saying Del Arden is one of the most potent male sex symbols to hit the music scene in some time, I won't disagree there. But that's no crime."

"Hey," Del said, laughing. "Now I'm a potent sex symbol."

"Yeah, right." Randall threw a crumpled-up napkin at him. "I can hardly control myself."

"As opposed to what?" Jud asked. "An impotent sex symbol?"

Anne choked on the coffee she was drinking. Del just glared. He could imagine what his family would say to Orin's comment. Then again, maybe he didn't want to imagine it. They might laugh. Or his mother would give him another lecture on the discretion expected of his "station." He had once infuriated her when, as a teenager, he had told her he wasn't a mag-rail train stop.

"It's unhealthy," Flume was saying.

"Why?" Orin had that Prime-Nova *We know so much more than you* tone. Del usually hated it, but when it was being used in his defense instead of against him, he liked it just fine.

"Because it leads to what happened in Wyoming tonight," Flume retorted.

"Nothing ever happens in Wyoming," Jud drawled. "No wonder this is such a big story."

Wyoming? Del had lost track of where they were on the tour. Yes, they had been in Wyoming. Tomorrow they were going to California. He was exhausted from all the traveling.

Laux turned to face the holocam. "There you are, folks. You've heard from both experts. Register your vote on the City-Time Hot Handle. Vote 'yes' if you agree Del Arden is popular because of his talent and 'no' if you believe his popularity comes from unwholesome qualities."

"What kind of wonky choice is that?" Del scowled at the others. "Can't anyone on this planet do anything without voting on it?"

"It's called democracy," Randall said.

"No, it's not!" Del said. "Democracy is a political system. This is—I don't know what it is. What happens if people vote that I'm unwholesome?" For all he knew, Prime-Nova might decide he was too risky to keep on tour.

"The polls supposedly don't have influence," Anne said. "But if it goes against you, our backers might worry."

"Here." Jud brought up another holo, a room with two doors. He flicked a holicon, and the right-hand door opened.

"You've just voted *yes* for Del Arden!" a cheerful voice announced. "Do you have any comments to include with your vote?"

"I sure do." Jud spoke into the mesh comm. "This poll is silly. Everyone knows Arden is brilliant. Just because Flume finds him threatening doesn't mean the rest of us will let Flume destroy our music."

"You know they can track who said that," Randall said. "They'll figure out it came from Del's morpher."

"I don't care," Jud said. "It's true."

To Del's amazement, Bonnie, Anne, Randall, and even Cameron voted yes. Then Jud flicked a holicon and a graph of the poll results came up. It was 88 percent in favor of Del.

"Do you think it will stay that way?" Del asked.

"It's too soon to say." Anne studied the stats below the tally. "About one thousand people have voted so far. So our four votes couldn't be skewing the result."

"Did you notice the way they phrased it?" Bonnie asked. "'Yes' came first, with a question almost guaranteed to make people agree. Of course Del has talent. The 'no' vote is second, with the unwholesome choice. Not yes/no on the unwholesome thing, but yes-talent and no-unwholesome. I think they set it up that way on purpose, to skew it in favor of Del."

"Huh." Del wondered why. "That's odd."

"Not really," Jud said. "Laux likes you."

"He hardly knows me."

"Yeah, but he brought you on his show when you were a nobody. Take my word; he likes you."

A chime came from the mesh. Jud flicked his hand through the *respond* holicon, and Mac's voice came out of the comm. "I'm on my way back from the stadium."

"Is everything okay?" Jud asked.

"It looks like the damage wasn't too bad," Mac said. "Some people got a few scrapes and bruises, but nothing worse than you all ended up with."

Not all of us, Del thought. He was still irked at Mac for refusing to let him help the others.

"What about the stage?" Jud asked.

"We'll have to pay for the damage," Mac said. "But all things considered, it could have been a lot worse." Then he said, "Del?"

Del leaned over the mesh. "Yes?"

"I want to talk to you. In private."

Del was aware of the others watching him, waiting for his response. He had told them they were all a team, not "Del and some other guys." Cameron looked uncomfortable.

"If you have something to say," Del said, "you can say it to all of us. And if you're going to tell me to stop touring, the answer is no."

"Damn it, Del!" Mac added some other choice words under his breath. "You're going to give me heart failure."

"No one was hurt. You said so yourself." Del smiled. "Actually, it was sort of fun. Why do all those women want to kiss me?"

"For crying out loud," Mac said. "I'll see you all in a few minutes. Good-bye!" With that, he cut the connection.

"I knew he'd be upset," Jud said. "But why would he want us to stop touring?"

Randall considered Del. "That's a good question. In fact, I've never seen a personal manager with so little desire to see his client succeed."

"That's not true," Del said.

"You have to admit," Anne said, "he's too protective."

"I'm Prime-Nova's investment," Del said. "They don't want me damaged."

"No one is that concerned about the rest of us," Anne said. She didn't sound angry, more puzzled.

"We're not important enough," Randall snapped. There was no mistaking *his* anger. "We can be replaced."

"No, you can't." Del looked around at them. "It isn't just me up there, it's the four of us, and Bonnie and Cameron. We're doing this together. Without you, I'm nothing."

Randall opened his mouth, then closed it again. While they waited, he took a breath. Then he said, "Del, I know I get testy. I'm sorry. I'm just not used to playing second in a band. But this all means as much to me as it does to the others."

Del hadn't expected *that*. He spoke quietly. "Thanks. I appreciate it."

He just wished Mac would appreciate his success more.

Staver invited Del to Muir Woods in California. The forest took Del's breath away. Lyshriol had no trees; the plants in the "woods" there were glasslike tubes and bubbles, all in gem colors that evoked the stained glass windows in cathedrals he had visited on Earth. But even after seeing trees in Maryland and other places, he wasn't prepared for the redwoods. They were *huge*. Magnificent. Centuries old. Just walking under them was incredible. A deep calm spread through him.

"I didn't know anything like this could exist," Del said.

"You've never visited here?" Staver asked.

"I didn't grow up on Earth," Del said. "I come from one of the rediscovered Ruby colonies. Earth just found us first."

"I had wondered," Staver said. "You have more interest in Skolian affairs than most Allied citizens."

"We hear a lot." In the serenity of the woods, Del felt more relaxed than he had in ages, except when he used his bliss-node. He eased down his mental barriers, curious about Staver—

And recoiled *fast*. But it was too late.

Staver raised an eyebrow. "Yes, I'm an empath."

"You *knew*? About me?"

"I wasn't certain until just now," Staver said. "But yes, I suspected the first time I saw you in concert."

"Oh." Del wondered how many other people had guessed. "I don't usually tell people." He rebuilt his shields to protect his mind even better than before.

"Nor do I," Staver said quietly.

They walked on, silent beneath the ancient trees. Even though Del hardly knew Staver, he didn't feel the nervous compulsion to talk that usually came when he interacted with someone who could affect his career. He had never needed to have such conversations before, and he didn't know how. Here under the redwoods, though, his stress trickled away.

After a while, Del said, "Did you mean that about the Skolian government locking up the Ruby Dynasty?" He kept his shields up so no hint about his identity would leak to Staver.

"I suppose not." The older man exhaled. "Of course you're right, it would make us no better than the Traders. And we just need two or three Ruby psions to power the Kyle web. But you don't realize how few of them there are. Only seven, I think."

"Twelve," Del said absently. People often miscounted the number of people in his family because no one really knew anything about him or those of his siblings who had never left Lyshriol.

Staver gave a wry laugh. "You're optimistic."

With a start, Del realized what he had said. Damn! He would have to be more careful. "Maybe it's wishful thinking."

"Why?" Staver asked curiously. "Why would you care if there were more of them?"

"I guess just the idea of psions having a larger community."

"I doubt it matters to them."

You have no idea. Del wondered if Staver could understand what it was like never to find a person outside your family you could fully share your love with. Staver could find other empaths; they were rare, but not one in a trillion. A Ruby could love someone who wasn't a Ruby, but they could never have the full link, two people become one, that miraculous bond Del's mother had known with his father—and lost the night his father died. Del had shared his mind with his twin sister from before their birth, but he had died and she had lived, and now they were no longer twins. Their connection had weakened.

"Do you remember what you said about the Trader Aristos the other night?" Del asked.

Staver met his gaze. "I meant every word."

"It almost sounds personal for you."

It was a moment before Staver answered. "Five years ago, their raiders kidnapped someone I knew and sold her as a provider."

No wonder he was angry. "I'm sorry."

"Why?" Staver asked. "So many of your people either don't understand or don't care."

Del decided to reveal just a bit. "A Highton Aristo nearly killed my father. He escaped, but he was never the same."

"Gods," Staver said. "I didn't expect *that.*"

Del stepped over a fallen log covered with moss, deep green beneath the high canopy of the forest. "It isn't something we talk about." Such simple words for a pain that went so deep.

"I understand." After a moment, Staver said, "I admit, my idea of locking up the Ruby Dynasty wouldn't solve anything. It's what you Allieds call a 'knee-jerk reaction.' But what would *you* do to protect empaths against the Aristos?"

Del thought of his mother, her eyes blank after the Traders had fried her brain. "Exterminate them," he said flatly. "Every last one. All two-however-many thousand."

"That's strong medicine from an Allied citizen."

Del shook his head, unable to explain. "They're too powerful. It seems hopeless that we'll ever be free of their brutality. I just wish I could *do* something."

"Aye," Staver murmured. "We'd all like to."

Del lowered his mental shields carefully this time, using more nuance so Staver wouldn't detect him. Staver's mood was difficult to read, but his wariness came through. He wondered if he should trust Del. Something to do with . . . what? Providers.

It hit Del in a flash, partly insight and partly empathy. Staver wasn't here just to find Allied talent. His job served as a cover for a very illegal project—he helped providers escape from the Traders, routing their path through Allied territory because it drew less attention.

Del pulled Staver to a stop. "I want to help."

Staver looked at Del's hand on his arm, then at Del. "Excuse me?" He pulled away his arm.

"Whatever you're doing, I want to help."

"What exactly am I 'doing'?"

"You're helping providers," Del said. "Getting them *out* of there."

Staver snorted. "You've an active imagination, young man."

Del couldn't just let it go. This was too important. "All right. You aren't doing anything. But if the anything you aren't doing needs financing, come to me."

Staver spoke kindly. "We all want to do something, son. It's frustrating to feel helpless against their tyranny. But we can't take on the Trader Empire. We're mice running at a huge monolith." He laid his hand on Del's shoulder. "I appreciate the thought, though."

Del frowned at him. "Right." He didn't believe for one moment that Staver didn't know what he was talking about.

Del turned over and stretched his arms. He was so drowsy, half awake and relaxed. His bed felt hard, though.

After a while, he opened his eyes. A woman was seated in a chair next to him, reading a holo-book. A braid hung over her shoulder, brown streaked with grey. She had a round face with laugh lines around her eyes, and she wore a blue shift. She was so unlike the glossy types that surrounded him lately, he wondered why she hadn't stood out more among his guests.

Except . . . what guests? He hadn't been at a party. He and Staver had gone to a café in a place called Sausalito. They had drunk herbal tea, whatever that meant.

Del's mind wandered, unable to focus. Cameron had once told him that people cooked with herbs. Anne claimed they were medical. Del had asked Randall, who told him "herbs prickled," a comment Randall clearly found hilarious. He told Del to go *smoke and have fun.* Frustrated, Del had consulted Claude, his EI. After some discussion, they figured out Randall meant "prickle" as in grass, an archaic term for marijuana, and also a play on a word referring to a certain part of the male anatomy. *Smoke and have fun* indeed. Del doubted he had been drinking marijuana tea, but who knew. He remembered zilch about whatever had happened afterward.

He was lying on his back on a stone ledge that jutted out from the wall. A smart-blanket warmed his body.

"Hello?" Del asked.

The woman looked up from her holobook. "Hello."

"Who are you?" Del was surprised how tired he sounded.

"My name is Lydia." She turned off her book. "Are you feeling better?"

"I got sick?" Damn. Maybe he had a reaction to the tea. He didn't remember pain, though, and he wasn't dead. At least, he *hoped* not. This would be a weird afterlife.

"You passed out." She leaned forward and smoothed his hair out of his eyes. "It's amazing. You really look this way."

"What way?" he asked.

"Like Del Arden."

"What an astonishing coincidence," Del said groggily.

She smiled. "I mean, the vids don't enhance your looks."

"Oh." He thought of asking her why would he bother, then changed his mind. Of course Prime-Nova would bother.

"Where's Staver?" Del asked.

"He'll be back." Lydia tilted her head. "Is that your real name? Del Arden?"

"Well, yeah. It's not a pseudonym." With horror, Del felt more words forming: *My full name is Del-Kurj Arden Valdoria Skolia.* He barely stopped himself, and holding back was a struggle. What was wrong with him?

"Staver said you're from a Skolian world," she said.

"Rediscovered world. A stranded Ruby Empire colony."

"Until the Skolians found you."

"Not Skolians," Del mumbled. "Earth. Texans, to be precise."

"Texans!" She chuckled. "What a combination. The ancient, enigmatic Ruby Empire collides with the Lone Star State."

"With the what?"

"Don't worry," she murmured. "It's not important."

Yeah, right. He was starting to see what was going on. Staver had drugged him with a truth serum. It wouldn't work, though. Imperial Space Command had given everyone in Del's family training to deal with interrogation. His siblings in the military even had specialized neurotransmitters in their brains that blocked them from answering certain questions under stress. But gods, what if Staver had given him something his body couldn't handle? Although as far as Del knew, his body wouldn't have a fatal reactions to a truth serum, it wasn't anything he wanted to test.

He had a good guess why Staver gave him a serum. However abhorrent free humanity might find the Aristo practice of keeping providers, it was legal among the Traders. What Staver and his group were doing was illegal on an interstellar scale. They could go to prison for a long time if the Allied authorities caught them. If the Traders caught them, they would be executed, except anyone like Staver who had more value as a provider. Del didn't doubt Staver would prefer the death penalty to a lifetime of slavery and torture.

Of course they wanted to know why Del had offered to help. Nor did he blame them for taking precautions. If they hadn't, he wouldn't trust the security of their organization. But he still didn't like being drugged.

"Del?" Lydia asked. "Are you there?"

"What?" He tried to focus. "Yeah, I'm here."

"You were telling me about your home."

"I was?"

"That it was one of the ancient colonies."

"Oh. Well, yeah. But that's boring." He tried to sit up, then sighed and lay down. His vision blurred.

"You'll feel better in a while," she said.

"I hope so."

"Staver told me your family had a run-in with the Traders."

"My father." Before Del could stop, he said, "And my mother."

She went very still. "What happened?"

The words hurt like broken glass. "An Aristo came to our world. He caught my father. My father tried to escape." The words wrenched out. "He was climbing a cliff. The Aristo shot it. It came down on my father. Pulverized his legs. Blinded him. The Aristo kept him like that for days, barely alive, with no treatment. *Nothing* for the pain." His voice cracked. "My brother Shannon rescued him."

"My God," Lydia said. "Did your father survive?"

"Yes. He—yes. Shannon killed the Aristo." The words tore out of him as if they were ripping his insides. "In retaliation, the Aristo's children kidnapped my mother. Our military eventually pulled her out, but—" He struggled to hold back the soul-parching words. "It took my parents a long time to recover."

"I'm terribly sorry," she said in a soft voice.

Del spoke unevenly. "In the meantime, I took care of the house, the farm, my father's duties as the Dalvador Bard."

Her brow furrowed. "Did you say a bard?"

The words, *The King of Skyfall* hovered on his lips, a specious title the popular media had given his father. But he managed to say only, "He was a historian for our village. They're called bards."

"He's lucky he had you to look after things."

The painful words kept tearing out of him. "After my parents recovered, I took one of the only offworld trips I've ever done. A vacation. I went to Metropoli. And I died there. Great get-well present, Mother and Father. Your idiot son killed himself."

Silence followed his words. Then Lydia said, "You did what?"

"I had a lethal reaction to a drug." Del didn't want to open his eyes and look into her confused face.

"But you're alive."

"They put me in a cryogenic womb."

"Until they could revive you?"

"Yeah, until whenever that happened."

Lydia exhaled. "No one should have to go through all that."

He finally looked at her, accusing with his gaze. "And I never tell that to anyone. What did you do to me?"

She stroked his head, her touch soothing. "It's nothing."

He shoved away her hand. "Like hell it isn't. You just ripped out very private pieces of my life."

A man walked out of the shadows behind Lydia. Staver. "We had to be sure," he said. "We gave you teracore."

Del recognized the name. "A truth drug."

"That's right." Staver took a chair by the wall, brought it over, and sat in it backward, resting his arms on the top. "That sounds horrific, what your family went through."

"Shannon was only fourteen," Del said. "He had never hurt anyone in his life. But he killed the Aristo."

"Tell me about him," Staver said.

"I don't want to."

"Why?" Staver asked. "Does he have something to hide?"

"Of course not," Del said, irritated. "He was gentle. I didn't think he was even capable of rage. But he found our father." He exhaled. "My little brother committed murder that night."

Staver stared at him. "How could a boy kill such a powerful lord?"

Del really, really didn't want to talk. But he couldn't stop. "The Aristo couldn't bring in weapons or shields without alerting our defenses. He barely got himself in." His voice hardened. "Vitrex didn't reckon with the fury of a boy who saw his father crushed."

"Vitrex?" Staver asked.

"The Aristo."

"How did he know your world had empaths?"

"Well, that's the priceless question everyone wants answered, isn't it?" Del said bitterly. Everyone in three empires knew the Ruby Dynasty lived on Skyfall. Exactly how Vitrex had infiltrated their defenses, they didn't know. Shannon had killed him before they could find out.

"Del?" Staver asked. "What is it?"

"Nothing." Del sat up slowly, his head swimming and his sight blurred. "Don't ask me any more. It hurts too much." He swung his legs over the edge of the ledge and regarded Staver. "Do you believe me now? I want to help you."

"I have no idea why you think we're doing anything that would require help," Staver said.

"Why would you have drugged me otherwise?" Then Del said, "And it was in your mind."

Staver shook his head. "You couldn't have probed my mind without my knowing. I'm an eight point four on the Kyle scale."

His confidence didn't surprise Del. That was a phenomenal rating. It meant Staver was such a powerful empath, he was rarer than one in a hundred million people. The scale didn't even go up much past ten, or one in ten billion.

"That's impressive," Del said—and dropped his shields, not slightly as he had done in the forest, but all the way. Then he politely "knocked" at Staver's mind. **Hello.**

Staver's eyes widened. *Gods, man!*

Del raised his shields again. He had made his point.

"That was *incredible*," Staver said.

Lydia looked from Del to Staver. "What just happened?"

Staver exhaled. "A tidal wave hit me and said, 'Hello.'"

"I didn't hear anything," she said.

"Are you a psion?" Del asked. When she shook her head, he spoke with an openness that didn't come naturally to him. "Staver reacted that way because he's such a strong psion. So we could set up a two-way link. But it's difficult to maintain that kind of mental intensity with another person even for short periods of time."

Lydia didn't look surprised, which made Del suspect she was used to working with psions.

"What is your Kyle rating?" Staver asked him.

"I'm not sure," Del said. Which was true. It was impossible to measure ratings for the Ruby Dynasty. The sum total of all humanity wasn't enough to determine how many Ruby psions occurred naturally in human populations. His family had ratings higher than fourteen, which meant they were rarer than one in one hundred trillion, and all humanity numbered no more than several trillion. The only reason more Rubies existed was because the Assembly had deliberately bred them, heirs and spares to keep the Kyle-mesh powered.

Del only said, "My rating is above nine."

"It doesn't surprise me." Staver considered him. "Suppose, for the sake of argument, we could help providers. Why would you join us? You know what would happen if the Traders caught you."

"I wouldn't go into their space. But I can offer you financial help." Del's gaze never wavered. "In the millions." For something like this, if Staver checked out, Del would gladly use his dynastic accounts.

Lydia's mouth opened. Then she caught herself and closed it. Staver had more success in acting impassive, but his astonishment trickled past even his formidable shields. What Del had offered didn't come their way often. To put it mildly.

"I wish we were helping providers," Staver said. "That we had this sort of 'underground railroad.' Except we are talking about escape across the stars. The Star Road, eh? If we had one, your offer would have been much appreciated."

Del waited. When Staver had nothing more to add, he almost said, *That's it?* They put him through all this for nothing? But he bit back the words. They were being careful.

Staver stood up. "Are you steadier?"

"Sure." Del rose to his feet. He had thought his vision was still blurred, but he felt all right. The room was just dark.

"We should get back to San Francisco," Staver said.

Del would have insisted on an antidote, except he didn't want to risk taking unfamiliar drugs twice in one day. Instead he frowned at Staver. "I shouldn't go anywhere with people. I might spill all sorts of embarrassing stuff the next time someone asks how I feel about being Prime-Nova's pretty boy."

Staver smiled. "The teracore should wear off in about thirty minutes. It will take longer than that for us to get back if we take the scenic drive up the coast."

Scenic indeed. Staver wanted to extract more information from him. Del had to admit, though, the view from that cliff-side road was spectacular. He had never seen an ocean so close before. It astonished him that humans had once taken vessels of wood, metal, and canvas out on that endless water. Starships seemed safe in comparison.

So he went with Staver and struggled to be patient. If they wanted his help, they would contact him.

The New Filmore didn't seem new to Del; the building was at least sixty years old. Mac told him it had been built on the site of something called Filmore West, so "new" came from that. Regardless, the acoustics were a dream, and his voice filled the place. The audience liked him from the moment he came on, after a warm-up from a local band. People filled seats and thronged the floor, dancing or standing, with girls sitting on the shoulders of their boyfriends so they could see over the crowd.

"It's great to be here in San Francisco!" Del called out. The audience shouted their agreement. Randall was morphing his guitar, coaxing out waves of music. Anne had turned on the echo engine for her drums, creating a resonance that gave them an incredible, rich, powerful sound. Jud sat in the center of his morpher like a fighter pilot in a cockpit.

Jud glanced at him with a questioning gaze. Del knew what he wanted to do. "Carnelians." Del never intended to perform it in public. But tonight he did sing "Starlight Child":

When the forever snows
Tightened their embrace
While my dreaming thoughts froze
You rose with newborn grace

Nothing ever will compare
Nothing ever will come close
Your eyes, your skin, your shining hair
Starlight child, my heart knows

He moved around less than usual because the song was more difficult than his others. The words were birds taking flight, soaring out of him with joy and pain, rising into the crystalline night of Earth until they found their way to the glittering stars.

XV

The Perfect Virt

The Los Angeles Coliseum was the largest indoor venue Del had played, and tonight people swarmed the place. The crowd poured into the lot behind the Coliseum as the band's hover-van pulled up.

"Are you sure the security guys will meet us?" Del asked for the third time. "They didn't in Chicago."

Mac was sitting across from him in the circular seat. "They'll be there."

"We should have used the underground tunnels," Del said uneasily.

"I thought you wanted to see your fans," Randall called from a seat up front.

Del felt trapped. "I didn't know it would be so many people."

Jud looked up with a start as the van jerked. "What the hell was that?"

The craft settled on the ground, and its turbines powered down.

"Van, why are you stopping?" Mac asked.

"If I keep going," it said, "I could injure someone out there."

"I'm glad we sent the instruments earlier," Anne said. They had learned their lesson at the Chicago Sports Fields.

Del stood up. "Let's just get it over with."

"I dunno," Randall drawled. "Could be rough out there. All those women might want to kiss you."

"Ha, ha," Del said. Although he did want to connect with his audience, it was no longer flattering when people pulled at his clothes, his hair, his body. Sometimes it had sexual overtones, especially with women, but often people just wanted to *touch* him. Maybe it all had subliminal sexual messages; he didn't know. He just wished it would stop.

The Coliseum was a mammoth circular structure that filled a city block and towered above them. Holos morphed up and down its sides, splashes of color mixed with giant images of Del's face, of Del leaping in the air, of Del shouting into the mike. Too much Del. He wanted to escape himself.

As Cameron opened the van, people surged forward. Four guards stepped out of the crowd, armor glinting, faces hidden by helmets. When Del and the band jumped down, the guards formed a bulwark around them. Their armor reflected faces from the crowd: a girl calling, a man tossing a crumpled paper, a youth craning to see. People pressed in, and the guards held them off as they escorted Del and the band forward. They couldn't stop every touch, not without getting rough, which would defeat the whole point of "meeting fans." A hand slid through Del's hair, another person brushed his lips, a third scraped his legs. He pushed away someone pulling his belt, *undoing* it. Someone else shoved a guard and knocked him against Del. The guard grabbed Del's arm, holding him up.

"This is too much," Del said under his breath.

"No kidding," Jud muttered next to him, pushing a dreadlock out of his eyes.

Then they were under the overhang of the Coliseum, in its shadow, the entrance looming before them. An airlock membrane slid across Del's skin as he went inside. The last guard stepped through behind him and flicked his gauntleted hand across his belt. The air shimmered, and when Del turned around, he saw the crowd pressing forward against an invisible barrier.

Del set his palms against the barrier while he looked out at the people. They stared back as if he were an exotic creature they had trapped. Then a girl at the front smiled shyly. Like the release of gas through a valve, Del's tension flowed away. He smiled at her and waved. A ripple of approval went through the crowd as people waved back at him.

"You all right?" one of his guards asked.

Del looked up. The giant had taken off his helmet, revealing a man with a rugged face and sandy hair.

"Yeah, sure," Del said, trying not to sound shaky. "Sure. I'm fine."

Submerged within ghostly holos that rippled throughout the giant Coliseum, Del crooned into his mike:

> No answers live in here alone
> No answers on this spectral throne
> Nothing in this vault of fears
> This sterling vault, chamber of tears

But his tears had never been steel, for he was vulnerable in a way his sterling vault would never know:

> Tell me now before I fall
> Release from this velvet pall
> Tell me now before I fall
> Take me now, break through my wall
>
> No answers will salvage time
> No answers in this tomb sublime
> This winnowing crypt intertwined
> This crypt whispering in vines

He sang, mourning the time he had lost in cryogenesis, in his life, in his soul, but he sang also with joy for his rebirth:

> No answers could bring me life
> Yet when I opened my eyes
> Beyond the sleeping crystal dome
> Beyond it all, I had come home

The audience listened and danced and tried to climb on the stage, but Del didn't think anyone really understood the song. Who among them had lost nearly half a century of his life while the universe went on without them? He had no answers because there were none. It had just *happened*.

Death had called his name, but by a fluke of luck, he had escaped its summons. Cryo had kept him alive, and if that rebirth had been a form of hell, at least he had survived. He had no answers for why he should have survived, but gods willing, maybe he would live long enough to find at least one.

After the concert, Del helped the stage crew take down the light amplifiers. Why, he didn't know; he was no tech or light expert. But he liked the manual labor. Princes weren't supposed to, but he was more farm boy than royalty. So he did whatever tasks the bemused techs gave him. When they finished, he walked back to the green room with Cameron at his side, his bodyguard silent, respecting his need for the privacy of his own thoughts.

The band had left a hover-car so Cameron could drive Del to the hotel. Mac surprised Del by approving of his staying late. He considered it even better than sneaking Del out of the Coliseum. People would believe Del was long gone, probably to a party, which was what everyone seemed to think he did all the time. What he really wanted was his bliss-node. He needed to untangle his mind.

Del had spent most of the night since the concert lost in thought. He kept wondering if he should talk to his family. He just didn't know what to say. *Look at me.* He had achieved his heart's goal, to have his music accepted. And it felt wonderful. But when he thought of telling them, it seemed trivial. They were making history, literally changing how humanity existed among the stars. And what did he do for a living? He yelled into a mike he didn't even really need.

As the Imperator, his brother Kelric was the greatest defense the Imperialate had against the Traders. For all that Del found it humiliating to have the "little" brother he had once babysat treat him as a defiant youth, he knew perfectly well Kelric offered far more to their people than Del would ever have to give.

Del longed to do something his mother admired. He wanted her to be proud of him. He knew she loved him, but he also felt her disappointment. Maybe it hit her so hard because he had turned away from the life of the Dalvador Bard, which had defined his father.

For the past year, since the Allieds had taken Del away from Lyshriol, no one had acted as Bard. Del was supposed to ask one of his brothers to do it, but he considered Chaniece a better choice. She was the best singer of their siblings still on Lyshriol, and she enjoyed the Dalvador music. She also served as guardian of the Valdoria estate and lands, and she had no desire to leave them, which was perfect for the Bard.

Del knew his family wanted him to assume the title. He had acted as Bard those first months after his father's death. He wished he could bear the thought of going home and carrying on his father's legacy. But if he forced himself to kill his dreams, he would die from a starvation of the spirit.

The voices of two women floated from behind a curtain by the stage, interrupting his thoughts.

"—don't see why everyone thinks he's so cute," one said. "He's not."

"I think he is," the other said. "I've always liked guys with brown hair. And he has a nice nose."

Del smiled, wondering if the subject of their attention knew he had a nice nose.

The first woman snorted. "He looks like a girl."

"What, a guy has to be Mister Blocky Chin to turn you on?" the other said, laughing. "I like his pretty face."

Del was about to joke to Cameron about the poor fellow under discussion when the first woman said, "That would make a great ad. Del Arden, the prettiest man in rock."

Del stopped smiling. Pretty? *Pretty?* He was not *pretty.*

Cameron laughed at his side. "Don't take it so personally. Not everyone has the same tastes."

Del glared at him. "Flowers are pretty. Not men. And my hair is red."

A woman came around the curve of the hallway. Startled, Del stopped stock-still, blocking the way. She was blond and buxom, dressed in a lacy pink dress that clung to her voluptuous curves. She looked like a younger version of Ricki. He didn't recognize her from any crew, and she shouldn't be here otherwise, but he doubted he had met every stagehand.

The girl smiled at Del. Remembering what the other woman had said about his masculinity, or supposed lack of it, he just tensed. Maybe this one thought he was too pretty, too.

"Hello." She sounded uncertain. "Is something wrong?"

Del mentally shook himself. "No! Not at all." He flashed his best smile. His best *masculine* smile. "I was trying to figure out why I hadn't seen you. Because I know I'd remember."

"I remember you," she said softly. "You sing like an angel."

"I've no halo, believe me," he said. He wished Cameron would go away.

"Oh, it's there," she teased. "A little tarnished. They're more interesting that way, don't you think?"

Del couldn't help but laugh. "What's your name, mystery girl?"

"Delilah."

"Are you on the stage crew, Delilah?" Gods, she was sexy in that flimsy lace. "Taking apart sets is a dull business."

She pursed her mouth. "Did you have something else in mind?"

Del knew he should say no. He thought of Ricki. Then he thought of waking up alone and how it hurt so damn much. She wouldn't talk to him about it. He questioned whether she would ever let him close enough to understand. He wasn't certain they even had a relationship.

"Well, I don't know—" Del started to say.

The girl stepped closer. "You don't?"

Del met her gaze and thought, *Why the hell not?* He was lonely, and she was lovely and willing. But gods, he was tired of Cameron knowing his private moments. He had to get rid of the Marine.

"Meet me here in half an hour," Del murmured.

"If you're not afraid to come back," Delilah said.

He smiled at her. "Come back, and I'll show you."

Her lashes lowered seductively over her eyes. "Promises, promises." Then she sashayed on, down the hall.

Del watched her go, her hips swaying, her long legs round and firm. Letting out a breath, he headed the other way, wondering how he would ditch Cameron.

It took Del too long to give Cameron the slip. When he finally returned to where he had asked Delilah to meet him, she was gone. Oh, well. Maybe she wouldn't have liked him anyway.

A rustle came from a side hall. Puzzled, Del went over and looked down it. Someone in a pink dress was going around a distant corner. It was hard to see because it was dark except for a spillover from this hallway.

"Delilah?" Del went down the hall. At the junction where it turned left, he stared down a new corridor. It was even darker, but he thought he saw a woman in a pink dress.

He followed her into the shadows. "Hey Delilah, is that you?"

Darkness closed around Del. He couldn't imagine why Delilah would go down here. He was about to turn back when someone grasped his arm from behind and swung him toward the wall.

"Hey." Del tried to pull away. "Cut that—"

He grunted as someone hit him across the back, knocking him into the wall. He barely turned his head fast enough to keep his nose from cracking against the concrete. A nozzle pressed his neck and a hiss whined in his ear.

"Don't!" He tried to turn, but someone large held him in place. A stink of sweat made him gag. His legs buckled and he slid down the wall, his palms dragging along it.

"You're such sweet mischief," a woman scolded nearby.

The world turned black.

Del lay on his back, swimming into consciousness, saturated with pleasure. Ricki had *never* gone down on him like this before. He wanted it to go on forever.

A sour note intruded into his bliss. Ricki couldn't be here. She had walked out on him after he had bared his heart to her. Hadn't he been at the Coliseum . . .

Del cracked open his eyes. Dizziness hit him even though he hadn't moved, and his vision blurred the way it did when he was drilled. He tried to think through what had happened, but his mind was sluggish, and blurred with pleasure.

He was lying in a dimly lit room on a mattress on the floor. Someone had opened his shirt, baring his chest. She had unfastened his pants, too, and her blond head moved up and down as she pleasured him, her hands cupping him underneath while her tongue did its wonders. It was *Delilah*, not Ricki.

Confusion washed over him. He should tell her to stop. But ah, gods, he never wanted it to end. Maybe this was her inspired way of apologizing for whoever had hit him. Had to find out . . . what was going on . . . he sank into the haze of lust. All too soon, it turned into an ecstasy that burst over him. With a groan, he lifted his hips and thrust deeper into her mouth. As he spent himself, he collapsed back, and dizziness swept him into sleep.

Del rose to consciousness like a swimmer through the ocean. It took a while, but gradually his thoughts formed. Someone had whacked him and shot him with an air syringe.

He lifted his head. "Delilah?" His voice rasped.

She was lying between his legs, her head resting on his thigh, her eyes closed, one hand under her cheek, the other resting on his other thigh. His vision went double for a moment, creating two Delilahs.

"Come here, sweetheart," Del murmured. Despite the bizarre situation, he felt a rush of affection for this woman who had given him such pleasure. And she hadn't left him to wake up alone.

She lifted her head, her face framed by silky blond hair. "Hi," she said softly.

Del reached for her, and just that slight amount made his head swim. She slid up his body, into his embrace, and he sank onto his back with his arms around her. She stretched out against him, her arm across his chest, and her leg tangled with his, wearing nothing except lace panties and a soft little top that felt as if it would fall apart under his hands.

Del stroked her breasts. "What happened in that hallway?"

"Darkman hit you."

"Is he your man?" It wouldn't be the first time a girl had come on to him and an angry boyfriend showed up to retaliate.

"He thinks so." She snuggled against him. "You're my man."

Del wasn't, but he did like her. He kissed the top of her head. "How did you get rid of that fellow?"

"I didn't."

He lifted his head with a jerk. "You mean he might come back?"

She watched him with her eyes half closed. "He never left."

What the hell? Del looked around, struggling to focus. "I don't see anyone."

"He's the other room, running the holo-cam."

"*What?*" He sat up, pushing her away, and groaned. His stomach felt as if it were about to heave up. "He's recording us?"

"Of course."

"No!" Del fastened his pants, though his fingers seemed too thick and clumsy to work properly. "You can't do that!"

She rolled languorously onto her side. "You can't go."

When he tried to stand up, his dizziness surged and he barely made it halfway to his feet before he lost his balance and fell onto his knees next to Delilah.

"There, there." She stroked his arm. "Don't get upset."

"Stop it," Del said. "What did you give me?"

"Just spikers and tranquilizers. Enjoy it."

"You can't give me drugs! It could kill me."

"Don't be silly. You'll have fun."

"*No!*" Using the wall for support, he tried again, and this time he made it to his feet. He sagged against the rough surface while nausea rolled over him.

The room had no door. No furniture. Nothing except the mattress and a mechanized commode against one wall. Del stumbled to it and fell onto his knees. Leaning over the bowl, he vomited as if his insides were tearing out.

"That's disgusting," Delilah said behind him. "That won't give us good material for the virt."

Del wiped his mouth on a paper-mesh towel that left a sour taste as it delivered enough soap to clean his mouth. He dumped it in the commode and watched it swirl away. "Who are you people?"

"I told you." She stood above him. "I'm Delilah. My friend is Darkman. You're our guest." Then she added, "For a while."

Del climbed to his feet. "You have to let me go."

Delilah took his wrist, but it wasn't in affection. She looked revolted. She held up his hand as if it were an accusation. "You're deformed."

"What? No, I'm not."

"Imperfect." She touched the hinge and her voice turned ugly. "When I first saw this in one of your live concerts, I felt sick. I don't like imperfection."

Del jerked his hand away from her.

With no warning, lights flared. Squinting against the glare, he peered across the room. A man was coming inside, but the light obscured any molecular airlock that might have appeared, and Del could barely make him out. He tensed into a *mai-quinjo* stance, preparing to defend himself, though he had never used the martial arts in self-defense, only as exercise—

Then the guy came forward, out of the light, and Del's stomach felt as if it dropped through the floor. The man held a giant Viper-IV laser carbine gripped in both hands.

"I think you should leave her alone," the man said.

Del lowered his hands, moving slowly. "Yeah. Whatever you want." The guy wore dark clothes, but he had spiky yellow hair and a blue laser-lit tattoo on his cheek. "You're Darkman?"

"Delilah calls me that." An edge grated in his voice. "You can call me Raker."

"Don't make a virt of me," Del said. Given that Raker had the gun, he could do what he wanted, but Del had to try.

Raker smiled, and it wasn't pretty. "Virts of you are floating all over the planet." He walked forward, his monster gun glinting. "All those cheap, unimaginative replicas of *The Jewels Suite*."

"Uh, sure, yeah." Sweat beaded Del's forehead. "Unimaginative." He felt sick.

Raker stopped next to Delilah, looming over her, huge and muscled. Del felt small.

"People will look for me," Del said. "A lot of them." Except he had tricked Cameron. It could be hours before anyone knew he had disappeared.

"They won't find you," Raker said. In a deathly calm voice, he added, "I used to be a mech wizard for a conglomerate bigger than your little Prime-Nova. Our security force was better than special ops in Allied Space Command. I know all the tricks."

Del pressed his hand against his stomach, willing it to settle. He stared at the gun, then lifted his gaze to Raker. "What do you want with me?"

"I have to do this," Raker said. "You're fresh, uncorrupted, new. Your genius isn't contaminated." His voice filled with righteous anger. "But it *will* happen. You'll get old too fast. Too much hard living. You'll sell out. You'll become a money-making machine. One day you'll wake up, and you'll be used up. All that talent? Tarnished. All that energy? Gone." A manic light glinted in his eyes. "My virt will immortalize your perfection before success destroys you."

"Sure. Okay." Del wanted to scream. "I'll always have that."

"You won't need it." A stern look came over Raker's face. "I can't have you ruining the perfection I create." He glanced at Del's hand, then put his arm around the scantily clad woman at his side. "Delilah wouldn't like that."

Del felt ill again. Only one way would ensure that the reality of Del's future never intruded on their "perfect" virt.

Get rid of the real Del Arden.

do we get Cameron out of this thing? I want to know why he's here instead of with Del."

"So Del dumped him." Jud was tired of Mac's constant worrying about Del, who was apparently perfectly able to take care of himself, to the tune of half a million dollars. "Maybe Del went off with some triller."

"I don't care how many girls he went with," Mac said. "He *knows* he can't leave Cameron behind. *Cameron* knows it."

"What is with you?" Jud said. "You're Del's manager, not his keeper. I don't care how much money Prime-Nova thinks he'll make them. It's his life. He shouldn't have cut it so close getting back here, but if he wants to go off, it's his business."

Mac spoke in a too quiet voice. "You have no idea what you're talking about." He indicated Cameron. "How do I get him out?"

"You have to wait until the session finishes."

"A way must exist to take him out now."

Jud almost said, *I have no idea.* But Mac's reaction was starting to unnerve him. "You need a neurologist. The helmet extends filaments into Cameron's brain. If we just pull them out, it could scramble his neural pathways."

Mac stared at him. "Then how does anyone get out?"

"You set it for a certain time," Jud said. "When it gets near that time, the node starts to untangle itself from your brain. It takes a while, but when it finishes, you come out of the session."

"Cripes," Mac said. "Why do you kids do that to yourselves?"

"*I* don't," Jud said. "I don't get any thrill out of locking myself into some fake fantasy world."

Mac studied Cameron's prone form. "Can you tell when he's due out of this one?"

"I don't know. He must have fallen asleep." Jud motioned at the glowing cube in the console slot. "But that's lit, so the session is still going."

"Talk about bizarre," Mac said. "A VR sim for someone to sleep in. What a waste of half a million dollars."

Jud stalked to the bed, then spun around to Mac. "It doesn't look like Del slept here at all last night."

"Damn," Mac said under his breath. He flicked a panel on his wrist mesh. A woman answered, her words indistinct. Then Mac said, "General McLane. Code Em-four."

Jud thought he must have heard wrong. McLane? As in General

Fitz McLane, one of Allied Space Command's top commanders? It couldn't be. Even Jud, who paid little attention to military matters, had heard of McLane. No reason existed for a rock star's manager to contact one of the most influential commanders alive.

Another voice came on the comm, a man it sounded like.

"That's right," Mac said into his mesh. "We may have an incident." He waited, then said, "He might have just spent the night with someone and overslept. No, I agree. I'd rather anger him than risk leaving him undefended. Can you locate him?"

Find him? Just like that? Jud didn't see how, unless they had a tracking device on Del. Or more likely, *in* Del, so no one would notice, not even Jud, who lived with him. Which was so crazy it might be possible in this suddenly bizarre situation.

"That's in the Sierra Nevada mountains!" Mac said. "Hundreds of miles from here." He listened. "I'm at the hotel. Yes, they have a flyer pad on the roof. I'll be waiting. We need someone to see to Cameron, too. Del's trapped him in a virt. His brain is hard-wired into it. Yeah, one of those." He paused. "Good. We will. Out."

Jud stared at him. "What the hell is going on? Why would Allied Space Command send a flyer for Del?"

Mac came over to him. "I can't force you to keep what you just heard to yourself. I have no authority over you. But I ask you please, for Del's safety, tell no one."

Jud was getting scared. "All right. But what's going on?"

"It's up to Del what he wants to reveal." He turned and headed for the door. "Stay here with Cameron," he called back. "Annapolis is sending an expert, but I don't want to leave him alone."

"I'll comm Anne. She'll stay with him." Jud came around and blocked Mac's way. "Take me with you. To help Del. I know him better than anyone else."

Mac spoke quietly. "Jud, you have to understand, if you get deeper into this, you'll be involving yourself in interstellar politics on a level you probably can't even imagine."

A memory came to Jud of Del kidding around with the band:

"Well, you know," Del said with mock solemnity. "I'm Skolian."

"Yet here you are," Randall said, "living in Baltimore."

"Actually," Anne said, "at the moment, he's in a van."

"Allied Space Command brought me here," Del said. "To Earth. To keep me in custody. Except they had to let me go because I hadn't done anything wrong . . ."

"My God," Jud said. "He wasn't joking."

Mac blinked. "About what?"

"He told us he was Skolian, that ASC brought him here."

Mac's gaze never wavered. "No, he wasn't joking."

"What could Del possibly have that the military wants?"

"Call Anne down here," Mac said. "Then walk with me up to the flyport. We can talk then."

Jud stood restlessly with Mac at the dark green doors of the lift to the roof. "Even if he is Skolian," Jud said, "that's no reason for a five-star general to notice him."

Mac spoke carefully. "Del is a member of a prominent family."

Jud found it hard to believe. Del acted neither rich nor important. "Would I recognize their name?"

Mac regarded him steadily. "The Ruby Dynasty."

Jud scowled at him. "Don't shit me."

"I'm not."

"Del isn't a Ruby prince." Jud was getting angry. What stupid game was this? "We both know that."

"No," Mac said with that oddly quiet tone. "We both don't know that. Del is the third son of Roca Skolia, Heir to the Ruby Throne."

Another memory came to Jud, the words to "Rubies": *Hiding deepest vulnerabilities/Cursed by your mind's abilities/For within you lies the hope for all days/Rubies must give their souls in all ways.*

"My God," Jud said. "He's a Ruby *empath*. No wonder he went catatonic his first time onstage."

Mac said, simply, "Yes."

The lift doors hummed and slid open. As they stepped inside the blue-carpeted chamber, Mac said, "That's why we never took the interview request from that undercity reviewer. We were afraid he would ask too many questions about the lyrics of 'Rubies.'"

"I don't get it," Jud said. "Why come to Earth?" Of all the places for a Skolian rock singer to make his name, he couldn't imagine why the home of the Allied Worlds would be on the list.

"Allied Space Command gave protective custody to some members of the Ruby Dynasty during the war," Mac said as the doors closed. "Except after the war, ASC wouldn't let them go. They're afraid the Skolians and Traders will go at each other until they wipe out the human race."

Jud grimaced. "They aren't the only ones."

"Skolians blast my mind," Mac said. "After that brutal, crushing war with the Traders, what's the first thing they do? Recover? Heal? Rescue people? No. The Ruby Pharaoh overthrows her *own* government. What the blazes was that about?"

"Hell if I know." Jud thought back to what he had heard about the coup. "I thought that takeover didn't work."

"Sure it worked," Mac said. "She just gave half her power back to the Assembly. They rule jointly."

"Why?" Skolian politics had never made much sense to Jud. Or, he suspected, to most people, including Skolians.

Mac spoke dryly. "You and every military expert we have would like that answer. She claims it's a better government. Maybe she's even right." He exhaled. "Afterward, Imperial Space Command sent a special ops team for the Ruby Dynasty on Earth. They were in Scandinavia, but we had Del here. So he didn't get pulled out with the others. Then Ricki saw him sing. The rest you know."

Jud couldn't put it all together. "Then why haven't I heard of this place Lyshriol where Del says he lived?"

"We have a different name for it."

"Yeah? Like what?"

Mac met his gaze. "Skyfall."

"*What?*" Jud couldn't process it all. "Are you trying to tell me that Del's father is the flipping King of *Skyfall?*"

"Actually," Mac said, "his father was a farmer and historian. When he married into the dynasty, the media dubbed him the King of Skyfall." His voice quieted. "He passed away a few months ago. Del's oldest brother left home, and the son next in line died in the war."

"Then who's the King of Skyfall?"

"Well, uh, Del, actually."

This was really too much. "Del. My sloppy, surly, don't-wake-me-up-until-noon roommate."

"Yeah." Mac smiled wryly. "That Del."

"So if he's a Ruby prince, why is he always broke? No, never mind." Jud knew Del well enough to answer that question. "He doesn't want to touch his family's money. Except for buying that damn bliss-node." Even that made sense. Being on stage had to be hell for a Ruby psion.

The lift suddenly opened onto the roof, and wind ruffled Jud's clothes. Far above them, a dark flyer was circling the tower, descending to pick them up.

Del ran.

The landscape buckled, black and glassy, a psychotic world with a red sky and distant volcanoes. This race was insane. He wasn't really running, he was strapped down in a virt suit and trapped in this sim, but if he didn't do what Raker wanted, the madman shocked him with electric jolts.

Until Del met Raker and Delilah, he hadn't really known what the term "virt-head" meant. They were addicted to bliss. Both were also virtisos, fans who followed an artist, trying to know him better so they could intensify the sessions they created about him. As far as Del had seen, most virtisos were harmless, like Talia and Kendra, the girls he had taken to dinner. But Raker and Delilah took it to a terrifying new level.

Sooner or later, Mac would realize something was wrong. But by then, it might be too late. Cameron wouldn't surface from the node until morning. He probably didn't even know he was in a sim. Del had told him that he had decided not to meet the girl after all. When Cameron asked if Del intended to do a virt session, Del said the suit was off-kilter and he didn't know why. Cameron had even offered to check it out without Del asking. Del had activated it while Cameron had it on, running a session that started with Cameron taking *off* the suit. Anne had come in, or at least Del's rendering of her, and things took off from there. All Cameron would know was that he and Anne had a great night together.

Del had thought he was so clever. Now he sincerely hoped he hadn't been anywhere near as smart as he thought, that Cameron had figured it out and found a way to contact someone from within the sim. The longer this went on, the less hope Del had that someone would find him before Raker decided he had enough material for his virt and disposed of the messy, imperfect Del Arden.

Del climbed into a cluster of black spears and collapsed in a pocket hidden within them. Breathing hard, he rubbed his eyes.

"You tired?" Delilah asked.

Del looked up with a jerk. She was leaning over a notch in the

crag that hadn't been there before, watching him curiously. She
was all in black now, from her boots to her skin-tight catsuit.

"Delilah, listen," Del said. "I can give you a much better time
if you don't keep me trapped here."

"But I like it here." She waved her hand at the sky. "Isn't it
dramatic?" Her smile dimpled. "And you look so cute, running
for your life."

Cute? *Cute?* She was as crazy as Raker. But they wouldn't kill
him until they completed their virtual Del Arden. He had to
convince them they needed him alive.

"If I get out of breath," Del said, "I can't sing my new songs
for you."

"I've heard all your songs," she purred. "I love them."

"Not these. I haven't sung them for anyone yet."

She straightened up. "You must sing them for me! We need
everything."

They needed everything—except the real him. He wiped the
back of his hand across his forehead, smearing away the sweat.
"Delilah, listen. I'm always thinking up songs. They're never like
the old ones. I can sing them to you forever."

Her face twisted. "You'll get old. Corrupted."

"Not in the virt."

"Sing to me," she said. "That strange song about a lagoon."

Del regarded her uncertainly. "Lagoon? I don't . . ."

Her face contorted into a hideous mask. "Sing it!"

Del jumped up, banging into the crag behind him. The sky
darkened, and one of the volcanoes spewed ash and flame. Fortunately, he realized what she meant before she decided to flood
him with lava. The verse in "Emeralds" about the lake.

"I'll sing!" Del waved his hand in front of his face as ash sifted
over them. "Whatever you want."

"Good." Her face turned angelic.

Del took an ashy breath. "Night darkens the secret h-hollows/
Within the silvered lagoon/Body rising from the water/Streaming
under the s-silent moons . . ." His voice trailed off. He didn't want
to remember that night, especially not now, when the person who
demanded to hear it also wanted to hurt him.

"Your beautiful body, all wet and sleek," Delilah murmured.
"Sing more."

Del could only stare at her, feeling ill.

"I can't hear you," she said in an ugly voice. "I like that part about how you didn't desert her. Sing that."

He sang dully. "I didn't desert you/Despite what they crowed." His voice cracked as he stumbled on the words. "Y-You still believed I was true/They learned what our love knows."

Delilah's voice took on an edge. "Who was she? Someone prettier than me?"

"No," Del lied.

"Your lover?"

"No. It wasn't that kind of love. I meant my sister."

"Oh." Her hard expression eased. "What does she look like?"

"She's skinny and plain and dull," Del said, though none of it was true. He didn't want a song about the killing effects of jealousy to end his life because of Delilah's jealousy. "Nothing compares to you." The words felt like sawdust in his mouth. He meant them, but not in the way she wanted.

"Good." She threw back her hair, and the volcano stopped erupting. Then she climbed into the hollow with Del and put her arms around his waist. "Hug me."

Del didn't want to touch her. It was all he could do to keep from shoving her away.

"Delilah, get the fuck off him," a voice said.

Del froze, then slowly lifted his gaze. Raker was standing behind the notch where Delilah had been leaning a moment before.

She pouted at the large man. "You're the one who wanted us sexing it up for the virt."

Raker ignored her and motioned to Del with his carbine, which had suddenly appeared in his hand. "Get out here."

Del had no idea what would happen if Raker shot him while they were in a simulation. In a normal virt, being shot would just throw him out of the session. But with his brain wired into the node, the experience could become so realistic, he might die even if Raker hadn't actually done anything.

Del didn't have to move Delilah; she vanished. Rattled, he climbed out of the pocket. Raker stood back, the carbine gripped in both hands. With no warning, he fired, blasting the crags where Del had hidden. Instead of turning to ash, the residue bizarrely ran across the ground and hardened into glass.

"You told Harriet you had new songs," Raker said.

"I told who?" Del asked.

"Me." Delilah appeared at Raker's side dressed in red lace panties and a little red top. "Harriet is my real name. I picked Delilah for you. Del. Delilah." She smiled. "It fits, don't you think?"

"Yeah." Sweat was gathering on Del's hands. "Sure."

"Sing something we've never heard before," Raker told him. "Something powerful."

Del stood with his hands at his side, instinctively poised to protect himself. He couldn't think of anything they had never heard except "Carnelians." He didn't want to give it to them, but he wanted even less to die. So he sang:

> I'm no golden hero in the blazing skies
> I'm no fair-haired genius hiding in disguise
> I'm only a singer; it's all that I can do
> But my voice is rising; I can sing the truth

"Oh, that's strong," Delilah said. She sounded as if she wasn't sure she wanted to approve or censure it. In the virt, Del couldn't pick up their emotions, probably because they were actually at consoles well separated from him. But he didn't think Raker liked the verse.

"Who's the golden hero?" Raker asked.

"My brother," Del said tightly. The Imperator. He even had gold skin. A metallic man.

"What about the fair-haired genius?" Raker brushed his hand across his bristly yellow hair. "You singing about me?"

"You certainly fit the line," Del lied.

Raker laughed harshly. "You're right, I'm a genius. And you're just a singer." He raised the gun. "What truth are you going to sing, hmmm?"

Then he fired point-blank at Del.

Mac stared out the window as the flyer circled, searching out a place to land in the mountainous forest. Maura Penzer and Jackson Stolia, the pilot and the copilot, were Marines trained for special operations, as were the four agents in the other flyer circling with them.

Jackson sat in a VR rig in his seat, the visor pulled over his head, his suit gleaming in the dim light from the controls. He was going through simulated walk-throughs of the mountains below, updating his assessment of the situation as the flyer's sensors monitored the area and refreshed his data.

Jud was in a passenger seat, looking out the window. He had been silent during the trip. It didn't surprise Mac, given what he had to absorb. *Oh excuse me, your roommate is a Ruby Heir.* Maybe it was good that Jud knew. Mac doubted Randall could handle it, and he didn't know about Anne, but Jud understood Del better than the others. He wouldn't take any guff from Del because his roommate turned out to be a prince, but Jud would keep an eye on him.

Holomaps in the flyer showed Del's location, a mountain cabin surrounded by fir trees heavy with snow, which also carpeted the ground. A quaint chimney jutted up from the roof, and a plume of smoke curled into the frosty air. It all looked innocently rustic. Maura brought them down in a clearing hidden from the cabin. The flyer had stealth capability, including shrouds that disguised it from radio, radar, optical, ultraviolet, and neutrino detectors. In silent running mode, it landed with almost no sound.

Jackson and Maura checked their armor and jumped out, followed by Mac and Jud. Mac sealed the front of his jacket, letting the climate controls warm his body. Jud watched him, then copied the gesture with an almost identical jacket that Jackson had lent him.

Maura stood facing Jud and Mac, and her voice came out of a mesh in the helmet covering her head. "Stay back. Let us do our work. Mac, I'm trusting your recommendation that we bring Mister Taborian. You're responsible for him."

"I'll stay out of it, believe me," Jud said.

"We'll hit the cabin with an EM pulse just before we go in," Maura said. "That's when your comm and the meshes in your clothes might stop working. Our optical and neutrino scramblers shouldn't affect you as much."

Mac nodded, and Jud said, "I understand."

"Good." She spoke into the comm on the gauntlet embedded in her armor. "Gregori, are you down?"

A man answered. "Two hundred meters north, Captain." Then he said, "Something's going on in that cabin. They've blocked all our three-D imaging sensors. I'm also registering a lot of optic-meshes, carbon fiber composites, and biosynthetics in there."

"Damn," Jackson muttered.

"Keep trying to get the images," Maura said. "We'll rendezvous at the cabin and go with Plan Delta." Then she said, "No lethals unless absolutely necessary. I don't want Valdoria hit by friendly fire, and if someone did kidnap him, we want them alive. But if you have no choice, I don't care what hostiles you blast. Just get Valdoria out of there."

"Got it," Gregori said.

"All right. Switch to internal."

Whatever other communication the team had went private among them, transmitted on a tactical channel from helmet to helmet. Mac had no doubt it was scrambled and encoded as well.

They slipped through the forest, their footfalls muffled by snow, Mac and Jud staying back a few paces. The pristine swaths of white on the ground and weighting down the firs reflected in the chameleon armor of the Marines until it was hard to tell where the land ended and the commandos started. It felt surreal to Mac.

Although it was out of character for Del to vanish this way, he wouldn't be the first of Mac's clients who went AWOL while celebrating the heady flush of success. They might discover Del had just come here for a tryst with some girl, but he would rather overreact than be unprepared. Given the cabin's defenses, though, Mac doubted they had overreacted. No normal person equipped a house with military-grade systems. Nor could the team's EM pulse, or electromagnetic pulse, affect the optical or bio-circuits Gregori had detected inside. The Marines had a Faraday cage that would protect their equipment against the pulse, but they couldn't put everything in it, which meant it might affect their nonlethal weapons. As a backup, they had semiautomatics, which were immune to modern tech, but in close quarters, the high-velocity rounds from those atavistic guns could end up hurting Del, too.

At least the team's armor included release ports for nanite gas, which could knock someone out without killing them. The nanites could be partially counteracted by an antidote gas, but it would take someone with a survivalist mentality bordering on psychotic to have stolen the military-issue gear and chemicals needed to give that protection.

Mac didn't want to think what would have happened if Del *hadn't* been a Ruby prince. Far more time would have passed before anyone found him. It brought home with a vengeance the price public figures paid for their fame. Nor did the tech advances of their mesh-saturated age guarantee celebrities would act with any more wisdom than in prior ages. Del had made a mistake, and he could die for that misjudgment.

Del became aware he was slumped against the wall of a darkened room. Immobile—but alive. *Alive.*

He couldn't move his legs. After several moments, he managed to raise his arm.

"Del?" Delilah spoke sleepily at his side.

With painful slowness, he lowered his arm and turned his head. He was sitting on the mattress, and Delilah lay next to him, just waking up, her body covered by a silvery sheet. He tried to speak, but only a whisper came out. "What do . . . to me?"

She pulled herself up until she was sitting, and the sheet fell around her waist, leaving her torso bare. Del didn't want to look, but his traitorous gaze dropped to her voluptuous body.

"You'll be all right," she said. "Your brain thinks you were blasted."

"Delilah, don't do this." His voice cracked. "Don't you want the real Del? You don't have to settle for some phony simulation."

"You'll never be corrupted in the bliss," she said in a surreally angelic voice. "You'll always be exactly as you are now." She touched the hinge in his hand. "Except better."

"It will get boring if you can predict everything I do," he rasped. "With the real Del, you'll always have pleasant surprises. New songs."

"Sing to me," she murmured. "'Diamond Star.'"

He sang raggedly. "Shimmering radiance above/Softening this lost man's love."

She sighed with pleasure, but something felt wrong. He didn't feel her enjoyment. With a rush of vertigo, he realized they were *still* in the virt.

"Make love to me," Delilah said, sliding down onto the bed.

Nausea swept over Del. He couldn't stand the thought of having sex with her.

A harsh voice spoke. "I don't think so."

Del jerked up his head. "No!" *Not again.*

Raker stood across the room with the carbine. He hadn't been there before, and Del hadn't heard any door open.

Delilah pouted at Raker. "You're always interrupting us. You'll get your turn."

"That's right." Raker raised his gun. "Good-bye, Del."

"No!" Del struggled to get up, but his legs were paralyzed from the last time Raker had "shot" him. "Don't—"

Raker fired.

Del barely managed to open his eyes. He was sitting against the wall in a dim room with no lights on, just dirty sunlight filtering in through high slits on the walls. As his eyes focused, he saw Raker crouched a few paces away, watching him, holding the carbine across his knees. A heavy metal ring hung around Raker's neck and lay against his chest. Delilah had put on an old shirt and mesh-jeans and was kneeling next to Del with a neural injector gun.

"What's that?" Del whispered. This time he knew he wasn't in the virt; he felt the moods of both Delilah and Raker with an intensity unmatched by anything in the bizarre universe of their bliss-node. What he picked up most was their avid fascination with him, as if he were a drug they craved. It scared the hell out of him. He tried to move, but his body wouldn't respond.

"This will act right away." Delilah pressed the gun against the base of his neck, and the cool tickle of its injection chilled his skin. "It'll kick the universe."

Del strained to push her away. "What are you giving me?"

"It's a theta-kicker," Raker said. "You'll see the world in whole new colors."

"No!" Panic swept over Del. Thetas weren't that different from taus.

Delilah twisted the top of the injector, resetting it, and poked the tip against his skin again. "We have lots of chem-candy for you."

This time Del managed to knock the syringe away. "Gods, don't."

"Oh, come on," Raker said. "Everyone knows you rock stars eat drugs like candy. Quit acting like it's going to kill you." He drummed his fingers on his gun. "We need more material. We need to know how you act under the influence."

"I'm allergic to kickers," Del said. "I'll go into something like anaphylactic shock." He prayed to every god of Lyshriol that his meds could counter thetas, or he was going to die a horrific death to entertain these two fanatics.

Delilah's face twisted. "You have *more* wrong with you?"

Del just looked at her. Nothing he could say would help. If he denied it, they would pump him full of more drugs. If he told her yes, something was very wrong with him, it would give them more reason to kill him.

"I want that edited out of the virt," Delilah told Raker.

"Why?" Raker said. "It'll make it more interesting to see what happens to him."

Nausea rolled over Del—an all too familiar nausea. It didn't slam him the way it had the first time; today it came more slowly. Gods willing, the meds in his body were fighting the thetas. But the sickness was building just like before.

"I need a doctor," Del rasped. "Please."

"This isn't fun anymore," Delilah said shrilly. "He's defective. I don't want that in our virt."

"Neither do I." Raker raised the carbine. "Good-bye, Del."

"Ah, gods." Del raised his arm as if that could ward off the laser shot. This time, if Raker fired, he would die. At least it would be fast, rather than the drawn-out agony of the kickers.

The world seemed to slow down for Del. Delilah pulled down his arm, and Del stared into the bore of the gun. From somewhere he heard a dim shout, something about, *Can't wait . . . move now . . .* The air crackled as if in a great pulse.

The laser flew out of Raker's grip, hit by some projectile, and flipped over as it arced away. Raker jumped up as if he were moving through molasses and spun toward the far side of the room. With a snarl, he yanked up the ring around his neck, and it molded into a mask over his face. A white cloud was swirling in the room, and its sweet, nauseating stench saturated Del until his head swam. Delilah sprawled onto her stomach, falling across his legs. But the mist had no effect on Raker. Moving in that eerily slowed motion, he reached behind his back and pulled out a huge, barbaric shotgun. He sighted on Del—

A rain of bullets hit Raker.

The virtiso spasmed, convulsing under the force of the shots. The bullets entered his torso in small holes and exploded out of his back, taking a substantial portion of his body.

"*No!*" Delilah's voice echoed as she struggled to her feet. In nightmarish slow motion, she grabbed the shotgun. "You can't have them both!" she shouted as she aimed the gun at Del.

Del raised both arms in a futile gesture of defense. But instead of shooting him, Delilah spasmed as if a massive, invisible hand had slammed into her torso. She arched with a drawn-out scream and collapsed onto the bed, falling so close to Del that her blood sprayed across him.

Gods help us. Del couldn't speak, he could only think the words. The thetas were kicking hard, both the hallucinations and pain. He doubled over, then fell onto his back and began to convulse.

"Del!" The word vibrated in his ears. Mac was kneeling over him, shouting, "Get the stretcher here! *Now!*"

Del's shaking eased just barely enough to let him whisper, "Help me—" His voice cut off as another convulsion started.

"God, no. This can't be happening." Mac literally picked Del up in his arms and carried him across the room.

Darkness swirled and encroached. Then a blast of cold air hit Del, jagged and sharp. Mac was carrying him outside. The sky heaved and buckled, turning red like a giant, laboring heart. Trees bent around him, heavy with snow, waving their arms, nauseating. The cold prickled Del's skin as it ran tiny feet over his body.

Mac laid him on something soft and people crowded around. Then they were carrying him, rushing through the cold air. The moments passed with jagged spurts. They were inside another place, setting him down. A woman leaned over him, and a mesh-patch wavered and popped on her military flight suit, then jumped off and ran across Del's body. He groaned as it gave him electric shocks.

Suddenly *Jud* was there, kneeling by Del, that familiar dark face, the dreadlocks threaded with yellow and blue beads. Ever since Del had seen Jud's hair, he had wished he could do that to his, too. Seeing Jud gave him an anchor in this theta-kicked madness.

Moisture showed in Jud's eyes. "I'll make all the dreads in your hair that you want if you promise to stay alive."

Del tried to say, *Did I tell you that out loud?* but no words came out.

A hum vibrated his body. An engine? Medics were attaching lines to him, their motions smeared across his sight. Mac had knelt on his other side, across from Jud.

"You'll be all right." Mac's emotions swirled around Del in hallucinogenic blurs. He feared Del would die. Jud feared he would die. And something else from Jud, too. Del didn't know. He had no strength to lower his barriers.

"Are you mad at me?" he whispered to Jud.

"No." Jud's voice echoed in Del's head. "I'm not mad at you. But don't you ever go off by yourself again."

"Is Cameron . . . all right?" Del asked.

"He's fine," Mac said.

Del closed his eyes. "I screwed up . . . royally this time."

Jud laughed unevenly. "It's the only way you *can* screw up."

It took a moment for Del's drug-soaked mind to absorb Jud's meaning. Then he slowly opened his eyes. "Mac told you."

"I was there when he called General McLane," Jud said.

Del felt sick. He didn't want to lose his best friend over this. "I'm not . . ."

"I know," Jud said gently. Tears were gathering in his eyes. "I'm not going to call your royal ass, 'Your Highness.' And now I know why you're such a slob. You're used to *people* picking up after you, aren't you? Not even bots, but humans. Well, it's not going to happen in our apartment. You have to do it yourself." His voice shook on the last few words.

Del didn't answer. His roommate knew what he needed to hear, that things wouldn't change. Of course it wasn't true; nothing would be the same. But it wouldn't take away Jud's friendship.

Del let go then and fell into oblivion.

Ricki stood at the observation window that looked into Del's hospital room. He was deep in his healing sleep, lying on his back with a silver sheet pulled halfway up his torso. As grateful as she was to Allied Space Command for rescuing him, she couldn't figure out why the hell they had done it or how they knew where to find him. Mac should have commed Prime-Nova. They had their own security force, which included operatives with military training.

At least ASC kept the incident out of the media. Unfortunately, they were also keeping it secret from Prime-Nova, including the virts those two sickos had created. From what Captain Penzer had told them, it sounded like "Raker" and "Delilah" had been whacked-out insane.

The records in the meshes showed they had followed Del from concert to concert until Delilah could get him alone. Delilah, aka

Harriet Delmartin, had altered her face and body to fit what they believed was Del's ideal woman. Ricki didn't miss that the girl had looked like her. She would have laughed if it hadn't hurt so much. She knew damn well she wasn't Del's ideal woman. She had no idea who lived in his dreams, but it wasn't her.

Del looked so young, sleeping in the hospital bed, his lashes gold against his face. He bewildered Ricki. When most holo-rockers hit it big, they plunged with abandon into the lifestyle. Del spent his nights quietly, preferring virts to parties. He made love to her like a maestro, sometimes gently, other times wild and rough, and always affectionate afterward.

In the past, when it came to lovers, Ricki had avoided rockers like the plague. They screwed around too much. Del wasn't as bad as most, but he was no angel, nor was he immune to how easy the women came. If he hadn't gone after that fanatical little tidbit in the first place, none of this would have happened.

The intensity of Ricki's response to him terrified her. She hadn't reacted with such strong emotions since her sixth birthday, the day her caustic father had walked out on her mother without even saying good-bye to his heart-broken daughter. Her mother had been no fucking saint, either. Seven years later, she ran off with that sleazy-assed cowboy with the scarred hand, leaving Ricki on her own. Ricki had sworn then she would never care about anyone again enough to be hurt, not her stupid dysfunctional family, not her glitzy friends, and most of all, never anyone she loved.

She had survived at thirteen by seducing her first holo-rock singer, who kept her in jewels and contraband furs while he slept with everything on the planet that had at least one x-chromosome. She dumped him when a gentler man wooed her away, but she left that one when he asked her to marry him. She became invulnerable, so beautiful they all wanted her, but none could have her, because if she stayed, even long enough just to wake up with them, they would hurt her.

"He looks so peaceful," someone said.

Ricki jumped and turned with a start. Mac was standing next to her at the window. She scowled at him. "Your commandos release those virts yet?"

"They weren't commandos," Mac said. "The Raptor squad is a unit assigned by Allied Space Command to deal with civilian crises."

"What the blazes for?"

"ASC doesn't just exist to fight wars," he said blandly.

Yeah. Right. "Don't shit me, Mac. They also don't exist to rescue philandering rock stars."

He shrugged. "I called in a favor from my Air Force days."

"What for? You could have called Prime-Nova."

"This unit could act faster."

"Maybe." She didn't believe him, but she had no plausible reasons to replace his. "Or maybe that's total horse manure."

Mac met her gaze. "Be glad he's alive."

She exhaled like a balloon deflating. There was that. A few minutes more, and Del could have been dead. Ricki had no idea how to deal with how much the thought wrenched her. She didn't know how to turn off the rusty, long-unused emotions Del jolted awake within her. She had been with him too long, over six months. She had even been faithful. But that surely was because she hadn't met anyone else who interested her. It had to be. She couldn't be falling in love with him, because she wasn't capable of loving anyone.

XVII

Rubies

The first person Del saw when he woke up was Staver Aunchild.

Del lay in a bed secured by flexi-metal railings. The room had blue walls with calming swirls of color. The subtle images would have soothed him if he hadn't felt like a star dock crane had hit him in the head. Lines of light went from his body to contraptions around the bed.

Staver was sitting in an armchair, studying a display of musical notes above a holobook. He was the last person Del would have expected to see when he woke up. Mac or Jud seemed more likely. Ricki, he hoped, but she probably never wanted to see him again. Him and his damn hormones and his stupid insecurity about being called pretty. Yeah, he had really proved his masculinity with Delilah. The gruesome image of how she and Raker died would stay with him for the rest of his life, as well as the knowledge that it could have been him, if his rescuers had been a few minutes later. He didn't want to feel remorse at their deaths, but the guilt flooded him.

The business with Delilah and Raker had an eerie resonance to what had happened with Lydia and Staver. In both cases, someone had knocked him out, and he awoke with a woman he didn't know. Both times, they had violated his privacy and forced his cooperation. Now here was Staver again. Panic flared in Del.

Calm down, he thought. *A coincidence doesn't make Staver guilty of anything.* But his fear didn't go away.

"Hi," Del whispered.

Staver looked up and smiled. "Hello."

"Good to see . . . you." Del wasn't sure that was true, but it came out anyway. Harv, his publicist, had coached him too well.

"I'm sorry it has to be like this." Staver spoke firmly. "You can be assured, Mister Arden, that at any appearances you do for Metropoli Interstellar, we'll provide you with full security."

"Thanks." Del wondered how Staver knew what had happened. He blanched at the thought of the news all over the meshes. "Have the m-casters picked up the story?"

"Nothing," Staver said, his voice reassuring. "Prime-Nova kept it quiet. I only know because I was expecting you to sign a contract that morning, so I was with Zachary Marksman when the message came in."

"What about my concert in San Diego?" Del didn't like to miss even a rehearsal. "I still had that one left on the tour."

"It would have been last night," Staver said. "You were here, in the hospital."

Damn. Del hated that people might think he had been unprofessional. He couldn't prove he was responsible about holding a job if he missed shows.

Del started to pull away the covers. "I have to reschedule—"

"Del, relax." Staver gently nudged him back. "Prime-Nova said you have bronchitis. They reimbursed people for tickets. Your fans are concerned. Not judgmental."

A flush heated Del's face. Like many empaths, Staver could judge his reactions all too well. "Do you know where Mac is?"

"He's been here non-stop," Staver said. "The doctors sent him home when he passed out from lack of sleep." He paused. "You'd think he was your father rather than your manager."

"I suppose." Del's mind was fuzzed enough from drugs that it lowered his natural emotional defenses, at least enough for him to say, "I lost my father recently." Mac had begun to fill that void.

"I'm sorry," Staver said. "It must have been difficult."

Difficult was such a weak word for that devastating loss. For all that he resisted his family, Del loved them. And his father had understood him better than the others.

"I took over for him after he died," Del said. "Except now I'm here . . ." His brother Vyrl would have been ideal to replace Del as the Dalvador Bard, except he couldn't carry a tune. His sister Soz had been a military genius, Imperator, commander of the Skolian forces. The thought of her staying home as the Bard was ludicrous. Besides, she couldn't sing worth spit. She made Vyrl sound good. Not that it mattered; the Aristos had made sure she would never do anything again when they blasted her ship into high-energy plasma.

Del pushed away the burning memories and closed his eyes, worn out.

"I'm sorry," Staver said. "I shouldn't keep you awake." His clothes rustled as he stood up. "Sleep well. We can talk later."

Del wondered if he would ever feel safe enough to sleep well again.

Denric Windward, or just Windar for short, taught reading, math, and anything else the children needed in the community where he had set up his school on the Skolian world Sandstorm. Today he took his students on an outing. They had nothing where they lived except water-tube ranches and sandstorms. So once a year he flew them to the starport where they could see the ships, visit the stores, and have a respite from the grind of their lives.

Sand blasted the fields outside the port, but the glossy malls inside gleamed. The eight teens he had brought wandered up and down the white Luminex concourses, gazing at displays, browsing the stores, and buying delicacies they could never get at home.

"Look!" One of the boys pointed to a marquee with red laser-torches. A gold sand-springer jumped up the wall and vanished in a wash of blue light. New springers appeared near the floor and dashed after the first.

"Sand-Springer Sounds," one of the girls said. "It's music!" She grabbed her friend's arm and headed into the store, followed by the others. Windar went with them, staying far enough back so he could chaperone without being intrusive.

The Sand-Springer brimmed with sound. Skolian music played everywhere, blending into a cacophony that was somehow harmonious. The store probably had AIs dedicated to creating that chaotic yet pleasant effect, matching it to whatever it picked up about customers from their conversation and body language. Colored lights reflected in the mirrored racks, and holos morphed in constant motion. The students spread out, exclaiming over the displays.

A tune jumped out at Windar, then faded into the din. The song sounded vaguely familiar, but he couldn't place it. He knew so little about what the kids listened to, though, and this shop clearly catered to a generation far younger than his own.

As he walked through the store, the music caught him again. He stopped, straining to hear.

"What's wrong, Genn Windar?" one of his students asked, Shainna, a dark-haired girl of about fourteen.

"It's nothing," Windar said, feeling a little silly. "I thought I heard something I knew. But it wouldn't be in here."

She gave him the winning smile that had helped make her so well-liked among her peers. "You never know. Maybe you're more on the ultra than you think. What's the song?"

"I don't—" Windar stopped as he caught another few notes. "There it is." He and Shainna followed the sound to a section where they sold imports—

Windar froze.

Surrounded by a small audience, a holo-vid was running on a circular dais. It showed a man singing, his curls gleaming in the lights. Drums played, morphers, stringers, a swirl of sound, with the Skolian translation of his words scrolling around the dais. The upbeat, danceable melody contrasted with the intense lines he sang in his rich voice:

> Look at all the widespread hate
> Comes from the anger that fuels our race
> Would you love me if I was somebody else?
> Would you hate me if I choose to be myself?

Windar's voice cracked. "Gods almighty."

"Isn't he ultra?" Shainna said. "His vids are the newest thing from Earth. He's absolutely the best Allied singer."

"From *Earth?*" Windar stared at her in disbelief.

She regarded him uncomfortably. "Don't you like it?"

He stretched out his arm, pointing at the dais. "That man isn't an Allied singer!"

Other people were turning toward them, frowning at the interruption.

"But . . ." She hesitated, clearly not wanting to contradict her teacher. "Why do you say that?"

Windar spoke incredulously. "Because that's my *brother.*"

Mac had seen General McLane angry plenty of times, but this was different. Fitz was furiously *afraid.* Mac understood the feeling, because he felt the same way.

"We were almost too late," Fitz said flatly.

"They might not have killed Del," Mac answered. He wasn't sure who he was trying to reassure, himself or Fitz. "They were threatening him to ratchet up the tension in their virt. They didn't go ballistic until we came in." Mac would never forget that horrific moment when he had seen Del crumpled on the ground with those two vultures hovering over him.

"How does he hypnotize all these people?" Fitz asked, incredulous. "It's like they can't get enough of him."

"He's good at what he does," Mac said.

Fitz spoke dryly. "A lot of us are good at our jobs. It doesn't send women into screaming ecstasy."

Mac gave a self-deprecatory laugh. "My singing would make them scream, but while they ran in the other direction."

The general shook his head. "It's odd, watching that virt of him with the girl. I would have expected him to be more—hell, I don't know. Jaded. Slicker. He was like an affectionate kid."

"Maybe that's part of his charm. No artifice." Mac had a more pressing concern than Del's charisma. "Did you destroy the virt?"

"All three copies," Fitz said. "Also the systems they used to create it. None of it will get out on the meshes."

Mac let out a breath. "Good."

"We still need to talk to his family."

Mac could just imagine Del's reaction. "He'll hit the roof."

"Tough."

"It's touchy," Mac said. "The Harrison Protocol is clear, and it's been in place for sixty years. Del is here with our permission. He's done whatever we asked him to do and obeyed our laws." Mac wasn't sure about the bliss-node, but so far he'd found no indication Del's license was fake. "He has no link to anything military or political. He's a private citizen we've allowed to work on Earth. We have no more justification for violating his rights than for anyone else."

Fitz gave him a sour look. "He's a goddamn royal land mine."

"His family knows he chose to stay here," Mac said. "Our providing him a bodyguard and constant security is already going beyond Harrison." When Fitz scowled, Mac held up his hand. "Of course we protect him. But it was his choice to trick Cameron. As much as I'd like to lock him up, he broke no laws. He's responsible for his bad decisions and for how he tells his family."

"And if he doesn't tell them?" Fitz said. "What happens when they find out, 'Oh, excuse me, your son nearly died, and Earth's government neglected to mention it.' You want to explain that to them?"

Mac didn't want to be anywhere near that explosion. "No. I'm not saying we shouldn't tell them. But let me talk to him first. See if I can convince him to do it himself."

Fitz snorted. "His Royal Snarkiness is more likely to tell you to go fuck yourself."

"Maybe," Mac said wryly. "But I have to try. I've always leveled with him. If we talk to his family without trying to work with him first, he'll never forgive me. So we'll still alienate the Ruby Dynasty."

"Only one of them," Fitz said. "Their least influential, least involved member. Better him than the Ruby Pharaoh or Imperator."

"Give me a day. Just one."

Fitz exhaled. "All right. One day." Dryly he added, "Good luck."

"Thanks." Mac didn't doubt he would need it.

"His vids just hit the Skolian outlets," Windar said. "But he's *huge* on Earth."

Roca, his mother, stared at him. "You're sure it's Del?"

"Of course I'm sure! No one else sings like him."

They were standing in the living room of the pharaoh's home on the Skolian Orbiter, a space habitat dedicated to government and military personnel. Windar's visits were sporadic, but his Aunt Dehya and his brother Eldrin lived here. His brother Kelric—the Imperator—lived in a huge stone mansion on a hill above the pharoah's house.

At the moment, Kelric was leaning against the living room table, his arms crossed, the gigantic biceps straining his shirt. He stood seven feet tall, with gold skin and molten eyes. Windar had babysat Kelric too much in their childhood to be afraid of him, but even he broke out in a sweat when his "little" brother was displeased. If someone had told him back then that his sweet-natured brother would someday be a military dictator, Windar would have laughed. Except it wasn't funny anymore.

Kelric took after Roca, their mother, in his coloring and facial features, but where he was hard, she was beautiful. Usually. Right now, she looked more annoyed than anything. She frowned at Windar. "Del never said a word."

"And you're surprised?" Kelric asked. Then he said, "Bolt?"

The voice of Kelric's military EI answered. "Attending."

Kelric glanced at Windar. "Tell Bolt where to find this holo of Del. He'll play it for us."

Windar gave Bolt the codes, then said, "Open all the Del-Kurj mods."

"*All* of them?" Roca asked. "How many did you find?"

"You wouldn't believe it," Windar said.

Before he could go on, a woman walked through the archway across the room. Dehya. His aunt. The Ruby Pharaoh. A slight woman in a white jumpsuit, she had a heart-shaped face and a mane of black hair dusted with grey. She was small compared to Roca, and next to Kelric, she looked like a child. Windar had always liked Dehya, but her delicate appearance didn't fool him. Her strength of will was as powerful as Kelric's physical strength.

"I got your message," she told Windar. "What's wrong?"

Roca gave her a dour look. "He's showing us a holo of Del."

Bolt spoke in his deep tones. "I have the holos ready."

"Play the one called 'Diamond Star,'" Windar said.

"I remember that one," Roca said, her voice lightening. "Some parts have a nice melody. But he does such odd things with it."

The screens around a dais by the wall glowed, and the life-sized holo of a man formed. Music filled the room, a melody they all knew, though with instruments they had never heard. But it wasn't the song that mesmerized Windar. It was *Del*. He sang with aban-don, his head thrown back. He turned around, crouched down, and jumped up, spinning in the air so he came down facing his audience. Then he ran forward and grabbed a stand. Snapping the mike into it, he stood with his feet planted wide, gripping the mike in both hands as he belted the chorus. His voice soared, and rainbow holos flared as if he were inside a diamond. Windar had never heard him sing this way before, wild and passionate, but the seeds had always been there. Now Del transformed them into a performance so intense, Windar couldn't stop watching.

"Gods almighty," Kelric said. "He's *dancing.*"

"Look at the audience," Windar said. "They're crazy for him."

"I knew he was singing on Earth," Kelric said. "But I had no idea it was like this."

Dehya smiled. "He looks like he's having fun."

"I don't believe this," Roca said. "He 'forgot' to tell us about this show? And what the blazes kind of music is that?"

"It's more than one show," Windar said. "I looked up their music charts. This is the top-rated holo-rock song on Earth."

Roca squinted at him. "On a chart for holographic stones?"

"No!" Windar smiled at her bewildered look. "On Earth, they have an entire genre with artists who sing like him. They call it rock. Right now, 'Del Arden' is one of their stars. The Earth meshes have holos about it everywhere. Newscasts of people mobbing him. It's incredible. Del! Can you believe it?"

Kelric spoke coldly. "Bolt, lower the volume." As Del's singing faded, Kelric said, "He has only two bodyguards, and Mac Tyler is a retired military officer. Who controls his career? Who pays his bills? Who looks after his health? Who monitors these 'mobs'? If he's that much of a public figure, who the *bloody hell* takes care of him?"

"He never said a word about it." Roca sounded stunned.

Windar felt his mother's hurt, and his anger stirred. She was already grieving over the loss of their father. Always Del caused her pain, with his brooding silences, his challenges, his sarcasm. He could have at least told her.

Dehya was watching him. "He told us last year."

"One message," Roca said. "And what does he say? He's staying to see some woman."

Kelric shook his head. "I want him back here. Immediately. No more 'rock star.'"

Dehya frowned at them all. "Maybe that's why he didn't say anything. Because he knew he would get this reaction."

"If he had told us," Roca said, "we wouldn't react this way."

"You would have said he was wasting his time," Dehya answered. "In fact, you *did* tell him that."

"He could do so much." Roca thumped her palm on the table. "Why does he throw away all that talent?"

"He doesn't see it that way." Dehya went over to stand with her and Kelric. "Roca, he can only be himself." She looked up at Kelric. "Legally we have no justification for forcing him to come home. He isn't breaking any laws."

"I don't care," Kelric said. "And we don't know what he's doing, legally or otherwise."

Dehya motioned at the holo, where Del had launched into another song. "If he's performing in a venue that large, with all those musicians, equipment, and effects, he isn't doing it for free. So he's earning a living. For the first time in his life."

Roca crossed her arms. "It's unseemly."

Windar stiffened. "Why? Because Ruby princes don't work for a wage? I do."

His mother's voice softened. "You've dedicated your life and personal assets to helping communities that couldn't even afford a school before you came. You've made a big difference there."

"I'm doing what I love," he said. "So is Del."

"He's making noise," Kelric growled.

"Actually," Windar said, "I sort of like his songs."

Roca regarded him with bafflement. "Why?"

"I always liked 'Sapphire Clouds,'" Windar said. "And the others sound better the way he does them now. It fits, somehow."

Kelric just grunted.

A rustle came from the entrance of the room as a man appeared in the archway. Eldrin. The eldest of the Valdoria sons, he had been the first to leave home, when he moved here to the Orbiter. Watching Eldrin walk toward them, Windar could see how much he looked like Del. They had similar features, coloring, and builds, though Eldrin was broader in the shoulders and chest. But no one would ever confuse them. Del looked like a farm boy, and Eldrin looked like a king.

Dehya's expression warmed as she saw Eldrin. "My greetings."

He came over to her, his face gentling. "I got your message." He glanced at the holo-dais where Del was silently singing. "I guess I don't have to ask what it's about."

"Your brother is following in your footsteps," Roca said dryly. "But opera, this is not."

Eldrin watched the holo with a bemused expression. "It looks like he's in front of a real audience."

"He is," Windar said. "He's done it all over Earth."

"*Live?*" Eldrin stared at him. "I could never sing that way."

"You do a lot," Roca said. "Just last year, at the Parthonia Arts Gala. It was exquisite."

"That was only a few hundred people." Eldrin gestured toward the holo. "That crowd goes on forever."

Windar could never imagine facing that many people. "Maybe it's not real, just a mesh-created audience to make the performance more exciting."

"Maybe." Eldrin didn't look convinced. "Look at his eyes."

"I noticed," Kelric rumbled.

Windar glanced at his brothers. "Noticed what?"

Kelric scowled. "He's drugged."

"Gods," Roca said. "Is he *trying* to kill himself?"

Windar's pulse lurched. After all those years they feared Del would die in his cryogenic tomb, it would be unbearable if he overdosed or had another runaway reaction now, when he was finally better. Windar had never understood his brother, but he loved him. He couldn't imagine losing Del again, not after all Del had gone through and survived.

Eldrin studied the holo. "I don't think it's drugs, unless you count his audience. I've seen that look before. When he's deep in his songs, he goes into this sort of empathic euphoria."

"I don't understand why he does something so inappropriate," Roca said. "If only he would really use that incredible voice of his."

"Mother, he's always sung like that," Eldrin said. "He's not going to change."

"We can't leave him vulnerable," Kelric said. He stood thinking, his gold eyes impossible to read. "I'll send an escort. If the Allieds refuse us access to him, we'll step up the pressure on their government. They know they had no business hauling him off to Earth and separating him from us."

Dehya was shaking her head. "Our relations with the Allieds are already strained enough. If he refuses to come home and we force him, it could turn into a diplomatic mess."

"His safety is more important," Kelric said. Frustration leaked around his mental shields. "Yes, I know what he'll say. He has a right to live his own life, and the hell with the rest of us. But damn it, he needs to think about who his behavior affects."

"It's called independence," Eldrin said dryly.

Kelric scowled at him. "It's called immaturity."

Dehya spoke quietly. "If you force him to come home, he'll never forgive you."

"I don't want to alienate him any more," Roca said. "But saints, we can't leave him there." She motioned at Del, who was crooning into the mike while his hips moved with the music. "It's not right. *Look* at him."

"What's not right?" Windar asked. He could tell the holo bothered her, but not why.

"The way he moves. Like a—" She cleared her throat.

Dehya spoke wryly. "Yes, Roca, he's a sensual, alluring man. He always has been. No matter how much it bothers you to see your little boy grown up that way, it won't change."

Windar blinked. Del looked like Del. He didn't see where "sensual" or "alluring" came into it.

"He's just a boy," Roca protested.

"No, he's not," Kelric said. "He's an adult, and it's time he started to act like one."

"He's not 'acting' any way," Dehya said. "He's being himself. It's not an offense against the throne, you know."

Roca scowled at her. "Women will get the wrong idea."

"For flaming sake, Mother," Eldrin said. "They've had that idea for most of his life. He's never objected. I'd say he's thoroughly enjoyed it."

"Don't talk about your brother that way," Roca told him.

"Dragging him home isn't the answer," Windar said. It would destroy what little détente they had built with Del.

"You have a better idea?" Eldrin asked.

It seemed obvious to Windar. "Let him sing."

Kelric gave him an incredulous look. "Until the media finds out who he is and turns it into a circus? Or until someone kills him?"

Dehya sat down at the table and rubbed her eyes. "I don't know. I say, just leave him alone."

That gave Windar pause. He hadn't thought *I don't know* was in his aunt's vocabulary. She always had ideas.

Eldrin sat next to her. "Are you all right?"

Roca was also watching her. "Dehya? What is it?"

"I'm just tired," the pharaoh said.

Kelric wasn't buying it. "There's more than that."

"You know," Dehya said wryly, "this business of living in a family of empaths has its drawbacks."

Eldrin regarded her, and she met his gaze. Although the two of them were guarding their minds, Windar caught the hint of a silent conversation between them. Something private, so he mentally withdrew and waited.

Then Dehya spoke to Eldrin. "Are you sure?"

He nodded, his face drawn. "Yes."

"What is it?" Roca asked.

Dehya looked around at them. She said, simply, "I'm pregnant."

Windar froze. *What?*

"Saints, Dehya," Roca said. "Are you all right?"

"I'm fine," Dehya said.

Windar didn't believe it, and he doubted the others did.

Dehya gave Windar a wry look. "Nor does the Assembly."

His face heated with a flush. He hadn't realized she was picking up his thoughts.

"You're just telling us?" Kelric rumbled. "But the Assembly already knows?"

"The Inner Circle, yes," Eldrin said. His fist clenched on the table. "Our doctor told the First Councilor before he told us."

Roca stared at him. "He had no right!"

Eldrin's voice tightened. "I put it far less diplomatically."

Kelric was watching Dehya. "The Assembly ordered you to abide by their decision about this pregnancy, didn't they?"

"And I told them to go to hell." Steel glinted in her gaze. "The days when they can force us at gunpoint to marry or do their bidding are over. We control half the government now."

Kelric's mind blazed with power. "And the entire military."

Roca spoke gently to Dehya. "What do the doctors say?"

At first she didn't answer. But finally she said, "The fetus is missing most of both legs. Some organs are in the wrong place or malformed." Her eyes were glossy with tears, the only time Windar had seen her cry. "But his brain is fine. His beautiful Ruby brain." She rubbed her palm over her eyes. "The doctors hope they can heal him. It will take years. *If* he survives. He could die when he's born. He could die *any* time. I could miscarry. It's—" Her voice broke, and Eldrin took her hand.

"Gods," Kelric said in a low voice.

"What are you going to do?" Roca asked.

Dehya met her gaze. "Whatever hells the Assembly forged by forcing our marriage, this is still our child. We're already linked to his mind."

"To end the pregnancy would end part of ourselves," Eldrin said.

"You'll go through with it?" Windar asked. It sounded torturous, yet he also wanted his nephew to survive.

"Yes," Dehya said in a subdued voice.

"I'm sorry," Roca murmured.

Kelric scowled at Dehya. "You should have goddamned tossed out the entire Assembly when you overthrew the government."

"The thought occurred to me," she said dryly. "But it's a good government, Kelric, despite everything. Without them, we would weaken ourselves. And we can't afford that with the Traders at our borders, waiting for us to stumble."

"Like hell it's a good government," Kelric said. "I would have pitched the whole contentious lot of them. Look at what they've done to the two of you. It never ends, even when they can't control us any more."

Roca spoke as if she were picking her way through glass. "Why would they pressure you into this? They know the danger, with you two related. If your children are so impaired they can't be heirs to the Kyle-mesh, it defeats the Assembly's purpose."

Windar wished he could help. A child should be cause for rejoicing, not grief. But they all knew the truth; Dehya and Eldrin should never have children. Years ago, a desperate Assembly had forced Dehya to obey an ancient law requiring the pharaoh to marry her own kin. It hadn't been because they cared about that obsolete decree. They wanted more Ruby psions. The scientists didn't yet know why they could neither create nor clone a Ruby psion; they knew only that a Ruby mother had to carry a Ruby child. But the recessive genes also carried devastating mutations. It could kill this child.

"Denric." Eldrin was watching him. "It's our choice. They haven't forced us."

It was startling to hear Eldrin use his real name, Denric, instead of his nickname, Windar. Eldrin did that when he wanted to emphasize his words.

Windar spoke quietly. "Then you should do it."

Dehya looked around at them. "We damn the Assembly, yet at the same time, we talk about forcing Del to leave his dream." She let out a breath. "He'll never be like us. Instead of pushing him into a mold he'll never fit, maybe we should let him alone."

Roca spoke with pain. "I won't watch my son kill himself."

"We can send him a bodyguard," Dehya said. "A Jagernaut."

"You know how he'll react," Kelric said. "He'll turn into a supernova."

"Have Chaniece talk to him," Windar suggested. Even when Del refused to acknowledge the rest of them existed, he always had time for his twin sister.

"She won't do it if she thinks we're intruding on his life," Eldrin said. Wryly he added, "She'll be the one urging him to tell us where we can put our ideas."

Roca glared at him. "Chaniece would never be so crude."

"Sure she would," Kelric said with a rumbling laugh. "She'd just do it with impeccable courtesy."

"She won't, though," Windar said. "She doesn't want Del in danger any more than we do."

"I hope so." Kelric considered the holo of Del. "Because if he refuses, I'm bringing him back no matter what, even if it convinces him I've become the greatest tyrant alive."

Del was lying on his bed, fully dressed but half asleep, when Jud sauntered into the doorway. His roommate leaned on the frame and grinned. "Haven't learned your lesson yet, eh?"

Del rolled onto his side. "What?" He squinted at Jud. "Why are you smirking? I cleaned up." It irked him that Jud thought he lived in a mess because he expected someone to pick up after him. It bothered him even more to realize Jud might be right. He had cleaned his room from top to bottom to prove he was perfectly capable of doing it himself.

"It looks great," Jud said. "I didn't mean your room, though." He waggled his finger at Del. "Don't you know yet to watch it with the women? It's karma, sent to you by Ricki. Mess around, and you get in trouble."

"What women?" His esteemed producer had been a block of ice since he had woken up in the hospital. "Ricki is ignoring me. I'm not seeing anyone."

"Yeah, well, the someone you aren't seeing is gorgeous."

Curious, Del sat up and swung his legs over the side of the bed. It had been two days since he had come home, after three in the hospital, but his body was still recovering from the theta-kickers.

"Did she give you her name?" Del asked.

"It was hard to understand," Jud said. "She has an accent like yours. I think she said Chaniece."

Del jumped to his feet and strode out of the room. Or tried to stride. Dizziness hit him, and he stumbled into the doorframe.

"That certainly got a reaction," Jud said, laughing as he grabbed Del's arm to steady him. "If she's not your girlfriend, will you introduce me?"

Del glared with his my-eyes-are-daggers look and yanked away his arm. "No. Never. Besides, what about Bonnie?"

"She can't make up her mind if she likes me or not." Jud lifted his hands, then dropped them. "I wish she would. She's the one I want."

"Good," Del told him. "Because if you look cross-eyed at my sister, I'll break your face into a hundred little pieces."

"Wow," Jud said. "That's your sister? Your family has some genes."

Del felt like growling that Chaniece never wore jeans, but he knew perfectly well what Jud meant. He pushed off the doorway and stalked into the living room. But he wasn't really angry, not if Chaniece had commed him. He missed her so much. When he had been in Allied custody, they hadn't let her contact him. Although he and Chaniece did talk now, he never mentioned his new life. If the rest of his family pressured him to quit singing, he could resist, but if she asked him to stop, he could never say no.

Del stopped a short distance from the console, where he could just make out a woman's silhouette on the screen. If he went closer, she would see him.

Jud came up beside him. "What's wrong?"

"What if she wants me to come home?"

A stillness came over Jud. "Will you?"

"I don't know." Del walked to the console and sat carefully, as if that could change how the conversation went. It was truly Chaniece. She regarded him with large eyes, violet like his, her eyelashes sparkling. Although her hair was lavender, it had so many sun streaks, it looked gold. The curls framed her face and spilled over her shoulders. Del felt as if he had come home.

He spoke in Iotic. "My greetings."

"Del!" Her luminous smile shone. "My greetings.

"It's good to see you." He was the prince of understatement today.

"How are you?" Her smile faded. "You look tired."

"A little. It's this weird twenty-four-hour day." Lyshriol days lasted twenty-eight hours. "*You* look great, Chani."

Her smile dimpled. "Guess what I did."

"I've no idea." She was always making him guess what she did or thought, which was easy when they were together but impossible across interstellar space. "Tell me."

"I watched *The Jewels Suite* vid." She beamed at him. "You look so handsome when you sing."

Del's face flamed with his blush. "I look like me."

"I know. That's why I liked it."

Homesickness surged in Del. "I miss you all so much. I was going to come home, but then my label sent me on tour."

She tilted her head. "Your what?"

"My label. Prime-Nova. They produce my holo-vids."

"Windar saw it in a store. He's the one who showed us."

Del felt as if the air suddenly left the room. "You mean *everyone*? Mother? Kelric? Eldrin?"

She gave him an apologetic look. "Everyone."

Del could guess how they reacted. "I'm not quitting."

"I certainly hope not."

Relief washed over Del. She understood. "What did Mother say?"

Chaniece laughed like a sparkle of water. "She thinks you look too sexy. She's afraid all those evil Earth women will try to compromise your honor."

"Hmmm." Del squinted at her. "So how are the boys?"

She pretended to look stern. "Changing the subject won't work. Just how many girlfriends do you have?"

"Only one." Del thought about the way Ricki was refusing to acknowledge his existence. "Maybe none. She's mad at me."

"What did you do?"

"It's a long story." He couldn't tell her. If Kelric found out, he would yank Del off Earth so fast, it would bust a hole in the fabric of spacetime. "It has to do with, um, another woman."

Chaniece sighed, but she didn't look surprised. "Oh, Del."

"I made a dumb mistake." To put it mildly. "I'm trying to convince her to let me atone for my sins."

Off to Del's left, Jud snorted. "Ricki Varento, let you atone? I doubt it."

"Hey!" Del swung around in his chair. Jud was standing in the doorway of his room, leaning against the frame with his arms crossed, unabashedly eavesdropping.

"I should've never taught you Iotic," Del said. "Go away."

"Iotic?" Jud stared at him. "*That's* what you've been teaching me this last year? The language of Skolian nobility?"

"Del?" Chaniece asked. "Who is that?"

He turned back to her. "My nosy, rude roommate."

"Should I—?"

"It's all right. He knows who I am." He knew why Jud had spoken; he wanted to remind Del he could hear everything. The rooms had no doors on them, and the apartment was too small for privacy unless Jud went outside.

Jud spoke quietly. "I can leave if you want."

Del almost said yes. But maybe it was better if Jud knew about him. He was worn-out from trying to compartmentalize his life. Besides, Jud never asked him to leave when he commed people.

"It's all right," Del said. "Just go in your room, okay?"

Jud nodded and withdrew from the doorway.

When Del turned to the console, Chaniece was watching him with concern. "Kelric is worried," she said. "He wants you to come home."

"No!"

"He's convinced people are going to exploit you," she said. "Until, as he put it, 'they wear you out and throw you away.'"

"Prime-Nova wouldn't do that." Del wasn't actually so sure, but he remembered Mac's lengthy contract negotiations. "Besides, I have good representation."

"You look so tired."

"Just from traveling. I've been doing live concerts."

She hesitated. "In some of your vids, you look—"

Del waited, then said, "Like what?"

"Drugged."

It troubled him to see her upset, especially for no reason. "Just on the rush of people liking my music. Nothing else."

"I can tell something is wrong."

Damn. She knew him too well. If he didn't give her a reason, his family would keep at it until they dragged out everything. So he said, "I snuck out without my bodyguard and got roughed up by some crazy fans." When she tensed, he quickly added, "But I'm fine."

"I wish you would let ISC protect you. I don't trust ASC."

"They're all right." Del preferred Cameron to his brother's minions any day.

"They aren't us," Chaniece said.

"You'd like my bodyguard." Del felt a wicked grin coming on. "Besides, I can't fire him. He'd pine away. He's hot for my drummer."

Chaniece frowned at him. "He should be paying attention to you. Not some woman in your band."

"He does pay attention to me! Constantly. He lives next door. He goes everywhere I go. He monitors my flipping vital signs. I can't do *anything* without him knowing."

"Even so."

Del could guess who had put her up to this. "Kelric wants to send a Jagernaut, doesn't he?"

"You would be safer."

"I don't want his damn guards. Jagernauts are so *obvious*."

"Not if they don't act like one." She regarded him with her large eyes. "I wish you would. Otherwise I'll worry about you."

"I'm fine!"

"You always say that. What if people find out who you are?"

"It doesn't matter. I'm of no use to anyone."

"Don't say that!" She leaned forward. "You matter to me. To all of us."

Del wasn't so sure. More than once, when Kelric treated him like a juvenile idiot or his mother castigated him, he had almost asked if they wished he had stayed in cryogenesis. He felt their anger, their conflicted emotions, their frustration. It swamped everything else. Maybe they loved him, but if they did, it was deeper than their surface emotions, deeper than he could feel.

He spoke reluctantly. "If I take a Jagernaut, will Kelric still try to make me come home?"

"He gave me his word that he wouldn't," Chaniece said. "I told him I wouldn't ask you unless he did."

"The Jagernaut has to blend in," Del said. "Cameron looks military, but a lot of techs dress that way. Jagernauts all look like fighter pilots." It was their main job. Special ops was another, but the ones he knew still acted like cocky pilots.

"Kelric will make sure they blend in," Chaniece told him. "He doesn't want to advertise who you are."

"I'm not going to fire Cameron. He stays."

"I think Kelric expects him to. Then you have more guards."

Del had run out of protests. So he mentally braced himself. "All right. I'll do it." He shifted in his chair. "Do I have to comm Kelric?"

"He said I could do it if you didn't want to."

"I don't want to comm any of them. They'll just criticize me."

"I'll talk to him." Her shoulders relaxed, and Del could see her relief that he had agreed.

"Are the boys there?" he asked, glad for a more pleasant subject.

Her smile lit up her face. "They want to talk to you."

A boy stuck his head into view of the comm screen. He had his mother's features, but his hair was darker, like merlot wine.

"I've been right here!" the boy said. "Father, when are you coming home?"

XVIII

Over the Moon

A sharply indrawn breath came from Jud's room. Del ignored it and smiled at the boy. "Jaqui, you've grown. Look how big you are!"

The boy beamed at him. "I'll be as tall as you the next time you come home."

Del couldn't help but smile. Jaqui had nearly two feet to go before he reached that goal. "You better hurry. I'll be back before you know it."

"Hoshma says you're making music. Can we come watch?"

Del's good mood dimmed. He didn't want the boys exposed to the glitzy, drugged-out world of holo-rock. "It's no place you'd like. Too much noise and nowhere to chase bubbles."

"Oh." Jaqui looked disappointed. "Hoshma said so, too. But she said those soldiers weren't holding you prisoner anymore."

Chaniece had moved to the side, but she was still in view. She spoke quietly. "Jaqui thinks Mac Tyler put you in prison."

"Mac!" Del wanted to laugh, but he didn't want to offend the boy's dignity. So he just said, "Mister Tyler would never hurt me. He helps me."

"He's one of *them.*" Jaqui looked as if he would whip out his wooden sword and brandish it at all of Allied Space Command.

"Not all people from Earth are bad," Del told him.

"Oh." Jaqui didn't look convinced. Then his face brightened. "Guess what?"

Del had no clue, but he tried. "You went somewhere."

"No. I learned fractions. One-eleventh plus three-eighths equals forty-one over eighty-eight. And I'm reading books with chapters."

"That's great!" It never ceased to amaze Del how easily Jaqui learned. "When do you start designing starship engines?"

"Oh, Hoshpa," Jaqui said, laughing. Then he said, "Delson learned to subtract. The chip in his brain helps him."

That sounded like good news. "Is he there?" Del asked.

"Here." Jaqui moved aside and a young man took his place. Although on Earth, Delson would be eighteen, Del thought of him as twenty-two, his age in the octal system on Lyshriol. He was taller than Del and more heavily built, with rugged features. He had the same violet eyes as Del, but with no glint in the lashes.

"Hoshpa." His smile, so trusting, lit up the screen. "I can subtract now. Do you want to hear?"

"Yes, please," Del said, with a familiar ache.

The youth thought for a moment. "Five minus three is . . ." He paused, his forehead furrowed. "Two?"

Del felt as if he had achieved a milestone himself. "Yes! That's excellent!"

The boy grinned at him. "I can run, too."

"You run?" This was new.

Chaniece spoke. "He's good at it, Del. He wins every race with the boys in Dalvador."

A quiet joy spread over Del. If they had found something Delson could excel at, it was reason to celebrate. A sport like running was straightforward. As long as someone kept an eye on him, Delson could do it fine.

They talked a while longer, and Del felt better than he had in weeks. After he signed off, he sat staring at the console, wishing he didn't have obligations that kept him away from home.

A rustle came from his right. He looked up to see Jud standing in the doorway of his room.

"You all right?" Jud asked coldly.

"Sure, fine," Del said, waiting for the explosion.

Jud didn't blow up. He spoke in a low voice, but that only made it worse. There was no mistaking his anger. "Father?"

Del looked down at his hands. "That's right."

"Your *sister's* children?"

"Jud, don't."

"Damn it, Del! *Look at me.*" When Del raised his gaze, Jud was gripping the doorframe. "How could you?"

"I didn't." Del had to fight to speak words he always kept to himself. "I came out of cryogenic stasis to discover I had an eight-year-old son."

"Cryo what?"

"I spent forty-five years in a cryogenic womb."

Jud looked as if he had just hit a brick wall. "Good Lord, why?"

"Because they couldn't keep me alive when they put me in the womb." Del suddenly felt exhausted. "That's another reason Mac is so overprotective. Certain drugs can kill me. And they're common with our crowd."

Jud pulled over a chair, then set it backwards and sat with his arms resting on its top. "You overdosed?"

"Not exactly." Del told him, briefly, what had happened.

When Del finished, Jud said, "And you woke up to find out you had a son?"

Del averted his eyes, unable to face Jud's too perceptive stare. He rarely talked about the boys to anyone outside the family. He had never even hinted to Ricki that he had children. He dealt with his fears of rejection by hiding the truth.

But Jud was his best friend, even after seeing Del at his worst. So Del took a breath and said, "The first time they took me out of cryo, they took Chaniece out, too."

"Wait a second. Your *sister* was in cryogenesis?"

Del looked up at him. "When she found out that I had died, she told them to put her in cryo too, until they took me out." Even after all this time, Del couldn't believe what she had done. "We were twins. Two halves of one mind. We aren't complete without each other." His voice shook. "If I had known, I would have never let her do it."

"If she was in cryo, those couldn't be her children."

"They're hers." Del's pulse leapt, fueled by an anger he had never come to terms with. "They thawed us out nineteen years ago. She was all right, but I died within an hour. So they put me back in. The Assembly got scared. They thought I would never survive."

His voice cracked. "Another Ruby spare, down the drain. So the bastards had the doctors impregnate Chaniece without telling her, using my DNA. By the time she knew, she was afraid she would lose me completely. So she had the child."

Jud stared at him. "Bastards hardly begins to describe it."

Del waited until his pulse calmed. Then he said, "The doctors told them that even if I lived, I had brain damage. I couldn't survive the powerlink for the Kyle web. Then my brother, Kelric—they believed he died in combat. He didn't; he was captured. But the Assembly didn't know. They panicked. They thought they were losing all the Ruby Heirs." With pain, he said, "So they made a replacement for me. Delson. I mean, hell, it wasn't like I was in a position to object."

"How could they get away with that? It must be breaking I don't know how many laws."

"They *make* the laws." Del was gripping the arm of his chair so hard, his knuckles ached. "After all, Delson doesn't need to be smart to be a Ruby heir. Just a strong psion. And he's a powerhouse." His voice broke. "So what if he has the mind of a child?"

"Del, I'm sorry."

"Don't be." Del tried to smile. "He's a wonderful kid. Sweet-natured, despite how tough he looks. He could flatten someone with one of those big fists of his, but he never would, unless they threatened Chaniece or Jaqui."

"Why didn't this Assembly just clone you?"

Del wished it were that easy. "You can't. The geneticists aren't yet sure why. We're rare because the genes that make us such strong psions also have negative mutations associated with them." Bitterness leaked into his voice despite his attempt to stop it. "Scientists don't have many of us to study, and oh, there's this little ethics question of experimenting on living people." He took a breath, calming down. "Kyle genes are recessive, so they have to come from both parents. If a Ruby mother doesn't carry a Ruby baby, it almost never survives."

Jud pushed his hand through his hair, clacking the beads. "But if they breed you to each other, doesn't that make mutations worse?"

"Yes." Del flinched. "Look at the great gifts of intellect I bequeathed to my son."

"Damn it, you're not stupid!"

"Jud, don't."

His roommate scowled at him. "You're the one who told me how smart everyone in your family is. His being slow may have nothing to do with you."

Del just shook his head. It hurt too much to talk about.

"No wonder your aunt overthrew her government," Jud muttered.

Del's anger trickled away. "Yeah, the Assembly used draconian methods. But Jud, they had reason. Without Ruby psions, we have no Kyle-mesh. And without the mesh, we would lose our advantages in speed and communications over the Traders. They'd conquer us."

Jud blinked. "You mean a few empaths is all that stands between your people and mass slavery?"

"Essentially, yeah. It's why the Assembly tries to control us." Del took a breath. "They should have *trusted* us more. We don't want to fall to the Traders any more than they do."

"I'm surprised your aunt didn't throw the whole lot of them into prison."

"I was too, at first," Del said. "But you know, the Assembly is actually pretty effective. If she had dismantled the government right after the war, Skolia might have collapsed."

Jud snorted. "Politicians only do what's in their best interest."

"She's not a politician. She and Kelric are mathematicians."

"Kelric?" Jud asked. "Is that someone in your family?"

"My brother." Del shifted his weight. "Imperator Skolia."

Jud blanched. "Oh."

"He's in the Dyad with my Aunt Dehya. I'm the idiot brother."

"Stop it!" Jud looked ready to shake him. "I hate when you do that. You're one of the most creative people I've met. So what if you're not like everyone else? You may not read, but you have one of the most impressive vocabularies I've heard, and you've hardly known English a year. I don't know anyone who can match what you do with music and words."

Del was floored. Mac and Ricki had told him similar. He had hardly listened to Mac, and he hadn't believed Ricki, either. But now three different people said almost the same thing.

He spoke awkwardly. "Thanks."

Jud hesitated. "That younger boy called you Father, too."

The second shock. "Nine years after Delson was born, the doctors brought me out and made Jaqui with my DNA. This time I survived a few weeks before they had to put me back."

"Did you know about him?"

Del shook his head, trying to push away the hurtful memories. "Not until three years later, when they took me out again." Dryly he added, "I managed to stay alive that time."

"So that was the last time in cryo."

"I wish." Del rubbed the tensed muscles in the back of his neck. "Over the next two years, I was in and out every half year or so, for a few months. And I had to relearn everything. But I recovered. The past five years, I've been fine."

"You say it all so calmly." Jud let out a breath. "It sounds like a nightmare."

Del just didn't want to hurt anymore. "The hardest part was having two children, and I couldn't be a father to them, even after I came out for good. Chaniece looked after us all. I was almost as helpless as an infant. Jaqui and I learned everything together. He was two and I was—well, I don't know how the hell old I am. Twenty-six, if you count the time I've been out of cryo. Some tests say twenty-five or twenty-four. It messed up my DNA."

"No wonder they worry so much about you."

"They're *suffocating* me. They want to keep me in this symbolic cryogenesis forever."

Jud spoke gently. "They're afraid for you. It's hard, when you love someone, to see things clearly."

Was it love? Del wanted to believe that. But he said only, "So I have more bodyguards." He wished he didn't have to inflict them on Jud. "I'm sorry. It's affecting your life, too."

"Are you kidding?" Jud laughed good-naturedly. "My life has never been this interesting. A hit single, and my roommate is a flipping prince. It's great."

"Hey, I only do flips when I practice." Del snapped his arms up in a *mai-quinjo* move. "I'll toss you over my shoulder."

Jud gave him an unimpressed look. "I've never seen you toss anyone. I think you made all that up."

"Don't tempt me, or I'll have to prove you wrong."

His roommate laughed. "Okay. But first let's get pizza. I'm starving."

Del grimaced. "I hate pizza. How about Thai?"

"All right." Jud jumped up. "I'll tell Cameron."

"You don't have to," Del grumbled. "He'll know the second I leave this apartment."

Jud hesitated, his face thoughtful. "You know, you're well enough known now that someone might recognize you if we go out."

Del just wanted to eat, without people coming up to him. "Let's get it in, then."

So they commed a restaurantio in the m-universe and ordered food, which they had delivered to Cameron since he would intercept it anyway. When he showed up at the door, holding dinner, looking confused, they unlocked the security mesh, altered the permeability on the molecular airlock, and invited him inside. Together, the three of them consumed six full dinners.

It was almost fun. Del tried not to dwell on how much he missed his family. But he knew the truth, as hard as it was to face. It was wrong for him to be in their lives. What example could he set for his sons, that their uncle was also their father? His third sister, Aniece, had married Lord Rillia, who governed the Rillian Vales. Rillia loved the boys and had taken them and Chaniece into his home. He was surely a better father figure than Del could ever be, and he had been a constant in their lives during the years their biological father had slept in cold storage.

But Del missed them so much, it left a hole nothing could fill.

Mac had spent so much energy dreading his talk with Del that he almost passed out when the prince called him instead.

"You want me to do *what?*" Mac gaped at the comm screen.

"Cameron and I are supposed to meet this person at the starport," Del said. "But Cam doesn't want me going into the terminal because people might recognize me. So we were wondering if you would meet her while we wait outside in the flyer."

"Who is she?"

Del glowered at him. "Hell if I know."

"And you really told your family what happened?" Mac was sure he had heard wrong. "Everything?"

"I told Chaniece. Sort of." Del raked his hand through his hair. "My brother Windar saw a holo of me singing. So of course, instead of contacting me, he took it to Kelric and my mother."

Mac raised an eyebrow. "Whereas you immediately contacted them when Prime-Nova gave you the contract."

Del regarded him with those deceptively innocent eyes. "I've been planning to tell them."

"For a year? That's a long plan."

"I needed to think." Del even said it with a straight face.

Mac wondered how Del could be so charming sometimes and so exasperating at others. He said only, "I'm glad you talked to Chaniece. Fitz McLane wanted to contact your family. I got him to hold off, but he wouldn't have waited long."

Del glowered at him. "General McLane can go drill—"

"Uh, Del, you know our conversations are recorded."

To Mac's surprise, Del laughed. "All right. I won't cuss anyone out." He mimed doing a salute. "Hi, General."

Mac struggled to hold back his laugh. Fitz wasn't going to find it amusing, and Mac didn't want to antagonize him.

"All right," he told Del. "I'll go meet your new Jagernaut bodyguard."

The Thurgood Marshall Starport that served both Baltimore and Washington was east of the Interstate 95 Air Lane. Mac rode with Del and Jud in a rented flyer while Cameron sat up front with the pilot, another Marine. They let Mac off at the gates for offworld flights, then headed to a flyer parking lot.

Inside the terminal, Mac strode along a fast-walk, which took him to the waiting area for Skolian arrivals. As he stood in the blue-carpeted lounge, the Jagernaut strolled out of customs carrying a smart-sack over one shoulder. She was far more convincing as a civilian than Cameron. He fooled people because holo-rock techs liked to act military; this woman looked like a tourist, nothing more. The only reason Mac knew she was an elite military operative was because he recognized her from the images Del had sent him.

He waved her over. "Tyra Jarin?"

"That's me," she said as she came up. "Are you Mac Tyler?"

Good Lord. Her English was perfect. "Yes, I am. Welcome to Baltimore." Mac offered his hand, and she shook it with complete ease, as if she had done it all her life.

"Do you have any luggage?" Mac asked as they headed into the gleaming white concourse with its many shops.

"Just this." She hefted her smart-sack.

"Good." He didn't know what to say. She looked so normal. Straight, dark hair brushed her shoulders and framed an aquiline face. She was on the tall side, with a lithe build. It was hard to believe she was one of the most versatile killers ever created.

Tyra glanced at him with the hint of a smile. "This way, no one notices me."

A flush heated Mac's face. He had forgotten Jagernauts were psions. "Am I that easy to read?"

"Only if you practically shout it in your mind. Your mental shields are otherwise very effective."

"I was trained to build them during my Air Force days," Mac said. "It's one reason ASC hired me to work with Del."

"How is he?" Tyra asked. "That business with those two fans sounded gruesome."

"He was pretty shaken up," Mac said. "But he's better."

"Good." She looked around the concourse like a fascinated tourist, but Mac had no doubt she was taking in every detail.

They rode a lift to the top floor, then went outside to the flyer lot, which consisted of landing pads rather than parking spaces. They were walking toward Del's flyer when its door opened and he jumped out. He stood in the sunlight wearing a ragged pair of mesh-jeans and a faded T-shirt with a rip in one sleeve. His hair spilled over his collar. He rubbed the small of his back, then stretched his arms while he looked around. When he spotted Mac and Tyra, he waved.

"He looks just like his holos," Tyra said as Mac waved back. "I had thought they doctored his images."

"They don't need to," Mac said. "That's all him." It was one reason Prime-Nova liked Del to tour; he really did look as good in person as in his vid.

"He shouldn't stand out in the open." Tyra increased her stride. "People could recognize him."

"There's no one up here," Mac said.

She nodded toward their right. Squinting into the glare, Mac realized four people were in a corner of the lot, half hidden by the shadows of an overhang, a teenaged girl, a boy, and what looked like their parents. As they stepped down from their flyer, they stared at Del.

"Huh," Mac said. "I didn't see them."

"I'm trained to sense people," Tyra said. "To me, their minds practically shouted their surprise at seeing Del Arden here."

Mac glanced at Del. He was watching Tyra curiously while he leaned against the flyer, soaking in the sunlight.

"I don't think Del realizes they're here," Mac said.

"He doesn't." Tyra said it without doubt.

When they reached the flyer, Mac said, "Del, this is Secondary Tyra Jarin of the J-Force, Imperial Space Command."

Tyra spoke in flawless Iotic. "I'm honored by your presence, Your Highness."

Mac couldn't help but smile. "His Highness" looked like a scruffy kid.

Del knew the protocols, though. He answered with regal formality. "We are pleased, Secondary Jarin, by your attendance." Then he lapsed into his normal voice. "But we shouldn't use titles, should we? It's sort of obvious."

Unexpectedly, Tyra smiled. In English, she said, "From now on, I'm just a bodyguard Del Arden hired." She tilted her head toward the family of four. "We have company."

With a start, Del looked over. The family had come forward, but they were hesitating about halfway across the lot.

"They probably want me to sign something." Del spoke self-consciously. "People do that here. They ask for your signature on a keepsake." Before she could respond, he smiled at the group and motioned them over.

Tyra spoke to Mac in a low voice. "First order of business: he has to stop doing things like this."

The teens came forward, looking shy and eager. The parents followed, clearly intrigued. Cameron appeared in the hatchway of the flyer, his gaze fixed on the group. When Del walked over to them, Cameron jumped down and followed. Mac was aware of Tyra moving forward as well, her posture tensed.

Del smiled at the teens. "Hi."

"You're Del Arden, aren't you," the girl said. She gazed at Del as if she had fallen in love.

"That's me," Del said. "And you're . . . ?"

The girl blushed. "Colleen." She indicated the boy, who was probably about twelve. "This is my brother Tommy."

The boy offered him a vid cube. "We watch this all the time. It's great! Would you—would you sign it?"

With his own eyes lit up almost as much as theirs, Del took the cube. It sparkled like a gem, with a glittering holo that read *The Jewels Suite* floating above one face. The other faces showed views of Del singing or dancing.

"Do you have a light-stylus?" Del asked. He was trying to look relaxed, but Mac could tell he had tensed up, as he did every time someone asked for his autograph.

At first, Mac had thought Del disliked signing because he feared someone would forge his signature. But he had soon figured out Del was illiterate. It wasn't that Del couldn't sign; he had learned a suitable scrawl. But it bothered him to give it away. When Mac asked why, Del couldn't articulate why, except to say that each time he gave an autograph, he lost a piece of himself.

He was a good sport about it, though. When Colleen handed him a light-stylus, he opened the cube and drew his scrawl on a light panel. He even wrote, "Love, Del." Although he had practiced the word *love* over and over, he still forgot how to write it sometimes, but today he had no problem.

After Del finished, he spent several minutes talking with the family, who were curious about the tour and his next vid.

"We heard you were sick in California," Colleen said. "It was all over the meshes. They said you had pneumonia from overwork."

"It wasn't that serious," Del said awkwardly. "Just bronchitis." He even pronounced "bronchitis" right. Zachary at Prime-Nova had made him practice it.

Finally Del said, "I better go. I have a rehearsal this afternoon. We're working on the new vid."

"Ultra," Tommy said. "We'll buy it as soon as it comes out."

Del grinned at him. "Thanks."

"You know, you're really nice," Colleen said. "I was afraid you wouldn't want to be bothered by us."

Del looked embarrassed and pleased, and Mac knew it was real, not an act he put on for the kids. "I'm just glad you like my vid."

"It's the best," Tommy assured him.

Del flashed his dazzling smile and waved as he boarded the flyer. "Have a good flight."

Colleen looked as if she were melting. "Bye," she said, her gaze rapt. "You, too."

Inside the flyer, Del strapped into his seat while Tyra and Mac settled on either side of him, and Cameron took the copilot's chair.

"It's still so hard to believe," Del said. "They like my singing. I can't get over it."

"You'll have to," Tyra said as their pilot took the flyer into the air. "You can't talk to people that way."

"*What?*" Del turned to her. "Why not?"

"It's too risky."

Del scowled. "Cameron lets me."

The Marine cleared his throat. "We need to talk about that."

Tyra glanced at him. "You're Sergeant Cameron?"

"That's right." He offered his hand, and they shook with a firmness that made Mac wince. If either of them grabbed his hand like that, they would break it.

"Pleased to meet you," Tyra said.

"Glad to have you on stars," Cameron said.

"What stars?" Del said.

Tyra smiled at Del, and it looked genuine. He didn't seem to irk her the way he did most military types. Maybe that was why Imperator Skolia had chosen her. Del wasn't likely to get along with any bodyguard his brother sent, but the arrangement would be more bearable if they didn't find each other intolerable.

"It's military lingo," Tyra said. "On stars. On the ship. Part of the team."

"If you two are done communing with each other," Del said, "maybe you could tell me how I'm supposed to meet my fans if you won't let me talk to them."

"You don't meet them," Tyra said.

Del glared at her. "Like hell."

Mac felt like groaning. It would have been nice if the "I'm honored to meet you" détente could have lasted more than ten minutes. "Del, they have a point."

"Et tu, Bruté?" Del said.

"Where did you learn that?" Mac didn't know which startled him more, that Del knew the Latin or that he understood the reference to betrayal implied by the quote, supposedly the last words of Julius Caesar when he saw his friend Brutus among his assassins.

"Claude is reading Shakespeare to me," Del said.

Tyra came even more alert. "Who is Claude?"

"He's my EI," Del said. "What, are you going to say it's too risky for me to talk to my mesh? Heaven forbid. He might bore me to death with soliloquies on quantum scattering theory."

"Del," Mac said. He didn't know whether to laugh or groan.

"Mac, listen," Del said. "I know I shouldn't go into crowds. And okay, I admit it." He gave Cameron a guilty look. "I shouldn't have tricked you and run off."

"No, you shouldn't have." Cameron actually cracked a smile. "Though I've never been avoided in such an entertaining way."

"If I were in a better mood," Del said, "I would tell you that she really does like you that much. But since I'm pissed at you, I'm not saying anything."

"You really think she does?" Cameron asked. Del just glowered.

"Who?" Mac asked, at a loss to follow this development.

"It's nothing," Cameron said, back in taciturn mode.

Del smirked. "A nothing named Anne." When Cameron glared at him, Del regarded his bodyguard innocently. "What?"

"Who is Anne?" Tyra asked.

"She's my drummer," Del said. "Gosh, maybe it's too risky for me to hang out with her, too."

"We're checking all your associates," Tyra said.

Dreading the response he was about to get, Mac said, "You'll have to clear all your friends with Tyra, too."

"No!" Del stared at them in undisguised disbelief. "I refuse to live like a recluse. How is this any different than my being a Ruby prince in the Imperial Court?"

"I don't know about the Imperial Court," Mac said. "But Del, greetings, you *are* a Ruby prince." He regarded the grumpy youth with frustration. "Pretending you aren't won't make it go away."

Del crossed his arms and looked daggers at them, first Mac, then Cameron, then Tyra, then for good measure at the pilot, who couldn't see because he was paying attention to his flying.

"This drills," Del said.

Tyra glanced at Mac. "He's learned a lot of English."

"Too well," Mac said. Although Tyra hadn't smiled, he had the impression she found Del funny rather than aggravating. Well, good for her. She hadn't been around long enough to want to strangle him. If Mac didn't have nanos protecting his stomach lining, he would have an ulcer.

Del continued to bedevil Cameron about Anne. Cameron pretended to have no idea what Del meant, which only spurred Del to try provoking him more. Although Tyra hardly seemed to listen, Mac had no doubt she was taking it all in, analyzing, developing who knew what models. Jagernauts had more extensive node systems in their brains than most anyone else alive.

He just hoped she didn't end up needing it all to defend Del.

✧   ✧   ✧

Ricki spent the day working with Jenny Summerland on her new virt. After Jenny left, Ricki stayed in her office, hunched over a console, listening to one of the songs. She didn't like the whine of the morpher.

"You're here late," a man said behind her.

Ricki froze. She would know that sensual voice anywhere. She gritted her teeth and kept working.

"Ricki, don't." Del pulled over a chair and sat next to her. "Talk to me."

She looked up with her most innocent expression. "Talk?" she asked sweetly. "Do you do that? I thought you just fucked."

Del jerked as if she had hit him. "That was low." He spoke with difficulty. "You left. In the morning. After my party in Chicago."

She tensed, remembering that night. Such a great night. And then he had ruined it all with crazy Delilah in her pink lace. "I have a job. I had to be back." Frustrated, she said, "You wake up at noon, Del. I don't have that luxury."

Ricki couldn't tell him the rest, that if she stayed with him in the morning, she left herself vulnerable. He would see her asleep and helpless. She still remembered her mother crying the morning after her father had deserted them. How the hell could her mother have done the same thing a few years later, leaving her own *daughter* to fend for herself? Ricki should have gone into foster care, but she had run away. God only knew what would have happened if that musician hadn't taken her in. He had been her first and—until Del—her only rock singer. No way would she leave herself open to being deserted and crushed again, especially with a damn singer who jumped from woman to woman.

Del was watching her oddly, as if he were straining to hear a barely heard conversation. He spoke softly. "I won't hurt you again. I swear it. Give me a chance."

She couldn't relent. He scared the hell out of her, and being angry was easier than admitting how she felt. "To do what? Let me watch you drill your way across America? Not a chance, sweetheart."

"Ricki, I'm sorry. I really am." He took her hand. "I mean it. No more screwing around. No more Delilahs or Kendras or Talias."

She pulled her hand away. "I'm sure the next one will have a different name."

"I'm a reformed man."

"Yeah, right."

"I mean it. Let me prove it to you." He regarded her with those huge, heartbreaker eyes of his. "I'll take you to dinner. And afterward I'll take you to the fanciest hotel in D.C."

"On whose salary?" she asked curiously. She knew how much money Del had; she had arranged his loan herself, and he hadn't been paid yet for the next royalty period.

"I saved up." He had that boyish look that always weakened her resolve. Damn, he was good-looking. It wasn't fair.

"I'm busy," Ricki said.

"You have to eat." He recaptured her hand and kissed her knuckles. "Come with me. I miss you."

Ricki wanted to refuse. She intended to. But somehow instead she said, "You'd take me to any hotel I picked?"

"The fanciest you want. No limit."

"Does it have to be in D.C.?"

He brushed her knuckle down his cheek. "Anywhere you want, love, is fine by me."

Don't call me love, she thought. Aloud, she said, "I want to go to the Royal Lunar Suites. That's on the Moon, babe." It was the most exorbitant hotel in the solar system, arguably among the Allied Worlds.

Del's gaze never wavered. "All right."

She couldn't help but smile. "Oh, Del. You could never even get a reservation there, let alone afford a suite."

"Claude?" he said.

Ricki peered at him. "What did you call me?"

A man's voice came out of Del's wrist-mesh. "Here."

"Please arrange a reservation for myself and Miss Varento at the Royal Lunar Suites. We'll take the Express Shuttle up, so the Lunar should expect us in about twelve hours. Mac can give you the info for my accounts."

"I'll contact Mister Tyler," Claude said.

"Is that your EI?" Ricki asked.

"That's right." Del slid his hand behind her head and drew her closer, his lips coming toward hers.

"Oh no, you don't." Ricki pulled away. "You can't get reservations at the Lunar. Even if you could afford it, they wouldn't have a suite available in just twelve hours."

"We'll see." Del tugged her back and kissed her, his lips warm against hers.

Ricki instinctively started to relax into the kiss, but she caught herself in time. Putting her palms against his shoulders, she pushed him back. "Stop playing with me."

"I'm not," he murmured, his lashes half lowered.

When he looked at her that way, her good sense went away. "I know a Thai place not far from here. Let's go there." She gave him a stern look. "But you go home afterward. Without me."

Del trailed his finger down her cheek. "If Claude sets up a reservation for us at the Lunar, will you come?"

"Sure," Ricki said with a smile. "Why not?"

"Good," Del murmured. "Because the shuttle to the Moon leaves at midnight."

This isn't possible. Ricki gazed at the view screen in the lounge of the Express Shuttle. A diamond-dust limo was hovering into the cavernous bay where the ship had just docked.

"That can't be your limo," Ricki said.

Next to her, Del stretched his arms. "It's not."

She still couldn't believe they were on the Moon. Where had he found the money for the exorbitant Express Shuttle tickets? They had slept during most of the flight, so she might have wondered if they had really left Earth, except they had been in free fall almost the whole time.

"I didn't think it was yours," she said.

Del yawned. "I rented it."

Ricki just smiled. He couldn't have rented it. She didn't really believe he had a reservation at the Lunar, either, but who knew. Maybe his name had become well enough known that they gave him a suite from a cancellation. If the reservations officer were human and female, that could explain a lot. Del might have taken another loan against the royalties he'd receive in a few months. With "Diamond Star" on top of the charts and *The Jewels Suite* climbing back up, he would see a good chunk of money. It bothered her to think he might have blown his earnings on this trip because of a suggestion she had never expected him to take seriously.

When the ship announced they were free to disembark, they stood up. Ricki hadn't paid attention to the other three passengers in the lounge since she had slept during the trip. They were business types in expensive jumpsuits, silver or blue, two men and a woman. The woman was tall, with aquiline features and dark hair brushing her shoulders. Ricki half expected to see the ubiquitous Cameron. She had even thought she glimpsed him earlier with the ship's crew. But that was absurd. Cameron was a roadie, not a crewman.

The passengers had space suits available to them, but travel to the Moon was so mundane, no one donned suits except in the rare emergency. Del was wearing a pair of old mesh-jeans, though at least these didn't have rips. His blue pullover was soft and worn. He looked more like a high school boy than someone wealthy enough to afford two berths on the elite Express. Ricki hadn't changed her work clothes; she had on a green jumpsuit with a gold belt, a nice outfit, sure, but nothing fancy. The two of them hardly looked like they belonged in a limo.

As soon as Ricki took a step, she stumbled. No gravity! No, that wasn't true. She had a little bit of weight. During the trip, she had been strapped in, so the free fall hadn't affected her, other than when her hair floated into her face and woke her up. Now she felt as if she were drifting out of the lounge.

They followed the two men, with the woman behind them. Ricki half-floated, half-walked down the ramp to the corrugated deck of the docking bay. Del came to her side, his steps languid.

"Think how high I could jump if I did a show here," Del said.

Hey. That was a thought. "Maybe we could set one up." She slanted a look at him. "But you already jump ridiculously high."

"That's because the gravity on Earth is so low." He gave the barest jump and floated into the air. "I weigh almost twenty percent more on my world than on Earth." He came down so gently, his sports shoes made no sound. "My muscles are adapted to that."

"Huh." It was an odd idea, that Earth had "low" gravity.

Del stopped at the bottom of the ramp. The execs kept going, and Ricki fully expected one of them to meet the limo. But they went by it, while the limo floated up to her and Del. Silently. Impressive for a hover vehicle, especially such a long one. It settled onto the deck, and a hatch irised open on the driver's side. A molecular airlock. Good Lord. It meant they could survive in the limo even outside on the airless Moon.

A man in a sleek black jumpsuit stepped out and bowed to

them. *Bowed.* This was getting bizarre. His fingertip glowed with a laser-light as he touched his belt. An airlock in the middle of the limo immediately opened. Even stranger, Del inclined his head to the man as if he had done this sort of thing all his life.

Del let her enter the car first. As he slid in behind her, the driver resumed his seat up front and the airlocks closed. The limo lifted off, deliciously smooth, and hovered across the docking bay.

Okay, this is definitely weird, Ricki thought. The black leather seats had gold trim. Real gold. A silver stand in front of them with diamonds inset in its rim held ice and a bottle of champagne. And look at that; a bed with velvet covers waited behind their seat. My goodness, wasn't Del optimistic.

Del settled back and put his arm around her shoulders. "Do you like it?"

"It's all right." She didn't say what she thought, that even Prime-Nova top execs didn't take this level of luxury for granted. Yet Del didn't even *blink.*

Del laughed softly. "You like it, Ricki. Admit it."

She slanted him a look. "What, you can read my mind?"

"Not your mind. But your moods, yes, especially when you let down your barriers." He even said it with a straight face.

"Uh, yeah. Right." Had he gone wonko? Next thing she knew, he would be claiming to be a telepath, or whatever the Skolians called their supposed mind readers.

She pulled the bottle of champagne out of the ice. "Peking Gold, 2105." She glanced at Del. "I've seen faked bottles of the aged champagnes before, but usually you can tell it's phony. This is the best imitation I've seen."

"It's not an imitation," Del said. "At least, it had better not be. I told them to give me the best that they had."

Ricki laughed. "Told who?"

"The limo company."

"You told them." She couldn't figure this out. "You, who can't afford to pay your rent, ordered a bottle of champagne that costs thousands of dollars."

His gaze slipped away from her. "I don't know what it cost." He ran his finger around the rim of the bucket.

"You didn't ask?"

"No." He wouldn't meet her gaze.

Unease swept over Ricki, and she put the bottle back in the

bucket. "Del, how did you get all this?" She took his chin and turned his head so he had to look at her. "If you're into some illegal biz, tell me. We'll get you out of it."

His strain disappeared, and he laughed. "Good gods, Ricki. I'm not in trouble."

"Why do you always say that? It makes no sense."

"Say what?" His alarmingly sexy smile flashed. "That I've done nothing illegal? I'm really not such a bad boy, you know."

"Yes, you are. But that wasn't what I meant." She mimicked his deep voice. "'Good gods.' You say it all the time. Never 'Good Lord' or 'Oh, my God.' It's always plural."

"Oh. That." He tried to look nonchalant. "We have a whole pantheon where I come from."

"Lyshriol." She crossed her arms. Despite what he claimed, he had to be in trouble. Your typical farm boy wouldn't even know how to talk to the driver of this limo, let alone rent it. "This planet I've never heard of, that *no* record exists of, and oh gosh, you don't want me to mention it in any public bio. I wonder why."

"It exists."

She studied his face, trying to understand his reaction. He seemed . . . curious, of all things. She would have expected him to be nervous if he were in trouble. He did seem scared, but of her more than anything else. Well, he *should* be scared. He was pissing her off. "Fine. Take me to Lyshriol. Let me see this supposed world of yours."

He shifted his weight. "I can't."

"I didn't think so."

"It's not what you think, Ricki. It's real." His gaze never wavered. "You just know it by a different name."

"Is that so?" She had never been one to believe eyebrows really could arch, but she could actually feel hers doing it. "What might that be?"

He met her gaze squarely. And said, "Skyfall."

XIX

A Desolate Landscape

Ricki wanted to sock him. Skyfall. Did he think she was that stupid?

Except.

So much made sense. The military's involvement in his rescue, their ability to find him so fast, the eerie way Del knew her moods, his ease with this wealth that even in her circles would be extreme, the complete absence of any mention about his world in any database.

No. That was carrying the absurd too far. She took his arm off her shoulders and practically threw it into his lap. "Don't shit with me, Del."

He winced and rubbed his arm. "I'm not."

"Mac Tyler would never audition a Ruby prince."

"I wasn't the person you were supposed to audition. The guy never showed. Mac found out later that he had been too drunk."

"So you pretended to be him?" Ricki wouldn't have expected a cheap move like that from Del.

"No. I didn't know it was an audition. Mac said maybe I could try out a studio. I thought I was doing that." He regarded her with that melting look of his. "Are you angry?"

"Yeah." She refused to melt. "I hate it when people make up crap. This is some stupid trick to push up your royalty rate on the next vid, right?"

"Royalty." He gave an uneven laugh. "Right."

The explanation finally came to her. "Oh, I get it. You come from Skyfall, but you really are just a farmer. You did something that put you in good with one of those princes and he bought you a ticket to Earth as a reward."

"No," Del said quietly. "Roca Skolia is my mother. Eldrinson Althor Valdoria, the man you would call the King of Skyfall, was my father. My full name is Del-Kurj Arden Valdoria Skolia."

A chill went through Ricki. She was good at telling when people lied to her, and she didn't think he was doing it. But his name couldn't be Skolia. That was the name of a dynasty.

The name of an empire.

"You know," Ricki said, "I think I need your twenty-thousand-dollar champagne after all." She fumbled with the cork on the bottle.

"Here." Del took two goblets out of the ice and handed them to her. Then he tugged the green and silver bottle away from her and opened it with a practiced gesture. A trace of froth bubbled over the top.

Ricki was having trouble breathing evenly. As Del filled the glasses, gold bubbles clung to the crystal and rose through the sparkling liquid. She couldn't imagine drinking it. As much as she wanted to enjoy this, she didn't believe it, and she didn't want to look like a gullible fool. When Del returned the bottle to the bucket, she almost grabbed it to make sure no drops of the precious liquid escaped. How much were those drops worth? Hundreds of dollars each? If this was all a farce he had cooked up, they were worth no more than her foolish moment of weakness when she thought he might be telling the truth.

"To us." Del hinged his hand around his goblet as if it were perfectly natural to fold his hand in half. He tapped his glass against hers, producing a chime like his voice when he sang. He was so *different,* and it never fazed him. Then he raised the glass to his lips, and while Ricki watched in disbelief, he drank.

Okay, if he could take supposedly thousand-dollar swallows, so could she. Ricki sipped her own drink. God almighty. She had drunk plenty of expensive champagne, and none came close to this.

"It's exquisite," she said.

"It is good." Del looked at his glass. "I don't usually like alcohol. But this is great."

"I noticed you don't drink much." Ricki leaned back and closed her eyes, sinking into the blissful seat. The leather adjusted to ease her muscle tension. A hundred questions rose in her mind, but she held them back. If this turned out to be a scam, the less she reacted, the better.

"It's not a scam," Del said.

Ricki sat up abruptly. "Why did you say that?"

"You thought it. Loudly." He spoke quickly. "And no, I can't usually read your mind. But if you relax your barriers and have an intense thought, I may pick it up."

No. It couldn't be telepathy. He was just good at reading body language and facial expressions.

"What do I have to do to convince you?" he murmured.

"Well, hell, how about an introduction to the Ruby Pharaoh?"

"All right."

"*What?*"

"I'll comm her when we get to the hotel."

"Right, of course." She spoke unsteadily. "I believe that."

She didn't know whether to laugh or run away.

Del watched Ricki, enjoying the sight of her in that clingy jump-suit. She stood in front of a floor-to-ceiling panel of reinforced dichromesh glass and gazed out at the starkly spectacular landscape of the Moon. The sun was setting, brilliant in the black sky. No erosion had ever softened those peaks or craters. No sunset, no colors. It was a world of black, grey, and white, where the night began with an abruptness that took his breath. It meant a lot to him that he could give her something of beauty that even she, with all her influence and experience, didn't expect.

He left the lights off, knowing the view would be even more impressive that way. And he wanted to impress her. These past days had been excruciating, with her ignoring him or being icily formal when they worked at the studio.

"May we live to honor God's splendor," Ricki murmured. "In the glory of his incomparable nights."

Del came up behind her and put his arms around her waist, looking over her head at the moonscape. The low gravity made him feel light-headed. "Did you write that?"

"Not me. A poet named Constance Herrera, about a century ago, after she visited the Moon."

"It's beautiful." The tension eased in his body. He had been nervous all day, worrying how to tell her about himself. It was funny. He had finally done it, and she didn't believe him! He wished he hadn't said he would comm Dehya. His aunt might insist he talk to his mother. He hadn't spoken with any of them since Chaniece had told him they knew about his singing. He dreaded it. His aunt didn't judge him, though, even when his choices puzzled her.

Del wanted to use his bliss-node. He hadn't for two days, the longest he had gone except in the hospital. Yet as much as he needed the virt, he needed even more for Ricki to understand. It mattered too much to him, but he couldn't turn off that emotion. He didn't know what to do with it, because he felt as if he had nothing to give her.

The Skolian Assembly had left him in an impossible situation. Although the rural culture of Lyshriol and the glittering society of Skolian nobility had few traits in common, both agreed in one respect: a man who fathered children should marry their mother. He could never have the relationship with Chaniece a man should have with the woman who bore his children, but that did nothing to change the sense of responsibility he felt. He couldn't let it go, and it interfered with his ability to love anyone else. Somehow, he had to find his way through all the tangled threads.

A discreet hum came from across the room. Del looked over his shoulder. "Come."

A panel shimmered away in the gold and ivory wall, and the lights came up. A man in a formal black jumpsuit entered, moving with slow steps in the low gravity. He bowed to them both. In a culture where almost anyone could afford robots to do everything, human servants became an exorbitant luxury.

"Your dinner is here," the man said.

"Thank you." Del indicated a gleaming table of polished wood that stood across the spacious room. "You can leave it there."

"Of course, sir." The man lifted his hand without looking behind him. Two more people entered, a man and a woman, guiding an airborne tray that held platters, crystal goblets, and goldware utensils. They led the tray to the table and set out the gold platters, uncovering them to reveal steaks, sauces, curry, and unfamiliar dishes that smelled heavenly. Then all three withdrew as discreetly as they had come.

"Wow," Ricki said.

Del smiled at her. "Do you like it?"

"It's great. But I don't understand." She had that same wariness as in the limo. "Why did you need to borrow money from Prime-Nova if you could afford this?"

"Because I earn what Prime-Nova pays me." Del motioned at the glistening suite around them, with its plush gold rugs and diamond chandeliers. "I can give you this for a night or a year, Ricki, but it isn't from me. It's a fluke of my heritage."

"Did you tell the people here you're a Ruby prince?" she asked. "Is that how you got this suite so fast?"

"No. I just paid them a lot." He hesitated, uncomfortable with the pragmatic details. "There are protocols you can follow that tell the people who run a place like this you're—" He stopped, at a loss for the word in English. In Iotic, he would have said, *behind the sun*. It meant a person had great influence, title, and wealth. He couldn't think of an equivalent in English, so he just said, "That you're a dignitary."

"Oh." She studied him as if he were a code she was trying to crack. "You said something about your aunt ... ?"

Del had hoped she might forget. "Don't you want to eat?" He gazed longingly toward the food. "It smells really good."

She frowned at him. "Don't try to distract me."

He could tell she still didn't believe him. So he resigned himself to the inevitable. He walked to a gold console in a corner of the room, his steps long and slow in the slight gravity. At his approach, a chair morphed out of the console. Del blinked at it, then sat down.

"Hello," a pleasant female voice said. "I'm Elizabeth. What can I do for you tonight?"

"I'd like a link to the Kyle-mesh," Del said.

"I'm connecting now."

Just like that. No refusals, no lengthy procedures, no codes, no requests for payment. Just *I'm connecting now*. More than anything else, that spoke of the stratospheric quality of this hotel.

Ricki sat in an armchair out of sight of the screen, though Del could see her in his side vision. Within moments, the hotel's system connected him to the Sunrise Palace. He gave it Dehya's private channel and waited. The screen shimmered gold, cleared—

And it wasn't his aunt.

It was Kelric.

Damn! His square-jawed brother stared out of the screen, impossible to avoid. Grey streaked his hair and lines showed at the corners of his eyes. He wore a tan pullover with no marks, nothing except the symbol on his right breast of an exploding star within a circle, the insignia of Imperial Space Command.

The Imperator's symbol.

"Why are you on Dehya's comm?" Del asked in Iotic, flustered.

Kelric answered dryly. "I'm glad to see you, too."

Del was painfully aware of Ricki listening. "Do you have a translation program for Earth languages?"

"Why?" Kelric asked. "What's wrong with Iotic?"

"I want to speak English."

Exasperation flickered on Kelric's face. "Look, Del, I don't have time for this. We need to talk. In a language I know."

"All right." Del flicked some holicons above his screen. "I'll do the translator." The console even had an option for directing the translation to Ricki's chair, where it would give her the words without interfering with Del's conversation. Not that he would have minded interference. A lot of it.

Kelric glanced down, probably at displays on his console. "You have someone there. A woman. About thirty-nine."

An irritated breath came from Ricki. Del hadn't realized she was that much older than him. He had no intention of telling Kelric, though. He gave his brother a satisfied smile. "She's an angel." In his side vision, he saw Ricki smile.

"No doubt," Kelric said, managing to sound unimpressed with just two words. "It's you I want to talk to."

Del had no desire to talk to him. "I commed Dehya."

"She's not here. She's on the Orbiter."

"Why are you on her line?"

Kelric crossed his arms, and muscles bulged under his sleeves. "I saw that the incoming message was from you. So I answered."

"Well, I won't take any more of your time—"

"Oh no you don't. You aren't slinking out."

Del bristled. "I don't *slink* anywhere."

Kelric scowled at him. "Of course not. You immediately told us about this rock thing of yours."

"It's not a 'thing.' It's a profession. And I don't report to you. I'm not one of your lackeys."

Irritation crackled in Kelric's voice. "Letting us know what you were doing would have been, at the very least, a courtesy. Or doesn't your family rate even that? And leaving yourself open to risk was irresponsible and immature."

Great, really great. Just what he needed, for Ricki to hear his brother lecture him. "Don't talk to me like I'm some stupid kid. I cleaned your butt when you were a baby. You've no call to treat me like a child."

Kelric uncrossed his arms and planted them on the console while he leaned forward. "Then don't act like one."

"I'm not!" Damn it, why did he have to get Kelric? He wanted to cut the connection, but if he angered his brother, Kelric might order Del's bodyguards to bring him home. Cameron had ridden up in the shuttle with the luggage crew and was staying in the staff quarters here. Tyra had come up as a business exec and checked into another suite Del had rented. She was monitoring him via implants ISC had put in his body years ago.

"I've been looking into this career of yours," Kelric said. "The more I learn, the less I like."

"Yeah, well, I'm not enamored of yours, either. So what?"

"These people are using you," Kelric said flatly. "Prime-Nova will make millions off you, and when you're no longer useful—when you burn yourself out on exhausting schedules, drugs, sex, and gods only know what else—they'll throw you away."

Del felt cold, then hot. One of Prime-Nova's biggest movers was hearing every word of this. But when he lifted his hand to cut off the translator, Ricki spoke in a low voice. "Leave it on."

"Was that your girlfriend?" Kelric asked.

"It's not your business," Del said. "I have to go."

"Damn it, Del, quit avoiding us. Keep it up, and I'm bringing you home."

"You can't!" Del clenched the console. "The Harrison Protocol says that as long as the Allieds allow me to live here, I have the same rights as any Allied citizen. You can't do a damn thing. It's illegal to force me to leave when I don't want to."

Kelric regarded him implacably. "Who's going to stop me?"

"This isn't Skolia," Del shot back. "Maybe you can do whatever you want there, Mister Imperator, but you can't on Earth."

A strangled sound came from Ricki. Del knew he should stop, but he didn't know how to untangle himself from the argument.

"So you're going to start an interstellar incident over it?" Kelric banged his console with his fist. "Just *once* can't you think about someone besides yourself?"

"I *always* think of everyone else." Del's voice cracked. "I stayed home while you were all off making war. I took care of everything when Father was hurt, ran our holdings, looked after the farm, and headed the family on Lyshriol. I was hardly more than twenty! When he got better, I just wanted a vacation. Just a few days. Well, I got it. Forty-five *years* of one."

"Del—" Kelric let out a breath. "It was terrible, yes. But you chose to take those drugs."

"Yeah, I kicked the taus. I made a stupid, stupid mistake. And you're all going to make me pay for it the rest of my life, aren't you?" Del's fists clenched on the console. "Because, of course, you never make those kinds of mistakes. Or maybe it's just that I got hit, and you never do."

Anger snapped in Kelric's voice. "I would never do the things you do."

"For flaming sake," Del said. "What have I done that's so terrible? Loved my kids. Harvested crops. And sung those stupid—" He struggled to stay calm. "I don't want to be the Dalvador Bard. You think I'm irresponsible? Why don't *you* go home and be the frigging King of Skyfall?"

A sharply indrawn breath came from Ricki. Del wanted to fold into a dot and disappear. The magical night had turned sour.

Kelric started to answer, then stopped. In a quieter voice he said, "Why stay on Earth? If you don't like singing, why do it there?"

Del didn't understand how his brother could be an empath and understand so little about how Del felt. "I didn't say I didn't want to sing. I like what I'm doing here. Gods, Kelric, I love it. And other people do, too. Everyone wants more and more."

"Until they use you up," Kelric said.

"Can't you *try* to understand?"

"We don't have that luxury." Beneath the rumble of Kelric's voice, he sounded as if he were struggling, too. "I wanted to be a mathematician. But I couldn't. I have duties, whether I want them or not. We had no choice about our birth, but we choose how we live our lives. Turn your back on us, and you're turning your back on your people. Is that what you want? To put your life ahead of the Imperialate?"

"How can you say that?" Del asked. "What more do I have to

give up to satisfy you all? My soul?" He thought of Chaniece and the family life he could never have. "Hell, my DNA is all that matters. We both know I have nothing else to offer. Except my singing. That isn't useless or trivial. You want to take away the one thing I'm good at. I'll never be a genius like you or Dehya. I *can't*. But I *can* do this."

"And if something happens?" His brother shook his head. "You aren't just Del Arden, Prime-Nova's latest sensation. What you do has interstellar ramifications regardless of whether or not you want to acknowledge that. What if you're hurt? The next time two insane fans grab you, you may not survive."

Del stared at him. "You know?"

"I have the best covert ops in three empires," Kelric said. "When I tell them to find details, they find everything."

Sweat broke out on Del's forehead. "I'm all right."

"This time." Kelric leaned forward. "If you *ever* duck your bodyguards again, I'm pulling you out."

"No." Del regarded him steadily. "I won't put myself or them at risk if I can help it. But you have to let go. Let me make my own decisions. And yes, if I make bad ones, I pay the price. But it's my responsibility, not yours. You have no right—legally or morally—to drag me away against my will."

Kelric met his gaze. "I don't give a damn about the Harrison Protocol. It wasn't written for someone in your position. You aren't just some citizen, Del. That you're a member of the Ruby Dynasty may mean nothing to you, but it does to everyone else. And don't argue morals with me. I have a moral imperative to make sure my brother doesn't get himself killed."

Del was gripping the console so hard, his knuckles turned white. "You aren't my keeper."

"If I say I am," Kelric told him, "I am. Period."

"You know what?" Del hurt too much to hold back. "You can go fuck yourself."

Kelric glanced at his console, undoubtedly checking the Iotic translation of a certain English word. Dryly he said, "I think that's anatomically impossible."

Del couldn't answer. He had to get off before he said more he would regret. Hotness filled his eyes, and he could never, *never* shed tears in front of Kelric. He would rather curl up and die. "You had your say. I listened. I have to go."

Kelric exhaled. "I don't want to leave it this way."

"What way?" Del asked. "Like this: 'Del, I'm going to control your entire life, but don't feel bad that I've ruined the only career you'll ever have.'"

"If I were going to control your life," Kelric said, "you wouldn't be on the Moon with your girlfriend. You would be here."

Del struggled to keep his voice even. "If you see Dehya, tell her I commed her. Good-bye."

After a moment, Kelric said, "All right. Good-bye."

Del cut the connection. Then he sat in front of the darkened screen, staring at nothing. How could the little boy he had carried around the house have become this massive, dominating stranger?

Ricki came over and stood next to him. She rested her hand on his shoulder. "I'm sorry."

He couldn't answer. A betraying tear escaped his eye and ran down his face. He wiped it away angrily. Ricki didn't push, she just let him be, her hand a gentle weight on his shoulder.

After a while, he said, "I used to dream they would accept me. I thought if I could show them, really show them, that I could succeed, it would matter." Del stood up and walked away from the console, moving slowly in the surreal gravity, across to the dais and up its steps to the bed. Then he faced her. "But it's useless. They'll never take me as I am."

She spoke softly. "It would never have occurred to me that a man from so powerful a family couldn't live his life as he chose."

"It's not that simple." Del felt the questions roiling within her. "Go ahead. Ask."

"That man—he was Kelric Skolia?"

"Yes."

"The Imperator."

"Yeah. The Imperator."

"My God," Ricki whispered.

He folded his arms across his torso, though he didn't know if the action was defiant or protective. "Kelric was born when I was a teenager. I used to baby-sit him."

"Del, that man is much older than you."

"I know."

He told her then about the cryogenesis, everything except about Chaniece and his children. When he finished, Ricki gave him a shaky smile. "All this time, I thought you were so young for me. Now it turns out you're almost twice my age."

He laughed unevenly. Then he held out his hand. "Do you still want me, after hearing what an irresponsible screw-up I am?"

Ricki came up on the dais and took his hand. "I don't see any irresponsible screw-ups in this room."

Del pulled her into his arms and held her close, laying his head on hers. A tear squeezed out under his eyelashes. His hands wandered down her back, each caress a healing balm.

He pulled her onto the bed, and they lay together. She was gentler tonight, helping him slide off her clothes and his own. He entered her with a sense of homecoming, but it wasn't real, because even his home was an illusion he could only see but never own. His legs moved against the soft skin of her inner thighs, her stomach firm beneath his, her breasts full in his hands as he thrust inside of her, slow and strong. He rose on the crest of their desire, the intensity of his pleasure drowning his emotions, yet no matter how high it took him, it wasn't enough. He loved her in the Moon's soft gravity, as if that reaffirming act of life could banish a pain within him that never disappeared.

XX

Rising Diamond

Zachary stalked into Ricki's office while she was working on a new virt for the Conquistadors. She looked up with a start.

"Zach," she said. "How's it going?"

"It's been better." He dropped into a console chair near her desk and brought up the holos she was viewing. "This is crap."

"Thanks," she said crossly. "You do good work, too." Unfortunately, he was right. She couldn't concentrate. She had Del on the mind. A Ruby prince? She didn't know whether to be thrilled or run the other way. Their interlude on the Moon two days ago had been a dream, both ethereally beautiful and heartbreaking. Del hadn't wanted to talk about what she had overheard, but she would never forget. Listening to his monumentally overwhelming brother dismiss the central passion of Del's life as if it were nothing had been one of the most painful moments of her career. Hearing the love behind his brother's words only made it worse.

The more Ricki saw Del create, the more she heard of his inspiration, the more she knew she was seeing the genuine article. As a child, she had loved music, the one joy she had shared with her father. Nothing she had ever done had seemed good enough for him, but he liked to hear her sing. And then he left anyway. She had never seen music the same after that, and over the years she had become so jaded, she no longer believed true artists existed.

313

Del proved her wrong. She couldn't love him, she didn't dare risk it, but it was happening and she didn't know how to make it stop. She had no desire to be a notch in his belt. It was too complicated to unravel. He always held back, even when he had loved her with such passion on the Moon.

"Ricki?" Zachary asked.

"Sorry." She mentally shook herself. "I've been cranking this virt all day and it's zeroware."

Zachary scowled at her. "Do you think you could talk in English for once? I have no idea what the fuck you just said."

"What, you like profanity better?" She let out a breath and spoke more calmly. "Zeroware. Like old-fashioned software. Or meshware. Except it's nothing ware. The band and I spent three hours looking for images, and none of us are happy with the results."

Zachary flicked through the holos of bullfighters swirling their capes into starry fields of nebulae. "These aren't bad."

"I was thinking a Spanish theme. The Conquistadors are hot right now."

He kept bringing up images, but Ricki didn't think he was really looking at them. Finally she said, "What's up?"

He swiveled the chair to face her. "Do you remember the Eubian act that Acquisitions wants to sign to our Classics label?"

"Eubian?"

"Traders."

"Oh. Yeah, vaguely," Ricki said. "Wasn't there some problem with who would sign the contract?"

Zachary shifted his weight. "The musicians don't have the authority to do it. An Aristo lord has to sign."

"All sorts of acts do that. For a while, I thought Del was going to delegate everything to Mac Tyler." Del had turned out to be a lot savvier than any of them expected.

"This isn't the same." Zachary regarded her uneasily. "The musicians *can't* sign. They can't do anything without this guy's permission. Because he owns them."

Ricki snorted. "A lot of managers think they own the act. And yeah, it can get ugly. But they have to work that out themselves."

"I don't think you understand. He owns them. Literally."

Ricki laughed. "You make it sound like they're his slaves."

Zachary didn't smile. "They are."

"That can't be." She wondered what was up. "They're an accomplished act. Phenomenal, that guy in Acquisitions said."

"They are," Zachary said. "Except for this one 'little' thing. I just finished going over the changes the reps from Tarex want in the contract."

"Tarex? What is that?"

"Tarex Interstellar. It's a Eubian entertainment conglomerate. Axil Tarex, the chief executive officer, owns the musicians." He pushed his hand across his silvered hair. "The alterations in the contract specify that Tarex has to sign all agreements, receive all income, and make all decisions regarding the act."

"Sure, it's rigid," Ricki said. "But it isn't unheard of."

Zachary shook his head. "I've never seen language like this. It refers to the musicians as products."

"We've been accused of the same," Ricki said dryly.

"I mean, *literally*." He stared at her. "That contract says Axil Tarex owns them. Legally owns. Slaves, Ricki."

She didn't want to hear this. It made her too uncomfortable. "But that's just a nomenclature thing, right? Traders don't really own people. Not the way we think of it. It's a label."

"I don't think so." Zachary shifted his weight. "I talked to Staver Aunchild. He's livid. He used words far less polite than 'label.'"

Ricki moved holofiles around on her desk. "He's Skolian. They're always upset with the Traders. They just had a war."

"I know. But he's gruesomely articulate when he's upset." He slapped the arm of his chair. "That group didn't *seem* misused when I met them. Just happy to sign with an Allied label."

"So how would our refusing to sign them achieve anything? If we sign them, they'll reach a new market. That should please Tarex, which would be good for them." A thought came to her. "If they're unhappy, they could defect to Earth after a concert or something."

His voice tightened. "Are you suggesting we encourage them to an action that's a political and legal bombshell? You do realize you could be arrested for that."

"Arrested by who?" Ricki demanded. "Axil Tarex has no sway on Earth."

"He's a powerful man," Zachary said. "On a scale far beyond anything we deal with."

Ricki thought of Del. *If only you knew.* But she saw his point. "Of course I would never encourage a Eubian citizen to defect."

"Make sure of it." He leaned forward. "Because if we sign the act, we have to deal with this Aristo."

"I don't know anything about Aristos." The only person in that stratum of power she had dealt with was Del, who probably had as much in common with this conglomerate king as a harp had with the cry of a banshee.

"Tarex is coming to Earth," Zachary said. "I want you to meet him. Tell me what you think."

Well, hell's pails. She could imagine how Del would react. Maybe she should send him on another tour. *Fast.* "When will Tarex be here?"

"I'll let you know as soon as we do." He stood up, brushing nonexistent wrinkles out of his jumpsuit. "We'll do dinner with him. You can bring a guest. And yes, that means Del. I'm sure Tarex will be looking at our other acts."

Ricki couldn't envision a bigger disaster. "Looking for what? To *buy?*"

"To sign. And no, they don't expect to own an Allied act. Just rights to sell the work, same as with the Skolians." He lifted his hands as if to say, *What can I do?* "It's a lucrative market, Ricki, bigger than the Allied and Skolian combined."

She didn't want to imagine the furor if Tarex tried to sign a Ruby Heir. What a nightmare. Realizing how odd her horrified reaction would seem to Zachary, she forced out a smile. "Yeah. Okay. Thanks."

After Zachary left, Ricki went to the mahogany bar in her office and poured herself a glass of good, strong whiskey.

By the time Del submerged into the virt session, his mind was twisted into knots. He had spent four days without the bliss. He couldn't think straight, couldn't concentrate, couldn't eat. He had trouble rehearsing. Headaches and disorientation plagued him, and he felt as if he were balanced on the edge of a convulsion.

The session took him to Lyshriol—his version, the home he created out of his longings. Except he had no home. His family would never accept him. They condemned him for not letting them know about his life, but why would he? They would just tell him that he would fail. Or die. Or screw up. Because of course he was inconsiderate, immature, and irresponsible. Nothing he did would ever be good enough unless he became exactly like them.

Even if he hadn't hated the idea, he didn't have the intelligence to be what they wanted. He *couldn't* do it.

Del had figured out how to program the node, though. He had to focus on what he wanted, directing the thought rather than letting his mind relax. He also had tags, like thinking "walrus" to alert the node he wanted to alter its code.

Today he deleted his family.

He took out his mother, who had told him here in his foolish fantasy that she appreciated his music. He took out Kelric and Dehya and Windar and his other siblings. He even took out Chaniece and the boys, because it hurt too much knowing he could never be a true father, for he could never join his life with their mother the way a man should with the woman who bore his children. When he finished erasing them all, he lay in the rippling plain beneath the soft sky and cried.

"It's a relic," Cameron said.

Tyra considered his comment. "More like a museum," she decided.

"Naw," Jud said. "A mausoleum."

Del ignored them. To him, the bookstore was exquisite. In the three months since he had taken Ricki to the Moon, he had looked everywhere for a real store like this. It evoked a simpler life, a time when people wrote songs with pencils, before the world became too complex to hold on a piece of ordinary paper. Everywhere he turned on Earth, people streamed their lives to consoles, picked it out of the airwaves, or lived in a virt. Only a few antique stores existed that sold that rare commodity, a book with printed pages. Permanent printing. No holos, changing fonts, living ink, hypertext, supertext, ultratext, or pretext.

Del loved the Almond Bar Book Shoppe in Baltimore. He loved holding the tomes with leather covers and gilt-edged pages. He listened to the AI guide on each shelf describe the texts and then picked out four: *War and Peace* by Leo Tolstoy, because it was huge and sounded like it applied to almost everything in human existence; *Plato's Republic*, because the sample the guide read impressed him; *The Rake* by Mary Jo Putney, because it was about a misbehaved playboy who straightened out his life and found love; and *Twenty Thousand Leagues Under the Sea* by Jules Verne, because it sounded fun. Jud wandered down another aisle, and Tyra and Cameron walked with Del, surveying the store and pretending they weren't bodyguards.

"I've never seen so many of these things," Cameron said, scanning the crammed shelves.

Jud rejoined them. "They cost too much. You pay all that money for something so crude, you can't even change the font."

"They're antiques," Del said. "Historical. Claude reads to me all the time from old texts. I like Shakespeare."

Tyra regarded him curiously. "I wouldn't have guessed you had such a scholarly bent."

"I don't." Del gave a dry laugh. "You can't be illiterate and a scholar at the same time."

"You aren't illiterate," Tyra said. "You're—I don't know what. You input information differently than most people. You process it differently, too."

Process it differently. What a euphemism. Del smiled. "You're a diplomat."

Tyra snorted. "I have the diplomatic skills of a fungus."

"Del, you have a good brain," Cameron said.

"Annoying sometimes," Jud said. "But smart, yeah."

"Huh." This was an odd development. It mattered a lot to him that the three people who spent the most time with him didn't consider him stupid.

Del went to a kiosk and gave his codes to its AI. While he waited for it to process his purchases, his wrist comm buzzed. He jerked, startled. He would never become used to wearing a mesh. On Lyshriol, he had mostly ignored the tech, but it was unavoidable if he wanted to function here.

He touched the receive panel. "Hello?"

"Del!" A familiar voice came out of the mesh. "Staver here. How are you?"

"Fine." Del glanced up as Tyra stepped closer.

"Zachary Marksman told me that you're working on a new vid," Staver said. "I was wondering if you would like to have lunch today and talk about it."

Del knew he should comm Mac to join them if they were going to discuss business. But he was starting to chafe at Mac's father thing. Del had enough authority figures in his life.

"All right," he said. "It'll be four of us, though. I'm with some friends."

"That's fine," Staver said. "Bring them along. Let's meet at the Sheraton in Columbia. They've an excellent restaurant on the lake there. It's quiet and beautiful."

Del glanced at Jud, who mouthed *Sure*. Tyra and Cameron, standing a few paces back, both nodded.

"I'll see you there," Del told Staver.

As Del left the bookstore, he ran into a group of people strolling down the street. They were chatting among themselves, but they stopped when they saw him.

"Hey," one of the younger men said. "You're Del Arden."

A woman smiled at him. "Hi!" She hesitated, then held up a holo-map she had been holding. "Could I—would you mind if I asked for an autograph?"

"Sure," Del said. "I mean no, I don't mind."

They crowded around him, about ten people. One of the women touched his hair. "I love all these curls."

"Hey." Del smiled uncomfortably as he pulled away his hair. He felt Cameron's hand under his elbow, drawing him back.

"You're the morpher, aren't you?" a woman asked Jud.

"Are you doing a concert here?" someone else asked. "I didn't see any advertised."

Del backed into the antique brick wall of the store with Jud, the two of them flanked by Cameron and Tyra. He felt trapped.

A youth offered Del a napkin. "Would you mind signing this? I really enjoy your music. No one will believe we saw you."

"Yeah, sure." Del didn't know what else to say. *Go away* would hardly sit well with anyone. He took the boy's napkin and the woman's holomap.

"Here." Someone offered him a pen, and he scribbled his name on the napkin, then traced his signature over a panel on the map, leaving a squiggle of light.

"What's going on?" someone asked behind the group.

Del strained to look over the heads of the people. Another couple had come over to see what had drawn the crowd. More people were coming out of a shop across the street.

"All right," Tyra said. "Enough." Although she didn't speak loudly, her voice carried.

"Who are you?" someone asked her. He sounded annoyed. Someone else asked, "Did they answer about the concert?"

Del was getting claustrophobic. Someone touched his arm and another person brushed his elbow. Tyra drew him to the side, but people blocked their way. There were too many, too close. Cameron grasped a man's arm and carefully pulled him aside.

"Hey!" The man jerked away from Cameron. "Back off, bud." The fellow did try to give Del more room, but someone back in the crowd pushed forward, making it impossible. Cameron stepped in front of Del.

"Don't hurt them," Del said under his breath.

"Who's that?" someone yelled from the back.

Someone else said, "Del Arden. He's signing autographs."

"Let him by." Tyra's voice snapped out with an authority Del had never heard her use before. A startled murmur came from the crowd as people moved aside.

Together, Tyra and Cameron escorted Del and Jud through the group. Del was having trouble breathing, and he inhaled deeply, trying to calm down. They were just fans. Nothing threatening. He should be glad they liked him.

Del wasn't sure who pushed who, but several people stumbled into him. He staggered and lost his balance. As he fell, Cameron grabbed him. More people surged forward, pushing so he couldn't regain his footing even with Cameron's support. As he slipped to his knees, the crowd pressed in.

Tyra reacted with surreal speed, her motion blurring while she moved people aside and pulled Del to his feet. As murmurs went through the crowd, she and Cameron pushed forward, protecting Del and Jud. Whenever they had to move someone out of the way, they restrained their force with a gentleness Del hadn't expected in his military-trained bodyguards.

Then they were free and striding down the street, the guards flanking Del, each holding one of his arms, with Jud striding next to Cameron. Del had to run to keep their pace. He didn't look back, but he heard people following them.

They sped around the corner and waved down a hover-taxi. As they piled into the car, several women from the crowd knocked on the window and called out his name. Del blanched, but he waved back, because Harv had told him never to piss anyone off.

"Get us out of this crowd," Tyra told the taxi. "Fast."

"I can't do harm to anyone," the vehicle said.

"Just take us away from here," Tyra said. "We're going to the Sheraton Hotel in Columbia."

It wasn't until they had left the crowd behind that Del sank gratefully back into the worn seat. "That was weird."

Cameron surveyed the street. "It can't happen again."

Del knew what they were going to say. "Cam, I can't—"

"He's right," Tyra interrupted.

"I *won't* be a prisoner in my own apartment," Del said.

He expected Tyra to say he had no choice. Instead she said, "Then get your own transportation."

"I can't afford a car."

"Of course you can," Tyra said.

"It has to be on my earnings," Del said. The only exceptions he had made were the bliss-node and taking Ricki to the Moon.

"We should be getting our royalty statements soon," Jud said. "Ask Mac about it."

"All right." Del took a calming breath. Sometimes he could walk down the street and no one noticed him. But he didn't want a repeat of what had just happened. Probably no one would have hurt him or Jud, but it had felt too much on the edge of violence. "I don't get why people want to touch us so much."

Jud snorted. "It isn't me they want, Dello boy. When I'm not with you, I can go in public without worrying."

Del could tell he meant it; Jud preferred privacy to fame. Del exhaled. "I suppose it's better this way than if they forget me."

"Believe me," Tyra said. "You aren't forgettable."

Del hadn't expected that. His ISC bodyguards usually hadn't much liked him. Tyra said nothing more, just focused on her gauntlet as she monitored the area. Curious, Del eased down his barriers. He felt Cameron first; the Marine was tense but relieved they had done their job and avoided trouble. A sense of Anne underlay his mood, nothing specific, just that unre-quited desire. Jud was thinking about music, an upbeat tune he was writing.

Tyra had a sharper edge. She perceived more danger than Del thought existed. He also caught traces of emotions she thought she had hidden. She saw why women found Del sexually attractive, and that response bothered her, because she hadn't expected to notice him that way. She considered it unprofessional.

Del smiled and raised his shields. He didn't mind Tyra noticing him, but his celebrity was no longer so flattering. What if he scarred his face, wore ugly clothes, or gained weight? He would still sing the same. As much as he wanted to believe only his artistry mattered, he knew that if he lost whatever it was about him that attracted people, his popularity would decline. He didn't know which bothered him more: that millions of people had virts of him they could program as they pleased, doing gods only knew what, or that he would lose his career if they stopped.

"It's funny," Del said. "Sometimes when you get what you want, it isn't what you thought."

"At least you got it," Cameron said.

Del had a good idea what had put his bodyguard in a bad mood. "Ask her on a date, Cam."

"I have no idea what you're talking about," Cameron said.

"I know," Del told him. "But I still think you should ask her out. I'll bet she would go. She likes you."

Cameron glared at him. "You're talking nonsense."

"Well, I don't know for certain," Del admitted. "But her mood always improves when you're around."

"Her?" Tyra asked with curiosity.

Cameron sat back and crossed his arms. "It's nothing."

"How can you not know?" Jud asked Del. "You're an empath."

"Yeah, but I only get surface moods," Del said.

Cameron was watching him intently. "Could you get more?"

"Not really," Del said. "Even if I could break someone's mental protections, it's wrong. I wouldn't do that any more than I'd commit theft or assault."

Jud spoke dryly. "You're more courteous about privacy than people I know with the empathic abilities of a rock."

"Most people feel empathy to some extent," Tyra said.

"You ever hear that saying, 'Walk a mile in my shoes'?" Cameron asked. "It means 'Show some fucking empathy, already.'"

Del smiled. "Maybe." His good humor faded. "I'd go crazy if I couldn't shield myself from it."

"That why you're such an introvert?" Cameron asked.

Del blinked. "You think I'm an introvert?"

"Sure," Jud said. "Look how you always stay home. Even on tour, you hardly go out." Wryly he added, "Of course, Randall more than makes up for you in the partying department."

"I suppose." Del knew the empathy made it hard for him to be in crowds. He could probably walk a thousand miles in someone's shoes. He often wondered if it was more of a curse than a gift.

"The new vid should be done in a few months," Del said.

Staver nodded, relaxed in his chair. The four of them were sitting at a table by a wall of windows that looked onto a lake. The décor was elegant, but in a subdued way, with only a few hotel patrons at other tables. Aesthetic silvery-blue robots delivered their orders with impeccable courtesy.

"'Emeralds' is doing better on the major Skolian charts," Staver said. "'Sapphire Clouds' is more popular in smaller markets."

Del noticed he didn't mention "Diamond Star," which was higher than either "Emeralds" or "Sapphire Clouds," and on the Skolian Stellar Hundred. Since Mac wasn't here, Del didn't intend to agree to anything. But he had learned a bit about negotiating. "*The Jewels Suite* is number six on Earth's anthology charts."

"Six," Staver mused. "Not the top five."

"Yet," Del said. The anthology's slow but constant climb seemed to bemuse industry insiders. His work hadn't hit with a bang, but it had an unusual staying power. A band could do a virtual concert in one hundred cities on the same night, flooding the market, and the next day be replaced by a different virtual act in every city. When so much music was so available with so little effort, songs became ephemeral, easily forgotten. Del's music stood out, he didn't know why, but he needed to believe it had to do with quality, that it wasn't as worthless as the buried thought within him insisted.

He grinned at Staver. "It'll bust out to number one."

Staver gave a slight nod, his true reaction impossible to read. He was obviously interested, or he wouldn't have asked Del to lunch, but he wasn't committing to anything, either.

"This steak is good," Cameron said, oblivious to the undercurrents at the table. He had practically inhaled the biggest cut on the menu.

Tyra was picking at some fish-rice thing, and Staver had a stew from an offworld recipe. Del had ordered one of his favorites, a spiced curry with a freaky side dish called "yogurt." He could eat a vat of both, all mixed together, hot and cool, chewy and smooth. Although life on Earth could be a real pain, people here really knew how to eat. Everything on Lyshriol was bubbles: big, little, sweet, sour, leathery, smooth, but all bubbles. It got really boring.

Staver seemed distracted. He watched Del intently, and with a start, Del realized Staver was "knocking" at his mind.

Del partially lowered his shields, narrowing his focus so he wouldn't also send his thought to Tyra. She was a powerful psion, at least one in a million, six on the Kyle scale, maybe a seven. She wasn't as powerful as Staver, but then, almost no one alive had a rating that high.

Yes? Del thought to Staver.

Staver stiffened as if he had been hit by a hammer. His thought came through, faint but clear. *Can you modulate that?* His response had a directional quality focused on Del, which meant Tyra probably wouldn't get any of this.

Del lowered his strength to the equivalent of a telepathic whisper. **Is that better?**

Staver's shoulders relaxed. *Yes, much.*

What didn't you want my friends to hear? Del asked.

You spoke to me once about offering help, Staver thought. *For those who live the nightmare of a provider's life.*

Del thought of how Raker and Delilah had reminded him of Staver and Lydia. He responded warily. **I would need evidence my help would be used as expected.**

And if that evidence was available?

If I were convinced, then yes, I would help.

Thank you. Staver's thought came with depth. This was no mask; what Staver felt went far down within him. Even those skilled at presenting themselves in a falsely positive light couldn't keep that façade in a telepathic link. What Del felt from Staver was genuine, a strength of character that, given Del's suspicions, he hadn't expected. The only "act" Staver put on was the subtly glitzy exterior he adopted as an entertainment exec; the real Staver was a quieter man with an abiding sense of spirituality.

Del carefully raised his shields. Such mental contact was only possible between strong psions, and it was a strain for more than a few moments. He glanced at Tyra, who was pushing her food around her plate. She smiled at him, but he caught no indication she had picked up anything.

Del sipped his java, which tasted like a rich coffee, but was apparently named after some antique mesh language no one except historians knew anymore. As he drank, he lowered his shields again, this time focused on his bodyguard. **Tyra?**

She blinked, her fork halfway to her mouth. But she continued to eat as if nothing happened. Cameron and Staver were talking about the hotel, a historical landmark from the twentieth century.

Tyra's voice came into Del's mind, well trained and clear. *Del, is that you?* she asked in Iotic.

Yes. It's me. Did you know Staver Aunchild is a psion?

Your brother has a file on him. It lists Aunchild's rating as eight point four.

So Staver had told the truth. **He may be part of an organization that frees providers. They route the people they help through Earth because the Allieds have less barriers to travel with the Traders than we do.**

Tyra raised an eyebrow. *That wasn't in his file.*

Interesting. Either Staver's people had remarkable secrecy, hiding even from Kelric's relentless operatives, or else Staver had lied about his activities.

It doesn't mean ISC doesn't know, Tyra thought. Her response had a strained quality. *They could even be helping him. That wouldn't be in his regular file.*

Can you check for me? I was thinking of backing them.

I'll look into it. She swallowed a spoonful of soup. *Del, I have to break this mental link.* Wryly she added, *Otherwise, you'll burn out my brain.*

Sorry! Yes, of course.

They spent the rest of the meal with small talk. But as they were leaving the hotel, strolling past a waterfall of laser-light, Staver sent Del one last thought.

I'll be in touch.

"It's broad daylight," Del said with frustration. "The Baltimore waterfront is perfectly safe."

Cameron stood like a bulwark, blocking the door out of Del's apartment, and Tyra was by the wall, deceptively casual, but right next to the security screen. Which meant Del could neither open the door nor tell it to open itself.

"I'm going crazy," Del said. "I need to get *out*."

"I'm sorry," Tyra said. She even looked as if she meant it. "Some festival is down there today. The place is full of tourists. But we could go somewhere else."

"Where?" Del asked grumpily. "You two nix everything."

"How about Life Million?" Cameron asked. "You'd love it."

"A *mesh* game?" Del couldn't believe Cameron had suggested it. "I want to talk to real people, not cartoons."

"It is real people." Cameron actually smiled. "In college, me and my friends used to hang out there when we couldn't get off campus."

"We used to do Life Million when I was at the Academy," Tyra told Cameron. "It was fun."

Well, that was great, his bodyguards were communing again. Good for them, they had so much in common. Del had never played the damn game. "Why call it Life Million?" he grumbled. "Why not Life Thousand? Hundred? Forty-two?"

"I think it was called Second Life when it started," Cameron said. "You know. You have your real life, and you have your mesh life. Except instead of mesh, they said Internet or some weird thing back then."

"Come on," Tyra coaxed Del. "Try it."

Right. His first life was hard enough to deal with. He couldn't imagine what he'd do with a million of them. He smiled, thinking a million Dels would give General McLane heartburn at a level he couldn't even imagine.

He lifted his hands in surrender. "Okay. Let's go."

The Baltimore waterfront seemed astonishingly real. But a real *what,* Del didn't know, because this sure as blazes wasn't the Baltimore where he lived.

He stood with Cameron and Tyra in a plaza surrounded on three sides by boutiques and cafés. Water bordered the fourth side and lapped against the piers there with a soothing, hypnotic sound. The bricks that paved the plaza were also somehow water, green and blue, with seaweed waving below the surface. Except it wasn't wet. Del's feet went in up to his ankles, and things swam lazily by his toes. A neon-bright fish sailed out of a brick, into the air, circled his knees, and dove back into the ground.

Del tried not to gape. Neither Tyra nor Cameron seemed fazed, and he didn't want to look like a rube, but honestly, who had thought up this place? Some of the shops glistened as if they were painted with sunlight. Strange, but pretty. He had a soundtrack, too; upbeat music played in the background, a fiddle and drums, just the way he liked. In fact, it fit his mood so well, he suspected the bliss-node was tailoring it to him.

The aroma of steak drifted past, delicious and inviting. Del wondered if he would feel full if he ate in a virtual café. Even more distracting than the smells were the *people.* They walked along, browsed shops, and flew in the air as if that were perfectly natural. A man strolled by Del wearing a translucent robe sewn from . . . starlight? A cat-woman covered with yellow fur ambled past, her ears cocked forward and her tail whipping back and forth across her shapely behind.

"Hey," a man said behind him. "Another Del Arden."

Startled, Del swung around. A man with black hair and an impossibly perfect physique nodded to him.

"That's a good Arden avatar," the man said. "Looks authentic."

"You think so?" Del even asked it with a straight face. He had come into the sim looking exactly like himself.

The man studied him. "The hair's not quite right."

Del blinked. "It isn't?"

"I have an Arden avatar, too. That's why I noticed yours. Here, I'll show you." The fellow blithely morphed into . . . Del. Except he was bigger, and his hair had more gold. Del had been inside so much lately, his hair was losing its sun streaks.

"Uh, yeah," Del said. "I see what you mean."

"You can get great two-tone work from Sean Cinquetti and Carolhyn Wijaya Shops Unlimited." The man blurred into his previous form as easily as if he were donning new clothes. "They're top-notch."

"Sure. Thanks." Del considered the man, who was half a head taller than him and a great deal more muscular. "I didn't think Del Arden was that big, though."

"Yeah, I know. I prefer this build." The man nodded. "Nice to meet you."

"See you." Del lifted his hand in farewell, and the guy went off.

"That was surreal," Tyra said, laughing.

"What?" Del asked. "You like the new, improved me better?"

"I prefer the original," she assured him.

"It's flattering," Del said. "Strange, though, that people want to look like me." He wondered what they did with their Del avatars, then decided he was better off not knowing. He motioned at the scene around them. "And all this. I like it, but it's odd. It's almost as if it was tailored for me."

"The basic sim is the same for everyone," Cameron said. "But if you have a good VR setup, its AI will mold what you experience to your personal tastes."

"I'd wondered," Del said. "What music do you hear?"

"Just the public feed," Cameron said. "Some Jupiter Heavy Hop thing."

"Is that what it's called?" Tyra asked. "I had no idea."

"I'm getting—" Del cut off as a holo formed in front of him showing city towers rising from an idyllic lagoon.

A female voice said, "Welcome to Life Million, Mister Arden. Extropia would like to extend you this invitation to join our community."

Del stopped, bewildered. He looked around to see if anyone else had cities floating in front of them. All the exceedingly beautiful people, animals, and cyborgs continued on their business as if nothing had happened. One man walked through Del's holo, then realized what he had done and apologized. No one else paid attention to the floating invitation, though one person did smile at Del, a female android with a dazzling figure, purple skin, and a blue harem outfit.

Del watched the android walk away until she went behind a building. Wow. Then he mentally shook himself and turned to his bodyguards. "Do you guys see that, too?"

Cameron grinned at him. "What, the hot android?"

Del flushed. "No. *This.*" He waved his hand through the holo invitation.

"Sure, we see it," Tyra said. "It must have been queued to activate if you came into Life Million."

"You rate high with someone," Tyra said. "Everyone wants to live in Extropia. It's so much in demand, it's impossible to buy land there now. It doesn't matter how famous or rich you are."

Del gaped at them. "You buy *virtual* land?"

"Sure." Cameron indicated the thriving harbor scene around them. "Baltimore has eleven harbor sims you can join."

"Oh." Del tried to get his mind around the idea of digital people living in digital land. "How does Extropia know about me?"

"I'll see what I can find." Cameron's gaze took on an inward quality. After a moment, he refocused on Del. "Their records are confidential. But if you accept their invitation, you'll be a member. Then you can ask whatever you want."

Del was going into overload. He rarely interacted with real people in his sims. He didn't feel ready for more, at least not until he knew more about who had offered the invitation.

"Let's just walk for now," he said.

Neither Tyra nor Cameron looked surprised. When he asked the display to store itself for later, it disappeared from view.

Del strolled with Cameron and Tyra along a path by the water. They were in a historical area, with ships and an old submarine in the dock. When Del focused on one vessel, a small holo of it appeared to his left and offered to transport him there. He was about to ask the holo to go away when he heard someone singing to herself.

"Hey." Del stopped. "That's 'Diamond Star.'" The girl was on a bench several yards away, reading a virtual paper that changed its view every few minutes.

"It's on the public stream," Cameron said.

Del focused on his bliss-node. *Public feed*, he thought. The acoustic music faded away, replaced by "Diamond Star."

"That's one of my favorites," Tyra said.

"You *like* my music?" Del asked, astounded.

"Sure." She smiled at him. "Shouldn't I?"

"No other military officers I know do."

"Maybe they just didn't tell you," Cameron said. "A lot of guys at the Annapolis base listen to it."

"I'm an empath, remember?" Del couldn't pretend the reaction from his previous bodyguards hadn't bothered him. "I could tell they wanted me to be quiet."

"Were you practicing," Tyra asked, "or doing the full song?"

"Just practicing. But it was the same music."

"It's different when you practice," Cameron said. "It drives me crazy, too. You experiment, change things, stop and start. You'll hit a part I like, and just when I get into it, you do something else. It can sound off-tune, too, if you're working on the melody."

"Huh." Del had never thought about it that way.

"It's the result of all that genius that matters," Tyra said.

Del gave a startled laugh. "I'm a hack!"

Tyra looked annoyed. "Cut the false modesty."

"It's not false modesty," Cameron told her. "He believes it."

"How can you think you're a hack?" Tyra asked Del. "Don't you listen to what people say about your work?"

Del had never forgotten his miserable first reviews. "Not much. I mean, even the good ones just call it pop. Only the undercity considers me a serious artist, and they're starting to say I've sold out." With a wince, he added, "You've never heard what Fred Pizwick has to say about me."

"Freddy is an idiot," Cameron told him.

Del couldn't help but smile. "You're a good bodyguard."

"Who is Fred Pizwick?" Tyra asked.

"I'll show you," Del said. "If I can find a public console."

The holo from the ship, which was still at Del's side, spoke up. "I can transport you to one."

Del squinted at the holo. At least it talked, so it didn't matter that he couldn't read. "Okay."

The world went dark. Just like that. Before he had a chance to wonder if he had agreed to something stupid, the scene re-formed, except now they were in a plaza on the other side of the Inner Harbor, across the water. A public console stood next to them.

"Wow." Del blinked at the console.

"Will it work?" Cameron asked.

Del bent over the console. "I think so." It looked normal—except for the fish swimming in its water-filled interior. It worked fine, though. He searched the mesh until he found some reviews of his work. He was about to bring up one of Pizwick's old pieces when he saw a new one. Damn! Pizwick had done him the "honor" of reviewing his anthology, a rare occurrence for a critic whose bailiwick was live shows.

Del hesitated with his finger above the holicon of a diamond. Pizwick probably hated the anthology. Then again, Del's first concerts had been disastrously raw, whereas *The Jewels Suite* was as polished as anything Prime-Nova could produce.

"Del?" Tyra watched him with that curious smile she gave only him, as if he were a fascinating enigma.

"I haven't heard this review," Del said. "This guy doesn't usually like my work."

"Maybe he's changed his mind," she said. "It's a great anthology."

"You think so?" Del asked.

He didn't know how he looked, but it made her laugh, not in

a way that hurt, but with a fondness he hadn't expected. "Yes," she said. "I think so."

Del grinned at her. Emboldened, he flicked the diamond.

The plaza vanished. Suddenly they were in plush chairs in a darkened auditorium. The stage had only one person, a handsome man with silvered hair sitting on a stool. A light shone on him from above, and the rest of the area was dark.

Del was getting seasick from all the zipping around. "That's not Pizwick," he grumbled. "He's nowhere near that good-looking."

Pizwick spoke with a deeper voice than he had in real life. "Hello, my friends. Welcome to Fred's Favored Review."

Friends, indeed. Del felt queasy, waiting for the ax.

"I don't usually cover prepacked material," Pizwick went on, his face sincere. "I prefer live concerts where you experience what the artist is really doing. But I made an exception in this case, given all the hum about Del Arden's debut. I figured with the entire mesh-tech services of Prime-Nova at his disposal, his anthology had to be an improvement over his live shows." Pizwick paused. "Unfortunately, I was wrong."

"We don't need this garbage," Cameron said. "Let's go."

"No." Del had a grisly fascination with Pizwick. "I want to know."

"In *The Jewels Suite*," Pizwick continued, "Arden still fails to hit the right notes. If you think a conglomerate can create talent where none exists, think again. Arden can't even properly rhyme his songs. He doesn't count the right number of syllables per line, and he depends too heavily on assonance. His music doesn't fit any accepted mode, either commercial or classical. This anthology is a mishmash of styles and who knows what else. My recommendation: don't bother."

Pizwick mercifully stopped then and went on to a Baltimore band. As much as his comments bothered Del, it didn't crush him like the reviews of his first concerts.

"He really doesn't get it," Del said. As he spoke, his bliss-node turned down Pizwick's voice. "Ricki once told me he was being malicious out of jealousy. I can't say; she knows him and I don't. But I think he just doesn't get what I do. It doesn't fit what he likes." Somehow that made it easier to take.

Cameron made a noise that sounded like "Hmmph."

"Cam is right," Tyra said.

Del smiled. "It's okay about the review." He realized why it bothered him less than Pizwick's previous slams. Before, Pizwick had ridiculed Del. This time, he said he didn't like the songs. Some people might consider it a minor difference, but to Del it mattered. "No one creates music *everyone* likes. Some people don't even like Debussy."

"Day who?" Tyra asked.

"Debussy." Del warmed to the subject. "He was an Impressionist composer, though he hated that term. His music is amazing."

"So quit acting surprised that we like what you do." Cameron gave Del an implacable stare. "We don't care if Freddy doesn't."

"That's telling him," Tyra said. She looked as if she were trying not to smile.

Del squinted at them, wondering how they had managed to turn around his doubts so that unless he agreed he had talent, he was offending their honor.

Tyra's look softened. "Ah, Del, you're such a poller-pi."

His face heated. "No, I'm not!"

"Poller-pi?" Cameron asked. "What is that?"

"It's a Skolian word," Tyra said. "For someone charming."

"It is not," Del said. "It's what adults call cute little kids." Just what he needed, for someone to hear her call Prime-Nova's snarling bad boy the Skolian equivalent of a "fuzzy bear." It was difficult to be annoyed, though, given the way she and Cameron were supporting his work.

"I still think you should join Extropia," Cameron said.

After Pizwick, Del could do with someone who wanted him around. "You think it's safe?"

"It's a protected community," Cameron said. "They have some of the strictest security around."

"Oh." Del considered the thought. "Okay. Let's go."

"We can't," Cameron said. "Only you were invited."

"But then I can't, either."

"Sure you can," Tyra said. "It's virtual. You aren't going anywhere. So we can still protect your royal behind."

Del smiled. "Only that part of my anatomy?"

"Oh, go," Cameron told him. "Get out of here." It wasn't very intimidating, though, given that he was laughing.

"But how do I—"

"I can take you, Mister Arden," a woman said. It was the voice that had given him the invitation.

"Oh," Del said. "Okay, you can—"

The scene darkened so abruptly, he caught his breath. Then he was standing on a lush swath of grass bordered by a white path.

"—take me to Extropia after I tell Tyra and Cam good-bye," Del added.

The scene wasn't what he expected. The hexagonal lawn floated like a giant lily pad on water that extended in every direction to the horizon. So much! Before coming to Earth, he had never seen anything bigger than a moderate lake. This endless "sea" was pristine and clear, and as still as a lagoon. A city spread around him, its graceful buildings either floating or rising out of the water in gleaming towers bright against the sky. The lapping of tiny waves soothed him, and a pleasing scent of flowers tickled his nose.

"This is gorgeous," Del said.

"Welcome," the female voice said. "What can I do for you?"

"Are you the person who gave me the invitation?"

"I'm a mesh code. But I can put you in touch with the resident who invited you."

"Sure—" He cut off as the world *whooshed*. Then he was on a balcony in one of the towers. A breeze ruffled his hair, and far below, the grass rippled in the wind.

Bemused, Del turned and found himself gazing into a bedroom. He started to enter, then paused, wondering if he was about to get himself into trouble again.

"Hello?" he said. "Is anyone here?"

The female voice spoke. "You can go in, Mister Arden."

"Noooo, I don't think so." Del stayed on the balcony. "This is somebody's private residence."

"I'm sure the owner won't mind."

"But I would."

"Hell's pails," a new voice said inside. "Del, is that you?"

"What the—?" Del strode into the bedroom. "*Ricki?*"

She was sitting at a blue table, relaxed in a chair that glowed with an inner light. A holofile lay on the table as if she had been reading. Now, though, she was gaping at him.

"Where did you come from?" she asked.

Del grinned at her. "Was it you who invited me here?"

"Well, yeah." She stood up. "I didn't think you'd ever show up, though. You never seemed interested in the m-universe."

He laughed with relief that it was her and not a virtiso. "You should have told me."

Her face relaxed as she came over to him. "It's my getaway. I don't tell anyone. You're the first person I've ever invited." She laid her palm against his chest. "I'm glad to see you."

Del drew her into his arms, and she felt just as good as in real life. "Yeah. Same."

Ricki slid her arms around his waist. Laughing softly, she said, "That was poetic. Where are all those romantic lyrics?"

"You're the poetry." Del down looked into her face. "Hey. Your eyes are purple."

"Blue is so ordinary."

"Not to me." He touched his eyelid. "I have violet eyes. Practically everyone where I come from does. Blue is exotic."

She closed her eyes, then opened them—to reveal a vivid blue color. "Then that's what they shall be."

Del felt his tensions melting. Gods, it was good to see her. "What else can you do here?"

Her look turned sultry. "Anything you want, babe."

A slow smile spread on his face. "Anything?"

Her lashes lowered. "Anything."

Del needed no more invitation. He bit at her ear and murmured, "I want to make love to you while we're flying. To sit with you on a crescent moon while I drive you mad because you want me so much." Crumpling her silk shirt, he pulled. Instead of loosening, it dissolved, leaving her torso bare. He cupped his hands around her breasts, then bent his head and kissed her. When he tugged her skirt, it dissolved as well, leaving her standing in his arms with nothing on but white stilettos with gold metal heels.

"I want to go above the sky," he murmured.

"I know a place." She kissed his cheek. "It's mine, just mine, made by me."

He brushed his lips over hers. "Let's go."

The walls faded, leaving them in a dark blue sky, much higher above the ground than before. The city was gone; nothing showed but blue water. The sky darkened until they floated in a tapestry of stars, far more than were visible from Earth, a wonderland of gems set in the black sable of space.

Ricki hung onto Del as if she believed she really could fall. She pressed against him, her body soft and bare in his arms, and he slid his thigh between her legs. She rubbed against him, a languorous movement of her pelvis that set his pulse racing.

Del slid his hands over her behind and bit at her earlobe. "We need a moon, too."

A crescent appeared in the distance, glowing gold. Del saw it over her shoulder. When he focused, they floated toward the moon. Ricki tensed in his arms, looking down. And for her, it was "down." Del didn't feel any gravity, but she was clearly being pulled toward the world below. He didn't know why they interpreted the virtual reality differently, but he suspected his bliss-node gave him much greater control than a typical setup.

Nothing was visible of the world except for a rim of sunlight on the curved horizon. Then even that disappeared, and they were alone in the starfield and the night sky.

"Don't let go," Ricki said. Her voice shook.

"I won't." Her fear surprised him. Then again, he knew from his own experiences that sims could be so convincing, they could hurt you. Ricki wouldn't really fall if he let go, but it might be so real to her that her heart stopped.

"Come here, sweetheart." Del put both arms around her waist.

She laid her head on his shoulder. "You're the only person I like to call me that." She hugged him close, squeezing his leg with her thighs, her breaths speeding up. It was incredibly erotic, having her want him this way, caught up here in the stars.

While they were kissing, they bumped into the moon. It hung in space, a diamond crescent about six feet long, haloed by gold light. Del settled Ricki on it so she was straddling the crescent. She watched him with her sleepy eyes and tousled hair like an erotica holo-movie goddess, all creamy skin and those sexy shoes. The halo limned her body in gold, glimmering on her breasts, her skin, and her impossibly high stilettos.

"You look like an angel," Del said. "A naughty angel I captured when she snuck out of the heavens."

Her smile curved. "Then you should climb up here and be a bad boy with me."

Del tried to slide onto the crescent, facing her, but it wasn't big enough, and he almost knocked her off. She grabbed him, clutching his biceps, and paled as she looked down.

"Don't be scared," he said. "I'll hold you." He tried to pull her closer, but their knees bumped. It was hard to stay balanced. In images he had seen of Earth folk tales, the person sitting on the moon always looked comfortable, but this just didn't work.

"We need a bigger moon," Del said.

"This is the only one in my inventory." She was swinging one leg, flexing her thigh in the most distracting way. "I'd have to shop for another."

Del stroked her thigh. "You didn't make this moon?"

"Well, no . . ." She sighed as he caressed her. "Most people don't do their own design. You need to write mesh . . . code."

"I do it." His bliss-node wrote the code for him if he interacted with it well enough. It had taken a while to figure out how, but he was always improving. "It's easy."

"Such a talented man." She lifted his hand and put his index finger in her mouth, teasing with her tongue. "Come show me what else you can do."

Gods. He pulled her against his body and let them fall off the moon. Ricky clung to him, her arms around his neck, her silken curves pressed against his as they spun through the starfield. Del kissed her, and she wrapped her legs around his waist.

He spoke against her ear. "Do you know how many men would like to be where I am?"

"Hmmm." She moved against him, sensual and demanding. "Come on, Del," she murmured. "Don't make me wait."

He fondled her breast, teasing her because it aroused him to see her so hot for him. "You look incredibly sweet, but you can break almost anyone in the industry. It's all that power wrapped up in this soft, sexy package. Do you have any idea how many men would like to have you naked and hungry like this?" He knew what they wanted, to have her helpless while they were in control. Because *no one* could have Ricki Varento that way. Except him.

She drew back, watching him with her large eyes. "Why are you telling me this?"

The wicked smile tugged his lips. " 'Cause it turns me on." He didn't tell her the rest, because he didn't want to scare her away. By bringing him here, she let him see her without the power she wore like armor. No wonder she didn't want him near her in the morning. When she slept, she looked like a child, trusting and innocent. She protected her emotions more fiercely than the military protected its secrets. Why, he didn't know. He couldn't break her mental barriers without hurting her, and he wouldn't force those secrets out of her any more than he would force her to sleep with him.

An incongruous tenderness mixed into the aggression that fueled his desire. He wanted both to take her hard and fast, and to caress her gently. She closed her eyes and laid her head on his shoulder while she rocked against him, rubbing in just the right place.

"Ah, gods . . ." Del's thoughts fragmented. He fumbled with his pants, but he couldn't unfasten them. Then they dissolved, just as hers had done. She lifted her hips and slid down on him, sheathing him inside of her while she moved her hips, slow and maddening.

Del groaned and thrust harder, his hands gripped on her behind. As they floated through the starfield, Ricki whispered things in his ear no decent Lyshrioli girl would ever have said, or even known what they meant, and it drove him crazy. He teased her with his body, pleasured her, enjoyed her, and it felt so damn good, he would have been happy to stay here in the bliss forever.

Finally they both let go, and their sensations flooded him. And when his control fell apart, he thought he whispered what he had sworn never to say, that he loved her.

Later, while he held a sleeping, sated Ricki in his arms, he looked at the record of their session and found no trace of the words. They had stayed hidden in his mind, keeping him safe.

Mac was standing by his office door, pulling on his climate-controlled sweater, when Del showed up.

"He wants to license the new virt I'm working on." Del paced across the office. Watching Del in constant motion, Mac felt old; he was tired and wanted to go home. But Del seemed troubled

"It makes sense," Mac said. "*The Jewels Suite* is doing well for Metropoli Interstellar."

"Staver bothers me." Del stopped to regard Mac. "What do you know about him?"

"He's high up at Metropoli Interstellar," Mac said. "He has a strong track record with the acts he exports. Socially, he's conservative. Other than that, I can't say."

"Can you find out more?"

"Sure." It wasn't the first time someone had asked Mac to check out a buyer. He had uncovered several scams by listening to the intuition of his clients. "I'll let you know what I find out."

"Thanks." Then Del said, "Oh, I almost forgot. Did you get my royalty payment from Prime-Nova?"

"Not yesterday." Mac walked back to his console. "But it should be soon. I meshed them about it last week."

Del scowled. "It was supposed to come a month ago."

"Well, yeah." It was always the same story; the conglomerate held out long enough to earn extra interest on the money but not quite enough to provoke the artist into legal action. Mac could estimate to within days when payment would come.

He checked the evoc, or evocative mail, on his node. "You do have something with a 'good mood' rating." Opening the file, he glanced over the first part. "Yep, this is it. I'll zip it to your account, minus my commission."

"Okay." Del came closer. "Do I get any money?"

"Wait a second, I have to open—" Mac stopped and stared.

"What?" Del peered at the grid of numbers and letters on the screen. "What does it say?"

Mac straightened up. "Yes, you made some money."

"Why are you grinning?" Del asked suspiciously. "My finances suddenly became funny?"

"No." Then Mac said, "Two hundred forty-three thousand."

"Two hundred forty-three thousand what?"

"Dollars."

"What about them?"

"Del!" Mac laughed. "That's the royalties after Ricki's cut and your loans are deducted."

Del stared at him. "Two hundred *thousand*?"

"Yep. That's it."

"Whoa." Del took a moment to absorb it. "I didn't expect it to come all at once."

"What to come all at once?" Mac asked.

"All my royalties for the album and singles."

"Are you kidding?" Mac liked giving good news. "That's the tip of an iceberg. You're going to see a lot more than that on your next statement."

Del let out a breath, half a laugh, half disbelief. "Hey! I'm really 'earning a wage.'"

"A good one."

Del's smile flashed in his handsome face. "I'm going to buy the fastest hover racer I can find."

Oh, well. Here it went. Mac almost didn't say anything. But no, he should at least try. "You should save some of it."

"Why?" Del asked.

"Invest it. Use it to make more money."

Del squinted at him. "I don't know how to invest."

"Then learn."

He expected Del to brush him off, like his holo-rock clients usually did. Instead, the youth said, "Can you help me?"

Well, how about that. "I'll be glad to."

"I have to go now, though." Del tilted his head at the door. "Cameron and Tyra are out there pacing like caged lions. And monitoring us. I hope you don't mind."

"It's all right." Mac expected as much. "Need a ride home?"

"Hey, thanks." Del pulled himself up straighter. "But I can afford as many taxis as I want now. I could buy the business!"

"Slow down," Mac said, laughing. "Don't spend it all before it's even in your account."

"Only for essentials." Del had an odd look. "For freedom."

Mac understood then. Financial independence. For all that Del resisted his family, he had the same pride that drove them all. In Del, it manifested in his resistance to the limits they imposed and his desire for independence; on a greater scale, it showed in the determination of the Ruby Dynasty to resist the Traders despite the losses Del's family had endured at their hands.

Fortunately, Del wasn't involved in the politics. He kept far away from the power struggles that were tearing apart his people.

XXI

Trade Off

The Jewels Suite hit number five on the anthology chart the same day Prime-Nova released *Starlight*, Del's second anthology.

Starlight had twelve of Del's original works, with the title cut, "Starlight Child," as a tribute to his sons. He also covered two other songs, including a classic from the long-ago twentieth century, "Because the Night" by Patti Smith and Bruce Springteen. Prime-Nova chose it for him. Ricki said, "you'll sizzle off the scale with it." Dell didn't know about that; he had never seen what he did that sizzled. But he liked the song, and when he sang it, the response from his audience was great. So he added it to all his concerts.

The second cover was "The Sound of Silence," written by a duo called Simon and Garfunkel. This one he chose. He had started to write his own song with that theme, then discovered these artists from Earth's past had done it much better. It described perfectly how the Allieds refused to see the truth about the Traders. They heard what the Skolian government said, but they never *listened*. Del wanted to shout his anger; his people were losing their freedom and their lives, yet the Allieds turned away.

Starlight debuted at number six on the anthology chart. Two weeks later, *The Jewels Suite* peaked at four, the highest position it would ever attain.

That same week, *Starlight* hit number one.

✧   ✧   ✧

The party was huge. Prime-Nova rented an entire floor of the Star Tower Sheraton. They created a starlight motif using tech Del didn't understand, "holo digicals," whatever that meant. The place looked as if it were floating in the stars.

They were one floor beneath the glass-walled room where he had spent his first night with Ricki. It had been over a year since then, and the confused farm boy had vanished, replaced by one of the best known celebrities in popular entertainment. He was still confused, but it was a lot easier to take when he was independently wealthy with no help from his family and everyone loved his music.

Except they didn't all really love it. That was the problem with being an empath. He knew what they felt. Some of those who raved about his work meant it, but others said the words as their ticket to his party. A vivid thought from one exec jumped out at Del; the man would rather be strapped across the exhaust vents of a launching starship than listen to Del's music.

Others wanted to use him. A holo-producer talked to him about doing a holo-movie virt. He acted as if he were Del's best friend, but he felt nothing of the kind. He saw Del as a commodity to exploit. He didn't ask if Del had acting experience; apparently movie techs were even better than music techs at creating stars out of nothing. Which was fortunate, because Del couldn't even read a script, let alone act.

Some people wanted to use him in other ways. He was growing used to the invitations from women, some subtle, some blatant. Just when he would start to feel cocky, as if he were some rock sex god, he would meet someone like the woman here who wondered if everyone had gone nuts or was suffering from some bizarre mass hypnosis, that they got turned on by a skinny kid with shaggy hair dyed a weird color. Del resisted the urge to tell her he did *not* dye his hair.

Very rich, powerful, married women discreetly indicated their interest. So did several very rich, powerful, married men. At that point, Del went on a desperate search for Ricki, who had vanished with Orin the Exec and some other glitzy types.

"Del, wait!" someone said behind him in the crowd.

Del almost didn't turn around. The pressure from so many minds in one place wore him down. It was even more difficult tonight because Prime-Nova had thrown this bash in his honor, which meant people focused on him, creating a greater pressure. He had enjoyed the party at first, but now he just wanted to escape back to his apartment and his bliss-node.

The man sounded like Staver, though. So Del turned.

Staver took his elbow. "We have to leave."

"Stop it!" Del yanked away his arm. If one more person touched him without his permission, he was going to lose it.

"You don't understand," Staver said. "We can't—"

"Del, here you are," an authoritative voice said. Someone laid a hand on his shoulder. "I've been looking for you."

Del turned around. "Zachary. Hi." He barely stopped himself from shoving the vice president away.

"I want you to meet someone," Zachary said.

Staver's face paled. "Del, no. Don't."

Del felt Staver trying to reach his mind. He shook his head, too agitated to answer. He couldn't lower his barriers with so many people here.

"What's the problem, Aunchild?" Zachary asked coldly.

"I have to talk to him," Staver said.

"I'll be back," Del said. "I just need some air." A year ago, he hadn't understood why people on Earth said they needed air when they were obviously breathing, but now it made perfect sense.

Staver tried to protest, but Zachary maneuvered Del away. The crowd parted for Prime-Nova's tech-mech king and closed behind him, blocking Staver's way.

"Over here," Zachary said. Although he smiled, unease leaked from his mind. "It looks like you may hit an even bigger market."

"Great." Del took a breath, trying to calm down. If this was a potential buyer, he wanted to make a good impression.

Zachary called to a tall man standing by the bar, surrounded by people. One instant passed between Zachary's call and Del's recognition of the name he spoke.

Lord Tarex.

An Aristo name.

Del went ice cold. In that moment, the man at the bar turned around. Del met his gaze and wanted to scream. Tarex's eyes were red—pure, crystalline red. Like rubies. *No, not rubies.* Never rubies. Carnelians. Like the Carnelian Throne of the Trader emperor.

Then Del and Zachary were in the midst of Tarex's retinue,

surrounded by Traders. The slave lord was a big man, broad-shouldered and powerfully built, with the shimmering black hair so distinctive of an Aristo. Del felt trapped, panicked, unable to breathe.

"Lord Tarex, let me present Del Arden." Zachary used the formal phrases expected for a dignitary. To Del he said, "Lord Tarex is the chief executive officer of Tarex Interstellar. He came here tonight to meet you."

Del stared at the Aristo, and Tarex met his gaze, his own as cold as interstellar space. Del felt as if he were falling into the void of Tarex's mind, plummeting, suffocating. Nor did Tarex miss that instant of comprehension. He stared at Del with a dawning realization of the hunter sighting his prey.

"Ah, yes," Tarex said. "I knew, when I saw you perform."

"Knew?" Del could barely speak.

"You're an empath," Tarex said.

Del backed away. He wanted to break into a run.

"Come on." A man grabbed his arm.

He looked up at Staver. "Get me out of here," Del whispered.

As Staver hurried him through the crowd, everything became a blur. The exec cut off anyone who tried to talk to them. At first Del didn't understand why people moved aside so easily; then he realized Tyra and Cameron were with them, clearing a path, had probably been there all along. Then they were in another room, an empty bedroom. Del collapsed against the wall and heaved in a breath. "Gods. It was like—like—"

"Like dying?" Staver asked. He dropped into a chair by the bed.

Another voice registered on Del. Tyra was talking to a console nearby. "—open a Kyle link. I'll give you the codes."

"No!" Del strode over to her, nearly tripping in the process, he was so shaken up. "Don't do that!"

Tyra stood up and swung around, facing him. She pointed her arm straight at the door that led back to the party. "There's a goddamned Silicate *Aristo* out there."

"Tarex doesn't know squat about me except that I'm an empath," Del said. "Which is probably obvious to any Aristo who sees me perform. Why the hell do you need to contact my brother?"

"This isn't some fan pushing you against the wall," Tyra said. "That Trader could turn your life into a nightmare."

"Only if you blow up the situation!" Del tried to calm his

voice so she would listen. "If I leave, Tarex will be offended that I walked out, but I'm probably not the first person on Earth to react that way to him. So he's insulted and doesn't buy rights to my work." He took another breath and let it out slowly. "If you bring in my brother, it *could* become a major incident."

"I have to report this," she said.

"Tyra." Frustration strained his voice.

"I'm sorry." She looked past him to Staver. "I'll have to ask you to leave."

Staver stood up. "You want me to go out there?" His voice shook on the last word.

Alarm swelled in Del. "Staver is an empath! He can't go."

Tyra nodded, her face pale, and indicated a door by the bed. "That leads to another bedroom. You can wait in there."

"I don't understand." Staver came over to them. "Who is your brother?" he asked Del. To Tyra, he said, "What did you mean, report?"

"She's my bodyguard," Del said. "My brother hired her."

"Do *you* want me to leave?" he asked Del.

Del had no desire for Staver to see him humiliated by Kelric. "Maybe it'd be better. I'm sorry."

The door to the party hummed, and the room's AI said, "Ricki Varento would like to enter."

Tyra glanced at Del. It was an unspoken question: did he want Ricki to come in? Tyra had no idea how much that one gesture meant to him. His previous bodyguards would have decided whether or not to admit Ricki without asking him.

"Let her in," Del said.

The door slid open, bringing a wave of noise. Ricki stalked inside in her high, high heels. Her red dress glistened with holos, left her shoulders bare, and was slit up the side from the floor to her hip. Any other time Del's pulse would have gone into overdrive at the sight, but right now even Ricki at her most devastating couldn't affect him.

As the door closed, she came over and spoke softly to Del. "Are you all right?"

"What the hell?" Staver said.

Ricki frowned at the Skolian exec. "What?"

"I expected you to be furious," Staver said. "We just insulted your biggest client."

Ricki studied him. "You knew how Tarex would affect Del."

"Staver is an empath," Del said.

"Staver's right, babe," Ricki told him. "You pulled a major drill out there with Tarex. He's not saying anything, but I can tell. He's pissed enough to launch off a lune."

Del wasn't sure what she had just said, but he got the gist of it. "I can't talk to him. I can't be in the same *room* with him."

She considered him and Staver, then turned to Tyra. "It gets to you, too, doesn't it? You just hide it better."

"If you mean, does Lord Tarex exert a negative effect on the neurological physiology of my cerebral cortex, the answer is yes." Wryly Tyra added, "That translates as 'He scares the blistering hell out of me.'"

Ricki didn't look surprised. "I have to tell him something. I can't leave it like this."

"Tell him the truth," Del said. "He knows I'm an empath. Say I was so shaken up, I panicked. He's probably seen it a thousand times from his providers." With disgust, he said, "Tell him that his magnificent presence overwhelmed me."

Ricki frowned at him. "Sarcasm doesn't help, babe."

"I'm not being sarcastic. That's how slaves talk to Aristos. It's what Tarex expects." Del had to make a conscious effort not to grit his teeth. "Tell him, and he'll believe you."

Ricki pushed her hand through her long hair. "I don't claim to understand all this. But he scares me, too."

Del touched her cheek. "Don't go anywhere with him alone. He can't take you by force with so many people around."

She stiffened. "What are you talking about?"

"You're so pretty. You look like a provider." Del's voice hardened. "To Tarex, we're all slaves. If he got you into Trader territory, he could own you."

"Why would he?" she asked. "I'm not an empath. And I'm sure he can bonk all the sexpot slave girls he wants. So why piss off a major Allied conglomerate he hopes to do business with?"

"If you offend him, he won't care who he angers with his actions," Del said. "Aristos are the ultimate narcissists. They think they're gods. Don't even hint to him that you might defend my actions. Convince him you're on his side."

"Don't worry," Ricki said. "I've been in this business a long time, as your hard-assed brother so rudely pointed out when we were on the Moon. I can calm down drilled-off clients."

Del smiled. Any woman audacious enough to call his over-powering brother names was worth the pyrotechnics in their relationship. He pulled her close and bent his head as he kissed her. "Just be careful, okay?"

"I will."

After Ricki returned to the party, Staver raised an eyebrow at Del. "I didn't know kissing was part of the producer-artist arrangement at Prime-Nova."

The AI in the console spoke, saving Del from having to answer. "I have a Kyle link."

Tyra turned to Staver. "You'll have to go."

He hesitated, but when Del just waited, Staver nodded and left the room. Cameron took a post by the door after it closed and checked his wrist gauntlet, monitoring Staver.

Tyra sat at the console and set up the link to Kelric. Del stood behind her, his hand resting on the back of her chair. He didn't realize he was gritting his teeth until a stab of pain shot through his jaw. He rubbed his neck and tried to relax.

It wasn't Kelric who answered, though. In the strange universe of Del's recent communication with his family, of course the person they called didn't come on. This time, his brother Eldrin appeared. He looked exhausted. Dark circles showed under his eyes, and his face was drawn. The elegant furnishings of his living room gleamed, light gold wood with blue and white accents.

"Your Majesty." Tyra reddened. "Please accept my apologies for disturbing you. I must have misentered a code. I was trying to contact your brother."

"No, you didn't make an error." Eldrin rubbed his eyes. "Kelric is working in the Kyle web. He set your codes to contact my wife if you set up a link while he was unavailable."

"I didn't mean to disturb you at home," Tyra said. "The message should have gone through to her office."

"She's not there," Eldrin said. "She's here, asleep."

Del stiffened. Why would Dehya set up her system that way? He leaned over the console. "Eldrin? What happened to her?"

"Del!" His brother smiled. "My greetings."

"And mine," Del said. "Is Dehya all right?"

His brother's smile faded. "This pregnancy doesn't go well."

"She's *pregnant?*"

"Yes." Eldrin spoke quietly. "Her doctors fear the baby won't survive if he's premature. We've almost lost him twice."

"I'm sorry." Gods, how could Dehya be pregnant, apparently for months, and he hadn't known? They criticized him for not telling them about the singing, yet he knew nothing about this?

Stop it, Del told himself. *You've avoided them for months. Why would they seek you out for something so painful?* If her doctors couldn't keep a premature baby alive even with all their modern medicine, the fetus's condition had to be terrible.

Eldrin was watching his face. "It's good to see you, Del."

Del hoped so. He had only been two years younger than Eldrin in their childhood, and they had been close as boys, but they had drifted apart in adolescence, and Del had seen little of him since he came out of cryo.

"It's good to talk to you," Del said. Gods, he sounded so stiff.

"I watched your concerts," Eldrin said. "I've never seen you sing that way before. It was interesting."

Interesting. Del smiled wryly. "They have a curse here. It's used when you wish truly noxious things on a person. You say, 'May you live in interesting times.'"

Eldrin smiled, his face lightening. "I didn't mean it that way. You look happy when you sing. That is good."

"It is." Del hesitated, unsure what to say. His brother sat on the Ruby Throne now as consort to the pharaoh, and Del no longer knew how to talk to him. "I wish I could do something to help Dehya."

"Knowing that will mean a great deal to her." Even exhausted, Eldrin sounded regal. "It's the baby we're most worried about."

"Those doctors can do anything," Del said. "Hey, they even kept me alive."

"That they did." The thought did actually seem to give Eldrin comfort.

"Your Majesty, I'm sorry to intrude," Tyra said. "But I need to talk to Imperator Skolia as soon as he's available."

"I'll tell him," Eldrin said. "Can I help with it?"

"I don't know," she said. "There's an Aristo here, Lord Axil Tarex, who is interested in licensing Prince Del-Kurj's music."

Eldrin sat up straight. "Del! You have to leave Earth."

Del made an exasperated noise. "That would be subtle, to

drop all my commitments and run off the week my latest release becomes the most popular anthology on Earth."

"It doesn't matter," Eldrin said.

"I already went through this with Kelric." Del wished he could make them see. "If I were a test pilot, like Kelric used to be, I would be putting my life in far more danger every time I went up in one of those fighters. Yet none of you would tell me to stop."

"This is different," Eldrin said. "You don't have to do it."

"No, it's *not* different. It's my job."

"What, singing like that?" Eldrin started to say more, then caught himself.

"Like what?" Del said.

Eldrin hesitated. "Live. Can't you give virtual concerts? When I sang those operas, I did it here on the Orbiter, in a mesh studio, with verification protocols that my voice wasn't enhanced. Billions of people watched. The virts have trillions of downloads. You wouldn't have to give up your singing."

"It's not the same." Del struggled to let go of his anger, for he understood the unstated pain beneath his brother's words. "You're the Ruby Consort. One of the most valuable people in three empires." He felt small. "I'm nothing, Eldrin. I'm no good to the Traders. I'd die if they tried to use me in a Kyle web. No reason exists for ISC to constrain me unless I ask for it. And I'm not." He hated saying that to his brother, who had been forced into his title. It was a mercy Eldrin and Dehya had fallen in love; otherwise, their situation could have been a nightmare.

Eldrin's gaze never wavered. "Don't say you're nothing. Those of us who love you don't feel that way."

Del had prepared many arguments for the next time someone in his family told him he should stop his singing here. He had been ready for any angle of attack—except *We love you*. He just stood, at a loss for words.

Eldrin suddenly looked down at his console. "Dehya's medical alarm just went off. I have to go." He glanced at Tyra. "Do you want Admiral Barzun?"

"Yes, please." Tyra sounded subdued. She had heard more of the internal strife in the Ruby Dynasty in the past few days than most people would ever know if they searched the interstellar meshes for every mention of the royal family they could find.

"Very well." Eldrin smiled at Del. "Be well, my brother."

"And you," Del said. "Always."

The screen went blank, then cleared to show a man with iron-grey hair in a blue uniform.

Tyra reported to the admiral. Barzun wasn't happy, to put it mildly. He didn't have the authority to make Del leave Earth, but Del agreed to cooperate with whatever other precautions they wanted, knowing that if he didn't, Kelric would have him hauled back home.

Of course he promised not to accept any contract from Tarex. Del would have rather cut off his nose than license his work to an Aristo. He knew it would mean a big loss in potential revenue to Prime-Nova, and he hated that he was going to look unprofessional, as if he had become arrogant with success. He could talk to General McLane about telling Zachary his real reasons, but ASC felt the same as ISC; the fewer people who knew the truth, the better.

The room's AI spoke. "Mister Arden's band wishes to enter."

Tyra signed off with Admiral Barzun and glanced at Del.

"It's okay," Del said.

As the door opened, Jud, Anne, and Randall spilled into the room, talking and holding drinks. Anne glanced around until she saw Cameron, then reddened and looked quickly away.

"Hey, Del!" Randall yelled, even though he was right there. He lifted his oversized glass of ouzo. "Why aren't you celebrating? It's a great party."

Jud's smile faded as he studied Del. "What's wrong?"

Del just shook his head.

"He had a fight with Zach," Anne said. "Ricki is smoothing things over."

Randall gave Del an incredulous look. "You argued with the tech-mech king on a night like this? Damn it, Del, we're flying as high as we can. Why fight with Zachary?"

"He wants me to sell our work to the Aristos," Del said.

Randall's alcohol-flushed face turned redder. "It's not just your decision."

"Wait." Jud came up to Del and spoke in a low voice. "I heard an Aristo was here."

"I met him." Del winced. "And I panicked."

"Panicked?" Anne asked. She and Randall joined them. "Why?"

"Del, come on," Randall said. "Don't screw this up. Eube is a *huge* market. Man, we could outshine a screaming nova."

"Randall, don't," Jud said. "He's an empath. He can't be around Aristos."

"Oh, cut the crap." Randall downed his drink, then spun around and stalked away from them. Pivoting back, he spoke furiously to Del. "Whenever you screw up, you pull this 'I'm so sensitive' shit. It isn't just about you. Can't you stop thinking about your own damn problems and remember that four of us are involved in this?"

Randall sounded so much like Kelric, Del wanted to sock him in the face. Another thought came from deeper inside: maybe everyone was right, he was nothing more than overwrought and immature, and he didn't deserve this success. He knew this much; he didn't want to ruin things for his band.

Jud spoke sharply to Randall. "That's enough."

"You let him get away with this garbage." Randall hit at the air with his glass, his fist clenched around it. "Maybe if you quit coddling him, he wouldn't be such a high-strung baby."

"Shut up!" Cameron said.

Everyone gaped at the guard.

"Leave him the fuck alone," Cameron told Randall.

"Great," Randall said. "Now your babysitter is mouthing off."

"Del." Tyra spoke awkwardly. "Staver wants to know if he can come in."

"Staver?" Randall's face turned a deeper red. "You better not have pissed him off, too."

"He's the one who warned me about Tarex," Del said tightly.

Anne walked over to Cameron. "Is everything okay?"

"Fine." Cameron kept his face impassive, but his jitters at seeing Anne leaked out of his mind. He glanced at Del. "Shall I let him back in?"

Del nodded, flushed and uncomfortable. "Go ahead."

The door by Cameron opened, and Staver strode inside. He faltered when he saw everyone. Then he came over to Del. "Did you talk to your brother?"

"One of them," Del said.

Anne gave him a startled smile. "You have brothers?"

Del had no intention of talking about his family. "I need to leave," he said. "Go home."

Randall watched him in disbelief. "It's *your* party. Haven't you ticked Zachary off enough already? I can't believe you'd walk out after they went to all this trouble for you."

Del didn't want to antagonize Zachary, but he didn't know what to say. Someone in the party was using a spiker, and the smoke affected Del even here, leaving him dizzy.

"Can you get home all right?" Staver asked.

"No, I—I don't—" Del rubbed his temples. "My head hurts."

Randall gave him a disgusted look and talked in a falsetto. "Not tonight, dear. I have a headache."

"You're drunk, Randy," Anne said shortly. "Lay off."

"I'm sorry," Randall said. "But this always happens. Del, our livelihoods depend on your keeping it together. Here we are, on top of the stars. Don't take it away."

Del felt how much Randall feared he would ruin their success. Cameron and Tyra were waiting for Del to decide if he wanted to go home. Del couldn't answer. He needed his bliss-node.

A spark of anger jumped within him: *Are you going to run to a fantasy world every time things get a little tough? How much of your life will it devour before you've had enough?*

Cameron joined them and spoke to Del. "I can bring your racer around to the front of the hotel."

"No." Del took a breath. "I'll stay." He went to the bed and lay on his back with his arm over his eyes. "Just give me a few minutes. Alone."

After a pause, Jud said, "We'll be outside."

Del listened to them leave. When it was quiet, he lowered his arm and saw Cameron posted by the wall. Tyra was still standing by the console, watching someone near Del. Staver. The Skolian man had stayed, slumped in the chair, his face pale.

"I can't go out there," Staver said when Del looked at him.

Del nodded. "You should stay."

They fell silent, and Del closed his eyes. After a while, he began to calm down. The spikers left him sleepy and nauseous.

Eventually Staver spoke. "Why did he call you Del's babysitter?"

Del opened his eyes. Staver was watching Cameron, who stared back, impassive. Knowing Cameron wouldn't answer, Del pulled himself up and sat against the wall at the head of the bed. "Cameron keeps people away. I can't go alone in public anymore."

Staver glanced from Cameron to Tyra. "Two bodyguards?"

"It used to be one, before Raker and Delilah." Del felt Staver's mental knock. Now that he had recovered some, he lowered his barriers. This time, though, he didn't cut out Tyra.

Does Tarex know you're a psion? Del asked Staver.

I'm sure of it, Staver answered. *He asked to meet me. And a woman with him offered to take me home. She was beautiful, but I wouldn't go anywhere with someone from an Aristo's retinue.*

Del shuddered. **Never.**

I knew Tarex was on Earth, Staver thought. *Some people want to help a provider he brought. A lot of security surrounds her. To break it—let's just say it requires specialists outside usual channels. Help like that costs more than my friends can afford.*

But I can, Del thought.

So you claim. Staver didn't say more, though. They might wonder if Del really had the funds, but if their background checks had found anything they considered suspicious about him, this exchange would never have taken place.

Del hid his Skolian identity from Staver with defenses he had spent a lifetime learning to build. He could tell Staver believed him to be Del Arden of Earth. Had Staver known the truth about Del, he might have shielded that knowledge from a less powerful psion, but concealing it from Del was impossible when Del lowered his barriers. He would sense the conflict in Staver's mind.

I'll let you know, Del thought. He hadn't finished checking out Staver. **Be careful. Tarex might use the provider to trap you.**

Any help you can give would be greatly appreciated, Staver said. *And believe me, I'll stay clear of Tarex.*

Good. Del raised his barriers, strained by their link, and his sense of Staver faded. When he glanced at Tyra, she nodded, letting him know she had followed the exchange.

The room's AI said, "Ricki Varento is here."

"Let her in," Del said.

As soon as the door opened, Ricki came over to Del. She spared a puzzled glance for Staver, but didn't ask him to leave.

"How upset is Zachary?" Del asked.

"Keyed up and beyond." Ricki sat on the bed. "He told Tarex that touring had worn you out." She looked ready to punch someone. "Tarex didn't care, not after I told him what you said about his 'magnificence.' He reacted exactly like you predicted. Asshole."

Del grimaced. "That's probably what Zachary thinks about me."

"He's not happy." She glanced at Staver. "Do you have a body-guard here?"

He shook his head. "I had no reason to think I'd need one."

Tyra came over to them. "Staver, you can't leave by yourself. Tarex knows about you."

Ricki gave her an incredulous look. "Tarex wouldn't threaten a major exec from one of the most powerful Skolian conglomerates."

"For a psion as strong as Staver?" Del spoke grimly. "Tarex would probably consider him worth anything." The Aristo probably thought Staver had a higher Kyle rating than Del. Although Staver's personal info wasn't public, it would be far easier to find than Del's ISC-controlled records.

Del doubted Tarex realized Tyra was a psion. Although strong, her mind was less powerful than what the Aristo would sense from Del or Staver. More important, as a Jagernaut she had the most in-depth psi training ISC offered. She could pick up strategies from Tarex without giving herself away, and she would recognize anyone with enough Aristo heritage to endanger an empath. She was also a human weapon; with her augmented strength and speed, and internal mesh systems, she could probably outfight even the best of Tarex's guards. Which was great for Del, but didn't help Staver.

"Staver needs a permanent bodyguard," Del told Ricki.

"I'll take care of it." She turned to Staver. "We've plenty of rooms here. You can stay. Or my people can escort you home."

"Why would you do all this for me?" Staver asked.

She tilted her head toward Del. "He says it's important. I trust his judgment."

"I'd like to leave, then." Staver spoke quietly. "And thank you."

Ricki nodded to him, then glanced at Del. "Would you like to go upstairs? The suite there is yours tonight if you want it."

Del knew she was offering him a cover story in case anyone wondered why he disappeared at his own party. If he withdrew with a "friend" to Prime-Nova's love nest, it wouldn't raise eyebrows. Knowing Ricki's crowd, no one would even wonder why Tyra and Cameron went with them. They would assume—well, he didn't want to imagine what they would assume.

He managed a wan smile. "Come with me?"

"Sure, babe." She took his hand. "Will you be all right?"

"I'll be great."

It wasn't true. He still had to talk to Kelric. He was here only on the sufferance of his brother and General McLane; no matter how much he resented it, they controlled his life. Despite what Kelric believed, Del had no intention of damaging relations between his people and the Allieds, which meant if Kelric ordered him home, Del would leave. Everything he had achieved would be over, and he would return to a life he couldn't bear.

XXII

Headliner

The comm message came from Philip Chandler, the doctor who had checked Del after his first convulsion: *Mister Arden, please contact me as soon as possible.*

Del stood at the console in his apartment and listened to the message three times. It didn't improve with repetition. Nearly a year had passed since he had seen Chandler, and he had forgotten about the doctor's concerns. Since the party a few days ago, Del's main worry had been avoiding Tarex and any deals he might offer Prime-Nova.

Jud was leaning against the wall. "What do you think it is?"

"I don't know." In Del's experience, when a doctor commed you with no warning, it meant trouble. "Maybe I shouldn't call back."

"Yeah, right," Jud said. "And maybe you should go jump off the Star Tower, too."

Del scowled at him. "Ha, ha."

"Comm him."

Del gritted his teeth, but he did sit at the console. "Claude, can you put me through to Doctor Chandler?"

"Yes. One moment, please."

"I'll just get his AI," Del told Jud. Doctors never responded in person. "I'll leave a message." Then he could put the whole thing out of his mind.

"I have his office," Claude said.

"Del Arden?" a man asked. "Is that you?"

Damn. That was no AI. "Hi, Doctor Chandler. Yes, it's me."

"Can we go visual?" Chandler asked.

"Sure." As Del spoke, his screen cleared to show Philip Chandler seated at what looked like an oakwood console.

"Thanks for getting back to me so soon," Chandler said. "I was worried."

That wasn't what Del wanted to hear. "What's wrong?"

"I've been in contact with the Skolian Embassy in D.C.," he said. "It took a lot of back and forth, but I've finally spoken with a Skolian expert on the neuroscience of empaths. From what she told me, it sounds like that convulsion you suffered may have been more serious than our tests showed."

Del wanted to push away the words. "I'm fine, Doctor Chandler. Really. I haven't had any problems."

Although the physician looked sympathetic, he didn't relent. "A psion's brain produces specialized neurotransmitters. The higher your Kyle rating, the more you produce. In a live show, your brain goes into overdrive trying to deal with the empathic input from your audience and releases an excess of the Kyle transmitters. Too many of your neurons fire at once. If it overloads your brain, you have a convulsion. I didn't register anything when I tested you because my equipment can't detect Kyle-active transmitters."

As much as Del wanted to deny it, that fit too well with what he knew about his father's convulsions. "I do feel wound up, especially after a big show," he admitted. "But I can relax by spending time in a virt. Since I started doing that, I haven't had any problems."

"A virt suit shouldn't affect your neurons," Chandler said.

Del regarded him guiltily. "I don't use a suit. My setup has a direct brain interface."

Chandler stiffened. "I assume you have a license for it."

"Yes." Del had insisted. He knew that among his people, any system that acted directly on a psion's brain required a long application procedure and came with many restrictions. Casper, the man who had sold him the bliss-node, had required nothing. He simply gave Del the license—at a huge price. Del hadn't asked for details, legal or otherwise, but he had the paperwork.

"It isn't a good idea to use a virt that way," Chandler said. "It interferes with the way your neurons fire. Yes, it can calm down those overloaded cells, but it could make the problem worse if you aren't careful. You can also become dependent on it, just like anything else that affects brain chemistry."

Del wiped his sweating palms on his jeans. "I can stop any time I want." He wanted it to be true. Yet even now he longed to sink into the node's merciful oblivion.

"Are you on tour now?" Chandler asked.

"Well, no."

"Are you using the node?"

Del stared at him, unwilling to answer. He used it every day, sometimes for hours.

Chandler spoke quietly. "Del, I'd like you to come into my office at the Johns Hopkins Medical Center for more tests."

"I'm fine. I don't need more tests."

"I think you should," Chandler said. "Methods exist to help you deal with performing in front of all those people. But we need to monitor the procedures. If you try to do it yourself, you could end up with brain damage."

Del felt trapped. His lengthy time in cryo had affected his brain. His memories had been intact, but he had needed to relearn everything that required motion. He had barely been able to talk, let alone feed himself, dress, or walk. It had taken years to struggle back. The idea that he could damage himself like that using the bliss-node was more upsetting than he could endure. But he couldn't bear the thought of losing the bliss, either.

"I'll check my schedule," Del said. "See what we can do."

Chandler looked relieved. "Great. Get back to me soon."

"I will. Thanks for following up."

"I'm just sorry it took so long. The Skolians are secretive about this whole Kyle business."

"I guess so." Del made himself smile. "Talk to you soon."

After they signed off, Del stood up and paused uncertainly in front of the console.

"You're going to blow him off, aren't you?" Jud said.

Del looked around. "Damn it, I hate the way you're always eavesdropping."

Jud hadn't moved from his place by the wall. "You spend hours every day in the bliss, Del. You're addicted. Strung out on virt."

"That's stupid. You can't be addicted to a simulation."

"Like hell." Jud uncrossed his arms. "Del, please, listen to him. You can't play roulette with your brain."

Del wanted him to get lost. He wanted to forget Chandler had ever called. But more than anything else, he wanted to use the bliss-node. And that scared him.

"When I was young," Del said, "I knew some guys on Metropoli who used vampers, those neuro-psillic amphetamines that slam straight into your brain." He still struggled with the memory. "They both died from overdoses within a few years after I went into cryo. Except they weren't Ruby princes. So no one saved them."

Jud spoke quietly. "And that makes you angry?"

Del sat at the console, feeling as if he weighed too much. "I had no more right to live than they did. I need to believe I survived for a reason. But I don't see one."

"For your music."

"Yeah, right." He looked up at Jud. "And don't give me that 'Del, you're an artist' crap. I've heard it." He thought of what Eldrin had said two nights ago when Del had talked to him during the party. *What, singing like that? You don't have to do it.* "No matter how you spin it, what I do isn't important."

Jud looked ready to sock someone. "You've been talking to your family again, haven't you?"

"Just leave it."

"You think running away in a bliss-node will fix it?" Jud punched at the air. "That's not the solution! It's not real."

"I don't care."

"I do."

Del stood up and spoke coldly. "I never asked you to. I just want you to leave me alone."

"Yeah, well, listen, you stupid asshole. I'm not going to leave you alone no matter how hard you push me away." Jud glared at him. "You got that?"

"Call me a stupid asshole again," Del said, "and I'll—" He ran out of steam. He would what? "I'll stop cleaning up around here."

Jud looked as if he didn't know whether to laugh or throw up his hands. "God help me. What other dire fates do you have planned?"

Del couldn't help but smile. "Give me time. I'll think of something terrible."

"Del, listen," Jud said. "Think of all the time you waste in the bliss. You haven't written any new songs since *Starlight*. What about "Carnelians?" We were doing great work on both versions. You haven't rehearsed either for months."

Del shifted his weight. "Mac doesn't want me to do that one."

"Mac isn't your keeper." Jud came over to him. "Do you really want the bliss to take over your life?"

Del felt as if he had run into a wall. "Nothing should stop the music. Never."

"Go talk to Chandler. What could it hurt?"

"He'll tell me to stop touring."

"That's not what he said. He claims treatments exist." Jud paused. "You're going to visit Lyshriol next week, right? Will you use the bliss-node there?"

Del had intended to bring the whole setup. Now he realized he probably couldn't get it through customs. He saw then how bizarre it was that he wanted to bring a virt to simulate his home while he was at home.

"I don't know." Del felt overwhelmed. "I'll stop using it, Jud. Really."

"Can you?"

"Sure." Del almost said, *I'll just do one last session.* But he didn't tell Jud. He could do it later, when Jud didn't know.

Just one last time. Then he would stop.

Two days later, Mac told Del the results of his check on Staver. The Skolian exec was everything he appeared. The next morning, Tyra told Del what she had discovered. ISC had a secret dossier on Staver Aunchild. He wasn't just involved in freeing providers; he had founded the movement. ISC considered him one of their top civilian operatives. He had a long record of service to the Imperialate. He could have won numerous awards for bravery, but his actions had to remain covert. He did it all with no credit, no acknowledgement, nothing.

Staver wasn't what he seemed. He was more. It was considered impossible to gain access to any of the few thousand providers kept by the Aristos. Yet he had freed over one hundred, at great risk to himself. The Aristos knew he existed, but nothing about his identity. They had offered a mammoth award for any bounty hunter who brought him in alive.

What drove Staver? The woman he knew, the one the Traders had captured and made a slave—

She was his wife.

That night, Del transferred ten million credits into an unmarked offworld account with a code Staver gave him.

"Here." Tyra pulled Del into the cobbled lane between two buildings as they ran. Jud and Bonnie were close behind, and Cameron brought up the rear. They raced through a wash of bluish laser-light, the overflow from holo displays on shops behind them. Tyra stopped at a door and smacked the *open* panel. When nothing happened, she kicked the door fast and hard, her motion blurring. She left a big dent in the metal slab.

"Whoa." Jud gaped at her. "How did you *do* that?"

"You can't go damaging property," Bonnie said.

"Better than if I have to shoot your overeager fans." Tyra kicked the door again, and it buckled inward, hanging from one edge.

Grabbing Del's arm, Tyra shoved him inside. He stumbled into the dark, then spun around while the others followed him. As Tyra wrestled the door into place, the pounding of feet grew louder. It sounded like the people chasing Del had turned into the lane. Bracing her knee against the door, Tyra wedged it into the frame. It could still fall inward, but only if someone pushed. They all stood in darkness then, breathing heavily while the rumble of feet passed the door.

"This is crazy," Jud said.

"No kidding." Del tried to laugh it off, but he couldn't any more.

"I've never seen anything like this," Bonnie said. "Not even on the Mind Mix tour. And people get really intense about Rex."

A light appeared around Tyra, coming from the belt on her black jumpsuit. They were in a storage area for a shop. Cameron walked around, scrutinizing the shelves while Tyra checked the area with her gauntlet systems.

Jud was watching Tyra with fascination. "You must have some righteous add-ons. How could you bash in that door?"

"I'm full of biomech," Tyra said. "Muscle and skeletal enhancement, hydraulic augmentation, bio-optic mesh, spinal node, and a microfusion reactor to power it all."

Bonnie smiled at Del. "You have impressive bodyguards."

"Destructive, too," he grumbled. "I'm the one who'll have to pay for that banged-in door."

"Hey, be glad she could," Jud said. "Otherwise those people would've caught us. Then you'd be paying for your banged-in body."

Del regarded him curiously. "What do you think they would do if they caught us?"

Jud smirked at him. "The girls all want to have biblical relations with you."

Del squinted at him. "What relations?"

"Can't you tell?" Tyra asked. "Good gods, Del, it's in their minds. They want to touch you. If my guess is right about what biblical relations means, then hell yes, they want that, too."

Last year, Del would have joked about his supposed sex appeal. But the euphoria of being craved had worn thin. "It's hard to sort out their moods, especially with my barriers up. They seemed . . ." He hesitated, not wanting to sound as overwrought as his family considered him. "Out of control." It was a mild way of saying they were going to come down on him like an avalanche.

Tyra didn't ridicule him. In fact, she said, "I'm trained in crowd control. You're right, that group wasn't far from losing it."

Jud did a karate chop on the air. "Del can do his fancy martial arts to stop them."

Cameron turned from where he was inspecting a canister of neon. "Yeah. So why haven't we ever seen him actually *do* these martial arts. He never does anything but dance."

Del shrugged. "It's called *mai-quinjo*. I'm no good at it." After that night at the lake, he had practiced rigorously, but he had suffered a "slight" hiatus, as in forty-five years, before he started practicing again. "I don't know. Maybe it is more like dance steps." He had always wondered if the masters who developed *mai-quinjo* had subconsciously sought an outlet for men who wanted to move in rhythm on a world where only women were allowed to dance. "I've never used it to defend myself."

Tyra was studying the miniature screen in her gauntlet. "I think it's clear outside. We should get going."

Del nodded, relieved to escape their scrutiny. Tyra edged the door open and checked the lane while Cameron monitored the area. When his guards declared it safe, they all walked back to the plaza where Del's fans had accosted them. They crossed it with no other excitement and entered their destination, the Prime-Nova building in Washington, D.C.

✧   ✧   ✧

"You're late," Zachary said as Del entered his office with Jud, Bonnie, and his bodyguards.

People packed the room: Zachary was sitting in a leather chair, holding a glass of amber liquid; Ricki was leaning against the wall with her half-filled glass; Mac was seated near Zachary, reading a holofile; and Rex Montrow from Mind Mix, of all people, was on one end of the couch with a glass of the drink, probably rum from the smell. No one, however, caught Del's attention as much as the man who sat behind Zachary's mahogany desk, someone Del rarely saw in person because the man worked in New York: Lantham Marksman, Zachary's older brother, Chief Executive Officer of Prime-Nova.

"Some fans chased us," Del said. "We had to hide."

"Just as long as they keep buying your vids," Zachary said, then laughed as if he had made a joke.

Del gritted his teeth, remembering Raker and his laser carbine. Mac stiffened and set down his holofile. Although Lantham chuckled, his smile had a predatory quality. A Roman nose dominated his face, and silvered hair swept up from his unlined forehead. He looked forty, but Del knew the CEO was over eighty.

"Good to see you, Del," Lantham said, rising to his feet as Del reached his desk.

Del shook his hand, aware that Lantham didn't acknowledge the others with him. He hated it when Lantham treated his friends as if they were nothing, but he didn't want to antagonize the CEO any further after he had turned down the lucrative offer from Tarex. If Lantham had called this meeting because he expected to change Del's mind, they were going to have a problem.

"You know Rex, don't you?" Lantham said.

"Yeah, sure." Del nodded to Rex. "How's it going?"

Rex lifted his glass. "Great." As always, his smile flashed, ready and polished. And fake.

"Have a seat," Zachary said, indicating the couch.

Jud and Bonnie pulled up chairs, but Del felt like he had to sit on the couch; otherwise, he'd look as if he were deliberately going against Zachary. So he sat on the opposite end from Rex. The Mind Mix singer nodded in a friendly manner, but his gaze could have frozen ice.

Tyra stood by the door, monitoring the room, and Cameron

took a post by the wall. Lantham and Zachary both glanced at Tyra, but neither asked why Del had a new guard. Del would have hired additional protection even if Kelric hadn't insisted. He still had nightmares about Raker and Delilah.

Zachary came over and gave him a glass of rum. Del took a sip, then set it on the table after Zachary turned around to go back to his chair. Lantham stayed put, relaxed behind Zachary's desk, watching them all as if they were chess pieces on a board he had set up for his entertainment.

"Your most recent tour was quite a success," Lantham said.

"Thanks." Del hoped they didn't want him to do another. The last had exhausted him. And why was Rex here? Del had no intention of opening for Mind Mix again. He had two anthologies in the top five and Rex only had one. Yeah, Mind Mix had two decades of solid sales behind them. It would be a long time before he could match that, if ever. But damn it, he shouldn't be their opener.

"Maybe we could do some virtual concerts," Del said. He was stalling. Artists gave virtual concerts all the time. It was easy to set up. They wouldn't call in the big guns for that.

"Yes, of course," Lantham said with a hint of irritation. "I'm sure our techs can take care of it."

Del bit his lip, feeling foolish. Mac shot him a warning look and tilted his head just slightly, which wasn't any help, because that particular nod could mean either that he approved of whatever Prime-Nova was cooking up or else he didn't like it at all.

Del eased down his mental barriers. Both Mac and Ricki were uneasy. Rex was pissed. Zachary was worried and feeling aggressive, which was one of his worst moods, the type that led everyone to avoid the tech-mech king. Lantham was cooler, sizing them all up, especially Del and Rex. Del felt about as comfortable as if he were rolling naked in a hill of stinging ants. His head began to ache, and he raised his barriers.

"If this is about Tarex—" Del began.

"No, not that." Lantham waved his hand. "We want you to do another concert."

Damn. "For my *Starlight* vid?" If the tour was for him, he wouldn't have to worry about Rex.

"Not exactly," Zachary said. "Just one performance." He nodded to Rex. "Mind Mix is the lead in the July Fourth show in the Capitol Mall in D.C. We'd like you to play as well."

Well, hell. They *did* want him to open for Rex. Sure, the concert would be huge, bigger than anything he had done, over a million people. Mind Mix was one of the best-established bands in the business. Of course they were headliners. But damn it, Del didn't want to play second fiddle as if he were a raw new act. Even worse, he would have to cancel his trip home. Again. He *needed* that vacation.

Unfortunately, his refusal to deal with Tarex had ticked off Prime-Nova big time. If he refused this concert, it would do even more damage. They put up with more from him now because he was making money for them, but he could only push it so far.

Del spoke carefully. "I wasn't invited to do the concert."

Lantham leaned back in his big chair and steepled his fingers. "Well, that's the thing, Del." He nodded toward Rex. "Mind Mix was invited. Top billing. But it seems their morpher can't play."

"Tackman?" Del asked. He could feel Rex simmering. "Why not? He's a good musician."

"He's a fucked-up musician," Ricki said flatly. "He went on a very public neuro-amp binge three days ago, tore up a restaurant, smashed a wait-bot, and shoved around several well-heeled patrons who are now threatening lawsuits. We put him in detox, but he is *not* going on stage next week for the July Fourth concert."

"Is he going to be all right?" Del asked.

Lantham shrugged. "Eventually. If he stays in treatment."

"The hum on the meshes is bad," Zachary said. "Some virt worlds are saying Mind Mix should be kicked off the Capitol lineup. We don't want that to happen. We need to bring in someone fresh, with no bad press. Someone new and popular."

"I can't play a morpher," Del said, bewildered. "I don't know anything about keyboards."

Ricki motioned to Jud. "But you have one of the best in the business."

Jud gaped at her. "You want *me* to do it?"

Del could have fallen over. The way Ricki always complained about Jud being undercity, he had thought she couldn't stand his playing. Maybe that had been yet another tactic. He had finished his two vids, so Prime-Nova had to negotiate a new contract if they wanted more. And he had a lot to bargain with this time.

"That explains why you asked Jud here," Del said. "Not me."

"You're going to sing with Rex," Lantham said.

"Damn it!" Rex burst out. "I told you. I won't sing with him. Put him on before me." He looked furious, but what Del felt from him was *fear*. It came through even Del's raised shields.

"Del isn't opening for anyone," Mac said. "Most of those acts you have playing should open for *him*."

"We aren't asking him to," Zachary said. "He and Rex will sing together."

"No," Rex said. "I won't do it."

"You really find me that offensive?" Del asked. It bothered him a lot, because he liked Rex. Sort of.

Rex clenched his tumbler. "If we sing together, Arden, I'll sound like a fool."

That he hadn't expected. "That's nuts. You're great."

"Yeah, I sound good," Rex said. "But I can't come close to what you do. The comparison will drill my career. Everyone will talk about how Prime-Nova's two male stars match up. Your voice is eons better than mine, you're twenty-five years younger, you can dance, and you could go for hours after I would have to stop." He turned to Zachary. "You want to kill my commercial value? Then sure, put me up there with him."

Del felt as if they had knocked out his breath. Rex thought Del would make him look bad? It was nuts. But Zachary just shifted his weight and looked at Lantham, then Ricki. None of them disputed Rex's words.

After the silence became strained, Rex pushed his hand across his close-cropped hair. "All right! Put him on after me. Just fix it so I don't look like I'm opening for him."

Del stared at him. He didn't know how to absorb the concept that Rex Montrow, one of the biggest stars in decades, would rather let Del headline a concert than risk the comparison of their singing together.

"You'd let Del go last?" Mac asked.

"Yeah." Rex sounded as if he were gritting his teeth.

Lantham looked Del over with an appraising stare. "Can you do it? You only have a week."

"Of course I can," Del said, irked.

"The last time you told us that," Lantham said coldly, "you plummeted. Miserably."

Del flushed. "I didn't know what I was doing. I do now."

"You think you'll play for a million people," Lantham said.

"Isn't that the projected number?" Del asked.

"In D.C., yes." Lantham leaned forward. "They won't fit into the mall. The show will be broadcast all over the city. And not just the city. It's the only concert we broadcast live. It will go out to the North American continent on our feeds. Mesh-media will pick it up and send in all over Earth. And offworld. Not just to Allied Worlds, either. The Skolians and Traders are going to pick this one up, too. If you bomb, you can't fuck up much worse than that."

Del's anger sparked. Lantham sounded like Kelric. He spoke coldly. "Thank you for the vote of confidence."

Ricki raised her eyebrows. He ignored it. Damn it, he had proved himself on this last tour.

"Right now, you're the hottest boy on the market," Lantham told him. "But you could go down as fast as you went up. The newer you are, the easier it is to fall."

Del remembered the last time he had said, *sure, one week, no problem.* They had reason for their doubts. And they were already angry over Tarex. He made himself speak with respect. "I won't, sir."

Mac blinked, and if the atmosphere hadn't been so tense, Del would have laughed. He doubted Mac had ever heard him act deferential, especially with an authority figure like Lantham.

The CEO rose to his feet. "Then we're decided."

"You have my word." Del said. He stood up as well. "It'll be a concert like none you've ever seen."

XXIII

A Country Home

Del lay on his back on the marble floor of the crypt. A domed roof arched above, and a haze of motes drifted in a beam of sunlight that slanted past the open marble door. His voice drifted in the background:

> No answers live in here alone
> No answers on this spectral throne
> Nothing in this vault of fears
> This sterling vault, chamber of tears
>
> Tell me now before I fall
> Release me from this velvet pall
> Tell me now before I fall
> Take me now, break through my wall

His voice wound through the air, full of grief, but also hope:

> No answers could bring me life
> Yet when I opened my eyes
> Beyond the sleeping crystal dome
> Beyond it all, I had come home

Del rolled onto his stomach and rested his cheek on his hands. The marble floor was smooth under his palms. Although many people considered the lyrics of "No Answers" dark, to Del they were as much about his return to life as his death. Usually the crypt in his virt had a sense of serenity, but today it felt suffocating. Yet no matter how hard he concentrated on changing the scene, the virt wouldn't respond. He couldn't get out of the simulation. He was trapped, *trapped*—

Stop it, Del told himself. *Take a breath. Concentrate . . .*

The building rippled and wavered, then blurred into grey mist. Bewildered, he sat up—into brilliant light. He was in a cave. A crystal cave. Light bounced around the crystals, reflecting and refracting, too bright.

"No!" Del shouted. He struggled to hold down his panic and change the sim. He had to flee the crystal cave. The cryo womb. No, not a womb. The *tomb.*

His cryo unit had always looked like this when he awoke. The doctors brought him out when they took his DNA for Delson, then put him back when his body shut down. Ten years later, when they took him out again, Chaniece had been waiting. Hers was the first face he had seen. She had held him while he shook uncontrollably, terrified he would be paralyzed, mute, and helpless for the rest of his life.

Gradually he had healed. His body hadn't been stable at first, so they had put him back in cryo for a few months. It had gone that way for several years, until he no longer needed stabilization. That had been six years ago. He had been normal since then, at least as normal as he could be after he had lost nearly five decades while life continued without him.

Del had gone into cryo just months after the Traders brutalized his parents. Not long after he came out, his half-brother Kurj had died in the battle that started the Radiance War. The Traders had tortured and killed Althor, the brother who protected Del that night at the lake. Del's sister Soz became Imperator and went to war, bringing two empires to their knees. She captured the Trader emperor—and his own people blew up her ship, killing him as well as her. They captured Eldrin and interrogated him for months before he gained his freedom. No one knew what had happened to Kelric, who had vanished for years and only returned home in the chaotic aftermath of the war, ravaged by age and illness.

For Del, no decades had intervened in those events, though over forty years had passed between what happened to his parents and his siblings. The Aristos had taken so very, very much from his family. Usually he pressed down the memories until he no longer hurt, but here in the crystal cave of his own mind, he couldn't escape. He was helpless to do anything for the family he loved. And he did love them, deeply and desperately, despite the way he fought them, struggling like a wild animal in a trap.

His brothers and sister had been leaders, pilots, heroes. Dehya and Kelric were geniuses, using their formidable intellects to protect their people. Windar dedicated his life to teaching, for he believed education was the road to peace. Vyrl had led a planet-wide protest that forced the Allied military to leave Lyshriol and return control of the planet to Del's family.

Del had none of the traits that made his family valuable, nothing except his DNA, which had left his grown son with the mind of a child and the younger one with Del's painful empathic sensitivity. He had slept for decades while his family weathered the brutality of the Traders. He could do nothing to help. Nothing. He didn't resent them so much as he hated *himself* for having nothing to give.

Rex worried about how he would look next to Del on stage, but he had no idea how brutal a comparison could be. Next to the rest of his family, Del felt worthless on a scale so huge, it was unbearable. The Ruby Dynasty—the ultimate prey of the Highton Aristos—defied the Traders on an interstellar scale. It infuriated the Aristos almost beyond imagining, and they retaliated by doing everything within their power to make the existence of the Ruby Dynasty a living hell. Del had escaped the long reach of their brutality only because they knew they had nothing to fear from him. He was nothing.

That was the greatest irony, that he, the weakest link of the Ruby Dynasty, was the one left standing, unscathed—except for his grief.

Jud's frightened face swam into view. "Thank God! I was about to call the hospital."

Del peered at him with bleary vision. After a moment, he realized he was holding his VR helmet. He must have taken it off, because Jud would never remove a brain-wired connection.

"What happened?" Del asked thickly.

"You've been in that bliss all night!" Jud said. "Eight hours. I thought you would never stop."

Del's voice felt creaky. "I wanted to . . . couldn't stop."

"You look like hell."

Del sat up stiffly and set the helmet on the console. "Why were you worried? You see me in the node every day."

"Not this long." Jud sat in the chair next to him. "Staver commed you last night. He sounded frightened."

Dismay swept over Del. Had he been trapped in his nightmares while something happened to Staver? He fumbled with the console, trying to activate its comm. His mind wouldn't cooperate. Eight miserable hours of reliving his worst memories had wiped him out.

Claude, his EI, spoke. "Del, do you want some help?"

"I need to comm Staver Aunchild," Del said.

"I'm setting up the link," Claude answered.

Del tried to stand, then sank back into his chair.

"You have to stop," Jud said. "You want to be Prime-Nova's next meltdown? Tackman got hit bad, Del. It'll be a long time before Lantham works with him again. If ever." He shook his head. "The whole band got hit. Now we're the headliner on July Fourth. You could lose it just as easily as Mind Mix did."

"The virt *helps* me perform." But Del was no longer sure of anything. Bliss was supposed to untangle his mind after a concert. When had pre-concert trips become his routine? In everything he did, he was always planning his next session. It interfered with his music. How was that any different from Tackman needing his next neuro-amp fix? Del had thought of Raker and Delilah as the virtisos, but he wondered just how much—or little—separated him from them. He had promised to quit, yet he had just done his longest session ever, and it had been a journey into his nightmares.

"Staver Aunchild isn't home," Claude suddenly said. "His house EI says neither he nor his bodyguard have been in since last night."

Del climbed to his feet. "Why would it tell you that?"

"Staver left a message," Claude said. "He wanted you to comm him. He was supposed to stay home. But he left. His EI doesn't know when; Staver erased part of its memory, and it can't reach either Staver or his bodyguard. His AI posted an orange code."

Del tensed. Orange meant it suspected a risk to Staver. "Why did he erase its memory?"

"It doesn't know. Probably to keep his actions secret."

Del turned to Jud. "We have to find him."

Jud regarded him uneasily. "You think this is about that Aristo?"

"I don't know." Del took a step and stumbled as vertigo swept over him. With a groan, he grabbed the console.

"You've been in some weird neural state all night," Jud said. "You can't just go running around."

Hanging onto the console, Del regarded Jud bleakly. "If Staver needed help, and I didn't because I was in the bliss—"

"Maybe he wanted to talk business."

"Yeah, sure. That's why you thought he was frightened."

Jud grabbed his net-sweater off a chair and pulled it on. Del would have normally razzed him for wearing clothes that turned him into a walking console, but today he was glad. If intelligent clothes could help, he was all for them. He went to his room, moving with care, and changed into leather pants with a mesh that was neither ripped nor damaged. He looped a chain belt on his pants and tugged on a black T-shirt with the arms cut out. His head was swimming. Usually after a virt session, he felt relaxed, but last night had been miserable. Bliss it wasn't.

Cameron was waiting in the hall outside. No surprise there. Although he and Tyra didn't eavesdrop on Del in his home, they monitored him so well, he felt as if ghosts haunted the apartment.

"Where are you going?" Cameron asked.

"To see Staver." Del said. "Where's Tyra?"

"Asleep," Cameron said. "You should be, too."

"I can't!" Del told him about Staver. "We have to check on him."

"Not without Tyra," Cameron said.

Del knew arguing would do no good. "Let's get her, then."

They went inside Cameron's apartment, a neater version of Del and Jud's place. Light sculptures glowed on columns, holo-panels on the walls showed forest views, and big furniture stood on blue rugs. As they entered, Anne ambled into the living room, rubbing her eyes, her long hair tousled over her shoulders and arms. She had on nothing except Cameron's pullover, which came halfway down her thighs. She froze when she saw them, and her cheeks turned red.

Jud grinned. "I thought I heard drums last night."

Cameron scowled at him. "No one was playing any drums."

"Hey, Anne," Del said, delighted. "Good to see you."

Anne cleared her throat. "Uh—hi."

Cameron went over and spoke to her in a low voice. "I have to take these meatheads out. You can stay here." He hesitated. "If you want."

Anne gave him a luminous smile. "I'll be here."

Cameron's face did the most amazing thing, something Del had never witnessed. It softened and warmed. "Make yourself at home," the Marine told her. "For as long as you want."

She touched his cheek. "Sure, handsome."

"Could you go wake up Tyra?" Cameron motioned to another door. "She sleeps in there."

Anne's soft look turned into a glare. It was hard for her to look tough, though, given her sleepy, tousled appearance. "I really don't understand why you *live* with Tyra, Sergeant Cameron."

"I don't. I mean, I do, but I don't."

"Hmmm," Anne said.

"It's our job." Cameron hooked a thumb toward Del. "Guarding his skinny butt."

Anne looked at Del. "How come you need two babysitters?"

"My brother sent Tyra," Del said. "If I don't go along with it, he'll make me go home."

Anne snorted. "Who does your brother think he is, the King of Skyfall?"

Del gulped and Jud made a choking sound.

"Uh, no, he doesn't, I'm sure," Del stuttered.

Anne bestowed him with an unimpressed stare. She turned the same look on Cameron, but her face immediately softened. Rising on her toes, she kissed his cheek. "Don't be gone long, big guy."

Incredibly, the looming, tough Marine blushed. Then she walked off, swaying in his pullover.

"Wow." Jud smiled at Cameron. "You like 'em dangerous."

"Don't get her mad," Del warned. "She wields a wicked drum stick."

Cameron ignored them and went to a silver column in one corner. Del had thought it was decorative, but when Cameron tapped the surface, a panel slid open, and he took out a gun. A pulser-pistol. It shot serrated bullets under high pressure, and it emitted an electromagnetic pulse that scrambled mesh signals.

"That's some heavy duty artillery," Jud said.

"It's nothing," Tyra said.

Del turned to see her walking toward them, sleek and dangerous in black jeans and a black pullover. Anne was with her.

"Where are you all going?" Anne asked.

"Staver Aunchild wanted my help last night," Del said. "Now we can't find him, and his AI went orange."

"Orange what?" Tyra asked, annoyingly alert for someone who had just woken up. Del could barely function before noon.

"It's the North American warning system for house meshes," Anne said. "An AI posts orange if it thinks the house owner is in trouble. On code red, the AI contacts the authorities."

Tyra's posture changed subtly, as if she were tensing to fight. "Lord Tarex is still on Earth. He's staying at the Star Tower as a guest of Prime-Nova."

Del took a breath. "Let's get going, before that changes." He didn't say what he knew Tyra was thinking; if Tarex had Staver and took him offworld, the Skolian would never see home again.

With Tarex as a guest of Prime-Nova, someone the conglomerate hoped to do millions of business with, even billions, Del didn't feel he could contact them about Staver or his suspicions. He had absolutely no intention of telling Ricki. He didn't want her anywhere near Tarex, like not even in the same galaxy.

Staver had rented a house in an area that had once been a city called Laurel and now was all countryside. To get there, Del linked his racer into the traffic grid for Interstate 95, and it whisked them south of Baltimore.

"I don't know why they call this a racer," Del grumbled as trees flashed past. "The grid won't allow anything faster than two hundred kilometers an hour." Although he was sitting in the driver's seat, the car was doing all the driving. Jud was in the passenger's seat up front, and Tyra and Cameron were in the back.

"Oh, come on," Tyra said. "Most untrained, unaugmented humans don't have good enough reflexes to drive at that speed, at least not safely."

"Race drivers do," Jud said.

Tyra waved at the stream of chromed beauties whizzing along with them. "They look like they're on a race track to you?"

Del grinned at her. "Oh, yeah."

"Remind me never to drive with you off the grid," Cameron muttered.

Looking back, Del regarded him innocently. "I would never do that. It's illegal to take a car off the grid." Cameron just snorted.

"Going off-grid isn't much harder than cracking vids," Jud said.

"Which of course you would never do," Cameron said.

"Uh, yeah." Jud cleared his throat. "Of course."

Del slanted Jud a look. Right. At least Jud was more discreet about it than some artists. Everyone wanted an inside look at the competition. Although many people illegally analyzed the creations of other artists, Del rarely felt the urge. Contrary to what his family believed, he intended to honor the laws of his host world. He didn't really want to take apart someone else's work, anyway; he liked to listen to it the way they meant it to be heard.

"You know, we could buy an estate out here," Jud said. "We're making enough money. Why stay in that little apartment?"

"It's a good apartment," Del said. "Besides, just because we had one good royalty check, that doesn't mean we're rich."

"Are you shitting me?" Jud said, laughing. "Wait until you see the next one. That last hardly included anything for 'Diamond Star,' and that was before *Starlight*."

"I suppose." Del was happy in the apartment. If he wanted opulence, he could live in the Sunrise Palace on the world Parthonia or the Ruby Palace on Raylicon. His best memories, though, came from the house on Lyshriol, which had been in his father's family for centuries. Although pretty, it was nothing compared to the palaces the Ruby Dynasty maintained elsewhere. But it was a *home*: warm, comfortable, filled with the life of a large, energetic family. He had especially fond memories from his childhood, before his arguments with his family had soured everything.

Del peered at the trees along the road, trying to see past them, but the leaves were too dense. The foliage on Earth confused him. Lyshriol plants consisted of tubules, from tiny rods to columns taller than a man, all in stained-glass colors. Green was one of the colors, but it was more like emerald glass. The beautifully strange plants here soothed him at a deep level, a reminder that his ancestors had come from this teeming world.

"I wish we could fly." Del touched a roof panel and the top of the car went transparent, letting him gaze at the cloud-puffed sky. Flyers soared, following air lanes over the Interstate. "Hovering takes so long."

"Once we get into the country, it'll be better," Cameron said.

Del looked around at him. "Isn't that backward, that it used to be a city out there and now it's not?"

"There are fewer people now," Cameron said. "Some industries moved offworld. And population centers change around."

Del turned restlessly to face front. "Claude, are you here?"

His EI's voice came out of the dashboard. "Right here."

"Try reaching Staver again."

"Connecting," Claude said.

"Staver probably just partied too hard and passed out," Jud said. He sounded as if he were trying to convince himself.

"Have you *ever* seen him drink that much?" Del asked.

Jud regarded him uneasily. "He really wanted to talk to you."

Claude spoke. "Mister Aunchild's AI says he's still missing. It wants to know if we think it should go to code red."

"If it goes red," Del asked, "who will it contact?"

"The police and the Skolian embassy," Claude said. "And it would file a missing person report."

Cameron leaned forward between the front seats. "He's only been gone overnight. He could be with a woman, on a binge, anything. The police won't act until he's gone twenty-four hours."

"Staver is a prime-rated telepath," Del said. "Do you know how rare that is? Tarex is an Aristo. The police would be fools not to act."

"How would you justify accusing Tarex?" Cameron asked. "We have no evidence."

"He's an Aristo," Tyra said flatly.

"That's not evidence," Cameron told her. "Axil Tarex is a powerful man. Regardless of what you think, regardless of what may be true, we *have* to be careful."

"We should let the police know Staver is missing," Tyra said. "That's not accusing anyone of anything."

Del spoke. "Claude, tell Staver's AI to go to red."

"Done," Claude said.

Jud regarded Del. "If Staver shows up, hung over and with some girl, we're going to look really stupid."

"Better stupid," Del said, "than sorry."

✧   ✧   ✧

The mansion was still empty when they arrived.

Del stood with Jud and Cameron on the porch and gazed out at the hills of central Maryland, which were dotted with glades of trees. In the distance, the sleek towers of the Laurel-Columbia metropolitan center gleamed against the sky.

"Why would an exec rent a house out here?" Jud asked. "You'd think he'd prefer D.C. where everything is happening."

Del could guess why. Staver needed a secluded base for his covert work. He said only, "Most empaths don't like the city."

Tyra walked out of the house, studying the mesh on her gauntlet. She looked up at Del. "Looks like he left you another message. I'll let you know as soon as I get into his account."

Cameron raised an eyebrow. "You think you can break Allied security codes?"

Tyra smiled dangerously. "Hell, yeah." She went back to her gauntlet, and a moment later, she said, "Okay. Here it is."

Staver's voice rose into the air. "Del, we've found out Tarex is investigating you. He's searching out your Kyle rating. Stay with your guards. Be careful. Comm me."

"Huh," Jud said. "He wasn't afraid for himself. He was worried for you."

"So why did he go out?" Cameron said.

Del had a sinking feeling he knew exactly why. Staver had gone with his people to free the provider. "Tarex has him. We have to help."

Tyra spoke firmly. "You're staying away from Tarex."

"We have to do something!" Del felt as if he were clenching up inside. "If you won't help, call in people who can."

"I'll contact ISC and ASC," she said. "But I doubt we can get a team in here before tonight."

"You're a Jagernaut Secondary," Del said. "One assigned to guard a Ruby prince. I know what that means, Tyra. You're high up in my brother's forces. You can get it done faster."

"The holdup isn't ours," she said. "Allied Space Command won't let us act against Tarex without evidence. Gods, Del, that's risking a major diplomatic crisis. They'll insist on proof."

"The hell with ASC," Del said. "Don't tell them."

Cameron stiffened. "Are you asking me to hide information from my commanding officers?"

Del balled his hands into fists. "So you're going to stand by while Tarex tortures Staver?"

"Del, listen," Tyra said. "We aren't going to just stand by. But we have to work with the Allieds. And we don't know that Tarex has Staver."

"He does." Del had no doubts. Staver was trying to reach him. It was why Del's bliss session had turned into a nightmare about what the Aristos had done to his family. Because Staver was enduring the same.

Then it hit Del. "I know where Tarex has him! Staver tried to tell me last night. I kept hearing "No Answers." Except it wasn't right. I was trapped in the crypt. The cryo womb. That's where Tarex has him! In a tomb."

They all just looked at him. Finally Jud spoke uncomfortably. "You've been spending a lot of time in the bliss—"

"I'm not imagining this!"

"You had a bad night," Cameron said.

"No!" Del said. "I know what I'm talking about."

"What he's saying is more likely than it sounds," Tyra told them. "Psions can sometimes pick up what other psions experience if they know each other, and it can happen more in the virt because it relaxes Del's mind."

"It doesn't make sense," Jud said. "Why would Tarex put him in a crypt? And what crypt?"

They all looked at Del.

"I don't know," Del admitted.

Tyra worked on her gauntlet, running through displays on its screen. "Tarex's ship is still in dock. So are his Escort ships. In fact, no Trader ships have left any local starport in the past two days."

Del didn't ask how she knew so many details about private Eubian citizens. She wouldn't tell him in front of witnesses. He just said, "He could have left in secret."

"I doubt it," Cameron said. "It's not easy to sneak a ship off-planet, even for an Aristo."

"Especially for an Aristo," Tyra said. "Right now, everyone and his mother is monitoring Tarex."

Del hesitated. Was he mistaken about the crypt and his bliss session? "Maybe I'm just mired in my own imagery."

Tyra's voice gentled. "Only an artist would describe it that way."

Del blinked. It was odd to hear his brother's hand-picked officer call him an artist, especially as if it was a compliment. "Maybe the crypt is how my mind interprets something else."

"A cargo hold?" Cameron asked.

Del hesitated. "Possibly."

"A starship cold storage unit!" Tyra said. "Those things look like tombs."

"But Staver would freeze to death," Del said. "Tarex will want him alive."

"Maybe they didn't activate the unit," Jud said.

Del felt ill. The storage units on star-yachts weren't that big. A man Staver's size would barely fit. "We have to go to the port before it's too late. Tarex could leave any time."

Tyra crossed her arms. "You're going home."

Del banged his fist on the porch rail. "I'm the strongest empath here, and I have more connection to him than any of you. I can sense his mind, but I have to be closer."

"That may be," she said. "But you aren't visiting Tarex."

Del stalked away, across the porch, then spun around to her. "All right. I won't. But let me go to the port. I might be able to tell you more. The closer I get to Staver, the better. I was going to go tomorrow anyway, for my trip home."

His bodyguards exchanged glances. Cameron said, "Our precautions against Tarex are already in place."

"I can go there to change my flight," Del said. "I have to anyway, since I'm doing the July Fourth concert tomorrow."

Tyra put her hands on her hips. "No one goes to the port for that. You could use any console."

"Yeah, but I'm a holo-rock singer." Del crooked a smile at her. "Everyone knows we're weird, right? I can ask questions as strange as I want, and people won't blink. I'm good at playing the temperamental, impulsive rock star."

Jud gave him a sour look. "That's because it fits you so well." When Del glared, he held up his hands. "Hey, I'm agreeing with you."

Tyra considered Del. "I assume you won't argue if we decide you need to leave."

"Not a single protest," Del promised.

Her knock came at his mind. *Del?*

He lowered his shields to let her see he meant it. **I'll behave.**

Tyra let out a breath. "All right. We'll try it."

XXIV

Port Reckoning

The Thurgood Marshall Interstellar Starport, also known as BWI, or Baltimore-Washington Interstellar, had an entire department devoted to dealing with wealthy clients. As star travel had shifted from the military to the commercial sector, corporations had leapt into existence solely to take money from rich people who wished to play among the stars.

"I don't want it housed outside," Del growled at the fellow showing him around the area reserved for star-yachts. "Rain is bad for the finish."

"The finish?" The man, Reginald Wharton, worked for Centauri Travel. "On a yacht?" He was a paragon of courtesy, but his reaction to them leaked past his natural mental protections. He thought Del was a kook. A trendy kook, though. His other clients never showed up in black leather pants with chains hanging off them, a black T-shirt with laser-light rivets holding together the seams, leather boots, and a belt of starship ring fittings.

"That's right." Del brandished his smart-mug of deluxo-java. When Wharton had offered it to him, Del had insisted he have some, too. So now their guide carried a cup of deluxo. So did Jud, who walked on Del's other side. Tyra and Cameron strode with them, minus the java. Wharton didn't seem the least surprised that Del came with bodyguards. Given the clientele he served, he probably saw guards hulking about all the time.

"I don't want scratches on the hull," Del told Wharton.

"No scratches?" Wharton looked bewildered. "You mean on a starship?"

Del glowered at him. "Yeah, *my* starship."

"We can arrange any type of docking area you like," Wharton assured him. "Indoors, outdoors, underground."

"But can you protect the finish?" Del insisted. He felt Tyra struggling not to laugh at him. Every ship took a beating from the cosmic ray flux in space and whatever else spun, floated, or radiated out there. Only a nut would try to preserve the finish. It was a little annoying how easily he convinced Wharton he was an eccentric, but it let him ask nosy questions without looking suspicious.

"Nothing will harm your ship in our facility," Wharton told him. "And if it's damaged in space, we can see to its upkeep."

"Good," Del said. "Can't have a cheap-looking yacht."

"No, absolutely not," Wharton said.

"I'd like to look at the docking areas," Del said. "To see if they match the yacht I'm buying. I don't want your décor to clash with my ship."

Wharton spluttered his sip of deluxo.

"You all right?" Del asked.

"Uh, yes. Yes, certainly." Wharton took a monogrammed cloth out of his pocket and wiped his mouth. The cup cleaned itself, absorbing the splattered java. Then Wharton indicated a gleaming white corridor that veered to the left. "This way, please."

Del walked with him, looking around, presumably to see if the décor clashed with anything. Mentally, he reached out, searching for Staver. He picked up a flicker, but nothing definite. He needed to be closer.

"I'm considering buying a yacht in the Dieshan line imported from the Skolians," Del said.

Tyra made a choked sound, and Del barely restrained himself from glaring at her. Yeah, all right, Diesha served as a military headquarters. Kelric's commanders there were about as likely to make yachts for rich playboys as they were to pull out their teeth without an anesthetic. But it was the first place that came to mind. So Del gave Wharton his best smile and added, "You've heard of them, of course."

"Ah—yes, of course." Wharton cleared his throat.

"Good. Then you know how to house Skolian yachts."

Wharton blinked. "It's different than housing Allied yachts?"

Del stopped smiling. "You don't know how to look after the ships in your care?"

"We do, yes, certainly," Wharton said quickly. "We have the best facilities on the Eastern Seaboard."

Del scowled at him. "Maybe I'd better see these facilities for non-Allied ships."

"We have several Eubian ships in dock," Wharton said. "We can look at that docking area if you wish."

Tyra shot a warning glance at Del. Damn it! She didn't want him near the ships.

It's safe, he thought. **I'd know if Tarex was here. I'd feel it.**

No, she answered.

Why not? he thought, frustrated. **Even if he was here—which he's not—what could he do? Just grab me? I don't think so.**

Her gaze had turned steely. *The answer is no.*

Del gritted his teeth. If he pushed, she would make him leave the port.

"I don't want to go close," Del said grudgingly. "Just see the place."

Wharton let out a breath. "I'll be glad to take you."

It didn't surprise Del that Wharton looked relieved. The last thing he probably wanted was a whacko rock star bothering the other clients.

A carpeted fast-walk whisked them down glowing corridors, past panels that showed holos of local attractions. When they came around the corner, Del found himself staring at a life-sized holo of himself wailing one of his songs from *Starlight*.

"Hey!" Jud laughed at his side. "Man, they'll put up any crackpot's picture."

Del glared at him. "Ha, ha." He could feel Wharton holding back a laugh. Bah.

"Right this way," Wharton said, escorting them off the walk.

They went under an archway of blue flexi-glass with lights darting within it like fireflies. It opened into a cavernous docking bay. Everything was gigantic, including the serrated doors and the clamps to hold ships. It looked like all the other docking bays Del's family used, but from what he had gathered about the commercial liner he had planned to take tomorrow, most ships docked outside a building, in far less protected areas.

Wharton brought them out on a platform that overlooked the bay. Del rested his hands on a metallic rail at its edge. In the distance, two Eubian Escort ships flanked a golden yacht. He reached outward with his mind, but he picked up only the people around him. Jud was having the time of his life watching Del make an idiot out of himself. Even Cameron and Tyra were amused, at least as long as Del stayed here, away from the Eubian ships.

Del reached out, searching, searching, searching . . .

Pain!

He slammed up his mental barriers so fast, he staggered and lost his balance. As he lurched to the side, Tyra caught his arm, and Cameron put a hand under Del's other elbow.

"Mister Arden, are you all right?" Wharton asked.

"F-fine," Del said. "I had a—" *What?* "A lot to drink last night." It was a weak excuse given that he could easily afford the nanomeds that would cure a hangover. But he couldn't think of anything else.

"Can I get you anything?" Wharton asked. "We have an excellent lounge for patrons. You can relax, put up your feet."

"Yeah. Ultra." Del straightened up. "Thanks."

A mental knock came at Del's mind. Taking a breath, he eased down his defenses. **Tyra?** he thought.

What happened? she asked.

Someone is here. In Tarex's yacht. In pain. Terrible pain. I think it's Staver. I recognize his mind.

Damn. That probably means Tarex is there.

I didn't feel an Aristo.

"Mister Arden?" Wharton asked.

Del nodded unevenly to him. "Lead on."

As Wharton escorted them though the port on a fast-walk, Tyra thought, *If Tarex isn't there, he has no reason to leave Staver in pain.*

Tarex probably isn't the only person with Aristo genetics on those ships.

You aren't going to stay here, Tyra told him. *We're leaving.*

Del stiffened. **Don't pull that authoritarian crap on me.**

You listen to me, Del, she thought. *If you blow off every person who reminds you of your brother, you'll get killed. You gave your word not to argue, and I expect you to abide by that.*

Was his resentment of Kelric that obvious? Del let out a breath. **All right.** Then he raised his barriers.

"Maybe it's better if I go home," Del told Wharton. "Thanks for the tour. I'll be in touch."

"Please do." Wharton handed him a glossy cube that fit into Del's palm. "That has my contact info, as well as displays about Centauri Travel. Feel free to comm me anytime, day or night."

"Thanks." He had to admit, Wharton did his job well. Del thought he might really buy a yacht; they had good facilities here, and it would make seeing Chaniece and the boys easier than if he took commercial flights. But he had a more important matter to settle first. Tyra expected him to leave Staver trapped in agony.

Del couldn't do it.

Jud paced the Centauri Lounge, restless and unsettled. "What's taking so long?"

"They've only been gone a few moments," Tyra said. "Even Del can't go to the bathroom that fast."

"I suppose," Jud said. He never knew what to make of Tyra. She wasn't anything like the women he knew. She looked feminine, but he had the feeling she could kill without blinking.

"Something about this doesn't feel right," Jud said.

Tyra tapped her gauntlet comm. "Cameron, are you with Del?"

His voice came out of the gauntlet. "Yes. Why?"

"Just checking." She sent Jud a questioning look.

"Del wouldn't screw around," Jud said. He wanted to convince himself as much as Tyra. "Especially not when we have that huge concert tomorrow night."

"Then why are you worried?"

He grimaced. "I'm always worried about Del."

"You don't usually bring it up." She took off across the lounge, striding toward the entrance to the men's bathroom.

"Hey!" Jud went after her. "You can't go in there."

By the time Jud caught up with her, she was in the spa that Centauri Travel modestly called a bathroom, with its marble stalls and tiled bathing pool. She was kneeling next to an unconscious man who lay sprawled on the floor.

Tyra looked up with a jerk. "I swear, I'm going to fry his damned royal ass!"

Jud stared at her. "Oh, shit."

It was Cameron who lay there.

With the fast-walk carrying him as he ran, Del flew through the port, speeding past everyone else. He knew Cameron would never forgive him. The Marine should have taken Del's *mai-quinjo* training more seriously. Del hadn't been sure himself what he could do in a real engagement. But the moves had come easily to him, honed by all his live concerts, and the mesh woven into his pants added intelligence to his actions, enhancing his efforts by contracting or releasing the leather. He had barely managed to knock Cameron out, but barely was enough.

Del had no doubt that when Kelric found out about this, he would pull Del off Earth faster than Del could grunt. But Del couldn't leave Staver condemned to a life of torture. As long as Tarex was on Earth, they could do something; once Tarex left, their chances of helping Staver were nil. The Star Road would die.

When Del had touched Staver's mind in the docking bay, he had caught only a hint of the exec—but given the intensity of what he found, that had been enough. Staver had commed him last night to talk about the rescue they planned for the provider. Del felt sure he could have convinced Staver not to go with the rescue team. Staver would be free now. But no, Del hadn't been available, because he had been submerged in his stupid, wretched bliss-node.

Del knew if he tried to help, he could become a prisoner. It scared the hell out of him. He was no good to the Aristos as a Ruby prince; if they linked him into the Dyad, he would die in a massive convulsion that made the ones after his concerts seem like nothing. But that would be better than the horror his life would otherwise become. All his instincts pushed him to retreat, seek protection, let the military take care of this mess. But he had felt the truth in his contact with Staver's mind; Tarex would leave today rather than risk losing the prize he had captured.

Del couldn't turn back. He had done nothing worthwhile with his life. If he were willing to admit it to himself, it was one reason he resented his family. It was easier to be angry at them than to acknowledge how useless he felt to help them. The Aristos had shattered his family, torn apart their lives, and turned them into interstellar pawns. He refused to let the Traders destroy a man who had fought them so well, a man Del might have convinced to stay in safety if he had been there when Staver needed to talk.

No more, he thought. *No more will I stand by.*

Del paused in front of the yacht, between the two Escorts, in full view of anyone within the three starships. They all had the circular shape of vessels that rotated in space, creating the effect of gravity, but they were too small to allow for much. He couldn't sneak into the yacht; they would catch him. More to the point, it would be obvious he was up to something they didn't want to happen. He had a better plan, one just bizarre enough, it might work, and let him get out with Staver, too.

So Del went up the ramp to the hatch—and knocked. "Hello?" he said in English. "Anybody home?"

Nothing.

Del knocked again. "Hello?"

A male voice came from within, speaking in the stilted phrases of mesh-translated language. "Who are you?"

"My name is Del Arden. Lord Tarex wanted to talk about licensing my work. I came to apologize for the way I acted."

More time passed. Del waited, his pulse racing. They would be monitoring his vital signs, which undoubtedly showed his fear. They probably assumed he was afraid of Tarex. Why wouldn't they? All "inferior" forms of life were supposed to fear Aristos.

Del was risking his freedom on his belief they wouldn't hold him prisoner if he came to talk business. They couldn't bargain with the Allieds if they grabbed the very people they wanted to work with. And Aristos liked one thing even more than providers: money. They were willing to deal with people they didn't consider human—which included everyone in the universe except themselves—if it would make them richer.

The airlock irised open. "Please enter," a voice said.

Taking a deep breath, Del went inside. As the airlock snapped closed behind him, an archway shimmered open in front. He stepped through into a gold and blue corridor with a lush carpet. A tall, strongly built man was approaching. He was larger than Del and wore an elegant black jumpsuit, a surreal contrast to Del's leather and metal. The man didn't have red eyes, but his hair shimmered faintly, suggesting he had some Aristo heritage. But he wasn't an Aristo. Although his jumpsuit hid most of his neck, the edge of a bronze collar showed above it. A slave collar. Nausea swept over Del.

"My greetings," the man said. "I am Bronzeson. Please excuse my English. I know only a little."

"Hey." Del smiled in what he hoped was a convincing manner. "I've never spoken it that well, either. I sing it better."

Bronzeson paused, probably listening to a translation in his ear comm. Then he chuckled. "Yes. Lord Tarex likes your music."

"He probably doesn't much like me." Del said, doing his best to look rueful.

"That you have come to apologize helps. I send message to him. He is here in an hour." The man lifted his hand toward a plush lounge ahead of them. "Please, be our guest. We have delicacy and fine wine." He didn't seem the least fazed to invite a man dressed like a thug onto the ship.

"Thanks," Del said. *An hour.* That was all the time he had. It didn't surprise him that Tarex made him wait. An Aristo would never let himself appear eager to meet someone who had treated him rudely. But he was coming, which meant Del had to finish his business fast.

"This yacht is great," Del said. He spoke slowly so the man's translator could keep up with him. "I'm thinking of buying one, too."

"Ah." Bronzeson beamed at him. "Take a look around. Lord Tarex has flawless taste and elegance."

Del had his own thoughts on that. Everything gleamed with too much metal, a stark blue and gold that seemed harsh to him. Whatever security measures were in place remained hidden. Given that Bronzeson had invited him onto the yacht, the ship would treat him as an honored guest. That was Del's only protection; it wouldn't immediately kill him when he started trouble. But that would only give him a few seconds to neutralize its defenses. It wasn't enough time.

As they entered into the lounge, Del lowered his mental shields. Bronzeson was easy to sense; Tarex would look with favor on him for hosting this guest, a man Tarex could make money from. Bronzeson couldn't imagine how anyone could refuse the Aristo. Nor could Tarex. Del's behavior at the party hadn't offended Tarex after Ricki "explained"; the Aristo took it as a given that empaths feared him. And of course Del crawled back to apologize.

Gritting his teeth, Del withdrew his awareness from Bronzeson and spread it through the ship. He didn't sense Tarex, but he did catch a sense of wrongness similar to what he felt around the Aristo. Where . . . ?

He hit the cavity.

Del froze. *No!* His mind reeled. He had slammed into someone part-Aristo, one of Tarex's officers. It said a great deal about how Tarex viewed him, that the Aristo had his most important crewmember elsewhere while Bronzeson met Del. But now that Del had found him, he couldn't avoid the mind of the officer. It pressed on him, suffocating, and Del mentally fled like a gazelle running from a lion.

"Are you all right?" Bronzeson asked.

"My apologies," Del said. "I'm not used to being on an Aristo ship." He didn't have to pretend to look shaky.

"A lord such as Tarex can be overwhelming even when he isn't present," Bronzeson said. "You are an empath, yes?"

Del tensed. "Why do you ask that?"

"Lord Tarex said you were." He lifted his hands as if to shrug. "I don't know how they can tell, but apparently it's quite clear from your performances."

That surprised Del, not that Tarex knew, but that he and his people openly acknowledged Del had the traits they sought in their most coveted slaves. Maybe he wasn't the only one playing the game of *Oh, isn't this all so normal?*

Del had nothing against Bronzeson, but he had to act soon or he would never get off the ship before Tarex returned. He couldn't search for Staver with Bronzeson here. Nor would Bronzeson let him near the bridge, and Del needed to go there to disable the security. Fighting Bronzeson wouldn't be easy; he was a great deal larger than Del. But Del wasn't without resources.

Sorry, he thought to Bronzeson. Then he spun around and kicked. *Fast.*

Mai-quinjo had two modes: kill and disable. Del knocked Bronzeson over with the kick, then dropped next to him and applied pressure with his mind and hands until his host slumped into a heap. Done! And now his time was running out faster than sand in an ancient hourglass.

Del ran through the lounge and a dining area beyond. The tiny bridge was next, the same place it would be on a Skolian yacht.

A male voice spoke in Highton, the language of the Aristos, using the clipped tones of a ship's EI. "You are identified as a valued guest, but please explain yourself."

Del inhaled with relief. *Explain yourself.* It didn't just attack. Tarex had probably told the EI to accommodate Del; otherwise, it would have denied him access to the bridge. It would never occur to an Aristo that an empath, which Aristos viewed as the lowest form of humanity, would attack the ship. Their arrogance about their power was also their weakness. But the EI was undoubtedly contacting Tarex right at this moment.

"Bronzeson needs help," Del told it as he strode to the controls at the pilot's chair. Hieroglyphics covered them, but he couldn't read Highton any more than Iotic.

"You knocked out Bronzeson," the ship said. It had to be an expensive EI, to use idiom so well.

"No, I was helping him." Del leaned over a panel with a menu of holos and started flicking them in sequences he would use on a Skolian yacht.

"Stop turning off my systems," the EI said. A siren went off, and other alarms were undoubtedly notifying the authorities. Even if Del had known the yacht well, he couldn't neutralize its security fast enough to stop the warnings. Redundancy existed in its systems to prevent exactly what he was trying to do.

He deactivated systems as fast as he could, and tied up life support and environmental controls so it couldn't use them to counteract him. But the EI soon locked him out, and probably also blocked the transmitter in his body. Del spun around and ran out of the bridge. He could feel the mind of the half-Aristo clearly now, which meant the officer was nearby, probably headed here to find out what the hell was going on. The yacht was big enough for Del to avoid him by sensing the man's crushing mental cavity. That worked because Del had turned off the monitors that would let the officer find him, but they wouldn't stay off for long.

Del found a small cargo bay crammed with crates, trolleys, and cranes, all in blue chrome and Luminex. He knelt by a hatch in the middle of the deck. Its menus were similar to those on a Skolian ship, and he went through them quickly. But when he flicked what he thought was the final holicon, a voice said, "You must unfasten the l-bars to open the hatch."

"The what?" Del asked. The hatch didn't answer, which probably meant he had just said something wrong.

It took him three more tries to release the hatch, precious seconds he couldn't waste. As the hatch slid open, he practically threw himself down the ladder. It was colder in the hold below. He jumped to the deck, strode to where the cold storage unit should be—and it wasn't there.

Damn! He saw nothing in the cramped hold resembling the heavy door and circular handle he expected. As he searched, his pulse ratcheted up so high, he felt ready to burst. He found a vacuum compartment behind a stack of crates, but no cold unit. He didn't have time! Even if he located Staver right this second, they would have trouble getting out of the yacht.

As Del ran to the ladder, he looked one last time at the bulkhead where he had expected to find the cold storage unit. It hit him then; it wasn't identical to the other surfaces in the hold. It looked heavier.

Del strode to the wall and pounded on it. If space existed beyond, he couldn't tell; the barrier was too thick to reveal any secrets. He ran his palms over it, his heartbeat racing. He was an idiot, wasting valuable time on a blank wall—

A menu popped up in front of him. He recognized it, yes, this one should open the door—

Nothing!

Del wanted to shout his frustration. He went through the steps that had unfastened the l-bars on the hatch above. A loud click came from somewhere—and a portal in the bulkhead swung open. A wave of icy air blasted Del.

"Gods almighty," a man whispered.

Del made a choked sound. Staver was wedged into the unit on his side, with his knees drawn up to fit in the cramped space. Del had no time to be gentle as he pulled him out, and he felt Staver's agony. He gritted his teeth, knowing that the Trader officer had probably been sitting down here, drugged out of his mind on Staver's pain.

Staver stumbled as he tried to stand up. "How—?"

"I knocked on the door." Del grabbed Staver as the exec crumpled. "You're too heavy for me to carry. Can you walk?"

Staver staggered with him to the ladder. "Anything." Alarms were blaring throughout the ship. "Where is Kryxson?"

"If you mean the sadist who was down here, I'd bet he just found Bronzeson in the lounge."

"Why no gas . . . knock us out?"

"I turned it off." Del started to help him up the ladder, but then realized Kryxson was probably headed back here. The Trader officer could reach this ladder faster than Staver could struggle to the top.

"This won't work." Del pulled him away. "Wait here."

Staver's face was ashen. "You're insane to do this."

"We *can* get out," Del said. He hauled himself up the ladder and scrambled to his feet at the top. In that instant, a man with shimmering black hair and a stark black uniform ran around the curve of a bulkhead. As soon as he spotted Del, he raised his gun, a medical stunner.

Del lunged to the side, and the shot just missed him. He rolled on the floor as the man fired again. Numbness spread in his ankle, and he stumbled when he tried to jump to his feet, but he controlled his fall so he barreled into the man. They crashed to the floor, wrestling for the gun, and in his adrenaline rush, it took Del only seconds to knock him out.

Gasping for breath, Del climbed to his feet and limped to the hatchway. "Staver?"

The exec was already climbing. He dragged himself out the top, and Del helped him to his feet.

"Can we get out?" Staver asked.

"I shut off the security robots," Del said. "It'll buy us a little time."

As they stumbled past the unconscious officer, Staver's face twisted with hatred. "We should kill him so he can't warn anyone."

Del kept going, pulling Staver with him. "If we don't get out of here now, we're screwed." As much as Del understood Staver's reaction, he had no intention of killing anyone.

"My people know Tarex has me," Staver said. "They got his provider out of his hotel, but he caught me."

"Gods," Del muttered as they half ran, half staggered through the ship.

"Yes." Then Staver said, "I've never heard an American man on Earth say 'gods' in Iotic before."

A chill swept through Del. He hadn't even realized he spoke in Iotic. He couldn't have deactivated every monitor on the ship, which meant Tarex now had a recording of that single damning word.

In the bridge, the controls were lit up like a deranged festival tree, red and amber blazing. The ship's EI spoke. "Your actions have overridden my orders to harm neither of you. Release my systems and surrender."

"Go drill yourself," Del said. They ran through the bridge, dining area, and lounge, past Bronzeson's unconscious form. At the airlock beyond, Del smacked the release panel.

Nothing.

Damn! Del slammed his fist against the hull and swore loudly about the deviant sexual practices of the EI that controlled the lock.

A clank came from the lounge behind them. Whirling, Del saw a robot-mech headed toward them, towering, all gold, with a smooth head, recessed slits for eyes, and a metal mouth without lips. One of its fingers was morphing into a gold syringe. It jerked to a halt, metal grinding metal, then took another jerky step.

"Hell and damnation!" Del swung back to the airlock and went frantically through its menus. Symbols he couldn't read flowed in a gold blur on the screen behind the holicons.

"Del, wait!" Staver said. "Go back! Read that last menu."

"I *can't* read." Del backed up the menu. In the lounge, metal ground against metal as the mech managed another step.

Staver scanned the glyphs. "It's a list of malfunctions. The EI couldn't override your tampering, so it kept creating errors until the airlock jammed." He flicked up a new menu and swore. "I don't know Highton well enough to read this one."

"I do, if you know how to get it on verbal."

Staver flicked more holicons. A voice spoke, androgynous and mechanical, different from the main EI that ran the entire ship. "The airlock is frozen due to instability. If I release the freeze, the airlock membrane might collapse."

Del pounded on the airlock. "Release it!"

"I cannot until the lock is repaired," it said.

"Check the air outside the ship," Del shouted. "This is *Earth*, for flaming sake. We can breathe the air."

"The lock must be repaired," the voice said. Then it added,

"Armed units have surrounded this ship. Police and port security. Also two unidentified people."

"The two must be my bodyguards," Del said. If it took his being a Ruby prince to get people here, his damn title had some use after all. "The armed units are no danger."

This time the ship's EI answered him, its icily human voice a stark contrast to the airlock. "You aren't leaving this ship."

Staver flicked through more menus. "It must be possible to override this. Nothing is wrong with the atmosphere."

Metal screeched behind them. Looking back, Del saw the mech take a step, forcing its legs forward despite its locked joints.

"I can't believe this!" Del hit the bulkhead with his palm. "Let us out!"

The airlock said, "I have no reason to override my freeze."

"I have to give a concert tomorrow for a million people," Del yelled, even though he knew it was ridiculous.

"Reason accepted," the voice said. "Freeze released."

"What the hell?" Del stumbled forward as the membrane opened.

The security codes must be corrupted, Staver thought as they crowded into the airlock. *Tarex is going to the concert. He wants your work, so getting you there is important. But the airlock should have known better than to open. You really must have screwed up security here.*

My family has a similar yacht, Del thought. **So I had a good feel for its systems.** Better, apparently, than he had realized.

Your family? Staver's thought lurched. *Who the hell—* He stopped as the outer surface of the airlock opened.

They were standing at the top of the wide ramp to the yacht. People surrounded the ship, staring up at them, police from the port and guards from Tarex's Escorts. Del and Staver stood in the hatchway, hanging onto each other, while inside the yacht, another clank came from the mech. Guards from the Escorts were coming up the ramp, and Tyra and Cameron were running forward with their guns drawn. As Del lurched forward with Staver, a blue metallic streak whipped by in Del's side vision and was gone.

"Help us!" Del shouted.

The cavernous bay suddenly went dark and the hum of engines died. Lights flickered, went out, flashed erratically, and died again. Then the Trader Escorts began to pulse with a steady green glow.

"What the bloody *hell?*" Staver said.

In the wildly fluctuating light, Del could just make out Tyra sprinting up the ramp with enhanced speed. A Trader lunged at her, and she countered him with a kick that made Del's *mai-quinjo* look like molasses. She fired point-blank at the officer—and nothing happened. With a snarl, she threw the weapon away and grappled with him in hand-to-hand combat. Del felt sick. He hadn't even known it was possible to neutralize a pulser-pistol that way. Nor was it only the gun; a ring of security bots from the port stood frozen around the ships. Useless.

"What's wrong with everyone?" Staver croaked as they staggered forward. "This port should be swarming with security equipment, remote operations vehicles, alarms, *something.*"

"Those 'civilian' Trader ships have military defenses," Del said tightly. "State-of-the-art, I'll bet, probably as illegal as all hell."

"They must've—locked down the bay." Staver stumbled and lost his balance.

Del grabbed Staver, holding him up as he jerked to a stop. In the jarring flashes of light, he could just barely see Cameron sprinting up the ramp. The Traders fired guns that flashed, Del had no idea why. It looked like shots were hitting both Tyra and Cameron, but neither faltered. The melee was beyond anything in Del's experience. He knew nothing about why the engines died or people couldn't get into the bay. Green light pulsed throughout the area, blurring his vision and disrupting his thoughts.

Tarex's people were fighting with Cameron and Tyra. People ran through the dim light below, weapons discharging with red sparks. Del felt confusion and fear all around. The fighting blocked the lower end of the ramp, trapping Del and Staver above.

The metallic streak darted through Del's side vision again. In that instant, a screech burst out of the Escort ships, a gut-wrenching siren that vibrated *within* Del. He screamed and sank to his knees, his hands over his ears. Staver cried out, his face contorted as he crumpled next to Del. Everywhere, port guards dropped to the ground, but Tyra and Cameron kept fighting. Whatever sound weapon the Escorts were using, it affected neither Del's bodyguards nor their Trader antagonists.

One of the Traders broke away from the fight and ran up to

Del. As the man hauled Del to his feet, Del cursed and kicked out, catching him in the leg. He grabbed the man, rolled the Trader over his hip, and heaved him over the side of the ramp.

The relentless scream from the Escorts never stopped. With a moan, Del bent over double. That sound was *killing* him. Air buffeted him, and he looked up through eyes bleared by the gusts to see an airborne platform with turbines hovering past the yacht. It was small enough that its spy shrouds could help it evade security, but that meant it couldn't hold more than three people. Two Traders stood on it, leaning over its rail as the platform swooped close to Staver.

Tyra was halfway up the ramp, still fighting. She knocked one person out with some sort of dart from a tube, but another of the Traders disarmed her. Cameron was grappling with more of Tarex's guards. Many people were on their knees or sprawled flat, bent under the horrific sound. How the Traders had isolated the bay, Del didn't know, but no gases swirled here, and no roar of rescue tanks, drones, or anything else cut through the noise.

Del groaned. He felt the sound in his body as if it were churning him into knots. The airborne platform shot past him again, blasting the ramp. It came back and hovered, knocking Del flat as hot air seared his skin. They were insane to land here, but they were doing it anyway.

Then it hit him: the people on the platform *weren't* Traders. One was Lydia, Staver's associate, the woman who had tended Del after the truth drug. The man with her was an exec from Staver's conglomerate.

The man Del had thrown off the ramp was climbing back up. Another man broke free from the melee below and lunged at the landing platform. In all the noise, confusion, and security alarms, Del barely heard Lydia shout, "We only have room for one!"

Del shoved Staver toward the platform. "Take him!"

They grabbed Staver and threw him on the platform. As it lifted off, Tyra raised her head and screamed, "*NO!*"

"I'm sorry, Kelric," Del whispered. "But it was my choice."

Then he passed out.

XXV

The Yacht

Del awoke screaming.

It was all he knew, the pain, fire across his back, accompanied by breaking sounds, as if brittle rods were snapping in two. He wanted to fold up and protect himself, but he couldn't bring down his arms. They were pulled tight over his head.

As Del's vision cleared, he comprehended that he was kneeling in the lounge of Tarex's ship. A hazy figure reclined in a seat a few yards in front of him. He felt queasy, the way it happened when he was on a small ship that rotated. He still had on his pants and belt, but his shirt, boots, and socks were gone. He groaned as the pain seared across his back.

"Stop," he said hoarsely. "No more."

Again. And again.

His sight cleared enough for him to see who was sitting in the chair. Tarex. The Aristo had relaxed back, a drink in his hand, his eyes glazed. He smiled as Del met his gaze. Then he languidly raised his hand, giving a signal to whoever was behind Del. The cracking sound came again. A whip. Del screamed as his tormentor increased the rhythm.

Eons later, or maybe seconds, Tarex raised his hand and the blows stopped. Del gasped and sagged forward, his head hanging down, his arms held over his head by restraints. Something wet trickled down his back. Blood? He hurt, gods he hurt.

"So." Tarex spoke English in a cultured voice. "I had a provider. I lost her but I gained a Skolian music exec. I lost him but gained an Allied singer who curses in Iotic. Isn't this all so interesting?"

Del looked up and clenched his fists in whatever cuffs held them. "Go drill yourself."

"Aren't we gracious today," Tarex said.

Del wanted to spit on him. "You can't hold me prisoner in the port."

"What port?" Tarex said. "We're in orbit."

Gods. Of course they were in orbit. Why else would the damn yacht be rotating? Del could barely talk through the pain in his back. "How many people did your ship kill when it blasted the docking bay?"

"Oh, don't worry." Tarex waved his hand. "It gave them warning. Only about twenty died."

"*Only?*" Del stared at him.

"You killed them." Tarex's expression hardened. "*You* vandalized my ship, assaulted my crew, and caused thousands of credits in damage." Contempt crackled in his voice. "They died because of your trespasses."

"You were in American territory," Del ground out. "If you want me arrested, you have to go through their authorities. By taking off and killing people, you commited a far worse crime."

"My crewmen were defending themselves," Tarex said. "And me. I barely got on board before they took off. Can you imagine the political fallout if an Aristo lord was killed on Earth? It would be a disaster." He leaned forward. "One you caused."

Del didn't doubt the Allied authorities were afraid of exactly that. But surely they wouldn't let Tarex leave Earth with a major celebrity imprisoned on his ship. They were probably holding Tarex in orbit while they figured out what the hell to do.

"Where is Tyra?" Del asked. She must have reported to Kelric and General McLane when she realized Del had knocked out Cameron and faked the taciturn Marine's voice.

"Tyra?" The Aristo regarded him curiously. "Who is that?"

"My bodyguard. The female one."

"You mean the Jagernaut?"

"I don't know what is a Jagernaut," Del lied.

"Of course you do," Tarex said in Iotic.

Del answered in English. "What?"

A muscle twitched under Tarex's eye. "Don't play games with me. Your guard is a Jagernaut. Who are you?"

"Del Arden."

"You have an accent." Tarex sat back and rested his elbows on the arms of his chair while he steepled his fingers around his drink. "My analysis codes can't identify its origins. It has Iotic components, but it's not pure. But you swore in pure Iotic."

"I've been around Staver. He says that word a lot." Del winced as blood ran down his back, over gashes left by the whip.

Tarex raised an eyebrow. "He doesn't come from a Skolian noble family."

"He has to deal with them. In their language."

"With Iotic curses?" Tarex gave a wry laugh. "Given the way people talk in this business, that actually makes sense."

"You didn't say what happened to my bodyguards." Del felt as if his pulse were going to burst his veins. "Are they dead?"

"I should say yes, just to make you suffer," Tarex said. "But no, only the woman died. The man is in a coma at the hospital."

Nausea swept over Del. Just like that: *The woman died. The man is in a coma.* He had ended Tyra's life and that of twenty other people, and the same could soon be true for Cameron. He had never believed Tarex would *kill* them. The Aristo was a sadist, not an idiot; even if he didn't consider his Earth hosts fully human, he knew the political mess it would create if anyone died. Del hated knowing Tarex would probably get away with it on a claim of self-defense. It killed Del even more to know he would live the rest of his life knowing he had caused their deaths.

Tarex exhaled, his eyelids half lowering as if he had shot up a neuro-amp. Watching him, Del gritted his teeth. Aristos fed on the emotional as well as physical pain of their providers. For all he knew, Tarex had lied to him to heighten Del's misery.

"How can you live with yourself?" Del asked.

"Only a lesser form of life would misunderstand the honor I've given you." Tarex leaned forward. "Through your exquisite suffering, you become part of something more than human. You become part of the gods."

"That's sick," Del said. "And you're no god."

"You have such fire." Tarex motioned to someone.

A rustle came from behind Del. Bronzeson walked into view, holding a blood-stained whip. He stared at Del with hatred.

"My crewman wasn't happy about what you did to him," Tarex said as if he were discussing mildly unpleasant weather. "So I told him he could help." He gestured, and Bronzeson walked back around Del, out of sight. Then Tarex said, "Proceed."

"NO—" Del's voice broke off in a scream as the whip came down.

"It's not enough!" Tyra shouted at Fitz McLane. She stood facing the general across his desk like a boxer in the ring. "As long as you leave Tarex in orbit up there, he could escape. Your people have to take command of his ship *now*."

"And if Tarex kills Del in retaliation?" Fitz demanded. "I have a Trader prince up there holding a Skolian prince prisoner. You better pray *no one* dies when I send in the Raptor squad."

"I don't understand," Ricki said. She was standing with Mac, back a few paces from Tyra and McLane. Mac had brought her as soon as Fitz notified him of what happened.

"What would possess Del to go after Tarex?" Ricki asked. "Del is terrified of him."

"An excellent question," the general said, his gaze hard on Tyra. The Jagernaut met his stare and said nothing.

"Ricki is right," Mac said. "It makes no sense. Del couldn't even endure being in the same room as Tarex."

Tyra still didn't answer.

"We have a need to know," Fitz told her. "A damn good one."

At first Tyra remained impassive. Then she exhaled and spoke. "Staver is the mastermind of a Skolian underground movement called the Star Road. They free providers."

"Holy mother shit," Ricki muttered.

Mac wanted to hit something. He could think of only one cause that could pull Del out of his apathy—and that was it. "How could Del have known? Staver had no reason to trust him."

"He and Staver are both powerful empaths," Tyra said. "I think Del figured it out from that."

"How is Staver?" Mac asked. "And Cameron."

"Cameron is fine," Fitz said. "He had a broken femur, but it's almost healed. No one else was critically injured. The hospital released Staver into the custody of two Marines we provided as guards." Frustration snapped in his voice. "Not that any of the people we're trying so blasted hard to protect will let us do our jobs. If Staver hadn't ditched his bodyguard when he went to see Tarex, he would never have been captured."

Tyra scowled at him. "Staver could hardly bring an ASC guard when he went in to free that provider."

"That's right," Fitz said curtly. "Because what Staver did is illegal."

"So is what Tarex did to Staver," Ricki ground out. "And whatever the hell that bastard is doing to Del."

"We need proof!" Fitz said. "Del walked up to Tarex's yacht and knocked, for God's sake. Tarex claims his people believed they were acting in self-defense when they blocked the port security. If we storm his ship with no evidence, this will all blow up in our faces. Literally. And then Del won't be a prisoner, he'll be dead. He should have left the rescue to us, damn it, not tried to go in himself."

Mac crossed his arms. "Del's not stupid. He knew you all wouldn't get to Staver in time."

Ricki spoke to Fitz. "Why couldn't you send someone to check out Del's story? If you had, Del might not be up in orbit."

"We were investigating," Fitz said. "But we had to be careful. Tarex has been a model citizen. We couldn't instigate a diplomatic crisis with an Aristo prince based on the unsubstantiated word of an emotionally unstable rock singer."

Ricki bristled. "Nothing is wrong with Del's mind."

"He's a virt-addicted mess," Fitz said.

"Fitz, wait," Mac said. "I know how it looks with Del. But he's a lot more stable and responsible than you think."

"Then why are we in this blowup?" the general demanded.

Tyra finally spoke, her voice no less powerful because of her quiet tone. "Because Del considers Staver's life worth more than his own. He sacrificed himself to free Aunchild because he believes Staver contributes more to humanity."

"What he did may be the greatest act of bravery this side of the Milky Way," Fitz said. "But we have to deal with the fallout. The Imperator is sending a detachment of the Skolian Fleet. The Skolian embassy here on Earth has an associated contingent of ships in orbit that they've put on battle-ready alert. The Trader emperor is sending forces because he thinks we're threatening one of his lords. The Trader ships associated with their embassy here are also on alert. So is Allied Space Command. We have to get Del out before this thing explodes."

"We have to get him out of there," Tyra said flatly, "before Tarex tortures him into insanity."

Ricki shuddered. "Don't say that."

Tyra started to pace. "If Tarex suspects we're trying, he might jump his ship into inversion and leave the solar system. We'll never see Del again."

"He can't," Mac said. "Activating a starship drive this close to a planet, at such slow speeds, could destroy his ship."

"It's slow, yes," Fitz said. "But he wouldn't be starting from rest. Inverting so close to Earth is more likely to damage other ships caught in his spacetime backlash. It's still a risk for him, a big one, but he might consider it worth the danger if he realizes who he caught."

"Del would never tell him," Ricki said.

An awkward silence followed her words. Mac doubted she had ever encountered anything like a Trader interrogation. Her crowd played games, but that was all. This was the real thing. He spoke with difficulty. "Del may not be able to stop himself."

"It's worse than that," Tyra said grimly. "He has a neuro-active pico-web in his brain with bio-electrodes. Everyone in his family has it, some much more than Del."

"I don't understand," Ricki said. "What does that mean?'"

Fitz spoke quietly. "The web destroys pathways in his brain. Under duress, it can prevent him from answering questions. If the interrogation is too intense, it will erase his memories."

Ricki's face went ashen. "His own people did that to him?"

"He asked them to," Tyra said. "It protects the people he loves. He wanted it redone when he came out of cryo."

"It isn't Del's memories I'm worried about," Mac said. "It's his health. Tarex could kill him in more ways than he knows."

Tyra hit at the air with her fist. "Damn it, I believed Del when he promised he wouldn't pull anything."

"I've no doubt he meant it when he said it," Mac said.

"He's always putting himself down," Ricki said. "I'd never have guessed he would risk his life this way."

"That's just it!" The usually stoic Tyra was furious. "He has this idea that he's worthless. He won't listen to anyone who tells him it's not true."

"If he were worthless," Fitz said tightly, "the militaries of three empires wouldn't be poised to fight right now."

"The problem," Ricki said, "is that you're all thinking in military terms."

Fitz gave her a look he reserved for sweet, clueless sexpots. "Given that it's a military situation, Miss Varento, that would be the logical approach."

Ricki returned his look with the one she reserved for big, clueless studs. "Even so. Let's just suppose we leave the military out of it for a minute. Del broke civilian laws when he damaged Tarex's ship. Of course our police want him. It's a civil matter with an Allied citizen. If they courteously but firmly tell Tarex he must surrender Del so they can put him on trial for his actions against Tarex, it removes the appearance of a threat from our people against the Aristo."

Fitz rubbed his chin. "If Tarex refuses to release Del to the police, it does weaken his claim of self-defense."

Tyra snorted. "Among my people, no one would ever believe the police would arrest someone for helping a psion escape an Aristo. They'd consider the idea ludicrous."

"Probably," Mac said. "But it could work here. A lot of my people don't even believe psions exist, and Tarex knows that."

"The police are standing by," Fitz said. "They've already charged Del for a number of crimes. They don't know he has diplomatic immunity." His eyes glinted. "If Tarex refuses to relinquish Del, our police will have to appeal to the Trader authorities for help."

"Then *Tarex* becomes the one creating the problem," Ricki said.

Tyra shook her head. "It won't work. Aristos consider us subhuman. They believe they have a right to do whatever they please to us. If Tarex wants to kidnap Del, enslave him, and force him to sing so Tarex makes billions, none of his people will blink."

"Usually, yes," Mac said. "But the emperor doesn't want his Aristos torpedoing his diplomatic relations with Earth."

"The emperor is a teenager," Fitz said sourly. "He has no power. He couldn't stop his own shadow."

Ricki blinked. "The Eubian emperor is a kid?"

"Jaibriol the Third is eighteen," Mac said. "His father died in the war, so Jaibriol ascended the throne."

"With less leadership at the helm, the Aristo lords have more power," Tyra said. "It's Tarex we have to deal with."

Fitz looked around at them. "We'll have the police notify him, then. Del broke our laws. We want to prosecute."

"It'll calm Tarex down," Tyra said. "Maybe take him off his guard. But not enough. He won't give up Del."

"Probably not," Fitz said. "But while the police distract him, we'll get the Raptors in there."

"Can you?" Mac asked.

"I sure as hell hope so," Fitz said. "Because we don't have a lot of other options."

The hours merged into a blur of agony. Sometimes Tarex watched Bronzeson work on Del with the whip. Other times Tarex used a neural dust that adhered to Del's skin and extended tendrils through his skin. When Tarex activated the dust, the tendrils jolted Del's nerves, setting him on fire with excruciating pain.

Tarex questioned him relentlessly.

"You speak Iotic," he said. "You're Skolian, aren't you?"

"No," Del rasped. He was sitting on the deck of the lower cargo bay with his hands bound to a rung of the ladder by his shoulders. "I only know . . . that word."

"Why do you have that hinge in your hand?" Tarex asked. "Can't you get it fixed?"

Del tried to say, *nothing is wrong with it,* but the anti-interrogation treatments in his brain wouldn't let him reveal even that much. So instead he said, "I like it."

"You shouldn't lie," Tarex said mildly—and touched a small disk he held.

Del screamed as his nerves burst into pain. He didn't think a human being could hurt that much and survive, but he had resources he had never known. He couldn't even goddamned pass out.

"Answer me," Tarex said. "Are you a Skolian nobleman?"

"No," Del whispered. He *wanted* to tell Tarex and make the pain stop. But he couldn't. If he tried, his mind blanked.

Tarex's half-Aristo officer, the man called Kryxson, had come partway down the ladder. He stood on the rung above Del and stared down at him. "He would have told you by now if he were a nobleman. He's too weak to hold out this long."

Tarex stopped pressing the disk, and the pain eased. "What do you know about Staver?" he asked Del.

Del's voice cracked. "He licensed my music."

Tarex frowned. "You can't sing with your voice so raw." He glanced up at Kryxson. "Go get the EI-doc to repair his throat."

"Right away, sir." Kryxson went up the ladder.

Del leaned his head against one of the rungs. "Why are you doing this to me?" He knew the answer, but he couldn't believe someone would deliberately hurt another human being this way.

"Tell me about Staver," Tarex said.

Sweat beaded on Del's forehead. "He's an exec at Metropoli Interstellar."

"Don't play the innocent." Tarex's voice hardened. "You know what I'm talking about."

Del met his gaze, though he wanted to look anywhere but at the Aristo. "I've told you everything I know."

"Aunchild hired someone to help him get my provider." Tarex leaned forward. "Someone who tampered with the EI at the Star Tower Sheraton. Help like that isn't cheap. Where did he get the money?"

"He's a conglomerate exec," Del said. "They pay well."

"Not that well." Tarex poised his hand above the disk. "Answer me, Del."

"I swear, I don't know—*ah, no.*" Del screamed as his nerves exploded with fire. He tried to hold back, but it went on and on, until finally he shouted, "*I'll tell you. Stop!*"

Mercifully the pain ended. And because it had never occurred to anyone in the Skolian military to program him against talking about Staver Aunchild, he said, "I gave him the money."

"I thought so." Tarex lowered the disk. "Why?"

Hatred edged Del's voice. "Because what you do to providers is twisted."

Tarex looked down at him as if from a great height. "You Allieds are so self-righteous." The anger faded from his face, replaced by satisfaction. "But those anthologies of yours must be even more lucrative than I realized, to finance Staver's little gambit. I'll make billions."

"I won't sing for you," Del rasped.

Tarex glanced up the ladder. "What do you think?" he said to someone above them. "Will he sing?"

Kryxson answered. "Of course." He was coming down the ladder. When he reached the rung where Del's wrists were bound, he stepped squarely onto the hinge in Del's hand. Del gritted his teeth, but he held back his groan, refusing them that satisfaction. At least the medical robot, or med-bot, that followed Kryxson stepped over Del's hands. It resembled the security mechs, except it was blue instead of gold and much less bulky.

When the med-bot reached the bottom of the ladder, it leaned over Del and passed its hand over his throat. Lights blinked on its arms and chest, but Del couldn't interpret the patterns.

"His vocal cords are inflamed," the med-bot said. Its finger morphed into a syringe. That one simple action told Del plenty about Tarex; it was extraordinarily expensive to build a robot that could re-form parts of itself with such fluidity. Yet this was the second of Tarex's robots Del had seen do it. Either Tarex was wealthy even among Aristos, who were probably the most avaricious group of humans alive, or else he wasted his money. From what Del had seen, he had little doubt it was the former. It scared the hell out of him, for it implied Tarex was even better at being an Aristo than most Aristos.

The med-bot set the point of its syringe against Del's neck.

"No!" Del tried to jerk away, but Kryxson held his head while the bot administered the shot. Del choked back his cry. The syringe hurt like everything else. It didn't have to; they could have used a method he didn't feel at all.

Tarex sighed and sat down on a crate, his eyes glazed. "You will be my greatest acquisition, Del. An anthology a year, eh?"

"You can't take me with you," Del said hoarsely. "I'm supposed to do a huge concert tonight. If I don't show up, everyone on Earth will find out what you did to me."

"I've permission to extradite you," Tarex told him.

"Like hell."

Tarex motioned to the med-bot. In response, it raised its hand, showing Del the syringe as it morphed into a knife.

"No," Del whispered. "Don't."

As the bot brought down the knife, all Del could think was that not only would he never see his family again, he had also let down Jud, Anne, and Randall, with all the intensity, friendship, and arguments they shared. Then the knife struck home, but instead of stabbing Del, the robot sliced the cords binding him to the stairs. With a gasp, he dropped his arms into his lap. He crumpled against the ladder, sitting with his knees bent next to his body and his head hanging. The med-bot's feet were visible, but then they moved away.

Tarex spoke gently. "Del, look at me."

He raised his head. Tarex was standing over him, staring down as if Del were an insect he had found on the floor.

"Kneel to me," Tarex said softly.

Del gritted his teeth and stayed put.

Tarex moved fast, probably with augmented reflexes, and backhanded Del across the face. Del's head slammed into the ladder.

"I said *kneel*," Tarex told him.

"No," Del ground out.

Tarex pressed the disk.

Agony erupted in Del's body. He screamed and screamed—and he *could* scream, because the medicine was already healing his throat.

The pain ended abruptly. Then Tarex murmured, "Kneel. And say this: I submit to your magnificence, glorious Lord."

Del met his stare. In slow, succinct words, he said, "Fuck you, Tarex."

The Aristo's lower eyelid twitched.

And he pressed the disk.

"Mister Arden has already been charged," the man on the screen said. "We have to take him into custody."

Tarex was watching the screen from the pilot's chair of his yacht. Del sat in the copilot's seat, out of sight. The med-bot had given him some drug that paralyzed him. The pressure of the seat against his back hurt, with all the welts, gashes, and bruises, but he couldn't do anything to alleviate it. His head was turned sideways, toward Tarex, so he had to watch as Tarex spoke with the officer, a man called Gregori. The Allied man looked familiar, but Del couldn't figure out why.

"He's being charged under Eubian law," Tarex said. "I'm taking him to stand trial."

Liar, Del thought. The moment they reached Trader space, Tarex would collar and cuff him, and file documents to declare Del his legal property.

"I understand," Gregori said, with a sympathy that made Del want to strangle him. "But he must stand trial here before extradition." He gave Tarex a sympathetic look. "You can't take him off Earth yet. It's against our laws even if he wants to go with you. You would be abetting the flight of a criminal."

What? They called *him* the criminal? They were crazy. Del fought to move, protest, anything, but he could barely blink.

"I'm sure our representatives can work this out," Tarex said smoothly. "Our laws require that anyone who offends against an Aristo must face a Highton tribunal." He tried to look apologetic, but he came off patronizing. "So you see, I can't give him to you."

"I have orders to bring him back," Gregori said.

"Yes, I understand," Tarex said with impatience. "I'll make sure you aren't held responsible."

The ship's EI spoke on the bridge channel, which wouldn't carry to Gregori. "Lord Tarex, an Allied space-pod is approaching the yacht."

Tarex didn't hesitate. "Cut transmission." As Gregori's image vanished, Tarex said, "Freeze controls on the pod and have the cargo cranes immobilize it. And have my Escorts increase their surveillance of that Allied police cruiser."

"Pod frozen," the EI said. "Alert status increased to gold."

Tarex spoke to someone out of Del's sight. "Get Arden moving."

The med-bot appeared, its blue metal reflecting the harsh light. It gave Del another shot in his neck. When Del winced, Tarex frowned at the robot. "Don't use that syringe."

As much as it relieved Del to have any reprieve, he didn't trust why Tarex would spare him from pain. Then it hit him. He was a *drug* to the Aristo. In a potentially dangerous situation, Tarex didn't want to be affected by a psion any more than he wanted chemicals to blur his mind.

"Bring him," he told the med-bot.

The robot tugged Del to his feet with unexpected gentleness, but Del flinched anyway. His welts burned. The low pseudo-gravity from the yacht's rotation made him dizzy, as did the Coriolis forces when he leaned in the wrong direction.

Tarex was watching him. "Cooperate," he told Del, "or I'll let Kryxson put you in the storage unit." When Del's lips drew back in a snarl, Tarex said, "Oh, never mind, you'll just use more of those quaint little cuss words. Try this, Del. If you don't cooperate, I'll let you watch me hurt whoever is in that pod. You're responsible for what happens to them."

Del blanched. He had already been responsible for who knew how many deaths, including Tyra and possibly Cameron. He spoke with difficulty. "I'll cooperate."

Tarex nodded, his eyes glazed. "Good."

Del wanted to break the Aristo's gratingly perfect face. Regardless of what Tarex intended, he was clearly savoring Del's pain, both emotional and physical.

Kryxson was waiting in the archway between the bridge and dining area. He glanced at Del with a hint of Tarex's drugged look. Then he spoke to the Aristo. "The Escorts are ready to fire, sir. The pod is trying to dock with this ship, but they can pick it off the hull if you want."

"How many people are in it?" Tarex asked.

"None," Kryxson said.

"Don't destroy the pod yet," Tarex said. "Keep the Escorts on alert. I'd like to avoid antagonizing these police, if possible. But have the security bots meet us in the cargo bay."

Del gritted his teeth. Just his luck, that Tarex was smart enough to put his ego on hold. If the Aristo had been willing to alienate the Allieds with his arrogance, they might have been more willing to help Staver in the first place.

Kryxson and Tarex strode down the corridor, and the med-bot followed with Del, holding his upper arm as it pulled him along. Although Del moved stiffly, the low gravity helped. But the nausea roiling within him came from more than the ship's rotation. His difficulty in walking was a painful reminder of the way he had struggled even to take one step when he first came out of cryo. The idea of being crammed in a cold storage unit terrified him almost beyond thinking. It would be like being trapped in cryo, but while he was awake, buried alive in the crypt of his nightmares.

Del didn't see why the Allied police had sent a pod. If they expected Tarex just to give him up, they were woefully naïve. Of course, the Allieds had always seen the Aristos though a rosy filter that denied the truth.

They stopped in the upper cargo bay, Tarex on one side of Del and Kryxson on the other while the med-bot waited behind them. Two looming security bots strode into the area, their gold bodies reflecting the curved blue bulkheads.

"Open bay doors," Tarex said.

Del went rigid. "There's no airlock!"

Everyone ignored him. He stood riveted as the huge doors in front of them pulled apart, their engines rumbling, their giant serrations reflecting the stars outside. Even knowing Tarex wouldn't open his ship to the void of space, Del waited for the roar of escaping air. The Milky Way moved across his view like a path of glitter. He stared in terrified awe at the spectacular panorama undimmed by any atmosphere. So many jeweled stars!

"Gods," Del breathed. "It's incredible."

"Aye," Tarex murmured. " 'Such majesty beyond the end of days would never compare to the dust of the gods.' "

"Did you write that?" Del asked. It wouldn't surprise him if the Aristos thought they were gods, with galaxies for stardust.

"It's from an opera sung by Vitar Carlyx." He smiled at Del. "His voice isn't as good as yours, though."

Del blinked, at a loss for a response. He motioned at the open doors. "How do you keep the air from going out?" He had only traveled in space a few times, and he had never been interested in starship design.

"It's a membrane similar to the airlock," Tarex said. "But much bigger." He gazed at the view. "I wanted it transparent so I could look out."

"I see why." With a rush of nausea, Del realized he was making small talk with his torturer. He shut his mouth and said nothing more.

A crane with a huge claw unfolded from inside the bay. When it swung toward the open area, Del tensed. "It'll break the seal." He instinctively tried to back up, as if that could save him when the atmosphere escaped. The med-bot stopped him, and held him in place.

"Relax." Tarex said. "It becomes part of the seal."

As Del watched, his pulse surging, the claw swung out into space, the shimmer of a membrane sliding along its gold surface. It moved out of sight around the edge of the doors, but within moments, it reappeared with a spherical life pod tight in its grip. The pod was barely big enough for two people.

Tarex glanced across Del at Kryxson. "What's in it?"

Kryxson was studying the mesh on his gauntlet. "Nothing, sir. No people, weapons, or supplies."

"Secure it," Tarex said. "Notify the Allied police we have it in the hold."

As Kryxson worked on his gauntlet, Tarex glanced at Del. "Do your people actually believe I'll put you in and send you back?"

"I don't know." He didn't miss Tarex's phrasing. *Your people.* Mercifully, the Aristo still believed he was an Allied.

"I have Lieutenant Gregori," Kryxson said.

Tarex lifted his own wrist gauntlet. "Lieutenant, did you send me this silly little pod?"

"I thought they sent a shuttle," Gregori said.

Del wanted to groan. Couldn't the police do any better than this? Maybe not, if they were clueless enough to believe he was the criminal here.

Gregori's voice came back. "I'm sorry, Lord Tarex. We meant to send a shuttle with one of our representatives to greet you and accompany Mister Arden back. However, you can send him in the pod. It's rated for prisoners."

"Good gods, man," Tarex said. He switched off his comm and glanced at Kryxson. "Close the doors. I want every picometer of the pod examined. Make sure it has no surprises." Grabbing Del's arm, Tarex shoved him toward the archway that led back to the dining area. "Come on. Enough of this."

Del stumbled on his lacerated feet. "Slow down."

Tarex laughed shortly. "Like the minds of your police?" He dragged Del into the dining area and pushed him at a bulkhead. "In here."

"What?" Del saw nothing but blue metal. He didn't understand the abrupt change in Tarex's behavior, but he had no idea what was normal for the Aristo.

Tarex smacked the bulkhead and it shimmered into an archway. The Aristo shoved him through the opening, and Del stumbled into living quarters with sumptuous furnishings, wooden cabinets, and panels painted with pastoral scenes. The green carpet was a balm on his ravaged feet. A bed was fitted against a bulkhead across the room, under a low ceiling where the ceiling sloped down.

"You live in here?" Del asked.

"Be quiet," Tarex muttered. It was the first time Del had heard him sound distracted. He dragged Del across the room and threw him down across the bed. "Rest. I'm going to have a drink."

Del sat up and swung his legs over the edge of the bed. Tarex didn't even turn around as he walked away; he just raised his hand, holding the disk that activated the neural dust on Del's skin. "Stay put."

Del froze, his gaze fixed on the disk.

Tarex opened a cabinet and took out a crystal decanter, tall and rectangular. He poured gold liquid into a crystal tumbler. The liqueur looked so odd, going slow in the low gravity. Then he set down the decanter and leaned against the cabinet, facing Del while he drank.

Del wondered what was wrong with Tarex. Maybe he was an alcoholic. He had certainly acted like someone who needed a fix these past few minutes. But he could afford nanomeds in his body to stop the chemical processes leading to addiction, and he didn't seem the type to forego them.

"Look at you, staring like an Earth gazelle." Tarex raised the glass. "I've acquired a singer. It's why I came to Earth, but I didn't expect it this way. Who would have guessed you were such an incredible empath?" He shook his head with a laugh. "You Allieds are so foolish. No one wants to believe psions exist. So they waste your talents and let you go crazy in a world that has no accommodation for you."

"You offer such a great alternative," Del said acidly. "Torture for the rest of my life."

Tarex's voice quieted. "Life as a provider won't be as bad as you think. I'll take good care of you." He even looked like he meant it. "You won't want for anything. I'll give you luxury you can't imagine. You'll never need to worry about anything." Tarex downed the rest of his drink. "And my conglomerate will make billions from your singing."

Del couldn't believe he was so blithe about it. "No free citizen will buy the music of someone you kidnapped and enslaved."

"Oh, don't be stupid," Tarex said. "It will titillate people no end. Besides, you'll tell the media you wanted to come, that the life I offered fascinated you, blah, blah, blah."

"Like hell I will."

"By the time I'm done with you," Tarex said softly, "you'll do anything I damn well want."

Del clenched his fist. "Go drill it, Tarex."

"Oh, be quiet. I'm tired of your filthy mouth." He set down his drink and walked over to Del. "You said it, so that must be what you want, eh?"

Said what? Del tried to jump away, but he mistimed his moves in the unfamiliar gravity and stumbled. Tarex easily threw him back on the bed, on his stomach.

"You want to drill?" the Aristo said, kneeling so he straddled Del's hips. "Fine. I'll give you what you want."

"Stop it!" Panicked, Del tried to throw him off. Tarex shoved him back down and yanked on his belt, loosening it. Del's memory of that night at the lake flashed in his mind. This time, his brother wouldn't rescue him—because the Aristos had killed him.

Anger snapped within Del. He wasn't a damned helpless kid any more. He jerked his shoulders to mislead Tarex, and when the Aristo shifted his grip, Del twisted into a *mai-quinjo* roll, hurling Tarex to the floor. As he and Del both jumped to their feet, Tarex backhanded Del so hard across the face, Del slammed into the hull. Tarex's face twisted with rage. Del didn't know what was wrong with him, why he didn't call for help or use the disk clenched in his fist, why the ship hadn't sent in the security bots. He tried to dodge past the Aristo, but he couldn't go fast enough. Tarex hit him again and again, beating his shoulders and arms.

Del leaned back and kicked, ramming his foot into Tarex's gut. The Aristo grabbed Del's calf and flipped him backward. As Del crashed to the deck, hitting his head, colors shot through his vision. Dizzy and off balance, he scrambled to his feet. His training couldn't help him adapt to this gravity, but it kept him going even when he could hardly see. He kicked again, spinning so Tarex couldn't grab his leg, and hit the Aristo in the hip so hard, he heard the crack of bone.

Tarex's face contorted with fury, and he clenched his fist *hard* on the disk. Del's nerves burned with an agony of fire. He screamed and dropped to his knees, doubled over. But he refused to let it stop him. When Tarex grabbed his shoulder, Del reacted through the haze of pain, and threw himself into a roll, knocking Tarex to the ground—

The worst of the pain stopped.

Del rose to his knees, swaying as he gasped. Tarex lay under the table, his head bleeding. Gods *almighty,* would the police add murder to Del's crimes? How much worse could this nightmare get?

But no, Tarex was breathing. As much as Del hated him, he gasped with relief. He struggled to his feet and backed out of the quarters. He dreaded what would happen when Tarex awoke. Del was trapped here, and no way would the ship let him near the controls again.

Del looked around, dazed. Surely Kryxson, Bronzeson, the robots, *something* had picked up the fight. He staggered through the ship, unable to think through his haze of pain.

Del found Kryxson and Bronzeson in the cargo hold, sprawled on the deck, bruised and unconscious. It looked like they had been fighting. Del turned in a confused circle, swaying—

And came face to face with Lieutenant Gregori.

"Ah, gods," Del whispered. He was hallucinating.

Gregori came toward him with several officers. Wait. That one, the captain . . . she was familiar. Hadn't she been with the squad that rescued him from Raker? Captain Penzer. And Gregori! He had been part of the squad, too.

Gregori was saying something. Del struggled to concentrate.

" . . . you ride in the pod?" Gregori asked.

"Anything," Del rasped. He would stand on his head and chant in ancient tongues if it got him out of here.

Gregori opened the hatch of the pod, and Del climbed in. When Gregori tried to help, Del jerked his arm away. He didn't want anyone touching him.

It was cramped inside, with two seats molded into the hull, a panel curving around one side, an icer for food, and nothing else. Del kept his head bent until he sat down. When Gregori started to climb in, Del stiffened, remembering Tarex grabbing him.

"No." Del pointed past Gregori to Penzer. "Her."

"You'd rather have Captain Penzer ride with you?" Gregori spoke carefully, as if he thought Del might break. Del had no idea what he looked like, but he felt like a jigsaw puzzle about to fall apart.

"It's all right," Penzer said. "I'll go."

Gregori backed out, and Penzer squeezed onto the seat across from Del. He moved his knees aside, giving her space, but they were still cramped. Gods, he wished Ricki were here. Not that he could hold her; he hurt too much. He felt insubstantial, as if his mind were apart from his body. His nausea hovered like a bird, ready to swoop down. He had a horrible feeling this was a hallucination, or that if it was happening, Tarex would recover and stop the pod. Del jerked as the closing hatch sealed them in.

Within seconds, they were in space. Penzer activated a screen so Del could look out. He watched, dizzy and ill, as they drifted toward the police ship, which gleamed silver and blue.

"What happened?" Del finally asked. "Why did Tarex and his crew go crazy? Why didn't his ship stop you from boarding?"

Penzer was watching him with concern. "The pod was doped with nanos targeted at Aristo genes. We got the codes from your Jagernaut bodyguard."

Del's pulse leapt. "Tyra is *alive*?"

"Well, yes," she said. "Very much so."

Emotions welled up inside Del that he couldn't describe. He wanted to laugh, then to cry. "And Cameron?"

"He's fine."

They were *alive*. He hadn't killed them. "How many people died when the yacht took off?"

"No one," she said gently. "They had plenty of warning."

Del wiped his palm over his eyes, smearing away the tears. He hoped Tarex rotted in a worm-world slum-hell. "I'm surprised Tyra didn't demand to come with you."

"She wanted to, but we couldn't risk it. Tarex's security monitors might have detected her biomech. His systems respond to Skolian tech far more than they do Allied." She paused awkwardly. "Since you all had that war."

Of course. The Traders were always developing counters to Skolian technology. "What do the nanos in this pod do?" Raggedly he asked, "Can they hurt us?"

"They act on certain brain centers. But not ours. Only Aristo. They were supposed to knock out Tarex and any crew he had with Aristo DNA. Which was apparently both of them."

"I think it made them crazy, aggressive too."

Penzer grimaced. "Apparently." She glanced at his bruised chest, which throbbed where Tarex had beaten him. "I'm sorry."

"You don't have to apologize for their inhumanity." Del couldn't say any more. If he talked about it, his anger would scorch him.

He stared at the screen, watching the police cruiser come closer. The Escort ships drifted in space beyond it. "Why aren't Tarex's Escorts trying to stop us?"

"They don't know what's going on," Penzer said. "Except that their vessels are in Allied custody." Her eyes glinted. "'Tarex' just told them that he sent the empty pod back to us."

Del still didn't understand. "Surely they can monitor the yacht and this pod. They must know what's going on."

"Normally, yes. But your Jagernaut bodyguard knew some of their security codes, including a neutrino pulse sequence that could scramble their systems enough to let us tamper with them. For the next few minutes, they should read this pod as empty and that everything is fine on the yacht." She pushed back a straggle of hair that had escaped her braid. "It won't last long. And we weren't sure it would work. We had to get close enough to these ships for the nanos and pulses to act, which meant practically on top of them. No way would these people let us near Tarex if they thought we posed a threat."

Their behavior was beginning to make sense. "So you acted a little dumb."

"A *little*?" She snorted. "We acted like idiots."

"It played right into his opinion of us." Del's pulse surged. "We need to get to your ship faster, before they figure out what's going on."

"If we go too fast, it will draw attention. The police have no reason to rush back an empty pod."

"I feel a little . . . strange." He couldn't focus.

Penzer spoke quietly. "You look like you went through hell."

Del probed a bruise on his arm. The neural dust on his skin felt slick against his fingertips. "Tarex and I . . . had a fight."

Penzer indicated mammoth doors of a docking bay opening on the police crusier. "We have doctors ready to treat you."

"I'll be fine." Del had no intention of letting anyone touch him. His injuries didn't matter anyway. No one could treat his rage. He had spent one day with Tarex. What about the people he loved who had been prisoners for so much longer, who had *died* in that agony? Hatred filled him.

He wanted the Aristos to pay.

XXVI

A Simple Choice

When the police cruiser landed at the port, more police met them, and this time they were the real thing. They demanded Captain Penzer release Del into their custody.

"This is absurd," Penzer told the sergeant. "This man is the victim, not the perpetrator."

They were all standing on the tarmac, including Del, who had on a shirt the doctors had given him. He left it unfastened in the front so it wouldn't pull across his back and aggravate his injuries. Although he had let the doctors remove the neural dust and treat the bruises on his face, he had stopped them when they tried to take care of the lash wounds. By then his bruises were healing, and their fast recovery reminded him of the way Tarex's med-bot had treated his throat. That had also healed fast—because Tarex had wanted him to sing even after Del had fucking *screamed* for hours.

Del was too angry to care what the police thought. He stood there in his leather pants with chains, his shirt open, his chest banged up, and his hair in his eyes. The police scowled as if he were a dissolute punk staggering home after a night of misdeeds.

"We have to bring him in," the sergeant said. "He's a well-known figure involved in a major criminal incident." The officer looked harried. "The buzz is all over the meshes. They say Prime-Nova bribed us to let him off. If we don't bring him in, the publicity could cause major problems for the police commissioner and the precinct."

"You don't understand." Penzer handed him an ID cube. "Comm the people here. They'll explain."

"Why can't you?" the sergeant asked.

Del knew Penzer couldn't breathe a word about his identity. If it jumped to the meshes, it would cause far more furor than the police were worried about. She glanced at Del, and he shook his head slightly.

Penzer turned back to the sergeant. "My CO can talk to you."

He lifted the cube. "I'll give this to the chief. But we still have to take Mister Arden in."

Del stiffened as two officers came over to him, one carrying a pair of magnetized cuffs. He couldn't take being manacled, not after everything else that had happened. "No!" He stepped back from them. "Don't put those on."

Penzer stepped past the police, ignoring their warning looks. She spoke quietly to Del. "What do you want me to do?"

He knew what she was asking: should she tell them he had diplomatic immunity? They would want proof. If it became public that she claimed he had a status reserved for foreign dignitaries, it could turn into a mess. She couldn't give details, and neither could Del, but that would just make it worse, deepening the mystery.

Del was tempted to tell them so he could get away from this. He had to do a concert tonight. He couldn't think past it, couldn't settle his mind. He felt too dizzy to make decisions. His family would be furious over what he had done. What if he said something he later regretted, when his mind cleared? He didn't know what to do.

"Call Mac, my manager," he told her. They both knew she would call General McLane first, but Del wanted Mac.

"We'll take care of it," Penzer promised him.

Then the police took him away.

Del panicked when he saw the cell. Three of the officers took him down a corridor with blue walls. The simple cell at the end was a white room with a white table and chair, and a bed against one wall. As cells went, it was innocuous—except it looked exactly like the room where he had awoken from cryogensis.

"No!" Del balked at the threshold. "I can't."

"You're in a jail, not a hotel," one of the officers said. "You don't get to choose."

Del was having trouble breathing. "You can put me in that room we passed up front."

"The holding cell?" That came from the man the others called Gonzales. "It has other people in it."

"I don't give a shit who's in it." Del knew he wasn't helping himself, but he was too agitated to stop. "I can't go in here."

"We can't put you in the holding cell," Gonzales said. "You're too well-known."

Del knew what they feared: bad publicity. It was probably the only reason they were discussing this at all instead of just dumping him in the cell. "I'll sign a release or something. I won't hold you responsible if anything happens."

"It doesn't work that way," one of the other officers said. He looked as if he wanted to shove Del into the cell and be done with it. "Why can't you go in here?"

"I—it—I get convulsions. When I panic. And being in small places makes me panic." Del made it up on the spot, but it was a lot closer to the truth than he had intended.

"Hell," Gonzales muttered. "We're screwed no matter what we do with him."

"Enough of this," the first man said. "He wants the coop up front? Fine. Put him in it."

The holding cell had six other prisoners. One was in for drunk and disorderly behavior. Another very large man was there because the police had caught him roughing up someone who owed a debt to somebody else. Del had no idea what the other four had done. He found out about the first two only because they knew each other and were talking when the police brought him into the cell.

"Hey, look at that," the drunk said. "We got ourselves a real rock star." He laughed idly. "You're that guy who gets all those pretty little peeps all turned on and then screws 'em all night."

"What?" Del was too edgy and in too much pain to figure out what the man said. He just wanted to hit something.

"He ain't no rock star," the giant man said.

"Looks like him," the drunk persisted.

"Looks pissed," a gangly man with acne scars on his face said. "What's wrong, pretty boy, got no one to bail you out?"

"Back off," Del said. He knew better, but he was too angry to think straight. He paced away, to the front of the cell. The wall looked like black glass, but when he pressed it with his palms, it felt like steel.

"It don't break," the giant said.

Acne came over to Del. "You're stuck with us."

Del shook his head and started to pace again.

"You look ready to blow holes in the sky," the drunk said. He sounded more curious than anything else.

"I need to get out," Del said. "I have to sing tonight."

"You *are* that guy!" The drunk grinned. "In D.C., right? I was going to the concert before I got cooped here."

"So was I," Del growled. He couldn't believe this, that he had escaped from an Aristo, one of the most powerful men in three empires, only to end up stuck in jail. Where the hell was Mac or McLane or *someone*?

It had been late afternoon when the police brought him in. Even with a flyer, it would take half an hour to reach the mall in D.C. where the concert had been going all day. If he didn't leave soon, he would miss his performance. He knew Mac would tell him not to do the concert, but he had no intention of staying off that stage. It would be Tarex's final victory over him.

Del didn't know how he would sing when he was so angry. His back hurt like hell. He kept hearing Tarex. *Kneel.* The Aristo was going to get away with everything. He had tortured Del and Staver, broke gods knew how many laws, sinned against human *decency*—and no one would touch him because no one wanted an "incident." Instead here was Del, in jail while people waited hand and foot on poor Tarex in his fucking yacht. The Aristo would raise hell over Staver and Del, throwing a spotlight on Staver that would probably end his Star Road and his hope of ever finding his wife.

"Damn!" Del shouted. He *needed* his virt. He had gone too long without the bliss. The only thing he hated even more was being so dependent on it.

"What are you yelling about?" Acne said. "And quit walking so much. It agitates me." He said it like *a-gee-tates.*

"Lay off," Del snapped.

Acne gave a dry laugh. "I ain't been laid in too long, pretty boy. You offering to help ease my pain?"

Del jerked, remembering Tarex slamming him down on the bed. He went over to Acne and spoke in slow, overly enunciated words. "Shut your fucking mouth."

"Not smart," the drunk muttered. "I don't think you're gonna sing tonight."

"Oh, he'll sing," Acne said. "Loud and clear."

Del took a breath. He didn't want to fight. "Sorry. I'm wound up."

"Oh gosh durn," Acne said in an exaggerated accent, parodying Del. "You're wound up. Wound up like what, boy? Like a whore? Oh, whoops. That's your mama."

Del froze. "What did you call my mother?"

"Now you're going to say she's not a whore," Acne said. "She just likes strolling the street when the boys come looking for fun."

"No one calls my mother a whore." Del was surprised how calm he sounded, because inside he felt ready to explode.

"Your daddy her pimp?" Acne asked.

Del hit his palms against Acne's shoulders, shoving him away. "Pull it back, asshole."

"I think you got a death wish," the giant told him.

Acne hit his fist against Del's shoulder, making him stumble back. "I'm getting sick of you." He hit Del's other shoulder with his other fist, pushing him back more. "Little boys shouldn't drill with big ones. Leave that to your mama."

That's it. Del snapped into a *mai-quinjo* move and threw Acne into the wall. For one instant the larger man gaped at Del. Then he lunged forward, raising both fists. Del reacted on instinct, spinning as he brought up his leg. He kicked with his body laid out in the air and caught Acne in the stomach. Then he whirled around and kicked again, catching him from the other side. Acne couldn't fight at all, even though he had obviously expected to win. His size and strength might take him a long way against untrained opponents, but within seconds, Del had laid him out on the floor.

Del was so worked up, he whirled to the other men. "Come on!" he yelled. "Fuck with me. Just try it!" He needed to *hit* something.

"Jesus." The drunk backed away. "I got no argument with you."

Del strode to the wall and slammed his fist against the glass. "Damn it, Mac," he shouted. "Get me out of here."

A harsh voice came over a comm. "Stand back."

Del took a breath and backed off. The other men gave him plenty of space. When he was in the middle of the room, an airlock shimmered and left a very large policeman in the opening. Two more stood behind him.

"Stay there," the big man said. He came forward, accompanied by an officer who kept a stunner aimed at Del. The third strode to Acne and knelt next to him, pulling out a medical tape. More voices were coming from the hall outside.

Gritting his teeth, Del stayed put, watching the doctor treat Acne. He had to get a grip on his anger before he started punching police officers and ended up in even more trouble. He was surprised they hadn't gassed the cell when he started to fight.

A deep voice spoke from the entrance of the cell. "Del, what the bloody hell are you doing?"

Del turned with a start. A tall man in a military uniform stood there, frowning at him. General McLane.

"Holy shit," someone said.

Del stalked over to McLane. "What the 'bloody hell' took you so long?"

"Definitely a death wish," the giant muttered behind him.

Their reaction startled Del. Although he knew the five stars on Fitz's shoulders meant he had a high rank, he didn't understand it at a gut level. But he didn't need empathic abilities to see everyone's shock. They recognized McLane. Apparently Fitz had decided getting him out of jail fast was even more important than the stir that would start if it went public that the military had sent one of their big guns for Del.

Fitz, however, was furious. "My people were right behind you, arranging your release. You've been here *five minutes*. How could you get into so much trouble so fast?"

Del bit back his retort. It was either that or lose his temper.

One of the policemen cleared his throat. "General McLane, are you in charge of this man?"

"Yes, he is." That came from the grey-haired police chief, who had come up behind McLane and was entering the cell. He regarded Del coldly. "You're free to go."

"He hit Vic," the giant protested, motioning at Acne, who was sitting up with the help of the doctor.

"I want to press charges," Acne said. "For assault."

"You think those little kicks were assault?" Del demanded. "Call my mother a whore again, and I'll show you assault."

"Enough!" McLane looked as if he wanted to shake Del. "You aren't going to kick anyone."

Acne crossed his arms. "I'm gonna sue."

McLane considered Acne, then spoke to the doctor. "How is he?"

"A few bruises." The doctor rose to his feet. "Otherwise he's fine."

Acne stood up as well. "I've been in the courts," he told Del. "I know the drill. You inflicted emotional trauma. I'm suing your rich rock star butt for punitive damages."

"Young man," McLane said. "Don't make trouble for yourself." He glanced at Del. "I'm sure reparations can be made."

"I don't want no one shitting me." Acne fixed Del with a hard stare. "I'll see you in court, asshole. Your mama, too, if she's rich."

"Pray you don't," Del said. He was the one who would take the brunt of his family's anger, but it wouldn't stop them from coming down on Acne like a ton of plutonium. Of course it would never get to court; the two governments would deal with it. But Del knew he had burned every bridge he had to the Allieds. No more concerts. No more vids. Kelric would drag him home.

And Tarex, gods damn him, would go free.

Del started to speak, but Fitz shook his head and jerked his chin toward the exit. "Now."

As Del went down the hall outside the cell with Fitz and the police chief, the general said, "What were you thinking?"

"I didn't fight to do harm," Del said. "Just to shut him up." The last thing he could take right now was censure from Kelric's counterpart among the Allieds.

"We're going to bring you to Annapolis base," Fitz said. "Doctor Chandler wants you in the hospital. We've also been in contact with your brother. He's scheduled a holo-conference for tomorrow, after you've rested."

"No." Del couldn't settle his agitation. "I have to sing tonight. I'm going to be late if we don't hurry."

Fitz stared at him. "You must be joking."

"No!" Del knew if he lost his temper, Fitz would never listen. He spoke in a calmer voice. "I signed a contract. I gave my word, General McLane. It's a huge concert. I have to show up. I'll go to Annapolis as soon as it finishes. I swear." He took a breath. "Please. It's probably the last concert I'll ever do."

Fitz answered in an unexpectedly kind voice. "Del, you're in no condition to perform."

"I'm fine." Del could hear a woman's voice. It sounded familiar. "Is that Ricki?"

"If you mean Ms. Varento," Fitz said, "then yes, that's her."

Del quickened his pace and entered a large room filled with people working at consoles. Except right now, most were pretending to work while they watched him covertly or stared outright. Del didn't care. He had one goal: the gorgeous blond standing in the middle of the room, arguing with two men in dark suits.

"He needs to leave," she was saying in her *Don't mess with me* voice. "Our people will take care of your forms. You just have to release him into my custody."

"Hey," Del said, coming up behind her.

Ricki spun around. "Thank God!" Her gaze swept over him. "Good Lord, Del, what did they do? You look like hell warmed over."

He gave her a shaky smile. "I'm glad to see you, too."

Her voice softened. "You okay, babe?"

"Yeah, I'm fine." He was too tense to embrace her. "Do you have a flyer? If we leave now, we'll just make it."

"You aren't going anywhere," Fitz said. His voice was low enough that it didn't carry, but that didn't lessen its force.

Ricki looked up at the general. Del expected her to turn on her barracuda mode or the wide-eyed innocent look. She did neither. She just said, "Sir, he has over a million people waiting to hear him, and that's just in D.C."

"I can't. I'm sorry." Fitz even looked as if he meant it. "Not without permission from Imperator Skolia."

"Well, hell," Del said. Like his brother would ever agree.

"Permission from *who*?" the police chief asked.

Fitz exhaled and just shook his head.

Ricki spoke softly to Del. "I'm sorry, babe. I want you to do the concert. But he's right." She looked almost as tired as Del felt. "You need a doctor. That's more important."

Del stared at her in disbelief. Of all the people he thought he could count on for support, she was the one.

Fitz's shoulders relaxed. "Thank you, Ms. Varento."

"Ricki, I'm doing great," Del said. "Really."

She laid her hand on his arm. "I know you were looking forward to the show. But not this time."

What alien had stolen his girlfriend and put this stranger in her place? Before he could protest, a bustle came from across the room and a small crowd of people swept into the station.

"Mac!" Del called.

Mac strode over to them, his legs eating up distance, Cameron and Tyra at his side. And Staver! Then they were all gathering around Del, everyone talking at once.

"We've already spoken to the concert organizers," Mac told Del. "They don't expect you to perform."

"I have to!" Del said. "Don't make me give this one up."

"You'll have others," Ricki said.

Del couldn't believe it. She had *heard* Kelric. She knew his brother would call an end to his career. His stupid fight in the cell had put on the finishing touch.

He turned to Tyra, but what could he say? She was Kelric's officer. Cameron stood next to her, his face impassive, his mind protected. When Del tried to speak to him, Cameron shook his head.

Del swung back to Mac. "Please."

Mac bit his lip, his face strained. Then he turned to the general. "Surely we can do something."

Fitz shook his head. "I'm sorry."

"Let yourself heal," Staver said. With a quiet eloquence, he added, "I owe you my life as a free man, probably even my sanity. You sacrificed yourself for me. I'll always be in your debt." He nodded to Ricki, who was standing with Fitz. "Listen to them. Take care of yourself. You'll have other concerts."

Del wished it were true. He wished a lot, that he could take away the pain his family had suffered from the Aristos, that Staver would find his wife, that Tarex would pay, that the Traders would goddamned leave the rest of humanity alone. But none of it would happen. He couldn't do anything. The Aristos would go on with their crimes against the human race, and the Allieds would look the other way because they didn't want to hear a truth that ugly.

General McLane glanced at Cameron. "Do you have a flyer?"

The Marine nodded. "Annapolis issued us one."

"We can all go with Del," Tyra said. "Ricki and Mac, too."

"No." Del regarded Ricki. "You and Mac go with someone else." As much as he knew they were acting in what they considered his best interest, it still felt like a betrayal. His bodyguards had to do their job, but Ricki and Mac could have given him support. Even if it hadn't done any good, it mattered to him.

Incredibly, Fitz looked as if he felt as bad about all this as the others. To Mac, he said, "Do you have another flyer?"

Mac spoke awkwardly. "Not here."

"I took a fly-taxi here," Ricki said.

Del wanted to say, *So take one home.* Instead he told himself to grow up. Then he said, "You might as well ride with me, then." He wasn't going anywhere, except to the end of his dreams.

"Annapolis, hell," Ricki said. "Cameron, get this flyer on the right course." She, Mac, and Staver were with Del in the passenger section while Cameron and Tyra sat up front.

"We'll only be twenty minutes late," Ricki told Del. "Jenny Summerland can play that much longer. Your band is ready to go on."

"What the flipping hell are you telling him?" Mac demanded.

Del stared at Ricki while his heart did a dance. "You were faking out McLane!"

"Of course I was faking McLane." She scowled at him. "You're an empath. You should have known."

Del had been too harried trying to control his own rage to concentrate on anyone else. "Why would you fake him?"

She leaned forward. "Because General Ramrod wasn't going to let us take you anywhere if he thought we'd override his orders."

"We *can't* take Del to that concert," Mac said. "Fitz would hit the roof. Del's family would hit the roof. God, Ricki, the president of the Allied Worlds of Earth would hit the roof."

"Interstellar civilizations don't have roofs," Ricki said.

Mac groaned. Then he motioned at Tyra and Cameron. "They won't let you do it."

"Tyra?" Del asked.

She gave him an incredulous look. "Do you have any idea what your brother would do to me if I disobeyed his orders?"

"Did he order me to stay away from the concert?" Del asked.

"No," Cameron said from the pilot's seat. "He didn't."

Tyra gave him a sour look. "He didn't know Del was scheduled to *do* a concert."

Del held back his protest. Even if he could push Tyra into letting him do the concert, which was as likely as his earning a doctorate in inversion physics, Kelric would probably have her court-martialed for it. Del couldn't ask her to risk that, especially after everything he had put her through. She was already in enough trouble with his brother.

Del forced out the difficult words. "I understand." To Cameron, he added, "I'm sorry I knocked you out in the port."

Instead of maintaining his stony silence, Cameron said, "You really *do* know martial arts." Incredibly, he laughed. "I can't believe you put me out. I should hire you as my bodyguard."

Del gaped at him. He had expected Cameron to be angry. Tyra was furious at someone, but he didn't know who she felt that way about; she kept her mind too well shielded for anything specific to come through.

"Del," Tyra said. When he looked at her, she spoke quietly. "What you did was brave. I've faced death during combat without a flinch, but I don't know if I could have made the choices you did when you went for Staver on Tarex's yacht."

Of all the responses he had expected, this wasn't even close. She thought he had more courage than a Jagernaut? That was crazy.

Tyra leaned over Cameron's seat. "You're off course, mister. You're going the wrong direction."

"Tyra, no." Del had to force out the words, because he wanted to shout *Yes, yes, yes!* "You can't."

Her eyes glinted. "It's true, you know. Your brother never ordered me *not* to take you to the concert."

"You can't argue semantics with Kelric," Del said. "Believe me, I know. He'll strip you of your rank and put you on trial."

"Maybe." Tyra said. "But if he isn't willing to listen to my reasons, he isn't the commander I've admired."

"That's nuts," Del told her. "If he's so hard-nosed even with me, he won't listen to you."

"Oh, Del," she said. "Don't you know? He's tougher on you than anyone else alive. Because he loves you."

Del couldn't answer. His relationship with Kelric was too complicated for him to talk about.

Tyra frowned at Cameron. "So fix the damn course."

"Cameron, don't do it," Mac warned.

Cameron looked back at him. "Sorry, Major Tyler." Then he changed course.

Mac raised his comm, but Tyra acted faster, grabbing his arm. She peeled the comm off his wrist, then laid his hand on the arm of his seat. Mac stared at her, his face pale.

But he didn't protest.

As the flyer banked in a circle toward Washington, D.C., Ricki said, "We've got a concert tonight!"

XXVII

One Song

The sea of people went on and on, across the Capitol Mall in Washington, D.C., filling streets, flowing into every open space. Jenny Summerland was singing with Rex and Mind Mix on the huge stage in the mall, their figures highlighted against clouds of billowing holographic color. Lights flared, their backup singers danced, and the stage glittered.

Del's flyer landed behind the stage in a flare of exhaust. The audience assumed it was part of the show, cheering in a tidal wave of noise. Del jumped down while the engines were roaring and ran through the steam curling around the flyer. Staver ran at his side while Ricki and Mac searched out the crews for Del's performance.

Del began to ease down his mental shields as he prepared to face the audience. With so many people, he had to take it slow.

Staver? he thought, doing a "sound" test.

Are you sure you're up for this? Staver asked.

I'm fine, Del lied. **Did you get the provider free?**

From Tarex, yes, Staver thought. *But we can't get her off Earth. His people are watching too closely, and the Allieds are searching. If they find out we've hidden her, they'll arrest us for kidnapping.*

Gods, why? Don't they know what Tarex did to her? To *you*?

Staver's face creased with anger. *The police analyzed his responses to their questions. He thinks he's done nothing wrong. When he says*

427

he honored me as his guest, he believes it. So it registers as truth. Before he put me in the cold storage unit, he had cleaned the neural dust off my skin, so even that evidence was gone. The police are investigating, but he has them convinced I started a smear campaign. He acts the perfect lord.

Del gritted his teeth. **Right. He just enslaves billions of people.**

The Allieds can't comprehend Aristos. And Tarex is far more powerful than you or me, enough even to pull General McLane into this mess. Frustration leaked into his thought. *Unless we can divert Tarex's attention, we're going to lose the girl back to him. And we're all out of diversions.*

Maybe not. They had reached the stairs up to backstage. Jenny's soaring voice came from above, muted by layers of wood and flexi-metal. Del took the stairs two at a time, driven by his urgency, until Staver fell behind.

Del! Staver thought. *You can't go onstage in that shirt. It has blood all over the back.*

Del hadn't realized he was bleeding again. He had probably torn open his wounds during his fight in jail. But he couldn't stop. He had to focus, prepare for the million minds he would face when he went onstage. He reached the top of the stairs, heaved open the door, and ran down the corridor inside.

A tech caught up with him. "Del! What do you need?"

Still running, Del yanked off his shirt. "My vest. It's the leather one with metal conduits. Ask Bonnie. She knows which one."

The tech took off with his shirt, running ahead. Jenny had stopped singing, and the crowd was applauding.

Another tech fell into step with Del. "Your band is all set. Jud Taborian played with Mind Mix, so he's already on stage. We have it all—" She stopped, her mouth open as she stared at his torso. "Good Lord, who worked you over?"

"It's nothing." Del was too wound up to say more.

The other tech came jogging back to him, carrying a black vest. "Bonnie said this is the one . . ." She trailed off as she looked at his torso. "What happened?"

"*Nothing.* The vest will cover it." Not his arms, but he was past caring. He pulled it on, wincing as it scraped his back, but it would bother him less than a form-fitting shirt. The techs tried to help, but he just shook his head and kept going.

They soon reached the scaffolding of a tower that rose at the back of the stage. Techs swarmed around the tower and toward Del. He joined them—and stopped. He sensed Ricki.

Del spun around to see Ricki running toward him with Staver. Del wanted to move, go, get on the lift that would take him up the tower. He forced himself to stay put. The techs around him were talking on comms, checking his clothes, checking the lift.

Ricki stopped in front of Del, breathing hard, with Staver at her side. "Del, what are you doing?" she asked.

"What do you think?" His tension was rising, matching the crowd. "I'm going to sing."

"I don't know what this is about," Ricki said. "But I want your word. You won't do anything but sing out there."

He met her gaze. "You have my word."

"I have people here," Staver told him. "Do you want me to put them in the control booth?"

"What?" Del asked.

"Do you want Staver's people in the booth?" Ricki asked.

"Why?" Del asked.

Staver regarded him steadily. "So they can keep out anyone who tries to come in. For whatever reason."

"Like to stop your performance." Ricki scowled at Del. "*Why* they would want to stop it, I have no idea."

Del didn't know, either. Why would he need Staver's people in the booth? But something was rising in him, a fury that wouldn't let go. His gaze never wavered. "Yes, I'd like his people there. Only them. And don't let anyone on the stage but the band. Not Mac. *Especially* not Mac. No matter what he says. Keep off Cameron and Tyra, too, if you can."

"Why would they want to get on the stage?" she asked.

"Just trust me," he said.

She looked at him as if he had grown a second head.

"Ricki?" he said.

She drew in a breath. "All right. We'll do what we can."

Del knew what a leap of faith it took for her to trust *anyone.* He hoped that after tonight, she wouldn't feel he had betrayed her trust.

A tech came over to Del and handed him a mike. "Jud Taborian wants to know if they should start 'Emeralds.'"

"Not 'Emeralds,'" Del said. Because he knew now what he was going to do. "Tell them the 'Carnelians Finale.'"

"Will do." The tech went off, talking on her comm.

"'Carnelians'?" Ricki looked relieved. "That's gorgeous."

Del knew she meant the music of the original. "You've only heard the first version."

"Why would anyone stop you from singing it?" she asked.

Del had no idea what would happen, and he wasn't calm enough to think it through. He was going purely on instinct. "Just keep them off the stage and out of the booth." With that, he strode to the tower. He felt Ricki watching him, felt her puzzled curiosity.

The lift in the tower took Del up through the dark. Only faint purple safety bulbs lit the way as the lift rose. When it reached the platform at the top, Del was far above the ground, high in the wind and the night. The introduction to the "Carnelians Finale" began, a relentless chord progression that repeated over and over. As the music swelled with power, the audience applauded. Del *felt* their response; this was new, strong, vigorous. They wanted more.

Del locked the controls so no one could call the lift back down. Then he raised his hand in a prearranged signal. Clouds of dry ice billowed as purple lights flared under the tower, shining on him from below. Lasers swept over him, drawing glints from the metal in his clothes and hair. The audience shouted their approval. Holo-cams swung around the stage on platforms and sound-orbs spun everywhere. They were sending the concert out on the mesh, across the planet, and into space.

The music swelled with its relentless beat. Del walked to the end of the platform—and kept going, down a ramp. It morphed as he walked, sloping before him, lowering him to the ground. Holos brightened around him, emerald at first, then shading into red when the techs realized he had switched to another song.

As Del reached the stage, the music hit its high point, driving him onward. He strode to the front of the stage and stood with his head lifted while the song crashed to its finale.

And it began again.

In the relative quiet of the opening, Del called out to the audience. "Are you ready? *Ready to hear some music?*"

The roar of agreement buffeted him, huge and full of power. It fueled his energy, and he sent it back out, riding the crest. "I've got something new. A song for those who share the stars with us." He lifted his chin and shouted, *"This is for you, Tarex."*

The drums joined the driving melody, and Del sang, his lyrics very much like the original. But he did this version hard and fast, one line after another, barely pausing for breath:

> You dehumanized us
> Your critics, they all died
> You answered defiance
> With massive genocide
>
> You hunt us as your prey
> You assault and enslave
> You force us bound to stay
> For pleasures that you crave

Listen to me, he thought to the audience. ***Hear me.*** He veered away from the original. Instead, he sang the words he had created in the deep of night, born of his worst memories, born out of the pain suffered by the people he loved. He sang hard and furious, filled with rage, sang to the Aristos, the sons of the Carnelian Throne, whose emperor presided over the most monstrous empire in human history:

> You broke my brother
> You Carnelian Sons
> You tortured my mother
> In your war of suns
>
> You killed my brothers
> You shattered my father
> You murdered my sister
> Expecting no others

Del heaved in a breath and sang what he knew, no prettied lyrics, just the truth.

> Well, I'm no golden hero
> In the blazing skies
> I'm no fair-haired genius
> Hiding in disguise

His voice rose, his anger adding power as he shouted:

> I'm only a singer
> It's all I can do
> But I'm still alive
> And I'm coming after you

The morpher thundered, Anne's drums filled the night, Randall's stringer wailed. And Del sang:

> I'll never kneel
> Beneath your Highton stare
> I'm here and I'm real
> I'll lay your guilt bare

When the music reached its crescendo, he threw back his head, his legs planted wide as he shouted into the mike.

> I'll never kneel
> Beneath your Highton stare
> I'm here and I'm real
> Your living nightmare!

He held the final note, his fist clenched around the mike and raised to the stars as the song finished in one powerful, crashing chord.

Mac was talking to a mech-tech behind the stage when the "Carnelians Finale" began. He stopped in mid-sentence, unable to believe he was hearing that ominous progression of chords.

"Mac?" the tech asked. "Hello?"

"I have to go," Mac said. He spun around and ran for the stage. By the time he reached the top of the stairs that led backstage, he was gasping for breath, his sixty-year-old heart laboring. But he didn't pause as he yanked open the door and ran down the corridor. "Carnelians" kept on, inexorable.

Mac grabbed the audio-comm hanging on a cord around his neck and shoved it into his ear. "Del, can you hear me? *Del!*"

No response. Del rarely answered during a concert, but Mac could always tell the comm was active because he could hear

Del breathing and the noise of the crowd. Now he was getting nothing.

He ran through a tangle of light-amps and morph engines, came around a looming pile of equipment, and plowed into a cluster of people standing around the base of the tower: Ricki, Staver, assorted techs, and four very large men from the stage crew.

Mac strode up behind Ricki. "Is he onstage yet?"

She jumped and spun around. "Mac! Don't scare me that way."

"You have to get him off the stage!" Mac said. "*Now.*"

Ricki met his gaze. "No."

"This isn't some special effect!" Mac tried to push past her. The tower lift was gone, but he'd climb the stairs if he had to.

Two stagehands caught Mac's arm, one on each side of him. "I'm sorry," one of the mammoths said. "You can't go up there."

"Let me go!" Mac struggled to pull away. "Ricki, listen. You can't let him do this."

She met his gaze. "I promised I wouldn't let you stop him."

"Where are Tyra and Cameron?" It was all Mac could do to keep from shouting.

"Checking the area," Ricki said. "Like they always do."

Mac raised his arm, but one of the stagehands stopped him before he could activate his wrist comm. They were young, big, strong, and not out of breath, none of which applied to him.

"Don't hurt him," Ricki told them. She spoke more gently to Mac. "I'm sorry. But you can't comm Tyra or Cameron."

"Ricki, you have to listen to me," Mac said. " 'Carnelians' is a fire bomb."

"Maybe," she said. "We'll see."

"Why does it upset you?" Staver asked. "Del's material is cleaner than what you hear from a lot of bands. It's *how* he sings that causes problems, not what he says."

Mac gave an unsteady laugh. "You think I'm worried about sex? God, I wish. He's about to do one of the most politically inflammatory songs ever written." He willed Ricki to listen. "You *hate* politics. Believe me, you *don't* want him up there."

With a comment like that, the Ricki he had worked with all these years would have immediately pulled Del off the stage. This stranger just crossed her arms and said, "He goes on."

Mac clenched his fists, straining against the stagehands. He couldn't fight these hulking youths. He had to depend on Tyra and Cameron. Neither knew the "Carnelians Finale," but surely they would stop Del, especially when they heard the lyrics. If they would just get back here. He wasn't far from the stage, only a few yards back, behind a bank of light-amps. The stage remained dark, but the music was working up the audience. Del was just barely visible in the dark, already at the top of the tower. He raised his hand into the air.

"That's the signal to start the show," a tech said into her comm, probably to someone in the control booth.

The lights came up below Del. As he stalked down the ramp, the music swelled and holos formed around him, first green, then red and orange like flames.

"Don't do it," Mac said to the solitary figure striding down the ramp. "Del, be wise. *Don't do it.*"

When Del reached the stage, he strode to its edge while the music crashed to its final ringing note. Jud immediately started the piece again. It could repeat as many times as the band wanted. In rehearsal, they played it over and over, improvising. Although sometimes Del sang a few verses, usually he left it as an instrumental piece.

Not tonight.

When the music quieted, Del's voice rolled over the audience. Desperate, Mac struggled with the stagehands. When Del shouted, "This is for you, Tarex," Mac swung around to Ricki. "You have to stop him! Don't you understand what he's doing?"

She answered quietly. "Maybe people need to hear him."

Mac stood transfixed as Del's vocals swept over the crowd, carried by orbs, holocams, the night air. *You killed my brother, tortured my mother, shattered my father, murdered my sister.*

"Gods," Staver said. "He sings as if that's all true."

Mac spoke numbly. "It is."

Light from the stage washed across Ricki's face as she watched Del. "I've never heard him do anything like this."

I'm no golden hero in the blazing skies. I'm no fair-haired genius hiding in disguise. I'm only a singer, it's all that I can do. But I'm still alive, and I'm coming after you.

"He's singing to the Aristos," Mac said.

Staver stood transfixed. "Why would the Traders devastate the family of an Allied citizen?"

Mac knew billions of people would soon be asking that same question. For every person who thought it was just a song, two more would wonder if Del were singing about himself. He struggled futilely with the stagehands. When Del shouted, *"I'll lay your guilt bare,"* Mac felt as if an avalanche were crashing down on them.

"My God," Ricki breathed. "He's magnificent."

"Magnificent?" Mac couldn't believe it. "Do you have any idea how the Traders react to criticism? With one song, he could shatter any hope we ever had of diplomatic relations with them."

"You want 'diplomatic relations' with monsters," Staver said harshly. "Listen to the first verse. It's all there. Your people need to hear it."

"Not like this!" Mac said. "It will destroy everything."

The music thundered to its crescendo and Del's voice soared into the final note. Finally the music dropped into the quiet opening, and Del stopped singing.

Mac sagged in the grip of the stagehands. *Thank God.* It was over.

"That was for all of you," Del told the audience. Then he raised his chin and said, "This one is for my people."

"What the hell?" someone said.

Mac started at the unexpected voice. A group of techs had gathered around them, all watching Del.

"My people?" one asked. "What is he talking about?"

The drums joined the chord progression, and Del sang—

In perfect, unaccented Iotic.

Staver's mouth dropped open. "Gods *almighty.*"

"No," Mac said dully.

Staver swung around to him. "He's a Skolian lord?"

"If you only knew," Mac said. "Ricki, *pull him off.*"

Tyra stalked up next to Mac, her gaze fixed on Del. "What the hell is he doing?" She looked at the stagehands restraining Mac. "What's going on here?"

"Tyra, stop him," Mac said. "Listen to what he's saying."

Tyra paused, her head tilted as she listened. Watching her, Mac feared she would refuse. Then she exhaled and strode toward the stage. The two stagehands who weren't holding Mac blocked her way. Although she countered them, whirling right and left, Mac had the impression she was holding back. Her fighting style looked like a cross between martial arts and street brawling. They kept trying to restrain her—

Tyra suddenly turned into a blur, like a black streak. She threw both hulks so fast, Mac couldn't even see what she did. One of Mac's captors let him go and waded into the fray, but it made no difference. Within seconds, all three mammoths were crumpled on the ground.

Tyra turned to Ricki. "Get him off the stage. Or I'm going out there."

"Look at them!" Ricki jerked her hand at the crowd. "You see how worked up they are? You pull him off, and we could lose control of the audience."

Mac needed no telepathy to read Tyra's thought. She could handle three stagehands, but a million people was another story altogether.

Tyra walked slowly onto the stage. When Mac strained in the grip of his guard, the man said, "I can't let you go, Mister Tyler. I'm sorry."

The stagehands that Tyra had knocked over picked themselves off the ground, brushing dirt off their arms. When they saw Tyra on the edge of the stage, they headed out after her.

"Take it slow," Ricki said. "If you start fighting onstage, it could cause a riot."

The men nodded and kept to the edge of the stage as they moved into the light. Tyra was about ten yards from the front. Del had seen her, but he kept singing, rising into the climax of the song. He held the last note longer this time, but finally, mercifully, he let it go. As the music dropped into the intro, Mac sagged with relief. Whatever damage that furious challenge was going to do, at least it was over.

Del watched Tyra while the music cycled. Then he spun around to the other side of the stage. It looked like a dance move, but Mac knew he had sighted Cameron, who was coming from that side, in front of where Jud sat at his morpher. Jud's gaze flicked defiantly from Cameron to Tyra as he continued the song. Anne and Randall seemed bewildered, but they kept playing, too.

Del took a deep, visible breath—and moved to the very front of the stage, right on the edge. He was standing above a sea of people clapping, dancing, reaching for him, their energy driven by the music. If he took one more step, he would fall into that seething mass of humanity. Mac understood then why Tyra and Cameron weren't going closer. If they spooked Del and he jumped, the devil only knew what would happen. He had provoked the crowd to the edge of rational thought; if he fell now, he could end up in the hospital. Or worse.

Then Del raised his head and shouted into the mike. "This one is for you, Jaibriol Qox." He began again—

In a third language.

The blood drained from Mac's face. He had never had cause to use that language, but he could never mistake the harsh words. Oh, yes, he knew. Del was singing in Highton, the language of the Trader Aristos.

Of their emperor, Jaibriol Qox.

Mac sank down to sit on a light-amp. His guard only eased his hold enough for Mac to move that much. The other stagehands were edging around the stage, closing on Tyra and Cameron.

And Del sang the "Carnelians Finale."

"He's going to start an interstellar war," Mac said dully.

Del *was* the Aristo's living nightmare, the prince everyone had overlooked, the survivor who came to fight them with one of the most powerful weapons in existence.

A song.

As Del finished the Highton version of the "Finale," he lowered his arm with the mike. This time when Tyra came forward, he stayed put. Mac didn't know what Tyra thought, but she was moving with caution, as if Del were a bomb ready to explode. She walked over and stood eye-to-eye with him. Then, slowly, she took the mike. The crowd was clapping like thunder, but quieter pockets of people were just watching. Staring. More and more, they were realizing Tyra wasn't part of the show.

The lights went out and the music cut off.

"Hey!" The protests swelled in a multitude of voices.

Mac laughed raggedly. "A little late, don't you think?" Why it had taken the concert management so long to cut the power, he had no idea. It was only when he looked at his wrist-mesh that he realized almost no time had passed. Del had blasted through the song three times in three languages in three minutes.

✧   ✧   ✧

In New York, the giant holoscreen that dominated Times Square showed a man singing with fury, his music filling the humid night air as a Manhattan crowd gathered below to watch.

In Peking, China, holoscreens constructed from the sides of entire skyscrapers showed the giant figure of the man singing, his music filling the city.

The song poured out into space, to Mars, the asteroid belt, the moons of Jupiter and Saturn and beyond. The Kyle relays the Allieds had licensed from the Skolians kicked in and hurtled the music across space.

Deep in the Skolian Imperialate, in the Amphitheater of Memories where the Assembly met, thousands of tiers rose up like a vertical city. The delegates of an empire convened to discuss, debate, and vote on the business of a thousand peoples. Giant screens all over the amphitheater showed the speakers. When a broadcast from Earth suddenly replaced the proceedings, protests rumbled—until people recognized the singer. He had never sat in Assembly or spoken at any government convocation. Almost no one had met him. But his resemblance to the man who sat as the Ruby Consort was unmistakable.

The man sang in Iotic, his voice soaring. On the dais in the center of the amphitheater, a woman with silver-streaked hair and a giant man with gold skin—the Ruby Pharaoh and Imperator—stood together, watching the screen as the man sang: *I'm no golden hero in the blazing skies, I'm no fair-haired genius hiding in disguise.*

And even farther across the stars, in the largest empire ever known to humanity, the Trader Aristos gathered in the Amphitheater of Providence to rule their glittering, brutal empire, tier upon tier of them, all the same, with shimmering black hair and carnelian eyes. Their emperor stood on a balcony, his hands planted on the railing. As one, they watched the giant screen where a young prince shouted in Highton:

> I'll never kneel
> Beneath your Highton stare
> I'm here and I'm real
> Your living nightmare.

XXVIII

Sunrise Eyes

Mac had never seen Fitz McLane this drained. The general sat in the large chair behind his desk and rubbed his eyes, then dropped his arm.

"Hannah Loughten will join the conference from Australia," Fitz said. "Via a holo link."

Mac nodded. They were fortunate the President of the Allied Worlds was here on Earth, but she would have linked in from anywhere. "Does she want Del deported?"

"She hasn't said." Fitz leaned back in his chair. "That's moot, anyway. When Del can travel, Imperator Skolia will pull him out of here faster than a starship can invert. We'll be lucky if the Skolians don't sever all relations with us."

"I'm not so sure," Mac said. "I've never seen Staver Aunchild so grimly pleased. His people resent our dealing with Aristos." Dryly he said, "I wouldn't be surprised if they think Del should be canonized."

Fitz gave him a sour look. "His family are the ones we have to deal with. Let's just say my conversations with Imperator Skolia have been less than friendly."

Mac could imagine too well. "Which of them will be in the conference?"

"The Imperator," Fitz said. "The Ruby Pharaoh. The First Councilor of their Assembly. Queen Roca, Del's mother. Naaj Majda, the General of the Pharaoh's Army." He paused, squinting at a display on his desk. "And some person named Chaniece."

Mac sat up straighter. "Chaniece is Del's twin sister."

"Oh, great," Fitz said. "Just great. Another hothead."

Mac smiled. "She's the opposite, Fitz. They probably asked her to join the link because she may be the only person alive who can consistently calm Del down."

"I hope so." Fitz restlessly smoothed his sleeve. It was telling of how rough his night had been, that the self-ironing uniform could no longer stay military-sharp. "How is Del this morning?"

"He was asleep when I checked with Doctor Chandler at the hospital." Mac would never forget how Del had collapsed after the concert. "He was in pretty bad shape."

"I saw the report." Fitz's grimace heightened the dark circles under his eyes. "Tarex did all that to him?"

Mac's anger surged. "He beat the crap out of Del, whipped the skin off his back, and gave him neural shocks all over his upper body." It was no wonder Del had exploded last night.

Now they had to deal with the fallout of that three-minute blast.

Del didn't want to leave his room at the base. To say he dreaded the upcoming conference was like saying he had slept a little in cryo.

Although his body still ached, he felt much better than yesterday, when he had escaped Tarex. Physically. Emotionally he wasn't ready for anything. But he had to face the consequences of his concert. He, General McLane, and Mac would link into the conference from here in Annapolis. President Loughten would connect from Australia, and Del's family from the Orbiter, except for Chaniece, who would use a console in their home on Lyshriol. As the eldest member of the Ruby Dynasty on Lyshriol, she was now head of the family there, in charge of their holdings and the Valdoria branch of the royal family.

Today Del dressed far more conservatively than usual, grey slacks and a white dress shirt with diamond cufflinks, the type of clothes his family wanted him to wear. He stood in the middle of his living room, looking at nothing. He had seen no one but Doctor Chandler since he woke up this morning. But no matter what happened, he didn't regret what he had done. Whether or not anyone had heard, *truly* heard, what he had sung, he didn't know. But it was out there.

Del craved his bliss-node. He wanted nothing more than to submerge in the forgiving euphoria of his dreams. The agitation he felt when he went more than a few hours with a session had plagued him all morning. How he would make it through the long days without it, he didn't know, but make it he would, because he had sworn to stop. The joy it offered was false, an escape that drained his life and his music.

Doctor Chandler was helping, giving him neural blockers that eased his need. But nothing took it away. The hunger always lurked in his mind. Yet no matter how difficult it became, he would keep the vow he had made to himself. No more would he waste his life in the counterfeit promises of a bliss that had never truly existed.

A chime came from his door. Del tensed. He had put off leaving for so long, someone had come looking for him.

"Claude, who's outside my room?" Del asked.

"Mac and Ricki," his EI said.

"Oh. Okay." His shoulders relaxed a bit. "Let them in."

As soon as the door shimmered away, Mac strode inside. "How are you?" He came over to Del, then stopped, blinking. "Good Lord. You look like a Ruby prince."

Del smiled. "Well, that's a coincidence."

Ricki came in more slowly. She spoke in a subdued voice. "You carry it well."

"Hi." Del wanted her to hurry over to him, pull him into her arms, say how happy she was to see him. She did none of those things. She did come closer, though.

"Are you nervous, babe?" she asked.

"I guess so." If only she would—what? Act like she loved him? Once he had told Mac he was incapable of loving a woman. So much had changed since then, but even as an empath, he couldn't tell where he stood with her. Either she didn't know herself or else she hid it so deep, he couldn't pick it up.

"You'll be all right," Mac told him.

Del just looked at him. They both knew it wasn't true.

The door chimed again.

"Guess it doesn't matter if I'm ready." Del's attempt to laugh sounded forced. "Claude, who is that?"

"I don't know," his EI answered. "I don't recognize the woman or the guards."

Huh. It couldn't be Tyra or Anne. It seemed odd McLane would send someone Claude didn't know, but they couldn't be here if the general hadn't approved their presence. "Let them in."

The door vanished—and left a luminous woman framed in the archway. Silken hair poured over her shoulders, streaked gold from the sun and pale lavender underneath. Her eyes were large and violet, framed by glimmering lashes. She had on a dress, blue and soft, its skirt brushing her knees, its bodice snug. She looked like an angel come to Earth.

"*Chaniece?*" Del's native language burst out of him though he hadn't spoken it in over a year. "Is it you?"

She smiled at him. "I hope so." She stood with two large guards, undoubtedly Jagernauts. "May I come in?"

"Yes! Of course." He sped over and drew her inside. "How did you get to Earth?"

"I took a ship, silly." She glanced at Ricki, at Mac, then at Ricki. Hesitating, she said, "I'm sorry if I'm intruding."

"No! Never." Del touched her cheek, then dropped his arm, self-conscious.

Her smile turned radiant. "I listened to *Starlight* on the trip here." Her face gentled, so familiar, the curve of her cheek, the delicate arch of her brows. "I do so like it, Del."

A flush spread through him. He put his palms on her arms, and she tensed, the easy camaraderie of their youth gone. Then he thought, *To hell with that* and pulled her into an embrace.

"Thank you for coming," he whispered.

She put her arms around his waist and laid her head against his shoulder. "I wanted to before. Kelric said it wasn't safe."

"He was right."

"We thought it better if the boys stayed home."

Del drew away so he could look at her face. "I'll see them as soon as I get back."

Someone cleared his throat. Del turned to see Mac and Ricki watching them. Mac looked as if someone had dropped a brick on his head. Ricki was angry, but also . . . scared? Why?

Del brought Chaniece forward. It felt unreal to have her here. Impossible. Incredible. He spoke in the style of the Imperial Court, first in Iotic, then English. "Chaniece, may I present Michael

Tyler, my personal manager, and Erica Varento, my producer at Prime-Nova."

Mac bowed to Chaniece and spoke in Iotic. "It is an honor, Your Highness."

"My greetings," Chaniece said softly.

Ricki should have bowed, but Del doubted she knew anything about court protocols. She returned Chaniece's curious look with a cold stare and spoke in English. "Hello."

Del translated, substituting "It's an honor to meet you" for "hello." He didn't fool Chaniece. Her curiosity bubbled around his mind.

She's lovely, Chaniece thought.

She puts together my anthologies.

Kelric said you have a girlfriend.

Del averted his gaze.

Ricki spoke coolly. "You seem to know each other well. Was that your native language?"

Del looked up, feeling so awkward. He wasn't prepared for this. "Yes. That's right."

Mac spoke to Chaniece in Iotic. "We'll have a translation program for you at the conference."

She inclined her head. "Thank you."

A hum came from Mac's wrist comm. When he touched it, Cameron's voice came out. "We're ready. Are you with Del?"

"He's right here," Mac said. "We'll be right down."

"All right," Cameron said. "Out."

Glancing at Chaniece, Del tilted his head toward her guards, who were standing back. **Two of them?**

Apparently one isn't enough, Chaniece thought wryly. An image of Tyra came into her mind.

That's because I kept ditching her. You're far better behaved.

You've done more than misbehaved.

The concert was something I had to do.

A sense of steel came into her thoughts. *I'm glad you did.*

Del suddenly felt lighter. He could handle censure from the rest of his family, but not her disapproval.

Tarex has a lot to answer for, she thought.

But he won't! The bastard left Earth right after my concert.

Del, that was good. It's why Staver's people could smuggle his provider off Earth.

She escaped? That's wonderful!

She has asked for Skolian asylum. Kelric is expediting the process.

At least some good came out of this.

Mac was watching them, waiting. When Del met his gaze, the older man spoke quietly. "We should go."

"All right. " Del turned to Ricki, uncertain what to do with her icy hostility. "Would you—you could wait for me. Here."

"I have to go to work," she said, as distant as if they were kilometers apart. "Deal with the mess from last night."

Del winced. "I guess Prime-Nova won't be offering me a new contract." After so many struggles to climb his way to the top, he had lost it all in one day.

Her chill thawed a bit. "I'm sorry, babe." She started to reach for him, then glanced at Chaniece. Her expression cooled and she dropped her arm.

Del didn't know what to say. He never knew how to tell a lover about Chaniece, so he ended up saying nothing, afraid of offending someone. He also felt Ricki's conviction that she would soon lose him back to his world. He didn't want this distance that separated them.

Something loosened in Del, a rusty lock on his emotions. Taking Ricki's hand, he drew her forward. "I'll see you tonight?"

She remained stiff in his arms. "I'm sure you'll be busy."

He leaned down and kissed her ear. "She's my sister, love."

"Oh!" Ricki drew away, her face startled. "Oh."

Del stroked her hair back from her face. "I'll comm you tonight?"

She started to respond, stopped, then said, "Zachary will be asking about you."

"You can tell him who I am. Last night blew off the cover." He kissed her again, hoping it wasn't the last time.

Then he left with Mac and Chaniece, headed for what felt like sentencing.

The techs fastened Mac into a virt suit, which linked him to the Kyle gateway provided by the Skolians. And just like that, he was standing in the virtual conference room. It had no furniture except gold chairs at a gold table on transparent columns.

Fitz McLane appeared next to Mac, by a chair at the table. He stood tall and broad-shouldered in his dress uniform, every bit a five-star general, the only one among the Allied military.

Across the table, one person rippled into view: General Naaj Majda. They had all agreed to the Harrison Protocols, which meant they didn't alter their appearances. Majda was an unusually tall woman with a regal face. Black hair streaked by grey swept back from her forehead, and the force of her personality came through even in a simulation. It was hard to believe Del had almost been betrothed to this woman's sister. Then again, if Del had worked the same spells on her that he did on most women, he could have turned even one of these formidable Amazons into putty.

A voice announced them by name. Mac heard it in English, but translator codes would give it in Iotic for the Skolians. They nodded to one another and took their seats, Fitz and Mac on one side and Majda on the other.

The air blurred near the end of the table and coalesced into two people. Del and Chaniece. They stood side by side, luminous and golden, oblivious to their own beauty, and everyone else in the room became drab in comparison. Across the table, their mother appeared, as golden as her children.

The EI spoke: "Her Majesty, Roca Skolia, Foreign Affairs Councilor to the Assembly; His Royal Highness, Prince Del-Kurj Valdoria Skolia; Her Royal Highness, Princess Chaniece Lyhalia Valdoria Skolia."

Mac, Fitz, and the Majda general each bowed, first to Roca, then to Del and Chaniece. One change in the protocols puzzled Mac. Roca was a "majesty" rather than "highness" because she had married a man her people considered a king. She was also heir to the Ruby Throne, which made her a "highness." That title actually carried far more weight, yet the EI had used the lesser form of address.

A monolith of dark gold light formed across the table—and then Kelric stood there, huge, massive, his gaze impassive, his face unreadable. His metallic skin caught glints of light. Grey streaked his gold hair and lines creased his face around his eyes. Although he had similar features to his mother and siblings, he was as hard as they were beautiful. It was surreal to Mac that this man had once been Del's baby brother.

The EI said, simply, "Imperator Skolia." No dynastic titles, nothing else. He needed nothing more.

The final three people appeared together: Hannah Loughten, President of the Allied Worlds; Barcala Tikal, First Councilor of the Skolian Assembly; and Dyhianna Selei, the Ruby Pharaoh. Loughten was a lean woman with dark hair turning silver at the temples. Barcala Tikal was her male counterpart, even down to his greying temples.

The Ruby Pharaoh mesmerized Mac. Among all these formidable leaders, she was small and fine-boned. Her long hair was swept up on her head, but black tendrils had escaped to curl around her face. Her eyes were unusually large, making her seem fragile. Mac wasn't fooled. This was the powerhouse who had overthrown one of the most bellicose empires in human history—her own—and then handed the conquered government half their power back, giving Imperial Skolia both elected and dynastic leaders. The Skolians clearly had no objection to the pharaoh retaking her throne. Skolia had called itself an Imperialate even when only the elected Assembly governed. The dynastic roots of the empire went deep in their cultural memory.

The leaders took their seats, the Skolian pharaoh and first councilor on one side, the Allied president on the other. Then everyone else sat. Mac doubted anyone missed the unequal balance of power: two Skolian leaders facing a single president who presided over a civilization one third the size of their empire, with both the Imperator and Skolian General of the Army facing a solitary Fitz McLane. Mac had never figured out if Skolians deliberately set out to intimidate or if it was just so ingrained in their psychology that they did it on instinct.

However, Mac also didn't miss that Del had sat on the Allied side of the table. Interesting. He wondered if Del even realized what he had done.

Hannah Loughten, the Allied president, spoke to the pharaoh and first councilor. "We are met to discuss Prince Del-Kurj's concert last night. Let me begin by extending our deepest apologies for any difficulties that may have arisen between your people and the Eubian Traders as a result."

The Ruby Pharaoh inclined her head, acknowledging the apology, though it was unclear whether or not she was accepting it.

Councilor Tikal spoke dryly. "It was certainly a surprise."

Fitz McLane didn't waste time circling around the subject. "How did the Traders take it?"

"Badly," Tikal said. "They want a guarantee the song won't be produced or spread." He met the general's gaze squarely. "However, many of our people feel just the opposite. Pressure to distribute it as widely as possible is coming from powerful sectors of our populace."

"And your people?" the Ruby Pharaoh asked Loughten. "We aren't getting a clear reading of their reaction from your meshes."

"I don't think anyone *knows* how to react," Loughten said. "Mainly people want to know who Del is."

"People think 'Del Arden' is an Allied citizen," Kelric rumbled. "But the Traders have dossiers on all my family, including Prince Del-Kurj. They've made the logical conclusion."

The pharaoh spoke wryly. "However, Del sang here, during a celebration of *your* people's independence. It's confused everyone."

Loughten let out a breath, just the barest indication of the strain she must surely feel. "Emperor Qox has asked if we're changing our neutral stance to an alliance with your people." Her gaze never wavered as she regarded the Skolians. "I've told him we have changed nothing. Our stance remains the same."

Pharaoh Dyhianna spoke. "It was never the intent of the Ruby Dynasty to put your government in such a sensitive position."

Fitz McLane leaned forward, his eyes blazing. "Then help us deal with the impact of that song."

"We've told the Traders we'll limit it as best we can," Loughten said. "Your help on the Skolian meshes would further establish that it wasn't meant as a declaration of hostilities toward the Traders by either of our governments."

Kelric spoke coldly. "You want us to help you suppress my brother's words."

Mac shifted in his seat. If Imperator Skolia took a hard line on this, it could leave Earth vulnerable to retaliation by the Traders.

President Loughten didn't back down. "We're asking for your help in minimizing the damage done by a member of your family to our relations with the Eubian government."

Roca spoke. "If you want a declaration from the Ruby Dynasty that my son's performance represents his own opinions and only that, we will provide that statement."

"If you want us to do more," Kelric said, "you'll have to convince some strong opposition." He nodded to Naaj Majda, and the general inclined her head, acknowledging his signal.

"Prince Del-Kurj gave powerful voice to our people's anger,"

Majda said. "We live with Trader brutality beyond anything your people have experienced." She spoke with an undertone of steel. "The Traders want Del's work silenced because it exposes the lie in the false image they present to you."

Kelric leaned forward. "The inhumanity Del sang about—our forces went up against it every day. They lived that nightmare, President Loughten. Millions died. I see no reason why we should help suppress that truth."

Loughten regarded him steadily. "To keep hostilities from growing worse."

Del was listening intently, his gaze going back and forth between the speakers. But he said nothing. Mac didn't recall ever having seen him so calm in such a tense situation, particularly when it was about him. If Chaniece always had this effect on him, it was no wonder the family had sent her to Earth.

Mac had to speak, though. "Realistically, we can't contain the song. It's everywhere. What's out can't be put back."

"Perhaps," Pharaoh Dyhianna said. Her voice had a distant quality, as if she didn't exist fully in the same space as the rest of them. "Perhaps not."

A chill went through Mac. People called Dyhianna Selei the Shadow Pharaoh for good reason. Supposedly the name came from the way she avoided public appearances, but Mac knew otherwise from his Air Force contacts. Her ability to create and manipulate the interstellar meshes was unmatched and mostly unseen. He doubted anyone knew the full extent of her ability.

"If you could contain the music, would you?" Loughten asked.

The pharaoh considered her. Then she turned to Del. "It's your song. What do you think we should do with it?"

Del regarded her like a startled deer. He obviously hadn't expected anyone to ask his opinion. But he was the unknown, and the key to everything. If he refused to stop singing "Carnelians," or even just let his fans know why it had become so hard to find, nothing would contain that song.

"I can't suppress my own work," Del said.

Fitz leaned forward with the tension he always showed around Del. "Does that mean you'll work against our attempts to limit it?"

Del hesitated. It was a long moment before he answered. Finally he said, "Not if the Traders agree to a condition."

Kelric was watching his brother with a mixture of wariness

and curiosity. Mac wondered if the Imperator realized he reacted to Del with more emotion than he showed anyone else.

"What condition?" Kelric asked.

Del took a breath. "That their emperor arranges the release of a Skolian woman who was sold as a provider."

Mac blinked. What the hell?

Kelric, however, didn't look at all surprised. "Jaibriol Qox. He may not know how to find her."

"Qox is the bloody emperor," Del growled. "He can find her."

"I'm glad you both know what you're talking about," Councilor Tikal said dryly. "Maybe you'd enlighten the rest of us?"

The pharaoh spoke. "I think they mean Staver Aunchild's wife."

"Lord Tarex claims Staver Aunchild kidnapped his provider," Fitz said. "No one can find her. Is she his wife?"

Mac tensed. Staver's *wife* was a provider? No wonder the Skolian exec had reacted so violently against the Aristos.

Kelric shook his head. "Tarex's provider has no connection to Staver. Tarex is using Staver as a scapegoat."

"Staver *and* Del," Mac said. Tarex had claimed he invited Staver Aunchild onto his yacht to discuss business and that Del caused Staver's injuries. But every doctor who treated Staver verified that he had taken all those wounds long before Del was on the yacht. It enraged Mac that the Aristo blamed his brutality on Del, another of his victims.

"Tarex is obviously lying about Del," Fitz said. "The police dropped the charges without even knowing Del has diplomatic immunity."

President Loughten spoke firmly. "The question of Prince Del-Kurj's presence on Earth remains."

"I've sent a squadron to escort Del home," Kelric said.

Loughten paused for a moment. Then she spoke again. "If His Highness agrees to help us lessen the impact of his song, we won't ask for his deportation or revoke his license to work here."

Whoa. Mac hadn't seen *that* coming. From the way Del's eyes widened, he hadn't, either. It wouldn't work, though. Del's family would pull him home regardless.

Kelric started to speak, then stopped when the pharaoh glanced at him. Nothing else visible passed between them, but Mac suspected they were communicating in some other way. Roca was sitting unusually still, as if she were also in the loop.

After a moment, Roca spoke to President Loughten. "We will discuss the matter with Prince Del-Kurj."

Del grimaced, though the look quickly vanished, undoubtedly edited out by his EI. Chaniece laid her hand on his arm, and he took a breath.

The meeting continued as they decided how to respond to the Traders. Mac wasn't sure what was up with the Skolians. They acted as if they didn't intend to help, but his gut instinct said they were bargaining. It didn't feel that different from negotiating a contract, except a great deal more was at stake than music vids. And gradually he realized what they were "bargaining" for. They wanted the Allieds to listen to the song. Just *listen*.

The Skolians finally agreed to help control the spread of the song among their own people if the Traders accepted Del's condition about the provider. But they declined to help limit his song among the Allied Worlds. Although they claimed it was an Allied affair, it didn't fool Mac. They knew the power Del had unleashed. The raw, pure force of the "Carnelians Finale" would affect people far more than any speech from the Skolians.

After the meeting ended, the president, first councilor, and generals withdrew, leaving Mac with Del's family.

Roca glanced at Mac. "Thank you, Mister Tyler."

"My pleasure, Your Majesty." Mac could recognize "get lost" as well as anyone. His virtual self stood up, a signal to the EI to release him from the session.

"No, wait!" Del said.

"Del, this is private," his mother said.

"I want him to stay," Del said.

Roca looked ready to argue, but Kelric just shook his head tiredly. "Fine. He can stay."

Del looked at Mac with an imploring gaze. Ill at ease, Mac sat down. He couldn't desert Del. But he had no desire to be anywhere near the argument that was about to happen.

Del wasn't sure why he asked Mac to stay, given the humiliating scene he was about to face. But with Chaniece at his side and Mac's support, he might make it through this without unraveling. He thought of a hundred ways to start and none were any good, so he just came out and spoke his piece.

"I want to stay on Earth," Del said.

"No," Kelric said flatly.

His aunt Dehya, the Ruby Pharaoh, answered in a gentler voice. "Del, they'll expect you to cooperate in suppressing your song."

Mac cleared his throat. "You might want to talk to Prime-Nova first, Del, before you make any decisions."

"I know I've killed my career," Del said. The words were like knives. "But I might find work on a smaller scale, maybe in the undercity." He didn't add, *And Ricki is here.*

"Why the blazes would we let you stay?" Kelric asked. "You constantly thwarted the people trying to protect you. A Raptor squad had to rescue you. Twice."

"It won't happen again," Del said.

Kelric crossed his arms. "So you've promised before."

Del's anger sparked. "No I haven't. I gave in to your attempts to control my life because I had no choice."

His mother spoke quietly. "What did you expect? If you wanted us to trust you, why didn't you show us why we should?"

"But I have." Did nothing else he had done matter?

"You call your behavior responsible?" Kelric asked. "You want to live as you please, but when you get into trouble, people have to pull you out."

"No matter how much you resist your title," Roca said, "you have a greater burden of responsibility because of it."

Del's temper was rising. But before he could lash out, he felt Chaniece touch his arm. He waited until his surge of anger cooled before he said, "Yes, my title matters. If I hadn't been a prince, the authorities would have taken longer to act when Raker and Delilah took me. I'd probably be dead. Staver nearly ended up as Tarex's provider because ASC wasn't willing to move as fast for him as for me. That doesn't make me irresponsible."

"You wouldn't have needed help if you had stayed with your guard," Kelric told him. "It's always the same thing. You get in trouble, but when we react to that, you snarl and tell us to let you take care of yourself. You *can't* take care of yourself."

"Yes I can! " Del said. "I have the entire rest of the time I've been here. I've been doing fine. Doesn't that count for anything?"

"You couldn't even get proper evidence for your age," Kelric said. "Your manager had to pay a doctor to say you were an adult."

"Mac didn't bribe anyone!" Del wanted to shout, but he felt Chaniece's hand, soft and subtle, on his elbow. If he lost his temper, that would be the end of it. He drew in a breath and spoke in a lower voice. "Did it ever occur to any of you that I didn't go to you all for proof because I felt humiliated?"

"Why?" Kelric asked. "We're your family." If Del hadn't known better, he would have thought that under Kelric's metal exterior, he was vulnerable, that Del's words actually hurt his implacable brother. But then Kelric said, "You have to stop putting all this emotional hyperbole ahead of logic."

"I'm not a robot." Every time Kelric talked this way to him, he died a little inside. Couldn't his brother tell what it did to him? "How can you be an empath and have no emotions?"

Anger flashed on Kelric's face, and something else. Pain? "You think I have no emotions? You're confusing your overwrought immaturity with empathy."

"Don't talk about me like that!"

"Then don't give me reason."

"You just see what you want. Not what I really am."

Kelric leaned forward. "You're coming home. Period."

"Yeah, well, fuck that."

"Del, enough!" Roca told him.

"Gods, Del," Kelric said. "Can't we have a civil conversation just once?"

Del's voice cracked. "Maybe if you would treat me like I deserved one. Then I wouldn't have to program a bliss-node to find a family that accepts me."

"Del, what?" Dehya was staring at him as if she were breaking inside.

"And of course you have a valid license for that node," Kelric said. "You would never bribe some slimy dealer to fake one so you could feed your addiction."

"Don't you have anything better to do than spy on my life?" Del shouted. "Is yours that miserable?"

"Stop it!" Roca said. "*Both* of you."

Del wanted to take back the words as soon as he said them. Kelric always seemed indomitable, impervious to any hurt, yet Del had no doubt pain had just flashed on his brother's face.

In the stunned silence that followed, someone cleared his throat. With a start, Del glanced at Mac.

His manager spoke with diffidence. "May I say something?"

Dehya let out a breath. "Please do."

"I've worked with many singers," Mac said. "Some are notorious for their behavior. Del isn't like that. Yes, he's made mistakes. He's not perfect, not by a long shot. But he *is* responsible, and that's even given his constant exposure to a lifestyle where he could be as wild as he wanted. He had no idea how to handle his finances when he started to work. He asked me to show him. Then he learned to invest. It's that way in everything. He jumps at the opportunity to manage his life. He learns from his mistakes."

Del stared at him. He'd never have guessed Mac saw him that way. He often picked up Mac's disapproval, but either Mac kept his positive opinion buried deeper, or else Del didn't recognize it.

Chaniece spoke in her melodic voice, though today it sounded like a song in a minor key. "Kelric, Del, it tears me apart to hear you two go at each other. Surely you can find a common ground."

Del averted his gaze. He hadn't meant to upset her.

Kelric spoke quietly. "Del."

He looked up at his brother. "Yes?"

"For what it's worth," Kelric said, "I'm sorry you can't stay to sing. It obviously makes you happy."

Del felt the betraying moisture in his eyes. He wiped his palm over his face, smearing tears away.

"Ah, gods," Dehya said. No one else spoke.

Kelric frowned at Dehya. "Don't say it."

Del blinked. What did Kelric mean by that?

"At least listen to him," she said.

Frustration creased Kelric's face. "Dehya, he couldn't spend five minutes in a police station without getting in a fight."

So they knew about that, too. Del thought of what Acne had said about their mother, and his anger rekindled. "That asshole deserved a lot worse than me knocking over his skinny butt."

Kelric spoke dryly. "Your language capability in English is growing by leaps and bounds."

"I mean it," Del said. "That guy had a mouth worse than mine. It's not always about swearing."

"I've been called worse, honey," Roca said. "He wasn't worth the trouble." Her face softened. "But thank you for defending me."

Del reddened. "He pressed charges."

"Actually, he's dropped them," Kelric said.

"He has?" Del regarded them uneasily. "What did you do?"

Kelric shrugged. "Our people settled with his. It was less than he wanted, but enough to finish the matter."

"I'm sorry." Del glanced at his mother and spoke quietly. "I thought you all would be angrier about my singing 'Carnelians.'"

"I could never make such personal matters public." Roca exhaled, stirring a tendril of hair around her face. "But what you sang— it needed to be heard. I think your father would have felt the same."

"I hope so." Del missed his father as much now, a year after his death, as the day he had died. "Would it be so terrible for me to stay? I know I used bad judgment when I tricked Cameron. I've learned." He spoke directly to Kelric. "With Tarex, I made a choice. I knew I could become a provider. I was willing to risk it and live with the consequences. Was it right for ASC to rush in for me when they wouldn't for Staver? That speed made the difference between hell or freedom for him. You may not agree with my decision, but it was mine to make."

Kelric pushed his hand over his hair, a virtual gesture he didn't let his virt setup edit out. "Del . . ."

Del waited for him to go on. When Kelric added nothing more, Del said, "I'm never sure what that means, when you just say my name and nothing else."

It was Roca who answered. "Your song, 'Carnelians'—I never knew you were so furious."

Del hadn't realized the full extent of his rage, either, until the words exploded out of him. He had suppressed so much, but it came out in other ways, in his behavior, his resentment.

"You all had decades between those events," he said. "For me, everything just happened. All those years I slept, you all did so much. Kelric, here you are, like some war god fired in the crucible of the hells you've survived." Bitterly he said, "And here's stupid, illiterate Del singing loud songs."

"Del, no," Roca said. "You aren't stupid."

"I can't—" He shook his head, unable to go on.

"Your father felt like that, too," she said. "But he was a miracle. What he did with languages was incredible. And when he sang—" Her voice caught. "You remind me so much of him. I had hoped you would carry on his work." Tears glistened in her eyes, and she wiped them away with the same motion Del always used, as if she were angry at herself for crying. "You have a gift. It isn't one I understand, but it's real. I can't ask you to deny it."

Something moved within Del, something big and painful. It had never hurt in his virtual world when his mother spoke this way. But this was real. She truly said the words. She called his music a *gift*. He ached inside, so much he thought he would burst.

Chaniece's thought came to him. **She's right.**

I can't— He didn't know how to answer.

Tell her what you feel. Her thought was a balm. **Let them know. They've seen so much of your anger and so little of the rest.**

Del spoke to his mother in a voice rough with emotions he feared to reveal. "You don't know what it means to hear you say that. I—it's—thank you."

Her gaze softened.

And Kelric. Chaniece's thought murmured.

Del knew too much separated him and Kelric for them to find their way back to each other. But for Chaniece, he would try. "Kelric—" What could he say? The truth, perhaps. "I wish we could fight less and talk more."

"I'm no good with words," Kelric said. "You say more in one song than I could in a year. But I—" He stumbled to a halt. Then he said, "Damn it, I don't want you to die because you're my brother and I love you."

Del sat in stunned silence. Kelric always seemed invincible, lofty in his strength. His emotional defenses were stronger than those of anyone else Del knew. But when Kelric let them down, Del glimpsed the brother he remembered from their childhood.

"I don't want to hurt any of you," Del said. "I just can't seem to do anything right."

After a strained moment, Dehya said, "I'd like to talk to Del alone, if he doesn't mind."

"It's all right." Del doubted the others wanted to leave. But none of them were going to naysay Dehya.

I'll talk to Kelric, Chaniece thought. **Maybe I can make him see how important staying here is to you.**

Chani, wait. Del didn't want her to get the wrong idea. **It's not more important than you and the boys.**

I know. Her thought came with a pain that would never fully leave either of them.

You could all come to Earth, he thought.

Is that what you want?

He almost said yes. But he knew the truth. **They wouldn't like living here. And they're safer on Lyshriol.**

Yes. Her thoughts flowed. *You need to find your life outside this guilt that's crushing you. What the Assembly did isn't your fault. You have to stop believing you harm the boys just by existing. You're a good father. You have to make peace with yourself, and it will never happen if you stay on Lyshriol.*

I don't feel whole without you.

It's the same for me. A tear formed in her eye. *We have to let go, Del. Let yourself love that woman. And I want to love someone. Not as a brother. As a man. A husband.*

He felt as if part of him were dying. **I miss you all so much.**

You can come see us all the time.

I will. I swear, Chani.

I'm glad. She touched his arm. Then she faded away.

When Del looked up, he was alone with Dehya. The air rippled, and she was sitting next to him. A year ago, that sudden shift would have rattled him, but after all the time he had spent—no, wasted—in the bliss, he no longer even blinked at the abrupt transitions.

Dehya watched him with green eyes overlaid by an inner lid that was no more than a glimmer of gold and rose. Sunrise eyes. She spoke softly. "What you said about your virt—do you really feel that way, that you need to escape us by creating a virtual family?"

"Not you," he said. "But the others—" He didn't know what to think anymore. "Maybe it can change. I never thought my mother or Kelric would say what they did today."

"Does it make coming home easier?"

"I wish I could say yes, Aunt Dehya. But nothing could make it easier. I like it here." His mood dimmed. "Maybe it doesn't matter. Prime-Nova doesn't want their artists involved in politics. It kills sales, and the censors hate it. They won't offer me another contract."

"Are you sorry you sang 'Carnelians'?"

"Never." He felt subdued. "But I'll have to start over."

"Even with that, you still want to stay?"

Del didn't hesitate. "Yes."

Dehya was watching him as if her ancient gaze could see through his armor into his heart. "I'll talk to Kelric, then."

Del stared at her. He must have misunderstood. She couldn't have just said what he thought. "About what?"

"Letting you stay." Incredibly, she added, "If it means this much, you should have the chance."

"But—why?"

"Because you're right," she said. "You need to make your own decisions. And yes, your own mistakes." She sighed. "We've all made them, Del. But fate hit you harder for yours."

"What happened with Staver wasn't a mistake."

"It took great courage."

The blood rushed to Del's face. "I was terrified."

"With good reason." Dehya pushed back the tendrils curling around her face. The familiar gesture made him suspect she was more worn out than the virt revealed. She didn't look pregnant, but surely by now she should be showing.

"Aunt Dehya—?" Del hesitated, uncertain what to say.

"Yes?" she asked.

He couldn't think of any subtle approach. So he just said, "Is your baby all right?"

A shadow passed over her face. "I—it's—"

"I'm sorry." Del felt as if the ground dropped under him. "I shouldn't have asked." Gods, had the baby *died?* He wished he could disappear.

"It's all right." She looked worn out, but . . . not grieving. "He was born prematurely. He's in a life-care mod. The doctors think he'll survive." Her voice softened. "We named him Althor, after your brother who died in the war."

His voice caught. "That's good." He had always wished he could have named one of his sons for Althor.

She exhaled. "I'll let you know what happens with Kelric."

Del nodded, afraid to hope.

XXIX

Carnelian Sun

Ricki went up to her office by a back entrance in the Prime-Nova building. That way, no one could catch her sneaking in before she faced Zachary. She dreaded the meeting; he had to know she could have stopped Del last night. She had tried to reach him after the concert and this morning, but he hadn't been available.

Her office console blazed with holicons. She winced and flicked one that showed Zachary's face.

His message was curt. "Ricki, come up as soon as you're in." No "Good morning" or "Hey, sweetheart." She hated it when he called her sweetheart, but anything was better than *You're fired*.

She took a private lift upstairs that let her out in front of the huge silver and glass doors of his office. No one was in the reception room, which was odd. Usually he had some gorgeously extraneous receptionist sitting at the curved desk. Music was coming from his office, though, several songs playing at once. She walked through the big archway into his office—and froze.

Holos of Del were playing everywhere, above consoles, in front of screens, over Zachary's desk. Most showed the "Carnelians Finale," but one was playing "Rubies" and another "Diamond Star." Zachary was standing in the center of the room, surrounded by holos while he spoke into a comm he was holding to one ear. "That's right!" He was yelling to be heard above the cacophony.

"Let me know how long it'll take." He motioned at Ricki to come in. "What?" he said into his comm. "No, that's too long! It has to be tonight. Yes! Good-bye!"

"What's with all the noise?" Ricki said as he lowered his arm.

Zachary grinned at her. *Grinned*. The man had gone crazy. "Haven't you looked at the stats?" He was practically shouting.

"Uh, no, I haven't." It had been too painful to contemplate. "Are they that bad?"

"Bad?" He burst out laughing. "*Bad?* Ricki, look!" He thumbed his wrist mesh and the holo of Del above his desk blinked out, replaced by a graph showing the sales of *Starlight*. The curves were, literally, off the chart.

"What the hell?" Ricki said. "That's against every truism!"

"The truisms are falsisms this morning." Zachary waved at the holos all around the room. "That song is *everywhere!* People are going crazy. Who is Del Arden? They can't get enough. They're buying his stuff so fast, we can't keep it stocked." He shook his comm at her. "The wizards at Wonder-Works are going double time to fill all the orders."

Ricki couldn't believe it. "This is good."

"Good, hell. We've never had an anthology sell like this. It was down to number six yesterday, but it jumped back to the big One this morning." He let out with a triumphant laugh. "With these sales, it'll stay there fucking forever. We *have* to get him back in the studio. Soon. Now. Today!"

Uh oh. Ricki walked over to him. "That may be a problem."

Zachary stopped smiling. "You think he'll play hardball?"

"No. I think the President of the Allied Worlds is going to deport him."

Zachary looked as if he had run into a wall. "What?"

"Imperator Skolia agrees with her."

"Over one song? *He has a right to sing it.* Free speech! Who the hell do they think they are?"

She regarded him with exasperation. "Well, Zach, the last I checked, one of them is the president of our government and the other commands the Imperialate military."

"So?"

"*So?*" She would have laughed if her job hadn't been at stake. "Zach, even *you* don't outrank them."

He crossed his arms. "I have a Skolian expert in our Foreign

Sales Division. He says Del was singing *perfect* Iotic. So who the fuck is Del Arden? He's Skolian, isn't he?"

"Oh, yeah." *Skolia,* to be precise.

Zachary put his fists on his hips. "He lied to us!"

"Actually, he never lied," Ricki said. "Everything he told us is true. He does come from a rediscovered Skolian colony. Developers from Texas did try to build a resort there. He just 'forgot' to tell us the Skolians threw out their sleazy butts and took over."

"What planet?" Zachary demanded. "I thought we made that up. Lishy-lushy or whatever."

"Lyshriol. It's real. You've heard of it."

He scowled at her. "Not so."

"If you translate Lyshriol into English, it means Skyfall."

Zachary snorted. "Sure, sweetheart. He's the freaking King of Skyfall."

"Uh, yeah, as a matter of fact, he is." She snapped her fingers at him. "And I swear, Zach, if you call me sweetheart again, I'm going to sic his Jagernaut bodyguard on you. I'd like to see you call *that* Valkyrie 'sweetheart.'"

He seemed more puzzled than angry. "You believe all this, don't you? He really threw you a line."

"Actually, his brother did."

"His brother?"

Ricki blanched. "Imperator Skolia."

And then she told him everything.

For a long moment after she finished, Zachary looked at her. Finally he said, "So his family doesn't like what he's doing."

"They're pulling him home."

"They can't do that. He needs to cut another anthology. One with this 'Carnelians' song."

Ricki didn't know whether to groan or shake him. "That song is a political nightmare."

"Does he want to leave?"

"I don't think so. But he has no choice."

"He's an adult. He can do what he wants." Zachary glared at her. "Or was that doctor's report a fake?"

"No, it was real. But it doesn't matter. He has to do what Imperator Skolia tells him to do."

Zachary snorted. "I'll talk to this Imperator."

The thought of Zachary doing his Prime-Nova routine on Kelric

Skolia was more than Ricki ever wanted to imagine. "I don't think that would work." Before her boss came up with more brilliant ideas, she quickly added, "I'll talk to Del."

He narrowed his gaze. "How long have you known about Del?"

"Since that trip to the Moon."

"And you didn't let me *know*? The King of Skyfall! Think of the promotion we could do!"

"I did." Ricki had more than her share of nightmares without that one added in. She just said, "Del didn't want anyone to know."

"Talk to him. See what you can do."

"I will." She knew it would do no good. It wasn't Del she had to convince, but his infamous brother, and no way would she ever have the chance.

Del was in the living room of his quarters on the base, dozing in an armchair, when the door chimed. He opened his eyes, disoriented. The console across the room said it was afternoon. Chaniece had left for the port, and Mac had gone to find out what was happening with Prime-Nova.

"Who is it?" he asked groggily.

"Ms. Varento," Claude said.

Del dragged himself up straight. It was too soon for Ricki to be back. He had wondered if she would even come. He had avoided checking the mesh because he wasn't ready to face the outcry over his song, and Claude had told him Ricki hadn't sent any messages.

"Let her in," he said.

The door shimmered, and Ricki stood there watching him with those big blue eyes. Del rose to his feet, uncertain. "Did you talk to Zachary?"

"Oh, yeah." She came over to him. "Did I ever."

Del winced. "He's that angry?"

"Are you kidding? He's having multiple orgasms."

He reddened. "What?"

"Haven't you *looked*?" She shook her head, laughing. "Your sales are going crazy. Everyone wants your songs."

Del didn't believe her. "It doesn't work that way."

"If your song was about my people, you're right, it wouldn't." Ricki waved her hand toward the sky. "But you were singing about Skolia and Eube. My people have no stake in it. It doesn't affect their political views, so they don't get mad. For them, it's like watching gladiators fight. And here you are, this wild, gorgeous angel in black leather singing about the wrongs done to your family. People are eating it up faster than Tackman zaps his brain with neuro-amps."

Del didn't know about the "angel" part, and given his struggle with the bliss-node, he had no call to criticize Tackman, but he understood what she meant. Interstellar politics mattered to Del because how the Allieds dealt with the Traders directly impacted his people and his family. But he knew little about the politics among the various factions on Earth and understood them even less. Seeing news holos about who was fighting here over what issue was like watching a fight in an arena where he had no stake in the outcome.

"Even so," Del said. "The censors must be furious."

"I think they're more confused than anything else. If you were singing about us, they'd ban it in a second. But you're not." She regarded him with satisfaction. "No way will they get you off the meshes now. No matter how far away your family hides you, nothing will stop your songs. Your music will play everywhere."

Something loosened inside Del that had tightened the moment he decided to act against Tarex. And he felt that sense of release for more than himself. Even if he couldn't benefit from the unexpected results of last night's concert, Jud, Anne, and Randall would reap the rewards. After Ricki and Mac, they were the ones he would miss the most when he left Earth, even Randall who, despite his many challenges, never gave up on Del. None of them condemned Del for his decision to sing the "Finale," though it affected them as much as him. They had stayed with him, playing until the end, and for that, he would always be grateful.

He pulled Ricki into his arms and laid his head against hers. "Thank you," he whispered against her ear.

She held him close. "I didn't do it, babe. Prime-Nova didn't create Del Arden, no matter how much it feels that way. It's you. Your talent, your gifts, your passion."

He had never had a lover who wanted both him and his music. Now he was going to lose her. He wasn't ready for what he had to say, but hell, he would never be ready. So he just said it. "I don't want to go without you."

"Your family won't give you any choice."

He drew back and looked down at her. "Come with me."

She regarded him with no artifice, just Ricki, straight. "I can't. My work is here. I love what I do."

"You can work for Prime-Nova anywhere." He held her arms and spoke intently. "I'll get you your own studio. You can run the whole thing."

She stiffened. "I won't be your mistress."

Del was as scared now as the first time he had gone onstage. "I'm not asking you to." He felt as if he were on the edge of a cliff. So he took a breath and stepped off. "Be my wife."

She backed away from him. "Stop it."

"Why? Don't you trust me?" As soon as he spoke, he felt like an idiot. "Okay, maybe not. But I won't hurt you again. I swear."

"Del, don't." She smiled wanly. "Besides, your family would never agree. Don't they arrange marriages or something?"

"They try. It never works. And I want you, not some matriarch I've never met." He spoke more quietly. "I can't promise it'll be easy. But my love life has been so convoluted anyway, my family will probably be relieved to see me start untangling it." He tried to pull her back into his arms. "Say yes."

She braced her palms against his shoulders, holding him at bay. "I can't."

"Why, Ricki?" Softly he said, "What were you running from all those mornings you left me to wake up alone?"

"Nothing."

He stroked her hair back from her face. "I'm afraid, too."

She looked as if she wanted to run, like the wind. But she stayed put. "I don't know how to love. I never have."

"Well, neither do I." He gave her a crooked smile. "Maybe with two brains combined, we can figure it out."

She spoke quietly. "I'm honored, Del. But I can't live as your consort in the Imperial Court."

"We could live on Lyshriol," he said, knowing it was absurd. Her life was on Earth.

An edge came into her voice. "With your sister?"

What could he say? "I guess not."

"Is she still here?"

"No. She went home." They hadn't wanted to leave the boys for long, but it had made his time with her much too short.

"Your song, 'Diamond Star'—it's about her, isn't it?"

He took her hand. "Let me show you something."

"Del—"

"Just come with me." He drew her out to his balcony. They stood looking over the river, he behind her with his arms around her waist. "Do you see how the sun sparkles on the water?"

"It's beautiful."

"I translated 'Diamond Star' into English out here. I think of it every time I look at the river." He bent his head and kissed the top of hers. "You commed me that night, Ricki. And then I went up to the Star Tower to meet you. Now, when I come out here, I think about you. You're the 'Diamond Star.'"

She leaned her head back against his chest. "I'm afraid."

"Who wouldn't be, at the prospect of being stuck with me?"

She laughed softly. "It would certainly never be boring."

"There's more." He gazed over her head at the water. "When I was in cryo, our government was scared. They feared they would lose their Ruby psions. So they made more of us."

"I thought Rubies couldn't be created in the lab."

"They can't."

She wasn't smiling now. "I'm not sure I want to hear this."

"You should know." Del took a breath. "Chaniece and I have two sons. The Assembly used both our DNA and her eggs. I didn't know about the first until years after he was born." He stopped, mentally bracing himself.

"Do you miss them?" Ricki asked. "Your children, I mean?"

Del blinked. That was it? *Do you miss them?* "Every day."

"How could your government do that? It's horrible."

"Do I disgust you?"

"Why? It's not like you had any choice."

It finally sunk into Del that she wasn't going to explode. "I got serious enough about a woman once to tell her. She left me."

Ricki snorted. "She's an idiot."

His smile curved. "So if a woman leaves me, she's an idiot?"

"Del! Cut that out."

He kissed her ear. "Marry me, beautiful."

"Stop being so charming," she muttered.

A chime came from the suite behind them.

Del swore under his breath. "Not now."

"You better answer it," Ricki said.

With a scowl, Del released her. Then he stalked into the living room. "Claude," he growled. "Who is it?"

"Your bodyguard, Tyra Jarin," the EI said.

"Oh." Damn. He hadn't seen Tyra since last night. She was supposed to come for him today when Kelric wanted to see him. He intended to argue her case as best he could with his brother, but he wasn't sure if his support would help or hurt her.

"Open the door," he said.

The wall vanished, and Tyra came in. She didn't hide her relief. "You look a lot better today."

Del shifted his weight. "Does Kelric want to see us?"

She grimaced. "He's already talked with me."

"No!" Del hadn't expected it to be over before he had a chance to speak on her behalf. "I was going to tell him it wasn't your fault."

Her expression eased. "I thank you. But it wouldn't have helped. He knows it was my decision." Grimly she added, "He's taken 'suitable disciplinary action,' as he put it."

Ah, hell. "What did he do?"

Tyra looked past him toward the balcony, and Del could hear Ricki coming into the room.

"We can talk later," Tyra said.

Del wanted to say she could talk in front of Ricki, but it wasn't his choice. "All right."

"Are you ready?" Tyra asked him.

"To see Kelric?" Del asked. "Never. But yeah, let's go." He turned to Ricki. "Give me moral support?"

She took his hand. "Always."

The three of them left together. But Del knew he would have to face Kelric alone.

The virtual conference room was empty when Del arrived, but Kelric appeared within moments. It was just the two of them, with no one to put out any flames they ignited.

Kelric wasted no time. "You'll have four Jagernauts at all times. No more apartment. We'll find an estate outside the city with better security. If you want roommates, they have to go through security checks. No live concerts unless ISC approves the venue *and* its security."

It seemed to Del as if the world went still. This couldn't be what he thought. It was impossible. "You're letting me stay?"

His brother's voice lost its crispness, which Del had begun to suspect was as much a defense for Kelric as Del's songs were for him. "Dehya and Chaniece can be very convincing." He gave Del a wry look. "We're outnumbered by all these women in the family. You and I need to stick together."

Del knew no one could sway Kelric when he set his mind, besides which they had a lot more brothers than sisters. Kelric had made a joke. At least Del thought it was a joke.

Del smiled for the first time with Kelric in he didn't know how long. "Thank you for letting me stay." He needed to find words to say what this meant. He was the writer; he shouldn't be so tongue-tied with his own brother. "It wasn't until I sang here that I knew how much I wanted this. Not having to give it up—I want to say—well, thank you."

"Just be careful." Kelric didn't go on; he had never been one for words. But his decision said more about how much he understood than anything spoken.

Del couldn't rejoice yet, though. He had an unfinished matter to tackle. "About Tyra."

Kelric frowned. "I should break her out of the J-Force."

"No! She's a good officer." Del hoped he wasn't about to ruin the tentative détente he and Kelric had just attained. "I pressured her into it. I'm the one you should 'break out' of something. Not her."

To his unmitigated shock, Kelric laughed. "I never thought I'd hear you say a bodyguard that ISC sent you is a good officer. You usually hate them."

Del didn't see what was so funny. "Tyra is great. She doesn't deserve a dishonorable discharge."

"Oh, I didn't. I gave her a worse punishment."

"You can't!" Del had to convince him otherwise. "Don't do that to her."

"She said the same thing." Kelric raised his eyebrows. "Is guarding you really such torture?"

Del felt as if he had slammed on brakes. "What?"

"I put her in charge of the unit that guards you."

"But that's good!" Del began. Then he absorbed what his brother had said. So instead he glared. "Guarding me is not a punishment."

"So don't get her in trouble again."

"I'm a reformed man."

Kelric smiled slightly. "I hope so."

"This turned out so different than I expected."

His brother's expression became more serious. "For decades, centuries, we've struggled to tell the Allieds about the Traders. They heard the words, but they couldn't believe them, maybe because they're incapable themselves of being that brutal. You convinced them to listen, truly *listen*. You achieved more with one song than we've managed in over a century of negotiations."

"Do you think it will change how they deal with us?"

"They've agreed to talk about forming an alliance. This is the most progress we've ever made with them." He spoke quietly. "You got to them."

Del had never imagined one song could make that difference. "I'm glad some good came out of it."

"I also." Kelric spoke awkwardly. "You know, I rather like some of those songs on your vid. 'No Answers,' especially."

"You do?" His brother was full of shocking statements today.

"Yes, I do." Kelric sat back against the table. "But you have to promise me one thing."

Del regarded him warily. "What?"

"The next time you get mad at *me*, don't write a song."

Del couldn't help but laugh. "Deal."

"Just take care of yourself, all right? No more wild stuff."

"I'll be so boring, no one will want to be around me."

His brother smiled. "I doubt that will ever be true."

Del knew his life wouldn't be easy. But it would be worth every difficulty.

Del found Ricki in his living room, sleeping on his couch. He stood just watching her. She looked so helpless like that.

He sat next to her on the couch. "Wake up," he murmured.

Her lashes lifted slightly. "Del?"

"That's me."

She curled drowsily against him. "You don't look upset."

"He's going to let me stay." Del still couldn't believe it.

Her eyes widened and she sat up. "On Earth?"

Del pulled her into his arms. "I'll have a lot of restrictions. But yes, here."

She hugged him. "That's incredible."

"We could live here, Ricki. Together."

"That's true, we could."

He smiled into her hair. "That doesn't sound like a no."

"I need time to adjust. Wait awhile, then ask again."

"I can do that." He hesitated. "I won't mislead you. I'm going to spend a lot of time with the boys, both in trips home and through the meshes. They'll be a big part of our lives."

"I've no problem with that." She laughed unevenly. "It's the marriage thing that scares me."

He stroked her hair. "I'll wait. Until you're ready."

She gave him her sultriest smile. "Hey, babe. I'm worth the wait."

Del laughed and kissed her. "That you are."

It had only been a day since Del's virtual conference with Kelric, but it felt as if far more time had passed. Today, when he "walked into" the virtual conference room, his pulse surged. He stood by the table, for all appearances calm and composed. Of course he wasn't "standing" anywhere. Sheathed from head to toe in his virt suit and lying on his back at a console, he was sweating like an asteroid jockey running out of oxygen.

The air rippled across the table—and a man appeared.

He was tall and broad-shouldered, perfect in form and feature, his hair as black as interstellar space, his eyes like red crystals.

Like carnelians.

Del bowed deeply and spoke in Highton. "My honor at your presence, Your Highness." His instinct was to say *Your Majesty,* but the Traders used Highness for their emperor.

Jaibriol Qox regarded him with a cold red stare. His voice was as chillingly perfect as the rest of him. "So. You are the one who claims to be my worst nightmare."

The blood drained from Del's face. It was hard to believe the man he faced was only eighteen; he looked and sounded much older. But sitting on the Carnelian Throne would age anyone. Jaibriol Qox, known to most people as Jaibriol the Third, could just as easily have called himself Del's worst nightmare.

Del wouldn't take back the words, but neither did he want to inflame the volatile situation he had created. So he said only, "President Loughten said you wanted to talk to me."

"She has told me of your request that I free a provider in return for your retracting your song."

Del gritted his teeth. It had been a condition, not a request, and he had never offered to retract anything, he agreed only not to resist efforts to suppress the song. But nothing of his anger showed; Claude was editing out all his responses except respect.

"The provider is Staver Aunchild's wife," Del said.

"Why do you care?" Qox said. "And why would a Ruby prince risk his freedom for this man?"

Del felt as if he were in a field of orbiting mines. One misfired word and he could destroy the Star Road. "He's my friend."

The emperor raised his eyebrow, nothing more, but that one gesture conveyed more disbelief than any words. "Indeed."

"Will you let her come home?" Del asked.

"I find myself unconvinced," Qox said, "that I should do anything for the man who accused me of mass genocide."

Del struggled to hold back his anger. He could bring up Tams Station or any other world. But Qox knew what his predecessors had done. This emperor hadn't been on the throne long enough to commit atrocities, but he carried the blood of his forefathers.

Del spoke quietly. "We each have our view of the universe, Your Highness. You and I won't change that here."

"Yet you would start a war," Qox said, "by performing this song during a politically charged event, a situation guaranteed to create a flood of propaganda."

Propaganda? He wanted to ask Qox how he would like to have his nerves fried by torture dust or his back shredded under a whip. The words strained to explode out of him. Somehow, he said only, "I sang what I knew."

"So you claim."

Del waited, sweating. Qox watched him with those unfathomable red eyes. Finally the emperor said, "Neither your leaders nor the Allieds wish another war. They have made it clear that they neither sanctioned nor encouraged your outburst."

Del refrained from saying the obvious. The Traders didn't want another war, either. The last one had drained them as much as it had worn out Del's people. "It's true, Your Highness. The decision was mine and mine alone. Those who knew the song strongly discouraged me from ever performing it."

Qox just looked at him. Here in the virtual universe, it was impossible to tell what he thought of Del's response. He gave no sign that it affected him at all.

"Very well," Qox finally said. "This time I will show mercy. In my benevolence, Prince Del-Kurj, I will overlook your paltry attempts to incite wrath against my people. If you fulfill the terms of your request, I will see that Staver Aunchild's wife returns to him."

Del hadn't realized how much he feared the consequences of what he'd done until Qox spoke that reprieve. As much as he hated feeling grateful to the man who embodied the worst of Aristo tyranny, he couldn't help the relief that poured over him.

He noticed, too, what Qox had said: *fulfill the terms of your request.* The emperor could have asked for a full retraction. He left it vague as to what Del agreed to do.

"Thank you, Your Highness," Del said. "You are generous." It was true, given how much worse Qox could have responded. Given that Qox also represented the most monstrous empire ever known to humanity, the "generous" part came hard to Del.

Qox regarded him steadily. "If you ever sing such a song again, I *will* consider it an act of war and act accordingly."

Del nodded stiffly. "I understand."

"Be careful, Prince Del-Kurj," the emperor said. "Don't run beyond your ability to catch yourself." With that, he disappeared with an abruptness that left no doubt as to his low opinion of the man he had come to see.

Del let out a breath and sagged against the table. It was over. At least for today, none of them would go to war.

Del stood on the balcony of his room and looked over the river, which caught sparks of light from the setting sun. He thought of Jaibriol Qox's last words: *Don't run beyond your ability to catch yourself.* Ironically, it reminded him of what his sister Soz had often said when they were children: *Don't run so fast, you can't catch up with yourself.* That was decades before the Traders had blown up her ship, killing her—and Qox's father. Del wondered what the emperor thought, knowing his own people had murdered his father rather than let the Skolians capture him.

"I ran home," Del said. He had almost outrun his life and family, but somehow he had found both before it was too late. Earth would be his adopted home for a while. It would never again be like that first year, when he had been no one except Del Arden, a struggling artist. That had been one of the hardest—and most satisfying—times of his life.

Del had found parts of himself here he had never expected. In signing his name, he had felt as if he were giving away pieces of his soul, but instead he had become more complete than he had been in years, perhaps ever.

He watched the light of the setting sun and sang softly to the world and star that had given birth to the human race:

> Brighter than the crystal caves
> Sunlight glancing on the waves
> Sol's child, timeless and whole
> Your gift was to heal my soul

Lyrics

Diamond Star

LYRICS BY CATHERINE ASARO

Angel, be my diamond star
Before my darkness goes too far
Splinter through my endless night
Lightening my darkling sight

You're, you're, you're, you're
A diamond, a diamond, a diamond star

Brighter than the crystal caves
Sunlight glancing on the waves
Swirling dance upon my heart
Longing while we're held apart

You're, you're, you're, you're
A diamond, a diamond, a diamond star

Take it slow, a daring chance
Swaying in a timeless dance
Shimmering radiance above
Softening this lost man's love

You're, you're, you're, you're
A diamond, a diamond, a diamond star

In Paradisum

GREGORIAN CHANT

In Paradisum deducant te Angeli;
in tuo adventu sucipiant te Martyres,
et perducant te in civitatem Jerusalem

No Answers
LYRICS BY CATHERINE ASARO

No answers live in here alone
No answers on this spectral throne
Nothing in this vault of fears
This sterling vault, chamber of tears

Tell me now before I fall
Release me from this velvet pall
Tell me now before I fall
Take me now, break through my wall

No answers will salvage time
No answers in this tomb sublime
This winnowing crypt intertwined
This crypt whispering in vines

Tell me now before I fall
Release from this velvet pall
Tell me now before I fall
Take me now, break through my wall

No answers could bring me life
Yet when I opened my eyes
Beyond the sleeping crystal dome
Beyond it all, I had come home

Tell me now before I fall
Release from this velvet pall
Tell me now before I fall
Take me now, break through my wall

Oh, oh I'm falling down
Oh, now

Emeralds

LYRICS BY CATHERINE ASARO

Green as the bitter nail
They drove into my name
I won't try to fail
Just to satisfy their game

Don't listen to their lies
I'll never turn my back on you
Never wait 'til someone dies
To promise my heart is true

Emerald drops, emerald tears
It's you they see
In their green-shaded mirrors
Emerald drops, emerald tears
The darkness feeds
On their green-bladed fears

Night veils the secret hollow
In the silvered lagoon
Body rising from the water
Under silent moons

They waited in whispering reeds
Green within, predators without
But my brother intervened
He answered my crying shout

Emerald drops, emerald tears
It's you that they see
In their green-shaded mirrors
Emerald drops, emerald tears
The darkness feeds
On their green-bladed fears

I didn't desert you
Despite what they crowed
You still believed I was true
They learned what our love knows

Emerald drops, emerald tears
It's you that they see
In their green-shaded mirrors
Emerald drops, emerald tears
The darkness feeds
On their green-bladed fears

Emerald drops, emerald tears
It's you that they see
In their green-shaded mirrors
Emerald drops, emerald tears
The darkness feeds
On their green-bladed fears

Sapphire Clouds
LYRICS BY CATHERINE ASARO

Running through the sphere-tipped reeds
Suns like gold and amber beads
Jumping over blue-winged bees
Don't catch me, please

Cause I'm
Running, running, running
Running, running, running
Running, running, running away

Flight of bubbles everywhere
Pollen dusting in my hair
No more troubles anywhere
Sapphire clouds above the air

And I'm running, running, running
Running, running, running
Running, running, running away

Memories fade in life's strain
Winds of age bring falling rain
Cornucopia of lives
Of years and joys and grieving sighs

Recall sapphire clouds on high
Drifting in an endless sky
Childhood caught and kept deep inside
To treasure after days gone by

And I'm running, running, running
Running, running, running
Running, running, running away

Rubies

LYRICS BY CATHERINE ASARO

Born to live in a Vanished Sea
Lost to seeds of a banished need
Caged in desperate hope for all days
Rubies must give their souls in all ways

Living bound by your empathy
Shelter found in your trinity
Love imprisoning hope for your days
Rubies must give their souls in all ways

Hiding deepest vulnerabilities
Cursed by your mind's abilities
For within you lies the hope for all days
Rubies must give their souls in all ways

Carnelians

LYRICS BY CATHERINE ASARO

You dehumanized us; your critics, they died
You answered defiance with massive genocide
Hunt us as your prey, assault, and enslave
Force us bound to stay, for pleasures that you crave

I'm no golden hero in the blazing skies
I'm no fair-haired genius hiding in disguise
I'm only a singer; it's all that I can do
But my voice is rising; I can sing the truth

They strangled our summers, your Carnelian Sons
You anguished the mothers in your war of suns
With a heart that freezes, you shattered my kin
You thought you were leaving no one who could win

I'm no golden hero in the blazing skies
I'm no fair-haired genius hiding in disguise
I'm only a singer; it's all that I can do
But I'm still alive; I'm coming after you

I'll never kneel beneath your Highton stare
I'm here, I'm real; I'll lay your guilt bare
I'll never kneel beneath your Highton stare
I'm here, I'm real; I'm your nightmare

Carnelians Finale
LYRICS BY CATHERINE ASARO

You dehumanized us
Your critics, they all died
You answered defiance
With massive genocide

You hunt us as your prey
You assault and enslave
You force us bound to stay
For pleasures that you crave

You killed my brother
You Carnelian Sons
You tortured my mother
In your war of suns

You shattered my father
You broke my brothers
You murdered my sister
Expecting no others

Well, I'm no golden hero
In the blazing skies
I'm no fair-haired genius
Hiding in disguise

I'm only a singer
It's all I can do
But I'm still alive
And I'm coming after you

➡

I'll never kneel
Beneath your Highton stare
I'm here and I'm real
I'll lay your guilt bare

I'll never kneel
Beneath your Highton stare
I'm here and I'm real
Your living nightmare

Starlight Child

LYRICS BY CATHERINE ASARO
(To my daughter, Cathy)

When the forever snows
Tightened their embrace
While my dreaming thoughts froze
You rose with newborn grace

Nothing ever will compare
Nothing ever will come close
Your eyes, your skin, your shining hair
Starlight child, my heart knows

You're starlight, starlight child
You're starlight, my lovely child

When your laugh stills the world
Miracles arise
Unexpected, a hidden pearl
Heals my stricken eyes

Nothing ever will compare
Nothing ever will come close
Your eyes, your skin, your shining hair
Starlight child, my heart knows

You're starlight, starlight child
You're starlight, my treasured child

The ices of sleeping death
Melt within your candle's light
Your trust, your smile, your lilting breath
Starlight child, my heart flies

You're starlight, starlight child
You're starlight, my starlight child

You're starlight, miraculous child
Streaming starlight, my starlight child

Boxcar Madness

LYRICS BY HAYIM ANI

This is the first day on your dimming stage
This is the last smile you'll ever see
Look at all the widespread hate
Comes from the anger that fuels our race
Would you love me if I was somebody else?
Would you hate me if I choose to be myself?

Turn away as struggles take me better learn to pray
Gone insane from crossing out this bitter memory

Leaving a loved one ignoring the pain
Holding your hand out despite all shame
Lying on cold stone rather than on dreams soft
Jumping high fences not to get caught
Scream to the whole world but nobody's there
Even if they were I doubt they'd care

Turn away as struggles come I hear you scream my name
Gone insane from crossing out just what you meant to me

I can't go home. I can't go home.

Love me.

Quietly you walk right in and out of my dreams
No need to sing I hear your eyes hum everything

I can't go home. I can't go home.

Would you love me if I was somebody else?
Would you hate me if I choose to be myself?

Etch-a-Sketch

LYRICS BY HAYIM ANI

Writing little notes on the Etch-a-Sketch of life
Carving secret hopes on sand dunes in your mind
Water will come now and wash it down the drain
Oh the sketch will shake and your thoughts will fall away

Leaves turn brown and fall to the ground
Fading lights you're all alone tonight

Well I want to be hated
That would justify my world of pain
And I know you feel like Satan
Protective hands watch the candles wane

Sliding slowly down on the slip-n-slide of time
Looking for footholds now on the glass wall passing by
Where's the lifeguard? Is that the sound of loneliness?
Coming from my heart, my heart of emptiness

Trees fall down without making a sound
Angry eyes lie

Well I want to be hated
That would justify my world of pain
And I know you feel like Satan
Protective hands watch the candles wane

Hold back the storm and close your eyes waiting for the light
You pawn away forgotten dreams for thought provoked misery

Always seem outnumbered against the star filled sky
But wait the late sun is rising when it shines begin to fly

So fight no more and raise your hands in the rain we'll dance
Turn to east with heads held high watch the new sunrise
. . . whoa in your eyes.

Breathing Underwater

LYRICS BY HAYIM ANI

Now I know, with all the blood that's on the floor
Things will never go back to the way they were before
And there may be a man who says tomorrow's not today
But I know no joy that will take this pain away

Yet when I close my eyes I feel the warmth of the sea
I fall into sleep but you're there to catch me
Your arms are outstretched, you're loving no other
Together we'll learn how to breathe underwater

Just a little boy left in a house of pain
Wondering where all the ashes went
Now I'm standing in a spotlight of shame
Staring at my black and empty frame

Yet when I close my eyes I feel the warmth of the sea
I fall into sleep but you're there to catch me
Your arms are outstretched, you're loving no other
Together we'll learn how to breathe underwater

And when I close my eyes I feel the warmth of the sea
I fall into sleep but you're there to catch me
Your arms are outstretched, loving no other
Together we'll learn how to breathe underwater

Your arms are outstretched as warm as the sea
Just hold me girl together we'll breathe

Characters & Family History

Boldface names refer to Ruby psions, also known as the "Rhon." All Rhon psions who are members of the Ruby Dynasty use **Skolia** as their last name (the Skolian Imperialate was named after their family). The **Selei** name indicates the direct line of the Ruby Pharaoh. Children of **Roca** and **Eldrinson** take Valdoria as a third name. The del prefix means "in honor of," and is capitalized if the person honored was a Triad member. Most names are based on world-building systems drawn from Mayan, North African, and Indian cultures.

= marriage

Lahaylia Selei (Ruby Pharaoh: deceased) = **Jarac** (Imperator: deceased)

Lahaylia and **Jarac** founded the modern-day Ruby Dynasty. **Lahaylia** was created in the Rhon genetic project. Her lineage traced back to the ancient Ruby Dynasty that founded the Ruby Empire. **Lahaylia** and **Jarac** had two daughters, **Dyhianna Selei** and **Roca**.

Dyhianna (Dehya) Selei = (1) William Seth Rockworth III (separated)
   = (2) **Eldrin Jarac Valdoria**

Dehya is the Ruby Pharaoh. She married William Seth Rockworth III as part of the Iceland Treaty between the Skolian Imperialate and

Allied Worlds of Earth. They had no children and later separated. The dissolution of their marriage would negate the treaty, so neither the Allieds nor Imperialate recognize the divorce. *Spherical Harmonic* tells the story of what happened to **Dehya** after the Radiance War.

Dehya and **Eldrin** have two children, **Taquinil Selei** and **Althor Vyan Selei.**

Althor Vyan Selei = **Akushtina (Tina) Santis Pulivok**

The story of **Althor** and **Tina** appears in *Catch the Lightning.* **Althor Vyan Selei** was named after his uncle, **Althor Izam-Na Valdoria.** The short story "Avo de Paso" in the anthologies *Redshift,* edited by Al Sarrantino, and *Fantasy: The Year's Best, 2001,* edited by Robert Silverberg and Karen Haber, tells the story of how Tina and her cousin Manuel deal with Mayan spirits in the New Mexico desert.

Roca = (1) Tokaba Ryestar (deceased)
       = (2) Darr Hammerjackson (divorced)
       = (3) **Eldrinson Althor Valdoria**

Roca and Tokaba had one child, **Kurj** (Imperator and Jagernaut), who married Ami when he was a century old. **Kurj** and Ami had a son named Kurjson.

Although no records exist of **Eldrinson's** lineage, it is believed he descends from the ancient Ruby Dynasty. *Skyfall* tells the story of how **Eldrinson** and **Roca** meet. They have ten children:

Eldrin (Dryni) Jarac (bard, consort to Ruby Pharaoh, warrior)
Althor Izam-Na (engineer, Jagernaut, Imperial Heir)
Del-Kurj (Del) (singer, warrior, twin to **Chaniece**)
Chaniece Roca (runs Valdoria family household, twin to **Del-Kurj**)
Havyrl (Vyrl) Torcellei (farmer, doctorate in agriculture)
Sauscony (Soz) Lahaylia (military scientist, Jagernaut, Imperator)
Denric Windward (teacher, doctorate in literature)
Shannon Eirlei (Blue Dale archer)
Aniece Dyhianna (accountant, Rillian queen)
Kelricson (Kelric) Garlin (mathematician, Jagernaut, Imperator)

Eldrin appears in *The Final Key, Triad, Spherical Harmonic,* and *The Radiant Seas.* See also **Dehya**.

Althor Izam-Na = (1) Coop and Vaz
                  = (2) Cirrus (former provider to Ur Qox)

Althor has a daughter, Eristia Leirol Valdoria, with Syreen Leirol, an actress turned linguist. Coop and Vaz have a son, Ryder Jalam Majda Valdoria, with **Althor** as cofather. **Althor** and Coop appear in *The Radiant Seas.* Vaz and Coop appear in *Spherical Harmonic.* **Althor** and Cirrus also have a son.

Havyrl (Vyrl) Torcellei = (1) Liliara (Lily) (deceased)
                           = (2) Kamoj Quanta Argali

The story of Havyrl and Lily appears in "Stained Glass Heart," in the anthology *Irresistible Forces,* edited by Catherine Asaro, 2004. The story of **Havyrl** and Kamoj appears in *The Quantum Rose,* which won the 2001 Nebula Award. An early version of the first half was serialized in *Analog,* May–July/August 1999.

Sauscony (Soz) Lahaylia = (1) Jato Stormson (divorced)
                           = (2) Hypron Luminar (deceased)
                           = (3) **Jaibriol Qox** (aka **Jaibriol II**)

The story of **Soz** at seventeen, when she enters the Dieshan Military Academy, appears in *Schism,* which is Part I of the two-book work *Triad.* The second part, *The Final Key,* tells of the first war between the Skolians and the Traders. The story of how **Soz** and Jato met appears in the novella, "Aurora in Four Voices" (Analog, December 1998). **Soz** and **Jaibriol**'s stories appear in *Primary Inversion* and *The Radiant Seas.* They have four children: **Jaibriol III, Rocalisa, Vitar,** and **del-Kelric.** The story of how **Jaibriol III** became the Emperor of Eube appears in *The Moon's Shadow.* **Jaibriol III** married Tarquine Iquar, the Finance Minister of Eube. The story of how Jaibriol and Kelric deal with each other appears in *The Ruby Dice.*

Denric takes a position as a teacher on the world Sandstorm. His harrowing introduction to his new home appears in the short story, "The Edges of Never-Haven" (*Flights of Fantasy,* edited by Al Sarrantino).

Aniece = Lord Rillia

Lord Rillia rules Rillia on the world Lyshriol (aka Skyfall). His realms consist of the Rillian Vales, Dalvador Plains, Backbone Mountains, and Stained Glass Forest.

Kelricson (Kelric) Garlin = (1) Corey Majda (deceased)
= (2) Deha Dahl (deceased)
= (3) Rashiva Haka (Calani trade)
= (4) Savina Miesa (deceased)
= (5) Avtac Varz (Calani trade)
= (6) Ixpar Karn (closure)
= (7) Jeejon

Kelric's stories are told in *The Ruby Dice*, "The Ruby Dice" (novella, *Baen's Universe 2006*), *The Last Hawk, Ascendant Sun, The Moon's Shadow*, the novella "A Roll of the Dice" (*Analog*, July/August 2000), and the novelette "Light and Shadow" (*Analog*, April 1994). **Kelric** and Rashiva have one son, Jimorla Haka, who becomes a renowned Calani. **Kelric** and Savina have one daughter, **Rohka Miesa Varz,** who becomes the Ministry Successor in line to rule the Estates of Coba.

The novella "Walk in Silence" (*Analog*, April 2003) tells the story of Jess Fernandez, an Allied Starship Captain from Earth, who deals with the genetically engineered humans on the Skolian colony of Icelos.

The novella "The City of Cries" (*Down These Dark Spaceways,* edited by Mike Resnick) tells the story of Major Bhaaj, a private investigator hired by the House of Majda to find Prince Dayj Majda after he disappears.

The novella "The Shadowed Heart" (*Year's Best Paranormal,* edited by Paula Guran, and *The Journey Home,* edited by Mary Kirk) is the story of Jason Harrick, a Jagernaut who just barely survives the Radiance War.

Time Line

Circa 4000 BC   Group of humans moved from Earth to Raylicon

Circa 3600 BC   Ruby Dynasty begins

Circa 3100 BC   Raylicans launch first interstellar flights; rise of Ruby Empire

Circa 2900 BC   Ruby Empire begins decline

Circa 2800 BC   Last interstellar flights; Ruby Empire collapses

Circa AD 1300   Raylicans begin to regain lost knowledge

1843   Raylicans regain interstellar flight

1866   Rhon genetic project begins

1871   Aristos found Eubian Concord (aka Trader Empire)

1881   Lahaylia Selei born

1904   Lahaylia Selei founds Skolian Imperialate

2005   Jarac born

2111   Lahaylia Selei marries Jarac

2119   Dyhianna Selei born

2122   Earth achieves interstellar flight

2132   Allied Worlds of Earth formed

2144   Roca born

2169	Kurj born
2203	Roca marries Eldrinson Althor Valdoria (*Skyfall*)
2204	Eldrin Jarac Valdoria born; Jarac dies; Kurj becomes Imperator; Lahaylia dies
2205	Major Bhaaj hired by Majdas to find Prince Dayj ("The City of Cries")
2206	Althor Izam-Na Valdoria born
2209	Havyrl (Vyrl) Torcellei Valdoria born
2210	Sauscony (Soz) Lahaylia Valdoria born
2219	Kelricson (Kelric) Garlin Valdoria born
2227	Soz enters Dieshan Military Academy (*Schism*)
2228	First war between Skolia and Traders (*The Final Key*)
2237	Jaibriol II born
2240	Soz meets Jato Stormson ("Aurora in Four Voices")
2241	Kelric marries Admiral Corey Majda
2243	Corey assassinated ("Light and Shadow")
2258	Kelric crashes on Coba (*The Last Hawk*)
early 2259	Soz meets Jaibriol (*Primary Inversion*)
late 2259	Soz and Jaibriol go into exile (*The Radiant Seas*)
2260	Jaibriol III born (aka Jaibriol Qox Skolia)
2263	Rocalisa Qox Skolia born; Althor Izam-Na Valdoria meets Coop ("Soul of Light")
2268	Vitar Qox Skolia born
2273	del-Kelric Qox Skolia born
2274	Radiance War begins (also called Domino War)
2276	Traders capture Eldrin. Radiance War ends; Jason Harrick crashes on the planet Thrice Named ("The Shadowed Heart")
2277–8	Kelric returns home (*Ascendant Sun*); Dehya coalesces (*Spherical Harmonic*); Kamoj and Vyrl meet (*The Quantum Rose*); Jaibriol III becomes emperor of Eube (*The Moon's Shadow*)